"*Rocker Heaven* jolts right off your lap! New author Tom Trainor is funny, irreverent and raw. Book's about the 60s, sex, drugs and rock and roll and lots lots more."

— *SF Nights*

"A daring, breathtaking book, written in a rapid paced style that is unlike any recent work of literary fiction I have read. *Rocker Heaven* provides a view of American culture from the 60s to the present that is broad in its scope and humor. Tom Trainor is fresh, his writing masterful, his characters vivid, and the satire underlying the outrageous fun razor sharp. I read it cover to cover in three days running."

— Liam Shaughnessy, University of Massachusetts

"Best read with a flashlight underneath the sheets."

— Michael Olendzenski, Cape Cod Community College

"…a bold new voice …wildly imaginative …might very well set the pace for twenty first century American fiction…"

— Oliver Hoyt, *London Underground*

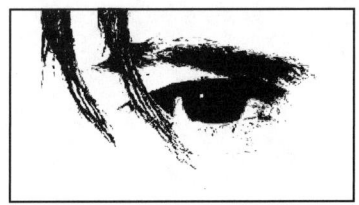

thewaryeye.com
press

TOM TRAINOR
ROCKER HEAVEN

thewaryeye.com
press

Published in the United States by thewaryeye.com press

Copyright © 2003 by Tom Trainor

First edition 2003

All rights reserved under International and Pan-American Copyright Conventions

No part of this book may be used, reproduced or transmitted in any form or by any means whatsoever, electronic or mechanical, including photocopying, recording, or by any information storage and retrieval system, without written permission of the Publisher except where permitted by law, as in the case of brief quotations embodied in critical articles and reviews. For information address thewaryeye.com press at www.thewaryeye.com

---

Publisher's Note: This is a work of fiction. Names, characters, places and incidents are either the product of the author's imagination or used fictitiously; and any resemblance to actual persons, living or dead, events or locales is entirely coincidental.

Cover design and graphics: Brian H. Gay at www.roguesjournal.com

Library of Congress Cataloging Number: 2002105653

ISBN 0-9720129-0-7

1 5 7 4 0 0 0 2

Dedicated to Brian, Katy, Betsy, Liza, Zephyr and all her brood without whose constant enthusiasm, humor and patience this work would never have ensued.

And special thanks to Dave, Bob and Barbara for nailing it down at the last minute and to all those who lent time over time.

Time but plays everyman for a fool

ALLIED FOR LIFE

...HEATHROW AIRPORT

...OUTSIDE LONDON

...SOMETIME IN THE TOO NEAR FUTURE

"Uut oof me way, yoo roody sod!"
"Nice mouth!"
"Stuuff it!"
Big girl, whole gang load of them push past everybody else — CLANK CLANK CLANK CLANK — clad in hefty metal and rough soled biker boots.
"Hey! Watch who you're shovin!"
"Shoove yoo, yoo poof!"
"Shove you back Sally!"
Wrong move — CLANK CLANK — gang load jumps the sorry bloke.
"Fuuk 'im uup! Fuuk 'im uup uugly!"
They do as they're told, these girls, with studded belts and steely toe plates, while the crowd around backs way off.
"That's that Cissy Coombs, that's who that is!" Someone snipes.
And the nastiest fatassed of the bunch flashes the finger, some sort of ribbed ring sheath t'poop uup yoor ruudy buum 'ole!
CLANK CLANK CLANK CLANK CLANK CLANK CLANK CLANK
Heathrow has been shut down. Scheduled flights have been rerouted to Gatwick. Concourses, escalators, lounges are mobbed. Kids. Millions of kids and rude and loud, and elite Brit SAS troops stationed in tight formation in front of the Terminal 4 VIP Pavilion. Throughout the day the traffic in celebrities has been phenomenal, jet loads of them — AK47, CRAM, Parson Nevilles and Jeb Latham, Arbie Riffendorf, Tom Scum, Child Bride, Constance Flit, Luther T. Wallop, Early Stook and the Kid

Squid. Later in the afternoon, Swag, Sore Losers, the Scupper Plugs fresh out of East Auckland, Ether Bib, Liz Croft, Rob Hart and the Red Hot Cherry Busters, Seattle's Orphic Gizzards — the list goes on. Not that the kids can catch a glimpse of a one of them. There's this fleet of helicopters lifting the stars directly off the tarmac and up over the crowd toward the stadium. Still, every whine of a jet engine, every whip of a rotor blade sparks this surge of excitement, this movement. Kids gain a few feet. Red berets step back. It's a standoff, but hey, they're here, they're part of it, and no way these diehard rockers can get within striking distance of Wembley.

Besides the day's not over with, not yet. It's near midnight and Chipper Stirbee's due in direct from Melbourne. He's on last and he's late, as usual.

Enough of a delay for Cissy Coombs and her girls to make headway. The stout ones up front storm the VIP gate. They're in no mood for no, no sir, no pardon me please, no step aside otherwise, No Admittance Beyond This Point Without Proper Clearance, no skirts to hike as they hurdle the crush barriers. Girls look stylish in slick black leather zip suits, punker hairdos, Cissy's is plum purple brushed up center and shaved along the sides, and she's got flared nostrils and pierced nipples on a pair of exposed double D's, and chains rankling anyone who dares step in her way as she marches straight through the metal detector — CRANK CRANK CRANK CRANK CRANK — gets everybody going.

Troops listen up.

Not that these biker babes have a gripe with the boys in fatigues, fact a rumble or a tumble with the likes of some broad shouldered British specials would be A-OK with them, no, it's Chipper Stirbee they're after, and if the Army's going to bar the doors, then the girls'll stomp through the plate glass shattering windows, thank you. Cissy Coombs and her sisters hop outside onto the darkened tarmac.

Troops pursue, hands on their holsters, although the damage has been done, scores of teenage travelers pour rapidly through the breach behind Cissy's gang to get a closer look.

Her timing couldn't be better. In the shadows is a Leeds Executive Supersonic gliding to a stop, a hundred feet from the charging beauties.

CHIPPER!

Crowd calls.

CHIPPER!

Rampaging kids being perfect cover for a paramilitary maneuver.

CHIPPER! CHIPPER!

Which could be a warning, which could be a greeting, at near hysteric decibels.

CHIP- CHIP- CHIPPER!

Like a shrieking mulch machine... while a compact yellow and red sea rescue craft hovers overhead, and sensing trouble groundside switches on its high intensity beam.

There's the slightest *whirrrr* as the cabin door of the executive jet slides open and a ramp descends. A pair of bright blue eyes peers out, curious, cautious — and a pair of black velvet ears — perked!!

Chipper?

A flash of the telltale platinum blond hair. A whip of a spiny black tail.

It's… the crowd grows closer, yes it is, it's…

CHIPPER! CHIPPER!

Cry goes shriller still! Blue eyes blink… black ears twitch… "Don't much like the looks of the welcomin pahty. How about you gihl?"

There's this audible gulp. Hers, his, who knows? They're both abruptly whisked back inside the jet, instead a detachment of QuotLink Inc Security types in uniform blue blazers with buzz cuts clamors down the ramp.

QuotLinks off the plane survey the crowded terrain. Right away they figure Cissy's not friendly, could be the needle tips, could be the mean sucker curl to her lips. Whatever. She's advancing and the elite paratrooper unit is lagging behind. Hence the best defensive posture for the private security squad is to close into a wedge formation around Chipper, who's toting his classic 56 Fenderbender in a gig bag. Two types on the edge cradle assault weapons. The rest are armed with double-handled batons. The one on point has his eyes aimed directly at Cissy. And a rigid black tail brings up the rear!

WHUPWHUPWHUPWHUP — rescue chopper is attempting to set down in between the opposing forces.

Cissy Coombs doesn't flinch, doesn't slow her pace.

Kids in the crowd do. Something about automatics and an improvised air show, they freeze in place. Gives the paratroopers the opportunity to squeeze through, reestablish a line — *hup hup*, might is right, plight makes for such a sight, it's flee, flip or fight when the scene suddenly goes silent.

Everybody's watching.

Only sound is the tread of Cissy's heavy boots, and the WHUPWHUP of the helicopter settling in closer.

Is there an ugly incident in the making?

What the kids inside the terminal can't see they don't know, so most join the trek out toward Wembley, site of Chipper's next earthy appearance where close to 2000,000 of them have jammed inside the stadium, while outside and spilling into adjacent neighborhoods, ten times their number have assembled, along with a full division of regular Army infantry.

WHUPWHUPWHUPWHUPWHUPWHUPWHUP — back at Heathrow the

helicopter descends — but that doesn't deter Cissy. With a hoist of her ribbed midfinger, she signals her squad into action. Confusion's the game as the girls start in scrimmaging. Looks like a snatch pass, pat on the ass, a long sweep to a wild receiver, a flame headed wonder running backwards open mouthed and hooting, "Who's here got the balls?"

Not the QuotLink Inc Security Corps, they doffed theirs for generous severance packages eons ago, which might explain why they misjudge the play, like entirely. They close into a shell while two of Cissy's tiny tight ends sneak along the wings. A dive, a tackle, and the girls take down the heavy artillery. Call it foul but two-fisted batons are useless when your enemy's on your back kicking and scratching. Seems these QuotLink lifers weren't trained for resistible wenches with finger spikes and spindly spurs that tickle. So when Cissy who's been saving her loveliest linebackers does a final rush forward, that is, hits full force head and shoulders and piles on rugby style, game's over, security detachment falls without firing a shot.

Paratroopers do a double take. Hesitate.

And if an armed bodyguard is no match for these babes, what chance does a lone rockstar or his pet Lab who's part Dobie have of surviving?

Plenty. Dog's gone a few rounds in her life and Chipper's still scrappy.

"Remembah the pahkin lot ovah at Hack's Bah that rainy Satuhday night Betsy?"

Remember? How could she forget, lug wrenches and a dozen Kanooks in mud up to their ankles, after Chipper has to go and say something disparaging about his quarter-French ancestry.

"Fihst to draw blood in a brawl's suhe to win." Some comfort that is as the two go back-to-back, face off the force encircling hem. "Go fah a throat and I'll try and knock some sense into one of theih pretty little heads."

Betsy bares her incisors, scopes for one her size or smaller.

WHUPWHUPWHUPWHUP — rescue craft is whipping up dust as Cissy's gang closes in tighter and tighter.

"Tough lookin bunch of bruisahs."

Betsy and he twist around, looking for a break in the ranks, which is at least two deep with more of the sisters moving in from the midfield.

"Spot a hole gihl, scuhry through it. I can take cahe of myself."

-rr-right! Betsy slinks low to the ground.

Chipper starts bouncing up and down, short hops, warming himself up — boy is Maine State Champion jumpy, can leap five, ten, fifteen feet at the slightest female provocation.

"Stook'em!" Cissy commands and the girls advance — CLANKCLANK CLANKCLANKCLANK.

"Looks like this is it Betsy baby!"

Chipper must have springs on his heels as he leaps — *h'yigh hoop* —

straight up in a high fly vault over the front line offensive. Perfect form. Arms. legs stretched, head ducked and ready to roll when he lands other side — *whoof* — but what's this? Something soft? Yes, a punker heavyweight on her back and unzipped. Chipper lands full flop on top a cushion of belly and breasts, but *-ee y'ouch!* — something sticks, a pair of nipple pins in the palms of his hands. It's Cissy Coombs leering lustily up at him.

"Help yoorself flybooy!"

Though Chipper's, "Nope, and I thank you kindly fah the offah ma'am," as he scrambles off her, "theah's this somethin else I've just got to be doin — BETSY?"

Betsy's spotted a hole in the line and gone squirreling through it — Cissy's girls tumbling all over themselves trying to block her.

"Whoa, theah you ah. Figuhred I'd lost you fah suhe this round."

Fat chance of that chum. So what's our game plan?

True. One play, no matter how spectacular, isn't going to finish this quarter, not as Cissy calls for a time out to regroup. But with the clock still ticking she's got to act quickly, so she fans her force across the field and comes running on the offensive.

Chipper starts in bouncing again. Betsy hunkers low. "Ahright, stay cool, they say theah's ahways a way out of anythin, long as you don't panic."

WHUPWHUPWHUPWHUPWHUPWHUP

"H'yep, ahways is! Lock on my hip pocket gihl, let's grab the elevatah."

-rr grab the what?

WHUP -UP -UP

Cissy's team comes charging, so... so... so Chipper goes for another soaring leap, vertical, the goal this heat being the skids of the small rescue craft fluttering some forty feet above him — *WHUPWHUPWHUP* — which might be slightly out of reach for someone not in training, but go for the gold Chipper — right about now!

Though just as Betsy readies to hitch a ride on his back pockets, someone stomps down hard on her tail — *cur-ripes!*

"Uut oof me way, yoo stuupid muutt!"

It's Cissy Coombs, offside, she nabs at Chipper's heels as he goes launching upward, arm over arm paddling, feet thrashing, up, up — *WHUPWHUP* — reaching — *WHUPWHUP* — until one hand... one hand overlaps... overlaps metal flange! Maine boy's made it! A new varsity record for broad jumping! Yes! His fingers grasp for the portal...

"Say mate, could you use a hand aboot new?" Pilot reaches over the spare seat.

Chipper's got his elbows in... his gig bag secure on his shoulder... "Crowbah'd be bettah!" While the rest of him's left dangling dangerously, and the helicopter's listing way to starboard... not to mention the pooch marooned below…

"Ball-peen hammer do?"

Because this fist full of knuckles is clutched on one foot and yanking, with all her weight. "Whatevah, othahwise I'm a gonah fah suhe!"

Instead his boot bops off, and he's mercifully free of Cissy as he does a final pull-up into the cockpit.

CHIPPER! CHIPPER!

Except Cissy's still clinging to the skids and a chain of her sisters has the chopper anchored to the ground.

TIP- TIP- TIPPER!

It's a mighty tug-o-war between woman and machine, with a black dog in between — Betsy's busily chewing the ankle of a crucial ground link — pilot's above trying manfully to lift when — *FWOOSH!* — an airbus locked on a glide path zooms in low.

"Mayday! Mayday! — Heathrow Tower, this is Skyhook XS90, South Bay 11, requestin emergency clearance fir take off, copy?"

Right, but how are you going to shake Cissy and her girls loose? They've got superhuman strength and not a lot of give — *KRANK KRANK KRANK* — pilot pulls up on his stick, as any normal guy would, and slowly, rotor shifting, straining, he's… he's… he's beginning to broach — *SNAP!* — rivets pop! Skid gives! Rips clean clear off the fuselage, with Cissy and her gang taking a plunge… while the helicopter does a gyro, which is *WHUP WHUPS* spiral up, then *WHIP WHAM* downward slam.

"Pissah maneuvah theah fella, pissah!"

"Go fir the thrills, do you?"

WHOOP -HOOP -HOOP

"Hope this burd hodds steady — name's Scott Burlap, n you'v got ta be noon other than Chipper Stirbee."

"None othah." Chipper offers a hand.

"Pleasure's mine."

"Appreciate the lift."

"Do wha ah can do. So tell me, how'd you git yirsell inta a scrap wi a bunch a'Sheffield razorheads?"

"Sheffield razahheads?"

"Heard tell it's the style thir ta git a sharp blade incised front ta back righ inta yir scalp."

"Whoa! Didn't run into one of those."

"N needles inserted inta the tips a'yir nipples."

"H'yep, can attest to that."

"So wha say we haul ou'ta hir? Had enough ruckus fir one ev'nin?"

"Can't just yet Scotty, we've got to drop back down theah, way stealthy like, go in fah a quick rescue."

"Tha's a quick what?" WHUPWHUP

Chipper does a downward motion with his thumb.

"Might be ev'ry bit the nutcase you a, r warse, but it canna be done." Helicopter is riding at a noticeable tilt. "Though ah do admire a bloke who'd go back ta save his mates."

"My who?"

"Yir mates, yir security escort doon thir on the ground."

"Hell with them, those ah QuotLinks."

"Qua-whats?"

"QuotLinks Scotty, QuotLinks."

Who still lie littered across the field.

"Those suckahs can suhvive on theih own anywheah, anytime, believe me. It's my gal Betsy I'm wohryin about."

"Ah see, thirsa wuman involved. Thasa dif'rent story."

"Best damn hound dog in Aroostook County, except I can't see hide noh haih of huh down theah anywheah."

WHUP -PUP -PUP

Hide or hair of her is about all that's left of her. Betsy's got the wind knocked out, lying flat on the ground with thousand pound butchbullies dumped on top, and she's *grr-rrum*-muttering mad about it too. Worst predicament she's been in since she got her front half stuck deep in that mama woodchuck's hole a few soggy springs ago. She tries a yelp — *elp!* To no avail. Squaws could give a squat. Which gets Betsy's dander up, something about solidarity and sisterhood as she begins spinning her heels in reverse — *grr-grrr-grrrrrrr* — got to kick up some dust, got to bust out of there — and up top Cissy's girls sense something, sense the sassy brat beneath them is about to blast backassed out from under them, and she does, in a flash, and lands scat scratch on her tailbone while the heap load of sisters collapses through a crack in the asphalt. Might not be the most dignified exit for a prize pup, but a lass packed fast in a morass has hardly any other way she can go.

-FWHUP -FWHUP -FWHUP — Scotty's lowering within range, although the helicopter's vibrating dangerously.

"Theah she is! That's huh doubled up ovah on the edge of the runway!" Scotty sights her.

"Betsy baby, hold on!" Chipper hangs out the open portal. "HELP IS ON THE WAY!"

Sure-*rr*, and anyway Betsy's busy, leg up and licking at her war wounds. But if Betsy's sanguine, Cissy isn't. Gang girl sees opportunity.

"Coo'moon, puut soome muuscle into it sistoors! We've goot t'dig oor way uut oof this bloomin 'ole!"

CLUMP CLUMP CLUMP CLUMP CLUMP CLUMP

WHUP WHUP WHUP WHUP WHUP WHUP

Scotty takes the chopper in low. "Any closer n ah could round up!"

"HEAH YOU GO GIHL!" Chipper tosses a rope ladder. "CATCH THIS!"

-rr right, that's catch what in the dark outside where — oh I see it, a stick in the air. Piece of cake!

A stick with some strings attached however, as the ladder stops short just as Betsy makes her famous leap — makes her famous leap and misses! Betsy, blue ribbon best and misses!

-rr rough, because now she's going to have to do laps around the warm-up track while the rescue craft circles.

"Whir yoo oof to in suuch a huurry, I want t'knoow?" Cissy's fast, fat or no, hustlin close behind her.

-rrooh!

"Take yoo doown single handed, I will."

-rr -ROW!

And do they ever! *Mano a mano*, nip you and nasty, with big mama on top, though only momentarily, Betsy going for the soft underbelly of the beast — but what's this, an arm block? No matter, wrist's not that bad to gnaw on either.

"Yoo bitch!"

That's a given sist-*rr*, as Betsy digs in. First leather, next flesh, then crunch until Betsy hits bone.

"And a diirty rooser as well."

-rr right, because clean's clearly a losing battle with your kind.

Cissy tumbles free, stands on her hind twos. She uncinches her waist chain, which granting the gal's girth is quite lengthy. She twirls it over her head — *CLANK CLANK CLANK* — lasso western style.

Betsy shrinks to the ground — *WHUPWHUP* above her.

"Yoo'r gooin to end uup minced buutcher's meat!"

-rr wrong, as Betsy springs for Cissy's kneecaps, which is why thigh highs though not as chic as the wellies afford the female biped so much better protection — brings Cissy buckling down to doggy dog level.

WHUPWHUPWHUPWHUPWHUP circles in closer.

Cissy scrapes the mud off her face and scowls, all sour and spikes and not a thing nice… *-rrr*

And that's an *-rrr* back at you while they square off, Betsy crouching low, Cissy lower yet, Betsy more, until the fatass can't get down any further and is forced to spring first, digs into the raised nap on Betsy's neck — *whelp* — like needle points *-ow! -ow! -ow!*

"Yoo'r doone foor it noow."

Maybe. Betsy does a rollover…

"Yoo roody looser!"

…Betsy's ears up and ready to spring

...plays dead, then when Cissy lets up a bit Betsy lunges for her throat — contact sports routinely requiring the stitches — and round and round they go at it, fur flying, flesh tearing, two black coated wenches in heat.

WHUPWHUPWHUP "BETSY!" WHUPWHUPWHUP

Just in time too because Cissy's girls are about to step up — CLANK CLANK CLANK — since there's no such thing as innocent bystanders in an unfair fight.

"BABYDOLL!"

What? Betsy pokes her head out of the scuffle.

WHUPWHUPWHUPWHUP "I'M RIGHT HEAH ABOVE YOU GIHL!"

Truly, and miraculous to say so, the helicopter is hovering close by, though not at a terribly reassuring tilt.

"Hold huh steady Scotty, steady!"

Salvation must be whatever's within grasp that last second because...

"READY BETSY?"

...Betsy's ears up and ready to spring.

Chipper tosses the rope ladder.

Maybe she missed the first throw, but a frisbee retriever of her class isn't about to miss the second. She's a six foot stretch from snout to hind paw, and with a leap — *rrr-rompf!* — she latches onto it!

"AHRIGHT NOW! AHRIGHT! HOLD ON!"

Chipper's hauling, Scotty's lifting, Betsy's climbing rung over rung, chomp over front paw -*hep* -*heft*, chomp again, paw...

"Hold on tight!" He hollers as he reels her in the final few feet. "Climb right on ovah me gihl!"

Which she does — *tromp tromp* — she might not be a chimpanzee, but -*huff* then -*puff* she's not about to miss this one last link on the great climb out of the slime and upwards towards mankind.

"You'h ahmost home, ahmost... ahmost..." — one last rung when there's some sort of a tug on the bottom of the line, so forceful that Chipper's arm is nearly wrenched out of its socket and Betsy has to spring for it, paws off and raw pup propulsion, through the hatch and slam dunk against the back of the spare seat.

"Hey theah babydoll, it's you, right heah in my evah lovin ahms!"

She's all licking and kissing...

"Missed you too!"

...and slipping and sliding...

"Watch youh step!"

...and trying to balance on delicately clipped toe tips while the helicopter banks steeply to race away from the action — WHUPWHUP WHUPWHUPWHUPWHUP.

"Scotty, this heah's Betsy, my all time favohrite hound dog."

"Pleased ta meet you."

Betsy gets a good scrub on the noggin, for which she is *grr*-rateful, besides she's always been fond of handsome young Scotsmen.

"We go'ta ge'tout of hir. Ah don'need a citation fir bein an operational hazard."

"Let's head."

"Buckle up mates, we could be in fir some rough seas ahead."

WHUPWHUPWHUP

Which is about when Betsy feels the breeze — *rr* like where's the doors, or more to the point fellas, where's the floo-*rr*? Betsy's never flown in a bubble cab with sky high open seating. Makes her wonder if the bash on the ground wouldn't have been a whole lot safer, some terra firma and none of this rolla coasta, because if dogs were designed for flight, they'd sprout wings and feathers, -*rr* right? And rocket farts for starters?

"Yoo think yoo'r free oof me, doo yoo?" Cissy Coombs shakes her sheathed finger at the heavens. "Think again yoo cloowns, I'll stalk yoo to the ends oof the earth I will!" **CLANK CLANK**

Cissy and her girl gang mount their armor-plated motorbikes and join the trek with the youngsters blocking the roadway out of Heathrow toward Wembley, though Cissy'll get through — *ROOM-ROOM-ROOOOOOM!* — you bet she will.

"Lay back Eminenze, vay back."

"-*gack*..."

"Vay vay back. Make yourzelv comvortable."

"'-*gack*... -*gack*..."

"Now open vide. Vider. I can't vix notzink iv I can't zee notzink."

"-*gaaack*..."

CHIPPER!

"*GACK!*"

"Vatch vitz ze vingerz, vill you, iz ze only zpare zet I've gotz!"

CHIPPER! CHIPPER!

"THAT NOISE! THAT INSIDIOUS NOISE!" His Eminence clamps tight.

"'Zo vhat'z in a noize?' Azked ze high ruffed Roozter..."

"No, not another of your barnyard fables, I couldn't bear it."

"Juzt zome idle jitjat, getz your mind ov your eggz un painz."

"Spare me the sympathy and try hurrying this procedure along. I have more important things I must be doing."

"Yez vell, iz not eazy zcrewink ziz up eitzer."

Seems his Eminence has developed a steady drip about the lip and his most trustworthy practitioner Queezac, has had to be summoned. Only flat surface available is the floor of the Executive Liaison's private sky box, situated high atop the home team bleachers at Wembley, so Queezac's asquat His Eminence's chest, has his shoulders pinned to the floor…

"-ga -ga -ga-ga"

…one large claw of a hand crammed down his throat and twisting.

"-gag -gag -gag -gag"

"Zorry, zorry, iz ziz tricky adrenal regulator vavle I've gotz to tighten up, un ov courze I didn't tzink to pack my torque vrenj."

"-gog -gog"

While it could be that his Eminence's bright white new dentures have shifted alarmingly out of alignment, there is a suspicion he has sprung a leak — anything's possible with hydraulic assists as stressed as his.

"-gog"

"Zteady Eminenze. I vaz never muj ov a dentizt."

"-goh"

"Un I grow tzumbz under prezzure."

CHIPPER! CHIPPER!

"GAAAAK! -GAAAAK!"

"'Zo vhat'z in a noize?' He azked, zat cocky eyed Roozter. 'Vor a noize only annoyz 'til iz over, zen you can zcoot under ze coverz un go back to beink your normal mizerable zelv.'"

"DON'T TRIFLE WITH ME YOUHUMPBACKGROTESQUE!"

"Zorry Eminenze, zorry. I vorgotz my plaze… az uzual."

"All the years of planning, all the effort, the billions in investment, everything we at QuotLink Inc have worked to accomplish unexpectedly pressed to the verge of collapse!"

"No time to getz ziz jawbone ov yourz out ov vwack neitzer. It'z ze ztrezz, ze ztrezz vill muck upz ze bezt machinery every time."

"Entirely on account of that dredged-up rockstar…"

CHIPPER! CHIPPER! CHIP- CHIP-

"…AND THOSE FILTHY ITINERANT TEENAGERS — LISTEN TO THEM! Riff raff off the streets with nothing better to do than stand around outside the gates of this stadium and brazenly chant his name over and over."

"Iz juzt ziz ztage zey go tzrough, zeze kidz today, bevore zey zettle down to ze zeriouz buzinezz ov havink babiez on ze dole."

"They are a threat to world order and prosperity."

"Zat too."

CHIPPER! CHIPPER!

"THAT NAME! THAT NAME!"

"Pleaze Eminenze. Relax. He'z not vortz ze vorry."

"Your fate's not tied to that infantile prankster as closely as mine."

"Ziz iz true. Now open up, vay up. Yez, zat'z good — tzough I muzt zay you takez ziz job you gotz muj too zeriouzly. Even zoze titan tycoonz in ze zky overhead, zey lay down nightz zo ze rezt ov uz can getz zome zleep."

"Easy for you to say, you're not fully vested."

"Lotz ov good zat bloated ztock iz goink to do you after ze buzt, bezidez ve're all goink to loze to invlation in ze end anyvay. You zave un you zave until ze day you guzzle zat lazt drop you gotz ztazhed in ze bottle — hold it rightz zere…"

"-gaa… gaa…"

"…I'm zmack dabz on topz ov it — *yezzzzz!*"

"ACHE!"

"Zere ve go, let me getz my vingerz out ov ze vay — now znap zat trap ov yourz zhut un ve'll zee."

CLAMP!

"Yez ziree bob! Tight az a pair ov alligator jawz!"

-pthut!

"Zat'z it. Zpitz it out…"

-pthut! -pthut! -pthut-pthut-pthut-pthut-pthut!

"…zat'z it, zpitz it all over my zleeve — all over me!"

Spit it is and dripping out of His Eminence's mouth worse than ever.

"Jezuz! All zat vork un notzink to zhow vor it! You must've blown a gazket in ze zump pump, boy-o-boy zat'll be a job un a halv."

"How bad is that?"

"Ve're talkink major zurgery un a painvul recovery in a zuper-zenzitive zpot — at leazt a veek vlat on your vace."

"I haven't the time for any of that!"

"Zen ze bezt I can do iz a qvick vix vitzout benevit ov anezthetic, try un apply zome pump greaze I keep in my bag vor zuj emergenzies."

"Whatever is required, but I insist on returning to work immediately."

"OK, drop trou-…"

"Do what?"

"Juzt bend over. Let me zee if I can adjuzt zat zticky nozzle by hand."

"I-… I-… I-…"

"You're ze vone who'z inziztink on no zurgery — downzpout'z ze only janz I've got to reach it."

"This is outrageous!"

"Zo go un complain to ze vokez in engineerink, ziz iz juzt a qvicky roadzide repair — zo bend over an zpread zem – vide!"

AAAAAA -HH!

Queezac barely has his beak inside along with a flashlight.

"AAH! AAH! AAH!"

"Vider vider… zay ah…"

"AAAAAAH!"

"Your Eminence." A QuotLink Inc QSS intelligence officer in pressed blacks clicks to attention as he enters the door to the sky box.

"What th-… HOW DARE YOU BURST IN HERE UNANNOUNCED!"

"Beg pardon Sir! But you insisted we inform you the moment we received confirmation that Chipper Stirb-…"

"NEVER — *chirpychapclapyourtrap* — EVER MENTION THAT NAME IN MY PRESENCE!"

"Beg pardon Sir! Sir, the subject of concern has landed at Heathrow."

"Finally!"

"Yes Sir!"

"Boy-yo-boy, vill you getz a load ov ziz! Everyzink down here iz copper vitz lead zolder, I mean iz ziz Cold Var vintage or vhat? No PZV nor zuper light weight tevlon, un manual zet zcrewz, no electronic controlz at all."

"Will you get on with it!"

"Yez yez, but zeze ruzty old pipez you've gotz buried in ze bazement aren't goink to lazt muj longer."

"Are you absolutely certain?"

"Who knowz notzink for zertain, but if you vant I can poke around zome vhile I'm down here, do a curzory inzpection."

"I was not talking to you Queezac! I was questioning the lieutenant!"

"Affirmative! Sir!" The QSS officer salutes.

"Talk to anybody you vantz, but ziz fix iz only temporary at bezt."

"Will you simply stick to business."

"Yes sir!"

"Not you! Him!"

The QSS officer stands at rigid attention, eyes perfectly forward.

"We must proceed according to plan without any further delays."

"Sir!"

"Let me remind you that our tactical options are severely limited by our need for absolute secrecy."

"Sir?"

"Should this mob become aware of our plan, they shall most certainly riot, and with the entire area rife with camera crews — the episode could leave us exposed to billions of home viewers. Hence, we must be circumspect in our actions, none of your hooded assassins this time around, no SQWAT squads, we must appear outwardly friendly and endeavor at all costs to take him alive."

"Yes Sir!"

"We should begin by sealing off the landing pad in the car park from the reach of the rioters."

"Right, ve don't vant no pezky vitnezzez ve'd have to deal vitz later."

"Tend to your own dirty business Queezac! — UH! UH! UH!"

"Hold ztill Eminenze, zere'z alvayz ze pozziblity ov a rupture in ze zirculatory hozez."

"We have already deployed our crack units to the backstage area Your Eminence, and we expect Army reinforcements for the outer perimeters of the stadium within the next quarter hour."

"Excellent, even though history has shown that a resort to armed force upon the general population takes generations to gloss over."

"We seemingly have no alternative. Sir."

"Zuj vondervul newz! Jipper Ztirbee, zave in our clutjez at lazt!"

"THAT NAME!"

"Zorry. Iz juzt I get zo exzited vhenever I tzink about zeeink him up cloze un toujink him, oh yez, toujink him in perzon."

"You can pack your wares for now Queezac. We shall finish with this procedure later."

"Zat'z inadvizable, bezidez I'm up to my elbowz in ziz zhit already."

CHIPPER! CHIPPER!

"YAK YAK! YAK YAK!"

"Zere you go again!"

CHIP- CHIP- CHIPPER!

"YAKITY YAK YAK!"

"You getz yourselv all exzited over notzink! Your adreneline zhootz vay upz! Un zuddenly ze vlood in ze bazement'z a deluge!"

"EXCITED OVER NOTHING? AN UPRISING IN THE STREETS NECESSITATING A FULL-SCALE INTERVENTION BY THE BRITISH ARMY IS NOTHING?"

"Zo maybe notz notzink, but notzink vortz burztink a gazket ove-…"

"IN THE MIDST OF THE LARGEST BENEFIT CONCERT EVER CONCEIVED, BROADCAST LIVE AS WE SPEAK ACROSS FIVE CONTINENTS?" His Eminence is more than leaking, he's seething.

"Lotz ov over expozure, ziz iz true, but ztill…"

"THE ENTIRE DEBACLE SPONSORED BY QUOTLINK INC, WITH MY NAME WRIT LARGE ALL OVER IT — AND YOU SAY I HAVE NOTHING TO WORRY ABOUT, YOUIMPUDENTMEDICALIMPOSTER!"

"…un lotz ov itjy aggravation too…"

"Sir! If I may spea-…"

"AGGRAVATION!" His Eminence spouts.

"Vow, zat'z zome geyzer!"

He spouts and he spouts, about the mouth and out the down spout too.

"My cripez! Ze main von't budge!"

"Aah aaah…"

"Guezz ve juzt gotz to go vitz ze vlow…"

"...*aaaaaaaaah*..."

"...un mop everytzink upz later."

"...*uh*..."

Except sudden fluid loss causes the Executive Liaison to lapse into shock. His tongue stops moving, his eyes glaze over.

"You must do something to stanch the flow doctor!"

"I'm tryink, I'm tryink."

"Might I suggest a tourniquet."

"Zat vould pop hiz old eyeballz clear outz ov zeir zocketz – un zinze vhen did you ezpionage typez become medical exzpertz?"

"The situation is obviously dire."

"Yez vell, I zuppoze I could cork him vone vitz my big toe? You agree vitz me, zat ve muzt rezort to suj an invazive prozedure, yez?"

The QSS lieutenant is non-committal.

"Zen ztand back my lovely lieutenant, here goez!" WHACK!

"AAACK!"

"Bullzeye!"

"YOU YOU YOU..."

"Zorry Eminenze, muzt've hit a zenzitive zpot, yez?"

"...YOU ...YOU SO ENJOY HUMILIATING ME, DON'T YOU? YOUGROVELING DEVIANTDRUDGE!"

"Ze lieutenant here, he agreed."

"Sir. If I may speak candidly."

"WHAT IS IT, YOUMEALYMAGGOTMOTTLEDMOLE?"

"Ye-yes Sir! I regret the untimely interruption..."

"Ze untimely eruption."

"...but I must inform you that while the subject of concern has indeed arrived, there has been a slight altercation at the airport."

"Back door plumbink vaz never my zpecialty, no ziree bob, vhat could be more dizguztink zan crawlink tzrough zomebody elze'z drain pipez."

"And?"

"He has escaped. Sir."

"ESCAPED!" His Eminence spits, spits all over the QuotLink specialist in his full dress blacks.

"Vhat vaz zat? Zaliva or more hydraulic vluid?"

The lieutenant doesn't blink, doesn't wipe. "Regrettably, the security contingent we had assigned him in Melbourne was overwhelmed at Heathrow by a heav-..."

"OVERWHELMED?" His Eminence swills about the mouth.

"...by a heavily armed group of terrorists... terrorist feminists."

"TERRORIST WHAT?" The Liaison launches another globular lob.

"Feminists Your Eminence!" The QSS officer is forced to wipe a direct hit to the eye.

"Jezuz, iz hydraulic. Meanz I've gotz to go poke my head in zere again!"

"Impossible. Feminism in all its disreputable guises — AAAAK! — has been dormant for decades."

"Ziz iz muj more zeriouz zan I had azzumed. Vhere'z my flazhlight — iz not like I can zee vhat I'm doink in ze dark."

"Not this particular gang." The specialist begs to differ. "They have been staging raids out of their base camp in Sheffield into the Midlands and East Anglia with increased frequency, engaging in various covert activities, most recently in the vicinity of Thetford…"

"Let'z zee, vitj valve iz it? I zhould have labeled zem. I tzink zat vone adjuztz ze filter function, un zoze two are kidneyz inz un outputz, but vhere iz zat ztinkink little zump pump I vantz to know."

"Thetford, what would revolutionary feminists be doing in Thetford?"

"Organizing local housewives into skeet shooting cells and overland biking brigades."

"Biking brigades?"

"Vhat'z vitz all ziz zhit! I'm a zurgeon, not a pipevitter."

"Motorbike brigades, to be more precise, and they have been quite successful, notably among single working mothers left alone with all the bills to pay, the noses to wipe and no husbands to wag a finger at…"

"Remindz me ov ziz zmug azz guy zittink next to me at ziz medical convention. He leanz over un he vhizperz, 'I've gotz myzelv a tzrivink little proctology practize.' Zo I repliez. 'About ze only zink I can tzink ov vorze zan a proctology practize vould be a tzrivink proctology practize.'"

"Although the incident tonight at Heathrow is purportedly their first excursion this far southward, cleverly exploiting the confusion occasioned by this ersatz rock concert to infiltrate London."

"Cut to the quick of it lieutenant, what are their specific demands?"

"'Takez a zpezial talent to be a good proctologizt,' he confidez. Un I had to agree vitz him on zat point."

"They seem concerned primarily with high retail prices and claim that consumer debt is the modern day equivalent to slavery. Their agenda is nothing less than the destruction of the credit card and the overthrow of the established male banking order with its replacement by an absolute cash-and-carry matriarchy."

"*SOMUCHDIMWITTEDSPECULATIVENONSENSE!*"

"'Tzink I'll ztick to zurgery myzelf,' I zayz to him, 'but oh zoze lawzuitz, zoze vill be ze debt ov me yet.'"

"What do these women want with- with-…"

"Jipper Ztirbee, spitz it out!"

"…him, ransom?"

"Perhaps."

"No one would pay a penny to ransom that reprobate!"

"He is a symbol of the times Your Eminence."

"Of the times. Of all that man has degenerated into since the social demise of the 60s."

"Precisely, and the publicity they-…"

"*Meddlesomemobofmuffdivers!* Publicity? Well if publicity is what they want in exchange for his remains, we shall give them publicity in abundance — what's one more wild animal act thrown into this circus? Initiate negotiations immediately."

"Sir."

"Their presence could provide us with the perfect cover — no one would blame us. Why we were attempting to provide protection against this very sort of contingency. Any harm that might come to him would in turn weaken their cause."

"To the contrary Your Eminence, we at QSS would advise restraint in negotiating with such groups, because giving into one seemingly innocuous demand from an organization this determined will only encourage more demands. Why if they had succeeded in capturing him, I tremble at the thought of what they migh-…"

"*IF?* Did I hear you correctly, did you say *IF?*" His Eminence sputters and spills, spills over his lower lip again and down his chin.

"Yipez!" Accompanied by spastic contractions. "He'z zhiftink into zpin zycle."

"Ye- yes Your Eminence, he was able to escape their ambush at the last second, in what I must say was a quite remarkable feat of daring-do…"

"WHY ARE YOU WASTING MY TIME DISCUSSING THIS CONSPIRATORIAL DRIVEL, YOUSPINELESSWHIPSHITEFFETEINTELLECTUALFOP…"

"Vill you qvit vitz ze zcreamink vor Chrizzakez, un me vitz my head ztuck inzide ziz gyratink ztink hole!"

"…WHEN ALL I NEED KNOW IS WHERE HE IS AT THIS PRECISE MOMENT!"

"Sir! We at QSS can only conjecture…"

"CONJECTURE!"

"He'z dilatink dangerouzly! Meanz he'z gettink ready to blow!"

"We have reliable information that after some acrobatics at the airport, he boarded a small helicopter, a common sea rescue and salvage model, which is more than likely making its way here toward Wembley… sir…"

"I sense a hesitation in your voice."

"The a- the a- helicopter is reported to be flying rather erratically."

"I had assumed that our own corporate security fleet was ferrying the celebrities to and from Heathrow."

"This over-zealous pilot from some small towing and salvage company unexpectedly intervened in the ground dispute."

"Walk me through this one more time if you will, step-by-step. You are telling me that Chi- *pp- pp-*..."

"Jipper Ztirbee!"

"...yes ...is aboard some small commercial helicopter which you cannot identify with precision and that in addition you are uncertain whether or not he is presently on course to Wembley. Is that a fair representation of the facts as you understand them?"

"Presumably. Yes Sir."

"Yez zir notzink – Hiz Eminenze iz about to unleazh a torrential tantrum!"

"WHILE THE ENTIRE WORLD AWAITS HIS ARRIVAL, WHILE A MARAUDING HORDE STORMS TOWARD THE GATES OF THIS STADIUM, WHILE THE FATE OF QUOTLINK INC HANGS IN THE BALANCE..." The Liaison is standing on top of the lieutenant's toes and showering him with invective. "...MY FATE IN PARTICULAR – AND YOU CANNOT STATE WITH ANY DEGREE OF RELIABILITY WHEN HE WILL BE ARRIVING HERE AT WEMBLEY?"

"We- we- we- we know he is heading in a general north, northeasterly direction." The QSS officer is drenched to the skin. "And we postulate that he would never willingly disappoint his fans, therefore we can assume with some degree of certainty that he will be arriving here at Wembley sometime in the very near fut-..."

"I gotz to popz myzelv outz ov here un qvick!"

"*YOUPRATTLINGINSUBORDINATETWIT!*" And with that said, the Liaison lets flow a waterfall of phlegm, or some such greasily green and gritty that flushes the unsuspecting QSS officer over the handrail from this uppermost balcony of the stadium and down a backbreaking cascade of bleachers into a pulp of plasma on the field below where groundskeepers at the ready with a pressure vac suck up his rheumy remains.

"Jezuz!" Queezac stares over the rail. "I guezz ve've zeen ze lazt ov him."

"YOU DARE QUESTION ME OR MY MOTIVES?"

"Zertainly not."

"THERE ARE MANY MANY MORE WHERE HE CAME FROM."

"Ziz iz true, but he had suj nize dimplez."

"AND THERE ARE MORE OF THOSE WHERE HE CAME FROM!"

"Yez vell, but none ov me, no ziree-bob, I'm vone ov a kind, yezzir, I'm a real original. Bezidez ve go back Eminenze, you un me, to anotzer time, to anotzer age, remember vhen ve firzt met in ze men'z room ov ze Hotel Grand Ziozity in Belgrade at ze end ov ze Greatezt Var in memory, vhen ze Zerb Reziztanze vaz burztink tzrough ze doorz to get at ze collaboratorz hidink in ze bazement un ve had to ezcape down ze zewer togetzer?"

"*Murkydunkinthedrink!* Somethings in life we can fortunately forget."

"Yez vell vell…"

"Are you about finished with your work on the undercarriage?"

"Almozt Eminenze, I juzt gotz to noze back in zere, zee exzactzly vhat it iz I'm dickerink vitz."

"THEN GET TO IT!"

"Yez yez, but you've gotz to ztay calm, take a deep breatz – un zhouldn't ve be talkink about zometzink extra in ze vay ov hazard pay?"

"GET!"

"I'll juzt be a zecond – incomink!"

"UUUUUUUUUUUUUUUUUUUUU!"

"Zo zorry."

"YOUDECREPITCRAYFISH!"

And truly Queezac bears a resemblance to a crustaceon, though more an upright snapping turtle, stubs for legs and for arms, large frontal molars better adapted to gouge or to tear than to chew, and a powerful vertebral shell to protect from any backside attacks.

"Then what do you inferiors understand of real power, the power to finance empires or reduce them to rubble with a midnight raid on their currency – uu uuuuu…"

"Vhoopz, juzt zcrewed ziz pinjcap in upzide down, zat'z all."

"…the power to buy and sell the future of millions, for billions…"

"Vone zmall tveek un you're goink to breeze zo muj eazier."

"…under the cover of international competition for global market share, with minimal government interference… -UUUCK!"

"Zat about doez it, zurprizink yez? A qvickie in un out vaz all it took."

"QUEEZAC!"

"Vhat can I zay, everytzink'z tvisted up nize un tight ze vay you like it, no dribz, no drabz, no zpitz, no zpaz, zo I guezz I'll go vash my handz ov ziz mizerable mezz un be on my vay, boy-yo-boy vill I ever be, gotz to ready mine zurgery vor our unzuzpected guezt, Jipper Ztirb-…"

"SOMEDAY QUEEZAC!"

"Don't go gettink yourselv upzet now. Remember iz all ztrezz. You've gotz to avoid ztrezz. Bezidez ziz vaz juzt a qvick vix, zat'z it, no extended varrantiez on partz or labor."

"SOMEDAY!"

"Here ve go, I can hear it comink. Virzt he ztartz in vitz ze tzreatz, no tzank-you notez vrom you, no dearezt doc, I appreziatez how you gotz me up un runnink vitzout too muj pain un zuvverink."

"YOUMUCKCOATEDMOLLUSK! YOUCLUBFOOTEDCRAB!"

"Next comez ze inzultz, no patz on ze back vor hiz loyal old var buddy, no ziree bob, Queezac'z juzt zome longtime convenienze ztore kickbag."

"WHY IS IT I ALWAYS HAVE TO COUNT ON YOU IN A CRUNCH?"

"Yez vell, zat'z a compliment ov zortz, izn't it, I mean a little zometzink to keep me cominK back vor more abuze."

His Eminence stands erect, the six foot plus of him, buckles his trousers. Queezac cringes. For this is no ordinary mortal, no, this is QuotLink Inc's Executive Liaison for the Entire Northern Hemispheric Region, a master of high finance, though schooled in the law, an alternate member of QuotLink Inc's very Council of Elders and their official representative at this evening's extravaganza. As such he is tailored impeccably in a double breasted gray silk suit of Italian design, a QL monogrammed silk shirt, silver engraved QL cufflinks, silver threads of hair, long and sparse and combed from one side across and woven into the other side, thereby to partially conceal a pointy bald crown, though this tonsorial contrivance of last resort serves instead to accentuate his skeletal features, his pale gray skin, his thin lips and slight jaw. Power lieth not in appearances however, which the Executive Liaison wields with utmost ease, a wave of his hand usually sufficing — yet of late he has been bedeviled by this dribble about the chin and an occasional drab down his pant leg.

"Nothing Queezac, I tell you nothing shall be permitted to slip out of my control, not this time." His Eminence dribbles and drabs some.

"Zat'z ze zpirit, ztick it to zem."

"I shall rain down terror if I must."

"Vell, you're goink to need a vull revill bevore you attempt zat trick."

"And destroy them utterly!"

"Like ze Vizeazz Old Vizard who had zcalez like a Lizard."

"No, no no, I shall not tolerate another of your ridicu-…"

"He ztirred up a Blizzard, zat Nazty Old Gizzard, un paid Holy Hell vhen it Vizzled."

"Fizzled? That doesn't rhyme — FIZZLED DOESN'T RHYME WITH GIZZARD! YOUSPITERIVENGARGOYLE! PROOF THAT YOU MAKE THESE STORIES UP ON THE SPOT, SIMPLY TO IRRITATE ME!"

That said, His Eminence plants a heel on the backside — NO -OOF -OW — hide of the creature, heel to toe to toe, heel, Queezac rolled up in his shell, kickball off the glass walls of the skybox — OW-OOP-OH-OOF-OFF…

Meanwhile QuotLink Inc's Corporate Security Corps, bolstered by newly arrived British regulars with water canon on half-tracks, tightens their formation outside the stadium where an updated estimate of three million teenage fans have now gathered to await the arrival of Chipper Stirbee, rock 'n' roll's last living legend, and the source of acute irritation to the Executive Liaison — OOF-OW-OFF-OLF — nobody whom anybody sane, savvy or sober would ever want to fuck with.

CHIPPER!

A cry of anticipation arises from the crowd, and how is it they know so instinctively, those inside the walls as well as the many more stranded outside and overflowing onto the North Circular, blocking traffic on the M1 clear to Northampton?

They know they know, and their cries reach to the furthest heavens.

CHIPPER!

Startles the giant QuotLink Inc blimp in the sky awake and sets a light display in motion — QUOT • LINK • INC • • PRE • SENTS • • CHIP • PER • STIR • BEE • • RE • U • NITED • WITH • • THE • LOOSE • NUKES • • AN • AL • LIED • FOR • LIFE • • BEN • E • FIT • CON • CERT — scrolling amidst the stars.

WHUPWHUPWHUPWHUPWHUPWHUPWHUP

"Nifty little machine you've got heah Scotty. Reminds me of the mountain buggies we use fah trail blazin back home in Nohthuhn Maine."

"Seahorse 2004, designed fir search n rescue operations, which is wha ah do fir a livin, except on a night like this when they need ev'ry bloke they can find ta do double-duty. But she's a sturdy burd. Ah've fished workmen off a'drillin rigs wi the North Sea blowin like a Bangkok pro."

"Must come in mighty handy fah prowlin around town nights too."

"Right you'a mate. Comfirtable, but compact, buil'ta maneuver in n ou'ta tight situations."

"That what you do best, maneuvah in and out of tight situations?"

"I've had mi share a'up n downer, spare time a'course."

"Bet. Bet you do. Hahd not to scohe with this contraption."

-hmmph! Betsy had mistook the young Scotsman for a gentleman.

"Ah cou'tell you a few stories. You say you fly?"

Fly! This guy's feet never touch ground.

"Well soht of. Couhse my mountain buggy can't lift off oah land as easy as youhs, hell no, get aihbohne in mine and you've got youhhself a heap of trouble. H'yep. I've taken some nasty spills tryin to hop a gully off a mowed-down pine ridge with no propellah, no wings, just a sawed-off truck frame and fouh tihes, engine, steehrin wheel, gas drum fah a seat, sometimes lights, sometimes no lights, no brakes, no nothin — flooh the suckah and go, switch off the engine and roll right up on some gal's window, oah pop it in geah and get away fast if theah's a dude inside theah with huh — head cross country, nobody'd evah know fah suhe it was you, just a fast pass and leave huh blinkin."

"Sounds like a fuckin good playtime craft ta me."

"You could say that, and cheap. Definitely low tech. Spahe pahts rustin in the yahd. Nothin like what you've got heah, no way, plus youhs flies. Why a fella could just kick back, crank up the tunes and take in the view." Chipper settles into his seat, adjusts the harness holding him in, rustles Betsy who's perched on his lap, albeit precariously.

WHUPWHUPWHUPWHUP -CH WHUPWHUP

"You got a rattle in the reah?"

"Somethin could'av broke loose in the rukkus, but nothin on the panel's flashin at me. Looks like we'a a'right fir new."

"So how about veerhin off couhse, see some London aftah dahk?"

"Strikes me the prime order a'the day is get yu ta Wembley, as soon as."

"Ohdahs. Have I had some ohdahs in my life, mahchin ohdahs, couht ohdahs – by the way, ah theah any rules against smokin aboahd this rig?"

"Thir's a'ways goin ta be rules."

"No rule that can't be bent some, right?"

"Wha can I say ta a celebrity like yurself?"

"Tell him to step out and hike like anybody else – heah, have a toke of this shit."

"Woul knock yu back if ah wisna flyin."

"Best homegrown evah."

-o moan...

"This is men's business Betsy, doesn't concahn you – stuff's totally ohganic, no pesticides, no chemical fahtilizahs, just loose moose shit and muddy Maine rivah watah, and sun, lots of hot sun whole summah long – have a sample? Couple of puffs'll set youh mind on cruise control."

"Got ta keep misell straight Chipper."

"Hey, man's bohn to fly high, play the dahedevil on the sly – I'll blow a little youh way. H'yep. That'll get you goin."

"Hodd- hodd-..."

"Told you so."

WHUP WHUP WHUP -UP

"...hodd on mates!"

As the helicopter swings way wide, wide high loop-the-loop in the sky.

"*Whoo-ee!* Guess I arrived just in time fah the aih show!"

"Somethin's naw right!"

"What, theah's mah to come?"

WHOOF   WHOOF

Cab starts in rotating.

WHOOF   WHOOF   WHOOF

Scotty rears back on his stick... back... rears back, back on his stick... "Fuckin grab on ta somethin. Ah'm tellin yu, wi'r headin inta a dive!"

Not to worry, Betsy has her claws dug in deep, into Chipper's thighs.

"Damn! This is bettah than a Fouhth of July cahnival ride!"

WHOOF   WHOOF   WHOOF WHOOF WHOOF
-row   -row   -row

"Ride'em cowboy!"

Scotty's holding… holding back…

"You've got to buck huh 'til you bust huh!"

"Appreciate the advice, ah really do, but ah think — naw that ah'm sure — but… but she migh'be kickin back inta shape…"

Helicopter levels off. Doesn't stall, not at all.

WHUPWHUPWHUPWHUPWHUPWHUP

"Awesome."

"Borin would'av bin better."

"Heah, I'll blow some mah smoke youh way, steady youh nehves."

"Must be somethin ou'ta balance." And without warning Scotty goes into another spin…

WHOOP   WHOOP

…round they go again, round and out at a tangent toward the center of London — see the sights: Buckingham Palace on your left, upside down, Parliament over there, floating along in its own reflection, and directly ahead — *whoa! whoa!* — the Tower of London looming square up at you.

"You suhe you'h not paht of some show-off stunt team Scotty?"

"Wish ah was Chipper, then ah would know what ah wis doin!"

Chipper doesn't mind, he's high on his homegrown and simply along for the ride, though Betsy's all wide eyed and restless, tongue hung out.

"I vote we flooh this suckah and soah…"

"Somethin's def'nit'ly naw right!"

"…see how high we can fly — cause you know we've only got so much time in this life befah somethin unexpected comes chahgin!"

whupwhupwhup -ch whup -ch -ch whupwhup

Could be the cabin clouded up with prime smoke, or the *chunk chunk* sound coming from back near the tail rudder.

"OK alright, I need footage gentlemen, I need filler — *snap snap* — replays, interviews, commentary from the field, whatever you can put your hands on. And let's check for volunteers to go on stage because after Sore Losers we are fresh out of talent — and Lou, my friend, what's that program clock there on the wall telling us — *snap snap?*"

"Time. Time is 23:07:26, that's 11:07 PM and 26 seconds."

"Which means we have fifty two minutes and thirty four seconds left before the Grand Finale."

"Cub, a man has got to have faith in the future, not everything in life can be timed to the sec-…"

"From here on in we're running on Chipper Stirbee time, right?"

"Chipper has never missed a performance, never in his entire career, and he'd never disappoint the band, c'mon, reuniting the Loose Nukes is a dream come true for him. He's been looking forward to this night for decades, and his fans, he loves his fans…"

"And he's never shown up on time for one goddamn thing in his life!"

"Punctual, no, I grant you Chipper Stirbee is not punctual, but what he brings to the occasion is well worth the wait, it's part of his persona, his celebrity, it builds anticipation, the crowd grows wild with excitement."

"We don't need a crowd as edgy as this growing wild with excitement."

"Cut the guy some slack Cub, he opened in San Francisco yesterday at dawn, set down for an appearance in Melbourne at noon and he's about to wrap it up for us here tonight at midnight, or… slightly thereafter."

"Can't be slightly thereafter, that's what I'm telling you — filler, I need filler gentlemen — a production like this is too big for adolescent antics — we need broadcast footage, something to fill gaps in airtime, let's go, let's go — *snap snap* — any of you characters into impromptu? How about commercials, anything in the queue, something we haven't played fifty times over already?"

"We have plenty of public service announcements left." One of the programmers down front shouts back.

"Stick with the payload first, OK? But line up whatever else you can find because we're definitely going to be winging it from here on in, right Lou — *snap snap* — that right Lou? You still with us?"

"Right, right right, I'm right here." In body if not in mind, for Lou is Louis B. Starcrave, the Loose Nukes' long-time manager, and he has been through it, years of it, good times and worse, dating all the way back to the late 60s when Chipper and the guys were lugging their own equipment around and playing basement clubs on the Lower East Side of New York City, when they cut *Getta Girl*, the hit that rocketed them to fame if not fortune, and Lou was there when they crashed and burned sixteen months later. It was Lou who kept the flame alive over time, collected the pennies in royalties and rediscovered Chipper buried alive in the deep Maine woods sixteen months ago to the day, today, tonight, midnight, with the whole world watching, and edgy, the kids amassed outside the stadium no more edgy than he, squirming around in his swivel chair, but goddamn it Lou Starcrave has earned the right to squirm around in his swivel chair.

"23:10:11 — *snap snap* — Chipper should be landing by now, but surprise surprise, let's take a look at the monitors in the auto park. See. Nobody's landing on that pad they cordoned off, which means the Loose Nukes haven't been reunited yet, no way, they're just standing around waiting like we are."

"I understand, honestly I do."

"Then there's me and the guys to consider, we've been working round the clock for three days now, patching together hundreds of sites worldwide so we can broadcast this tricky live five continent simulcast you creative folks dreamed up, thousands of the world's celebrities marching shoulder-to-shoulder in solidarity and lip-syncing this freeging Grand Finale for what is it… what's the in cause for tonight's benefit?"

"The environment?"

"The environment, like one song's going to solve that in a *SNAP!*"

"Bringing so many world leaders together in a show of unity on this issue is a giant step forward Cub, maybe not the end-all, of course not, but a beginning, a new initiative, a commitment among concerned people everywhere in unison with their cultural heroes, their spiritual leaders, a commitment that until tonight would have been considered impossible, I mean even you have to admit that one of the few, if not the only celebrity on the planet who could pull this feat off is Chipper Stirbee."

"Please. Hype is lost on a guy like me. Why? Because I've sat in this chair too long, I've seen too much, close-up. It's you creative guys that thrive on illusion. Reality's not virtual for me, it's real, it's right here in front of me every night, I'm front line all the time."

"I understand, yours is the newsman's perspective, you see the blood and the guts, history in the making, but-…"

"Stop. I've got a job to do, me and my crew have been up for 72 hours."

"I sit here amazed with what you fellows can do, and make it seem as easy as a left-handed pass."

"AND TIMED TO A MILLISECOND LOU, TIMED TO A MILLISECOND — *snap snap snap snap* — DO YOU HEAR ME?"

He hears, his ears are ringing, Cub rising slightly from his seat and shouting into his ear. How can he not hear?

"TIME, I NEED TO KNOW THE TIME! *SNAP! SNAP!*"

"11:14:58." Someone down front shouts out while someone else closer by shoves a cola in front of him, which Cub chugs, one big gulp because Cub McCluff's a sugar user, along with caffeine — Copa Colas by the cartons, man thrives on his liquid lube jobs, and coffee too, sick black with ten-packs of sugar — *synap synap* — Cub's body chemistry in constant alert mode, hyper-active from infancy through to middling age, Type-A type, heart attack type, and a chain smoker to boot, non-filtered Slug Rites, a lung full of which sits him back down on his swivel chair with a crunch.

While Lou swallows, chokes actually, restricted about the thorax because he is another type altogether, a phlegmatic B type, gloomy with an acid vat for a stomach and no sweet tooth. Man hardly eats at all. Thin, intense, with dark circles under his eyes, Lou's been through it too, and he's going through it again tonight, caught between Chipper and a clock. Poor fellow's nearly bent over double with anxiety in his swivel chair, and besides that he is smoking, which a man in his condition shouldn't be doing, Cub's cigarettes, which a man in his condition shouldn't be doing.

"So tell me, calmly, quietly, concisely, just so I know, just so I can plan – about how much longer do you figure this boy of yours will be delayed?"

"I-*hi*, I don't know, half an hour?" Truth is Lou hasn't a clue. Chipper doesn't clear his plans in advance with him, nor with anybody, and like what plans does Chipper have anyway, another toke before nightfall and he'll be off to another lights out adventure.

"Half an hour – GET REAL!" And Cub rises slightly out of his seat.

"Alright, maybe an hour."

"TRY TWO HOURS, FOUR, DAYBREAK IF HE FEELS LIKE IT, THAT'S AFTER A SEX AND DRUG BINGE WITH A BUSLOAD OF UNDERAGED CHEERLEADERS!"

No no, not that again, banging on Lou's brain. Decades pass and people can't forget, photographs, the lurid worst grainy kind, naked on front pages of hometown newspapers coast-to-coast, and nothing he could think to say could make a difference. 'Hell, he's only a teenager himself,' he'd argue, but who in a courtroom cares to listen when the law is aligned against you and consent's not the issue...

"LOU – *SNAP* – YOU'RE OUT OF IT!"

"Wha- wha- where am I?"

"SAME PLANET YOUR BUDDY COMES FROM, THAT'S WHERE!" Cub's standing over him, Cub's bearing down on him.

"Cub," a techie shouts, "Sore Losers finishing up their set."

"OK alright, no need to panic – *snap snap* – we need filler gentlemen, we need filler – *snap snap* – FILLER, WE NEED FILLER!"

Techies on their consoles scramble. Lou breathes deep, breathes a mouthful of smoke deep deep.

"AND WILL SOMEBODY EXPLAIN TO ME WHAT IS IT I'M LOOKING AT ON STAGE RIGHT NOW?"

"Crew moving equipment."

"THAT'S WHAT WE'RE BROADCASTING ON LIVE SATELLITE AT $20 MIL A MINUTE?"

"I've got a couple of interviews with the fans almost lined up."

"ALMOST'S NOT GOOD ENOUGH!"

There's a rustle around the control truck.

"WHERE ARE ALL THOSE DIGITAL READICAMS WE PAID THE BIG BUCKS FOR?" As Cub leans over his desk and peers into the layered array of seventy some monitors flashing before his eyes.

There are stationery line-fed cameras placed strategically on platforms all over the stadium, but the production tonight depends on thirty readicams, palm-sized ultra-HD remotes with infrared feeds that a slew of free-lance crews are using to cover every angle of the performance, on-stage, backstage, roaming through the crowd and outside the stadium too.

Techies are all over their consoles trying to trace some of these dudes. "Must be out back Cub. You ordered everything we could spare to head for the parking lot to cover Chipper's landing, remember?"

"REMEMBER SHIT, THAT'S WHAT I PAY YOU GUYS FOR!" Cub is pounding a fist on his desk and bellowing. "I NEED FILLER GENTLEMEN, SOMETHING LIVELY, SOMETHING SNAPPY — *SNAP! SNAP!*"

Someone slips Cub another cola.

One of the stationery cameras panning the stage picks up a rustle of a skirt in the wings, curled auburn hair.

"Hold on, that's Molly Dawkens!"

"WHERE?"

"A-3."

Sure enough. The auburn hair. Must be Molly Dawkens. One of the Loose Nuke originals. Famous for doing those gruff throated back-up vocals and the guys too.

"OK, alright gentlemen, heads up, looks like we've finally caught something worthwhile. Zoom in on her — *snap snap* — closer, get a readicam on her — closer, closer — get a readicam right up on that pouty mug of hers and fast before we lose her — SNAP SNAP SNAP SNAP — FAST FASTER — ANY OF YOU MORONS EVER DONE A LIVE ROCK CONCERT BEFORE?"

The roar gets the young guys with the remotes running here, there like a fire brigade, while Cub McCluff slumps back in his swivel chair, crushes the cola can in one tight squeeze and tosses it over his shoulder, sprawling big bear of a man, thick dark beard and patient neither with himself nor with anybody else in the control truck parked center field at Wembley. But then Cub can't afford to be easy, he's QuotNet's premier location man. Has two convoys of Boeing 1107 wide-bodies loaded with crew, cameras, and sound equipment that can leapfrog him anywhere around the globe on less than an hour's notice. Last few weeks he's had to cover the President's disastrous tour of Far East Asia, next the World Series back again in Toronto, and right as he's coming off another major oil spill in Prince William Sound, QuotNet orders him to London to manage the largest benefit concert ever staged, a forty two camera set-up at Wembley with slightly smaller scale productions at companion stadiums in Melbourne and San Francisco, and broadcast into an estimated five billion living rooms — an alignment of thirty seven satellites in the largest celestial network ever assembled for a live worldwide telecast — a resounding first in video tech history — but it isn't happening if Cub McCluff and his crew aren't there to witness it, loyal hard-drinking rib-thick buddies, everyone of them, and if Cub cracks the whip above their heads, they hunker over their consoles and they row the harder, each command punctuated with a couple of sharp finger snaps — *snap snap* — "Broadcast!"

And sure enough it's close-up on Molly Dawkens, peering out from behind a curtain, the green-eyed beauty who drove the early Loose Nukes to rift and to ruin, but who can still belt it out back-up and raise catcalls from the stalwart young gents in the rear of the hall.

But a glimpse is all you get. Molly's a restless spirit and so easily distracted. She turns her pretty head and wanders off out of sight line.

"WHAT'VE WE GOT NEXT IN THE QUEUE — *SNAP SNAP?*"

"I've got footage of the early Loose Nukes in the archives."

"WE'RE MAKING HISTORY FREDDY, NOT REPLAYING IT!"

"Check out the zoom Cub, we've caught Will Cook off guard."

Sure enough there's Will Cook on a monitor, Loose Nuke keyboardist and tunesmith who in partnership with Chipper gave the world some of its all time greatest rock 'n' roll hits, that's back in the 60s, but who's best known today for eluding all close contact, with a camera, with a reporter, with any warm-bodied human or less than which is why he's perched alone way high up above center stage on his own specially raised platform and banging out some sort of song for his own amusement. You can hear him, but you cannot see him.

"OK, alright. Cue on the zoom…"

Zoomocrane™ rises up slowly, imperceptibly, rotates — a 360º remote attached to the tip of a forty foot boom that runs along a track in front of the stage — sucker rears up and catches Will Cook mid-act.

"…that's three, that's two and broadcast — *snap snap!*"

Head bobbing up and around, earphones plugged into a jack, man's in a trance behind stands stacked with keyboards, Kurzweils and Korgs, synthesizers and samplers, all controlled by an antique Mac — when he abruptly comes eye-to-eye with the nosy remote — he flips, damn near goes careening backwards off his stool!

"Hooked him — *snappity snap snap!*"

Though the last laugh's on Cub, Will Cook recoils, roils and rolls out what's got to be the longest tongue in the business, flaps it smack at the intruding lens in a come-lick-me manner.

"Yuk! Ready on commercial?"

"Stand by on commercial!"

"Ready and counting three, two and *snap snap* cut!"

It's a panoramic view of a picnic scene from Northern California. Sheep grazing on hilltops, giant redwoods in the gullies, mud slides and washed out highways, a youngish Silicon Valley couple out for a romantic afternoon on a fault line, basket, blanket, Napa Valley wine, and she's tapping something on her user-friendly laptop. She smiles. He peers over her shoulder. It's *"I love you."* squiggling on the liquid green gelatin screen, but wait, hold on the kiss... there's another message emerging — *"Eat me!"* the machine advises — and they do, they both chomp delectably away at the keyboard for it's Dexter Rob's most ingenious invention yet, the wafer thin, completely biodegradable portable computer, one that's entirely edible, smack down to the crispy rye CPU, and available in four additional energy packed whole grain flavors from the local wheeler-dealer nearest you.

Although nothing, not television history nor rambling rockstars nor teenagers barraging the arena, none of it ruffles HRH the Queen, nary in the least, Her Ageless Majesty in attendance and taking the parade in stride, one of the remote cameras permanently encamped at the foot of the Royal Box She shares with Her grandsons, the randy Windsor heirs, Wills and Harry, and their newly arrived half-brother Izzy. For all eyes, those of the young, those of the wary, wait in anticipation of Chipper Stirbee's imminent arrival and the historic Loose Nuke reunion, and after that the Grand Finale which will bring together a thousand of the world's truly rich and famous, whether in person or electronically, rock stars and movie stars, religious leaders, the Pope Himself standing by in Rome, Imams and Rabbis and shaved-headed Tibetan monks, preachers and politicians, presidents, sovereigns, rogue generals-for-life, greatness and glitter gathering by satellite — all on screen live and timed to a millisecond — this night of nights at midnight (or slightly thereafter) on the giant stage at Wembley — AL • LIED • FOR • LIFE • • BEN • E • FIT • CON • CERT — the most spectacular event ever, with proceeds (minus production and management costs) dedicated to restoring the environment and to eradicating hunger and poverty among humankind forever, along with noisome peasant uprisings and pesky sexually transmitted diseases — the entire undertaking brought to you via QuotNet, a wholly owned subsidiary of QuotLink Inc, the only network licensed to broadcast without political interference into every nation, every city, every hamlet and hut on the face of the planet.

TIMES PAST

Lou stumbles out of the windowless control trailer center field for a breath of fresh air. He feels the ground pound under his feet and he's instantly engulfed by throngs of teenage partygoers. They dance around him and laugh and shout. The sights, the sounds remind him of another age, when he too was young. It was the 60s and things weren't so bleak for him, things were better, easier — an era of boundless opportunity and Lou Starcrave raring to take advantage, although Gertrude was around then as she remains today, lingering in spirit, the will power of one woman enduring throughout time in the embodiment of her one son.

Poor guy, desperate for at least one success in his what-seems-to-be-forever drifting Baby Boomer life, and making it happen if not for himself, then for Gertrude, his freshly dead mother who in Bayonne, New Jersey with final fits of wheezing had summed up her son as a "lump of a loser if ever I've seen one — *kuff-kuff* — and believe me I have because his father wasn't so much neither — *kuff-kuffkuffkuff...*" -THUD!

Certainly, if mothers can drive their sons, Gertrude Starcrave had driven hers, and where? To maniacal lengths to disprove her apt and oft repeated assessment.

Lou gaped at her face frozen into eternal disappointment and vowed he would not leave this earth without one notable achievement, and that is how his fate came to be linked with Chipper Stirbee's, not once but twice. And were apoplexy not to have overcome him at the moment of his greatest triumph, he would probably have told any reporter handy, almost anybody handy, that ambition too must learn its limits. But that powerful inspiration came late for him, much too late.

"Lou, you're not listening! You don't understand!"

The words resound as clearly as yesterday.

"The key in show business is to discover the new, search out the untested. Catch people's attention with something they don't expect."

The young Lou is running alongside Mel Nebberstoff, the founder of Askantics Records, and he is breathlessly trying to explain: "But I've got this great little act Mel, you have to see them to belie-…"

"I don't have time to audition everybody in the city."

"Yes but these three sisters, these three beautiful black girls, they're into church choir harmonies about innocent young love lost and found, they're from Hoboken, see, they work in a grocery store over there and I've named them the Superettes — I thought it was cute, but the name can be changed — and there's nothing in the world like them, nothing."

"You think not? How about the Primettes?" The older man keeps speeding along.

"OK name, I suppose — sounds a bit racist, but if you think it's bet-…"

"No you dummy, the Primettes? The Supremes? You've never heard of the Supremes?"

This is New York City, not Detroit, and no, he has never heard of the Supremes nor *Where Did Our Love Go?* — with the Baby / Baby refrain?

"How about *Stop In The Name Of Love?*"

And Lou has to acknowledge sadly yes, he has heard that on the radio.

"See, that's it! That's the problem!" The older man turns on a dime to face him. "You haven't been listening! And you have to listen! You have to be on top of everything — and to get on top, you have to take a chance! To catch a star, you have to take a risk! You have to reach for it, overreach!"

Risk? Reach? Lou has risked and risked again. And he's overreached, numerous times. And he has missed. He almost missed Chipper Stirbee and the Loose Nukes. Fact is he saw them many a night at the Green Pagoda in the East Village when they first began and paid scant attention, but then the Green Pagoda did have its distractions.

While the Loose Nukes went touring out west in Danny T's VW bus — that's after the drug bust at the pagoda in the East village — Lou was busy searching through the south in a rent-a-car. Refined hillbilly, or what those in the know were to call bluegrass was beginning to hit big, along with civil rights protests. Lou was in Okra County in Western Tennessee and he met Briar Daniels on the porch of a general store, one with a gas pump out front, one that somebody had to hop on a bicycle seat and pedal to prime. and Lou is pedaling and Briar is a'askin questions. "What's what that brangs yu down her'abouts, city boy?"

"Music. I'm a record promoter from New York." Lou is pedaling his heart out and in the hot sun.

"Recurd permoter, yu say?"

"That's ri right." He is pouring sweat.

"From New Yawk?"

"Tha-s, tha-s righ-t…"

"Don't need ta look no fu'tha boy, yu done found the best act round about these parts, and sittin right up har in the shade."

"Yeah?" Lou has to stop, and his tank is no more than a quarter full. "Are you sure, sure ther-'s... ther-'s any ga-s... in this pum-p?" He is already beginning to sound like one of them, with the heat and all, too much energy to enunciate.

"Don't much look like it, now does it?" Briar lights up a pipeful. "Guess yu'r gonna be stickin by ta har us do some singin ta-night."

The stage is the porch of the general store, and folks come from all over the county to see the show, bearin a stiflin heavy load of wet heat and drawin a crowd of mostly mosquitoes along with them. The older folks stand round, chattin or spattin. A few of the women sit in their car seats with the doors open and their feet stuck out, so they can hear even if they can't see, and the kids squat on the hoods of their roadsters, waitin.

Lou doesn't feel out of place there, nor time, just entirely alien. And people stare at him without blinkin or turnin away. But then he could be one of them eastern lib'ral activists they've heard tell about, comin down here where they don't belong an mindin ev'rybuddy else's business 'cept their own an complainin 'bout the rights a'colored folk who ev'rybuddy knows ain't got no rights ta begin with, so why go an give'em ta'em now, jus' goin ta stir'em up more'n they are a'ready.

There is one black in the crowd, a young kid attending the band and putting out jugs of something on a table on the porch for the band to sip, whenever it is they're plannin on showin up an beginnin.

Lou simply stands there. What else can he do? He has his arms folded in front of him, protective like, challenging if need be — not that he is a big guy, no way, Lou is skinny and intense, as then so now, with the striving and the driving using up all the energy most kids would apply to filling out. He is good-looking however, tie-dye, alert brown eyes, with an easy pleasing smile. The local young belles dripping in the heat glance over and lick their lips, but the young gents keep steppin in front, holdin him at bay.

With no signal at all, a few in the audience stop talking long enough to climb up on the porch. One is Briar Daniels. Another is a brother who looks just like him. Another a cousin. Each of various ages. But the last is a young girl, and before Lou can even think to ask her name, the crowd breathes out *Celestia*, and that she is, Briar Daniel's nach'ral daughter.

Briar picks up one of the jugs and blows across the head — *WHOOP!* The relatives dive in too, each liftin a jug an'a'blowin cross it — *FWOOP A'FWOOPA-WHOOP A'WHOOPA-HOOPF HOOPF* and *TOODA FROODA* — before long they'r'all a'huffin an a'puffin out a tune, the beautiful young girl's a'clappin an a'tappin her foot. After an opener with lots of wind and spit, a fiddler, a banjo picker and an old chin whisker who keeps rhythm on bones jump up on the porch, they start to play wildly. The young girl steps front, demurely waves the skirt of her dress, head tucked down, peekin up once in a while, and begins to sing in an angel sweet soprano:

> Buds on the vine / Butterfly wings
> Feel the breeze / Through the trees
> Waters in the falls / Whippoorwill trills
> Can't hold back the spring in its season
> Can't hold back the spring in its season

There's a heel-to-toe rhythm about the song that can't hold Celestia back from steppin. Few kicks at first, a lift of the skirts, then kick around, kick around, back around side, *click kick, click kick* 'til she's front and center.

> Fish in the pond / Frogs in the bog
> Chicks in the coop / Squirrels on the loose
> Girls in their prime / Boys dressed up fine
> Can't hold back the spring in its season
> Can't hold back the spring in its season

And round she jigs again

Crowd is breathless, as is Lou. The singer, this vision, the rhythm, the instrumental back-up — like nothing else Lou has ever heard. The new. The unexpected. Plus the millions that dance through his head, millions of records, millions of fans, millions of good ol' Yankee dollars.

He has a standard contract packed in his suitcase, and damned if the Daniels don't sign it, the whole family, cousins and all. They drive to Memphis to make a demo in a studio, and Lou mails it off to New York. He also makes a move on Celestia only to rouse the ire of her cousin Jasper who is plannin on marryin the girl once she turns of age, not that Lou gives up trying entirely, not at all. One night while they are pinin alone together on a screened porch in a motel in Memphis and waitin for a call from New York, he tries again. He touches Celestia's shoulder and plants a quick kiss on her neck. She doesn't seem to mind, so he slips a hand around her waist and up a little. She doesn't say no — so, so, soooo he handles a handful. She swats him right 'cross the back a'his head.

"Wha-da-ya thank yu're doin thar city boy?"

His head is a'jiggin, has he misread a cue?

"Whar I come from, boy's gotta get a girl good an liquored furst."

"Oh? Well. Whatever the custom." Lou eyes the glowing welcome sign of the County Line Liquor Store conveniently located across the highway.

"But then I don' drank, narry a drop." She smiles at him sweetly.

"*Ah-ah-* what's a guy got to do?"

"Run and buy me a candy bar. I like milk chocolate, never the too dark kind, with almonds and car-a-mel and white nougat fillin, yu know what brand I mean?"

He bounds out of that screened porch and across that highway. "You got a candy bar that is milk chocolate with almonds and caramel and white nougat filling, ah- fillin?" He shouts at the old geezer behind the counter.

"Take yur pick," the shopkeep waves at the candy array, "whatever's thar is what's I got."

He grabs a handful, and a pint of sour mesh whiskey too, local label, slaps a ten spot on the counter and bolts out the door.

Celestia's a'waitin for him when he gets back. She has pulled off her shoes and her socks and some white pair of somethings, and she tears into the candy like a kid, a'chompin, a'chewin an a'lickin her fingers, mouth full of a gooey sugary mess.

Lou slugs down the sour mesh, offers her a gulp, "Just to wash that crap down with."

She indulges a taste. "Whew, couldn't yu a'got nothin sweeter'n that?"

He is up and ready to shoot across that highway one more time when she pulls him down to the ce-ment floor. "Don't go runnin off again when I'm most al-ready." And she lifts her dress way up to her neck. Lou is writhing around on the ground trying to unbuckle his belt, untie his shoes, all the while tugging at his socks, when who, WHO, WHO do you expect walks in? Just Briar, his brother, old chin whiskers and her about-to-be betrothed cousin Jasper.

"CELESTIA!" Briar hollers. "Pull that dress a'yur'n down! T'ain't seemly. An city boy, pack that pecker back in yur pants. Thar ain't gonna be no baby makin ta-night."

It might be a bit humiliating, him on the floor unzippin and zippin up again, but he knows the time is a'ripenin. Yes ma'am, his chance is about to come. Next day the telephone actually rings — Mel Nebberstoff at Askantics Records. "You've got yourself something hot down there friend."

Does Lou know that, or does Lou know that?

New York is ready to take Celestia, Briar Daniels and all the tooters to their collective heart. Mel Nebberstoff is ready to record the song afresh with added electric guitar back-up and distribute it nationally. So Briar decides to drive his red Dodge pick-up all the way from West Tennessee up to New Yawk City, the black kid trying to stay awake in the front seat with him. But Briar gets lost somewhere on side roads in the wooded hills of Pennsylvania, while Lou and Celestia are finally, but oh so soundlessly making it in the back on a foam pad under a tarp, her uncle and her cousin Jasper a'sleepin an a'snorin on either side, chin whiskers barely breathin by the tailgate. Lou and Celestia feel the spark dance between them when all of a sudden the pick-up plunges off a narrow bridge and into the Delaware River. It's cold sludge water that pulls them apart, and Lou who is the only one who can't swim miraculously survives, he and the black kid who tends the jugs. And worse when he awakens from this long night of deep sleep, it's his mother Gertrude's hawk eyes he meets. They are glowering down upon him and she is repeating, loser, over and over again, loser… loser… He can only wish he had drowned along with the rest of them.

But Gertrude and Celestia — and that kissin cousin Amy at the Jersey seashore — they weren't the only women in his young life, no, there was Elli, during the heady days when he finally hooked up with the Loose Nukes.

There are feet rushing down some steps, and others bounding upwards two at a time — THUF- THUF- THUMP! — an artist's portfolio bursts and charcoals and pastels go cascading down the gum bespotted steps.

"Oh my God, I'm sorry! What have I done?"

"YOU'VE KNOCKED MY DRAWINGS ALL OVER THE STAIRS — THAT'S WHAT YOU'VE DONE!"

"I'm sorry, I'm really sorry, I was jus-…"

"Forget the sorrys, help me pick them up — HEY! WATCH WHERE YOU'RE STEPPING! — I'll get these, you get that one, and grab those over there before someone steps on them! HURRY!"

"I'm sorry, I'm awfully sorry."

"It's, it's — OHHHHH! — it's nothing really. I'm only an amateur anyway, and these weren't that good, they really weren't. It doesn't matter."

"Of course it matters, everything matters, and these drawings look great to me." Lou is holding a sheaf of pastel sketches, nudes, a woman sprawled back, another curved over, one standing from the rear. "These are great, wow, really great!"

"No they're not, you only like them because they're pictures of naked women!"

A young girl with horn rimmed glasses, straight brown hair, long legs and a long neck is straddling the steps down into the IRT subway station at Astor Place and explaining art theory to him. "If you look more closely, you can see. See the arm?"

"Yeah?"

"And the shoulder?"

"Yeah?"

"Well, they're all out of proportion. No shoulder would be that big with such a little arm."

"Picasso."

"But these aren't abstractions, these are representational, don't you know the difference?"

"Maybe not, I'm not an artist, I-..."

And her eyes catch his eyes, and he does have these brownies, gaping intense, his whole body intense sped-up metabolic, everything he eats generating energy, immediately expendable, a faster eater, walker, talker you could never meet, a real New Yorker, but an easy smile.

"My name is Lou, Lou Starcrave."

"Elli Vandenhook. You've ruined two weeks' worth of my drawings."

"I- I'm sorry, I'm really sorry. What can I do?"

"Nothing! You can't do anything."

"I could get you a new pad, some paint, some pencils."

"These are from my live drawing class."

"I'm sorry, I can- can't, could pose- pose nu-... whatever I could do to make up, I'd do gladly." He's breathless.

"Boys, always the same, and I'm going to be late — OH MY GOD, I'VE GOT TO GO! BYE!" She grabs her pages from him, crams them into her portfolio as she darts down the steps around him.

He's running fast behind her. She has a token, she's through the turnstile. He doesn't have a token, and the train is already in the station.

"Wait! Wait a minute."

"I can't. Bye!" At least she waves.

Lou hesitates, he does, he glances around quickly and then jumps the gate, mad dashes it toward the train.

"Hey boy, what the hell you think you'a doin. You gots to pay a toll jus' like ever'body else round here." This large fellow in a blue uniform with a flat little conductor's cap is charging after him, but somethings in life happen right in time, the train doors close in on Lou as he and the blue uniform meet face-to-face. There's a snarl through the window, but that's it, and the train rolls out of the station.

"I made it. I can't believe it. I made it! I MADE IT!"

Elli is clinging to a strap and watching him. After a minute more she smiles. "What did you say your name was?"

"Lou, and I'm sorry, I am, about your drawings and everything."

"They weren't that good."

"They looked great to me."

"Naked women, adolescent boy."

"No, that's not it, not at all."

"Yes it is, all adolescent boys think about is naked women and sex."

"No, that's not true."

Elli throws an impatient glance up to the ceiling, at a fan doing fits and starts at spinning in the overheated car — *whirr wh -ir -ir* — while he seizes the opportunity to look at her chest which for a young girl is developing amply. "I-... what I want to say is..." Lou attempts bravely "...is that you clearly have talent. Even you'd have to admit that."

"Even me, what do you mean *even* me?"

"Well I mean, I mean clearly... I mean you clearly don't value your own work, not sufficiently."

"I don't? Well for your information it so happens I do. I'm not negative about my work, not in the least. I simply know when I've done my best and when I haven't."

"So you have to admit you're good."

"I wouldn't have been invited to attend the Saturday Scholarship Program at Cooper Union if I didn't have *some* talent."

"No, you wouldn't, so see, you're good."

"I can get by." She takes her eyes off his eyes and glances back up at the fluttering fan blades – *wh- wh- wh* – she even stands up straighter, pokes them out. Lou zooms in again on her blouse, and smiles while he's doing it.

"What are you grinning about?"

"You, you're funny, I like you."

"You like my body."

"I- I- I-..."

"You don't have to be embarrassed. All the adolescent boys in East Islip are the same. That's why I never go out with any of them. They ask a girl out on a cheap date, some hot dog and a second run movie, they talk all evening about their buddies on the team, then they want to make out with you and feel you up. It's disgusting."

"You don't like to make out?"

"I didn't say that. I said I don't like cheap dates and the adolescent boys from East Islip. They're a bunch of jock heads anyway. All they talk about is sports and how athletic they think they are, but they're really wimps. What sports do you play?"

"I'm *uhm*- graduated, I graduated already and now I'm a musician..."

"A musician! You didn't tell me that!" The train lurches to a stop mid-tunnel. Elli about falls into his arms. "I love musicians. What type of instrument do you play – string, brass, reed?" The car goes dark, except for some mysterious reason the fan keeps whipping in its uncertain orbit.

"I don't play an instrument, I manage a band called the Loose Nukes."

"How can you say you're a musician if you don't play an instrument?"

"I didn't say I played an instrument."

"You said you were a musician."

"Well I am, in a way, I manage musicians."

"Carting around a band's instruments at night is not the same as being a musician."

Their heads accidentally collide in the dark. *Wirrr - er - wirrr* continues above them.

"Sorry."

"Sorry."

"I don't cart around the band's instruments, I find bookings for them, rep them, promote them. I have contacts in the record industry."

"You do not."

"Yes I do."

"How can you? How old are you?"

"I'm twenty. I'll be twenty one in November. I'm a Scorpio."

The lights blast back on and the train jerks and jolts its way again through the tunnel.

"You're what?"

"Twenty. A Scorpio. What are you?"

"I'm a Libra, I suppose, but I don't take that stuff seriously — how old did you say you were?"

"I'll be twenty in-…"

"Twenty. You still look adolescent to me."

"Adolescent! So how old are you anyway?"

"Sixteen — O MY GOD! BROOKLYN BRIDGE! — I have to switch." She is out the door and across the platform into an express.

Lou is directly behind. "You're the adolescent."

"I'm mature for my age."

They make the express, find seats on the bench, and he can't help but glance down the neck of her blouse. She is mature for her age, very mature.

"Where are you from anyway?" She asks as she adjusts her collar.

"Bayonne originally, but now I live in Manhattan."

"Where in Manhattan?"

"I have a studio over on 2nd Avenue and 3rd Street."

"In the East Village?" Her voice lilts.

"Yeah!"

"Is it safe at night?"

"Sure it's safe." A stabbing right outside my window a week ago, but… "If you know which side of the street to walk on, anywhere in New York is safe. Do you want to come by and see my place?"

"No! Besides I couldn't anyway."

"Why not?"

"Because my mother would never allow it, and my father doesn't want me talking to strangers in the city. He says you never know. And my parents only let me come into the city from East Islip on Saturdays if I promise I'll come directly back home after class and arrive promptly on the 5:24 — otherwise they'll ground me."

"Oh?"

"Yes. My family is very strict, and then there's my brother Kirk, and he gets so uptight whenever I talk to a guy, which *infuriates* me beyond belief, as though he's going to have to *fight* to protect my *honor* or something."

"Kirk?"

"Kirk."

"Is he a big guy?"

"Bigger than you are."

"Wh-why I'm bigger than I look, tougher."

"*Pu-lease!*"

"No I wrestle — and you sure know how to put a guy down, don't you?"

"Why, are you self-conscious about being skinny?"

"I'm not skinny, I'm- I'm thin, trim!"

"You're skinny, but so are rockstars and they're very sexy, besides all my girlfriends think skinny guys make the best lovers, you know why?"

"N-n-no, why?"

"Because there's no fat between their nerve endings and the surface of their skin, that way they can feel sensations more keenly than some muscle-bound doof, is that true? Does sex set your nerves on edge?"

"I-*y*... *yii*... yeah sure- you bet it does — nobody's ever complained..."

"Nobody's ever complained, hah! As though there have been hundreds of girls, or guys — are you into guys too?"

"NO!"

"You sure?"

"Yeah I'm sure." his mouth is going, and he's getting upset. "First you put down my body, then you call me a fairy..."

"You're very thin skinned, very sensitive."

"Yeah, well you'd be sensitive too."

"And sexy."

"H-iyy..."

"Sorry, but if it's somebody I like I ask questions, that's all. I'm uninhibited — *oops*, my stop — I have to go."

The doors open again. Elli leaps off the train and walks rapidly down the concourse. LIRR⇒ the signs say. Lou races fast behind her. "Hey, we were just beginning to like each other, you can't go running off." He shouts.

"I can too," she shouts back, "I have to catch a train home, or I will have a lot of explaining to do." She looks back at him. "I don't want to get grounded over you, and besides you wouldn't want my brother Kirk beating up on you, would you?"

They run along the platform together.

"I'm not afraid of your brother Kirk, I'm not afraid of any guy."

"You should be, Kirk's very protective."

"… kind of cute… especially when you get flustered."

"*Uh*-do you *uh*-come into the city every Saturday?"

"Yes."

"How about we go have coffee together next Saturday? I know this great little expresso place over near Washington Square Park."

"I can't"

"Why not?"

"Because I arrive on the 8:10 from East Islip, it takes me approximately 20 minutes to reach school on the subway from Brooklyn, and my class begins promptly at 8:30. I eat lunch with my classmates at 11:30, and we go back and draw until 3:00. Then I rush to catch the 3:10. So I don't have time for coffee with you — OH SHIT! DAMN IT! SHIT!" Elli slams her portfolio case on the floor. "DAMN IT!"

Lou is down on the ground again, retrieving the contents. Her drawings have scattered all over the platform, women in every pose imaginable, curves, lines, details, delicate shadings, along with footprints and smears and blotches. He lovingly collects each one of them — "*Uh- uh-* what's the matter, what's wrong?"

"I missed the 3:10 to Long Island!"

"Yeah well- well, there'll always be another one or we could take a cab — hey, I'll pay for it. I'll pay for your cab, and that way we can talk more and maybe stop and have something to eat on the way, you know, pull over for a while, get to know each other." He hands her back her drawings.

"Oh, I suppose, but DAMN IT! I'm going to get grounded over YOU!" She stuffs her drawings into the portfolio, and she's mad, madder than mad.

"Let's…" He leads her by the arm back down the concourse. "Let's get a hot dog, with sauerkraut."

"Adolescent boys and hot dogs, AUUCK! You've messed everything up!"

"Sorry, I-…"

"Don't say you're sorry, I hate that word. It means nothing."

"I'm sorry."

"I hate that word!"

"Hot dog."

"Oh alright, let's go upstairs and have a hot dog. You are nice, and kind of cute." She blinks and smiles at him, and he blinks and smiles back.

"Kind of?"

"Kind of…" Her portfolio is swinging freely as they climb up the stairs. "…especially when you get flustered."

"Flustered?"

"Let's get something to eat at Nathan's. I had to skip lunch today. We had this nude guy for a model, first time I've ever done a guy."

"N-no, you nev-never have, never?"

"It really wasn't all that big a deal, but guys are different. Proportion is easier with a guy, there are more angles and big shoulders, and muscles. Do you have muscles?"

Lou is damn near choking on something, like his own tongue. "So- so let's eat, ho kay?" They stand at the yellow and orange counter, and a guy in a wife-beater shirt with muscles and broad shoulders asks what they want — "Wha'daya want?" — but he's muscles all over, so he can't be anywhere near as sensitive, no way, and probably no good at conversation either.

"Order anything you want, I've got four bucks, two bucks apiece, OK?"

"FOUR BUCKS! AND YOU WERE GOING TO TAKE ME ALL THE WAY HOME IN A CAB TO EAST ISLIP!"

"Well, I would've needed to borrow a few dollars from you, or from your father, but I would've paid you back, honest."

"So, wha'daya want, hunh?"

"I'll have two of the Superdog Specials with relish, mustard and extra sauerkraut and a giant coke." Elli perks up.

"Yah, dat's for da lady, wha's for da gent?"

Lou is feverishly poking through his pockets, hunting for loose change, anything. He is quick with figures, and she has just ordered between $2.80, $3.10 worth. He counts what he's got. "*Uh- uh-* I'm not hungry, really, just thirsty, just a coke, small coke, 70 cents, thanks. Thanks!" Which doesn't leave him more than two dimes for carfare and a long walk home from Brooklyn, unless he wants to try jumping the turnstile again.

The muscle head moves away.

"So tell me something more about your life, other than you're being a rockstar." Elli's at least back to gazing into his baby browns.

"Like what?"

"Important stuff. Nothing else interests me."

"I like to read, and I- *uh- uh-* I ran track for a while in high school."

"Adolescent boys! What do you read, the sports page?"

"No, I read the *Times*, every day, and I read books."

"Books about sport car racing?"

"No, *The Kool Aid Acid Test* , have you read that? And Kurt Vonnegut?"

"Sure, who hasn't? Do you have a girlfriend?"

"No, I mean I did…we just broke up, we weren't right for each other."

"What was her name?"

"*Uh- uh-* Carol-… Carolyn."

"I bet you weren't right for each other, you can't remember her name."

"She went by both names — Carol is short for Carolyn."

"You didn't just have a girlfriend."

"Yes I did."

"No you didn't, you don't know the first thing about girls."

"Yes I do, I've been around."

"You sure you're not gay?" And she has to say that, doesn't she, just as the muscle man behind the counter delivers the Superdog Specials, and he has to look straight at Lou, wait for his answer?

"No I'm not gay. I like girls, I just don't happen to have a girlfriend right now." He stares at the Superdogs, wondering why Elli doesn't eat, why the big guy doesn't disappear.

"You going to pay him with your four dollars, or do I have to pay him?"

"No, right… no, here…" Lou spreads his money on the counter. The guy takes four dollars, leaves two dimes. $3.80. Lou was right to the penny, but he is face down on the formica counter top and almost as orange.

"Here, one's for you." And Elli passes Lou one of her Superdogs.

"No I'm not hungry." He slides it back.

"Yes you are, and I ordered two to make you face up to being honest."

"I'm always honest." He has his face buried.

"No you're not. I can tell by your eyes, the way you look down when you fib, and if we're going to be friends, you have to be honest."

"Are we going to be friends?" He lifts his head.

"Are you going to be honest?"

"Yeah!" His eyes sparkle. He's standing up again. He bites deep into his Superdog.

"And you're still a virgin too, aren't you?"

Lou gags on the Superdog, as the lug returns with the drinks.

"*Uh- uh-…*"

Everybody awaits his honest answer.

Lou, the aging Lou, is standing in the middle of a rainy block on Broadway near 96th Street, shouting foul language into a telephone receiver. Elli is on the other end of the line asking, "Hello? Who is this? Hello? Hello?" But the mouth piece on the street phone is missing, or some damn thing — the same damn thing that infects four out of five public telephones in New York City. Lou hurls the receiver against the box. It whips around — *smackwhack* — indestructible as well as inoperable. He tightens the collar on his trench coat, marches the last few blocks to Elli's.

Manhattan's Upper West Side is menacingly deserted at one in the morning. Grated boutiques border brightly lit all-night bodegas on the easterly side of Broadway, but otherwise, for all the hype in real estate prices, things haven't changed that much in the neighborhood. Broadway remains fixed as the dividing line. West side toward Riverside is intellectual New York, but east toward Central Park, Hispanola. The drizzly nighttime Broadway divider a no man's land.

He waits for two deadheading cabs *thud thumping* by at nearly ninety then crosses Broadway toward West End Avenue. Two dark faces in dark clothes are talking in a dark doorway. He glances at them, never varying his pace. They stop talking, watch him pass.

The tension of being this close invades Lou's body, this close to making a really big deal, this close to redeeming himself in the eyes of men, and women, particularly in the eyes of Gertrude, a mother, and in the eyes of Elli, an ex-wife — two formidable forces in a more than middle aged man's life. SHREE-REE-REE-REEEK! Screams. A *crashclank* of a trash can lid. His stride quickens. Alley cats, he reassures himself, but he's perspiring in the rain anyway, sweating. That and his intestines are tied in knots. There's a lot at stake, too much, and that's the way it always is. When the stakes are piled high, that's when there's opportunity. That's the way of nations and history, as well as with individual entrepreneurs like Lou. You risk. Sometimes you win, sometimes you lose. You give, you take. You let go, you grab back. Compromise, then wage war. If anything in life is simple, or simpler, he doesn't know about it, at least not when he's about to jump the biggest puddle he has ever encountered — and if he doesn't make it, he's going to get his socks soaked.

He dashes across West End Avenue and quickly enters the sanctuary of Elli's lobby, with its hollow high domed gilded ceiling and heavy creaking wrought iron doors, no doorman in sight. He pushes the intercom button, 9-H. Eventually, there is a "Yes?"

"It's me, it's Lou!" He shouts.

"I knew it would be you." Then there is a cranky drone as he pushes through the door.

His heels click as he crosses the marble floor, no doorman anywhere to be seen. He presses for the elevator, the door sliding open immediately and revealing a body slumped in the corner of the cab, the stench is beyond foul. He steps in and presses 9. The cables strain, the drum churns, and up they ride at a leisurely dowager's pace, no motion to the body at all. Lou breathes through his mouth and gasps as he steps off. 9-H is conveniently located next to the elevator shaft. He buzzes.

"Lou?" He hears through the door.

"It's me." His nostrils pinched, his voice muffled.

"Lou?" An eye at a peephole, the door opens a crack, and over a small chain a mouth appears. "You don't sound like you." The door slams shut so that she can undo the chain. He hears the clank as she removes the pole off the policeman's lock, then the door opens again. Elli. She betrays no emotion, simply stands her ground. He slips by her, gasping for air. The comforting potpourri smell of Elli's place at once overwhelms him.

"I have to be careful. There have been two muggings in the lobby in the past month." She explains dryly.

"I noticed there were no doormen in the lobby."

"They're on strike. A new group of trustees in the building decided to hold the line, not raise co-op fees again for the fourth time in four years."

"And where'd that get them?"

"Two muggings in the lobby."

"And somebody dead in the elevator."

"Poor fellow has been sleeping in there lately."

"Smells rotten."

"I agree, but somehow I feel safer with him around." They both stand and stare at each other, door wide open, Elli still holding the iron bar to the police lock in her hand.

"Sorry to come by so late, and no call. I tried, bu-…"

"I knew it had to be you, I knew it."

There's a rumble in the hall, and the elevator starts to descend. Elli reluctantly closes the door, Lou inside. "I suppose you have something you have to talk about." She doesn't wait for a reply. She repositions the police lock and bolts up everything on the door, including the little brass chain. She squeezes by and leads him down a long hall to her flat. She has the back quarter of a once large four bedroom apartment that stretched the length of the building. "Why are you out prowling at one in the morning?"

Lou is Elli's ex-husband. Someone she neither loves nor hates. Lou is simply Lou in her life, and he comes over once in a while, once in a great while, and always late at night, always unannounced, always after a vain attempt at phoning from a stand around the corner, and always — always, always — in the same goddamn trench coat and dripping wet.

"Do you even own an umbrella?"

He peels off his beloved trench coat. He hangs it on Elli's coat rack where there's never room, and over one of her coats, which will get wet, as will the floor underneath the rack where he kicks off his shoes.

"Why bother? Six bucks, ten bucks, you loose it or somebody takes it or it snaps apart in the wind."

"Your socks are soaking wet." Elli sits down on the sofa, the same sofa they bought together forty years ago. "I could fix tea or there's some bottled water in the refrigerator." She pulls her feet in under her.

"No, nothing for me, I'm fine." He sits in the wicker chair they found on the street, up the street, forty years ago, when the Loose Nuke sensation made them all heady and hopeful, when Elli's mother and her brother Kirk insisted that if the two of them were going to move in together, they had better be married. Elli had turned eighteen and was willing to give up a full scholarship to Oberlin to live with him.

But nobody at the time could argue with the success of the Loose Nukes. They were in the newspapers almost daily, some chart breaking release, some exploit, something Chipper said or worse, something he did. The full two inch headlines out of Cincinnati were to come later, two months after the barefoot June wedding. And among the guests was Gertrude, along with the two relatives on the groom's side who still spoke to her or even knew she had a son because Gertrude could be bristly, although she was on her best behavior with the Vandenhooks. Elli's father, Arthur, was a man of art and wit, a newspaper editor and respectful of traditional values. Gertrude Starcrave was neither arty nor witty, she read *The Daily News* and packed her own notions of what was valuable. Gertrude was born direct, and Elli's father knew instinctively to avoid tangling with her, a trick Lou never learned, and Gertrude obliged her son by saving her best barbs for him. "He resembles his father, believe you me, smells like him too." One *fwoosh* with that spiny tail and she could pin Lou up from eyeball down to peanut shell.

Gertrude never tangled with Elli, although she had a comment or two she shared with her new daughter-in-law naturally. "I'll never understand what you see in him, he's such a stump, but then his father was a horny toad too, always jumping at me from the behind."

Beryl, Elli's mother, heard that one and narrowed those eyes of hers at her daughter. But no matter, Elli was the portrait of a bride, technicolor through a gauze filter, a lacy plain dress, high waisted and leggy, a straw bonnet on her head, spring tall grass and flowers in the meadow. It was 68, blue skies early in the morning, storm clouds by late afternoon. The bride and bridegroom danced through the evening in the striped tent with the guests, and only as they were readying to flee to Vermont, did Gertrude sling her last. "Make sure he leaves his muddy shoes on the back stoop, because if he ever comes through the front door, you'll have a load on your porch you'll never get swept off." Some thought it a quaint Ukranian marriage proverb, but Beryl Vandenhook knew a threat from Bayonne when she heard one. Luckily there was no issue, and Bayonne and East Islip remain separate and entire unto this day.

But Elli was a 60's child, butterflies and beads, long hair and lithe limbs, she could dance through sunflowers and munch on figs. She was artistic, she sketched and she painted, she penned love poems in her diary and she played flute. She was pretty if plain and mostly she sat backstage like somebody's kid sister. Once she was portrayed in a pop magazine as a groupie girl, along with Molly Dawkens. It was a hoot, since Elli and Molly couldn't have been more different, a lone woodwind amidst the brass. But Elli was the charmer, she won everyone's heart. Molly had charms too, though it was hard-ons not hearts that Molly favored.

"You look well. Everything going along fine?" Lou fiddles with the figurines, cats blown out of glass, cats preening, cats stretching, cats curled up and napping, cats wide awake, watchful, getting ready to spring.

"What are you after?"

"Nothing really, simply dropped by to see how you were doing."

Elli is cautious.

"It's been a miserable April, hasn't it? Never stops raining."

Suspicious.

"Cozy in here."

After the cataclysmic descent of the Loose Nukes, and the demise of the Starcraves' wedded bliss, Elli held onto their rent-controlled apartment. In the financial frenzy of the 80s the building went co-op. Elli borrowed the money for the down payment from her brother Kirk since she earned only drabs from her drawings and part-time teaching – her art both her passion and her pension.

"Was always cozy in here."

And only when it rains does she miss him, or rather the misty romantic springtime fantasy of him – she has the Vandenhooks to remind her of that fiasco at every holiday dinner – but bottom line Elli is happy with her lot. Although once in a while she feels not remorse, but outrage at Lou and at mankind generally, and she stabs charcoal on a large sheet of paper, sketches out an anguished woman's face, one of those that seems both angry and expectant, one that over the years has become deeply lined, though not wrinkled, and she hauls it over to the West Side Woman's Art Collective where it sells almost as soon as it's hung up.

"Place looks the same."

The place. She hated it at first, rent-controlled or not, because it wasn't sunny. No sun comes through any windows in Elli's three spacious rooms. She has no plants, not a one, and Elli loves green. When, whenever, if ever her art goes mainstream, she is going to use the proceeds to find a place with sunshine so she can have plants, plenty of plants. She has to, they are the roots of life, and any time a grayer mood is about to overtake her, she will ride the subway deep into Brooklyn to the Botanical Gardens. She will wander through the Arboretum and examine each plant, deciding which would thrive in her sunny new apartment. For she has tried everything, grow lights, plants that don't require all that much sun, spider plants, ivy, ferns – *hah!* – ferns need plenty of light! All living things need sunlight to flourish. But in the darkness of her Upper West Side back half, nothing flourishes. Still, she does have Gilda, her blue point Siamese and old, who has curled up beside her on the sofa, and Topsy, a younger black cat with one white paw whom she found abandoned as a kitten in back of a trash barrel down 102nd toward Riverside. Topsy has this aversion to Lou, so she doesn't come out from under the bed when he drops by. Gilda has an aversion as well, but Gilda remembers him. Gilda glares at him when he drops by, and her glaring makes him feel mighty uncomfortable.

"Nice kitty."

-*nack!* Gilda shows what nice is.

"Amazing how things never seem to change in here." He tries a smile at Elli and Gilda. "Never."

"Are you trying to be snide?"

"No no, not at all. I mean- meant... meant it sincerely. That's what I like about this place. It feels comfortable to me, even after all these years."

"Things change. Things are ready to change for me. I've finally found a simpatico agent who likes my work. She specializes in women's art and she's had encouraging things to say about mine, that it's maturing."

"I'm sure, I'm sure it is, I'm sure you're going to be famous very soon, make it big. All you need is the right gallery, I know that." He fidgets in his chair, the rattan squeaks.

"So what's so important in your life that you have to come running over here after midnight in the rain when you know perfectly well I'm up early in the mornings drawing?"

"Well, I..."

"Come on, you only bother me when you can't figure something out. Who else would listen to your schemes?"

"It's not a scheme this time Elli, no way. This time it's big, it can happen. You're right though, you're right... I need some help thinking it through. And it's breaking fast, otherwise I wouldn't bother you about it."

"You'd bother me about what to eat for breakfast if I'd let you in here to discuss it."

"No Elli, listen, this is foolproof."

"It had better be if you're handling it." Elli reaches down and strokes Gilda with her fingernails. Gilda loves it. Dig right-*innnnnn,* she purrs, scratch down to the sc-*alpalpalp.* "I suppose you can tell I'm on the edge of my seat waiting to hear."

"You're going to flip over this one, you really are."

Elli sharpens her stare.

"I dropped by the restaurant to talk with Bubba, and he agre-..."

"How did he look?"

"Fine, he looked fine. He asked how you were doing, and-..."

"He asked about me?"

"...anyway I had dropped by to tell him about my idea..."

Elli relaxes back in her chair, she reminisces. Bubba Bonnanza, the lead guitarist, was the image of the dark male, the mysterious, the sensual, the overpowering, the unbridled, and yet he was so gentle and caring and warm and soft, and that name, why would anyone have ever called him that? Admittedly, there was a swagger, a stud code he was sworn from puberty to uphold, but that was attractive somehow, it fit, but not the name, Bubba was no bubba.

"...releasing a CD on late night TV, He agreed. He said he'd even be willing to appear, pitch it, but somehow I can't see him doing it, he's so out of shape."

"Bubba the Bod!"

"Gone to fat."

And why, why among Italians is age more than catastrophic? Is it some immutable law of nature that the most beautiful must succumb so early and so utterly? For this is the race of the Renaissance, their beauty extolled for centuries, their youth surely the most inspiring, the skin, alabaster smooth, the hair, carved ringlets, the sculpted bodies that excited Michelangelo to the heights of artistry — so how is it that the statuesque can fall to fat so soon after its flowering? For by twenty five all is lost, irretrievably. The Nordic types somehow mantain, their fair charm frozen to endure. The Thais stay trim, languid. The true blue blacks of Nigeria, ageless in grace and form. Why then must Italians waste so young?

"He's always had an appetite, and he works the restaurant every day..."

"Not Bubba! No! I don't believe it!" Elli narrows her eyes.

"I'd say 400, 350 easy."

The dark curly hair, those big beautiful eyes, the bright white teeth, he was probably a plump cherub when he was a baby, but Bubba, those broad shoulders, those muscles, trim waist, and hands, oh so soft, so gentle.

"...had an idea of how I can find Chipper, he couldn't pinpoint the town or even remember the name, but if I drove up there and looked around long enough, I know I could find him."

"Chipper? Why would you want to find Chipper even if you knew where to look?" And the cat scowls along with her.

"Why? Be- because — weren't you listening — they're going to re-master a CD of the Loose Nukes' greatest hits, produce an infomercial on late night cable. It would make a bundle, people would go crazy to see Chipper again, see what he looks like, hear him sing the old songs."

"No one wou-..."

"People are paying big bucks these days for nostalgia. All the old stars are making comebacks, and they've started playing Loose Nuke tunes on the radio, you know, for the over-50s crowd like us."

"Really?"

"Yes really. And Askantics Records called me last week — guess they've been bought out by some mega-conglomerate called QuotLink Inc — anyway, they wanted to know where to mail the royalty checks. Royalty checks! Like it's been forty years since we've received a royalty check!"

"How much?"

Every girl Elli's age wanted to lose her virginity to Chipper...

"Not so much, not yet, but it's a star-…"

"I actually could see where people might…"

"Where people might what?"

"…where people might be curious." Elli is curious. She's digging in on Gilda, going at her haunches — *brurr-burrr*, and deeper — every girl in Elli's graduating class in East Islip would be curious. Certainly they would remember Chipper, and how envious they were when Elli married into the band, so to speak. Every girl Elli's age wanted to lose her virginity to Chipper, or to Bubba the Bod, or to cute little Danny T, 'Drummer Dynamo,' even to weirdo Will Cook. The girls would sit on Elli's porch or they would lounge around her room afternoons and sigh over her collection of record covers, and Elli had an enviable collection of 8 x 10 glossies, mostly of Chipper, though some of Bubba, and signed. These were to become her most prized girlhood possessions — *burrow-burrow*, deeper and deeper.

"So what do you think? When you get quiet, I know you agree."

"I'm considering the possibilities — you're certain he's still alive?"

Elli remembers Chipper at the wedding, and Bubba and Will Cook, Danny T *and that Molly Dawkens woman!* Even the Vanderhooks were ready to forgive, waiting for Chipper to arrive. He didn't show for the ceremony, but that was expected. Will Cook did. He was always so dependable, on time for everything, modestly waiting in line to be seated, taller than everybody else by a foot, everybody staring at him, so serious, with his face down, buried in all that long black hair. And thankfully *that Molly Dawkens* didn't show up for the ceremony. She would have outshone any bride. Some women are like that, they do it purposely. They wear red, they wear yellow, they wear something too tight, too loose, they talk too loudly, laugh like a truck driver, get drunk and let a strap fall, corner the groom in the janitor's closet — women like Molly are full of cheap tricks! But if Chipper had shown up before the wedding, Elli was afraid she would have thrown herself into the janitor's closet. It was this thing she had, this girlish giddy feeling that would almost overtake her, almost, not quite, never completely.

"And Bubba knows where to find him?"

"I wouldn't say that, he remembers the landscape — woods, dirt road — see, he was the last to drive up to Maine and visit him."

The ceremony went along without a hitch, well, with a hitch, the wrong hitch as it turned out, but at that moment everything seemed perfect. That's what all the celebration is about, isn't it? Perfect day's start for a perfect life's ending. Which would work, if a couple could forget about the years in between. "And Danny T and… *and that Molly Dawkens woman?*"

"They're still married, I hear they're living in Staten Island."

"Staten Island!"

When Molly finally did arrive, swathed tight in Kelly green and her ravishing auburn hair loose down her back, arm-in-arm with Danny T *and with Bubba*, the guests did indeed forget the bride, the catering staff forgot the bride, the groom forgot the bride. There were suddenly celebrities at the wedding, reporters and cameras shooting, people talking excitedly. But Chipper slipped in through the kitchen, soundlessly, and across the patio around to the back of the tent. He waited until the bride and groom finished cutting the cake, and then the shrill cry went up, even the Vandenhook family was breathless — Chipper Stirbee standing alone and unattended in their midst. It was as if an angel of God had descended, his platinum hair like a halo. Smiling. He listened to each name and shook each hand. Elli's mother Beryl put hers to her lips after the touch, she kissed it. Sure, she denies it, "That's silly, he was simply a boy," she says, and brushes her lips to this day. Other women kissed Chipper's hand, and he'd laugh. He kissed the bride on the lips, and Elli remembers the kiss. She remembers Lou's kiss. Elli remembers kisses and she remembers hands. Chipper's hands were around her waist, and the dress was high waisted. Chipper Stirbee's fingers were mere inches from her breasts, his lips upon her lips. A slightly moist kiss, moist to the dry. Lou's a wet kisser and clingy. Chipper touches. Lou clutches. Some things in life a woman never forgets.

"Look. I know Chipper's alive. I know he's somewhere up in Maine."

"Maine's a big place, and that visit by Bubba was forty years ago."

"I know I can find him."

"What, with psychic vision?"

"It's time, it's time. I can sense it. I know I can get him interested...."

"Interested?" Elli is distracted and going at that cat, *-scrr-ratch, -ratch-ratch*, cat is eating it up, fur undulating, purring pruriently.

"...in a revival. That's where I fit in!"

"A revival! I thought they wanted to remaster a CD?"

"It's the logical next step. I'd bill it as a once-in-a-lifetime event, one night only, at first anyway. The Loose Nukes Reunited! Maybe Madison Square Garden, maybe the Meadowlands, I don't know yet, but make it big — REALLY BIG!" He is on the edge of the chair with excitement.

"You're daydreaming. Even if Chipper is alive somewhere up in Maine, Danny T and Molly would never agree to appear on a stage with him, not after what happened."

"Oh I think Molly might... might be very interested in seeing Chipper — see, he's my ace in the hole, without him there's no chance of a revival, but with him, with him, there's the sweet smell of success — big bucks."

"Besides everybody's too old now."

"They're not that old. They're no older than we are."

"That's what I'm saying." Sometimes Elli feels it, sometimes, age creeping slowly up from her toes.

"It's our last chance at fortune and fame." Lou is insistent.

Age always shows around the eyes, when Elli looks in the mirror in the morning and the lines that emerge on paper when she sketches a face. "I don't know Lou, not everyone wants to be reminded of their age, maybe you should do a market analysis first, find out who would be interested in a revival of the Loose Nukes, how many people would actual-…"

"You would, wouldn't you?" He is hanging off his seat, almost panting. "Wouldn't you enjoy being up on that stage again?"

The suggestion horrifies Elli. At her age? Sure, she's kept her figure, but all those people staring and the glare of the lights, cameras, the most dreadful invention ever, the uncompromising unvarnished gaze, the hideous detail… "No! I would not!"

"But-but-but you'd enjoy seeing Chipper again, wouldn't you?"

"I'd be intrigued, yes, to see Chipper… after all these years… see what he looks like now…"

"You'd get to see your picture in *People*! You'd enjoy that."

"Never! I'd never want anything to do with *People*!" Spoken with the true arrogance of an Uppity West Sider.

"Once we get everybody together, spark some miracle…"

"Have you talked to Bubba about this revival scheme of yours?" Bubba. His eyes, his hands, hands so adept, hands that strum with passion. Talk about a wedding kiss and a sizzling touch! Elli gets to going at the cat with a vengeance, and the cat is yowling with satisfaction — RR-OW-OWWW!

"It's not a scheme, it's a deal, but no, I only mentioned the CD. I thought I'd wait, come talk with you about it first."

"In the middle of the night?"

"I got up late, everything's been busy, I- I thought you'd be excited."

Maybe she is, she's got Gilda by the haunches — *rrow-rrow-rrow…*

"You don't know how excited I am, I mean, I can feel this one, this is the big one I've been waiting for! If only my mother were ali-…"

"Gertrude would be horrified."

"She would, that's true, maybe it's better she's gone — I shouldn't say that, should I? It'll jinx everything. But I'm so glad you're excited because I need you to go along with me and smoo-…"

"Go along with you on what?" Elli's eyes narrow again.

"I-I-I've got to head over to Brooklyn, sell, see… see Will Cook. He lives over in Park Slope now and… you remember Will Cook?"

"Who can forget Will Cook?"

"True. Weird sort of guy, moody."

"Perhaps, but I found him attractive in a way too." What Elli saw was something in a strange and private... strange, private, sensitive... so sensitive, and talk about hands... "Does he still have that long black hair?"

"It's clipped a bit and gray, mostly gray. Otherwise he looks the same."

Long thin tendrils that can stretch octaves, trying not to touch, but touching *hohh- hohh-...* Stroking the cat is not going to calm her down.

"If we played our cards right, we could get him interested."

"We?"

"You and me."

"You and I and no way Lou. Don't try to involve me in this scheme."

"It's not a scheme honey, it's a dea-..."

"And don't you dare call me honey!" RAA-AANH, the cat squalls. "My only interest is in seeing Bubba or Will Cook for old time's sake, nothing else. You have no idea, and you know you have no idea where Chipper is or how anyone of them would respond to this preposterous idea of a revival!"

"People forget."

"They never do, and Danny T hates you, after you humiliated him, and *that Molly Dawkens woman!*"

"Molly and I got along."

"She detests you."

"Alright. You've made your point. There was a misunderstanding."

"A MISUNDERSTANDING!"

"That was a long time ago. I realize I have my work cut out convincing them, OK? But we're talking about money here, not love eternal or peace now. And I can feel it, I can get to Chipper, and in a way he's all I need."

Lou had attempted to remake Molly Dawkens and Danny T into a Cher and Sonny Bono team, this was a few years after the Loose Nukes' disappearance, talking Molly into baring her lungs in public, Danny T buried back behind his drums. The premature TV exposure wasn't Lou's fault, not entirely, a blown-out bra had something to do with it.

"Always a scheme, always an impossible scheme." Elli suddenly stops massaging the cat — WANH?

"Why? Why do you say impossible? Even you said you were intrigued with seeing what Bubba looks like now, and Chipper? Every woman in her fifties alive toda-..."

"What about the scandal?"

"Times have changed, people accept more than they used to, and they're playing Loose Nuke songs all across the country."

Elli is not convinced.

"I have to find him, nobody knows where to send the royalty checks."

"Lou, be realistic."

"But if it's a great idea and I'm the only one who can find Chipper..."

"Even if you do get lucky and find him, and even if you could convince every member of the band to join, nobody in the music business will take you seriously. People remember. They remember all your deals, all the acts you've dreamt up, flop after flop. You're not their favorite person." And Gilda whispers concurrence on that one, muzzling up under Elli's hand.

"Thanks Elli, thank you. I knew I could count on you for support. That's why I braved the elements and came straight over to see you."

"I'm the only person on earth who would open my door to you on a rainy Sunday night."

"Elli, Elli, listen. You've got to help me. You're the only one, I admit it, and I'll cut you in, I will, I'll give you a commission, I'll..."

"What can I do? I can't even get my own drawings shown anywhere permanently, I can't... oh no Lou Starcrave, no way! I will not, no sir, never, I WOULD NEV-..."

"Just ask him, leave my name out, test the waters, see if he'd be interested in the concept. Tell him what you believe, be sincere, tell him how you reacted, how your old girlfriends in East Islip would react, how women your generation all over the country would react."

"No way, never, I would never — and that's why you came to see me, YOU SNEAK, YOU WRETCH, YOU-..."

RANH RANH RANH!

"Just tell him what you told me, that you'd be intrigued. Elli, every girl, woman — every woman your-our age would be intrigued — they all loved Chipper Stirbee and the Loose Nukes. Even you have kept a scrapbook full of pictures — Elli, please."

"No. No. I am being assertive No, I will not do this! Leave!"

"Elli, I'll cut you in, it'll be in writing, 5%, 10% of box office net, Elli, you've got to."

"No. Leave!" Elli stands abruptly. RANNNNNNH! The cat gets bounced out of her lap onto the floor.

Lou's instantly out of the wicker chair, he's pleading, he has his hands clasped, he's begging. "Elli, please, *please!*"

"NEVER NEVER NEVER!" Elli is stamping her foot, she means it.

"But think of the fun, think — imagine! Imagine the lights coming up on the stage! The music! Will Cook first, a tinkle on the keyboard! Danny T pumping the drums! Bubba touches his guitar, when WHAM! The crowd suddenly goes wild, screeching and jumping! He bounds out of nowhere, lands front and center — CHIPPER!"

Elli stops stamping. "Chip-..."

"Chipper! We're talking about Chipper!"

Elli's body begins to tremble, involuntarily, and her eyes flash, her mouth moves. "Chip -per..." She suppresses an urge to shriek.

ROW-OW? The cat is incredulous.

"I don't know why I let you do this to me!"

And he has the good sense to stop talking, the good salesman's sense, yes, let the customer sell himself, herself, whomsoeverself.

Chip -per... you have to pucker to say it... the way it slips off your lips... like a wedding kiss... that kiss and another kiss, one night late kiss, everybody else gone home, gone somewhere, Atlanta, the Paramount, Elli and Chipper alone backstage in the dark... he reaches over, removes her glasses, brushes her hair apart and back... "You know gal, I nevah realized you wah so beautiful." And he did, he kissed her, lightly, slightly sliding those hands of his down her neck, across her shoulders... she trembled... it was like an angel's kiss... fulfilling... "I-*hh*... I-*hh* admit I-*hhhh*... I would find it... intriguing... to see Chipper again... and Bubba and Will Cook of course and..."

ROW ROW...

Elli is sold — sold solid!

"I'll pick you up at noon."

"Noon?"

"We'll head over and visit Will Cook."

"You had this all planned."

"If Chipper has kept in contact with anybody, it would be Will Cook. Between Bubba and Will, I know I can find him."

"You simply assumed I would acquiesce."

"I had to call Will, I had to set up an appointment to discuss royalties, I dropped a hint or two."

"Noon."

"Perfect, and remember to call your brother Kirk in the morning, tell him you need to see him."

"Kirk?" Elli snaps out of her trance — and way to lose the deal, push on details, a textbook example of closure interruptus.

"No. I won't. Kirk would be livid with rage. My entire family would be livid with rage. They hate you, hate you — after what you did to me."

"What did I do to you?"

"What? You persuaded me to marry you, and I've never told them, never, I've never mentioned one word about your coming over here to visit once in a while, I couldn't."

"I really don't know why they dislike me, I always tried to be nice, I-..."

"Don't blaspheme. You were never nice to my family, my mother! My poor father! You were the death of him, and Kirk."

"Your father, Kirk, your mother, maybe them, but the rest of your family..."

"The rest of my family! Who's left?"

"That cousin of yours, the pretty little one, what was her name?"

"Lena, you bastard! You tried to put the make on Lena that Thanksgiving, and in my father's house!"

"I'm sorry, sorry Elli. I didn't mean to bring her up."

"Mean? You never mean anything!"

RANH! RANH!

"Elli! Chipper! I promise I can deliver Chipper!"

"And 25% on licensing tie-ins as well as 30% of box office *gross*, and a signed agreement."

"Elli..." *choke, cough,* colital burn... "10, 10 percent, *net*, on the condition you can secure financial backing, but 30! 30 will eat away all my profits. Your brother will want a chunk, the others in the band, we don't know what they'll demand — Elli, be reasonable."

"20."

"15."

"Gross."

"Net."

"On paper. Signed. Kirk will read over the contract."

"Kirk?"

"Kirk. Deal?"

"Kirk?"

"Kirk!"

"Deal. Shit. Kirk." Poor Lou's head swims. Kirk. Kirk Vandenhook is a lawyer, a damn good one, contract specialty, fastidious, tenacious, he is also the Deputy Commissioner of Cultural Affairs for the City of New York.

"Kirk will hate me." And the reality of what she must do overcomes Elli. She drops limp down to the sofa, Gilda scrambles back into her mistress' lap. Gilda understands. Kirk despises rock 'n' roll, has chosen to forget his sister's brief indulgence, but he also happens to know everybody in the business, knows their private numbers. "No, I can't. I'll never be able to hold my head up. I'll never be invited home for the holidays, an outcast from my own family."

He plops down on the couch next to Elli. Gilda wedges herself tightly in between.

"It won't be like that, only at first, a little shock at first. After that it will be easier, and successful. Success makes everybody forget, forgive. And Elli, you know it will work! Women Elli, women lust after Chipper Stirbee!"

Elli buries her face in her hands. "But they will laugh at Kirk, they will scorn him, throw him out of their offices if he dares mention your name — and besides he won't do it!" Elli unburies her hands. She sits upright on the sofa. "Lou! You have to listen to me on this one, you have to be realistic."

"Elli, I-..."

"LISTEN!"

He listens, he may not like what he's hearing, but he's listening. Besides Elli is shouting, he has to.

"We must be realistic. I know Kirk won't do it. And he will hate me forever for asking. My mother will never speak to me again, never. Every Thanksgiving she sits there staring at my father's empty chair and she says, 'Thank God it wasn't a proper marriage.'"

"Not proper?"

"Not properly religious."

"What do you mean?"

"No rabbi or priest officiating."

"We had a license and that Utilitarian minister."

"Don't quibble, they will disown me for even talking to you again, and it won't work anyhow. He won't do it." Elli gets serious. "Kirk won't. Nobody will. Nobody trusts you any more, nobody."

"But Elli, I can deliver Chipper Stirbee."

"You-you-… you will have to deliver him first. Yes. I insist on that. Find Chipper first!" She's adamant, that's obvious, she has put her foot down — she's also palpitating visibly.

He notices. Good salesman notices. "Alright. Alright. That's do-able. I can deliver on that. But we have to convince Will Cook, he might still be in contact with Chipper."

"And if not?"

"Then I'll scour the Maine woods and find him. Either way, tomorrow at noon?"

"Tomorrow. Noon."

"Oh Elli, honey bunch, we're in, we're on our way — BIG MONEY BIG TIME!" And he reaches over to hug Elli, to kiss her a big juicy wet one, but the cat rears up, Gilda, and — SCRAW-AL — swats him across his face before he can smooch her, a couple of deep claw marks along the cheek bone, right below the ol' eyeball.

BENEFIT CONCERT

"Lieutenant!"

"Sir!" A duplicate QSS intelligence officer clicks to attention at the door of the stadium observation box.

"Inform me the moment this so-called rescue craft sets down."

"Sir!"

"And bring that band manager of his, that Lou Starcrave up here to see me at once!"

"Sir! Yes Sir!" The officer clicks and exits.

Whereupon His Eminence resumes his pacing, back and forth, back and forth, his patience fraying with every step.

WHUPWHUPWHUPWHUPWHUP -CH WHUP

"Damn. Could suhe go fah an icy cold one about now Scotty."

"Thir's a cooler in the caddy mate, lift the lid n help yurself."

"Appreciate it. Been gettin wicked dry mouth from my homegrown, last batch in pahticulah."

"Wouldna mind a pint misell."

"Long dry summah can do that to a crop — let's see, what've we got in heah, ohrange soda, gingah ale, root beeh, gettin closah — whoa, what's this? Bahtlett's Aged Bittahs, 1987, that sounds intahrestin, got some sludge on the bottom too, and a Glasgow Sour Brown Ale that's good and cloudy — what's youh choice?"

"Prifer the Bartlett's, sludge n all."

"H'yep, definitely looks intahrestin."

"Brown ale's a pirfect chaser."

"Theah's only one of each. Can't take a man's resahve."

"Yu'r welcome ta either, I've got plenty more a the same at home."

"You'h not goin to join me?"

"Yu don'wan me flyin round in circles jus yet. Besides they'd pull mi permit if they caught even a whiff."

"Sayin goes though, man's a wastah who drinks alone."

"Ay, but when yu'r thirsty yu'r thirsty."

POP! "Whoa, thick foamy head... tasty... mite too heavy on the hops."

"Yu'r a reg'lar connisseur, a yu?"

He's a regular alright.

"Thir's salted nuts in a bag somewhir doon on the floor."

"You've got all the comfohts Scotty, contouh seats, moon roof, spectaculah view, even looks like theah's room in the reah fah a mattress... what've you got stashed back heah undah the tahp?"

"Regulation safety equipment mostly, life vests, inflatable raft, flares, radio signalin devic-..."

"Y'OUCH!"

WH   UH   HUP

"Wha is it mate? Wha's the trouble?"

"Just got clawed by somethin wahm and fuzzy — you suhe you ain't got a tigah kitten stowed away undah heah?"

"Naw the las I chec-..."

"SO KEEP YOUR BLOODY HANDS TO YOURSELF YANK!"

"What the flyin fuck!"

"AND NOBODY MOVE!"

-grr-rowl-rowl-rowl...

"YOU TOO! KEEP YOUR MOUTH SHUT!"

-rowlp.

It's this girl sprung out of nowhere! Mite of a thing, the size of an elf. Must be one of Cissy Coombs' gang, the tiny tickly tackler variety, shaved head, black leather biker's jacket, slim hips, snarl to her lips, pointy teats, toothy zipper running from throat to crotch, big silver round pulltab, and she's screaming she is — "THIS IS A HIGH JACK! YOU TWO DO WHAT I SAY OR YOU'LL BOTH BE HURTING HERBIES IN THE MORNING!" — and jumping and gyrating.

WHUP   WHUP
    WHUP   WHUP

"Don know who yu'a miss, r precisely how yu got in hir, but yu'r goin ta have ta sit doon somewhir n buckle up. Yu'r creatin a commotion!"

WHUP   WHUP   WHUP   WHUP

"DON'T GO ORDERING ME ABOUT SAILOR!"

"Don'take it person'ly miss, it's merely a matter a'proper load balance on a craft this compact."

"Oh?"

"THIS IS A HIGH JACK! YOU TWO DO WHAT I SAY OR YOU'LL BOTH BE HURTING HERBIES IN THE MORNING!"

"No offence intended."

"I don't suppose either of you gentleman will offer a lady your seat?"

"Suhe, take mine."

"DON'T YOU MOVE!"

"Whatevah."

"Best a hodd onta mine fir the time bein, don'yu think?"

Besides, she's busy keeping a watch on the both of them, on the dog too, although Betsy's more ears back and panting curious at this point.

"If yu could stand ta the center, distribute yur weight more evenly."

"There." She straddles the caddy between their seats. "That better?"

"Much."

"So you're Chipper Stirbee, like I need to ask or something."

"In the flesh."

"You look different up close."

"Fah bettah? Fah wohse?"

"Just different. Younger than I expected, whole lot younger."

"Try and keep fit."

"But you're almost my grandfather's age, right?"

"60's stud, what can I say?"

"No wrinkles, not even around the eyes, and your hair…" She reaches instinctively to touch the platinum.

"It's what's in yuh jeans that counts babydoll, all packed in theah tight." He nuzzles her hand some.

"BACK OFF! I'M TITANYA! SOUTHEAST COASTAL BRIGADE COMMANDER FOR THE SISTERS OF FIRE! I'M SEIZING CONTROL OF THIS AIRCRAFT!"

"Sisters a'Fire, a'yu?"

"Sistahs of fihe?"

"You havna been keepin up wi the local news Chipper. Sisters a'Fire's this wumen's counter-revolutionary terrorist group who've been kickin up quite the ruckus up north. They interviewed thir leader on BBC 2 las'week from some safe house near the border, big girl she was, solid."

"Cissy Coombs is our national spokeswoman."

"H'yep, Cissy Coombs, met up with huh myself."

"Hope you two took notes because the Sisters of Fire aim to take our men back — by force if necessary!"

"Hey, I'll join, no fohce necessahry."

"This is serious Stirbee!"

"Bet. Good lookin gals always ah."

"You're my hostage, understand, and you're not off to some drunken bachelor bash either. The regional chapter has had its eye on you for a long time." She leans down, hot breath in Chipper's face.

"Whoa! Whole bunch of you flame throwahs back home, ah theah?"

"Enough."

"Then snoht some smoke gal, tie me up and tohtuhe me silly — *skoobie doobie do do do!*"

"QUIET! I'M ASSUMING COMMAND HERE!"

"How's that? Yu'r unarmed?"

"Oh no I'm not sailor! Take a look at these!" And Titanya unzips, she does, one quick yank on the pulltab and there's a swell pair of hand sized C-caliber zingers with taut bullet tips. "YOU'LL DO WHAT I SAY OR ELSE!"

WHUPWHUPWHUPWHUPWHUPWHUPWHUPWHUPWHUP

"OK, alright, how are we doing on time? Lou? How are we doing?"

"*Uh*, eleven fifteen or so?"

"Clock on the wall says 11:27:45 and still no sign of your boy Chipper."

"He'll be here! I know it. He'll be here."

"Wish I shared your faith — meanwhile let's keep rolling with the commercials — *snap snap* — what've we got cued up?"

DESTINY... a fragrance to prepare man for the world to come... the wholly unimaginable... the immensely mysterious...

A shaft of light sears through the darkness and a cylindrical crystal vial rises slowly, a silver sliver of a vein projecting upward along the seam of the glass to a prong at the tip and topped by a pearl globular cap — OBSCURE reads the sub-text — DESTINY OBSCURE — as the vial mingles with these physically indistinguishable, though distinctly sexual body parts, some soft and round, others hard and angular, squirming all over one another on the home screen... Vivaldi playing in profusion, gauzy soft purple focus, audible gasps and gurgles... God alone knows what it is these people are doing, except that you feel like squirming around yourself some and squirts, spurts of DESTINY OBSCURE — for men who must struggle alone naked in this world or for women who must wear men's underwear... scantily clad with a scent that doesn't expose even the smallest laboratory critter to testing abuse.

DESTINY OBSCURE — *parfum pour l'homme solitaire.*

New this season from whom else — Ricky Ryme.

"Eminenze! Eminenze! You vouldn't believe vhat I've juzt dizcovered – iz injeniouz, even iv I muzt zay zo myzelv."

"What are you doing back here, *yourepugnantgardengrub*? I thought I was rid of you."

"Hold on a zecond… I'm all out ov breadz… zoze stairz all ze vay up here are killerz, but I couldn't vait vor ze elevator."

"I will not tolerate your barging in on me unannounced!"

"I tried callink a vew timez, but nobody anzered."

"That was you? I felt this insufferable buzzing between my ears!"

"Like electric zhockerz zappink vrom eyeball to eyeball?"

"More a dull throb across my forehead."

"Could be ztatic vrom any vone ov zoze high tech gadgetz you gotz crammed in zat cranium ov yourz – un don't zay I didn't varn you. Iz alvayz bezt to go vitz ze bazic zervize, by ze time you reconvigure all ze add-on veaturez, you might az vell tzrow ze whole contraption avay, ztart over vrom zcratj."

"Why do I continue to put up with you?"

"I can't help it iv you vere my virzt vorkink model, my darlink, my baby, I brought you kickkink un zcreamink back into live, avter zat overzealouz KGB apparatik tzought he had gotten rid ov you vor good vitz hiz Karazhnikov – remember Eazt Berlin in ze vabulouz viftiez?"

"Why didn't you leave me in peace, why do you continue to torment me *youovergrownwhitecoatedlabrat!*"

"Zat'z no vay to addrezz your maker."

"YOU- YOU- YOU-…"

"Carevul carevul, you don't vant to provoke anotzer rupture, have me go crawlink back up ze crack ov your azz."

"Whatever your role in my reconstruction, I have made myself what I am today, thank you, and that despite your continual interference."

"Yez vell, I guezz ve each revrite ze hiztory bookz to zuit our own zpezial interetz."

"Why are interrupting me with more of your nonsensical babble?"

"Becuz I juzt had a brilliant idea zat I vanted to run under your noze bevore I gotz myzelv all exzited."

"Your Eminence!" It's the replacement QSS lieutenant clicking his heels at the door.

"What now, *youfeyfesteringbootlick?*"

"I have a certain Lou Starcrave with me, per your request. Sir!"

"That despicable rockstar's handler and feeder, show him in."

"Sir!"

"Real qvickly, vhatz I tzoughtz ve could do vonce ve gotz our mittz on Jipper Ztirbee vaz…"

"THAT NAME!"

"...vhoopz, zorry... but iv ve could yank him azide vor a qvik vew zecondz un exztract a zimple core zample ov hiz genetic material, I could vork miraclez clonink him vor spezivik vunctionz..."

"Your Eminence. Good to see you." Lou offers a hand and a smile, neither of which is reciprocated. "*Uh-* rushed over the minute I got word you needed to see me, believe me, anything I can do to be of service, and naturally I regret the delay, but that's our boy Chipper..."

"ACK!"

"Did I say something to offend?" Lou ducks instinctively.

"Iz OK, hiz Eminenze zufferz vrom occazional migranez. He'z ezpezially zenzitive to zertain zoundz."

"That will do Queezac."

"Iv you vould zpeak zovtly, very zovtly."

"THAT WILL DO QUEEZAC, YOU MAY REMOVE YOURSELF FROM VIEW!"

"Zorry Eminenze, zorry zorry... no need to get ztrezzed, go zpillink your gutz outz all over ze vloor again."

"GO!" And His Eminence winds up for a good bootkick.

"Yez, I can zee you're buzy. Zientivic progrezz can alvayz vait. I'll getz back vitz you later on ze matter ve ver dizguztink."

"GO!"

And he crawls as he goes out the door, one huge claw of a hand pulling a shell of a body behind, each inch in slow excruciating pain.

Lou tries not to stare, though everyone does when seeing Queezac for the first time. "I hope I'm not interfering with anything imp-..."

"Not at all Starcrave, not at all." The Executive Liaison slams the door shut behind Queezac, then turns to stand his full six foot plus over Lou, who is of the slightly shorter persuasion himself and must perforce gaze up at his superior. "We have received word that your client is aboard a helicopter and making his way here, albeit circuitously."

"I knew he wouldn't disappoint us Your Eminence. Chipper Stirbee's never disappoi-..."

"Ack!"

"Sorry. Let me speak more softly, see he doesn't really mean anybody any harm, Chipper's simply spontaneous by natu-..."

"Ack! Ack!"

"Should I not speak at all?"

"Mister Starcrave, permit me to be perfectly frank."

"Please do Your Eminence, be as frank as you lik-..."

"IF THAT BASTARD FUCKS UP ON STAGE IN FRONT OF SIX BILLION HOME VIEWERS, I SHALL HOLD YOU PERSONALLY RESPONSIBLE – DO YOU UNDERSTAND ME CLEARLY ENOUGH?"

Lou bobs and grovels, signaling understanding.

"BECAUSE IF HE DOES I SHALL GNAW THAT PIN HEAD OF YOURS DOWN TO A QUIVERING STUB!"

Which is when Lou notices the Liaison has finely honed incisors…

"DO YOU UNDERSTAND WHAT I AM SAYING?"

…and a suspicious yellowish drip about the lip.

"I ASKED IF YOU UNDERSTAND WHAT I AM SAYING?" *Drip. Drip.*

"Per-fec-… perfect-ly…"

"GOOD." The Executive Liaison towers long tooth over him. "Then let me advise you and your band members to stay out of the way, way out of the way, hidden out of the way, when he finally does arrive at the stadium. QuotLink Security shall provide him with an escort to the stage, and they shall stand by until he completes the very last song of the very last set — DO YOU UNDERSTAND WHAT I AM SAYING?"

"Per-fec-…"

"Good. It has been a pleasure doing business with you Starcrave." The Liaison spews a bit.

"Thank you… Your Eminence…"

"You are dismissed."

As something slimy splashes on his shoulder, Lou has to scramble to get his pin head away out of sight.

ROOK! ROOK! Betsy's up on all fours in Chipper's lap and barking.

"What is it gihl, what's the mattah?"

Ears raised and tail flagging, she's got her nose pointed out the cab portal at something down on the ground.

"Wha's she lookin at?"

"Don't know Scotty, can't tell from way up heah. Only thing I can make out is a big traffic jam on the freeway."

"That'd be the North Circular headin ut t'ward Wembley."

"People wandahrin on foot all ovah the road, like thousands and thousands of them, cahs ain't movin an inch."

"Yur kids mate."

"My kids!"

"They've bin invadin London in droves all week from ev'ry corner a'the globe, millions a'them n millions more arrivin ev'ry day. They'r loungin in the rail stations, pitchin tents in the public greens, parkin thir vans along the roadways."

-ROOK! -ROOK!

"I'll drop doon so yu can have a closer look."

WHUPWHUPWHUPWHUP

Kids there are, millions, and autos stalled for miles in every direction, while threading through the throng, a string of hefty motorbikes.

"Can you see any better new?"

"Damn, that's that Cissy Coombs theah leadin the pack."

CRANK CRANK CRANK CRANK

A six year old is locked in her playroom, surrounded by Farfie dolls in dozens of different dress-ups, from full length mink to bikini pink, black mesh hose and negligee, the wedding dress, the business suit, a pony tail and sweater — and still Margot's not happy. She crashes over teeny teacups, upsets Panda, rips through closets full of Fab clothes. Margot's having her afternoon tizzy.

Nanny's not near, she's out on her umteenth cigarette break. Mother's way in the west wing while maid files at her nails. Father's in Hong Kong closing a property deal, and brother's off to boarding school in Switzerland.

Doesn't daunt Margot, she's shrill to piercing on the Lipper scale and high on Kidophen, screeching her head off, literally, it bops off and rolls, gets lost in the mayhem of playthings.

No one's near to hear poor Margot as the whine in her severed skull turns to a drone — and that's the second one the Naymores have lost to bad nannies this year.

PAID FOR BY THE SALVAGE THE KIDS FOUNDATION, WESTPORT, CT

WHUPWHUPWHUPWHUPWHUPWHUPWHUPWHUP

"So tell me Titanya, how'd a good-lookah like youhself evah get caught up in the tehrohrist trade?"

"Flattery won't work with me Stirbee."

"No honestly, I'm intahrested."

"It's a familiar story, a childhood wasted fending off the advances of drunken louts like yourself and nothing but a second-rate secretarial school to look forward to. A future of low wages and constant touch-ups. So I decided a working girl had to join with her sisters and make a stand. But what's my plight to a superstar whose life's all cushy?"

"Wasn't ahways that way. I stahted off pooh and unfohtunate like most evahrybody else."

"Don't go waving fantasies of fame and fortune over my head. I'm no dreamer. I realized what my fate was going to be when I was a schoolgirl!"

"I figuhe so long as folks can make an honest liv-…"

"You're one of the enemy Stirbee, singing about stupid lust and women succumbing to men's sickest desires, but we all know what happens when the song is over."

"What's that?"

"She's stuck bringing up the brats after he's run off with the au pair."

"Was it some neighbahhood lad who tuhned you so souah?"

"I'm warning you, don't go prying into my personal life. I'm the one asking the questions here!" Titanya tugs on her zipper, her pinkies tickling her terrific triggers.

"Hello Wembley, this is Skyhook XS90, requestin clirance fir landi-…"

"You can forget talking to them sailor." Titanya snatches Scotty's headset. "You won't be landing at Wembley this trip."

"Miss. This prank a'yurs is goin too fir."

"You don't take me seriously, do you?"

"Ta be perfectly frank, ah'v got no set opini-…"

Titanya cocks her erect C-calibers.

"Is it ransom money you'd be after, because I'd be more than willin ta radio in yur demands ta the proper author-…"

"YOU REALLY DON'T TAKE ME SERIOUSLY, DO YOU!" And to add emphasis she presses her hot 'n' handy pistol pup up to Scotty's temple. Poor lad, has his career, the rest of his life ahead of him. He starts in sweating profusely.

"That's better. I like my men hot."

-*rrowl!* Betsy, she's hot, fact she's up and defending. Who does this *brr-*razen tidbit think she is anyway, ordering everybody around, and if these *wu-wu*-wusses aren't going to take her on, Betsy will.

"HUSH YOUR MOUTH!" Titanya turns and lets go with a breast mounted zinger, grazes the pooch on the tip of her tail.

-*cur-ripes!* Wherewith Betsy plops back down on Chipper's lap.

"CONSIDER THAT A WARNING!"

"You ahright precious?" He strokes her bruised behind.

She's fine. Stunned. This sis must not be a member of the international.

Titanya blows on her fiery teaty, tries to cool the fool thing down, before nuzzling it back into Scotty's ear.

"Take me seriously now, do you?"

Man's quaking he is, can hardly keep his hand steady on his stick.

whup-pwhup-puppup

"Listen closely." And she leans in so they both can hear, and smell, and taste and touch. "You're to circle the stadium for awhile, dispel any suspicions. After one or two rounds you're to radio in and tell them you're experiencing mechanical difficulties and that you must return to Heathrow – mechanical difficulties, is that clear? Then we will chart a new course north to Sheffield."

"Sheffield?"

"I said, is that clear?"

Scotty nods his head, he comprehends, Sheffield, but Scotty's also a defiant cuss, he clinches down hard on his jawbone.

"Stirbee." And Titanya aims squarely at him. "You're going to sit tight until we arrive at Sheffield, where under my sole command you'll proceed to impregnate me."

"Whoa! That what you'h aftah, life-time child suppoht?"

ZIPPPPPPPPPPPPPPPPPPPPPPPP!!! – She pulls the ripcord on her jumpsuit.

"Mama!"

"Miss!"

-whulp!

Titanya's all arsenal, from chrome plated support bra down to electrified mesh bikini – stuff's sparkin.

"Don't look like I've got much choice!"

"Say, mate, if-… if you-… if ah-…" It's the young pilot, being brave. "If yu need the back-up, ah'll do whit a'hav ta."

"Appreciate it Scotty."

"Can the macho heroics – and Stirbee!"

"Yes ma'am?"

She plants a thick boot between his legs, a boot with a – *huff huff huff* – spindly spur.

"For your information, the Sheffield branch is not alone. The Sisters of Fire have organized chapters from Newcastle to Liverpool and all along the eastern coast in East Anglia."

"No sirprise thir Chipper, a traditional hotbed a'dissention."

"We are a vanguard army of proper British women who intend to reclaim our rights to a tidy home and to the uninterrupted joys of motherhood, which misguided feminists of past generations have irresponsibly handed over to wimp hubbies and socialized day care!"

"I thought women everywheah wanted to eahn theih own way, you know, equal pay fah equal laboh?"

What a piece of progressive propaganda that is! Name a woman who really wants to work side-by-side some scraggy boozer?"

"None I know of."

"No! We, the Sisters of Fire, demand as part of our social agenda separate but superior workplaces. We demand the best in housing and schools for our children, more fresh fruits and vegetables at the corner market and new churches where we can worship the She-God without interference from wonkers the likes of you two!"

"If that's how you feel, how come you'h highjackin us?" Chipper's cheek inadvertently slaps up against Titanya's leathered thigh.

"We unfortunately need worthy sperm-carriers to achieve our goal of a totalitarian matriarchy!"

"Whoa, how many of youh sistahs will I be ohdahed to do?"

"Miss?" Scotty must interrupt. "Sure'n it's noon a mi business, but wha's wrong wi sterile injections from anonymous donors in the privacy a'yur own local clinic?"

"How demeaning!"

"Simply a suggestion."

"Who are you sailor," and she stomps her other boot mere inches from his proprietary glands, "to deny a woman's right to romance and to the raptures of natural re-creation?"

"Di- dinna intend na harm miss."

She spins her spurs. "For the truly enlightened woman, the bitter betrayal of our cherished female prerogative is entirely unacceptable!"

"Which is wha?"

"The almighty multiple orgasm!"

"Thir's naw use attemptin ta reason with hir kind," Scotty whispers to Chipper, "these Sisters a'Fire hav bin linked ta maternity ward mix-ups n numerous kindergarten snatchin's."

"LIES! Deliberate distortions and media misspeak, disseminated by old-style back-stabbing female politicians who have been attempting to discredit our message in order to cover up their decades of traitorous collaboration with mankind!"

"So let me get this straight, you gals ah achin to get laid in the traditional fashion?"

WHUPWHUPWHUPWHUPWHUPWHUP

"I'd be careful in wha yu say mate, yu wouldna wan'ta tread on hir heightened sensibili-…"

Chipper dares lift a finger to feel the softer underlining of Titanya's leather britches.

"I admire that about a Yank. He doesn't mince his words — nor conceal his contemptible intentions!"

"Bettah fah the thrush to fluff his feathahs in the open than hide out alone in the rushes — so you get sweaty, do you, undahneath this cowhide?"

"Let's make this clear right off Stirbee!" She snarls so sensuously. "I don't believe one word of what I read in *Vanity Fair*…"

"Nope, neithah do I."

"…about there not being a woman alive who can't resist your charms."
"That fact howevah, has been reliably repohted elsewheah."
"Because I could if I wanted to, but I won't because I have to."
"That's reassuhin, h'yep… come again?"
"I'm not the kind of woman who repeats herself."
"Hey, I'm only askin cause I wouldn't want you doin nothin you don't want to do. Consent's such a big thing in the couhts these days."
"You're simply a prime specimen male-type as far as I'm concerned, and your celebrity status enhances our cause!"
"Anythin fah a cause."
Fingers trip from leather dry to drippy skin.
"We assume that an offspring of yours will certainly be male, and we plan to raise him with a regimen that will be most beneficial for this new century of the woman!"
"Pity the little crittah."
"He will be instructed in the fine arts of carpentry, masonry, plumbing and electrical work…"
"Whew, that's a relief, wouldn't want him brought up a lawyah."
Chipper nips at a 38 caliber nipple.
"…as well as those of cooking and cleaning so he will be prepared to build a white painted cottage by the sea and care for his sisters."
"Lots of men like that these days ahready, why go and bake one up from scratch? Besides, what do you intend to do with me, you know, aftah?"
"If you're good…"
Tongue touches sweat.
"Don't wohry none about that, I'm the champion ball carriah in the league of he-man dribblahs…"
"…if you're cooperative, you will be ransomed and returned intact."
"Intact?" Tongue retracts.
"Because if you're no good, you're useless anyway."
WHUPWHUP
"Hahsh tahms."
"It's the way the world works today, clan against clan, woman against man – and don't think for a second that I'm one of your rodeo girls either."
She slaps at his fingers.
"Y'ouch! Rodeo gihls?"
"Those teenage screamers who mindlessly tramp around after you from continent to continent."
"Hey, those tykes don't mean a thing to me."
"I've heard what goes on late nights in the dressing room trailers."
"That's all newspapah talk, grocahry stohe press distohts everythin they print so they can sell mah copies."

"But we have received secret reports about what your crew says."

"Rumahs, all gossip and envy, bunch of hohny guys on the road with theih radiatahs ovahheated — and so what if I enjoy lightin up once in a while and havin some fun with the fans, nothin mah to it than that."

WHUPWHUPWHUPWHUP

"Disgusting."

"Nevah cry foul until you try faih."

"I am motivated solely by my desire to reestablish the natural female order. It is the nuclear family I fight for, guided by the executive wife who shall rule with a stern hand and forge with her sisters an entirely new and incorruptible civilization — and Stirbee!"

"H'yep, I'm listenin."

"I assure you I cannot fall victim to the mad sexual impulses that drive many unfortunate women."

"That's a relief, cause those gals have got to be the wohst, whoa don't I know, all ovah a guy without wahnin, rippin his clothes off befah he's even had a chance to considah his options."

"I UNDERTAKE THIS OBLIGATION OUT OF DUTY FOR MY SISTERS AND OUT OF LOYALTY TO MY QUEEN — OH$_{OH}$ — GET A GRIP SAILOR!"

WHU$_{HUH}$HIP^{HOP}

Scotty banks too fast into his turn, upsets Titanya mid-protest.

"Ah tried warnin yu miss, yu'a goin ta hav ta sit doon somewhir n buckle up, fir yur oun safety."

"Move bitch!"

-rwhro?

"YOU! MOVE!"

Betsy's forced to jump off Chipper's lap and retreat to the -*humph* back slab bench.

Titanya slips in quickly, sits face front on Chipper's lap. *Yahhhh*, she licks her lips and she takes her dips.

"Wait babes!" Chipper feigns restraint at his belt buckle. "You suhe this is fully consensual?"

"I do what I must."

"Guess that frees me from any liability — Scotty, you be my witness?"

Scotty can't help but be a witness.

"Ah these fah real?" Chipper reaches for Titanya's shoulder holsters.

"Hold on!" Titanya can unsnap her own, thank you. "A girl can never be too careful, she must arm herself in the most inconspicuous of places."

"Ain't nothin inconspicuous about these!"

"Beware mate, she might be a minefield below."

"I'm mere flesh and blood!"

"And heavy metal in between, but hey let's get it on — *syruppyslurp* — I mean, I could ahways plead duhress — *zippidyswift* — oah flee south of the bohdah — *slipperyslit* — 'cept I'd have to hide out fah a *lon -ong -ong...*"

"May my mother forgive me!"

"...h'yep, fah a *lon -ong -ong... time!*"

"To do my duty I shall sacrifice my virginity..."

"Sohry gal, but that's been gone fah a *lon -ong -ong...*"

"...to a monster of mankind!"

"...h'yep, fah a *lon -ong -ong... time!*"

"STIRBEE!"

"Yah gal?"

"I have this feeling, oh yes I do, I have this wonderful feeling..."

"H'yep."

"...that it's going to be a boy — A GREAT BIG BOUNCING BABY BOY!"

HUP HUP HUP HUP
HUP HUP HUP HUP

"Scotty, what's the mattah now?"

"Ah canna take it, ah'm only huuman!"

"He's got a point theah gal."

"How can ah concentrate on wha's hir in front a'me?"

"True. Man can only drive himself so fah, besides, maybe we should ease up a bit, you know, with us bein so close to the stadium."

Like zeroed in low on the approach, searchlights and millions of eyes watching — CHIPPER! CHIPPER! — and stomping and cheering.

Scotty starts circling.

"Least let me wave so-long to my fans."

"You two men aren't attempting to take advantage of me while I'm in a vulnerable position, are you?"

"Nevah."

"Never."

Titanya is torn, but she eases up some. "I might be willing to acquiesce this once Stirbee, for a final wave, but only this once!"

"Just a shoht recess, promise, we can hop back on latah — right Scotty?"

"Right!"

"Something tells me I shouldn't be trusting. Men can be so deceitful!"

When without warning — "Whoa! What the flyin fuck!"

-rr awe!

Light, ghostly white, engulfs them.

"Is this fah real oah am I dreamin?"

The rescue craft glides in between a brilliantly illuminated umbrella shaped dome covering the nine story stage set below, while above there's a massive translucent blimp, so close it seems Chipper could reach out and touch either marshmallow side — he even tries — at which the blimp begins to rotate — QUOT • LINK • INC • • PRE • SENTS • • CHIP • PER • STIR • BEE • • RE • U • NITED • WITH • • THE • LOOSE • NUKES • • AN • AL • LIED • FOR • LIFE • • BEN • E • FIT • CON • CERT – scrolling amidst the stars.

"Quite the show, wouldna yu say?"

"These mastah magicians don't miss a beat!"

"These who?"

"QuotLinks! Bastahds ah evahrywheah, evahrywheah you don't evah want to be."

Not a light unto the darkness, no, nor omniscient as much as ever-present, no matter which way you turn they're square in your face, flashing some bloody advert on and off at you.

"Ah'll bank a bit so yu can lean out n wave, but don go hangin out too fir. The doonwird thrust a'the blades could suck yu right out a'the cockpit."

WHUPCUTCHUHUPCHIPCHIP

Of course Chipper hangs out too far, the intense light rendering him ghostly in appearance, the downward thrust tugging at his long white hair.

"Can't see much down theah with all the glahe Scotty!"

CHIPPER!

"Clearly they can see you!"

"HELLO! HELLO MY SWEET LITTLE DAHLINS, HELLO!"

"Disgusting."

"No it's not, it's excitin — HEY! HEY! HELLO DOWN THEAH!" Chipper leans way away out so he can see through the intensity, way away out into the danger zone, waving both arms widely.

CHIPPER! CHIPPER! CHIPPER! CHIPPER!

They gaze up at their hero, blond and beaming ablaze in all his airborne glory.

CHIP / CHIP   CHIP / CHIP

Outside and in they chant antiphonally, nearly three million on the ground and still gaining. Never has he seen so many fans and friendly.

"Whoa!"

Even Titanya's swept up. She leans out over his shoulder.

"Why don't you join in, show off those nifty knockahs?"

"You would enjoy that, wouldn't you?"

"Bet!"

"Men so enjoy displaying their women!"

"Same game plays both ways sistah."

"Yu two ready fir a closer dip?"

"C'mon gal, loosen up! Have some fun!"

Yes, she starts to throb, the bright lights, the applause, Titanya the Terrific could indulge a trifle.

CHIPPER! CHIPPER!

But the poor girl is torn, there's the excitement on the one hand, party discipline on the other — duty/thrill, duty/thrill — what to do?

CHIP- CHIP- CHIPPER!

"I could, couldn't I?"

"Do it! Hang out heah with me! HELLO! HELLO GUYS AND GALS! LOOKIE SEE WHAT I'VE GOT SO EAGAH TO PLEASE! HELLO! HELL-... *Whoa! Whoa! Oh!* $_{Oh!}$"

"Hodd on mate! Wi'r runnin inta some unexpected turbulence!"

CHIPPER!

The cry rises up, engulfing the helicopter, drawing it downward into its orbit, dangerously close to the high glowing dome of the stage set, and jostling the thin-skinned QuotLink corporate blimp as it too is pulled into the vortex — SPIN SPIN — thankfully Scotty's at the controls! He pulls up, doesn't know how he does it, but he does, those years of coastal training, iron discipline under fire and a proverbial Highlander's brawn, while the Olympic-size stadium explodes underneath in one great voice:

CHIPPER!

Bolts the helicopter skyways.

WHUUUP^{WHUUUP}

"WHOA -HOA -HOA!" Which is when the turbulence trips him. Thrust hooks him. Chipper's head's being sucked out the portal!

"STIRBEE, BE CAREFUL!"

"Nothin much I can *controlllllll*—"

But Titanya's quick, she is, all arms clutched tightly around his waist. She hauls him back from the brink. "DON'T SCARE ME LIKE THAT!"

"Scahe you?"

"I can't lose you now that I have you!" And she locks her limber legs around his, clamps her ankles fast under the seat.

"Jesus H! Even a revolutionahy feminist can get possessive!"

"Can I help it if I am a woman first?"

WHUPWHUPWHUPWHUPWHUPWHUP

Then there's her sisters, cranking along the highway. "Hoorry oop, yoo sloow pookes, we've goot t'git there befoore midnight." With over twelve kilometers left to go — *RONK! RONK!* "Moove it oover yoo loosers, git it oof the rood if yoo can't hack the traffic!"

"See, I told you. There he is Cub. I knew he wouldn't disappoint us."

"What time is it?"

"11:46:18."

"Right on time for his set — and what a spectacular entrance!"

"OK alright, but what the hell is he doing, and who's that riding on his lap! SNAP SNAP! Get me a telephoto shot on that copter!"

MORE! MORE! MORE! The galley slaves in the truck are revolting, they're out of their chairs, craining their necks at the monitors, cheering the bare chested sweetie on.

"Look! It's some tart! He's hung us up for half an hour over some goddamn tart!"

"Can't!" Lou's eyes go blank, this is the night of nights, the Loose Nukes' reunion, and his too.

Then's when the telephoto cuts in, zooms tight onto Titanya's teats, both barrels smokin.

Lou slumps in his seat in shock.

HEY HEY! RIGHT ON! MORE! MORE! Techies are out of control.

"BACK! BACK YOU INGRATES! SNAP SNAP!" Cub lets go with the lash. "KILL! KILL THE BROADCAST LEAD! — Do you morons have any idea what a ten second exposé like that could cost us in audience share? — CUT! CUT TO... cut to what?"

"We have hundreds of public service announcements in the bin Cub."

"THEN LINE'EM UP AND LET'EM RIP! SNAP! SNAP! SNAP! SNAP!"

A nearly extinct black sarcophagus beetle is seen munching on a paralyzed tree termite underneath the large floppy leaf of a rare remaining radyam tree while a Carnegie-Mellon entomologist sitting on a camp stool in the spattering rain peers through a microscope and takes notes...

"Eminenze!"

The Liaison tears down the stairs from his skybox, two steps at a time.

"Vait! Ve vere dizcuztink my amazink dizcovery!"

The grumbling, this rumbling from behind.

"Ziz vill zolve all our problemz! Guaranteed!"

Fast as fast can His Eminence descends when — E-ME-NEN-ZE! — something goes rolling past him like a rock ball.

...on a rise a kilometer behind the bespeckled specialist, a battalion of bulldozers bowl over the scorched trunks of hectares of other eons-old radyams to make way for the long-horned cattle herds that will soon trample the last of the lush green vegetation into a mudden mulch prior to slaughter and shipment to a chain of orange and green gringo taco stands throughout the Southwest....

"How you holdin up gal, you look a little dazzled?"
WHUPWHUP
"I don't know Stirbee, I've never- I-..."
"What don't you know sweetiepie?"
"My sisters, the struggle, I-..." Her voice wavers, some doubt perhaps she might backslide into raw residual feelings of a recidivist libertinism, though not when the future of the woman's at risk, still... "Who am I in all this madness?"
"Just a girl out havin a hell of a good time, why has theah got to be any mah to the moment than that?"
"I feel the moment, you, me, flying high – I feel the fire."
"Was smokin myself some, h'yep, and it ain't that I'm unwillin noh unable, no way, I'm a-..."
"You're a superstar!" There's glitter in her eyes.
-gro-ro-ro-roan. Betsy's heard these lyrics before, knows them by heart.
"A supahstud supahstah."
"But beneath the gruff exterior a kind, a gentle giving man."
-roh – must be the altitude.
"But no mattah how fine it feels, theah's this somethin each of us has got to do, each individual on his own, and theah's this somethin I've got to do tonight – besides I've nevah been to Sheffield befah."
"Na a stop on most tourists' itinerary."
"Was I wrong?" Titanya's back to doubtful. "Or didn't I feel a spark jump between us?"
"Real scoahchah."
"A special feeling that could be nourished and grow into a beautiful life for the both of us."
"Probably, I mean you nevah know fah suhe..."
"I can see that white painted cottage by the sea."
"...no mattah what happens between a gal and a guy, fact remains..."
"Children, our children, running in the sun."

"…wait now, hold on, truth is a guy's ahways got that somethin else he's got to be doin — gal does too, pahticulahly a true believah like youhself — see we'h alike like that, you and me, we've both got these somethings we've just got to be doin, and soon."

"What? What could be more important than two lovers together by the seaside forever?"

"How aboot three million kids preparin ta storm a stadium?"

"Plus fahevah's a long time…"

"What would you know about love sailor?"

"…fahevah's a lot longah than anybody alive today will evah see…"

"I may na have slipped on every slut in the shop, but I kniw wha fits me off the rack jus fine."

"Who's a slut? Who's a slut?" Titanya instantly remembers herself, remembers her mission, who's who in this bloody battle of the sexes — so naturally she reaches for her pistols.

"Hold on, hold on you two, no need to bickah."

"Don't lie to me Stirbee!" She straps back on her studded holster. "It's another woman, isn't it?"

"Prob'ly a string of other wimmen."

"Stay out of this sailor! I'm warning you! — So tell me," and she turns on Chipper, "how about it, how about love everlasting?"

"You mean like serious?"

"I mean commitment."

Both men shudder. "Com-commi-commitment?"

"Right!" She cups her sockers.

"Serious commitment — whoa let me see, I've got to remembah."

"Hoo aboot las night Chipper?"

-*roh-roh-roh* This Scot's a corker.

"Now no need to provoke the little lady unnecessarily. I do seem to recall a meaninful relationship, you know, like you heah about on aftahnoon TV, h'yep, I remembah once way back, seems like only yestahday… Mary Ann, oah was it Mary Sue? Healthy gihl, could make a moose blink in a stahe down, that one. Nevah cross huh, oah if you did, bettah beat a fast path towahd the bohdah. Like the law she won't go chasin aftah you into anothah state, woman had huh pride, don't you know, but come sneakin back some spring and you'd find huh luhkin behind a tree. Mary Sue, maybe Mary Ann. Wanted to be the mothah of my children in the wohst way. Even jumped my half-brothah Eben, he was an Indian guide, fled by canoe with huh runnin aftah him along the rivah bank. We didn't see him fah a couple of summahs, but me, what did I know, I was youngah and paht French, the paht that'll fuck anythin breathin if nothin else nohmal's around, and she was hot undah the covahs in a snowstohm, *whoo-ee* did we evah! What that mama couldn't dream up has nevah been concocted — anythin to please huh man — oah huh boy, hell fihe, I wasn't even out of juniah high yet, but she put it to me bluntly aftah the fihst frost. If I had a hankahrin to stay wahm through the wintah, I'd bettah delivah on the family. That's the soht of true love you'h talkin about?"

"So? Did you?"

"Did I what?"

"Did you deliver on the family?" Titanya demands to know.

"Don't know. Could've been me, oah mine, some of them I suppose, could've been a few othah fellas too. Mary Sue — suhe it was Mary Sue…"

-mm-rrr-rry-roo-roo…

"…h'yep, Mary Sue — she had half of Aroostook County promisin huh a bundle. I might have been huh favorite, she always said I was, but with a gal that's got to be a mothah, you nevah know, leastwise not up wheah I come from in Nohthuhn Maine. Woman wants somethin wahm and cuddly to nourish huh cleah through to the spring thaw, she's got to fry up whatevah she can root out the cellah."

WHUPWHUPWHUPWHUP

…and in the mountains beyond the plateau, indigenous native children enslaved at below subsistence wages extract gold by washing rock dust in a mercury and sulfur solution that rushes downstream and over the Emerald Falls into a soapy yellow pool of irredeemable chemical pollutants…

"Time? Time check — *snap?*"

"11:53:27."

"Did you hear that Lou? Did you hear that?"

Lou must. He moans.

"The clock is ticking and that son-of-a-bitch is still up there circling!"

At the base of the bleecher stairs, the Executive Liaison must contend with the standing room only crowd who are pushing and shoving about the stadium floor, though not in a rude unfriendly manner, no, they're simply making the best of it, while His Eminence is intent on making it worse. He is joined by three burly QuotLink Inc Security corpsers who run interference for him as he rushes along the playing field.

The nappy Liaison stands out starkly against the unwashed – his entourage, his judicial tonsure, the slick silk suit, the dribble stains on his monogrammed tie, the pronounced overbite – all the better to gnaw on you my lovelies – "OUT OF MY WAY!" There's simply no excuses with this guy, just *ooff!* – "YOUSOULFOULOAF!"

"Kiss me arse toppe'!"

"Yeah, buzz off hook face."

What's this? Resistance? Which is when the security goons step in, when the havoc begins.

The Liaison quickens his pace.

"Eminenze!" Someone shouts amidst the crowd. "Eminenze!"

Without warning the Liaison stumbles, kicks against something, socks it solidly a few yards down field, but it's a shin splitter and he's hopping mad about it. "Damn it! Damn the nuisance!"

"Eminenze?" Whatever it is, it crawls back for more, and the Liaison is about to sock it another one. "Eminenze, iz me, iz Queezac!" And it's afraid, dark doubled-over and trembling, this thick shell of a creature, all shoulders and bone, its pink belly exposed, quivering, with a huge protruding head and a monstrous beak.

"Queezac!" The Executive Liaison peers down and recognizes it. "What are you doing out here in public!"

Indeed! And drunk too. Seems that QuotLink Inc's bio-engineering mastermind, who has been intentionally excluded from the official receptions, has been gratifying itself by guzzling alone in the basement of the home team's locker room.

"I have to zpeak vitz you, iz urgent."

"Can't it wait for later, and not in full view?"

"Iz about you know who un grabbink him at ze helicopter pad vhen nobody'z vatchink."

"Quiet you idiot, someone will hear."

Not the sort crowding the Liaison, they're all blown out on some specialty imported Turkish hashish, though they are staring at Queezac, I mean, is this an hallucination or what? Can we pet it?

Queezac snaps at them.

"Wow! What if this thing gets loose man?"

"Shouldn't it be on a leash? It might have rabies and bite somebody!"

"'At's right, wha' if it piddles on me ankle?"

QuotLink patrols rapidly enclose, form a tight phalanx around the Liaison and his encrusted friend.

"Quite the spectacle you are creating Queezac, what do you have to say for yourself?"

"Vhy'z Jipper circlink Eminenze, vhy dozen't he land?"

His Eminence is seething, about the mouth and down, so much drabble and drool abound.

"Vhat'z ze matter? Doezn't he vant to come down un play vitz uz?"

"Quiet Queezac! What is so important that you must interrupt me now. I have official duties I must perform."

"Yez vell, you remember ze debate ve've been havink ovv and on about ze benevitz ov clonink up againzt zoze ov proztzetic rehab?"

"Vaguely..."

"Vitz clonink, OK, you getz a duplicate ov yourselv, but you gotz to go tzrough ze baby ztepz, ze virzt googooz, ze terrible twoz, ze demandink fourz, zoze adolezcent zitz un fitz, un in ze end, iz not really you, juzt a cloze vaczimile?"

"Why is this discussion of any importance at this precise moment?"

"Patienze Eminenze, patienze vitz your poor Qveezac — un on ze otzer hand, rehab meanz montz, yearz iv you add in all ze zeparate zurgeriez, ze painvul recoveriez, plaztic partz zat zqueek when you getz up, electronic devizez zat go buzz ovv in ze night, un zen zoze outrageouzly exzpenzive organ tranzplantz, right, vrom anonymouz Jineze donorz?"

"Not to mention expense."

"Un in ze end, you're lookink in ze mirror at ze zame mizerable zelv you began vitz."

"I am beginning to take offense."

"Yez vell, vitz regardz to Jibber..."

"WHY DO YOU TAUNT ME WITH THAT NAME!"

"...zorry, zorry but zat'z ze point ov ze dizcuzzion, I had ziz miraculouz inzpiration vhile I vaz enjoyink a nightcap in ze bazement..."

"You reek of inspiration, *youlickspittleloquatiouslizard.*"

"Vhile ze zolution iz admittedly exzperimental..."

"You have experimented enough in your career, look at me, I have to live forever with the results of your surgical bungling!"

"Look at you? Look at me! You tzink you've gotz handicabz, I vaz my own vorzt lab rat!"

"But you have made a fortune for yourself in the process."

"Vor you, un vor zoze uppitzy mucky muckz vloatink overhead in zat luxuriouz boardroom blimp. You botz conveniently vorgetz zat ze Body Partz Divizion iz QvadLink Inc'z biggezt provit zenter, yez, un even more important, vitzout me none ov you, not a vone ov you, vould be alive today or az rij az rajaz, no ziree bob, you'd be notzink but pennilezz duztballz zwept into ze clozet!"

"YOUR POINT QUEEZAC!"

"Le'z juzt zay I'm on ze treatzhold ov an amazink genetic dizcovery, vone zat vould bridge zat big gap between zlow clonink un coztly reconztructive zurgery…"

"No, no more of your illusory promises of life everlasting. No sale. I am definitely not interested."

"Don't be zo hazty. Ziz technology might zimply zolve ze dilemma you faze ziz very night vitz Jibber — namely, how to keep him goink ztrong until avter ze Vinale un zen quietly rid ze vorld ov hiz kind vonce un vor all."

"How? How would you do that?"

"I zee you're zuddenly interezted."

"DON'T TRIFLE WITH ME *YOUDISGRUNTLEDGARDENGRUB*!"

"Yez vell, you heard about ze Irizh lad vho vaz high on zome halluzinogenic zubztanze un tzought he could vly, ze vone vho leapt ovv ze top ov ze zcoreboard earlier ziz eveninck?"

"A left-over football fanatic more than likely."

"Vell ze vall vaz vatal, he znapped hiz brain ztem zmack in ze half. Zere vaz notzink ze medicz could do exzept zcoop him ovv ze playground un haul him downztairz to my makezhift zurgery."

"My sincerest condolences to his family, *thepuddlebrainednumbskull*, now what's your point?"

"Zeemz ze poor lad haz no relativez cloze by to claim him, nor any friendz anyvhere in ziz country, zo…" Queezac opens the slit that is his mouth to reveal a wart-knobbed tongue. "…zo I inherited him un dezided to put hiz body on ize, un boy-o-boy vhat a body I gotz on ize! Muzzlez un zo muj more zocked in tight!"

"Queezac. Please. I need know nothing of your medical perversions."

"Yez vell ztick your noze vay up in ze airz iv you vantz, but ze Irizh lad'z a dead rinke vor none otzer zan Jibber, down to ze mozt exzquizite detailz."

"And?"

"Un." Aspirated as with a begrudged grunt.

"Un?"

"Un I gotz ze power to rezuzitate him." Knotty tongue laps zipzap contentedly.

"Resuscitate him? Resuscitate a double of Chip- Chip-…"

"Zat'z right, you gotz it — pluz in ze prozezz inject him vitz a tiny bit, ze tiniezt tiny bit ov Jibber'z ezzenze, un bingo, ve gotz a grown-up clone who'z zkipped tzrough ze detektible teenz un vill do only vhat he'z told."

"What makes you certain this facsimile would be so cooperative?"

"He'z Irizh, vor Chrizzakez, zey popz zem outz pre-programmed to be dozile."

"Or outright cantankerous! And what if that little drop of Chipper Stir-… Stir-… THAT NAME! THAT NAME!"

"Ztart again, zpeak zlowly."

"What if those errant chromosomes of his predominate?"

"Up against good Irizh ztock, no vay, ztadizticz vould be in our vavor vor vonce."

"It is much too risky a chance to take."

"Iz no good beink zkeptical, bezidez how many optionz have you gotz right now?"

"And none of this could be accomplished within the hour, which means this entire discussion is irrelevant — YOU ARE WASTING MY PRECIOUS TIME AS USUAL!"

"Not at all. Ze hunk'z juzt lyink zere on live zupportz. I've already ztijed hiz head back on, even vigured outz ze mechanicz to make him jump like a bullvrog in a bog. No vone vould ever zuzpect, he lookz juzt like Jipper up cloze or long zhot."

"How? How are you going to work this medical miracle?"

"Iz a trade zecret, mine own genome mappink zcheme, vhich I might be inclined to lizenze to QuotLink Inc vor a vone time only application, zat iz, iv ze prize iz right." Queezac rubs his beak along the Liaison's shin.

"I see, and what might that price be?" The Liaison resists an urge to reciprocate with a boot chuck at Queezac's exposed underside.

"Yez vell zome ztock optionz vor openerz, a cozy ovvize zvuite on ze top vloor ov ze new QvotLink Battery Park Headquarterz, one vazink ze harbor tzough, not ze Brooklyn dockz, a vat golden parazhute zhould I zuddenly dezide to bail outz, or bevore vone ov you creepz puzhez me outz, zen zome ov ze uzual perkz, a modezt corporate jet vould be nize, paid-up green veez, my own zecretary, a male verzion, tall, blond vitz nize bunz, blue eyez un a golden ta-..."

"This is blackmail."

"No iz not, iz high level negotiatink."

"But what would our Executive Committee have to say about the fact that you continue to perform surgery without benefit of a license nor even a mail-order medical degree?" The Liaison gets to dripping again, about the fangs.

"Zat'z notzink compared to ze vayz zoze zcoundralz un zere accoutantz have been zcramblink ze bookz in zoze boguz qvarterly reportz."

"Then there are the numerous arrests for malpractice and general misanthropy, prison records from both the east and the west sides of our beloved Iron Curtain!"

"All vaz vondervully vorgiven vitz an act ov international amnezia."

"How about the alleged Minigrade fraud?" Liaison's downright drooling about this. "Referring patients to your own laboratories for reduplicative testing, refusing to prescribe generic brands of medication when practicable, performing unnecessary sex organ transplants?"

"Nozink vorze zan vhat mozt Park Avenue practitionerz in today'z competitive healtz care vield are doink!"

"While you were double-billing the government and QuotLink Inc's own home office HMO!"

"Yez vell maybe iz bezt to leave zome zinkz outz ov ze perzonnel vile."

The slavering Liaison goes nose-to nose at Queezac. "I alone decide what goes into those files — so you tell me how soon can you refurbish this fresh frozen Irishman into a Chipper Stirbee look-alike?"

"Zo it comez down to a dizplay ov brute vorze, doez it?"

"I REPEAT, HOW SOON?"

"Yez vell actually I've been dabblink zome already, zimbly couldn't rezizt ze urge…"

"HOW SOON?"

"…I vould probably need anotzer hour minimum in ze lavoratory splittink ztrandz ov Jibber'z DNA."

"I'll give you half an hour after he lands from extraction to replacement."

"No vay, I have to izolate ze digital dexterity nodez iv you ever vant ziz guy to play ze guitar…"

"Why bother? Chipper doesn't play well at all?"

"Ziz iz true, but I ztill have to invuze ze Irizh hunk'z blood ztream un getz him up un kickink — how am I zuppozed to get him jumpink az high az Jibber in halv an hour?"

"By wit Queezac, and by grim determination." The two are more than none-to-nose, they are mouth-to-mouth, dripping fang to curdled tongue, and any lambkin knows the bigger the bad wolf's bite, the faster his curly little head's going to disappear out of sight. "FORTY FIVE MINUTES MY FRIEND, THAT'S DEADLINE, RUNS YOU FLAT UP AGAINST THE FINALE!"

"But zurely you can delay ze pervormanze a vew minutez longer?"

"DELAY!" Which mere mention sends the Executive Liaison into a frothing rage, great billows of it, slushy and sticky, glue gruel goo with Queezac flapping desperately to get his head above foam line.

"Bu- but iv I ruzh it, zere'z an awvul jance ze Irizh hunk vill come out alive, yez, but brain dead!"

"All the better for an ersatz rockstar!" The Liaison bellows blightly on. "SO SEE CHIPPER STIRBEE!" He arises gleefully out of the muck. "YOU MIGHT CIRCLE HIGH ABOVE US NOW, BUT YOU HAVEN'T A CHANCE ON THE GROUND, NOT AFTER OUR CRACK MEDICAL TEAM FINISHES WITH YOU — YIKKITY-YUKYUKYUKYUKYUK…"

"Jezuz! Vill you look at me, I'm zoaked!"

"…YUK YUK!"

> ...fish float and speckled tree frogs, birds of exotic plumage, monkeys and assorted corpses of other creatures drifting along the great river banks past construction camps and leveled villages, past trading posts and abandoned missions, out toward the sea and civilization, port cities, squatter slums, the promise of prosperity...

QuotLink Inc's vaunted Corporate Security Corps has managed to restore order in the auto park. Flogging batons and a mounted cavalry unit have finally driven the crowd away from the landing area, but it's a stand-off and tense. Kids, fearless, armed only with their youth, clustered in the corners. QuotLinks, lean, mean and totally mercenary, outfitted for a fight, in a solid ring around the copter pad, with camera crews and reporters barred from the scene. But all eyes are on the skies anyway, cameras and troops and the groupie groups, all gaze upwards without comprehension as the helicopter dips and climbs, whips and whines...

CHIPPER! CHIPPER!

They scream. They swarm. They stream. They storm. Three and a half million and more every minute, in the prime of their youthful exuberance, with a remnant of another age, a 60s crowd mixed in, generations beautiful in mind and body, friendly, colorful with tie-dyed shirts and skirts, bare midriffs and chests, long-haired, long-waisted, long-wasted, arms stretched up swaying to the staccato beat of the chopper and waving.

WHUP / WHUP WHUP / WHUP

CHIP /PER! CHIP /PER!

Chipper Stirbee, a still living legend from the early years, a backwoods boy who along with his trusty band of Loose Nukes slugged it out in the rut and rumble days of rock 'n' roll, back when Elvis was King, Buddy Holly, Fats Domino, back when the Beatles were born, the Stones, Jim Morrison, Haight-Ashbury, Vietnam, Woodstock, psychedelics, protests, back before the lush dubbed sounds of multiple overlays and the lurid spectacle of MTV, back when sex was banned from the airwaves and a sex scandal like Chipper's in Cincinnati, Summer of 69 could cost a star his career. Eternal banishment. But Chipper wasn't as dead as they said, from some long due overdose. Chipper never did hard drugs. He had his bad habits, God knows, and some close calls with the law, but he has survived and made a comeback in a tough business — and after half a century of seclusion in Northern Maine, his is surely a return from the grave.

WHUPWHUPWHUPWHUPWHUPWHUPWHUPWHUPWHUPWHUPWHUP

...though far from the devastation of the forests, in the nation's spectacularly modern glass and concrete capitol, a mustachioed Army Colonel turned El Jefe Presidente-For-Life counts his greenbacks and declares his country free from the tyranny of participant democracy and open, pried wide open to the marvels of foreign market speculation...

"Cub. Take a look on the remotes, there on G-5 — something's up outside on the landing pad."

Indeed. Cub watches on the monitor while one of his readicam remotes rushes into the middle of a melee. QuotLink Security types are advancing upon a group of Chipper's camp followers, a whole tribe of them, men, wom-... boys, girls with little children in tow — *WHUPWHUPWHUP WHUPWHUPWHUP* – QuotLinks spinning numb-chucks above their heads. Yet the kids seem entirely unaware of the assault, all gazing upwards at the approaching helicopter — *WHUPWHUPWHUPWHUPWHUPWHUP* — when suddenly there are screams, the realization, dull thuds and panic.

"I don't believe it."

"It was bound to break sometime."

"Broadcast it Cub?"

"No." Cub sips on a copa cola. "Stow it. Let the newsboys decide what to do with it later — *snip snip!*"

"What? What's up what?" Lou blinks alert, long enough to notice.

The erstwhile Carnegie-Mellon entomologist, having completed his observations, claps the beetle with its mealy victim inside a jar, folds his field stool and ambles off, searching for additional specimens of a rapidly dying era.

All's in flux and a frenzy as His Eminence plows through the crowd, paying scant attention to the commotion he leaves in his wake, absorbed as he is with matters of far higher significance, such as the enormous blimp fired up bright with QuotLink's corporate titans aboard, suspended there beware directly above his slightly stooped shoulders.

Yet it is a tribute to his diplomatic skills, and singular cast of mind, that the Executive Liaison can readily put these petty intrigues behind him in order to represent the multiple interests of QuotLink Inc before HRH the Queen. For if he is mostly merciless toward his underlings, he can be oily ingratiating to an upperling, unless, that is, he gets nervy and mutters something unseemly under his breath. Tonight especially he must endeavor to button his upper lip, he must play the charmer as he sits by invitation at the left hand side of Her Majesty. For His Eminence is the official host, QuotLink Inc the sole sponsor of this evening's festivities.

He steps into the Royals' box and bows obsequiously in the Queen's direction – *stuckupcrustycunt!* – or some such slips out involuntarily.

Which causes a stir to Her Highness' skirt.

Whereupon the Executive Liaison attempts to control himself, although he is growing increasingly impatient with every second's delay. And if foaming at the mouth isn't unsightly enough, his scratching at his sore butt borders on impropriety, and why? Mobs of kids and rockstars and threats of revolution in the streets, while that imbecilic Chipper Stirbee does loops overhead – "*I'llbusthisbuttonceandforall!*" – he coughs into a QL monogrammed silk handkerchief.

The Queen fidgets in her chair.

He swallows whatever sticks quite quickly, for much weighs upon this occasion, His Eminence being the first QuotLink ever permitted an audience before the Crown. Why the slightest indiscretion, even grumble of indigestion, could cost QuotLink Inc untold damages to its newfound image of corporate benefactor, this after decades on the expansionist prowl – swift unkindly takeovers, predatory pricing practices, pouncing on unsuspecting midwestern workers in their sleep, dragging their carcasses off to windowless Chinese factories, finance schemes and security frauds too numerous to mention, but sloughed off as mere technical violations, agreements to pay record fines with neither the admission of guilt nor the denial of allegations – but take a look at QuotLink Inc now, you quibblers, you naysayers, $1.34 trillion in gross profits this past quarter alone!

QuotLink Engineering, with their hot new line of portable nuclear reactors, the Biomedical Division's express transplant organs, QuotLink Inc's sweetest revenue stream, Quell Integrated Financial, surely Wall Street's most carnivorous, QTV, the biggest pay-per-view rip-off cable network in the States, Quot Records, Quot Publishers, Quot Movie and TV, Q-City Industrial Theme Parks, the NFL championship Jersey City Jackals, the LoveLink on-line weather and dating service – and these merely its most recent North American acquisitions!

QuotLink Inc's international holdings are equally alarming: QuotNet, the largest private satellite system in the world, QuotTrek airlines and container ships, oil tankers and cruise boats, aircraft carriers and submarines under long term lease to land-locked expansionist countries, then there are the numerous nameless offshore banking interests and arms trafficking and drugs, and the infamous QuotLink Corporate Security Corps — because QuotLink means *security*, the source from which all else subsidiary has been spawned, from QuotLink Inc's modest beginnings on the bucolic shores of Lake Geneva as a small arms manufacturer to a Wall Street takeover specialist, with the Corporate Security Corps alone employing a greater standing army than the German Bundeswher and the Japanese Self-Defense Force combined. A powerful ally for anyone in the business of government, this Executive Liaison, who can't restrain a grunt under his breath — *youchronicobsolescentcrone!*

Which perforce startles the Queen! There's a slight turn of the head, an inquisitive arch to the brow?

The Executive Liaison smiles, sharp sheared daggers and breath fresh from the kill.

Her Majesty is appropriately appalled.

Whereupon he attempts an apology of some such stuck in his throat as he gropes forward to joke: The lateness of the hour, the various dalliances and delays, the unpredictable nature of a rock concert generally, the playful behavior of the evening's feature in particular — "Chipper Stir- Stir-..." — something about that name, he can't quite get it out.

The Queen nods before she turns away.

He has tried, poor bastard, to be liberal and show a lofty forbearance toward the foibles of the common man, toward the upstart rockstar cavorting in the sky above. He sighs — *siiiiiiiiigh* — he chuckles — *yukyukyukyuk* — and he checks his hand crafted Swiss time piece, wondering to himself when if ever this nonsense will end, how soon he can withdraw to a chilled bottle of Wobbles Gin.

WHUPWHUPWHUPWHUP

"Skyhook Rescue XS90, this is Wembley Ground Control..."

"Hey, listen up!" Titanya has Scotty's headset. "They're signaling us."

"...this is Wembley Ground Control, do you read me? Skyhook Rescue XS90, you are presently cleared for landing, repeat, you are presently cleared for landing. Please prepare your descent. Copy?"

"Mechanical difficulties sailor." She tentatively hands them back. "Remember you have to divert to Heathrow."

Scotty has a cocked metal tip inserted into his other ear.

"Skyhook Rescue XS90, this is Wembley Ground Control, you are cleared for landing. Do you read me?"

"MECHANICAL DIFFICULTIES! IT'S NOT ALL THAT DIFFICULT TO REPEAT!" Piercing to the tympanum.

And to demonstrate to the world below that she is firmly in charge, Titanya leans out the cab and brandishes her chrome plated breasts.

CHIPPER! CHIPPER!

Searchlights and a cheer, then the guys in the audience spot her…

CHIPPY! CHIPPY!

…tantalizing Titanya, that is, until the adulation turns to catcalls…

CHIPPY CHIQUITA

"YOU- YOU LUMPEN LOSERS! CAN'T TRUST A ONE OF YOU, SO HERE, EAT YOUR HEARTS OUT!" Whereupon she takes aim and she lets go, strafing the stadium — FIRE! FIRE! — and she fires some more! Hot flashes of fresh grown terrorist teats on view for the consumer masses!

CHICK- CHICK- CHICK- CHICK- CHICK- CHICK- sends the guys on the ground scrambling for cover.

"DISGUSTING!" As she turns and zips up. "I MAY HAVE FORGOTTEN MYSELF ONCE STIRBEE, BUT BELIEVE YOU ME, IT WON'T HAPPEN AGAIN — SET A COURSE FOR SHEFFIELD SAILOR, AND SAY SO LONG TO YOUR CRONIES ON THE GROUND!"

So it's farewell to the fans, farewell to the Security Corps too, to the bright beacon atop the stage set adieu, and as Scotty steers away in a northerly direction he brashly buzzes the QuotLink blimp, bumpin the blinkin advert off and on again — QUOT • STINK • INC • • RE • SENTS • • CHIP • • STIR • BEE • • NITE • • • LOOSE • NUKES • • LIE • FOR • LIFE • • BEN • E • FIT • CON – scrolling amidst the stars.

The Executive Liaison startles in his seat — EYESOREMOTHERPUCKER! — the helicopter is flying off! This cannot be! Everything is in place at the landing pad, with no allowance for further delay!

He's abrupt — "*Stuffedtoomuchlunch!*" – he announces to Her Majesty as he hurries down the carpeted steps of the Royal Box. She, while initially inquisitive as to his disposition, seems relieved at his rapid departure.

Cameras too track the vanishing aircraft, dozens of readicams scan the skies, and inside the control truck Cub *snaps* – "LOU! I WARNED YOU!" — he's up, he's out of his swivel chair, this great bearded Santa Bear, not cuddly, no, not anyone anyone would want to hug or to wrestle with. Nobody wants Cub McCluff to squeeze them nor chuck them up under the chin, chuck them up and toss them across the room, no no, most people would run for their lives if this bear wanted to dance with them.

And Lou would too if he could, but he can't. He's trapped in his matching swivel chair while Cub stands *glow-rr-rrow-ering* down at him — and Lou who's minimorphic in physique, who underneath his slight frame has this stomach and some bowels, not much of his bowels left, but some, and acid drip dropping from his stomach into his bowels, acid running cross-hatched rivulets into his intestines, rivulets which cause him to ache and to wretch and to shit his pants if he gets really frightened, which he is about to do now as the bully bear stands *tow-rr-rrow-ering* over him.

And if that's not enough, there a loud *BAM* as the Executive Liaison for the Entire Northern Hemispheric Region comes storming through the trailer door — "WHERE'S THAT *PEANUTSIZEDSIDESHOWHUCKSTER*?"

His reference of course being Lou, hidden as it happens under bare hands, but the sudden intrusion diverts Cub's attention long enough for Lou to slip out of his swivel chair and go scampering down along the chained ankles of the galley slaves and in and around the consoles...

Cub's immediately after him, but a man of great substance does not move gracefully, upsetting consoles, dispersing crew — "WHEN I GET MY CLAWS ON YOU, I'LL…"

And right behind Cub comes the Liaison, so where are the fire exits or a window Lou can hurl himself out of?

"I WILL EAT YOU UP, *YOUSLICKWITHERINGWEASAL*, AND SPIT OUT THE PITIFUL PIECES!"

The both are chasing after him, His Eminence and His Immensity, when Lou trips — *oh no* — *ah yes* — trips through a trap door stuffed with routers and cables. He slithers down where only a mite size guy can go, disappears under the floorboards where he can hide out for a while, thank you, until the stratospheric storm above him blows over.

"WHERE'D HE GO? WHERE'D HE GO?"

The crew maintains silence, there being this unspoken code among sweatshop prisoners never to rat on an escapee.

"I'LL SQUEEZE THAT SPINDLY NECK OF YOURS WHEN I FIND YOU, UNTIL YOUR TONGUE TURNS PURPLE!"

"AND I'LL PECK YOUR EYES OUT OF THEIR SOCKETS!

Whew! Lou listens to the thunder and cradles his precious head in his hands, why, why is he the target of so much antipathy? He didn't invent Chipper. Chipper invented himself. Chipper lives by his own rules, which he surely must make up as he goes along, and who or what force on earth is going to stop him? Or who or what force or what combination thereof should even try and stop him? Not Lou. He can barely breathe.

Upstairs the Executive Liaison has reversed his guns, begun a barrage at Cub and his crew.

"WHAT ARE YOU STARING AT, *YOUMUCKRAKINGUNIONIZEDINGRATES!*

YOU ARE ALL PLOTTING TOGETHER, EVERYONE OF YOU, CONSPIRING TO SUBVERT CORPORATE EARTH!"

The workers shudder: NO! NO! NO! NO! ROW! ROW! ROW! ROW!

"BUT MARK MY WORDS, WE QUOTLINKS SHALL PREVAIL!"

Maybe, probably, but not while hemorrhaging from every orifice – "*YOUDUMBBUNCHOFDINGLEBUNGLERS!*" – frothing at the mouth he is, great gobs of green ghoulish gushes, something which even the older guys in the room have never seen before, and they're hardened, they've filmed plenty of animal eat'em-ups on jungle location for *National Geriatric.*

"WE SHALL PREVAIL AGAINST THE LIKES OF YOU DEGENERATE ROCK 'N' ROLLERS, HEAVY MEDDLERS, BIKERS AND STRIKERS..."

Fact is His Eminence is about ready to blow, which signals a serious design flaw in the circulatory system, for although QuotLinks have been designed to undergo enormous stress, they seem to frazzle when faced with humankind's needling foibles. Their sufferance-to-intolerance ratio accelerates at a hyperchronic pace, resulting in an observable neural circuit overload about the frontal lobe, complicated often enough by a rapid rise in arterial pressure with the possibility of rupture and a dangerous discharge of their nutrient green-label plasma – and the accompanying stench! Hey, it's every man for himself in the rush to wretch overboard!

Leaves Cub alone at the wheel in his attempt to withstand the siege.

"...AGAINST YOUR ATTEMPT TO DESTROY ALL THAT IS MORALLY DECENT IN AMERICA, GOOD AND LOYAL AND PATRIOTIC, GOD-FEARING, HIGHLY PROFITABLE AND MORE OR LESS LEGAL..."

Hence it is Cub who must endure wave upon wave of gagging grog, the volume of which astounds him. Sure, he has had to tolerate a mild spit-up from one of these upper-management clones time-to-time, but he has never had to witness a complete QuotLink techno-psycho breakdown – why these guys were deemed fail-safe because QuotLinks can never forget, never forgive, tossing and turning in their sleep while their tandem processors reconfigure teratons of data throughout the night.

"...AND REPLACE CIVILIZATION WITH WHAT? WHOREMONGERING, DOPE DEALING AND UNCENSORED INTERNET PORNOGRAPHY!"

QuotLinks are composed of 19% state-of-the-art computer electronics, 15% recyclable plastics and 76% off-the-shelf anatomical parts, mostly battlefield salvage from their original fabrication as forward line espionage agents, at which they proved enormously successful during the many hot and cold war generations throughout Eastern Europe, wherever they could be converted to resemble the indigenous population by using stockpiles of readily exchangeable body pieces. Rarely were they recognized for the impostors they were, and even if exposed most of their scraps could be cost effectively reconditioned to meet or to even exceed new factory specifications.

"YOU DELUDE YOURSELVES IN THE FUTILE HOPE YOU CAN OVERTHROW OUR KIND WITH YOUR PATHETIC SLOWDOWNS AND WORK TO RULE..."

QuotLinks are only slightly mechanical in their motions, however, because they are biomechanical and infused with this patented protein-enriched drive fluid which is many times more durable than human plasma, although the human cardiovascular system can tolerate more internalized stress than the comparable QuotLink brand Hyper-Flo™.

"...BUT DREAM ON, *YOUCAREERRABBLEROUSINGCAROUSERS*, BECAUSE WE QUOTLINKS SHALL SOON OWN EVERYTHING FROM THE CARS YOU DRIVE TO THE FACTORIES WHERE YOU WORK TO THE 500 CHANNEL TV SET THAT LULLS YOU TO SLEEP! WHENEVER YOU EAT, SHOWER OR SHIT, YOU'LL BE WORKING FOR ONE OF US!"

The only external manifestations of a QuotLink's mechanochemical origins are the characteristic creaking of their speech apparatus, puppy dog bad breath, inbred myopia and these ferocious temper tantrums.

"FOR WE SHALL BE SLAP-HAPPY PORKERS WHEN WE FINALLY CAN WATCH THIS RENEGADE ROCKSTAR MAKE HIS REQUISITE DEPARTURE FROM LIFE'S GREAT STAGE!"

But if anybody understands the downside of the QuotLink's more delicate mechanisms, it's Queezac, who has inobtrusively stuck his snoot inside the Liaison's motor room – "Vhere'z zat ztinkink breaker box?"

"WE QUOTLINKS SHALL STAND AND SALUTE WHEN THIS LAST BASTION OF RECALCITRANT INDIVIDUALISM GETS HIS BUTT BLASTED OFF INTO OBLIVION!"

Queezac is working feverishly for even he has never observed a tirade of this magnitude. Sure, the diplomatic model is old-fashioned, rahther old-school, but classic Geneva, built to withstand the extreme conditions of a direct nuclear hit with nary a ripple of the lower lip, and Queezac should know, he designed and constructed the original prototype back in 43.

"THEN WE CAN FINALLY TURN OUR ATTENTION TOWARD THE REST OF THE INSURGENT REMNANT OF YOU LEFT-HANDED 60S LUNATIC FRINGE!"

"Everybodzy betzer duck! Here comez ze lazt tzroez ov low vlung junk!"

Whosoever's left standing dives under his console, Queezac too, he tumbles down along the floorboards ahead of the flood, rolls up against a trap door and bounces underneath, startles Lou crouched in the dark – but then calamity can acquaint stranger bedfellows – as Queezac nods hello, then listens aghast while his august Eminence gusts out of control, utterly, with green globules of grease streaking down the front of his gray tailored suit – *gook-n-gunk gushes-n-gums-n-clumps-n-chunks they do* –

with language every bit as gritty!

"YOU SHOULD ALL HAVE BEEN LINED UP AGAINST THE WALL AND SHOT FORTY YEARS AGO!"

The Liaison is pretty much spent fireworks, yet even in a dissembled state, he has the capacity to rave on for hours and most likely mean every word of it without shame or embarrassment at heaving all over somebody else's carpet, although mercifully, two stout QuotLink Security linebackers hoist him up on their T-bar shoulders and carry him out of there spouting.

Queezac bids a bug-eyed Lou adieu and goes bounding back up behind his prized creation, as fast as his ingrown toenails will carry him.

Two longhairs outside the trailer watch as the Liaison is toted by.

"YOU TWO TOO! BLOWN TO SMITHEREENS!"

"Wow! Dude's havin a bad trip!"

"Must be a rancid batch of crystal meth."

"Somethin chemical they cut it with."

"Next stop's detox."

"Mandatory. And a mornin mouthful of methadone."

"Can't ever kick that shit."

"Get a meth monkey on your back and you've got guaranteed nightmares for life."

Next Queezac limps by.

"Looks like he's been there already."

"Yeah man, and goin back for more."

"Titanya, listen, a cause is a cause, can rub you raw, but…"

"We're past the discussion stage, I want action Stirbee!"

WHUPWHUPWHUPWHUPWHUP

"I can appreciate that too, I mean, if it wahn't fah you mothahs, theah wouldn't be any kids down theah kickin up a fuss, now would theah…"

"To think I was falling in love with such an emotional basket case!"

"…see, what I'm tryin to tell you is life's mah a mattah of timin than about anythin else – bihth, death, makin good, goin bust – you'h nevah suhe when things'll jibe just right."

"The quiet hope in a young girl's heart that love shall conquer all."

"H'yep, love can be beautiful, good beat, two folks meet, get to groovin, but wrong timin, both get out of sync and damn, along comes a disastah."

"But I'm the stronger woman for it Stirbee."

"Packed, stacked, but what I'm sayin is this has got to be the wohst time possible, like I've got othah things I've got to be doin."

"What, jump up and down on a stage and act like a fool?"

"That too, but it's this thing I've got inside me, this cohe soht of feelin."

"Core?"

"Cohe. You know, that somethin way down deep inside you that you can nevah control, that thing that's stuck in youh gut, drivin you nuts?"

"Everything for you is reduced to sex, isn't it?"

"Wish this was sex gal, it'd be a hell of a lot easiah."

"I watched the TV biography Stirbee, I understand how you have struggled these past sixteen months and climbed back again from obscurity to the very pinnacle of success."

"Needle point."

"What?"

"Pinnacle's like a needle point. Fact if a guy stops dancin fah half a breath while high up like that, he'll slip and skewah himself cleah through."

WHUPWHUP

"That's why you've got to release me, so I can head back to Wembley, got to try somethin befah it's too late."

"Too late for what?"

"Way too late, befah the real show is ovah, befah everythin we love around us in this wohld gets fried up in shoht ohdah."

"Like what, the environment?"

"Fah stahtahs, and time's runnin out on that act fast, that's fah suhe, fah you, fah me, fah everybody on the planet."

"You're going to save the planet? You? Give me a break!"

"Whoa no, ain't nothin one lone guy can do, even though he's a kick-ass supahstud, but right guy, right time, might spahk a mighty upheaval."

"But what about us Stirbee, what about me?"

"You know, I've been thinkin about that, and when it comes to baby-makin, Scotty heah, he'd be a prime candidate, steady, ready…"

"I'd be willin ta give it mi best shot."

"Don't trifle with my affections!"

"Nope. Nevah. It's just that I've got this one oppohtunity with billions of people watchin, and I've got no mah than a split-second to pull it off."

"Pull what off?"

"Don't know fah suhe, don't know."

"Then I'm not going to reconsider — to Sheffield and to our future!"

"Titanya please, considah my boy Scotty heah…"

Scotty gives her that craggy Highlands profile.

"…aftah he drops me off, he could do fah you 'til he runs out of gas."

"Go to it mate," Scotty's reduced to a pant, "bloke's got ta be brave!"

"Man can't shrink!"

"Can't shirk!"

"Answer the call."

"Rise to the occasion."

Disgusting!"

"No mah than most guys gal."

WHUPWHUPWHUPWHUP

"Ever think you might need some help Stirbee, someone to stand beside you, someone who could share this experience with you?"

"Whoa maybe so. A road warrioh like youhself might come in handy."

"I would agree, if... if you would be willing to link our fates together."

"How togethah?"

"I must insist on a living reminder of our union — come on Stirbee! Fuck me silly!"

"I'd- I'd love to gal, it'd be a distinct pleasuhe, *whoo-ee* would it evah be, and the way you ohdah me around makes my tendahs tingle, bu-..."

Before he can object, she's zap strapped back on his lap and flapping.

"Whoa gal, this has got to be the *wron -ong -ong...*"

"Let's make it happen — for posterity!"

"...definitely the *wron -ong -ong... time!*"

"You off to war..."

"Which might last a *lon -ong -ong...*"

"...me home minding the baby."

"...h'yep, fah a *lon -ong -ong... -wrong! -wrong!*"

"What is it, Stirbee? What gives?"

"Good stahtah doesn't necessarily win evahry race."

"I'm not going to permit you to mock my love..."

"Babes, ain't noth-..."

"...although I do intend to stand by my offer! For this is our one moment of glory together!" Titanya rises from her roost, and her stance is the thing, legs spread apart, head held high, eyes fastened forward, each hand clasped at a chrome-clad breast — Twenty First Century Female Heroic! — "Because my clock is ticking!"

"My clock is tickin too."

"Wha? Wha's tha yu go'tickin?"

"Clocks Scotty, and that's why you've got to tuhn us around."

"Roger."

"No! I've decided I won't let you go, not after we've finally found each other and flown this far!"

"Listen gal, lesson fah life. The wohse, and I mean the wohse thing a woman can do is to try and keep a man from doin what he's got to do — not his mothah, not his gihlfriend, not a wife, not even a terrohist bombshell like youhself can talk him out of..."

"Bombshell?"

"No Scotty, not that soht of bom-..."

"I can't wait, I'm ready to explode!"

"Yu'r na wired ta some sor'ta plastic device, a yu miss?"
"Search me Sailor, I'd never let anything artificial invade my body!"
"That's not a bad idea Scotty. Maybe you should pat huh down, you know, check huh out — heah, trade places, let me try drivin fah awhile." Whereupon Chipper tackles the tiny terror and gives her a toss in the air.
"STIRBEEEE!"
-*rr row,* and about time too.
From whence she lands in a couple of practiced Scot hands.
"What is it you do Scotty, just jiggle with this suckah stick?"
WHUP   CUP
      PUP   PUP   PUP   HIC
"STIRBEE!"
-*rr* there might be a bit more to it than that pal, let me have a look.
"Don't mind me, you two, I'll get the hang of this soon enough, right Betsy? Paid plenty of quahtahs fah an intensive Satuhday aftahnoon ahcade couhse at the mall in flyin genuine simulated space fightahs."
Helicopter immediately goes into a spiral.
WHUP   WHUP   WHUPEEE
"STIRBEE!"
"Wait and see, things'll wohk out fine fah us all — plus Scotty's not such a bad lookin dude, I mean you could suhe do a lot wohse."
"Thanks mate. Ah appreciate the vote a'confidence."
"OH NO YOU DON'T — no man alive is going to trifle with me!"
"Nothin wrong with bein a relief pitchah, so long as you get to play in the game."
"Save this game."
WHUP   WHUP   WHUP
"Steady mate, hodd the burd steady."
"LET ME GO! LET ME GO!"
"Damn, this suckah's a trip!"
-*rr* maybe those petals on the floo-*rr-rr* have something to do with it.
"LET ME GO! LET ME GO!"
"Betsy! What the fuck ah you doin, you'h right smack undah my feet!"
Relax chum. I'm on top of it. Apply a little paw pressure and…
WHIP WHIP WHIP WHIP WHIP WHIP WHIP
"Don't know gihl. we'h just spinnin!"
-ROH!
"What's this, the emahgency brake?" — YANK!
WHU- WHU- WHU-
"And a way up we go!"

"GET YOUR MITTS OFF ME YOU PUNTER!"
Scotty does have his hands full.
WHUP   WHUP   WHUP
As does Chipper — "Steady. Steady."
"I should never have let my guard down and indulged my romantic instincts…"
Scotty's a strapping six two, but the diminutive miss is all fists.
"…still, I have my principles intact, I'm a Sister of Fire!" She kicks, she scratches, she bites and she bashes.
He canna hodd onta her.
"I INTEND TO REASSERT MY CONTROL HERE!" Wherewith she unzips. Scotty loses his grip. And Titanya slithers out of her leather, stripped to the skin, revealing a body of death — muscles honed and toned, arms that could bend men's limbs, legs that could do more damage than that, and she leaps she does, straight at Scotty's throat — *HOAK!* — she squeezes without mercy. "IT'S NOW OR NEVER STIRBEE. SUBMIT OR WATCH IN WONDER AT THE FATE OF YOUR FRIEND!"
Poor Scotty, his face is red, bloody red, and he's *choak-haok-hoaking*.
"THE TIME IS NOW STIRBEE! THE CHOICE IS YOURS!"
"What happens if I pull back full on the stick?"

WHOOP!
¡dOOHM

"STIRBEEEEEEEEEEE!"
"Nevah figuahed you could fly one of these contraptions upside down, did you Betsy?"
-ro -ro
"Proves that simulation ain't half the stimulation as the real thing!"
Which trick saves Scotty's neck as Titanya comes unclutched, gets flung very top of the cab.

¡dOOHM
WHOOP!

Round about right side they roll, and while the boys might be buckled in safe, down comes Titanya for a great fall — see, always snap in tight for the drive, save on the backaches, save on the lives — and Scotty's on her, pins her down prone pronto before she has time to get her legs up.
"OHHHHHH…" She wrestles, she struggles, and *mm*-mad? Mean lovin mama is furious.
Betsy too, flipped like a flapjack herself, lands slap on the back bench, decides to fasten down the hatch, she's done what she can do, she'll ride the rest of this storm out 'til it's blown over.

"Listen gal, I've got somethin impohtant to tell you." Chipper leans over close for Titanya's benefit. "See, folks keep talkin about time, like time is somethin they can grab and hold onto fah a while, put in theih pocket, cahry around like spahe change, spend a little heah, spend a little theah, but time, youh time, my time, everybody's time is wohth mah than that."

"OHH! OHH!"

"See time defines who somebody is, wheah you've been, what you've done, what you'h about ready to do. Time/enahgy, it's this continuum, time *is* enahgy, they'h the same thing. Like life and time ah the same — lifetime, that's how much life you've got ovah the time you've got, and when youh one brief breathin spell is ovah, you'h ovah. Theah's no pie in the sky. Time's up. Lights out. Blink and wave bye-bye to the fans fahevah."

"OHHHH!"

"Whatevah you did is whatevah you could do. Whatevah you didn't get done nobody else is goin to fix fah you, I mean, some folks say, hey, let's live fah the moment! Let's do it up right tonight! Live like theah's no tomohrow?"

"OH! OH! OH!"

"I say no, now is tomohrow. Futuhe is present, futuhe is right heah wheah we ah, nowheah else. And if we don't staht doin what we've got to do now, and right now, do what we feel down deep in ouh cohe is the right thing to do — you, me, Betsy, Scotty, everybody doin the best we can do — then nothin wohth nothin is evah goin to get done, nevah evah."

"-H! -H! -H!"

"Folks can gripe about it all they want, say I've ahready done my paht, thank you, oah I'm savin myself fah somethin greatah, h'yep, they can try to stash time away on a shelf somewheah and fahget it, but that's not time, that's history maybe, time past, time gone and lost and mostly wasted from what I've read — but real time, that's what we'h talkin about heah, real time ahways stahts from jump, a fresh flash every mohnin and we've got to be sun up at the gun, sprintin fah what's impohtant to be done."

"-*hhhhhhhhhh...* -*hhhhhhhhhh...*"

"You bettah let up on huh some Scotty, she's tuhnin blue."

Mistake. Ever see two bobcats mate, tails up corkscrew and flailing at one another? Love is like that, born in battle, grown into open warfare, buried in bickering. But as Scotty and Titanya fly off to their Sheffield rendezvous, it's Chipper who bails out, free style, slips out the open portal and downward toward earth he tumbles...

"What the flyin fuck?"

...with a wave stay back at Betsy...

Betsy hesitates, deliberates, that's her Chipper, that's... that's... she pants... because if dogs were designed for flight, they'd have wings and

… it's Chipper who bails out, free style

feathers and rocket farts for starters, as she dances all fours at the threshhold — plus he's left his gigbag behind, his 56 Fenderbender which is more precious to him than life itself, and Betsy, he's left Betsy stranded with only a wave farewell — so she's got to do the one thing any loyal Maine hound would do, she grabs the strap on the gigbag, clutches it tightly in her teeth, tucks back her ears, closes her eyes and leaps... *yeeeps...* goes straight into a nosedive...

CHIPPER! CHIPPER!

Chipper? Crowd is dumb struck. That's their leader taking a tumble before their very eyes, and streaking fiery white through the night betwixt brilliantly lit blimp and the reflected glow of the stage dome — and that's something else riding right behind him, paws retracted, tail straight out, gigbag trailing...

CHIPPER¡

He's about to plunge into their open arms...

CHIP- CHIP-

...though not really, no, he seems to be drifting away out of everyone's reach... floating... this way and that... wafting in the breeze...

CLIPPER! CHIP!

...but how can this be, doesn't this defy some immutable law of nature, that solid mass must fall unnervingly fast, unswervingly splat — like Betsy is, on a dead-head gravity dive downward?

Not so. Proof is there for all to see. Chipper's hand gliding *sans glider* and aiming toward the umbrella above the nine story stage set... but with no raised flaps to brake him, grandslamming directly toward the luminous scaffold dome — blinding bright and beckoning blight, moth to fame —

B-bomber Betsy's first to the finish though — *whooooopf!* — does a noseplant into a section of the stretched nylon.

But he's a close second after her — stroke of midnight!

SPLOOOOF!   SPLUNGGGG!

Chipper's arrived, on time, splayed face first on the metal mesh, and while wobble spongy it might be, soft spun wire absorbent it's not — and any flyboy hitting crossbar has got to be hurting.

WILL COOK

From the archives there's a flickering kinescope of the such young Loose Nukes — Chipper in long hair and ripped jeans, Bubba The Bod bursting a muscle shirt, Will Cook shaggy in a black turtleneck, and the little crew cut cute Danny T 'Drummer Dynamo' in a polo — all looking very mod and performing their first hit *Getta Girl* on Rick Spark's US Bandstand.

> Getta Girl / Gotta, gotta
> Need a girl / Alot alotta
> Gotta gotta / Gotta getta girl
>
> Wanna girl / Really wanna
> Need a girl / Any girl
> Gotta gotta / Gotta getta girl
>
> Need a girl / Feel a girl /
> Gotta squirrel / Alot alotta
> Hoppa hoppa / Hop a little girl

Except the last verse was adapted to appease home viewing sensibilities:

> Need a girl / Feed a squirrel
> Getta girl / Really oughta
> Gotta gotta / Meet a pretty girl

But it was all nonsense verse anyway, and on and on the song went in the same vein with these JD muppets bounding up and down in front of the cameras, Chipper the born crowd teaser and Bubba muscling in on lead guitar.

Noon the next day and a sunny May first. Lou and Elli set off on their new adventure, take the IRT to Grand Army Plaza and walk past the stately mansions facing Prospect Park to President Street, a turn down a tree lined block of four story brownstones. They're almost touching hands.

Children are playing stickball in the street, a mixed tribe, black, white, girls, boys, all ages, religions and opinions. Park Slope is a liberal sector. Young families, husband and wife professionals, singles with some cash, artists who can afford it, open windows with no shades, plants in those windows, plants in pots on stoops, spring green everywhere and Volvos parked along the curb, lots of Volvos. Stone steps go up a flight to grand entrances.

"This is the house." Lou starts up the steps toward a huge scrolled wooden door with a brass knocker, the windows all glowing clean with intricately knotted macrame hangings.

"Wait a minute. What do you want me to say?" Elli a few steps behind.

"Just be yourself." He rings the bell. A chime sounds inside.

"Just be myself?"

Someone is heard approaching slick slippered shuffles. The door opens and a small woman, quite thin, quite quite thin and with blond long straight hair tucked back behind her ears meets them. "Hello." And no voice could be more absent from the reedy body.

"Hel-…"

Woman turns with no more greeting than that and steps back into the entry. Lou follows her through the doorway. Elli is more reluctant. Was that an invitation to come in?

The entry is sparse. A stripped bare wood floor, but polished to a high sheen. The little woman is clean, she wears slippers and beckons to a mat on the floor covered with rows of additional slippers in various sizes. Lou without saying a word kicks off his shoes — *flunk flunk* — and eases himself into an oversize pair. Elli does likewise. Her eyes roam. A long staircase, all turned wood with delicately carved lattice work overhead curves upward floor after floor. At top a skylight. Elli cranes her neck and peeks up. Pastel paintings cover the walls, longing eyed children with scrubbed faces and stringy blond hair, pale cheeks and pale pinks, yellows and greens. Elli thinks jelly beans and Easter bunnies.

The little woman precedes them through a tall wood archway and seats herself in a maple rocker by the mantle. Elli hears the rocking commence almost instantly. She follows.

Lou seats himself opposite the rocking little woman on a sofa of sorts. It's a wooden bench with spindle arms. Elli sits down beside him. The bench isn't cushy or comfy, but it's the only padded seat in the room. And the room is massive, yet furnished with sticks for furniture, spots of pallid colors, sparse — or for Elli who is eclectic and a collector, void.

The elaborate wood mantle reaches from floor to ceiling, some sort of crêche collection of figures in the bare brick fireplace, one seated, one bent over, two little ones kneeling, no swaddling however. Over the mantle another pastel portrait, the little woman and two littler women stare out and at nothing in particular. Elli stares everywhere, at everything. Light streams in through the bow windows, the room glows, but there are no green plants to soak up the sun. And everywhere woven rugs and tapestries and blankets spread across polished floors, hung on bare walls, slung over backs of chairs, straight back chairs, Quaker, Shaker, and oh yes, there it is, the loom, how could she have missed it, and next to it the spinning wheel. The loom and the spinning wheel and the little woman who rocks by the hearth.

More slip slipping is heard and from between two massive slider doors, a dining room no doubt, in skate two little girls in socks, identically dressed in Easter bunny colors, jumpers. They are wide-eyed and towheaded expressionless. Are they in from play outside with the other children? Seems not for they are much too clean to play in a street.

The girls neither introduce themselves, nor does the woman of the house. The two miniatures seat themselves cross legged on the floor, flanking their mother before the hearth. The three look entirely alike and entirely like the pastel portrait above the mantle and like the figures stashed in the crêche inside the fireplace.

Elli smiles hello, but even Elli cannot speak, her lips pursed closed and her mouth dry, a jelly bean stuck in her throat.

The little girls gape at Lou and Elli, some recent migrants from another planet surely. Manhattan perhaps. And do they speak English or merely blather in some odd foreign tongue, ignorant of our ways?

"Hello girls." Lou sings out.

There is no response.

Curiously there are no musical instruments about. No no. They are collected on the top floor, far away from sight or sound, Will Cook collected high and away in an aviaratic atelier atop, up the grand staircase on the fifth floor where he has his own soundproofed studio so he can be alone to play undisturbed, Will's solitary self-confinement. Though he has been roused. A rumbling is heard on the stairs, not shoes, but rather some rude heavy feet descending, male, an irregular rhythmic cascade, like a rock slide gaining momentum as the feet hurl themselves downward on the unsuspecting travelers seated below... the tumbling draws closer, closer... it resounds throughout the house, echoes off the barren floors and walls... the very weavings flutter...

Elli feels a strange anticipation reverberating within her. She is seized with excitement, the jelly bean sliding down her esophagus. Will Cook. Will Cook. Soon she will see Will Cook. Her mind flips pages in a girlhood scrapbook, Will Cook, one of the four skinny boys she and her friends wanted to ravage entirely and nightly. Will Cook! The boulders roll near range until they stop... abruptly... and there he lands, Will Cook, high arched barefoot huge in front of her. Elli marvels at the length of his toes!

"Will!" Lou's up out of his seat to greet him. "Good to see you my man, and you remember Elli, my ex-wife?"

Elli stands.

"And I don't think Elli has ever met your wife, Cloe? Elli. Cloe. And these are their two lovely daughters, let me see if I remember, Cissy and Crassy... I mean, Crissy and Cassy Cook-House-... House-Cook-... no, Houselander-Cook – right?"

Is there a lapse, a silence after the mountain falls? No one says a thing, not the Houselander-Cooks who have stayed seated and are staring suspiciously up at the Starcraves. The Starcraves! Elli beside herself for never in her life has she been referred to as an ex-wife and besides beside her stands Will Cook. His eyes bug as he does a fast sidestep around both Elli and Lou. She sees a dense head of hair spin by, graying some at the temples on the end of a long neck with a distinctive beak extended. He falls *faw-loomp* down on a simple three legged stool, some distance from his wife in the rock rocking rocker and some distance from the girls on the polished hard wood floor, closer actually to Elli on the cushioned bench. And his wide hands slap at his thighs as he does it.

Lou retakes his seat, and Elli – "Elli?" He tugs at her skirt. She sits. "So." Lou begins of course. "How have you been Will?"

Will actually opens his mouth to answer when out of nowhere the rocking chair quits its creak. "We have considered the proposal you outlined briefly over the telephone Mr. Starcrave, all of us, the entire family." Cloe Houselander-Cook chirps on. "We did not include our attorney as we would normally do in matters such as this because quite frankly we reached an agreement quickly, to wit, that we are not in the least interested in what you have to offer. The decision was unanimous, with no dissent." And she ceases to chirp quite curtly.

Lou is taken aback at this. Not Elli, she scoots further forward on the bench. Her mouth is dry, her tongue stuck to her teeth. "I can't help but mention how beautiful your weavings are, all these soft wool blankets."

"Cotton." The little woman corrects.

"Cotton, of course cotton."

"Will is highly allergic to wool." The rocker rocks, the blades coming dangerously close to splayed little fingers on the floor.

"But so brightly colored and textured…" Textured they are not, they are quite skimpy things really, and so Elli has to stop herself mid-sentence.

"Will suffers from many allergies. That is why we are not allowed kittens or plants, nor any dust from the street on shoes or playclothes."

Cats, dust, why certainly, but… "Why no plants?" Elli always the foil.

"Possible bacteria." Cloe Houselander-Cook is patient with her explanation, but the rocker whaps back and forth furiously. The little fingers backtrack oh so slightly. "We were never quite certain as to why, even after the exhaustive tests by the bacteriologists, but once we were rid of them, Will's wheezing ceased immediately."

With Elli's love of greenery, she must inquire further. "R-rid of them?"

"The bacteriologists took them, dissected them carefully, trying to isolate some fungus, some parasite, some microscopic discharge or pollen."

Elli envisions the house filled with filthy plant effluvium or creeping moss or wormy loam. She herself needs warmth, some accumulated dust to take root in, but she glances at Will who is shuddering at such a thought, his fingers tapping impatiently on his kneecaps.

"But to return to the discussion of your proposal, Mr. Starcrave" – the little woman is determined to fumigate all vermin and quickly before another of Will's wheezing fits occur – "the two or three items uppermost in our deliberation included the disruption that publicity around such an undertaking would mean to our small household and particularly among our young children's school friends. None of them need have any knowledge of Will's scandalous past – the firmer we tighten the lid on that putrid jar of preserves, the better. Secondly, Will has an impeccable career presently as a studio musician which we dare not sully with a return to the banality of rock and roll. He most recently provided keyboard tracks for Sabra Brastrain's newest album, *Can Never Cry Enough*, among many other notable releases. This is how our daughters perceive the musicianship of their adopted father. Thirdly and finally" – Cloe Houselander-Cook can speak at a rabid rapid rate, and she seems to require no intake of air while doing so – "we weighed Will's delicate constitution up against the rigors of rehearsing for an exhausting on-stage performance. We concluded that no amount of money, and certainly not in the low ball range you were suggesting, could adequately compensate for the demands on his energy and time. And noth-…"

Lou – and what whim so seizes him? – that he dares interrupt her with what could only be termed a squawk.

"Permit me to finish. You will have your time to rebut. And nothing" — the woman rocks savagely in her chair — "could be more disgusting to imagine than our Will appearing on a stage with that deranged pervert Chipper Stirbee!"

Did she say that word? Did Cloe Houselander-Cook say that word, and in front of the floored littler ones? She must have, because the chickies' eyes bulge as mom warbles on. "Nor could we countenance Will's playing with those inexcusably untrained musicians once called the Loose Nukes. As a matter of fact, their names have been left unmentioned in this household for decades, and I vote to let them remain so!"

The last phrase or two Cloe Houselander-Cook sucks through her tightly clinched teeth, her jaw drawn up and the tendons of her neck strained. The two girls raise their necks in a similar manner, and snap their teeth too, little birds fed from the same sharp caw.

"*Uh-uh-* Will..." Lou starts in, and all eyes turn upon him, but he's not up to it, strange to say, words completely fail the man.

"You mean, you really wouldn't want to play with your old gang one last time Will?" Elli opens her mouth even before she realizes it. "Wouldn't it be fun to hear those wonderful old songs you wrote once again?"

The poor guy is flailing about on his three legged stool, hair, neck, beak, and like any musician his hands always in motion. Fact is the entire time his wife has been speaking, Will has been pounding out some complicated fingerings along his extended femur bone, with both hands actually, Will being nearly ambidextrous after all these years of self-practice.

And those wonderfully warm eyes of Elli, and the way words form in her mouth — something awakens inside Will. He jolts on his stool.

"I mean the kid inside you," Elli continues earnestly, "you and the Loose Nukes were one of the early greats of rock 'n' roll. Why I remember as a teenager in East Islip, we girls would sit an-... "

"He has developed beyond that." Cloe Houselander-Cook interrupts, and the chickees concur. "Look at him!" *Rock Rock* and *BAM!* Damn if Cloe Houselander-Cook doesn't smack up against the mantle. Sends the chickadees flying.

Fact everyone's ass is astir after that.

And behind a hedge of hair Will Cook's eyes have receded, only his nose pierces the veil. He flaps those enormous hands of his against his thighs, some *concerto grosso* galloping through his mind no doubt.

"Well I'm quite certain Will has developed beyond that," Elli smiles and continues bravely, "as have we all hopefully. I no longer listen to rock 'n' roll myself, or to be entirely truthful I never did — naturally I made an exception for the Loose Nukes — but I loved classical, I played the flute as a child and I-..."

"What is your favorite period?"

What? What was that? Where did that voice come from? A low, deep, hidden away voice, redolent, resonant. "Who is your favorite composer?" Will's nostrils extend upward and sniff out Elli.

"Baroque," she chokes, "I really love Baroque."

"I love Baroque also. Bach."

"Bach, oh Bach and Vivaldi!"

"Yes Vivaldi," and Will Cook parts his hair and gazes wild eyed dilated into Elli's soft hazels. "It was Vivaldi who inspired Bach, you know. The earliest Bach is in comparison vapid, but after Bach memorized the works of Vivaldi, his own music erupted."

"I didn't know he memorized Vivaldi."

"Yes, he had never heard such joyousness in his solemn German soul."

"It makes sense, but I never knew — and Scarlatti, Domenico and Alessandro, I simply adore the Spanish intensity."

"Rodrigo in our own time."

"Yes."

"I share your passion. I play Scarlatti to relax," Will confides, "and Bach's organ concertos when I feel contemplative. There is a true divinity to his works." He is smiling, and he still has his innocent boy's face, a longing Elli notices, and a lusciously full mouth, large tongue. Though what Elli feels is entirely inappropriate because it was Lynn Neufinger next door in East Islip who always had the crush on Will Cook. No one else did. No one else could understand while Lynn Neufinger would extol Will Cook's mouth, what parts of her anatomy she would press against his large succulent lips, and sometimes she got right down and dirty about it. "I- I agree, Scarlatti can be aggravating yet relaxing and Bach, Bach inspiring."

"I was just playing Scarlatti." Will admits, his eyes now fixated on the waxed floor.

"Upstairs? Before we arrived, before you came down?" Elli can hardly restrain her excitement.

"No, here, now," and unconcerned about the opinion of others, he begins again to rhapsodize up and down his leg, thigh bone to ankle, with a vigor that would shame any less a man, and right in plain sight of his little wife and children.

Elli is so moved by the man, by the boy, so secretive, so exclusive to himself, so hidden away behind the hair, the eyes, the mouth, and the hands — THE HANDS! Everything liquid in her surges, freely. She radiates. She extends her hand out to him, proffers her touch — GOOD GOD ELLI! NO! NO! NO! — and she so so slightly taps Will Cook's kneecap, and just as he reaches a high sharp G, and what they have always said about tall skinny guys and their hypersensitivity, well it's true! If it's not an orgasm Will

Cook has on his three legged stool, then it is something so similar, an autistic reactive *gran mal* seizure — his spine bolts backward — WHIP-PLASH! Off he flips, that is off the stool he whips and down around circling in a vortex, upward and then downward — JUMPY! JUMPY! — nobody knows what to do, not even the three fluttering Houselander-Cooks. And poor Will ends spinning way across the slick floor, bare feet and hands extended up, foaming at the mouth, tongue extended and flapping, much like a plucked flamingo who's just been dipped thin skin into ice water!

Some tourist chanced upon a Kodak color 8mm film of the four kids cavorting around a swimming pool somewhere out west, cactus and desert and clear skies forever, and the only shots of them sunburned and bony chested, even Will Cook, shot when *Getta Girl* was still at the top of the charts — and why that's Lou in there too, cavorting around with the band, the young Lou, see, startled brown eyes and *whoops*, they're picking him up, all four by all fours, they're swinging him back and forth, and yes, there he goes — SU-PLASH into the pool — Lou who can't swim, and now they're turning on each other, Will Cook — SU-PLASH — and Bubba the Bod and Danny T 'Drummer Dynamo,' one on each end of Chipper — SU-PLASH — they dunk Chipper, and it's match point between six plus Bubba the Bod and five three Danny T — though between them there's no contest, a slight scuffle and a small *su-plash!*

Wait! There's still more: All are out of the pool dripping wet and ganging up on Bubba the Bod, four against one is almost a fair fight except Bubba manages to dip Chipper again, then Lou, then Danny T, except damn if it isn't Will Cook who finally manages to shove Bubba in, or does Bubba take a dive? Anyway, Bubba the bully is finally bested.

Elli hangs limp from a strap on a tight packed D train, mouth open and gasping for air. "What can I say… I don't know what to say…"

Lou's folded over on the bench beneath her, head between his knees.

"…I can only say I'm sorry Lou, that's all I can say."

Crowd around doesn't say anything either, each to his own business on a subway, except they sway together as the train takes a curve.

"No matttter."

Crowd sways back the other way.

"Of course it matters, you're slipping into obvious denial."

Woman seated next to Lou looks over, scrutinizes him.

Lou mumbles something indistinguishable.

"What? What did you say?"

"I said it's OK, shit happens. Past is over."

"You can't afford to become negative about this. Negativity begets negativity and before you realize it you're clinically morbid."

Woman stares. Other people stare. Lou's hunched over, doesn't care.

"You give in too easily, that's your problem. Then you isolate yourself, lash out at anyone who attempts to get close."

Woman scoots away.

"So what positive steps are you going to take to avoid becoming desperate about this? You have to nip these feelings of helplessness in the bud. We can't have another one of your episodes."

Episodes. People stare, fact they glare — this guy forgotten to take his meds, has he been sprung too soon out of Bellvue?

"It doesn't matter."

"You say that and you know you don't mean it. You lose the Loose Nukes, you lose your life."

"Time to get a new gig."

"Lou! You're fifty seven! There's not many gigs left!"

"Roll over, play dead."

"Suicide is an inappropriate solution."

Woman's out of her seat and moving quickly down the aisle.

"What?" Lou lifts his head, looks at the woman racing away, looks at the crowd, looks at Elli. "It wasn't your fault, Will was always like that, no joke, it used to happen all the time. We'd make bets before a show…"

"Bets on what?"

"…how far Will would make it through the performance before he'd go into a spin."

"You certainly can't be serious. You would mock someone with an unfortunate illness?"

"It wasn't illness, it was inspiration."

"You know, I have never fully realized, not until now, how incredibly insensitive you are! As in verging on the sociopathic!"

Crowd backs way off at that diagnosis, gives Lou lots of room.

"It was ecstasy. Will played his best licks while he was tripping."

"Tripping!"

"Whatever it was he was into it, especially if there was an overflow crowd and the pressure was on, he'd do this flip out…"

"I can't, I don't- I don't believe it!"

Crowd believes it, they've seen countless incidents of it, especially on the D-train.

"Hey I'm telling you, he thrived on it. Those were probably the happpiest, the most productive moments of his career."

"Will Cook did not strike me as particularly happy this afternoon."

"No, not this afternoon, but back when we were kids, he'd whack away at that keyboard, this big crazed grin on his face and pump out music like a madman. We'd race right along beside him, fast as we could, hope we'd remember enough to score another hit. Will Cook was our inspiration."

"Sick Lou, you're sick, terribly sick!"

People agree he must be. Whole train load bolts for the exit at Grand.

It's patched black and white newsreel footage, a mob scene outside a theater and lit up on the marquee — THE LOOSE NUKES — inside no better, police arm-in-arm across the stage, kids screaming. Nobody in those days knew what these crazed bobby soxers might do, with their sweet pouty faces and pony tails as they clambered pleated skirts over one another to reach the stage.

> Really oughta / Gotta poppa

Chipper's out front egging the girls on of course, and Bubba's right there beside him doing a twist of sorts, Danny T so excited that his banging drowns out the music. Will Cook has receded into the backdrop with near terror in his eyes, barely fingering his keys. Now while some say Chipper exposed himself that night, most reliable witnesses deny that happened, although Bubba did pull his shirt off and flex some, which was not done in those days, but whatever the proximate cause, the result was a previously unidentified form of teenage mayhem

> Wanna poppa / Poppa lotta little girls

The newsreel was introduced as state's evidence, ostensibly to prove that the police had used appropriate restraint in quelling a riot, but what caught the court's attention had nothing to do with crowd control and much to do with mid-century American notions of propriety. The focus of the flick was Chipper, so naturally he got charged, although the jury found the shy towhead in person guilty of mere misdemeanor. The precedent was set however, and stationhouses across the nation prepared themselves for the next Loose Nuke onslaught.

Getta Girl stayed at the top of the national charts thirteen weeks over the late summer, the teen romance season. The judge's stern rebuke notwithstanding, the incident did teach Chipper and the gang a hard won lesson, that lewd along with the rude sells well.

Lou gets off the train at West 4th, doesn't even mention dinner with Bubba at Ristorante Bonanza. Elli has to decide whether to pursue or not. All the years of playing nurse, not a career she wants to resume. But he looks so despondent, she melts and pulls herself off the train behind him.

A series of hit singles play — *Fightin For Her Luv, Lazy Lovin, Maine Boy* and the infamous *Love Baby* — each simply structured as befitting songs written by a bunch of jerky seventeen year olds in the early 60s, the same refrain repeating itself over and over for exactly three minutes, building in intensity with each repetition until the donut-holed forty five spun *whup-up* off its spindle!

The original record jackets spin into view, with Chipper's visage growing proportionally larger than the others, his shirt open, his pants bursting, hair tousled, and something about the mouth, this cultivated image of a street kid, a bike type, musky, scruffy, snarling and ready to snatch.

Additional rampage scenes from those months have been preserved, girls mobbing the guys at hotel entrances and in theater lobbies, chasing them into lavatories in most major cities across the Midwest, even before the tour reached its culmination that fateful Cincinnati Summer of 69.

That most infamous page one *Tribune* photo of Chipper and Bubba late at night, crawling out the back of a yellow school bus up from Our Lady of Mercy Academy in Joliet, Illinois for a cultural tour of the city. Whatever else there was cultural in Chicago, an after hours concert for a select few of the girls was not on the itinerary, and

Chipper's platinum blond hair naturally stands out better in flash photography than Bubba's dark wavy locks — one of those immutable laws of nature, that he who is most visible will most certainly get blamed.

When news attacks hit, and they did with increasing regularity, Chipper was the lightning rod, although Bubba was only a step behind. Fact the competition between the two was legend, over girls, over the spotlight, top billing, song credits. Bubba could not sing however, not a note and Chipper could barely chord, which is why Bubba played lead and Chipper a simple strumming bass. Whatever satisfaction Bubba might have felt was lost anew every performance as Chipper grabbed the mike, lapped at it, spat at it, then softly kissed it goodnight.

Neither music nor musicianship was ever to blame for the Loose Nukes' fame, everyone except Will Cook knew that. It was also a toss up between Bubba and Chipper who was the better looking, dark draught or sparkling light, depending on your taste for the night. Then there was Danny T, 'Drummer Dynamo,' sneaking around behind the stellar attractions, he might appear little league all-American, but those are the guys who can steal a base, slide silently in to score, and Danny T did, life-time. Will Cook, well, where's there to hide on a well-lit stage? Thick black hair passed his shoulders, stretched long limbs, fingers trembling as he reaches for the keys, tasty bait for a deviant age.

There were predictable alliances too, though they could shift. Bass player and drummer should have been a natural, but not often between Chipper and Danny T. Then the lead guitar is usually in sync with the keyboardist, but not Will Cook, when he wasn't locked away somewhere off by himself, he'd back Chipper.

The Loose Nukes didn't make millions, Lou can attest to that, but they kept on truckin city after city in Danny T's yellow Volkswagen bus. Lou doled out the proceeds from royalties and kept a tight budget, but he neglected to allocate bail money, and those big hits ultimately took the Loose Nukes down.

Elli catches up with Lou, takes him by the arm. "Think of this afternoon as round one. You have to stay on your feet and keep slugging."

He's grateful. He pats her hand. "You know, I don't know what I'd do without you."

"Don't doubt that, not for a minute."

Had some blizzard rolled across the Great Plains that ill-fated night and stalled their VW bus along I-74, rock 'n' roll history might have had an additional chapter on raw native creativity. Scat Cat, with its jazzy improvisations and philosophical reflections, or Alleyway Woman, which despite its title and Molly Dawken's bellyachin' back-up, were early indicators of what these kids could have created if left to flourish on their own. But it was a clear starry night when the kids blew in from Indianapolis to Cincinnati O – though that's a tale best told later.

The real news-breaker was Molly Dawkens, the busty auburn-haired tornado who took up residence with the band in their final months of youthful fame and fury, Molly, bellowing out back-up vocals and transforming the Loose Nuke sound from East Village brat to San Francisco mod, and more, for Molly's very presence on the stage served to disperse the mob of school girls from the stage door since one of their own had finally snagged a Nuke – snagged more than one Nuke if the truth be told – Molly glowing triumphantly in one telling glossy as she swings arm-in-arm between both Chipper and Bubba. The slut, she had succeeded where every teenage girl in America would have willingly consented to be, and leering ear-to-ear about it too.

But that's simply the cast of characters. For the story behind the story, the rivals, the romances, the grit, the gore, the scores galore – log on at www.loosenukes.com. That's www.loosenukes.com where you can grab a shopping cart and toss in your very own illustrated coffee table edition of *Chipper Stirbee and The Loose Nukes,* each chapter chock full of prurient details – yours for the low low price of $49.95 (plus $4.50 for shipping and handling) – "A must have," says Al Slaverly of *Random City News* – Visit today! Don't delay! – and have your credit card handy. www.loosenukes.com. (You must be 18 years or older to order. Sales void where prohibited by law.) Log on now!

WEMBLEY 12:01

"'E'yal'right, this is Indian Chief. Attention climbers. Looks like we've got trouble above. Let's move some help up there and fast — Eddie, Swag, Red Feather — hightail it on up that stage scaffolding. Copy?"

"Red Feather to Indian Chief, we're on our way. Copy."

"'E'yal Red Feather, remember that canopy web is delicate, won't support more than one man at a time. Copy me on that?"

"One man at a time. Copy."

Hand over hand, the climbers run the rungs of the ladders. It's the roughneck construction crew ready for any emergency, like the sound tower that nearly collapsed on the centerfield crowd a couple of windy hours ago or the lights out, no cameras, no action when let's-hear-it-for Yank, the head electrician, got excited over some number and threw the wrong switch, unplugged the base grid for the entire complex, plunged everybody into two minutes of stunned silence. But stands can collapse, speakers can crash, fans can flash, and Yank can dance in his pants, this time it's the star of the show stranded a way up where even a pro risks a go.

"Taken a nasty spill, have you — *YOUSPUNKLESSIMPUDENTPUNK* — you haven't a chance of surviving this catastrophe — *yukyukyukyuk!*"

"Eminenze?"

"Don't disturb me Queezac, can't you see that I am gloating?"

"Notzink zo nize az an enemy'z mizvortune."

"You have no idea how I have longed for this moment!" The Liaison even smiles. "Bye bye to Chip- Chip-..."

"Jipper Ztirbee — for Chrizzakez!"

"'E'yal Red Feather, do you copy me? Looks like you're the closest climber. Can you apprise us of the situation up there?"

"Almost. I'm almost in position Chief." Red Feather pants into his headset as he completes his ascent.

The dome is an aluminum ribbed half sphere with a high peaked center, a giant umbrella covered entirely with taut stretched nylon that glows luminously in the dark. Though now the dome's been dented and hangs precariously off its moorings. Red Feather jiggles it with his fingers.

"'E'yal, see anything?"

Climber's on the back side, Chipper's on the front. Light so intense Red Feather has to squint, but he can see indents on the snowy slope opposite. How to get there is the question. Up and over seems the only answer.

"'E'yal, careful crossing that canopy, one slip and it'll rip if the bridging doesn't collapse underneath you first. Thing wasn't designed to bear any load. Copy me on that?"

"Copy. Copy." Red Feather's going out. His fellows cinch a line to his climbing belt as he steps gingerly onto the slippery surface — *pip -pip* — he can feel the nylon give each inch he goes, crouched low, fingers, toes, slow slow, like treading across ice, a snap crack across and he'll sink asunder.

The audience is hushed, spotlights trained on the climber clad in soft-soled mountain boots and cutoffs, leather tool strap, radio headset on one ear, a hardhat propped on top of his long hair with this bright red feather swept back. He's all daring and dash.

"Red Feather? Can you apprise us of the situation?"

"Chief, I'm doing the best I ca-…" Climber slips slightly, almost loses his footing but catches himself, his fingernails scratch at the nylon. "…things take time, take the time that they take…"

"'E'right with the advice, but time's what we've got the least of."

The ascent to the top is at a steep incline and no foot holds, the aluminum framing as slick as the skin — *pip-pip-pip-pip* — Red Feather slumps to his stomach at the peak, peers over. "OK Chief. This is Red Feather." He speaks softly so even his voice won't vibrate. "I can see a-…" He falls silent as a monstrous shadow looms within an arm's reach overhead. It's the QuotLink blimp hovering close to, dark now and no helping hand, a lense in the nose cone reconnoitering the situation for itself. It eyes the climber, it eyes a wayfarer splayed across a support rib face down. After a few seconds additional dilation, the blimp shoves off, its curiosity apparently satiated.

"…I- I'm within range and about to begin my descent. I can see… I can see a-… I can see something black and spindly with arms or legs, something sticking up, no head…"

"E'yal Red Feather, we're looking for a rockstar, not a space alien."

"Whatever it is Chief, it's moving, like spastic…"

"Leave it be, we'll alert the animal leaguers – any sign of Chipper?"

"Yes! I see a body, long blond hair, human, definitely human! He's lying flat out about 20 feet to the left of me. There's no movement and I'm too far away to tell if he's breathing."

"'E'right, copy you on that, no on the movement, iffy on the breathing – you understand there's no way we can get a medic up there, you're going to have to do what you can and bring him down alone."

"Alone. Copy."

The blimp parks some distance overhead and blinks the circulating advert back on – QUOT • LINK • INC • • PRE • SENTS • • CHIP • PER • STIR • BEE • • RE • U • NITED • WITH • • THE • LOOSE • NUKES • • AN • AL • LIED • FOR • LIFE • • BEN • E • FIT • CON • CERT – scrolling amidst the stars. While below, Red Feather, Chipper, an alien, feckless specks clutching onto a naked lightbulb, but not insignificant to the crowd packed in at Wembley, it's their leader who's up there and a heroic rescue in the making.

CHIPPER – they dare to whisper.

"Listen to them all, the RAGTAGREMAINSOFTHEPROTESTGENERATION, hoping against hope – *yukyukyukyuk* – we shall soon be burying you!"

"Lookz like ve can turn ze page on zat whole zorry ztory."

"So few appreciate what I have endured these past sixteen months because of him – SCUTTLETHECUDDLEBUTT – his infantile antics and coarse remarks, the drugs, the sex, his self-righteous posturing and the preaching! Why if the true story of his derelict life were told, people would laugh, not applaud!"

"All zat iz yezterday'z bad newz in ze mornink."

"Yet here I stand, alive to see it – witness with my own eyes while my dearest, my loveliest of enemies is lowered to earth all broken bones in a body bag – *yukyukyukyukyukyuky!*" The way the Liaison throws his head back, his mouth open, a gargley guttural flush the bowl sort of sound, the noise unsettling even Queezac – *yukyuk yukyukyuk glug gluk gluuuu…*"

"Jezuz! Go eazy on ze vluidz, a revill runz uz $37.50 an ounze."

"Good gin is decidedly cheaper – *spu-spuu-uluu-guu…*"

"Zix qvartz ov zat un you'd be ztumble down drunk on ze zidevalk."

"A nap in a club chair."

"Vor ze rezt ov ze zentury – Eninenze, you've gotz to vorget ziz guy, he'z hiztory. Ve zimply ztazh him away zomevhere on a zlab un vorry about anotzer day."

The Liaison slobbers up soberly. "Bury him and we bury a most *slupslup* unfortunate chapter in our own corporate annals as well."

"Yez vell, zat viazco vaz no lavphink matter."

"A most regrettable incident, that despicable little island of Ste Cécile. Not that QuotLink Inc was responsible, nor in any way liable, not for a nickle! It was simply a high risk venture gone awry, a one time quarterly charge against profits."

"Rizky? Zat venture vaz inzane!"

"Keep your snout out of business that doesn't concern you creature!"

"But I varned you time un time again…"

"MUMBLEJUMBLEYOURUNTYTHUMBNAIL!"

"…I zaid vhatever you do, don't popz zat nuclear reactor on ze edge of zat volcano! Volcanoez only znooz, zey never zleep. Vhat zeemz inert today can explode in your faze bevore breakfazt, un explode in your faze, did it ever! Juzt look at you. Iz a vonder you gotz eyez levt in your head, or a mouze to zpitz up vitz, boy-o-boy vaz zat a neurozurgical jallenge! Vivty zix hourz on ze operatink table ze virzt night, un vhat a bill ve vracked up in ze IZU. You vere lucky I vaz nearby vitz a zcapel."

"You didn't get my chin right."

"Vhat jin? I do reconztructive zurgery, not phyziognomical miraclez."

"At least the one man who could tell the whole morbid story lies crushed on that canopy, silenced forever."

"Un tonight ov all nightz, vhen he vaz coaztink zo cloze on ze cuzp ov mortal zuczezz!"

"Revenge!" The Liaison manages a dry *yukyuk* chuckle. "The sure cure for the soul!"

"Ze exziztenze ov ze zoul iz mere idle tzeological zpeculation, but ze body, zat'z a divverent ztory. Iz real. You can zee a body, veel it, cut a big tazty junk outz ov it — zpeakink ov vhich, do you zuppoze you could arrange vor me to go pokink tzrough Jipper'z remainz after ze zhow iz over? Maybe I could zalvage zome of hiz juizier piezez? Pleaxe zay yez Eminenze, becauze I vould enjoy zat zo muj!"

Out along the roadways the news doesn't delay the progression, millions more kids clog the city's circulatory system, pushing their way inexorably toward Wembley and there out front, heading up the procession is Cissy Coombs outfitted in black leather, hair dyed that mournful deep purple.

"*Ohh-…*"

There's a twitch to the body. Red Feather freezes. A sudden motion could cause a shift, a rift in the canopy. Eddie and Swag, Red Feather's fellow climbers, rush to shore up the edges, installing extra clamps to hold the nylon in place.

"Ohhhhhh-..."

"Listen, you're going to be OK. Just don't move, don't hardly breathe."

"Ohh-... ohhhh-..."

"Everything's going to be fine. I'm working my way down to you, but whatever you do, don't move — can you hear what I'm saying?"

"Mama, my achin head!" Chipper lifts up his head, sees a hard hat and a red feather moving towards him. "What is it, wake-up call ahready?"

"Sorry to disturb you."

"That's ahright, but could you douse the lights fah me pahtnah, they've got to be blindin!" Until he realizes it's his pillow that's aglow, whereupon he does a flip flop, gets the whole bed to springing — WHOMMM! WHOMMM! WHOMMM! — and this Injun next bunk over, bouncing up and down on a trampoline.

"Lie still! Lie still!"

"My stomach. I'm goin into the spins." Dude has no idea where he's passed out, bare mattress somewhere strange after a hell of an all-nighter. "They've got to be the wohst."

Red Feather has to hug tight to the nylon, ride out the ripples — *pip-pip* — Eddie and Swag pulling tight on the edges.

"Say, wheah am I anyway..."

Chipper peers into space, sees the malign underbelly of the blimp holding above — QUOT • LINK • INC • • PRE • SENTS • • CHIP • PER • STIR • BEE • • RE • U • NITED • WITH • • THE • LOOSE • NUKES • • AN • AL • LIED • FOR • LIFE • • BEN • E • FIT • CON • CERT — scrolling amidst the stars.

"...must be the pahkin lot of some all-night dinah, oah no, wohse..."

Red Feather's squirming downward on his belly. "Hold on. I've come to get you out of here."

"...nope, *nopenopenope*..."

"Don't panic, but I'm afraid you've had a terrible accident."

"...I remembah cruisin on my way somewheah... I was drivin, oah somebody else was drivin, and this gal... came out of nowheah... brunet divebombah with shahp teats..."

"Always is."

"...next thing I know I'm way up heah... but no way, could nevah be..." Chipper quick checks around, bright lights, all whites? "This can't be the endin everybody's been prayin fah... floatin alone in the middle of no place nowheah on a cloud of ahtificial fibah — Betsy? Betsy, wheah ah you gihl? Wheah's my babydoll when I need huh the whost!"

"Best thing you can do for yourself is stay calm."

"Tell it to me straight fella, what ah my chances and wheah am I exactly? Heaven oah Hell oah some holdin cell in between... I didn't do whatevah it was, you've got to believe me!"

"You're at Wembley."

"Wembley?"

"Wembley Stadium. Don't you remember falling?"

"Remembah?" And this Injun inching closer is surely no angel. "So who ah you, one of those all-weathah EMTs?"

"Climber."

"Climbah?"

"Been a climber all my life."

"Climbah? Like a regulah down-to-eahth cahd-cahryin climbah?"

"Out of the Iron Workers' Hall in Providence. I've walked steel since I was sixteen, except for a six year stint with the 82nd Airborne."

"Screamin Eagles got me, did two touhs in Nam, one because I had to, the othah because I was young and dumb."

"Same way with me."

"So you'h real, flesh and blood soht of thing?"

"I eat, I drink, just like you." Red Feather's a few feet away.

"Pahty?"

"Big time!"

"Ahright then, that's settled. I'm still alive. I know I'm still alive. I'm just stuck somewheah else momentahily."

"OK now look, how many fingers am I holding up?"

"Two, two and a stub."

"Good. Lost one a year ago constructing a scaffold in Minneapolis, lateral bar sprang out of its fitting, whipped the sucker right off."

"Y'ouch, don't you know. Lost the tip to my strummin fingah same way, some on the job drinkin accident as I recollect... Say, have we evah met befah?"

"Red Feather's the name."

"Injun?"

"Penobscot."

"Whoa! Cousin!"

"Say what?"

"Must be a maniac Mainah like me, have brothahs who ah Micmac."

"Born and raised in a town called Millinocket — all of us proud of our county homeboy made good."

"Made good. H'yep. Fame's like bein rebohn, lohdy lohdy, sins of youh youth all fahgiven — Millinocket, that'd be off Route 11 neah Endless Lake, one of my favohrite spots fah fly castin."

"That's it."

"I'm from Ottah's Ledge myself, fuhthah nohth, evah heah of it?"

"On the St. John's River, up the road from Fort Kent. Bear country."

"Beah and of couhse moose — that damn neah makes us neighbahs, but I don't hold that fact against nobody, not fah long anyway — glad to make youh acquaintance." Whereupon Chipper extends a hand, but even a friendly gesture can set a delicate dome to rocking — WHOMMP! WHOMMP!

"Lie still! Don't move!"

"Frisky little missus."

WHOMMP!

"OK let's take a second, back off. We've got to figure the best way to get you out of here."

Which is when Chipper rubs his eyes and realizes he's been sleeping on a ski run, a steep one, within a few feet of a sheer ninety foot drop.

"Whoa! Don't suppose we could wing it?"

CHIPPER! CHIPPER!

"What's that…"

CHIP- CHIP- CHIPPER!

"…sounds like crickets in late August, don't it, the way they get to goin at it… whiddlin theih hind legs togethah… despahrate… like they've got one last chance to get it on befah it's ovah… fahevah…"

"But it's not over for you. You've got a song or two to do, remember?"

"Remembah…"

"You feeling OK? You hurting anywhere badly, arms, legs, back?"

"Nowheah wohse than usual… guy like me has gotten pretty used to bruisin's… though my head's cloudiah than usual…"

"You strong enough to hold onto my hand?"

"'Couhse, why?"

"Because I'm going to try to reach over, slowly, and I'm going t-…"

-rr-rr-rrrrrrrrr-rrrrrrrrr

"That's no cricket."

Not at all, some hydra-shaped creature with long spindly limbs, planted upside down in a snow bank on a ridge a ways to the right out of sight.

"Don't be alarmed, OK? We can't identify exactly what it is yet, but we're certain we can get you off here without disturbing it."

-rrrrrrrrrrrrrrrrrrrrrrrrrr

It's snorting, it's contorting, and Chipper's trying to hone in on the sound which is somehow familiar, a bit muffled but…

-rrr R'OUCH!

No buts about it. "That's Betsy!"

"Betsy?"

"That's my babydoll! I'm suhe of it." Chipper twists around in the direction of the sound — WHOMMMMP! WHOMMMMP! — "Wheah ah you little gihl? Can't see fah shit with the glahe!"

"E'yal Red Feather, any update on the victim's condition, copy?"

"Copy Chief, copy. Victim is mobile and speaking coherently, seems disoriented however and might be hallucinating, he keeps repeating some girl's name over and over."

"'E'right, vital signs seem normal. Let's get him down fast as we can?"

The blimp radios an update to the Executive Liaison, a modular receiver inserted into one of his spare cranial slots — *sputsput* — "What?" The QuotLink is incredulous. "It cannot be!"

"Vhat? Vhat cannot be?" Queezac not being privy to encrypted executive level communiques.

"They have observed movement, he might be alive up there!"

"A zlight jance, ztatiztically zomevhere betveen a long zhot un gonzo."

"Either way is unacceptable."

"Don't give up hope, live haz a vay ov alvayz vorkink out vor ze vorzt."

"*Sucksucksucsucksucksucksuck!*" His Eminence is hardly reassured

"Zere zere, don't vorry, he'z not goink to make it." Queezac tries his best to comfort his old friend, nuzzles at his elbow.

"If he makes it, I am finished, washed up, kaput!" The Liaison raises his eyes to the blimp overhead.

"Zem again," Queezac snarls at the skies, "bunj ov panicky old codjerz. I zhould never have zalvaged zem vrom ze duzt bin ov hiztory. Don't vorry, ve'll getz to Jipper — exzept vhat'z vitz all ziz gunk runnink out your noze, un your moutz, eyez un earz!"

But there is no consoling the wicked. They must perish in their own seep of despondency.

"Pleaze. It painz me to zee you like ziz, un vor no good reazon."

"For no good reason?" The Liaison oozes all over Queezac, an oily yellowish green, soaks the crab from furrowed brow down to draggy claw, which could be spittle, which could be much worse because the Liaison is pissed is what he is, at Queezac, at anybody within spraying range.

"You can't go gettink yourzelf upzet over ziz nonzenze — un look at ziz mezz on my lab coat!" Queezac wipes and wonders why there's not a single drip on the Liaison, not on his starched shirt, not on his pressed shark skin suit, not on his snazzy silk tie, but Queezac, he'z a greaze ball. "I muzt advize you az your perzonal vyzizian zat zere von't be muj more medical zcienze can do to help iv you keep zpillink your gutz outz like ziz."

The Liaison is oblivious to health concerns. "There I was, with my first promotion into the ranks of the QuotLink Board of Elders, an Alternate Member and the newly appointed President and CEO of the Nuclear Engineering Division, spearheading our break-through technological advance for recycling used Siberian plutonium, which we could purchase in bulk for pennies on the black market in Baku then hawk to hungry Third World countries for millions — we had the world's first portable nuclear reactor — pull it up, park it in somebody else's backyard, and before they even get wind of it, you were operational — 'Atoms For Spite' — throw in a six months' supply of lead lined trash bags and you had a program applauded for its innovative concept, its compact design, its built-in cost containments, its inimitable deception — what a resounding commercial success it could have been!"

"Could've. Vould've. But vhat did you do? You vent un tried it out on zat unjarted izland in ze Caribbean — firzt miztake, big miztake — all zoze jildren un zere grandmotzerz roazted alive on cable newz, I mean vhy not in Rio, vipe out ze zlumz in caze ov accident, un ze vorld'z governmentz vould have applauded you, paid plenty to zolve zeir own hard core unemployment problemz. Next inztallation could have been a vacant lot in ze Zoutz Bronx or ze courtyard ov one ov zoze immigrant houzink compoundz outzide Pariz, but oh no, you've gotz to locate it zmack dabz on ze edge ov a volcano in ze middle ov ze ozean."

"They assured me, those deplorably underpaid geologists, that El Snorro was extinct, last heard from over ten thousand years ago."

"Yez vell he voke up, didn't he, ze old grouj, un vitz a bellyache heard round ze globe?"

"And all because of Chipper Stirbee — how was I to know he had chosen serene Ste Cécile as a vacation getaway?"

"Makez zenze, an unzpoilt virgin vildernezz, pervect vor hiz peculiar predilectionz."

"Next I'm demoted to this position, the Executive Liaison for the Entire Northern Hemispheric Region -*HUK!* Lofty title, but no real clout, and now this, with me so close to retirement!"

"Un zere zey are, ze Elderz zirklink above in ze blimp — AL • LIED • VOR • ZE REZT OV YOUR LIVE — zoze uppizty mucky muck antiquez on ze QvotLink Exzecutive Commiztee, vatchink over your every move."

"You don't have to remind me, you ingrate! Besides, you're involved in this as deeply as I. Who designed the test reactor? Who wrote the specs?"

"Yez vell nuclear engineerink vaz never muj my bag anyvay, bezt to ztick vitz vhat you know, un zere'z more dough in bio-medical zeze dayz anyvayz, un none ov ze potential lonk-term liabilitiez."

"Advise me of that fact now — *GUT! GUT!*" Has the Liaison blown out his intestines, or what? There's this gush of putrid slush down a pantleg!

"Zo muj zewage under ze bridge, az zey zay." Queezac tactfully moves his shoe. "Ve ztill gotz to get up un zhit zome more ze very next day."

Which ellicits another gush from the Liaison.

"Good God, control yourzelv, you're vaztink your zpleen!"

But a blast of bile is what the Liaison thrives on.

"Relax, becuz even iv he doez zurvive, vhat'z he goink to do, zink zongz un dance live vrom zome hozpital vard — ve've gotz to look at ze bright zide, behindz every criziz lurkz anotzer opportunity."

"The man's mere inches from a microphone, billions watching, millions outside the gates ready to revolt!"

"Calm down. Iz no good overreactink, exaggeratink ze tzreat!"

"OVERREACTING! EXAGGERATING!"

"Iz problematic, yez, but we've survived worze. you un me."

"I AM SURROUNDED BY IDIOTS!"

"Zurely zat doezn't include me, not when I'm about to unleazh my amazink Jipper II, ze Irizh look-a-like, into ziz vondervul world ov celebrity un big buckz!"

"Who only exists in the deep folds of your imagination."

"Not true. He'z already up un kickink hiz healz — vell he'z tvitjink anyvay, vitz a vew azziztz vrom a ztun gun."

"Why aren't you underground somewhere attending to this matter?"

"Had to zee vhat vaz goink on. Vouldn't vant to mizz all ze exzitement. Bezides, I levt my azziztant Zmitzy in jarge, he getz ovv on high voltage, vhile I prever a more delicate touj myzelv."

"A phantom rockstar and a charlatan scientist, what must I contend with in a day — and if I do survive this test of wills, be forewarned I shall mount your stuffed shell on my wall!"

"Az a memento ov our long yearz togetzer?"

"*YOUSTITCHEDTHICKSKINNEDCROCODILE!*" And he kicks at Queezac, menacingly, at the crusted raw hide of him.

"Vhy take it outz on me, I'm juzt zome innozent byztander."

"Innocent, my backside, you delight in my ruination."

"You're juzt mad becuz you need me."

"*YOUGROVELLINGRIVERRAT!*"

"Alvayz vitz ze inzultz. Vhy I zought you'd velcome my zympazy. I zaid to myzelv, Queezac, go to your vriend, he needz you, let'z let ze bygonez be ze bygonez, zettle old allianzez, zign on vor a newer tomorrow, getz vitz ze program, do vhat'z gotz to be done…"

"*YOUPRESUMPTIOUSGUTTERSNIPE!*"

"I love you too — zo lean on over Eminenze, give your old comrade-in-armz a big zloppy zmooj."

The Executive Liaison gags at the thought, neck, gizzards and giblets he does, spit splatters everyone within earshot.

Kids aren't so pessimistic, they spring of hope eternal, rise from their seats, stand on their toes, shout encouragement…

CHIPPER! CHIPPER! CHIP- CHIP- CHIPPER!

"Theah they go, stahtin up again. Chippuh Chip? — Hey, that reminds me, I'm ahmost suhe I've got some soht of gig goin tonight."

"I guess you do, like big time benefit. You've got to be the most famous star on the planet."

"Whoa, not suhe about that."

CHIPPER! CHIPPER!

"They seem to think so."

"Folks can be easily confused, don't you know, mahketin schemes and advahtizin blitz, hellfihe, even I get disohriented by a special offah, oah like now, I mean somethin in my head's not clickin — Betsy?"

"Betsy? Who's this Betsy?"

"Betsy? Betsy? —BETSY!"

"Man, don't shout."

"BETSY BABYDOLL, WHEAH AH YOU?"

"E'yal Red Feather, this is Indian Chief. Hate to interrupt the heart-to-heart, but we've got to get moving. There's a QuotLink medical team standing by and the clock's ticking, some dude named the Executive Liaison is breathing down my neck, as in heavy. Think you can engineer a way off that thing any time soon? Copy?"

"Hear you Chief, and I'm working on it best I can, it's just-…"

"BETSY!"

"…Chipper, you've got to stay still, keep quiet."

"But Betsy's my babydoll."

"I'm going to try and tie this line around your wai-…"

-rrr-roo-roo-roo!

"That's Betsy! She's around heah somewheah — WHEAH AH YOU GIHL?"

"We'll have you down from here in no time and attend to those head injuries. You're going to be OK."

"That's ahright, theah's no rush, not without Betsy — BETSY?"

"Help me get this this line around your waist."

"Whatevah — did I mention I've done some climbin myself — did crew fah The Who back in 86 when they wah last touhrin with *Tommy*. Had my haih shaved off then so nobody'd recognize me — BETSY! BETSY!"

"I've got it, almost got it…"

"Funny how you can disappeah and then reappeah in this old wohld, ain't it, without most folks evah suspectin?"

-grr-row-row…

"BETSY BABY? THAT'S GOT TO BE YOU, OUT THEAH SOMEWHEAH!"

Betsy's buried in nylon from the nip of her nose to the nape of her neck and -*row-row* she wants out *now-ow!*

"WHEAH AH YOU GIHL?"

Dogged, she digs in her heels and *row-row* two front paws yanking that snout of hers out of the ground — *r'ouch!* — she's out, she shakes herself off, head quake to tail, sets the dome a'rockin — **WHOMMM! WHOMMM!**

"BETSY!"

-*ruff?* Her master's call!

"BETSY!"

She must brave the elements, make her way across tundra, but carefully, since it's a slippery slope and slow going, wobbily side-to-side as well, I mean she's seen snow in her life, like Northern Maine? But not the whole mountain shake each step she takes?

"BETSY? BETSY?"

She's doing the best she can without snowshoes, each clawprint leaving pinhole punctures in the nylon — *pip-pip-pip* — and she's getting nowhere fast, has to take a roundabout route to retrieve the gigbag and then there's this rip ripping sound following along each step behind her.

Whereupon this monster flying football with an eye attached comes zooming in — *rowlp?* — but Betsy being Betsy, she snaps right back, nabs at it. Only thing anybody earthbound can see on the screen is the insides of a jaw that can tear squirrels asunder. Blimp retreats, so does she, but the excitement gets her going into a backward roll — *plop plop plop plop* — gigbag and her gathering momentum with a minimum of friction — one of those immutable laws of nature that a mass when unexpectdly detached can tap an avalanche — *ploploploploploplop…*

Clamps give! Eddie and Swag lose their grip!

Dome tips! Chipper starts to slip!

PLOPPLOPPITYPLOPPLOP FLOP! FLOP! Betsy bounding heels over head, plows into Red Feather, sends him bobsledding toward Chipper…

"Hold on Chipper! Whatever you do, hold on!"

Whatever Chipper's doing, he's not holding on. Red Feather bumperheads into him — *Whoaaaaa!* — Chipper goes right up and over the rim…

CHIIIIIIP!

Audience gasps. Damn fool's dangling upside down from his last loose boot lace, nine stories from doom.

Billions shudder!

One mutters.

"OK alright, let's zoom in on that dome with anything we've got telescopic — *snap snap* — I want a close-up shot on Chipper's raw white knuckles — C'MON GENTLEMEN, LET'S MAKE IT HAPPEN! — and ready some takes on the crowd, I want pictures of millions of horrified faces! Let's go! Let's go! *Snap! Snap! Snap! Snap!*"

"What the flyin fuck!" Boy might be clinging to life by a boot strap, but what a sight he sees hanging upside down from a nine story trapeze, millions of horrified faces staring up at him — "Wembley! Right! It's all comin back to me!" — fine time to remember as he twists there in the breeze and notices that he is suspended directly in front of the giant projection screens, his figure imposed one upon another in an endless succession of mirrored images of himself — "Whoa! Not lookin too shabby!" — no, the ageless mythic troubadour might be hung by his heels precariously, yet he's not undone, not totally, and perhaps the wiser for it.

"'E'yal, let's get a catch pad under him, fast, he's about to come tumbling!" Copy! Copy! Red Feather, can you hear me? You OK up there?"

"Been better Chief, been better." The sweat washing around his thick eyebrows and pooling into his sockets as he tugs — Eddie and Swag in turn attempting to hold the tow they've got on him — Red Feather, brute forearms, inches along the incline, reaches over, nabs Chipper by the heel and drags him, brute forearms, up, up over the edge while scooting himself backwards, damn near deadweight dragging back *-ack-ack-ack* almost to the crest when — *Whoa! Whoa-oh -oh-oh* — both go sledding down that icy slope again — *rip-pipipipipipipipipip* — right through that nylon skin, sweep the chute, when *fwunk!* — Red Feather's ankle catches on something sharp — piercing man, piercing — but enough to anchor him, this time the both of them dangling over the edge.

"I can't pull you up Chipper, no way, I'm stuck here myself."

"Then hold on Red Feathah, time fah one of my high wihe flips."

"One of your what?"

"Don't let go!" Chipper starts in swinging — SWINGING??? Back and forth, back and forth, a couple of Maine boys looking to all the world like a practiced circus act.

"Evah notice how things get wohse, just befah they get bettah?"

"YAHH! YAHH!" Red Feather is lockjaw, croaking about his ankle.

Chipper swings wide to gain momentum — *hup/hup hup/hup* — hard back and forth until he can engineer this *hip whip* backflip — ladies and gentlemen, an unbelievably rare inverted double helix — clears Red

Feather, almost tugs Eddie and Swag off their moorings, but lands him with a thud on the rim bar and once he's got his own grasp onto stability, Chipper reaches down and yanks Red Feather up by the mangled leg — *aaaaaaaugh!* — brings him bottoms up to safety.

Below there's a collective sigh of relief — Chipper Stirbee! Superhero!

And in his own special niche a few stories below, Will Cook picks up on the crowd's excitement, feels it pulsing through his fingers -*zip-zip-zip-zip-zip* keys a playful chord and sets the kids to chirping…

CHIPPER! CHIPPER!

"*DUMBCLUCKERSLUCK!*"

Spotlights intersecting at the apex, a glint off Chipper's platinum blond hair, a wholly natural occurrence by the way, as Red Feather and he sway above arm-in-arm and wave back bravely.

CHIPPER! CHIPPER! CHIP- CHIP- CHIPPER! CHIPPER! CHIPPER!

"So what'h we do fah an encohe pahtnah?"

"Get the hell off this rig, *pronto*."

"H'yep, any ideas how?"

"I'm going to rig up a sling and lower you down."

"Sling?"

"Don't want to be accused of endangering the life of a superstar."

"Don't know who's endangahrin who, you'h the one who's limpin. Besides it wouldn't look right, a supahstah lowahed down in a sling."

Near death experience and you're going to worry how it looks, chum? Any way fast off this contraption is my advice.

"Betsy! BetsyBetsyBetsy…" Chipper bends down, hugs his babydoll. "…whatevah possessed you to try flyin through the aih aftah me?"

Same foo-*rool* thing that possessed you!

"Thought you wah a gonah this time fah suhe."

Hold on the smooches bud, where-*rr* is this slingamathing? I wouldn't mind taking the chair lift off this ski run.

"'E'yal Red Feather. Indian Chief. Enough of this trapeze act, time's running out down here. Copy!"

"Chief." Red Feather whistles into his headset. "We're about ready to descend — Chipper, you know how to rappel?" He unhooks the line he has attached to his belt.

"Rappel nothin, this looks mah like a free fall to me."

And one smile recognizes its fellow.

Fr-*rr-eee* fall? You two jokers have got to be kidding! *Fr-rr-reak* fall is more accurate, like take another look over that edge, not a pretty sight!

"You're a hot shit! And you know something Chipper Stirbee, you're partying with us tonight after the show." He thumps his stump on Chipper's chest. "You hear me? I don't care who's here or who's so important, before this night's over you're going to be down there under the scaffolding partying with the climbers. And I won't take no for an answer."

"Answah's yes, hell yes, I'll be down theah imbibin on those spihrits you fellas guzzle. Construction crew's the best drinkahs in the business."

That's even more reassur-*rr*-ing!

"E'yah'll Red Feather, you on your way down, copy me on that."

"You're sure you can handle a rope?"

"Don't wohry none about me."

"Here's a spare figure-eight." He unhooks a clamp from his rigging.

"Appreciate that." Chipper loops the rope through the large eye of the eight and tightens it. "Theah, that pass mustah?"

"Looks good, but you had better go ahead."

"Nope, it's ladies fihst tonight."

I'll *drr*-ink to that!

"OK, we'll lower the dog in the sling, then you go nex-..."

"No way. Stah always hits the stage last, that's one of those immutable laws of natuhe."

"You're something else, you know that?"

"H'yep, takes guts to be a showstoppah, but you'h no slouchah in that depahtment youhself fella!"

"Second string compared to you."

And while they volley back and forth with the heroics, Betsy decides to go fetch.

"Betsy? Wheah you headin off to?"

-*step-step-pp-pp* — she does her tip-toe best uphill.

"Damn fool dog! Get back heah!"

Nope. Girl's on a mission, search and retrieval.

"'E'yal Red Feather?"

"Copy. Copy Chief. We're almost underway."

As Betsy disappears over the crest.

"Nevah will undahstand that dog."

"Seems to have a mind of her own."

"BETSY! BETSY! Plain contrahry, that's what she is. Should've hauled huh off to obedience school when she was a pup."

-*hrrumph!* Black tip of her tail reappears first, then full haunch — listen to the county's reformatory class valedictorian talking, will you — and she's dragging... backwards...

"What?"

-rumph -rumph... by the teeth.

"Whoa, she's got my gigbag! My prize 57 Fendahbendah!"

"Go easy on the nylon dog, real easy."

Not to *wor-rr*-ry. Simply follow along the perforated path.

"Don't know what to say gihl, thanks heaps."

Better than listening to you moaning over the loss night after night.

"You'h about the best."

-mmm

Red Feather reaches to secure her into the sling. "Got to strap you in real tight, OK?"

Just low-*rr* away.

"Don't look down!"

-rrulp! Of course she's looking down, neck stretched, eyes round, ears spiked!!

Crowd is rooting her on.

She roots back, hey, walk-on or major role, we're all part of the show, although next time she'll let some other mutt do the stunts — as she drops into the catchpad where — **WHOMPP!** — one bounce on her backside and she's safe in the muscular arms of the construction crew — lady is grateful, she is, gives each one a syrupy lick and wonders what all those hounds back home must be saying about her now.

"Way to go pahtnah."

The two wave arm-in-arm once again for the benefit of the audience.

YAAAAAAAAAAAAAAAAAAAAAAAAAAAAAAAY!

"SPAREPAIROFBIRDBRAINS!"

"OK, I'm out of here." Red Feather takes the rope. "And remember you're partying with us tonight, down under the stage scaffolding — *wowwowwowwowwow!*" He fakes a war chant and dives off the dome in a free fall, slowly feeding and braking the rope through his hands, gliding gracefully down to the stage.

Chipper watches from on high as Red Feather lands and waves back up to him. The audience cheers, and lights, eyes track back upward: There he pauses, this tall lean figure, golden, balancing legs and arms wide apart, awaiting the moment for his descent. He waves with a hand, the Mighty Chipperinni, and the crowd stills, not a voice, not a cry nor a whisper. When all is quiet Chipper tosses his gigbag across his back, wraps the rope around a shoulder and down around his middle, loops it up front, tightens up on the eight. He smiles and steps off the canopy, there's a lurch, a

bounce — hearts below cease to beat as he settles into a swing and begins his descent, slip sliding slowly earthward…
> SOLO
> HERO
> NINETY
> EIGHTY FEET

He passes by Will Cook who pauses to shout over — "Man, don't you ever do anything easy?"

"'Couhse not, how about youhself?"
> TWENTY
> TEN FEET
> THEN FIVE
> FOUR
> THREE
> TWO
> ONE

There's this squeek as bare toes and booted touch ground.

The crowd erupts — shouting, clapping, stomping…

CHIPPER! CHIPPER! CHIP- CHIP- CHIP- CHIP CHIPPER! CHIPPER! CHIPPER! CHIPPER! CHIP- CHIP- CHIP- CHIP- CHIPPER!CHIPPER!

Will Cook captures the moment by pounding out a resounding last-of-the-ninth big organ grinding crescendo. The crowd calls: *PLAY BALL!* While Chipper hops around one leg tugging at the boot, flings it out into the crowd — some dude snags it — then he's off barefeet, springs into a series of cartwheels — a ONE and a TWO and THREE — lands him in front of his sound gear, spotlights chasing after him. Is he exhilarated, charged, sparking or what?

"Eminenze! Look! I mean iz ziz guy unbelievable, or vhat?"

His Eminence doesn't answer, he's stomped off, left Queezac muttering amazement all to himself.

"Zo beautivul, zo grazevul, zo blond, un zoze vlipz, boy-o-boy vhat a zpectacular entranze!"

Outside the stadium, along highways and byways the kid mass is expanding, as in exponentially, at least four million maybe more, bringing the total to completely unruly, and in the lead it's Cissy! "Sistoors, dismoont! Prepare t'stoorm the gates!"

CLANCLANCLANCLANCLANCLANK —CLUNK!!!

With Betsy there by his side, Chipper grabs his Fenderbender and strums one. "That sound about in tune to youh eah gihl?"

Anything's fine by her, since she howls on another scale altogether.

"HEY! HEY! ANYBODY OUT THEAH READY FAH A HEFTY SLICE OF OLD-FASHIONED ROCK 'N' ROLL?"

HEYYYYYYYYYYYYYYYYYYYYYYY!

Whap / whack / whack wham -ammmm -ammmm — Chipper whaps out a chord — *maa maa maam / mammmmmm!* — who knows what key? Though Will Cook can second it. Chipper quick shifts to another. As does Will Cook. This catch-as-catch-can duet having lasted these two odd school buddies over their musical lifetimes together.

Maam maam -mack'k'k'... Chipper catches his sawed-off strumming finger under a string and snaps it — "Damn!" — but six strings, five strings, he goes at it — *Whack / ack / ack /-am -maam -ammmmmmmm...*

Say hey! I say hey!

HEY! Comes back in response.

SAY HEY!	SAY HEY!
SAY HEY! HEY! HEY!	HEY! HEY! HEY!
WHAT'H WE GOIN TO DO?	WHAT'H WE GOIN TO DO?

Right / What'h we goin to do my friends?
What'h we goin to do?
Whack / whammmm
Stand by? /
Let it all run down the drain?

SAY HEY!	SAY HEY!
What'h we goin to do?	WHAT'H WE GOING TO DO!

Chuhn all this acid into rain?
wham / wham / wham / wham
What'h we goin to do?
Squat down upon ouh hands?
Watch fahests rot
The icecaps melt
And fahmlands tuhn todust?

whack / wham
Nucleah waste stuck some place
To buhn a million yeahs?

While Chipper hops around one leg tugging at the boot

SAY HEY!
WHAT'H WE GOIN TO DO!

SAY HEY!
What'h we goin to do?

Oah ah we just some race
Without a face
Too fah gone to shed some teahs?
I say HEY!
whack / wham
WHAT'H WE GOIN TO DO?

The crowd is instantly standing on their seats, arms lifted above their heads in long armed Vs.

"What sorta riff's he playing here?" Bubba Bonanza dances over and asks Danny T.

"Don't ask me. I'm just the dumb drummer, remember — a one, a two, a three and four."

Bubba's over questioning one of the back-up guitarists. Entire team's trying its best to play catch up with whatever Chipper is pitching, stunned too that the SOB finally made it, standing center stage, stabbing fitfully with one blunt finger at his one sprung guitar.

Will Cook's got a hold of it if nobody else has. He's up on his platform head back and laughing, man's as loony as Chipper and that's why he can do it, keep up with Chipper, even stay a step ahead of the ball. He's hands all over his keyboards, doing improvs in and around Chipper. He ups the volume, joins in with a synthesized brass section.

But before any of them stumble too badly, there's this revelation — a breath, a pause — everyone's all at once aware they're there on stage, the Loose Nukes, reunited — crowd's only been waiting eighteen hours…

LADIES AND GENTLEMEN, IF YOU PLEASE, THE THREE LOOSE NUKE ORIGINALS — CHIPPER STIRBEE, WILL COOK AND DANNY T 'DRUMMER DYNAMO' — WITH BUBBA BONANZA JUNIOR JOINING IN — THE ROCK 'N' ROLL RAGE OF THE 60S REUNITED HERE TONIGHT ON STAGE AT WEMBLEY! AN ALLIED FOR LIFE BENEFIT CONCERT! LET'S GIVE THESE FOUR FELLOWS A GREAT BIG WARM HAND OF WELCOME!

YAAAAAAAAAAAAAAAAAAAAAAAAAAAAAAAAAAAAAAAAAAAAAAAAY!

Bubba Two, son of the legendary Bubba Bonnanza, can bask in the applause too. Danny T, forgive and forget it, let's play some tunes! And Will Cook? He's hanging from his fingertips and laughing like crazy! But no mistaking it, there they are reunited after forty five years, three men who despite their youthful looks and energy are far, far away into their fifties, with the one young stud as a reminder of how they looked way back in their glory. Even Danny T skips a beat. It's an emotional moment for these guys who have had their share of troubles, women in particular and particularly one woman, Molly Dawkens, who lingers backstage for the suitable moment to make her entrance, but tonight all is right, for long time buddies have got to be forgiven, that's an immutable law of nature.

YAAAAAAAAAAAAAAAAAAAAAAAAAAAAAAAAAAAAAAAAAAAAAAAY!
"Whoa!"
YAY! YAY! YAY! YAAAAAAAAAAAAAAAAAAAAAAAAAAAAAAAAAAAAAAAAY!
"Don't know what to say fellas."

Nor do they as Bubba Two gives Chipper a big hug, and Danny T trips down from behind his mound of drums to do the same.

YAY! YAY! YAY! YAY! YAY! YAY! YAY! YAY! YAY! YAY! YAY! YAY! YAY!

The three Loose Nukes stand out front, take their bows, and look! They point skyward toward Will Cook who honks this off-key reminder of his lofty stage presence.

"HEY! HEY! About all we can say…"
HEY! HEY! HEY! HEY! HEY! HEY! HEY! HEY! HEY! HEY! HEY! HEY! HEY!
"SAY HEY, what'h we goin to do, my friends? What'h we goin to do?"
"SAY HEY!" Danny T repeats the refrain into his mike, and Bubba Two, "Say hey, like what'h we doin?"

Chipper grits his teeth, jams his nipped tip under the low E-string and works his way up the struts, in agony, wring wire wrenching the attenuated spines of everyone in speaker range — and on live world-wide satellite hook-up, that's five billion at least people wincing while he does it — finally resolving on a *D- D- D- flat flat*, and soul wretching he wrests it out.

I say I say I say — HEY! WHAT'H WE GOIN TO DO?

Some beautiful body in the crowd shouts back: "Beat the bastards!"
Somebody else bare, but audible: "Reach out, touch hands!"
And from somewhere else entirely: "Jump up!"

Chipper's finger's crammed in there on that D-flat minor, taunting, that same hair raising single sound over and over. Brave Will Cook joins in, glues his hands to his keyboard, his feet pressed to the pedals. Danny T whipping at a cymbal relentlessly — SAYASAYASAYASAYASAY — HEY!

> What'h we goin to do?
> *whack / whack / whammmm*
> With no mah whales to watch
> No dolphins to jump through hoops
> No mah giant redwoods to drop
> Nah mighty elephants to loot?
>
> I mean / they'h tearin down the jungles

The Indians got to flee
It's all a game of fumbles
A BUHNT-OUT LAND SCAM JAMBOREE -*ee* -*ee*

'Cept it's rahe bihds and buttahflies
Who've got no place to roost
Cah emissions foulin up theih skies
And coal plants belchin soot

So I say // Hey! // What?
What'h we goin to do, my friends
What'h we goin to do?

"Fuck'em!" Some hardass out front shouts.
"Fight'em!"
"Vote them out of office!"
"Join'em" is fainter and isolated.
"JUMP UP" comes across the strongest.
 Chipper's listening, he's rolling back and forth from heel to toe, full body into it, the calls from the wild, the pounding drum, the mezmerizing repeating chord, he slides his finger tip up and under that E-string again, an agonized foreboding — SAYASAYASAYASAYASAY HEY!

HEY!

WHAT AH WE GOIN TO DO?

JUMP UP! answers in volume from the millions in the vicinity who start bounding up and down, the entire stadium, the entire industrial park a'rocking and a'rolling, dangerously, all youthful vigor in motion, their loving arms stretch -UP -UP in suppliant V- VVVVVVVVVVVVVVV!

"OK OK, are we up and running with this one, let's get a readicam smack up in Chipper's face, how about B-14 — *snap snap* — I want to count his pearlies, and ready on A-2, bring A-2 around center stage, that's A-2 center stage, let's go! A-2! What's the hold up? *Snap? Snap?*"

"A-2's down Cub, that's a dead feed you're getting on the monitor."

"Thought the operator was dead, so thanks for telling me different — alright then get me A-9, front and center stage, and get a techie over on 2, we're going to need everybody alive and working, and I want a readicam parked next to our boy Chipper, catch him biting into that mike — LET'S GO! LET'S GO! WE'RE HERE TO DO A SHOW, REMEMBER? *Snap! Snap!*"

"Here Cub, have a cola."

"OK alright…" He claws off the top bear handed, chugs it.

"Cigarette?"

Grabs one of those too, even though he has four or more burning up in ashtrays around him, and maybe he doesn't even notice that it's Lou who's handing them to him, who's snuck back into the swivel chair next to him, no nor the fact that Lou has been lighting up Cub's cigarettes all evening, but then ten-pack-a-day men don't notice much, *smack smack!*

"Let's get another readicam focussed in on Bubba's fingers, B-8, B-8's in line, *snap snap* — I see some fancy finger work about to materialize and we're set up to miss it as usual!"

B-8 snaps to, and there's the prize Loose Nuke lead guitarist, Bubba Bonnanza, doing digitals and flexing a bicep while he's at it.

"OK hold it steady and broadcast, that's it, and ready for a wide-open shot center stage on whatever whatever."

"A-9."

"A-9, *snap snap*, and let's bleed it, bleed it to broadcast. Now we're sparking! So OK Lou, what's with this song, this *Hey What?* they're doing? It's not on the playlist. This some kind of last minute switcheroo?"

"I'm not sure."

"OK OK! What do you say? Let's do an overlay! How about Chipper's mug again, B-14, let's put it up against something out there in the audience, maybe C-11 or C-16? What am I looking at?"

"C-11. Those are the girls in The Pit."

"Then make it C-11! Why not the pits? *Snap! Snap!*"

Chipper's profligate grin is thereby layered atop dozens of pouty fresh preteen faces and broadcast thusly throughout the civilized world as well as projected high up on the three giant video screens, and when the little darlings with the special passes who are jammed into The Pit directly in front of the stage see themselves on telly, they get to going at it, saucy and sassier, yelling themselves silly!

CHI-HIP-PER! CHI-HIP-PER!

And you've got to wonder what attraction this guy holds, the way these teeniteens purse their impertinent lips and thrust their hips and make slight sucking sounds that can only be described as disgusting!

"So you didn't answer my question, why's this song not on the playlist?"

"Don't know."

"So what are we now, forty three minutes behind schedule — and what's with this scene I'm seeing? It's getting gross!" Indeed. Chipper's thrusting his hips back and forth in time to the misses in The Pit and tossing slobbery kisses, gets them climbing all over themselves trying to get to him, which only gets him going, climbing all over himself trying to get to them. "*Snap snap*, let's cut to the Queen!"

Who is royally shocked at what she is witnessing, subversion outside the gates is one thing, but perversion on the stage quite another.

"OK then, let's try a long shot on the stadium and back off everybody on stage, *snap snap!*" Which is always a safe bet, long shots a lot less risky than those tell-all close-ups. "So Lou, what's with this song, it's dragging way beyond three minutes? Look at the clock! We've got to get on with the Finale — and maybe if we're lucky we'll get it on air before dawn!"

"Cub, the girls have grabbed C-11, our man in The Pit."

"Don't bother me with trifles, I'm trying to make a point here with my man Lou. We've got to snap it up some, *snap snap snap snap!*"

Lou twists in his seat.

"Because we can't keep the Pope, these kids and six or more billion people at home waiting up past their bedtimes, now can we, not while your born-again rockstar is hogging the mic?"

"Cub! They're eating him alive!"

"Who?"

"C-11!"

Truly. The readicam technician's caught alone in a war zone. *Chomp. Chew.* And when the little girls are through, the line gets sliced, the monitor in the control trailer goes blank.

There's a second of silence among the crew.

"Where was I? *Snap?* Right, it's A-9, let's dolly up front, get Chipper up there gryrating! *Snap! Snap!* A-9, keep it wide, but ready for a rapid pull-out when he starts with the acrobatics, and you know he's going to do it — better to be prepared, isn't that the scout's motto? — that's good, you've got him in your sites, stay on him, let's see if our boy gets to jumping!"

More than a dozen cameras go racing around stage, vying for the best angle on the athletic star.

"Ready for A-1 on the Zoomocrane™, *snap snap,* let's do a scoop, start with Bubba on lead and ride right around all of them fast, sweep across, then narrow on Will there, cooking in his catbird seat! Let's go!"

"Are you ready?"

"Ready."

"Ready ready?"

"Ready ready."

"Then cut to A-1 and ride it out! *Snap! Snap!*"

Maneuver works well, too well as Will Cook notices his face loom up on the giant screens he's hiding behind — and he does what any man that averse to publicity would do — he ducks!

"So Lou, talk to me, we sticking with the playlist or what?"

"Hey Cub!" Some voice calls out from the galley benches below. "Take a look at D-17. Look what we've got hooked on a remote!"

A young lady is showing off a full-front see-through top for a marauding camera crew. *Whistle thistle!* The techies shout encouragement, not that she can hear them, but then what is it that explains her smile as she obligingly turns to show a peek-a-boo slide-slope view?

"Looks great guys," Cub *snaps* and laughs, "guess we can spare a few shots to make sure you heavy breathers are still alive and working."

Another remote crew knee deep in the crowd has an up angle on two young lovelies jumping along with the song. *Hi-hup* they go, and underneath they show. *Hi-hup* they go again, tickly pure sweet tasty skin.

"We need broadcast footage gentlemen, not take-home videos. Let's keep scouting the stadium for photo ops, *snap snap*."

Like eight to ten to twelve — the camera opening up — to fourteen to more and more a dressed-up American fraternity crew kicking arm-in-arm in a chorus line, doing fine South Sea islander style, beer smeared smiles, a few of the Fiji bros out having a blow.

Or back to the Royals seated in their box primly enough, the Queen, gloved hands folded on a purse in Her lap, slight parting of the lips, a smile and wide wide eyes. The Heir Apparent leans over to make a comment, and Her lips part further, a downright regal guffaw.

Other crowd shots show clumps of people shouting, jubilantly jumping, nubile and dewy, all the while waving their hands away above their heads and laughing daftly — kids and kids of kids having a hell in a lifetime good time.

"WHAT ARE WE DOING WITH THE AERIAL REMOTE, PANNING THE STARS?" Cub shouts above the confusion.

A radio-signal remote camera, G-7, capable of rotating 360 degrees, is suspended above the stadium by guide wires. Designed for soccer games, it can back up to focus wide on the entire crowd, narrow down to track a running pass, whiz overhead for the fastest zoom on the stage imaginable, much like a guided missile.

"Are you ready with the aerial?"

"Ready."

"Ready ready or about ready?"

"Ready ready."

"Then fire away at that stage — *SNAP!*"

And damned if there isn't a sky rocket swooping down on Chipper Stirbee at exactly the right second — luck! — G-7 catches his legs leaping and arms reaching, jumping up!

"WILL YOU LOOK AT THAT BOY FLY!"

He's a good fifteen feet above the stage, yet lands with all the grace of a gymnast. And the crowd, well…

YAAAAAAAAAAAAAAAAAAAAAAAAAAAAAAAAAAAAAAAAAAAAAAAAY!
Man's into it.

> SO- SO- SO- SOOOOOO...
> So what'h we goin to do / my friends?
> What'h we goin to do?
> *whack / whack / whack / whack*
>
> I SAY I SAY I SAY — HEY!
> What'h we goin to do / my friends?
> What'h we goin to do?
>
> JUMP UP!
>
> That's ahright by me. Let's jump up!
>
> JUMP UP! JUMP UP!

And Chipper does, a short one this time, fewer than ten feet.

> Cause it's up to you / you know
> Folks like you and me
> Cause...
> No cohporate type oah bankah bloke
> Is goin to do nothin fah free
>
> No Senatoh's wife nah movie stah
> Is goin to push that fah
> No / No
> No king / no queen / no priest nah preachah
> No TV anchah and suhely not youh high school teachah
> SO HEY! // HEY! HEY!
> WHAT'H WE? // YOU AND ME?
> WHAT'H WE? // GOIN TO DO?

...about all this mess? I mean folks, let's get real we can't-...

> JUMP UP! JUMP UP!
> JUMP UP! JUMP UP! JUMP UP!

Can't huht — LET'S ALL DO IT! C'MON — JUMP UP!

And they do, the entire stadium quakes with the weight.

> Cau- *h'au-h'au-h'auauauauauauauau -ause* /
> All these celebrities want is applause
> Youh taxes oah youh vote

He's a good fifteen feet above the stage, yet lands with all the grace of a gymnast

wham / wham
So no sih oah madam
Bewahe of theih pleas — PUH-LEASE! PUH-LEASE!
And it ain't just the French and Japanee-*ee-ee-ee-ese*...
Shippin theih nucleah waste ovah *se-ee-ee-ee-eas!*
NO NO NO... NOOOOOOOOOOOO!

JUMP UP! JUMP UP!

Every country's got a stake in it
It's a UN done dued-up deal
Make no mistake of it /
Everyone of them's in theah fah the steal!

wham / wham / wham / wham
Cau-h'au-h'au-h'ause...
They'h playin on the othah side
Ain't the same team as you and me
Which leaves it up to us / you *see... see... seeeee!*
Since they haven't even tri ...-*ried* ...-*ried* ...*ried!*
So it's you! // It's me!
YOU! // ME! //
SEE? SEEEEEEEEEEEEEE?

JUMP UP! JUMP UP! JUMP UP! JUMP UP!

The sight of all these kids jumping, well it must inspire Chipper, youthful exuberance especially, because he does one of his back flips, lands standing on his hands and then flips front again. But how can the dude do it, age and there's also all those years of seclusion and hard Maine winters in between which can take their toll on a guy despite rural pleasures of the flesh — homebrew, homegrown and homespun neighborly daughters — though he looks good, close-up and long shot, maybe not 19 anymore, but he could easily pass for early 30s, that critical age for a guy, and he shows it, exposes it — though hopefully not tonight before the Queen, the Pope and such — but blond hair, tanned skin, raw muscle, packed pants, a scar over the left eye from a wheel buggy spill and a bit of talent, mostly for guts and self-promotion which in total have made him into a still living miracle, a 60s legend and a hero for the 2000s. And he is jumping around up there for the world to see. AND JUMP HE DOES! — ONE MORE TIME OFF THE DIME! — free style, twelve feet, sixteen feet, twenty feet straight up in the air, legs spread, slapping at his ankles with those long wing fingers of his.

THAT'S RIGHT!

Cause we've been sittin on ouh duffs too long-*ong-ong*

Wait! Wait! Wait! / Wait up one doggone minute…

HEY!

Nope folks! This is serious business. I mean…
whap / wham
We've eithah got to clean / it / up
Oah give / it / up /
Theah's no time in betwee-*ee-ee-een*
Fah what's done is gone fahevah
And lots mah's in dangah too!

wham / wham / wham / wham
A UN - I - VEHSE OF DIS - GRACE
OUH GLOHR - I - OUS - WOHLD - UN - DONE!
SO-SO-SO-SOOOOOO… WHOA!
WHAT'H WE GOIN TO DO, ME MATES?
WHAT'H WE GOIN TO DO?

JUMP UP! JUMP UP! JUMP UP! AND UP! AND UP! JUMP! JUMP!
AND UP! UP! UP! UP! UP! UP!

"Not bad fah stahtahs, but…" And Chipper is up once more himself! Guy is airborne this time! Arms in the trademark V! And from center field it looks better than twenty feet, lot better, thirty, forty maybe, has to be because he spring dunks up on Will Cook's hidden platform, slaps hands with the musical maniac — G-7 on the guide wires is doing a fast back — captures him on camera as he does a flip back and rebounds to the ground, landing standing, arms up in a V — kids are jumping ecstatic, which means they're diving off their seats and moshing into the crowd, same in billions of living rooms in front of TVs — WHOOPF / WHOOPF / WHOOPF — the entire arena, in fact the entire planet bounces up and down once or twice which with a full moon tide means a typhoon size surf because…

SAY HEY! THAT'S WHAT WE'AH GOIN TO HAVE TO DO!

Chipper bows, turns and does cartwheels off the stage. The band sprints after him, except for Will Cook, the aloner up in his protected perch, for one among the many must remain behind to tell, or at least to entertain, and the crowd loud lungs it, stretches high-armed vs.

YAAAAAAAAAAAAAAAAY! - YAY! - YAY! - YAY! YAAAAAAAAAAAAAAAAY!

"*GRUNGYSONOFASUMPPUMPER!*"

"Keep on that boy, track him, track him right off the stage, *snap snap!* Right off, off he goes, bye-bye, bye… bye… and ready, ready on the commercials… line them up… that's three, that's two and one and go to broadcast — *SNAP!*"

Two hands from on high scoop out sand from a bleached white beach and let the granules run through fingers — "Do you worry about the financial security of your family?" An almighty voice intones. "Where to invest for your children's tomorrow?"

Tanned tow-headed twins skip by, a boy and a girl, and the camera follows them until they reach a huge sand castle, dug out and piled high. The two children run round and behind the mound, laughing, playing, and the hands from on high stack more sand on top, another turret rises upwards, while more and more sand is scooped away from the perimeter.

"INSTITUTIONAL LIFE offers the highest return for your investments — Blue Chip Growth Stocks, Riskfree Treasury Bills, Solid Goldbrick Futures, Early Retirement Funds, B-School Education Trusts, Bankruptcy Credit Renewals, Pre-Term Birth Insurance — make your money work for you… in a new age of financial vulnerability… and for those you care most deeply about…"

Two tykes seem to take it all for granted. They jump feet first on top of the castle, roll giggling into the moat which swiftly fills with rising surf, and the camera freezes on their trusting innocent little faces: "Buy a handful of sand, INSTITUTIONAL LIFE — off-shore pay dirt that endures forever!"

"OK alright, let's keep on line with the commercials gentlemen, while we run checks on each of our downlinks for the Finale — that's Melbourne, that's San Francisco, Rome and the rest, all the way around the world to the snowy mountain caps of Tibet — because it looks like we just might be able to call it a wrap — *snappity snap snap snap!*

There's a cheer from the control room crew — WAY TO GO! — one final push and this long night might finally be over.

"OK and remember, it's out back of my trailer for thick Iowa corn-fed steaks and plenty of ice cold brewskies. We'll pack tomorrow afternoon."

"You mean late this afternoon Cub."

"Whenever. After everbody's been fed and tucked into bed – so Lou, level with me," Cub lights up a cigarette, "this song, this *Hey Say* or *So What* — what was that all about?"

"Genius."

"Speak up, I can't hear you."

"*Uh-humm*, creative genius Cub…"

"Genius. Right. Here Lou, sit up straight, turn up the volume. You're looking tired or worried. Relax. Have a soda. Have a smoke."

"Thanks… Thanks." He passes on the soda but lights up another one of Cub's cigarettes. "Appreciate it."

"I've got to hand it to you and your boy Chipper, that entrance was all show, open jump out of a helicopter, classic cliff-hanger, next the acrobatics, an exciting new song — what was it a cut off a new album?"

"N-no I don't think so."

"I wonder if anybody in the world left their seat for that entire hour and forty minute sequence?" Cub rolls his swivel chair close over to Lou's swivel chair. "I've never seen anything like it in all my time in the business."

"No?"

"You guys are too clever, you see an opportunity, you grab yourselves a bundle of free airtime, right? To announce what, the release date — you have a press conference scheduled for later this morning?"

Lou's a bit uncomfortable with Cub so close, Cub being a big guy, burly, bearded and breathing fire out the mouth, while Lou's this little guy who's shrunk some over the years, smaller and smaller, and worse tonight by the hour — still he struggles bravely. "Spontaneity, see Chipper needs plenty of room for spontaneity."

"Spontaneity, is it?"

"Spontaneity, creativity, the mark of the true performer, his ability to be innovative, responsive to his audience on the spur of the moment…"

"Right. On the spur of the moment."

"…and deliver this message on the crucial issue of our age without anybody expecting it!"

"No. None of us expected it."

"This is genius. The art of the surprise!"

"Wait… wait…"

"Cub?"

"…I'm not catching on, am I? I'm some sort of dummy?"

"No. Not you…"

"This sideshow wasn't a plug for a new album, was it?"

"No… no…"

"You don't have a new album?"

"…no…"

"So what you're not telling me is that Chipper Stirbee simply made up this song while he was going along?"

"I- I- I've never heard it before, but that doesn't mean…"

"WITH MOST OF THE WORLD WATCHING, THAT BASTARD TOOK UP MY TIME ON LIVE SATELLITE TV TO MAKE UP A SONG!"

"Y-y-yes…"

"DO YOU HAVE ANY IDEA WHAT INTERCONTINENTAL TRANSMISSION COSTS AMOUNT TO BY THE SECOND?"

"N-n-no…"

"Twenty nine grand, let's see, round that to thirty multiplied by one hour and forty five minutes — so thirty thousand times sixty times one hundred and five — call it an even $190 million! THAT'S WHAT YOUR BOY'S SPONTANEITY COST ME OVER BUDGET!"

Must come down to a matter of money because Cub's up from his seat — and a grizzly standing on his hind twos is a frightening sight — and that's before he plunges down on top of Lou — "NO WARNING! NO PREP, NO NOTES, NOTHING! SPONTANEITY! CREATIVITY! GENIUS! TOAD CRAP! YOU'RE AN INGRATE!" *BWAP BWAP BWAP BWAP!*

"I'ke- I'ke- I'ke-…"

"Cub, man-o-man!" A couple of techies are out of their chairs. "You're losing it.."

"You've got enough problems. You don't need a corpse on the floor of the trailer."

"TWO CORPSES: LOU'S FIRST, CHIPPER'S LATER!" *BWAP BWAP* and *BWAP BWAP* some more!

Lou is kicking fitfully.

Cub is squeezing with all his strength, his teeth clinched, this mean sucker snarl on his big bear face.

"*I'gg-gggg-gggggg-…*" Lou's face is purple and his tongue is hanging out, it's purple.

More of the switchers are away from their consoles and up on the platform, they're tugging at Cub, trying to restrain him, one more time, because it's just another uproar in the control trailer, uproar upon uproar, delay upon delay.

"YOU MISERABLE SON-OF-A-BITCH, I'LL SEE YOU WASHED UP DEAD ON THE SHORES IN THIS BUSINESS IF IT'S THE LAST THING I DO!" — *BWAP BWAP!*

They finally manage to pry Cub off and back into his swivel chair. They placate him with a two liter jug of the real zing, classic sugar and caramel-colored caffeine, which he pours down in one continuous stream. Seems to sedate him. Leastwise he belches.

Lou however, he's left bent over and gagging, though one of the techies hands him a cup, cold coffee — *gluck!* But what is it he has done exactly, Lou wonders as he strokes his sorely stretched neck? He can't help it if he's saddled with a Chipper. He didn't ask for it, not initially, he started out to make a buck like every other Boom Baby, when suddenly he found himself part of a cause, no bucks but plenty of non-profitable headaches, yet he can't quit can he, walk off, wave goodbye to a nuclear sunset or worse, floods, famine and little world wars for what's left to feed the burgeoning billions?

Not to worry. A sky pan of grain fields that stretch on across townships and counties, across state lines of harvest and bounty. Wheat. Soybeans. Corn. Granaries. Cattle. Hogs. Chickens. Rail yards. Feed lots. Slaughter houses. Packaging plants. Every once in a while a homestead with a few scraggly sharecroppers, but mainly not, just lots and lots of motorized equipment and labor-saving devices — GIGAGROW, the entirely automated feed and food conglomerate — plant it, pick it, pack it, chop it and stack it on a supermarket shelf nearby anywhere on the planet and never touch it, not with human hands, not until you buy it, cook it, stuff it in your mouth. For nobody need starve so long as they have coupons aplenty or cash to pay for it — though without jobs, how do people pull that act off? Since there's laws on the books saying they can't simply pocket it. What to do? What to do? GIGAGROW can't make it donating it? And so far folks aren't eating off the internet.

Even so. That's somebody else's problem, isn't it? Meantime GIGA GROW is bagging it, $3 trillion gross annually, the biggassed export business in the U.S. and unless you want the starving masses to purge your palaces, you foreign potentates had better pay the grim reaper the balance.

GIGAGROW. The subsidiary that wholly owns QuotLink Inc.

The Liaison is rushing across the playing field in a desperate attempt to find cover, Queezac dragging along behind him.

"Vait Eminenze, I can't hardly keep up vitz you."
"It is everyman for himself in a thunder storm."
"Yez butz it'z not even rainink."
"Soon Queezac, soon!"
"No cloudz in ze zky zat I can zee, juzt ze overzized blimp!"
Two freaks standing off the path watch the odd couple pass.
"That the dude with the football?"
"Yah, and the football."
"Two don't look so good."
"Drag man."
"Think they'd want a hit?"
"Be a waste of good weed on those two."

CRR-RACK! The QuotLink Inc lightship berths itself directly above the Executive Liaison as he runs along. The eleven octogenarian Council of Elders inside have met in conclave and reached a unanimous decision. Seems the Executive Liaison has become a liability, a disgrace before Her Majesty as well as wholly ineffective in dealing expeditiously with one Chipper Stirbee. Their recourse is instant termination of the Liaison's position in conjunction with a reversal in corporate strategy – the failed diplomatic mission replaced henceforth with open intervention by the military – a certain Colonel L. L. Peckler assuming control of all QuotLink Security forces on the ground.

"Eminenze, vhat's vitz zoze pinvheel zpinz in your eyez!"

CRACK-KUR-AX! The Elders rain down a lightening strike straight to the skull of the the Liaison. He falls face forward into his own spittle.

"EMINENZE!" Queezac tumbles to his knees. "Vhat have zey done to you, to me, my prize dezign, my only vriend in ziz vorld un liege."

The two longhairs are witnesses.

"Did that dude just OD on the spot?"
"What a time to exit."
"Yah, right when there's a drop-dead party in progress."

Queezac is distraught, though his rage turns quickly to cunning. "Yez vell, I've gotz zecretz untold un vengeance to unvold. I've been zere you zmug old baztardz, I know all ze endz un outz ov your operationz, un bevore I'm tzrough I'll vry your brainz to a zizzle, you betz I vill!" An ugly glance upward must suffice for now, but in time the resident genius will surely shake QuotLink Inc to its very junk bond foundations.

But whatever might constitute appropriate revenge, the proud on proud Liaison is left a puddle. The groundskeepers soon come to sponge him up and carry away his remains in a bucket. A parade of mops, brooms and dust bins crosses the playing field followed so slowly by a loyal grieving ingrown three-toed turtle.

"Man, take a look." The one longhair nudges the other. "There goes that rolled over troll."

"Wow. You suppose he's some sort of throwback to the past?"

"Maybe, or a sign of what's comin.'"

Mercifully a hot breaking news flash preempts the brouhaha.

BULLETIN: WEMBLEY STADIUM: JUST IN:

There's a crisis out front, someone, it looks like a young guy with a close crop and black leather has climbed to the top of one of the tall sound towers, no, look closely at the legs in the shorts, shaved smooth, could be a cross-dresser or a bi-cyclist, but no, it's a young girl, yes yes, angle the camera up to see better, look at that unzipped jacket, definitely female not silicone imitation and she must be high on something, she is... a cause she is, one of those revisionist feminists, a Sister of Fire... and she's hanging from her hands, suspended mid-air, now from her toes, dangling it, but up the scaffolding goes a climber, cutoffs, boots, hard hat and a bright red feather — oh no not Red Feather again! — indeed it is, look he's limping, but he doesn't care, oblivious, no gain no pain, he's the closest climber and there's a job to do, a girl to be undone.

The crowd's attention switches from the **GigaGrow** commercial projected on the three suspended video screens above the stage to the hot and ready action on the single tower — *fickle fickle.*

Is that a dive the girl is doing? Mid-air and no bungee cord attached! "I can fly, fly!" She squeals. Monkeys see, monkeys do. She's out of her cage and flinging in the tree-tops.

-hohhhhhhhhhh! The whole stadium startles, but she catches on something, something snags her leather jacket — *rrrrrrr-rip* — what she's got she shows — though at least she's still hanging in there.

Red Feather's gaining on her. He's breathless, especially as he closes in. He's on top, coming on slowly, saying something softly to her, probably attempting to calm her fears. She doesn't seem to react, she has a giddy grin on her face even though she hangs by a tender hook. He reaches — my God, look what the guy has got to do, and stretched out precariously himself to do it — first by her ankles, then by moving up her calves, it's the thighs next and around the curve of her buns, he's holding her close, yes, and a hand, delicately slipped across her midriff and another locked on one breast — what a man does when he has to!

Yet she's resisting?

The crowd, the males start to hoot and to holler, no respect, egging one of their own on to daring exploits in public — and let's hear it for Yank, head electrician's gone groping for that wrong switch again, there go the lights — *BOO BOO BOO BOO* — then up again.

When the girl slips from Red Feather's tenuous grasp! Down she goes! And are those fingernails tearing through his tank top, latching onto his tool belt? Yes. He's both hands shackled back and hanging on dearly for himself. It's his buckle that bursts first and shreds of stripped jeans. She's locked on to his hips, poor girl, it's all she's got left between life and limb — but what is it she's doing now? Life's last act and without a gasp for air. She's clinging on and giving high wire head, no mistaking it! — *BOB BOB, BLUB BLUB, BUBBLING BUBBLES IN THE TUB!*

She is hanging there solely by her crusted upper lip — only one thing on earth can save her now! Can Red Feather hold tight for a second coming?

His fellow climbers gang for the scaffolding — Eddie, Swag — ready at the line should Red Feather fail — an immutable law of nature, where one buddy succeeds others shall necessarily follow — and they do, ferocity ascending — Eddie snags her by the ankles, Swag by her wrists, slowly they relieve their work mate, and what a man he is, bravely holding. They carry her off strapped to a stretcher and screaming, the crowd gone wild outdoors and howling.

YAAAAAAAAAAAAAAAAAAAAAAAAAAAAAAAAAAAAAAAAAAAAAAY!

For is there no end to what one lost Injun can do?

For is there no end to what one lost Injun can do?

MAINE BOY

"Hey Sally, toss anothah quahtah in the jukebox! Let's heah that old-time song about one of ouh own!"

O moan, the regulars groan.

"Toss in youh own quahtah Scootah, and leave me the hell out of the ahgument!"

-SKLUNK — *whipf whipf whipf whipf…*

> Rumah is that BOY's been spendin NIGHTS OUT
> Sniffin tracks back DEEP theah in the WOODS
> Can't seem to lose the SWEET SCEN / h'right SCOUT?
> Got that wet NOSE of youhs rub'd in real GOOD!
>
> MAINE BOY / SHAME BOY
> Wheah'd you lose youh PANTS?
> MAINE BOY / SHAME BOY
> When you goin t'leahn t'DANCE?

The search for Chipper can't be that bad, Lou reasons, simply a matter of heading north northeasterly up into the Maine woodlands beyond Bangor where vast tracts of pine forests have no names, simply plantation numbers, where mountains, streams and winding roads go, no towns for miles nor people, and early spring rains that bring mud, rivers of mud, and dense low lying fog that leaves winding roads impassible unless you hang your head way out the window and run your eye along the broken yellow line in front of you, praying you don't bump up against a moose nine feet or taller or a frost HEAVE — but hey, Welcome to Vacation Land early — least the black flies haven't hatched yet, nor has the sun begun to shine.

Lou's got tunes cranking on his stereo, old Loose Nukes tunes. He has a brightly colored Starco road map on the seat beside him, that and a New York City boy's inborn sense of direction. So outside of Portland he pulls off at a scenic overlook bulldozed into the trees. He makes a list of likely towns. He can cross out the Deer and the Swan Islands and Bucks Harbor and Seals Cove since they are coastal, and Bubba had said distinctly that the town wasn't near the ocean. Lou can cross out Moose River and Moosehead. Animal wasn't a moose. There's no Raccoonsburg or Possum Hollow, at least not on record, and while Foxcroft is a possibility, it seems simply too main road for Chipper. That leaves four likely lonely suspects: Badgersville, Caribou, Eagle Lake and Otter's Ledge, all located on some lake or stream or river, but then what town in Maine isn't located on some lake or stream or river? Badgersville is the closest of the suspects, center state on Highway 6 and 15, while the other three are way away up north on 11. So mere proximity dictates that Badgersville goes top of the list.

It takes Lou six hours to reach Badgersville because he's driving full face into a gale — *whish whap, whish whap, whissssh wha-aa-ap!* — the wipers a waste. Finally a sign breaks through the density: Badgersville: Incorporated 1762, Pop. 307 — the 7 with an X through it and a 6 affixed. Where the 306 live though is a mystery because there are no more than four two story gray clapboard buildings encircling what must be the village green, a grassy patch with a low black chain fence and a Civil War cannon pointed at a World War I gattling gun.

There's a boarded up grocery, a locked Town Meeting Hall, an out-to-lunch U.S. brand Post Office and a white steepled First Church behind closed doors, one with a walled graveyard adjoining and all the headstones overturned. Town seems to have gone out of business. Best Lou can do is pull over and try to decipher a bronze plaque bolted to the pedestal of the cannon, a list of local heroes of the many wars, but there's no ancestor named Stirbee among them.

Down the road out of Badgersville, there's a sign of life, a Racoon Lodge R.P.B.O. — Regulah Payin Brothahood Only — a racoon's head nailed over the doorway. Lou cuts across the gravel parking lot — *grattle grattle* against the tire wells. He parks and ducks underneath the head. Inside's a musty place, but lit up by at least two forty watt bulbs. There's a beefy bald fellow behind the bar, so Lou blurts out a loud howdy and would he happen to know the whereabouts of one Chipper Stirbee, a musician?

"Can't say I've evah heahd of nobody round these pahts named Stuhbee, but then can't say I knows everybody round these pahts neithah." The bartender draws a bead on Lou and doesn't flag in holding it steady.

"Lives by himself far back in the woods." Lou presses.

"H'yep, lots of woods round heah fah folks to live in, don't you know." If there is any humor implied in the man's answer, he doesn't betray it.

Nor can Lou argue the wisdom of the man's observation either. The drive after Skowhegan was lots of woods, nothing but woods, with an occasional glimpse of a house or a car back off the highway and into the trees, though no roads Lou could discern to reach them, nor any electrical poles linked up to them either.

"Used to be a rock 'n' roll star, lead singer for the Loose Nukes back in the 60s."

"Betcha he was, but fact is I ain't nevah heahd of him." Bartender doesn't move, just keeps Lou in his sites.

"No? Well- well thanks… thank you…" Lou waves thanks and goodbye in the same grand gesture and backs toward the door, checking out each of four additional sets of eyes aimed straight at him. Anybody else here never hear of Chipper Stirbee, he wants to ask as he steps butt backwards out of there. All eyes watch him go. No eyes betray the whereabouts of Chipper Stirbee to this stranger than stranger a way h'yup heah in snowman's land.

Lou jumps into his new four door Korean-engineered Ultimatum, one of those swell sport-utility imports that undercuts American models by at least five thou fully equipped, four wheel drive, imitation leather seats, electrocuted windows, a spurt of power at the touch of the accelerator and that thrill of a spill when you speed into a curve — Lou loves his Ultimatum and damned if he doesn't pick up speed going into a curve — *scramble scramble* — tilts right out of that parking lot, gravel to gravel, asphalt to asphalt — *ei-yeeee* he whistles through his teeth, but it's worth a bounce to say so long to Badgersville, Pop. 307 minus 1.

> What's he chasin round NIGHTS in such a HUHRY?
> Looks like he's done TREE'D himself some fancy TAIL
> Got somethin UP THEAH lookin mighty fine 'n' FUHRY
> 'Cept one fast WHACK 'n' even a Maine boy might FAIL!

The CD has jammed playing the same Loose Nuke tune over and over.

> MAINE BOY / SHAME BOY
> Wheah'd you lose youh PANTS?
> MAINE BOY / SHAME BOY
> When you goin t'leahn t'DANCE?

Eagle Lake, Caribou and Otter's Ledge are hours plus to the north, and although it has stopped raining the air continues to hang low down heavy, which throws the carburetor off enough to cause a chugging sound in the advance design inverted six cylinder fossil fuel infected engine. Lou wonders what to do and decides that a speed trial over 80 might blow whatever gunk's accumulated out the exhaust, and thus and fast he cuts across 6 and 16 toward Foxcroft on a flat four laner. Maybe Chipper lives in a civilized area after all, or leastwise where there might be a lone motel with color TV and hot running water.

The cold is gnawing on Lou's bones, and in his hurry he does as many these days do, he mistakes speed for progress. His miscalculation is set right just as rapidly by a Maine State Trooper, seems vacation state revenues are down, this being off season, and what's $230 cash out-of-pocket to teach a New Yorker about the north country where early spring is anybody else's late January.

> Hit sixteen like he'd NEVAH get anothah CHANCE
> Climbin in through WINDOW / livin without FEAH
> Boy's lookin WHUPED out / in some soht of TRANCE
> Keeps it up at this RATE he'll nevah last the YEAH!

There are no Stirbees of record in Foxcroft either, according to the roadside folks Lou meets first night out at Tally's Truck 'N' Stop — what the locals call Sally's Suck 'N' Pop — and there really is a Sally, Sally Tally, and Sally distributes the beer in the bar by the metal bucketfuls.

"Ovah heah Sally, we'ah ridin puhty neah empty — right strangah?"

Lou must agree, the bucket in front of him is almost empty, and he has at least a half dozen times introduced himself to Hutch Stevens, a long haul trucker, but if the stranger he is, then the stranger he is, and in a rainstorm with reported flooding of the St. John River up around the Canadian border, a beer drinking companion who forgets your name is better than no beer drinking companion at all.

"What the shit was it we wah talkin about?" Hutch's short term memory has lapsed entirely.

"Chipper Stirbee."

"Yeah right — Sally, baby! You've got to get us mah brew!"

"I'm huhryin fast as I can Hutch, you'h goin to have to sit theah and hold youh watah."

"Ain't the only thin I'm holdin fah you Sally!"

"Yeah, well hold whatevah it is you've got a hold on tightah!"

Tally's whatever 'n' whatever is crowded to overflowing rowdy on this particular Tuesday night because the roads are deemed impassible by those who know, those who drive them endlessly, and so a good laugh on Sally is welcome. Not that she minds. As long as they pay, Sally could care what they say, and if one ever tries to grab her, she wears four inch high heels with a pointy toe, and that toe has crimped many a trucker, and that heel if he has a randy buddy handy. Though three at once and Sally Tally's got more trouble than even she can foot.

"Anybody heah remembah a Chippah Stuhbee?" Hutch calls out.

There are nahs and nos and whos ho hos, but there are also a few yeahs and suhes and why's that you'h askin? A few of the younger fellas, the under 70s, do indeed remember the Loose Nukes and the infamous *Love Baby* and one of their very own singing out front.

"That fuckah's still alive, you say?" Somebody hollers over.

"That's what I hear and that's why I'm here." Lou reminds him.

"Damn, nevah would've thought it." Somebody hollers back.

"H'yep. Old rock 'n' rollahs nevah die."

The concern for Chipper sparks a discussion throughout the room.

"Rick Nelson, he's gone, and that theah Buddy Holly, and Elvis though my wife don't believe it none."

"King's gone but not fahgotten."

"H'yep, she's made the trip to GraceLand fouh times now, drives down to Memphis with huh gihl friends, plops posies on his grave."

"T'ain't nothin, my gal damn neah ran off with a Elvis' impahsonatah!"

"Yeah well mine run off with a female impahsonatah."

"Why's that? He look bettah in huh bra than you did?"

As usual, the mere mention of Elvis sparks a bucket fight, beer billows and soaked flannel, which is normal business for Sally, easier to mop up bucket beer than sweep up bottle glass. Which is why she bans Elvis from the jukebox eventhough there's still one of Chipper's old 45s on the charts, *Maine Boy*, a lasting tribute to his woodsy heritage. Anybody got a quahtah they can spahe?

> What's that MOM'S BOY upstaihs theah DOIN
> Spends all his time LOCKED TIGHT inside his ROOM
> Scrawny jehk's only got HIMSELF fah FOOLIN
> Eahly mohnin oah ANYTIME from dusk 'til DOOM!

"I heahd rockahs got a special heaven wheah they can go."

"Yeah wheah's that?"

"Right round the cohnah from hell, don't you know."

"Hell, you say? Why that's the only place theah's goin to be any aftah houhs action from what I've heahd them preachahs tell."

"H'yep, and you know Sally'll be down theah runnin the show."

"Good Jesus! You mean I'm still goin to be cleanin up aftah you jokahs when I'm dead?"

"Could be wohse Sally. Suppose you had to sing in the Lohd's choih every Sunday mohnin eahly?"

"Prefah to haul beeh fah the likes of you Satuhday nights, thank you."

And she hauls a couple of fresh buckets up to Hutch and Lou's table, clangs them down with a bang. "Eithah of you plannin on payin?"

Lou digs down for a twenty.

"What's this?" Sally holds it up to the light. "Haven't seen one of these in a few yeahs? Folks round heah-abouts make do with singles and fivahs, an occasional ten spot if they win the lottahry."

Lou almost tells her to keep the change, but thinks better of it — because with everybody having stopped talking and started gawking, there's no need to appear the rich New Yorker in poor man's Maine.

"Sally? You evah heahd tell of this singah named Chippah Stuhbee?" Hutch eases one of the new buckets his way.

"Suhe have. That boy could've stuffed my tuhkey any time he wanted — 'scuse my French — but he was a lookah when I was youngah. We'd travel many a mile if he was singin — remembah that trouble he had out west somewheah, was the Summah of 69."

"You heard Chipper sing after the Summer of 69?"

"H'yep, graduated high school in 66, heahd him lots aftah that."

"How long after? Do you remember any dates?"

"Let me see, let me see…"

"Huhry up ovah heah Sally, we'ah plum dry."

"Hold youh hohses, I'm tryin to remembah somethin — was like a national calamity to folks up these pahts, he was ouh only local hero, Maine boy made good, brought this state some pride."

"When? When was the last time you saw him?"

"Must've been 78, 79, I'd've still been with Buck Huhley about then, and I remembah us drivin ovah to…"

"Where, what town?"

"Sally? We'ah gettin awful damn thuhsty!"

"…it was eithah in that Chevy Malibu of his, oah was it the Dodge Aspen? Memohry ain't as good as it used to be…"

"Which direction?"

"Nohth from heah, some way out-the-way joint ovah on One, Highwayman's Hut oah such — best I can remembah.

"So he's alive, you're certain he's alive?"

"I'd 'spect he is. Ain't a lot else to do in this state 'cept stay alive. He's just buried back in them woods somewheah with lots of othah folks. You look long enough strangah, and you'h bound to run into him."

"Sally! We'ah gettin awful tihed of waitin!"

"I'm comin, don't go havin a hahnia ovah it."

Lou makes a motion with his hands for Sally to keep the change from the twenty, might jog her memory back. Because that's certainly the most encouragement Lou's had all day, Sally too. "I knew it, I knew it," he coos to Hutch, "I knew he was up here somewhere."

"Him and Bigfoot!" Some clown at the bar adds his mouthful.

"H'yep strangah. Now all you've got to do is track him." Hutch tosses his head back and drains his bucket. Time comes in a night when a thirsty fella can't tolerate much more beer, about the same time Hutch decides to slip under the table, bucket and all, and Sally's got to get the mop.

"Hutch hasn't been the same since his gihlfriend up and left him," she confides to Lou, "but could you blame the pooh gihl, fifteen and how'd you like to be cleanin up aftah a man three times youh age? About makes you want to run off with the fihst woodsman who'll ask you, which is what she did, a Frenchman" — Sally whispers — "and that's somethin you just don't do heah in these pahts."

Half the bar must be speaking French, so Lou's confused.

"See French is French, then theah's everybody else. Bettah not to mix the ducks up with the chickens, that's what my mothah advised me, and I've lived by that rule my entihe life, and look wheah it's gotten me." Sally shakes her head sagely.

And Lou wonders where it has gotten her, but he knows it's better in a foreign land to save the questions and sip silently.

"Though I've heahd rumahs that Frenchmen make the best lovahs" — something about Sally, the stick straw blond, the spread red lips, the ample thighs and bust suggests she wouldn't need to rely on rumor, and the way she leans close in over the table when she talks — "true of dahk and musky men the wohld ovah."

It's better also not to be the one man in the room the one woman in the room showers with attention.

"Sally? You stahtin to sweep up oah what? Cause the rest of us ah gettin rusty."

"Fella who lets his tongue droop down too fah to the ground is goin to get it stepped on." Sally stamps her heel.

Lou has at most a minute to make his final move.

"Sally..."

"Yeah strangah?" She brushes her hair back off her forehead.

"...has anyone told you they've seen Chipper Stirbee around lately?"

"Nope, but then he ain't the only attraction at the state faih neithah." At which Sally snatches another one of Lou's twenties, doesn't even bother to make change. Tucks it in her blouse and struts off. "Now who's doin all the hollahrin ovah heah?"

Lou searches the bleary eyes of the regulars seated around the bar. Doesn't anybody in Maine know anybody else? They all nod no. He even tries, "Vous savez la whereaboots du Chipper Stirbee?"

"Non. Non." Two bearded drivers of the opposite persuasion repeat.

"OK then, has anybody here ever been to Caribou or to Eagle Lake, Otter's Ledge?"

A shaggy haired student, probably a poet or a philosophy major over at

Orono, who can parlez-vous the Français, walks over. He's dressed like the rest of them, uniform plaid shirt with suspenders, 501s, Red Sox ballcap and hairy chest. He rests his hand on Lou's shoulder. "Are you lost?"

Yes, that would be Lou's most existential answer, but Lou's a ready realist, he braves a "No, not yet."

"Well, I'm originally from Eagle Lake and I certainly don't recall a family named Stirbee. Perhaps that was a stage name?" And the young man takes over Hutch Steven's vacated seat. Sally promptly replaces the downed bucket with a freshly filled one since the buzz is that students still have cash, from them govahnment backed loans they hand out, or if the student doesn't, the talky New Yorker does.

Lou had never thought about Stirbee being a stage name, but would anybody take Stirbee as a stage name? He ponders that in his beer, with the concerned gaze of the student in the plaid shirt beaming over at him.

"Could be." Any explanation being logically possible.

"Well, my bike has broken down and I need to hitch a ride up to Eagle Lake for a spare part. Maybe I could point you in the right direction."

Lou does need a guide, and a student poet biker might be the best guide for him, for any of us into life's wide wilderness. Besides this kid has crisscrossed the state on a classic flat-twin BMW 90S, he must have seen a few things in his flight. So Lou is delighted to accept the offer. Can he buy the young man another beer, or dinner?

Both yes, and thank you for asking.

About an hour and a half after the official two AM closing, the student has propped his elbow on the table and gone snoozing, while everybody else in the room who hasn't passed out is quietly sipping. Good time, Lou figures, to try and sneak out of the trucker bar. He mumbles thanks and nice meeting everybody, or thinks he does, though what you say and what you thought you said after beers by the bucketfulls are often at variance, but best to leave a foreign place friendly, so Lou also leaves another twenty on the table as a tip — that Lou remembers distinctly — which sets Sally Tally to wondering if there could be a tighter wad deeper down his pocket, and for no more than a ten minute work-out with the sauser before he rolls over to sleep it off — she puts her proposition to Lou directly, "You plannin on askin a lady to join you fah some aftah houh room sahvice?"

While the bar might be mostly blotto, no guy's ever so bad off he can't smell somebody else scoffin the puddin.

"I have to be up really early." Lou tries to plea bargain.

"I can do breakfast in bed if you'd rathah."

"Sally," calls out one of those cut off from the feed trough, "ain't faih you givin out unadvahtised specials."

"Pop youh nose back in youh bellybutton." Sally reprises.

"Man's got a point Sally," says somebody else with an interest, "bettah tend to youh regulahs befah you dish out to some strangah."

"Ain't none of youh business whose suppah I wahm up in the oven."

Even a lost New Yorker can understand that this scene is quickly developing into an incident, particularly when two regulars who are sober enough to stand decide the best way to even up the competition is by taking out the lead runner.

"Just a good night's sleep works wonders for me." Lou explains as he does his Maine brand back walk toward the door.

"Don't let these pinewood bullies go scahin you away honey!"

Amazing how a gal like Sally can deflect any animosity off herself and onto anybody else, anybody male and about to be rodent roast..

"Best to feed the family first Sally, though I appreciate the invitation."

"You mean you been leadin me on all evenin strangah?"

Lordy! Lordy! Now he's got Sally ranged against him too! Better do the quick turn head first dash as fast as you can, which he attempts, but Lou is no seasoned sprinter, not as he bangs into a bucket, wakes the student out of his semester slumber, kid half awake wondering what century it is and the barmaid and two bouncers headed his way, or so he thinks and so he stands, he's young, he's only had a halftime to learn what the old pros can sock you with if they come charging, or maybe he's already beginning to realize because he rubs his eyes and inadventently elbows one of the fellows, chop under the chin, he turns to apologize and cuts the other one at the swollen gut, so down two and only Sally to contend with — only Sally! Watch out friend, she's got her stiletto heels off and coming at you — when it's Lou who comes to the rescue by waving two more twenties, puts Sally off the scent immediately, like how much was she going to make carting her leftovers down the hall anyway?

"Couple of queeahs!" She yells as Lou and the student book it out the slamming storm door, which won't be the only instance during the next twenty four hours when Lou gets interrogated about his tender gender preferences.

After a back of the neck aching nap in a bucket seat and with the student poet as guide, Lou Starcrave has his blunt nosed Ultimatum pointed north on Highway 11. He's psyched, he can feel it. Chipper's actually been seen by a Sally in a roadhouse on U.S. 1 — twenty years ago — but no matter, a sighting's a sighting to a true believer.

"Stirbee, Stirbee," the young man keeps repeating, "could be a corruption of the original French. But then some of the early English settlers had strange names themselves that they bequeathed to their descendents. I've met Hoggs up here, Pennypackers, Oldcocks, Athols, Mavericks, Wigglebottoms — early settlers, late arrivals, all with strange names, strange accents and customs, strange people everyone of them, everywhere, strange land, strange country when you really think about it. Americans forget that. Whole country full of strangers, all trying to be neighbors. Hell, if the mix can't work here in the land of plenty, where is it going to work? Yugoslavia? The Middle East? Everybody speaking strange languages and not enough interpreters to go around, though on the other hand, if everyone did know for sure what the other guy was saying, or what he really meant, it could be worse. Maybe it's better that no one knows what his neighbor is saying, or thinking. Maybe it's better that people do live off by themselves in their little corner plots, their little house with a pointed picket fence, their little acre of woods…"

Lou could appreciate the philosophical ramblings of his poet sidekick if he didn't have such a hangover

"…while the polar ice caps melt and flood the entire Eastern seaboard, all because of the hole we've ripped a hundred miles wide in the ozone layer…"

Along with the drone of thick rubber tires against asphalt.

"…just so we can fill'er up and go driving anywhere we damn well please — take for example this thirty grand piece of molded junk metal we're driving…"

High 20's is all, plus Lou is proud of his Ultimatum, a *Consumption Guide's* Best Buy despite the recent expiration of the Hypnophonic™ CD player. But no need to contradict the fuzzy cherub, Lou advises himself, let the boy rant and rave, as long as he knows where he's going.

"…depleting the world's readily available supplies of crude oil within the next forty years while we rush to convert food crops to cornfields so we can produce enough ethanol to make up for the shortfall…"

Though thankfully in between musings there are uniterrupted miles of woods and silence.

"Even up here in these hundreds of thousands of acres of woodland, the trees and lakes are choking to death, fish floating to the top of the water, wild animals with cancers, trees blackening. We have fouled our planet's lungs with midwestern carbon monoxide while we wait for the Seabrooks to implode and poison what remains with radioactive particles that'll take millenniums to become inert, unless the whole scenario is preempted by some heavy handed potentate igniting the gaseous mess with a misdirected plutonium bomb."

Lou keeps his eyes on the road. His passenger crosses his arms and squints ahead through the interminable spring rain.

"Caribou would be off to the right, see the sign to Ashland, 163?"

"How far is Eagle Lake?" Lou's eyelids are weighty.

"Another two hours."

"Think we had better pull over and have lunch. You a vegetarian?"

"No, I too must kill to live."

Lou goes to pull into a Roaster Coop, then quickly gets a grip on himself, pulls out again fast.

"Plastic food packaging that will take decades to disintegrate, and even when it does will leave particulate matter behind that remains toxic to plant life a half century longer, ultimately climbing its way up the food chain to humans, the same formaldehyde used in household insulation, bedding and packing materials with no regard once so ever to its environmental impact — there's a BeefJack's up the road. They use plain plastic coated paper to wrap their ground up cow's flesh. Only takes a few years for that to decompose."

"Well," Lou sparks over lunch, "I'm really happy I ran into you, and I appreciate you're helping me find my way up here."

"*Mmm*," the poet munches, "I'm sure there are no Stirbees in the Eagle Lake area, but my father is the postmaster there and he'll know for sure. He could even call up to Otter's Ledge or over to Caribou for that matter."

"I would be much obliged. Another coke?"

"As much caffeine as four cups of black coffee, enough fructose to wire you for an entire day, not to mention the carbonic acids added to your stomach's stew — sure, why not?"

Lou gets out of his molded fiberglass seat (read: nondisintegrating asbestos fibers), and orders two freshly microwaved blueberry turnovers. He also orders a sulferized decalf for himself, though no hormone treated cow's milk please, and no B-vitamin depleting processed sugar.

"Sehve youhself on the drinks mistah, that way you can make it anyway you can take it."

Which is a consideration for Lou, he's burping beer and his stomach's swollen into a bubble. Lou's not a beer drinker, he's not much into alcohol period. Maybe a line or two of finely granulated cocaine once in a while. Though it may waste the mucous membranes, it leaves the delicate lining of his stomach untouched.

"But doesn't everyone burn out on something in their life?" Lou asks, sitting back down across from the brooding seer. "Doesn't everyone have his own special addiction?"

"While it's certainly true that everyone does have their something, and loses something of themselves in the doing, ultimately whatever you are decomposes into a handful of mostly useless chemical compounds…"

Why did Lou bring the subject up? Isn't a microwaved turnover with more preservatives per serving than proteins enough to digest after lunch?

The young man chews his food reflectively, "I must inevitably agree with you — but why, I ask, is it a necessary consequence that man must waste everything he can get his hands on during his strung-out lifetime? Must he consume the entire earth? And why? Simply to prove he was here? Are we doomed to become a desolate rock pile circling the sun, stripped of all higher forms of biological life, simply because man must have an enduring mausoleum dedicated to his historic inability to control himself! Is that the inevitable?"

Lou swallows, he nods, he agrees. He lived through the heady 60s, the lost 70s, the greedy 80s, the frantic 90s, and he's coasting into another century along with everyone else. He's part of the new age enlightenment. He votes liberal and he's into ecology, astronomy, anatomy and stuff like that. Just because he cares more about a buck than anything else doesn't mean he's a cultural heathen or insensitive to third world issues, no, he likes dark-skinned women almost as much as he likes lily white lovelies.

The poet's postmaster father looks an older and even wiser version of the poet, white bearded but young faced, the both of them together look as though they have gaped at life through the glassy eyes of idealistic youth forever, and no, no Stirbees in Eagle Lake, nor Stirbay nor Stirbois nor Stirbonne, no Stir-nothing. A call to Caribou to the east is fruitless as well. Otter's Ledge doesn't answer.

"How much further to Otter's Ledge?" Lou whimpers to the father.

"You could take Highway 11 straight through back country to Fort Kent, or you could circle around on scenic U.S. 1, that's the same One that follows the Atlantic coast all the way to the Florida Keys — see U.S. 1 begins or ends in Fort Kent, depending on which way you look at it."

Lou holds no firm opinion on this nor on most issues.

"Now Fort Kent's where you cross the bridge over the St John's River into New Brunswick — that's if the bridge hasn't been flooded over — except that's nothing you need worry about because right before the bridge is where you want to take a left, west, on Route 161."

Lou nods, he understands perfectly, 11 north, better to go straight than to circle, don't cross the river, left on 161. He jingles his keys.

"But watch out for moose."

Everybody up Maine way worries about moose, he notes.

"If one's on the road during daylight, best thing you can do is stop dead and wait until he gets out of your way. Don't honk or try to slide by him, I've seen them jump on top and trample a car, and at night switch off your lights and slow way down. Flash of light and a moose will freeze, then come charging at you."

OK, back off a moose. Anything else?

"Now there might not be a sign for Route 161, so as you approach the bridge, keep a lookout for Delaney's Feed Store, follow along the river. Keep going past St. Francis, past Allagash, through Dickey. Road's marked clearly enough, and you can always stop and ask one of the locals. In the end you have to reach Otter's Ledge. You'll know you're there because you can't go any further."

11, left, avoid the bridge and any moose, and don't stop until you get there. What could be simpler.

"Don't worry, I'll ride right along with you," the young philosopher offers, "I can't abandon you up here in the woods all by yourself now — besides I enjoy talking with someone who listens."

Lou is appreciative, he does listen, and thanks but no thanks, no way he could tolerate the kid's litany of worldwide woes. He waves good-bye. He is outta there and on to Otter's Ledge, alone.

> MAINE BOY / SHAME BOY
> Wheah'd you lose youh PANTS?
> MAINE BOY / SHAME BOY
> When you goin t'leahn t'DANCE?

> Gihls all claim he's NASTY / theih mothahs sweah he's CRAZY
> And most his friends AGREE he's def'nit'ly actin ODDAH
> Neighbahs think he's CRIM'NAL / teachahs say he's LAZY
> And coach / he's about to DOUSE him in a cold SHOWAH!

Otter's Ledge Maine is indeed where Chipper Stirbee was born and where he lives today — the original, it so happens, was Soirbie, French from a wayward Quebec trapper who was waylaid by a mother bear from an old tribe of Maine indigenous. That was back in 1644, and Mildred's a direct descendant, the last of a long line to bear the family name. Woman grew up determined to repopulate the Maine woods with more of the same, and succeed at that she did — had nine Stirbees in a line, all sons, each from a different unnamed father, hence mongrels everyone. Now despite the neighbors' gossip and their unreserved scorn, Mildred lived an otherwise modest and sober life, raising her sons in a strict fundamentalist tradition, plenty of hard work and a whupping if one of them stepped out of line, with Chipper stepping out for most of the whuppings. Well, Chipper was her eldest and his grandfather's favorite. Pappy as the kids called him was well known throughout Aroostook county. He had this distinctive long white blond hair, the Nordic, the Viking, and a fierce temper. Chipper had his granpappy's hair, but was more mellow, more French, and certainly a chip off the old stock his granpappy was hewn from. Seems Pappy spent most of his time scattering his chips wher'ere he'd be, and plenty of chips went flying because the northern woods are full of cousins, kissin cousins, girls every one and all within wood splitting distance of one another, though none of the clan, blood brothers or distant cousins, would claim kinship with Chipper even when he was famous and had some cash. And the few other Otter's Ledge locals who weren't related to Pappy didn't like Chipper much either. Hence, with all the incestuous hostility, Chipper had to settle back in Otter's Ledge after his sudden fall from fortune in the Summer of 69 — proving some immutable law of nature that man must live only where he is most intimately despised.

But why is it that Chipper has come to deserve such universal enmity? The answer has partly to do with Chipper's boyhood attempt to best Pappy's record for chip splitting, cousins among them, that and also Chipper's last single, the infamous *Love Baby* which failed to make it anywhere on any chart, and for good reason — sadomasochism and devil worship are one thing, so is necrophilia and parental chainsaw massacres, but consorting with minors, comely or otherwise, is simply not yet acceptable to the public at large, not even in rural Maine, though up thereabouts the woodsman rule does prevail, if it has a tail and can stand high on its hind legs, you don't need a license to shoot at it.

Not that any of Chipper's neighbors are really going to press the issue. Live and let be, fah in the woods man can crap free behind a tree. What gets done gets done, what doesn't wouldn't anyway, cause nothin's wohse doin than wohkin fah free. Which aphorisms combined constitute the basic tenets of a Northern Mainer's philosophy of survival — seems the only real responsibility a man has is to pile up wood for the winter, that he must do, drunk or sober, famished, naked, clothed, crazed by the cold or dazed by the sunlight. For freezing is easy this far north.

With his neighbors preoccupied by the cold, Chipper continues to do with impunity the two things he was born to do, screw and sing, both of which he does best in the local roadhouses, the same off-key catterwalling that gave his records the plaintive edge his audience once found appealing. One such place is indeed over on U.S. 1, on the outskirts of Fort Kent, a place called the Highwayman's Hut where Sally Tally and her like go. The Highwayman's Hut is a WWII quonset style pick-up joint with a *Le Best Le Blast's* neon sign flickering in the window. Sample's Diner is another stop that can appreciate Chipper Stirbee, over in Wheelock. Though sometimes he crosses the border to Edmunston where he is considered a bit of a novelty act at Boyce's Tavern. Any one of these places, and a few more further distant, if Chipper has a mind to travel, will cordially switch off the jukebox and let him hook up his guitar and play. People will stop their complaining and sit contentedly while he sings those mournful woodland ditties he feels from his soul. *Home Comin* is new, but has already become a local favorite.

> Come on home to you aftah weeks on the road
> Find you haulin down that othah man's load.

The woe and the worry play right to a truckerman's heart. *Startled Raccoon* sounds a variance on the theme and never leaves a dry eye in the place, Chipper's nasal Down East drawl to the contrary. He whines out each word and folks perk up and listen. Lyrics are important to Chipper, he has a message he's got to get across.

> Those black masked eyes you once thought wah so cute
> That face of mine so fuzzy and fine
> Then right on the behind you give me the boot
> I'm just a stahtled raccoon stunned caught with the loot.

Some day some Cambridge affectionado will comb these far northern Maine woods, tracking down every sad paean to lost young love Chipper has written, some day after Chipper is buried under a tree or locked up in a back county institution for doing God knows what to somebody's underage daughter — underage though still willing — but then Chipper won't derive any benefit from the discovery, will he, only the Cambridge student who will write a dissertation or have a connection on public radio. Student will strum old Chipper's tunes on the air, mocking his nasal twang and making a bundle on native Maine blues and rock because that is what Maine has in abundance, blues and rocks, and woods and dirt, and dirt poor people with the blues scattered deep in them woods and trying to pound a living out of them rocks. But that's where Chipper lives, has lived and will live, on the furthest outskirts of Otter's Ledge.

"Excuse me?" Lou shouts. "Excuse me. Sir? *Excuse me?*"

He's using the proper New York form of direct address, applied either informally to solicit information from a passerby or more formally to tell a passerby to get the hell out of the way — whichever is deemed appropriate to the situation.

"*Excuse me!*"

The emphatic form is vocalized as though one is about to spit, as Lou is presently using it, and correctly, and spitting it out the rolled down window of his Ultimatum. He is doing this in order to solicit information from a man in uniform who is taking a leak alongside a truck stamped with the Maine state seal of approval.

"HELLO! EXCUSE ME!"

"What's that you'h sayin?" The man turns.

"Yes… excuse me… but…"

"You talkin to me strangah?" The man twiddles a little Lou's way.

"Ye-ss…" Who else would Lou be talking to? He is on this narrow mud slide of a road in the middle of the woods, having slid passed no other living persons for at least twenty miles nor any identifiable vehicles nor any mud covered dwellings of such persons. "Sorry, don't mean to intrude, but I seem to be lost."

"H'yep." The official shakes and zips and saunters up to Lou's open window. "I'd say by the looks of you and this vehicle of youhs, you ah."

"Yes, yes I am. I'm trying to reach Otter's Ledge before nightfall. I'm trying to find a Chipper Stirbee? Am I on the right road?"

"H'yep, this road'll get you to Ottah's Ledge, eventually, 'specially if you keep followin it and don't go and get youhself lost completely."

"So, straight ahead then?"

"About as straight as a man can go." Official smiles some, unlocks his jaw, twicks his tongue.

"And *ah-* how far would you estimate Otter's Ledge to be?"

"Well, let's see, as the crow fli-…"

"No no," Lou's patience with the Maine countryside is wearing thin, "as the road goes."

"This heah road?"

"This road."

"I'd say about anothah houh, houh and a half strangah, dependin on how fast you dahe drive this faheign thing on slippahry mud." Man is now grinning in the window at Lou, his hand still lingering on his zipper, and Lou has no idea what the man's idiotic smirk might mean, there being only the two of them alone out in the mud woods, no traffic, nobody else around, the sun descending — there's this sudden flashback to a movie scene with a catchy banjo picking soundtrack — and that gets Lou *nerrrr-vous*. Which the face in the window can plainly see. Grin. Grim. So he has to think fast, what- what to do? So what does he do? He waves, fast as he can, five fingers up, OK bye, thanks and see you later. A flick of a button and up goes the window, and he's peeling away, hand still waving, shaking, visibly shaking, as he stabs at the CD player.

> Gettin youhself in TROUBLE boy, that paht's EASY
> Hits fastah than a BLIZZAHD as Maine old timahs KNOW
> But cleanin up the MESS you make / that'll keep you BUSY
> The lesson's in youh BIBLE / whatevah you reap you sow!

Lou's bouncing around in his seat, the Ultimatum tilting to and fro, swerving widely to avoid the mud piles, though he can't entirely, clumps of it flip up under his tire wells — *flumpflumpflumpflump* — then there's the relevance of the music, the primitive rhythmic ritual percussion finally hitting home — *flumpflumpflumpflump* — repeating and repeating the same refrain, and that's what triggers the fear in the over-wrought store-bought psyche of the American male caught stark alone out there in the dark woods — *flumpflumpflumpflump* — also the road is getting narrower and narrower, the slime level rising, so much so the woods, the rocks, the mud are all converging in the dark, leaving Lou with a wheezing shortness of breath and this frightening premonition that there probably won't be a Holiday Inn in Otter's Ledge! No! No place for a stranger to sleep, unguarded. Plus he's running out of gas. These dusky bleak images feed Lou's panic, with the lure of a back track country banjo picking up his ass!

Even so, it's a pity Lou didn't linger longer roadside and speak frankly with Ranger Eustus W. Dorbs about Chipper's whereabouts, because Useless, as he is affectionately called by those who know and despise him, is the regional surveyor for the Maine State Department of Forestry and Fisheries and he must be the only person *on earth* who knows the exact whereabouts of Chipper Stirbee, to the minute, to the second — 69° 20' 45" longitude and 47° 25' 32" latitude — and how to get theah from heah directly, like about ten minutes over a rutted back country loggah's road.

Lou however, is destined to go the long way around.

> MAINE BOY / SHAME BOY
> 'Bout time to take a CHANCE!
> MAINE BOY / SHAME BOY
> Theah's diff'rent ways to DANCE!

Useless Dorbs still fingers his fly. H'yep. Frightening the wits out of a New Yorker gives the guy a rise. Seems Useless Dorbs spends most of his surveyor evenings, mud or no mud, waiting along abandoned logger's roads for abandoned loggers, or for lost drivers or for solitary hikers or for an isolated deer or other large, largely unsuspecting warm-blooded mammals. Seems it all has to do with personal preference, an employee of the State being no exception, except tonight Useless has an appointment with none other than Chipper Stirbee, which is why he's parked on this particular logger's road that mere ten minute trek to Chipper's, that is, if it were a dry trek, half a day if it's a muddy one, and muddy might explain why Chipper's late by over an hour, but then Chipper being a Maine boy learned early about forestry rangers and Useless Dorbs. H'yep. Long ago.

And Useless can wait a good long while down there on that abandoned logger's road because Chipper is busy. He and his hound dog Betsy are shovelling the mud away from the foundation of their dugout basement home. Big spring runoff can do that. Stream swells up, overflows on

Chipper's acre. Bottom land. No good for nothing except shovelling although it's surrounded on all sides by an untouched Maine State wooded preserve, poplars mostly, thousands of spiny ones and dense, and muddy and marshy and great for ducks and frogs and black flies. Plus deep mud is like deep snow, keeps people away, and rangers and other State paid purveyors of perversion. Not moose. Moose migrate down with the melt. Fact is Chipper sees moose more often than he sees people, and not many moose. Chipper is content with that. The density of tree coverage is a comfort to him. And on the sunniest, the warmest day of any August, light hardly penetrates the leaf shield surrounding his lone little acre. And if the density of the forest doesn't afford him enough protection, Chipper will only venture out late at night. It's then when he scurries around and does what he has to do for his survival.

"No way! I'll pick food out of gahbage cans befah I'll pay these prices!"

That's what he concluded when he ventured over to the Grand Nohthuhn, Fort Kent's brand new all lit up, all night super food warehouse. The intensity of the lights startled him at first, how everything glowed in the middle of the night like that — since he went in at 3:30 in the A.M. when the only other people in the store were stockers pulling around pallets of cereal and soda pop and baby diapers, and one bored bleached blond freckled girl at the check-out counter who must have recognized him. At least she blinked something like recognition when he walked up to her. For Chipper appeared to her as he appears to everyone who meets him, as a miracle of human preservation. Guy looks exactly the same as he did forty years ago when he first took to the stage.

Chipper struck a pose for her, a jutting chin profile to help jar her memory — head tossed this way and that, blond hair glistening in the glow of the fluorescent tubing that flooded the entirety of the store with its unremitting iced blue reminder that all light man makes is artificial.

She had to know it was him, she snapped her gum and she stared.

He also mouthed greeting types of sounds at her, because whether she recognized him or not, he recognized her, instantly, as the only fool in the place who would have the least understanding not so much of who he was or had been, but of what he was, lost and out of place in this illuminated illusion of plenitude. For what need had he of microwave jello or of a giant box of biodegradable sex-differentiated diapers, a bag of sun dried dog food pellets or a packet of azure-brilliantly-wrapped sugar-coated oat bars or a special six pack of indisposable plastic razors — get six for the low low price of seven. What did Chipper need of these? He fries everything he eats in one crusty black pan, and Betsy eats squirrel meat fresh off the limb. He has no babies that he knows of, and besides he is himself one of these perennially infantile smooth faced kids who shave less than monthly and look innocent, or young anyway, be they fourteen or fifty five. He doesn't eat sugar because sugar doesn't mix well with the beer he drinks, either the Old Swaukeegan in 48 ounce cans because it's cheap up hereabouts or his own homebrew because it's even cheaper, though sometimes he does indulge in hollowed out wood spirits with proofs that would power race cars in fierce desert time trials, and drugs generally, whatever he can scrounge, mad as hell that no street gang or road gang is selling crystal meth up in his neck of the woods, not yet, though he has heard that freebasing gives the same high, but nobody he knows knows how to pull that act off, and wasn't there some entertainer in Las Vegas, some comedian no less, who blew half his face away trying to light up one night before the show, but pot, well that he has in abundance and growing back a ways behind the house in the only grove he knows of for miles around where the sun hits all day long, granting him the one great asset which ties him permanently to his Maine landscape, and also to Useless Dorbs – Chipper's got the best homegrown he or anybody around has ever tasted, celebrity endorsement without reservation, h'yep – and so what did he do in that glowing arcade of pre-packed and bar-coded sustenance? He rolled his hand across the counter at the little missy, she being no more than sixteen and hopefully less.

"Heah hon, check this shit out."

She giggled some and diddle dallied with his fingers.

"Thanks fah letting me take a look at youh stohe, but I'm out of heah. Ain't my kind of place, don't you know."

Hey, not so fast, she smiled. A touch is a touch, state law or no, a wink a wink, and what's this, a joint! A JOINT! She shrieked, the kind of sound only a Chipper can provoke from a teenager, and she latched onto his hand – hey, where there's some there might be more.

Chipper fired her up with his free hand and she started to puff, all the while craning her neck and twisting around to make sure nobody was watching so she could suck in on that bone big time, and did sweetie suddenly go into a spin, did sweetie suddenly go into a swoon? She landed *su-plop* backside atop the counter, crush down on Chipper's fingers. Not that he minded. No. No. He oh so delicately let the babydoll test taste his tick pickler up the center of her butthole – *heave-h'yup* – her puffing in one end and poofing out the other. No care. All in an open all night's day's work anyway, but with her keeping a constant watch out between tokes and pokes, though for who or whom was unclear, because it was only kids like herself working the late shift. Girl was into it, corkscrewing like crazy, with Chipper about to shift digits when she thought to mention, demurely. "I got me a husband who's the night managah, and he gets awful jealous."

"YOU GOT YOUHSELF A WHAT!"

Chipper popped his pinky stickler out of her so fast she spit the joint into a cart loaded with sex-differentiated diapers, and they let off a shit house load of an explosion that brought some guy out of hiding — some guy older than she who looked exactly like a night manager/hubby would, mustache and glasses with a pencil parked behind his ear — and it didn't take the dude much time to assess the situation, disposable baby britches burning, his wife churning and Chipper turning tail and racing out the door. Grocery shopping probably being more hazerdous to people's health than driving or flying, because that's what Chipper did, he flew, did a running jump into the driver's seat of what could be called a Subaru pick-up, when it was a hatchback originally, but a sawsall can do customized wonders and after the local junk yards ran out of Subaru doors and fenders, they suggested Datsun which fit sort of, and some kind of a Ford import hood with an old Impala trophy screwed on, but whatever he's driving has got to be a next generation type of car, when everybody finally goes bust and the banks plain ain't got no more money to throw around and even the government can't peddle bonds without putting up the White House furnishings as collateral — pick-up runs, damn it, which is more than they can say about the economy. Subaru started up in the grocery store parking lot after a few whining cranks of the ignition, but then there was the problem of the slip clutch and getting it into gear.

Betsy was in the back bed baying. She could tell there was trouble, always was when Chipper went out late driving, but she was unprepared for this night manager rushing after and hurling what the whats? Fiery bales of baby diapers at them, at her! Chipper had the cab to protect him, but there she was out in the open. Give-*rr* the gas, she yelped, get us out of *h-rrrrr!*

Cantclankcram and away they went barrelling down the highway at night, too dark for anybody to notice that there's this trail of black smut blowing out the tailpipe, which bothers Chipper because if there's one thing in this world that he and most of the folks in Maine are concerned about, it's the environment, you bet, for while he might thrive under the cover of darkness, he knows his furry little animal buddies won't, nor those very tall trees that protect him, nor that beautiful patch of green plants flourishing in the one sunny grove, no, all that will be gone.

They made it home safely that night as they had most others, if home this humble can be named such. For Chipper and Betsy reside in what the locals call a dugout. A dugout is a house where only the concrete foundation got poured. That's as far as Chipper got when the meager earnings from his royalties gave out in 1969. Mel Nebberstoff, the president of Askantics Records, he built a house with a swimming pool in La Jolla on his earnings from Chipper's songs, but then he knew what he was doing during the 60s, and he sent all his kids to Stanford for as long as they could pass those advanced communication arts courses, but the star, Chipper Stirbee barely got his basement excavated. Chipper nailed down the sub-floor himself when he was on what he thought would be a short break from touring, and only when the break lasted forever did he cover the first floor to his dream bunker with asphalt in order to keep the rain out. But Chipper Stirbee is content therein, don't mistake it. Betsy too. Might be musty and ten degrees cooler in wintertime, but hey, at least they own what they live in — the bank eventually got Mel Nebberstoff's. Chipper's taxes amount to $28 a year, and he has no phone. He has electricity because he had to plug his amplifier into something, despite the threats of the electric company that they will shut the remnants of his career off if he doesn't pay the bill, that is, if they can ever remember how they got a line back there in the first place, and few employees of North Maine Power dare to take on one of these loner backwoods types over something as paltry as a ten year overdue balance, and particularly if they are dispatched single handily and unarmed. The upshot is that North Maine Power leaves Chipper Stirbee plugged in and alone, which is what anyone with half a brain would do. Lou? Well. Which is what anyone with half a brain would do… then there's Useless Dorbs…

"Damn man! Toke of this shit's goin to take me mah'n two days to get straight again."

Useless hands Chipper back the lit joint.

"Then why'd you drive up heah in the rain and bothah me fah a sample of my eahly spring pickins in the fuhst place?"

"Cause you've got the best weed available, and I've smoked a bundle," which is why Chipper gave Useless Dorbs a bundle at Christmas, so he'd haul back down that abandoned logger's road and leave him be the rest of the winter.

"You know, this is plain ohdinary big govahnment extahtion."

"Extahtion, why you say that?"

"Because that's what it is Useless, legalized extahtion."

"Legal, *ee*-legal, what the fuck ah you talkin about. Pahtakin in the proceeds is what the lawful practice of the State is all about, and don't you go thinkin it's evah goin to be no ways diffahrent. You give them a little and they get out youh way. You hold back and they'll come gunnin fah you, take it all, set you up in front of a judge — you know what a judge is? — judge is a man, sometimes a woman who ain't nevah wet his pants and who sits up theah enjoyin watchin you wet youhs, that's what a judge is."

Chipper knows what a judge is — Cincinnati, there was a judge, mean sucker scowl on his face, the long shot Summer of 69.

"So fohk ovah anothah bale of that homegrown befah I radio in a helicoptah full of Feds fah a bahn buhnin."

"OK, but you ain't touchin my wintah supply noh my seed crop, a man's got to be able to live off the fruits of his labah, don't you know, that's enshrined in ouh Constitution somewheah."

"Sovahreign powahs of the police is in theah too."

Whatever. Chipper whistles to Betsy to follow and to cover his trail because even Useless Dorbs doesn't know exactly where Chipper's grove is or where he stashes his supply, and Useless Dorbs knows pretty much near the backside of every damn tree and deer in Northern Maine.

Not that Useless cares where Chipper's stash is — well, he cares — not that Useless can do much about it. State read the same fairy tale when it was young, the one about the goose that lays the golden eggs? The moral of which is that Chipper does grow the all-round best ganje in Northern Maine, so don't go messing with successful entrepreneurship, particularly when jobs are migrating at the fastest rate in decades to the sunny south. So Useless contents himself with scratching his balls and watching Chipper's and Betsy's butts slosh off into the woods.

Chipper returns Useless' interest with a Sicilian salute and makes his way slowly back down the slippery logger's road. Uniforms do not intimidate Chipper, military or police or marching band style, although he generally does his best to avoid all contact with ohdah and the law, except when it's a really boring Saturday night and getting higher than high's not fun enough. Then's when he races the local patrols over the back roads seeing who can out do who, and they're Dorbs too, family has all the local government no-show jobs locked up, and they go crazy wild about Chipper on Saturday nights because Chipper loves driving his souped up Subaru down the roads where the Dorbs thugs hang out. And they chase after him like bloodhounds after skunk, bother him about some cockeyed head light he hasn't got or a tail signal flickering contemptuously at them, license plate not lit up, hell, no license plate to light up unless you count the 1976 collector's item he has rusted on there, and no sticker on no windshield, plenty of stickers on all the other windows though. The window on the driver's side has parked for years at the Augusta General Hospital, the Datsun on the left went to U.N.H. and belonged to Phi Gamma Delta — a fucking Fiji man! — the Ford import front bumper is a member of the Audubon Society, which is why Chipper bolted it on instead of the Honda that listened to WFCK and admired the Bruins. The back bumper has climbed Mount Washington and wants no part of Proposition 2, to avoid something that peeled off long before Chipper got it. But properly identified and labeled with his places in the universe, he'll fire himself up with devil weed and hurl himself thusly down dark roads past parked Dorbs who wasted on the same weed will gladly play dodge cars with him til dawn.

And although Betsy privately abhors violence, her breed of hound dog is universally renowned for its enjoyment of the breathless chase.

"You suhe this is a full bale?" Useless kicks at it, delicate like — *thud, thud, thud* — with the boot of his reserve unit issue.

"What, you want me to caht along a scale and weigh it fah you?"

"Nope, but I don't want you cheatin me none neithah."

"Nevah cheat you Useless, though I should, might weight justice back in my favah fah once."

"Don't say. — Oh, befah I go, I should tell you, Hugh Fahmah down the road is lookin fah whoevah it was pluggin his wife while he was away beah huntin."

"I wasn't down doin Hugh Fahmah's wife, she can attest to that."

"That's just it, she's attestin to just the opposite, says you've driven down that rutted road plenty of times and nevah used no brakes at all."

"That's a lie, I ahways slow down and wave when I see huh."

"Well, I'm simply advisin you of youh rights, he's lookin fah you, so you and Betsy had bettah be on the lookout."

"Why Betsy?"

"Because she can sniff trouble comin soonah than you can."

-mmm...

"Aanothah thing, ran into this New Yahkah up on the main road?"

"H'yep?"

"Well he was askin out his cah window how to find you."

"What'd he look like?"

"Insuhance salesman."

"They'h the wohst."

"Don't you know."

"They staht in makin you feel scahed the sky's goin to drop right down on youh head and wipe out youh cah, youh house, youh wife and youh family in a single blow, plus give you lung cancah and flood youh cellah."

"You ain't got no wife to lose."

"Still I wouldn't want to have no financial consolation if I did."

"Yah, well be on the lookout. I sent him loopin round to Allagash and back, give me time to wahn everybody in the neighbahood to douse theih lights and hope he passes by in the night."

"Thank you fah the mention."

"Think nothin of it, thank you fah the smoke. See you pooch." Useless tries yet again to pat Betsy gal on the noggin, but Betsy doesn't take kindly to perverts and official sorts. She snaps right back at him.

"Mean disposition youh dog's got theah Chippah."

"Naw, not really, she just doesn't like the way you smell."

"What?" Useless turns on his heel.

"You know what I mean, youh scent, you've been hangin round too many othah animals recently and that offends huh sensibilities."

"You had bettah watch that mouth of youhs, it's goin to get you in mah trouble than youh dick."

"Same advice you should follow, and like my grandpappy used to tell me, man's dick's his last line of defense."

"How's that?"

"Cause if a man can't put it to his enemy dihrectly, he can ahways put it to the daughtah."

"Youh grandpappy gots lots of enemies."

"Dohbs fah the most paht."

"I'm goin to hold back from takin offense, but if my brothahs oah Hugh Fahmah finds you any time soon, you'h goin to be stuffed ovah with youh nose up youh butthole." Useless starts to walking again.

"Ah you suhe you didn't undahgo some soht of medical convahsion and try puttin it to Hugh Fahmah's wife youhself?" If Chipper were the kind to let well enough alone he wouldn't be where he is now — where? Face-to-face with an agitated officer of the State. "C'mon at me Useless, give it youh best shot! Take that chance you and youh family of retahds have always been spoilin fah." Chipper is leaner than the spilt-gut Dorbs clan, so he has more advantage than his mouth. Still, he's only one, and the Dorbs are many. Plus this feud's been going on for centuries, which must explain why Betsy with a fight about to break out yawns and sits down on the ground, licks her privates. Chipper meanwhile spits in his hands and starts circling Useless, making mouth motions as to what the State can do on its knees to Chipper's male member. That in turn upsets Useless because he's a devotee of suck delights, the offer half taunting, half tantalizing him.

"Ain't takin you on just yet Chippuh, but you'd bettah know I'm lined up and waitin fah my chance."

"And a long line of Dohbs it is, if my grandpappy did it right."

"We'h goin to get you Chippah, we'h goin to get you good."

"You've been sayin that fah three genahrations, and we Stirbees still got ouh asses intact."

Useless Dorbs turns, slings the bud over his shoulder and marches out of there, fast though, fast for a Mainer, and like he says, he's in line and in Maine time's enough, for there's not much of anything that can't wait.

Chipper and Betsy watch Useless fade into the brush, probably because both are blinded on the homegrown, Betsy from the ambient air, Chipper from direct hits. "C'mon gihl, let's go make suppah."

Betsy obliges. There's a hind quarter of a moose that got too close in the freezer, and who knows, Chipper might be into an early summer cook-out. Grilled squirrel with a piquant barbecue sauce would be nice.

Chipper's not thinking food, he's wondering who it might be that's been doing Hugh Fahmah's wife. Not a bad lookah, short though, real short, four two, but young still and nice nipples. H'yep, he wanders as he wonders what she might be like all fired up on some homegrown and a hot poker, which Chipper will supply gratis to the younger wives around – cause Chipper's got nothing against marriage so long as a woman can momentarily forget who she's hitched up to and why, money being a more common motivator for intra-marital liaisons than good sex anyway – plus what woman in an emergency minds being routed out by an unexpected plumber, hey, at least he's interested, what with so many fellas into male bonding these days, the local churches ought to be condoning old time adultery as a virtue, not a vice, husbands too, because a back-country housewife gets bitchy when she gets itchy.

> Ain't no FOHCE on eahth can hold HIM
> Waitin fah all his HOHMONES to EXPLODE
> Boy's 'bout READY to jump cleah out his SKIN
> Bettah try and slow DOWN son / least take time to RELOAD!

Lou is doing endless loops through Alagash and around again on a mud-paved one laner – when without much warning, these bright yellow lights come boring down on him, truck, state truck, wrong side of the road, blade down plowing mud, ranger at the wheel leering at Lou, motioning him left, left, sharp left off the highway Lou goes, clips a pole with a yellow metal sign attached, something about MOOSE X-ING – watch out for moose, right? – as he careens down a gravel road which runs alongside a steep ditch, *whoa whoa,* slow slow, there's a bump and a scrape to his muffler while he bounces by a mobile home sitting on top of a cinderblock foundation, but not quite squarely. Where is he? Where is he going? Somewhere where he's got to go, got to keep going, because where else can he go, can't keep driving on instinct and fumes when he has to slam on the InstaLock™ brakes a bare few inches before he's about to roll over a log, a log with long spikes upstanding!

"JE-SUS H. CHRIST!" He shouts. The mud's up to the floor boards so he tries reverse, tries forward, rocks back and forth, his steelbelteds spinning, finally shifts into four wheel drive and begins to creep slowly around the log, half way slipping down the ditch when suddenly a mixed variety pack of large dogs comes snarling out of nowhere and hurl themselves full body against the sides of his SUV, one dog reaching the hood long enough to growl savagely through the windshield at him – and scratch the shit out of his paint job – but a flick of the wheel and down that mongrel goes – "So the rest of you won't give up easily, eh?"

-grrrrowl -rrr rowl! rowl! bow-rr rawl! brawl!

Guess they're a tenacious lot.

"Well then have a dose of this!" He snarls back. Then's when Lou really lets them have it, with his HandiAntiHighJack Alarm Set™ — horns, hazards and an air-raid siren sound simultaneously, and at such a high pitch the pooches cannot resist — *shreee-ee-ee-eeeek! -rrr? -rrr? Reetreet!*

Naturally the noise of a dog fight brings the next door neighbors out of hiding, *en masse*, the DuChamps brood. And if the rickety trailer of the Corker family rocking sideways on its foundations fascinated Lou, take a look at the DuChamps residence. Rooms upon rooms, garage, barn and chicken coop, all attached, New England farmhouse style, except each addition is constructed out of entirely different building materials — mostly filched from the condominium complex some fellow New Yorkers are building over in the next valley — but none of it holding up well, chimney crumbled, wood shingles blown off, cardboard insets instead of glass in the windows, and the whole thing wrapped Christo style in azur blue plastic tarps, winterized so to speak. Home to the DuChamps however, the eleven or twelve of them teenagers who haven't run off yet to Portland. And if there's a mother or a father inside there, nobody's saying, because to any stranger, sheriff, bill collector or nosy welfare worker, the both of them have been long gone — but how then how do you explain a spanking brand newborn every nine months or so? Genes runnin wild, that's what it is, mothers begettin daughters begettin sisters and cousins generations beyond generations of DuChamps, all tucked into their beds in that same bahnyahd fahmhouse.

Lou has to pull to a stop for this one. His insurance doesn't cover steam rolling over children, also he hasn't a clue where in the hell he might be.

"'Lo!" He sings out. None of them even nod — one girl, blond startled eyes smiles back interest. "I'm looking for Chipper Stirbee's house, you kids have any idea where he lives?"

The kids, various aged versions of the same, male or female, wide-eyed and malnourished, garbed in blue jeans and T-shirts with unfamiliar allegiances printed on them, stare. At Lou. At the Ultimatum. They're variously unfriendly, except for the one girl Lou is smiling at. The rest, little to biggest, swarm about his car, and kids, being kids, recognize expensive instinctively. He can hear a fingernail test the resilience of the enamel, while the oldest boy, anyway the tallest one glowers at him through the half rolled window. "Jist who is it wants to know?"

At least he can speak, and English. Now, does the kid really know the whereabouts of Chipper Stirbee? Does he have a concealed weapon? Will he take money, not much, in exchange for a little information, and let Lou escape relatively unharmed? Can he rent the sister for a while? These are the concerns that race through Lou's head as he introduces himself as an old friend of Chipper from ages past.

"Chippah ain't got no friends, new oah old."

Lou must be close. The kid has intimate knowledge of Chipper's habits.

"Wheah'h you from?" The girl with the moon eyes asks unexpectedly.

"New Yahk, can't you read?" Another little boy answers for Lou. "Yeah, look at this funny license plate."

Funny? Depends where you're not from.

"What kind of a truck is this?" Yet another little boy shouts.

Lou glances over to see who might be asking the question, but whoever it is doesn't acknowledge himself.

"An Ultimatum," Lou responds to the crowd of little faces, "it's Korean."

One of them is assessing its durability, kicking it, right side toward the back, Lou can hear the pounding and feel the slight rocking. He quickly turns to the tall older boy. "Give you a dollar if you point me toward Chipper's house."

"Dollah ain't wohth much these days." The smiling girl responds.

Not for you, Lou imagines, for you five dollars.

"Chippah don't like nobody distuhbin him, not duhin the eahly evenin noways. That's when he takes his nap. You tell me who you ah and what you want, and I'll find out if he wants to see you."

Before Lou can respond, another one of the many voices shouts out, "You a undahcovah fed?" Along with the question there's this prying noise off his back bumper.

"No," he shouts, "I'm a record promoter. Take your paws off my car!"

Well! Record promoter! Why didn't you say so first off? That's got to be better than the ding-a-dong candyman.

"My sistah can sing real good." A younger version spits up at Lou.

"Oh? Which sister?"

And wouldn't you know, a little finger points to the friendly, wide-eyed, expectant one. And ain't it always the way, and ain't it always easy. Lou wants to say, get in, we'll drive down the road a ways for an audition, but with the brother standing right there and an army of filthy elves for reinforcements, he hesitates on the offer. "If I can get something going with Chipper again, I'm certain he is going to need back-up talent. Any of the rest of you kids play or sing?"

Can they play or can they sing? No, but when does the chance of a lifetime pull up in your front yard, rural Maine and in an Ultimatum? The kids start sca-*reaming*, singing anything they can think of, and simultaneously. The girl starts gyrating suggestively, her hands tugging up her T-shirt, a few would be drummers start pounding on the car. Only the oldest boy remains aloof. Lou is stuck in between the fear of anarchy and the desire to clutch at the little girl's writhing body when the oldest boy shouts, "Shut the fuck up, all of you!" And he bats his sensuous sister side of her head. The clatter ceases instantly. "You give me twenty bucks fah expenses and meet me back heah in a houh. I'll get you what you want."

The offer is made starkly, without guise or guile, and Lou has precious few seconds to consider it because the drumming on his car begins again, lowly at first, but distinctly and with a mounting crescendo — *what you want... what you want...*

Lou whips out a twenty, two twenties, one for the boy, the other for the girl. Both snatch at them like practiced iguanas, swallowing into pockets quick before the naked eye can catch them at it.

"I'll be back, now don't you kids let me down. Could be the chance of a lifetime for some of you" — for one in particular.

Lou edges forward in the Ultimatum and backs slowly around, the kids pushing like hell to get him out of his puddle — Mainers are like that, not so glad handy to see you come, but willing to strain painly a back to see you go. Lou waves at the boy and winks at the girl, then retraces his path out of there, slow around the spiked log and fast past the pack of dogs.

"So what was his name?" Chipper can't stand to be awakened out of his early evening slumber, his head clogged with spun webs of stickily smooth smoke.

"Don't know, fahgot to ask." The oldest DuChamps boy answers. The sister, the one sprouting out of her shirt just smiles, says nothing as usual.

"So why'd you go and tell him you knew me?" Gradually the speck of concentration is making its way along the precarious strands of Chipper's brain.

"He asked." The kid is sullen.

Consciousness sneaks back center. "But shit, this guy could be anybody. Could be a Fed."

"Said he wasn't. Had a new kind of cah, a Ultimatum, New Yahk plates."

"Been wahned about him, could be sellin insuhance oah could be a real estate speculatah who's goin to buy up all ouh propehty, sell time shahes to othah New Yahkahs. They'll be up heah vacationin, diffahrent ones every two weeks, with all theih relatives visitin from Jahsey, pissin in ouh streams, playin golf in ouh fields, eatin un-American food and movin us out of heah like they did folks ovah in Vahmont." Chipper is leaning up against his Subaru, supporting himself against something solid.

"Good," the girl finally speaks, "wouldn't mind movin somewheah else, like Flohida."

"You wouldn't like it once you got theah, believe me." Chipper remembers boot camp in the swamps with a shudder, the matrix of his mind emerging into semi-lucidity. Vague outlines of faces, he blinks, h'yep, DuChamps, just like he suspected. OK kids, long as they keep their distance, don't come snooping around too much. Chipper knows the older boy Lloyd is searching the woods for his prize plants and one of the middle girls, could be this one, is always looking at him in a longing way, probably tired of doing it with her brothers. "Which one ah you anyway?"

She flushes red.

"This heah's Belinda."

"Belinda."

She gives him a glance.

"Nice name, sounds soht of musical."

"Ain't no reason to get mad at me. Fella said he was a recohd promotah, that he'd make Belinda heah into a stah."

"You got a hankahrin to be a stah?"

She sparkles at the mere mention, steps closer, her thigh resting right up against the back of his hand, the hand he strums with.

Betsy's laid out on the stoop, catching the day's final rays, she's half snoozing, half eyeing the neighborhood soap opera — entirely predictable characters, same repetitive plots, which is fine because if she blinks out and misses an episode, she can always tune in later.

"Recohd promotah's wohse than a real estate speculatah, speculatah only takes youh propahty, promotah walks off with youh creativity."

Belinda squirms around. She's getting bored with all this talk.

Which is just what Chipper likes, young and jumpy, not knowing what's normal and what's not. Get her high and do whatever comes to mind, and Chipper Stirbee has one hell of an imagination, especially when it comes to sex.

"So I'll tell him I don't know wheah you live."

"He'll want his twenty bucks back." Belinda warns.

"Twenty bucks! You sold me out fah twenty bucks?"

"Didn't sell nobody out, just took twenty bucks." Boy doesn't back off a bit. Neither does Belinda. If anything, she moves in closer, Chipper can feel moist heat against his leg.

"You told him to come back latah tonight?"

"H'yep. Aftah sunset."

"How's he going to find his way back in heah in the dahk?"

"Dunno. That's his problem."

Belinda is pressed up against Chipper's hand — and that spider in Chipper's head starts in weaving another cocoon.

MAINE boy / SHAME boy /

"Well could be wohse. 'Spose theah ain't no hahm in talkin to him, see what's his angle."

Betsy lifts an eyelid, his angle, that would be obvious, he does a buyout, everything you've taken years to write for a pittance, you do a sellout, everything you've taken years to write for a pittance.

"I'll have Belinda meet him down at the main road and lead him up to ouh place."

"You'h goin to put youh kid sistah in a cah seat next to a recohd promotah from New Yahk!" Chipper is shocked.

"She's got to get huh staht in life some way."

Belinda slithers up along Chipper's arm and down his leg. "You'h a cold dude Lloyd, you'd considah sellin youh sistah fah twenty bucks!"

"Man already gave me my twenty, 'cept Lloyd heah took half of it."

"Half a twenty! You sold youh sistah's pride fah ten bucks!"

"No, half my twenty, ripped it cleah in half, said that way I'd need him along when I meant to spend it."

"What, you demented oah somethin?"

Whole family's demented, Betsy moans.

"I'd sell huh pride fah some decent smoke." Boy adds without a twinge.

The spider is spinning inside poor Chipper's head now, gobs of cobs, and his arm is twitching badly.

"I'll spot you some smoke, but you make suhe that recohd promotah pahks his cah in youh front yahd. Walk him back heah real sneaky like, round about, as only you'd know how to do, cause I don't want him knowin how to get back heah on his own, no way."

"What about Belinda?"

"Goddamn it, I'll take cahe of youh sistah…"

'Bout time to take a CHANCE!

"…like I did youh oldah sistahs, just cause I feel you folks ah sohta like family." He and Belinda are entangled anyway, in a common neighborly embrace, hands on each other's private property. "So heah, heah's some fresh smoke. Go get youhself wrecked and steeh that guy around in cihcles 'til he gets dizzy, you heah me?"

"I heah you." The boy accepts a plastic bag of glistening green buds that Chipper has stashed in the ripped upholstery of his truck and starts to wander off. "You comin Belinda?"

She chokes and looks to Chipper expectant like.

He wraps his arm around her shoulder, protective like. "Might as well be somebody she knows, staht huh off on the road to stahdom, not some strangah from New Yahk."

She slips her hand appreciatively past Chipper's zipper, and her brother heads back home by himself.

> Good lesson to REMEMBAH / write it in youh BOOKS
> Sixteen is when they'ah LEGAL and up to EIGHTY FIVE
> Anytime along through FIFTEEN they'h only good fah LOOKS
> Once could get you TWENTY / twice'll do fah LIFE!

Betsy's been listening and she's worried, not about the fledgling because buds do burst for bumble bees in springtime, but a tourist this early in the season is decidedly unnatural. And Betsy being fiercely territorial figures it's her duty to go scout out the situation.

She lopes along behind the DuChamps' kid, wants to make sure he's headed home. Something about the DuChamps, like their skanky reek, makes her highly suspicious, particularly this boy Lloyd, worst of a bad litter, one any self-respecting mother would have drowned straight away.

While Lloyd stumbles along the path, Betsy cuts cross country, her nose knows the way, though just in case she has to head back late, she lays dabbles of fresh scent amidst the pine needles.

Roof! Roof!

That'd be the Corker brood in their cage — *rr rough!* Strays mostly, all unrelated and -*ru-ru-rude!* Can spoil a lady's night out if she's not careful. Betsy curves wide to avoid their likes, decides she'll do sentry duty down by the highway, see what she can see.

Ranger Dorbs is the first sight of the night, he keeps passing, the same section of highway over and over, not that that's anything unusual, he's a thermos-to-lunch-bucket-after-dinner-overtime type of state employee. Otherwise there's not much else happening, unless you count some snorts of sorts. Betsy's ears rise… could be one of the mongrels from Corker's kennel gone mad and fled over the wall.

-*SMOOTS-SMOOOOOTS*

Could be a horse…

-*SMOO-SMOO-SMOOTS*

That's no horse, by God that's *a moo-moo-MOOSE!!!* Betsy dives into a crevice in the rocks, thereby displacing a porcupine who declines the challenge, ambles off to kick some rabbit's ass — *SMOOT? SMOOT?* — Betsy sneaks a peep. It's a large moose, eleven footer with three feet more in trophy antlers, what's he doing loose on the highway and some foreign kind of 4x4 steering mindlessly towards him, brights on…

SPOOK!

…stuns the sucker in his tracks, leastwise that's the initial reaction, and don't flip off the lights whatever you do, and don't slow down, keep coming at him, the buck's in your way, right — *ROOK! ROOK! MOOSE!*

Bark in the night, large anmial in sight, Lou does what's only unexpected of him, he honks. Only makes a bad situation worse — *honk honk* — worse than worse, moose goes charging. Lou has to swerve, too quick, swerves to the left and does what an SUV does best in a ditch, rollsover, and if that's not bad enough, there's this enraged hoofed mammal stomping on undercarriage — KLAP! PLOOK! PLOOK! KLAPLOOIE! — the plastics they're using in imports these days simply can't hold up!

ROOROOROOROOROO... Rowdy bowsers are out of their cages as well, rampaging through the woods — ROOT! ROOT! ROOT! ROOT! — they've heard the ruckus, now it's gangway for the road kill.

And there's nothing anybody can do to save him, not Betsy, one lone lady can't stand up to all these brutes.

But what about Lou? He's surrounded — when suddenly, without much warning! — the beating on the rooftop stops? Seems the moose has to contend with a pack of wild dogs nipping at his ankles. SMOOT! A head down scoop one up, fling it into the treetops — *rr -rooroo-reeeeeee!* — stomp on another then another after that, whereupon the remainders beat a tasteless retreat.

There in the darkness surrounding, Lou listens, damn well listens, hears more snorts, more clod clomps too close for comfort, huddled as he is in an overturned bucket seat, quaking, when — what's that? — STOMP STOMP - STOMPSTOMPSTOMP — moose trots off.

Whew, he's over that nightmare and only eight hours til dawn, although he's trapped inside a Korean Ultimatum at the bottom of a ravine, with no lights, no stereo and water trickling in, which triggers a panic — when *knock knock*, who's there? Lloyd DuChamps, that's who, see the flashlight in his monkey face? Blown cold stoned out of his mind Lloyd is, eyes wild and glazed over and he's staring in at Lou who's turned blue, heater's not working either, shines that flashlight right in on him, see, he's asphixiated.

"Hell-*pp*..." Lou manages. "Please! I'll pay you."

What more could the good Samaritan ask for. Lloyd reaches down and opens the unlocked door. "You ahright strangah?"

Lou manages to unbuckle his seat belt and tumble out the door, one foot slops into the cold runoff, then another.

"Good thing I came looking fah you aftah you didn't show up."

"I-..."

"How'd you get youhself pahked upside down in a stream?"

"I-..."

"You suhe you'h ahright? Look like you've seen a ghost — and what about youh truck, this mess is goin to cost you crazy — you out of gas too?"

"You- you don't think, not for one second, that I carry that much cash."

"Lot mah'n I got, lot less than you'h goin to need — but I'll tell you what I'm goin to do fah you. While you'h in theah talkin with Chippah, I'll tow you out, salvage what I can. So hand ovah youh keys and youh wallet."

"My keys? *My wallet!*"

"You think I'm goin to help out a New Yahkah fah free?"

"You-... you-..."

"Ain't no good squawkin about it. It's eithah me oah the state who's goin to be pullin you out of heah, and they'll throw in a ticket fah recklessness and drivin to endangah the wildlife, they'll compound youh vehicle until you can pay off the magistrate with unmahked bills — heah, let me smell youh breath — *pew-ee* mistah, what've you been drinkin, cheap beeh by the buckets? Hand ovah those keys... and the wallet."

"Why-why, why my wallet?"

"Cause youh wallet's the only secuhity I got against you runnin off and not compensatin me fah my labah."

Kid's as deft as a Park Avenue lawyer. Case looks bad, real bad, my friend, about how much do you have in savings? Anything parked in a municipal bond account? What's the worth of your home on today's market? Think you can borrow from relatives? No? Then how exactly do you intend to wiggle out of this jam you're in?

"You got any mah twenties on you strangah? And don't go tryin to pawn some plastic off on me, MisahCahd's wohthless heahabouts."

Kid has to repeat the question. Seems Lou's too stunned to answer. He stutters to gain time to think. Offer too little, the kid won't do it. Offer too much, why should the kid do it. Just enough. Just enough. "About how much would it take?" Lou braves.

"Can't give you a accurate estimate right off, plus I'm goin to need some help, maybe a wreckah, lift this suckah up, see how much damage's been done to youh frame."

"I-... you- you do this sort of thing often?"

"Whenevah some fool touhist tuhns off the main highway, not watchin wheah he's headed and cracks into a fencepost oah creams a stray kid, but that's the way it is, ain't it? I mean, soonah oah latah everybody's got to pay off somebody fah what nobody evah suspected would happen?"

Lou considers that observation, he considers it well — with all its financial implications. "I'll give you one hundred to pull my car back on the road and forty to fill it up with gas."

"What about youh battahry?"

"Sixty."

"Theah fouhty five fah a decent diehahd."

"Sixty five — all I need to do is make it to Fort Kent."

"Emahgency road sahvice is extra, then theah's the mattah of my tip — total $300 with the usual guarhantees."

Lou is baffled. Could this kid make it on Wall Street? Up along the

Khyber Pass? Inside the Iron Triangle?

"So we got some soht of deal, oah you just goin to leave this clunkah heah in the ditch?" And in the distance the sound of reproaching hounds. Lou is stupified. "I'll walk you round to Chippah's fihst, ain't that fah. Then I'll come back and see what I can do about the truck, get the kids to help."

"No no, don't let that gang tou-…" Lou can't spea-…

"Just who the hell else is goin to haul you out of heah, the AA? Besides, you ain't got no cell phone to call fah help."

No, not for $69.95 monthly service in addition to roaming charges.

"Hand ovah the keys strangah, I can't spend all night waitin. I got to sleep late tomhorow."

Lou is slowly comprehending what is occurring, and he does not like it. After all Lou is a New Yorker, and New Yorkers do not like handing over their car keys and their wallets to wise-ass back-woods kids.

"You don't huhry up and Rangah Dohb's goin to be ovah heah checkin out the crack of youh ass!"

"Ahh!" And it's not that Lou understands fully what a Dorbs is, not yet, but he has met the ranger, and Lou's quick, he can imagine the rest — a bit of spine tingling banjo — so over goes the wallet — no quick, think it through, dickhead! — Lou snaps it back. He hands over all his cash, not quite $300, but close, then there's the two folded hundreds he keeps hidden behind his American Excess card. Kid takes the cash and waits for more, palm uphanded. Lou is quizzical.

"Keys." Kid demands.

"They're in the ignition."

"Right." Kid slips in behind the wheel, snaps out the keys, slams the door locked. "Bettah be safah than sohriah in this neighbahood."

Then there's the matter of the dogs closing in.

"Bettah staht walkin towahd Chippah's place. Heah take my hand, and don't go gettin queeah on me."

He takes the kid's hand, something about this kid could never make Lou feel queeah.

The kid is of course, stoned silly on Chipper's dream weed, and while he may live nearby, he too can get turned around in the darker than dark — like all those fairy tales about the child getting lost in the dense woods while trying to make it to grandma's house? Well, there's nothing fairy tale about a Maine woods in the dark, and there you are following this kid you distrust entirely, by the hand no less, but who now has the keys to your twenty grand plus car and all but $200 of your cash reserve, because what the hell else are you going to do anyway as you wander in what seems to be endless circles through brambles and brush, wading across a cold stream not once, but twice, and finally arriving at a hovel dug into the ground, a knock, and from inside some moaning that sounds like early death. The kid, impatient as kids are today, knocking and getting no answer, he shoves the door open to reveal this tall gaunt blond guy sitting up straight on a gouged out sofa, naked, with a young girl plopped down on top of him, naked, and doing her up and down to ecstatic moans on both their parts.

"BELINDA?" The brother yells, letting go of Lou's hand.

"Lloyd! That you?" She calls back without turning away. "Chippah heah likes it the same way you do!"

MAINE boy /

"Come on, we got to head home."

"Why? It ain't even close to my bedtime."

"Will you huhry the fuck up!"

Chipper shrugs, and she takes her own sweet time dressing, then dawdles at the door, head down, like a naughty puppy – sneakin peeks up at him.

SHAME boy /

"Damn gihl, looks like you and me got a long hot summah ahead."

She smiles at Chipper, glares at her brother who's waiting by the door.

"H'yep, plenty of time fah us to get to know each othah, but right now daddy's got business he's got to attend to."

As she passes she stares daggers at Lou – cause ain't it ahways the way, company comes, spoils all the fun.

Guess you took that CHANCE!

Chipper closes the door behind them. "Puhky little spud, ain't she?"

Lou must nod, indeed, for it is a familiar scene to him, hillbilly rockstar walks off with the girl, slick city manager's left holding a beer, like some immutable law of nature, all of the bucks, none of the fucks.

"Damn! I didn't realize it was you the kids wah talkin about, no way! Lou Stahcrave! Ah you a sight fah sohe eyes! My buddy from back befah I got slammed into solitahry!" Chipper throws a hug on Lou, a tight one, both arms. "But why sneak around? You could've told them right out who you wah, left a cahd."

True, in retrospect, that would have been easier, and a lot less costly.

"What'd you want to do, suhprise me?" And Chipper squeezes the harder. "Well you did, big time!"

Lou is squeezed speechless. He can only marvel at the man he has journeyed these many miles to see, same raw bones, almost skeletal, his muscles hanging on him like he was a dismantled skeleton for an anatomy course, but permanently youthful, teeth, skin, eyes — incredible — plus he has achieved the impossible, he has kept all his hair and still platinum blond, an almost perfectly preserved young Chipper Stirbee. "I- I don't believe I-..."

"H'yep, it's me. In the flesh."

Which is why he should put some clothes on.

"Everyone in New York thinks you're dead."

"Hahdly. One thing folks ought to know about us Mainahs is we nevah go easy, noh quiet fah that mattah." Chipper's rummaging through the refrigerator. "Let me grab us some of my homebrew, celebrate."

Lou's stomach could do without it, but when a friend you haven't seen for forty years offers, the answer's got to be sure.

"Let me look, what've I got left from my select? Hey how about 97, that was a yeah!" Chipper serves up an unlabeled green bottle, a dark thick liquid grainy malty, which tastes fine though there's this rancid smell to it and something with many legs floating in the settled brine at the bottom.

"Fuckin spidah, that's what that is, fuckin spidahs all ovah this house because it's so goddamn damp, cellahs ahways ah. Moistuhe seeps in and spidahs, everywheah you can imagine — you try and filtah them through aftah you've scooped out the mash, but they end up disintegratin on you befah you can pick them out whole."

Lou peers into his bottle.

"Leastways this way you can see what you'h drinkin and avoid swallowin most of them most of the time, 'cept if you do, you know they'h dead and any gehms oah such they'd be cahryin ah dead too. 20 proof. So watch out, a guy can get pretty pickled." Chipper chugs and who knows, maybe this is the very elixer of his youthfulness.

Lou gurgles. He'll try anything once, twice.

"Ready fah anothah?"

No no, Lou sips, he doesn't guzzle.

"So what brings you all the way up heah anyway? You on the lamb oah somethin?"

Lou *bel*-ches. The fumes escaping his mouth but precede the fire he feels fuel forth from his gut.

Chipper pounds him on the back. "Somethin stuck in youh throat?"

Lou shakes his head no.

"Don't tell me they want me to recohd a new album?"

Lou's raised eyebrow answers that question.

"No? Then what?" Chipper plops himself down on the couch next to him, bangs Lou's back a good one.

Clears Lou's throat. "Fir-fir-first, I can report that I have started receiving royalty checks again. Surprise, yes? I have one with me for $187.45. It's not much, but they're playing the old Loose Nuke hits on the classic rock stations, nationwide."

$187.45 is jackpot for Chipper. "Damn, that's mah than my monthly disability."

"There'll be more where this came from."

"Whoa. Nevah thought I'd strike it rich. Look at that Betsy, told you I was famous once. Heah's proof, check with a signatuhe is prima facie. Maybe I should frame it."

Particularly when you don't happen to have a bank account.

"Thank you Lou, I appreciate you'h drivin all the way up heah to delivah it." And there's a glimmer of a tear in Chipper's eye.

"I-I'm so happy to see you alive."

"I nevah knew you wah so sentimental."

Chipper goes gets them both another. "Will still cookin?"

"He has a wife…"

"Say no mah, how about you and Elli?"

"No more."

"Hey, single life suits me fine, long as I have a string of neighbah daughtahs — won't ask none about Danny T, but wouldn't mind heahin somethin 'bout Molly."

"Live in Staten Island, right by the ferry. I've never been invited over."

"H'yep, old friends ah just that, ahn't they? And Bubba?"

"Had dinner with him just last week."

"What's he got, nine kids by now?"

"Eleven."

"Man was ahways a stokah — anothah?"

"Why not?"

Well for one, there's the state of his gut, those lower intestines which become inflamed and cause him to writhe about on the floor doubled up, but then a long trip, a car in a ditch, that's something to get tanked about.

"Theah's got to be somethin I can do to reciprocate Lou, aftah all youh trouble to drive up heah."

"Well I- I did come up for a reason, see, I think it's about time-…"

"Got lots of that."

"…time for a revival."

"Whoa!"

"Now I don't want to promise anything I can't deliver."

"You wah always cautious. Plus you ahways leveled with me — usually when we wah knee deep into it and needed bailin."

"Maybe one joint appearance of the Loose Nukes, a nostalgia bit, and who knows, let's not get our hopes up, but a successful appearance might buy us another, then maybe another, then maybe a tour…"

"About how much cash up-front?" Chipper's no longer the starry eyed seventeen year old he was once.

"Don't know yet, don't know, and to be honest I don't have the financing in place yet, although I have one good lead…"

"Reason I ask is it suhe would be great if I could make enough money to put a house on top this foundation." And he looks around at the stark gray concrete walls that encase him.

"That I think we could do." Lou sighs. Yes, that he could do if that's all this man wants, but then somehow his incredulity breaks forth. "That's all you want out of life, an upstairs to your basement?"

Chipper is sitting there, entirely naked on a caved-in couch, downing his homemade beer, and in such a state of inebriated undress a man can become unusually honest, with himself if nobody else. "Lou, I've sat up heah in these woods fah mah'n fohty yeahs, time enough to reflect on what's what in life, what's impahtant and what's not, and I've leahned that a man who wants too much from life is doomed to fail. So me? All I want is a house on top my foundation, that's it, to get out this damn damp cellah once and fah all. If I wanted mah, I'd be a damned fool, damned fool not to be content with stayin right heah in these woods, because everythin I need is handy neahby, as you might have noticed." Chipper winks and elbows Lou, right aside that inflamed gut.

Lou tries to reflect on what Chipper has learned over the years, on his words, on his woods, on his spidery brew, and naturally on his young neighborly neighbor — yet he knows not what to answer.

"Anothah thing I could suhe go fah is a new album." Chipper pulls on a shirt, his trousers." Been feeling real creatve lately, gots lots of new songs buzzin through my head."

-*roh no*, Betsy buries her nose in her paws.

"Don't know what you'h ovah theah muttahrin about gihl, but I can tell you'h bein critical as usual, like I've got to lead my life to satisfy some dog."

Some d-*rogg!*

"Anothah beeh Lou?"

"Why not?" Lou shouldn't, he's near blotto, and Chipper seems content to carry on a conversation with his dog — God knows musicians are loony, but have all these years of seclusion pushed him ever closer to the edge?

Chipper's unconcerned, he's stands there in the stove light stuffs a fat bud into a wood pipe, flares it up and sucks down a lung full. Offers it to Lou who waves it away, sensing the dangers therein — drugs to contend with and the neighbor kids, shades of Cincinnati Summer of 69.

But Chipper insists, "How can I trust a dude who won't blow dope with me?"

"How can I trust a dude…

Lou reflects on this, and he is weary, the long drive up, his encounters with the locals, his new SUV rolled over in a ditch...

Chipper presses the smoldering pipe into Lou's hand.

...Lou sniffs at it. Remembrances of mild feelings of euphoria as a teenager — so he sips on it, lightly, quickly passes it back.

"Man, take a heavy hit. You ain't goin nowheah tonight, plus Belinda said she'd be back up aftah huh brothah's fell asleep — child's insatiable."

Lou chokes. The idea of the lovely pubescent girl's return catches him offguard, he hauls in a mouthful, his mind momentarily mightily distracted, and if things get too dicey, he can always crawl under the sofa and have a chat with the dog.

"Seems all the gihls in that DuChamps' family get the yeahnin eahly." Chipper adds as a matter of fact. "She might pahsuade one of huh sistahs to tag along fah you."

Lou chows down what's left in the pipe, the trip suddenly worth not only the effort but also the loss, particularly when the man's blown out on dope — these Chipper's prize pickins, not some mild sophomoric euphoria — all that is reality coalesces into a blur, a swirl really, things blending one into another, events, faces, bodies, hopes and expectations, words and promises, even money amounts, fantastically futuristic visions of show business grandeur, shrill sold-out crowds, startling visual effects, monster sound systems, shrieking young girls — there's this knock on the door and Lou hears voices, more than one, and giggles — and dancing in circles, dark beer in green bottles, spiders' legs swimming in the dregs, hands touching exposed body parts, Chipper's plaintive voice cutting a ragged edge through the cloud, some moaning about how good things too must past — Lou attempting to stand and tripping over his own belt down around his ankles. His need to pee, and young girls clapping while he tries, cheering him on and with some success as he attempt to recycle into a green bottle what he has taken from it, and the nasally lyrics of...

> Without his wings a man can't fly
> Without his wings a man won't even try
> Witsout his swings high heaven's too fah
> Witszout his swigs a man can't be a stah!

The significance of the song goes unnoticed as more of Chipper's homegrown is passed around, and more homebrew. Lou is not conscious, no conscience at all, seems the whole neighborhhood's been alerted that a smokefest is in progress, footsteps in and out the door and stepping over him — and is that that kid's voice, the Lloyd kid returned with his keys? Lou's not sure, not sure of anything, and Chipper's singing is becoming indistinct in the fog as well.

"... who won't blow dope with me?"

> Whissou'his winks man's goin to fall
> Whissou'his winks man's so small
> Whissou'no swinks man ain' god no shance
> Whissou'no swinks man can lose his pants...

Andeverybody blaring back-up vocals, loudly.

Then, afterwards, an orgy of words, deepfelt, an expurgation of the longings within both souls, Lou's for money and Chipper's for...

"What is it you want out of the deal anyway?"

"Immah'l'ty man, I wanna be immah'l. I don' wanna die Lou, don' wanna be fahgodden up heah nowheah in some stinkin cellah in Oddah's Letch man, I wanna sink again, I wanna fly, fl-, man, fly, sink an fly. You godda helb me man, you godda helb me sink an fly, h-OK man? H-OK? You gonna helb mesink an fly ha'gain?"

"Yeah yeah," Lou burbles on his back. "We'll get you a fucking pilot's license if that's all you want."

"Good! Good! You'h a good man, a good man, cause you know why? You know why you'h a good man?"

Lou doesn't know why, and what's a good man anyway? But he does remember Chipper Stirbee standing over him, his blond hair, every strand of it aglow, the flare off the woodstove highlighting it, these who knows how many young cherubs chirping away in the background and Chipper trying to enunciate as clearly as he can: "Cause you still know howda dream, tha's why, you still know howda dream, and you can have all the money, i's yuhs, all the money, don wohry none about me, i's all yuhs cause all I wan man, all I wan is immahl't', tha's all I wan, I wanna be immah'l, tha's all, tha's all I wan man, tha'sz all, I wanna be him- hi- immah't... him- himmah't'l... tha's h'all, h'OK?"

> Ain't no use MOM, tryin to stop him NOW!
> No good to PRAY fah him noh PREACH!
> Any hahm the BOY's been doin he's done by HOW!
> And what he's LEAHNIN them schools don't TEACH!

> Hey hey, say say...

> MAINE BOY / SAME BOY /
> Did you evah find those PANTS?
> MAINE BOY / FAME BOY /
> Looks like you fin'ly leahned t'DANCE

1968

St Mark's Place / A gypsy space
Lots of loose cats hangin round
Stray mates
Playin safe
With loads of drugs goin down

68

Save the date
Earthquake
Shots fired round the globe / Signal the
Outbreak of a brand new brand of
Revolution

Vietnam's still crankin up / Up
Gettin washed and ready for sup-
Purr- purrrr- purrrrrrrrrrrrrrr
On TV
There / Where / The whole world can see
Mom / Dad / Big brother Dave
Little sis / Sittin on the sofa
Watchin a whole family
Take it in the face / *But hey!*
That's some other place
Simply say grace
Father in heaven / Right up above
Tell the rest of the world
They can shove
It

Over there / Over there
Let's declare
Keep it there / Over where
They ain't got a prayer

Listen to me / Attentively
Want you to eat
Sleep
Don't make a peep
Other people's problems are theirs to keep

Martin Luther King
Gunned down
From a roof top in
Memphis town
But hey!
That's Tennessee
Where they wiped out the Cherokee
We're secure / Tucked states away
In a cozy heartland suburb / Where
Fifty feet of grass
Keeps us safe from enemy attack

Kiddies under cover
Can't sleep
Got to take a peek
OK / Alright
Tonight
Facts of life / See
Everybody's got rights
So long as they're whites
Besides
Those in the know know
Black folks were created to hand out
Towels / Though
They're man enough to fight
Every boy / Even white
Stripped to his skivvies joins
The Army
Better enlist / Before you get drafted
Resist / You're gonna get shafted

Boot camp

Stamp! Stamp!
Teach these smart-ass brats
A lesson in civics
No recess / Until after
The President's address
Salute / The Commander-In-Chief
Squirmin in his seat
I will not seek / *Hell No!*
Nor will I accept
We won't go!
My party's nomination for
58,128 of our boys dead
And more / Spent
One hundred fifty billion
For a dirty little war
He cannot win

From the halls of Montezu-U-ma
To the shores of TRIP-o-li
We will fight our country's ba-A-tles
Mired in the mud
Hup! Hup!
Hut to hut / Except for Tet
From high in the skies / B-52s will
Bomb these slanty-eyed gooks into
Oblivion

Pop! Pop!
RFK just got shot!
With TV hot on the spot so
All of us can watch
Fascination / With
Assassination
The Kennedy tragedies
Violence on the air as the children
Stare
Don't gulp / You'll choke
Break fast for a commercial
Gleem / Listerine
At least twice a day / Brush those
Nasty germs away
While our affiliate in LA joins the fray

68

No time to waste
Psychedelic's passé
Moody Blues / Pink Floyd
Popped in Monterey
Beatles too
Sgt Pepper can't compete with
Troops on the streets
Doesn't phase Jim Morrison / Though
Boy wanders the stage / In a daze
Flash of cock sends the country into
Shock
And his dad's an admiral!

Even Dylan's deserted / Converted to
Jesus
Heavy metal's in
Led Zep / Steppenwolf /
Born to be wi-i-ild /
While Mick quick switches to a
Street fightin man
Got to livin up the
Act / As
A civil rights rally suddenly goes
Bloody
In Belfast /
Troubles begin / And last and last
Riots in Paris / Students bring down
DeGaulle
Who's who?
The last living legend of World War Two
Then there's Prague /
Workers / Students / Tanks
Take to the streets
But what's the beef?
That's some commie country's business
Beyond our reach
Still
Crack! Crack!
Did you hear that?
Barefoot on the stairs and
Terrified

Hurry back to bed / Scouts
Lay awake while you do a head count
That's a one / A two / A three
Lightning strike's at least an ocean away
While we're home safe
So why are you staring up at me?
Can't you see / I'm too busy
Fending off ants in the grass to
Intervene

Chicago
The Democrats convene
LBJ *won't go* /
Nor will I seek / *Hell no!*
Outside the walls of the
Convention hall
Tear gas / Our boys in uniform
Marchin in time behind
Halftracks / Armed and ready to
Resist
A domestic insurrection
Civil War
Brother pitched against another
Innocent / Or with intent
Tanks on city streets
First time ever in America
Kids the cops are bashing
Could be yours / If not mine
Our own sons and daughters
On the line
Shame Shame
Shake your finger in the face of
Democracy
While
THE WHOLE WORLD IS WATCHING!
THE WHOLE WORLD IS WATCHING
Along with history

Nixon / He's the one
Law and order from
Border to border
With the wider war to come
Laos / Cambodia

Million more innocents / For the
Warlords to slaughter

Hey! Hey!
Ain't that Jackie K
Shipping off in a two-piece
With some old tycoon
On her very own Aegean
Honeymoon?
What a hoax
Even Camelot's a joke

68

Wide awake / Truth or fake
At stake
An entire generation / After
All we've worked so long / so hard
To attain
Prosperity / Propriety / Posterity
Authority / Conformity
Backed up by our unassailable
Military superiority
Only thanks we get is
A headache
Of migrane proportions /
Quick! Quick!
Take two / Speed relief / Or at least
Click! Click!
Switch the channel / Although
Woodstock's not due til
Summer of 69
Jimi Hendrix headlines
Ho ho say can you see
Squeak! Squeak!
Neil Armstrong's walkin on the moon
So what's in store / Beyond more
Of this not so cold
Cold War?

Plenty / And not very pretty
Plague / Fire / Famine / Pestilence or
The Bomb!

Fate's worse than worse / So
Better brace yourself
Stash the kiddies in gramp's abandoned
Air-raid shelter
Because
The USA's been targeted for an all-out
As in a far out
Cultural revolution

Stray cats /
Meteoric brats / Out on a
First date in the
Universe
Little Adam / Little Eve
Unsupervised
Teaming up in the back seat at the
Drive-in / Hold tight
Don't let go
Next feature's The Big Burst in
Cinemascope and stereo
Burnt stars /
Birth of a brand spankin new
Baby Galaxy!
Damp grass under the thick cover of
Darkness
My goodness / Ain't it but
Beautiful to behold!
Mass / Energy / Timed right for a nuclear
Attraction / That's
Lights! Camera! Action!
Instead of God's finger in the mix
There's this heavenly
Flash!
Asteroid attack!
Bright streaks in the night sky with mutual
Combustion / On
Impact
Planet's about to blast off into a
New age of ready-to-aim-to-
Please / Mama / Papa's home grown recipe for a
Fresh baked / Hot chunk of
Rock 'n' roll!

East Village
New York City

St Mark's Place / A gypsy space
Lots of loose cats hangin round
Stray mates
Playin safe
With loads of drugs goin down

SCREEEE-YEE-YEE-YEE-YEE-YEE-YEEEEEEEEEEEEECH!
"'Scuse me, 'scuse me — I say ezcuse me puh-lease! — dumb honky motha-fucka, move yo ass out a'the doo'way!"
"Who? Me?"
"Yah! Yo! Yo is standin directly in the way an blockin my legal access on to this public conveyance — so move ova!"
"Sorry, I didn't notice."
"Didn't notice shit!"
"Sorry."
"Sorry shit! Subway's been fillin up with all so'ts a'riffraff lately."
SCRE-SCRE-SCR-SCR-SCR-SCREEEE SC… SC… REEEE-REEEE-REEEE -CH!
"Sorr-…"
"What is yo anyway, musician?"
"Yes, I play violin, piano, trumpet, dru-…"
"'Spect yo do, by the looks a'all these hea instruments yo is totin. Yo some kind a'one man travelin bandstand?"
"I just arrived in New York City."
"That a fact?"
"I've decided to become famous."
"Famous. Everybody I's eva met in New Yo'k City came hea t'be a famous somethin."
"Wow! You must know lots of famous people?"
"Sho do, famous waita's, famous cab driva's. Why look round yo, what d'yo see? Whole ca load a'famous people."
"Really?"
"Really. Whea's yo from anyway?"
"Pennsylvania."
"Philly?"
"No west of Philadelphia, a town called Motherly Love."
"Motha'ly what?"
"Love. Motherly Love, Pennsylvania. It's a farming community."
"Why ain' I su'prised none."

"I was born and raised there. This is my first trip... away..."

SCREEEE-YEE-YEE-YEE-YEE-YEE-YEE- YEE YEE YEEECH!

"Step aside boy, yo gots t'let all these fine folks get off the train — then move ova hea and let all these otha fine folks get on. Betta still, move away from the doo' an sit down, take a load off. How fa is yo goin anyways?"

"I don't know, I just got here."

"Yo don't know, *unh hunh*, so 'spose yo tell me all what it is yo do know, say fo esample, bout New Yo'k City?"

"Well let's see, a friend of mine back home told me to go to Times Square on 42nd Street, he said he saw lots of people there on TV once on New Year's Eve, but-..."

"But what?"

"I don't know, I was just there and I kind of became confused."

"Yo kinda became confused, I'll bet yo kinda became confused — 42nd Street at midnight when thea ain't no New Yea's Eve — and did that same friend a'yos tell yo anythin else bout New Yo'k City? Like bout what neighbo'hoods yo goes inta nights an what neighbo'hoods yo don' go nowhea nea nights no daytimes neitha?"

"No, no he didn't know anything about that kind of stuff, he only knew about 42nd Street, so I decided I'd explore for myself."

"Well let me tell yo somethin, yo friend back home thea, he don' know jackshit bout New Yo'k City."

"Maybe so, see he's never... nobody ever from my hometown has ever been to New York City, except me."

"Yah? An thea's good reason why nobody from yo hometown ain't neva been t'New Yo'k City."

"Why's that?"

"Cause they gots betta sense than yo do, clea'ly, that an they's still alive t'talk bout it."

"You mean I'm risking my life being here?"

"If it was just yo life friend, that'd be easy. Yo is riskin yo body an yo soul, yo futua an everythin else yo holds nea an dea."

"Oh no, that's what my mother told me the night before I left."

"Bet. Bet she did, but think yo'd listen t'yo mama? No. An kids like yo should definitely be listenin t'theia mamas — so yo gots any place special yo is plannin on stayin fo the night?"

"No. I just got off the bus and I saw a sign that pointed to 42nd Street."

"Yah?"

"And I walked around for awhile trying to follow the signs, and..."

"An?"

"...and I got tired of walking around, and it was getting awfully late and... and people kept asking me all sorts of strange questions."

"Like what?"

"If I wanted to buy things or… or try things."

"An I don't 'spose yo wanted t'buy nothin no try nothin?"

"I said no thank you, maybe some other time. I was scare-…nervous, sort of nervous, I went down these stairs that said train… I thought if I could get back to the bus station, I could find my way."

"Way whea?"

"Somewhere."

"Well 'spose I told yo that right now yo is on the Broadway Espress an yo is headin way deep inta Ha'lem, what would yo say bout that?"

"Where?"

"That's ezactly what I thought yo'd say. Ha'lem? Ha'lem? That name don' ring no bells, don' set no ala'ms off in yo head?"

"No, should it?"

"Yah it should! Plenty a'bells an whistles an sirens – an I don't know why I should be the man tha's got t'explain the facts a'lives t'yo, I mean, bein yo is a honky white motha-fucka an I's a bad ass black motha-fucka!"

"Explain what?"

"Ezactly how big is that town yo say yo is from?"

"Not big at all, maybe 300 people."

"Yah, an do they gots a newspapa thea o radio o TV – o ee'lectricity?"

"No."

"N-no? – Did yo say no?"

"Yes. No."

"So yo don' know nothin bout no race riots no neighbo'hood organizin no freedom marches no back-a'the-bus rides, no nothin bout lootin no bu'nin no lynchin an shootin shit?"

"No… No?"

"An white folks tryin t'exclude us black folks from theia neighbe'hoods, stompin on ou rights t'vote an walk the streets afta da'k?"

"No! See people in my town, they… they're… we're this community of brethren, you know, selected by God who led us to the New Jerusalem and out of the old Germany where we weren't much tolerated because we believe that war is immoral and that machines are the inventions of the Devil and that hard work by hand wil-…"

"Yah, sounds like they is pretty much right so fa. What else do they believes in?"

"*Uh-uh-* men and women should live separate after *uh-*, after we boys and girls start to grow up, and dancing is bad, and smoking and drinking and being lazy and day dreaming and…"

"An?"

"…and music, because music makes people, mostly young people have evil desires to…"

"To? To what?"

"…to want to procreate outside the bonds of most holy matrimony, and *uh-*… what I want to say is they don't like music very much."

"*Hmmm*, an hea yo is a musician."

"Yes sir."

"So how'd yo learn t'play?"

"I'd sneak into the church late at night, see they had these instruments locked in a room in the basement, and I used to jiggle the lock and play."

"An nobody neva caught yo sneakin in t'the chu'ch basement an jigglin the lock an playin?"

"Elder Hubert did once."

"An what did he do?"

"He beat me with a birch branch across my backside and told me if he ever caught me playing with the Devil's tools again, I would have to confess in front of the assembly, and- and probably never be able to get married."

"Tha's no punishment."

"It is in our church because… because… because that's all there is, if you know what I mean."

"Tough ass religion yo belongs t', an anyways, yo neva did it again, right? Play music?"

"No, I mean yes. I did it lots. Almost every night."

"An I 'spect all these instruments yo is carryin is chu'ch propa'ty?"

"They didn't want them! They are the Devil's tools!"

"But did they tell yo yo could go ahead an take the Devil's tools wi yo t'New Yo'k City?"

"No."

"So yo is a thief."

"I- I-…"

"A'chu'ch propa'ty? An a incor'igible sneak too, cause yo prob'ly didn't go an tell nobody yo was leavin Mo'thaly Love, now did yo?"

"No, that's not true, I told my mother I was thinking about leaving, but she didn't believe I would actually do it."

"But leave yo did."

"On the morning bus, but you don't really think I'm a thief, do you?"

"I don' care if yo is a thief o not o if yo is a sneak, o that yo goes an lies t'yo own mama, but one thing I feel I gots t'tell yo is that yo is definitely headed in the wrong di'rection."

"I know, I know, life is filled with temptations and…"

"Temptation boy, tha's easy. It's discrimination we is talkin bout, an white boys like yo, musicians an such, yo should be headin downtown t'the East Village. Tha's whea yo belongs. Colo'd boys like me, the black brotha's, we belongs uptown in Ha'lem — is yo beginnin t'get the pictu'a?"

"*Uh-* I don't see what difference color makes where you live."

"Was thea any colo'd folks livin thea in Motha'ly Love?"

"No."

"'Nough said."

"But everybody who lived in our town belonged to the same religion."

"Tha's true, can' see none a'the brotha's, sista's neitha, puttin up wi that much religion — but tha's not the issue. See, yo is white, an hea in the big city... Hey, it ain' like I gots lots a'time t'esplain all this stuff t'yo, so let me ax yo somethin basic?"

"OK."

"Yo gots no place yo is goin t'be sleepin t'night, right?"

"Not really. I thought maybe I could find a deserted barn, or a field somewhere I could hide out for a while until I..."

"A ba'n?"

"Or a hayloft."

"O a chicken coop?"

"If I had to... yes."

"Chicken coop — *whoo-ee* baby boy — yo su'a gots lots t'learn bout New Yo'k City, an life in gen'ral, but the first thin I clearly gots t'do is break yo the bad news: Thea ain' no ba'ns in New Yo'k City, an no chicken coops neitha, pigeon coops, an why folks keep pigeons in a coop I don' wan' t'know, but one thing's certain, yo ain' neva goin t'wan' t'crawl inta one a'those t'sleep, no way — which means the best advice I can give yo is — yah well first, don't go talkin t'no mo crazy ass nigga's like me, tha's first — an second, tu'n yo own crazy ass round an heads yoself down t'the East Village next station we stop at. A'right?"

"East Village. Alright."

"Good. Now give me a dolla fo all my trouble — man'o'man, I done exhausted myself talkin t'yo, I'll say."

"A dollar?"

"Yah a dolla'."

"A dollar."

"A dolla. What? Yo wants my brotha's sittin hea on this train, the ones who's been keepin a eye on yo an all this good shit yo is carryin round with yo — yo wants them t'think I wasn't the one t'go an take advantage a'the situ'ation when I had the oppo'tunity fo free?"

"I don't understand..."

"Yo wants my brotha's hea takin yo shit, o yo wants t'walk off this train easy like?"

"I- I-..."

"I- I- nothin, now give me a dolla out a'yo pocket an then we's both goin t'get off at the next station real cool like, an I is goin t'hurry yo white ass across that platform an out a'Ha'lem — an when yo gets on that train headin downtown, don't go pa'kin yo ass an all this music shit yo stole in no doo'way on no train because that makes fo a pa'fect oppotun'ity fo somebody t'go an take advantage a'the situ'ation — yo listenin t'me cause yo gots a strange look in yo eyes?"

"Yes, yes I am, but I don't understand why I have to give you a dollar?"

"Why yo — hey! — let me ask yo a question: Is it betta yo gives me one dolla than yo gives me ten dolla's, is that betta?"

"Yes I guess…"

"Is it betta yo gives me one dolla than yo goes an gives all the dolla's yo gots plus yo watch plus yo violin plus yo trumpet t'the brotha's sittin hea on this train an eyein yo shit, is that betta?"

"Yes, yes I suppose it is… is it?"

"Yah it is, an yo is clea'ly sta'tin t'think logical like, yo is learnin a few thin's bout New Yo'k City a'ready."

SCREEEE-YEE-YEE-YEE-YEE-YEE-YEE-YEEEEEECH!

"A'right, hea we is. Now pick up yo shit an follow me. We is goin t'go up the staia's an cross the tracks t'the otha platfo'm, an yo don' have t'pay no additional fare, yo follows me?"

"I'll follow, yes, sure."

"Is a good thing I ain' no mo than a petty two tima cause otha'wise yo'd be a'ready wand'rin the streets cryin fo yo mama."

"Pardon me? What did you say?"

"I'm sayin when yo gets yoself back t'42nd Street, yo finds the shuttle t'Grand Central Station whea yo gets on the Lexington Avenue Loco, Downtown — yo listenin t'me? Yo is starin off again!"

"Yes yes, shuttle to Grand Central Station, Downtown, yes?"

"At 42nd Street."

"Right."

"Maybe yo ain' as slow a learna as yo looks."

"No, I earned good grades in the church school."

"Which is whea yo should've stayed in the fi'st place, like how old is yo anyways?"

"Fif-, six- sixteen, I'll be sixteen in November."

"This is May."

"Yes."

"So yo is fifteen plain an simple an tha' makes yo a runaway."

"I'm… no, I left home because I want to be a famous musician, and New York is the only…"

"Right right, I mean brotha, little white brotha, I has heard it all befo, an if yo is fifteen an a runaway, the last place yo wants t'be is on 42nd Street cause if yo hangs round thea mo'n a minute, yo is most definitely goin t'get yo ass plugged, yo hea' me?"

"Get my ass plugged?"

"Yo jus' don' know nothin, do yo?"

"I-… No."

"Bet! Now yo takes my advice, yo gets yo runaway ass down t'the East Village an yo stays thea 'til yo grows up an learns what's what bout this city, yo hea' me?"

"Yes, I… thank you for the advice sir."

"Thank yo fo the advi-… yo… I don' believe this! — So anyways, repeat those directions back t'me."

"Get my runaway ass down to the East-…"

"No, not those, the directions a'how yo is goin t'get t'the East Village, cause one thing I ain' definitely goin t'do is take yo down thea myself cause I gots things I gots t'do t'night!"

"Right yes, thank you, *uh-uh-* at 42nd Street I get off the train and look for a shuttle bus…"

"Ain' no shuttle bus! It's a shuttle train! Yo stays right down unda the ground! Don' go wand'rin up the staia's an gettin yoself lost an found in some gutta on 42nd Street — now what do yo do when yo gets off the shuttle *train*?"

"I take it to Grand Central Station."

"Grand Central is full a'trains goin every which way, so yo makes ca'tain that yo takes the 6 Train, 6, S-I-X, the Lexington Avenue Loco, an yo gets off at Asto Place — yo goin t'rememba all this? It's somethin bout those eyes a'yo's makin me na'vous as shit."

"I take the 6 Train to Asto Place."

"A'right, yo gots it, now give me that dolla."

"Alright, thanks for everything, here's a dollar… twenty five, thirty, thirty five, thirty six, thirty seven… *uh-uh-*…"

"Tha's all the money yo gots?"

"I- I didn't know, I didn't bring… I figured I could get a job in a store stocking shelves, sweeping up, sleep in the back room…"

"Maybe yo had betta get off at 42nd Street — no no, tha's a joke, but yo best keep the change, white boy, an hea… I's goin t'give yo a dolla — wait, turn round…"

"Why?"

"Cause I don' wan' my brotha's on the platfo'm t'see me givin no white boy no dolla, they'll think I let yo blow me o somethin…"

"Blow you?"

"Boy, yo su'a don't know too much bout nothin, do you?"

"I-…"

"Motha'ly Love, eh?"
"Right. Pennsylvania."
"Religious folk."
"Yes, founded by Semenites from Westphalia back in the…"
"Don't matta none t'me which one a'them did it t'yo, but they got it t'yo real good, tha's clea. An believe yo me, nothin an nobody yo is goin t'meet up with in New Yo'k is goin t'do it t'yo no wo'se than they done yo back home. Ree'ligion — *whoo-ee*, talk t'me bout that will yo! Hea, takes two dolla's — an don' let nobody see me doin that! No idea what they might think we is up t', dealin pu'ple microdots o some wo'se curse."
"Purple microdots?"
"*Ohhh*, jus' take the money boy, an study New Yo'k ha'd! Make me proud a'my investment! City's gots lots t'teach yo!"
SCREEEE-YEE-YEE-YEE-YEE-YEE-YEE-YEEEEEEECH!
"Tha's yo train, now get on it."
"Thank you, but I can't take your money, I don't even know you."
"Hell, I was goin t'take yo money an I don' know yo!"
"Right, OK, bu-…"
"But nothin, yo gets yo white ass on that train an yo keeps yo white ass on tha' train all the way til yo gets t'Asto Place, yo hea me?"
"Yes, I-…"
"And when yo gets thea, yo follows one a' yo own look-a-likes out a'that station, follows them close til they leads yo t'whea yo belongs."
"One of my own look-a-likes?"
"One a'those boys o girls who looks a whole lot like yo does, yo knows, pale white with long hair an scraggly clothes an that same glazed ova look yo gots in yo eyes because they been smokin way too much reefa!"
"Reefa?"
"Marijane! Yo… yo su'a yo didn't jus' spring up out in the middle a'some co'nfield, yo is so tall and skinny and green and dumb…"
YEE-YEE-YEE-YEE-
"Thank you. thank you sir, I appreciate your-…"
"Yo betta."
"And thank you for the two dollars."
"Will yo keeps quiet bout them two dolla's an gets yo shit inta that train! Trains don't just pa'k hea fo'eva waitin while yo makes up yo mind bout whea yo gots t'go — in New Yo'k City boy, yo jus' goes!"
SCREE-SCREE-REE -EEEEEREE-EEEEE REE-EEEEE
"Say, wha's yo name fo futu'a ref'rence, jus' in case yo does go an gets yoself t'be a famous musician?"
"Will, Will Cook, and I'll never forget you."
"'Spect yo won't, an I'll rememba that name — can't ha'dly fo'get a name

as simple as that an Motha'ly love, PA, now can I?"
"WHAT'S YOUR NAME?"
"SALAAM, BROTHA SALAAM KAREEN KAB-..."
SCRE-SCRE-SCR-SCREEEEEEEE-SC... SC... REEEE-REEEE-REEEE... -CH!

Will Cook... "Excuse me sir, ma'am, excuse me!" Will Cook... "Sorry, real sorry, excuse me." ...makes his way through... "Excuse me, excuse me!" ...through Grand Central Station with all his cases and bags strapped to his back, more under his arms ... "Excuse me, sorry, excuse me — is this the train to Asto Place?"
"Yu wan Asso Pwace?"
"Yes, that's it."
"Yu wan go otha side o pwa'foam, Dwontwon."
"Thank you, thank you ma'am."
SCREE-YEE-YEE-YEEEEEEEECH... 'CH'CH'CH!

...SCR, SCR, SCRSCRSCR-SCREEE- REEEE-RE-RE-REEEE -YEE-YEE-YEECH!
Astor Place and Will Cook's follows close step-step-step on the heels of this girl, he thinks, maybe a guy, but somebody who looks a lot like himself, all hair wild and frazzled with only a nose protruding like some mole blindly digging along behind some other one with a decent scent when she/he abruptly stumps to a full stop — "Back off, will you buster!"
"Sorry I-... Excuse me, sir/ma'am — ma'am!"
She's a look-a-like alright, but with some fairly significant differences. "I'm looking for the East Village."
"Yah well, this is it."
"Thank- thank you — oh wow! This is it?"
"You're new in town, aren't you? Like where're you from?"
"Pennsylvania. Motherly Love, Pennsylvania."
"Yah? I'm from Jersey myself. Exit 11 off the Garden State."
"I can't believe this is it!"
"What's all this shit you're lugging?"
"Instruments, musical instruments. I'm a musician — are you?"
"No, I'm a model."
"A model!"
"Artist's model."
"Wow!"
"Which means I'm willing to pose naked for money..."
"W-oh?"
"...but I like musicians OK, they're normally kind of kinky."

"Kinky?"
"So you a guy?"
"I-'m a guy."
"Let's see."
Good thing he has his hands full because she reaches over and parts Will Cook's hair back. "Cute for a guy – you don't shave yet."
"N-no."
"You can stay at my place."
"What?"
"You need a place to stay, right?"
"Yes ma'am, I do, bu-…"
"And you're a guy, right?"
"Yes, bu-bu-…"
"So you can sleep with me, c'mon." She leads and Will Cook follows, and she doesn't brake for traffic – BE-BE-BE – nor does traffic brake for her – BEEP! BEEP! BEEEEP! BEEEEP!
"Watch where you're walking you fucking creeps!" Cabby calls.
"UP YOUR ASS!" She raises her middle digit in defiance. Cabby returns the gesture with one of his own, from the elbow.
"Whole city's full of creeps! CREEP! – C'mon."
Will Cook and his look-a-like cross from the Astor Place kiosk and head down along St Mark's Place – a gypsy space, lots a loose cats hangin round – out windows, off fire escapes, down steps, across sidewalks and along the street. It's way past two in the AM, though summer time, and the police have conveniently set up barriers to keep the traffic out.
More people than Will Cook has seen in a lifetime, and all look-a-likes, anyone of whom he could as easily follow home – *whang* – as he bangs into a low slung hydrant. He tries to right himself and slips off the curb.
"Here, let me carry a couple of those."
Music is blasting from all sides, and all kinds of music blasting, people are smoking, smoking and joking and laughing and shouting, they're posing and they're parading, girls and boys and boys and girls and boys and boys and girls and girls…
There's every sort of color, smell, sound, sight, light, light everywhere, whole street lit up for blocks like daylight, all the shops wide open neon, record shops and clothes shops and poster shops and shops that sell beads and incense and flowers and pizza and Copa Cola and ice cream and pipes, wood pipes and stone pipes and glass pipes in funny blown shapes and…
"Wah!"
…devices clearly designed to frustrate the sacred ends of nature…
"Cheryl!"
"Joycee!"

Will Cook's guide sees another like herself and starts in shrieking. They clutch at each other and jump around — SHRIEK! SHRIEK! — as though they haven't seen each other since at least noon.

"What are you doing?"

"Hanging."

"With anybody special?"

"No, nobody — oh, I found this one in the subway station."

"What are you going to do with... Are you a her or a him?"

"I- I'm a him!"

"Yah, well I'm a her — a woman!"

Which is very apparent since all Joycee is wearing up top is a halter, a tie-dyed bandana that's not tied too tight, and Will Cook is gawking at her, as he has been gawking at everybody all along the way because in hometown Motherly Love, PA, folks, kids, boys, girls don't go crowding into the streets half naked, and Will Cook has seen more human flesh in the past fifteen minutes than he has seen over the past fifteen years — his particular sect disdaining mirrors and any nakedness, even during bathing, which makes bathing quite a formidable task, what with the special button up underwear, the stitched pockets, the crevices that never seem to get washed properly, but then they are filthy dirty to begin with, aren't they, the roots of all evil and strange tingling sensations, although not if you buckle the Founding Fathers' leather strap contraption on properly and cinch it up tight around your middle, sure, it might hurt at first but it certainly can keep carnal matters under control, except sometimes a buckle gives and SNAP! — thing'll bulge on you and start in leaking, about like it is now.

"What are you going to do with him?"

"Take him home and sleep with him."

"Just the two of you?"

"Why, you want to come along?"

"If I don't find anything better."

"Well I'm tired of looking and he's handy."

"OK OK, let's get going."

Will Cook follows along behind both Cheryl and Joycee. What does he know, or what alternative does he have? With no knowledge nor forethought and no escape available, there can be no sin, certainly — and besides this is his first night in New York City, something's got to give.

"Should we stop and get some pizza?"

"Sure, why not? You got any money?"

There's a delay before Will Cook realizes Joycee is asking him. "Ye-yes, this man on the subway train gave me two... two..."

"Two what?"

"Two dollars…"

"That's all you got?"

"…and thirty seven cents."

"Never go that cheap kiddo!" Joycee is genuinely shocked. "Always go for premium price, especially if you're young and can play innocent — how old are you anyway?"

"Six- fifteen?"

"Same age I am — believe me you can do a lot better than two thirty seven, even on the subway. Guess we're gonna have to teach this guy how to hustle 42nd Street Cheryl."

"Hustle?"

"It's a groovy new dance step. C'mon. I'll spring for the pizza, made a hundred and fifty off some banker — want me to carry your piccolo?"

"Violin?"

"Whatever, bongo-bongo, let's go make some noise."

"Th-thanks, and… my name's Will Cook."

"We will kiddo, we will."

There's a stop at a pizza stand on the corner of First Avenue and Third Street, and Will Cook's first sight of a pizza — might look like hog puke on a giant slice of bread, and smell like it too, but the taste is decidedly better — and what's this *sip sip*, never have drank black fizz water before.

"Want another slice?"

He nods, he should say no thank you, but he's so hungry he could eat a dozen more.

"Did you go over to Paul and Eddie's?"

"They had all dropped acid, but no way I could do another hit, not after last night, so I left, wandered over to the square, hung out for a while and bumped into you."

SHRIEK! SHRIEK! — on the street as the two girls walk along. SHRIEK! SHRIEK! — as they round a corner into an *outre* neighborhood, one of those avenues nobody in New York City ever walks nights without a police escort, the ABCs, the very edge of civilization, which is apparent even to Will Cook — this woman with blood gushing from her nose goes running by shouting, "Watch out! He's got a knife!" A knife. Big deal. Doesn't slow down Cheryl and Joycee, they keep on shrieking, Will dragging his shoes because he has stepped into some sort of muck on the sidewalk while he's been gawking around — dark entryways and thin passages between tall buildings, a gruff shadow staggers out bumps him. Will almost topples over, all the stuff hanging from his shoulders, but the girls grab him and step up the pace — the New Yorker double step, brisk stride and nary a glance side-to-side. No shrieking now, not as a car load of guys slows — "Chic chic, wanna ride?" — and the girls break into a race for their very own doorway. Up a set of steps, and keys, lots of keys and locks, lots of locks! More stairs, narrow stairs — *bump clunk,* damn near *dump* — up Will Cook treads with his cases bouncing off walls, five flights of tenement walk-up and then more locks and dead bolts, chains and latches, but finally they're in. In where? No lights, no hot water and sporadic heat, but no matter, it's May and what windows aren't broken are open, and Joycee or is it Cheryl? One or the other lights a lighter, and what's that funny smell? Incense?

"The roach guy must have been in here today and sprayed."

"No shit! Place smells definitely chemical!"

"I hope he didn't get my plants or my cat!"

Me-yew, me-yew-too. No Cheryl, cat's fine, but why are the plants drooped to the floor — and a flip of the light in the kitchen reveals that the roaches have survived swell.

Will Cook's transfixed in another room however, the only other room, where there is light, this bit of purplish haze that's almost sufficient to illuminate a fright bright color fresco of nightmare creations clinging to the walls, orange eyes, blue fangs dripping cherry ripe saliva, unisex nubiles in the claws of wolves badly in need of shaves, especially their teeth — Hold on there Whisker Face, while I take a file to those incisors!

Cheryl notices Will Cook staring, mouth open, hair parting of its own volition. "You like my art? I did it while I was tripping."

"Tripping?" Will Cook notes as he is struck dumb, but not blind, no, Will Cook sees too too clearly, it's the flesh that's chilling, bluish.

"C'mon, sit down, take off your clothes" — an invitation that Cheryl means sincerely, for with a few tugs and a zip she's at her imposing reposing artist model's best, not much for breasts but she's definitely a girl and willing. "What's the matter? You never seen a girl naked before?"

Will Cook has seen women, he was raised with women until age twelve brought about unintended changes. He has a mother of course, and a grandmother, two aunts, both unmarried, what are called spinsters in his sectarian farm community, old maids elsewhere, bachelor gals out West, professional women along most of the East Coast, but co-unattached females in New York City, closet lesbos in Jersey — it's all a matter of inappropriate usage, although Will Cook wouldn't know about any of these dialectic variances. It was simply Auntie Leah and Auntie Rachael who shared the room off the kitchen. Will Cook also had sisters, seven of them, all older, a typical knit-tight rural Pennsylvania religious family, of which Will Cook was the youngest and the only boy — what is today called a love child, but what in those days was called a period child, a surprise in polite circles, an accident in those more coarse — OH MY GOD IN HEAVEN! LOOK WHAT YOU DID TO ME ON PERMISSION DAY, OLLIE — I AM WITH CHILD

AND I DIDN'T EVEN NOTICE!

Nor did Ollie notice, because by an essential canon of his faith he must reside in the men's barracks down the twisting road, although as a signatory to a marriage contract, notarized by God Himself, Ollie has certain monthly privleges, so-called visitation rights, when he can do what nature perforce, not God, demands he do. And he did it, dutifully, and in accordance with the procedure writ in the Olden Semenites Book of Rules For Divine Copulation. And his Sacred Partner has a right to be upset. She is long past the age when women should bear Divine Droplings, and Ollie should have known about her irregularity since he's the sole apothecary in Motherly Love. But then who could have predicted that Permission Day would fall on a second Friday when he was under the influence of the one glass of barley ale permitted him monthly — with the relieving benefit to the bowels that God surely intended man to have on occasion — although some of the brethren eschew even this rare indulgence in barley ale, and also their monthly rites of copulation, but then they are of a firmer conviction, one that requires that men should never celebrate nor shower, for levity or a bath of any kind shall only incur more of the like — laughter, excitement, accidental brushing, one thing leading to another, and sorry, I must have tripped for I seem to have inserted my male member inside your female opposite and I can feel God's punishment making the most of it — steady Nellie, I must have popped the cork and what a dry hole gusher that was — IT'S GOD WILLING GOT TO BE A BOY THIS TIME ROUND!

And oh yes Ollie was so proud of his having a son because untutored farmyard prejudice or not, a man with only daughters — and two maiden sisters — lives his life under the snickering suspicion that he hasn't got much more than a toothpick in his toolbox. But birth is joyous in the community of the True Religious Brethren even if creation itself must begin in funny smelly places, what else can be said, lower level instinct, procreation or amateur, makes no difference, Pennsylvania is rich farm country, God's Green Earth down there below the waist, though the strictly religious never get to appreciate the scenery, always plowing in the dark — and so Will Cook who has never seen anything like a Cheryl before, except the nape of the neck of his next oldest sister, once, the rest of the women in his life sewn up the back tightly, and down the arms and legs — they don't shave limbs either, probably against God's law and man's best interest — so that only the hands show and once in a while the feet in a steaming bucket of epsom salts and water because when you don't want to lie back and like it, you had better stay standing on your toes doing dishes, sister, hanging laundry, toiling over a hot stove, because the Lord knows that by the time night falls, a poor woman's too tired to do one more thing, sorry Ollie — and so Will Cook has no idea what it is he's gaping at except the last time he looked he had something far different hanging in his valley of darkness than Cheryl does and he's jerking uncertain now about how to react, what to do, finger fucking being expressly prohibited too, can't waste good seed on fallow ground, Good Book says to save it all for a rainy Sunday afternoon after meeting.

And if the sight of Cheryl is not enough, there's the she-devil with multiple crimson breasts lurking on the walls in the glow of flickering violet lights – and Joycee – who strips down too, flings that halter to the walls. Joycee's bigger chested so Will Cook has to face up to what those are all about, and the combination, two, four, six, eight, twelve, he starts to swoon, but the girls catch him and relieve him of everything he's been clutching, bags, bongos, shirt and trousers, down to zero except for his peculiarly hand-tooled leather underwear, the aforementioned that the Divine Founder mandated his male followers wear in order to frustrate unnatural acts like urination and defication as well as crack scratching and the unmentionable manipulation of the thing-a-ding, though Joycee and Cheryl know nothing of divine invention and they view this most peculiar pair of briefs as definitely a turn-on, which in a way Will Cook is – he's not your every day gardener variety come to market his wares on St Mark's Place, no, he has bloomed elsewhere and so is quite unused to this sudden exposure to violet light, whereupon, unto and before only the small town doctor, a close friend of his pharmicist father, who has seen as much as these two young ladies are viewing, and the good doctor touching where Will Cook thought the Bible said nobody should never, and coughing and probing, Will Cook thought he was surely going to expectorate while standing there upon his hind legs, his male member erect for inspection, and then the lecture the old doctor gave him about the abuse of the flesh and his being young and formidable, Will Cook pulsing red from head to head to toe and finger tips, Sodom and Gomorrah, something about a salt shaker and never try tossing it high over your shoulder.

"Will you get a load of this!" Joycee is shrieking – and you will hon, you will.

"Far fucking out!" Cheryl is shrieking as well.

And they are both fingers all over the contraption.

"You definitely found us a hot one!"

"I told you, the late night subways are packed with them."

"What are we waiting for?"

"Nothing, but… what do you think this strange thing is?"

Well girls, it's a more ingenious device than you expected. It's inspried as well as laboratory tested. Getting it off the poor boy won't be any easier than what the Elders had to go through getting it on. Those are hand-stitched leather straps you're gaping at and forged iron rivets, why it's a harness that the religious founders prophesied could restrain a mule of a boy if necessary.

"You're good at buckles and stuff Cheryl, you do it."

"Try, why not?"

Does anybody have a blowtorch handy, and can she use same with surgical accuracy?

Pull! Tear! Bite! The girls are doing the best they can, and the Elders in their accumulated wisdom surely did not foresee such a predicament, where two sharp toothed girls from New Jersey would need to tear into one of their prize colts and in such a hurry, but — WHAMMM BAM! — damned if the young girls don't succeed where the old boys have failed, though right when they're about to spring Will Cook loose from the last of his shackles, there's this loud knocking at the door.

"I'll get it!" Joycee shrieks — her attention easily diverted — "Ramon!"

"Si seester, ees me! Am I on time for the partee?"

"Cheryl, it's Ramon, the cute new guy I was telling you about from across the hall!"

"Great! Come on in!"

"Wha's thees?"

As Will Cook scampers around the room, retrieving his possessions.

"He's a musician Cheryl found in the subway, and kinky."

"Maybee, but wha's he do-eeng?"

Will Cook? He's into one of his spins. Started up inexplicably when he turned twelve. First he runs in circles, then suddenly he's on his back, all fours, fives, up and twitching, foaming.

"Tastee tempteeng teemper tantrum, grab hees tongue."

Cheryl and her roommate are daring, to say the least, but neither have the nerve to go close in Will Cook's mouth with their feengees.

"Here, le' me." Ramon places a ballpoint in between Will Cook's uppers and lowers while the girls restrain his arms. "Bite on thees cowboy, hard."

Will Cook needs no encouragement, snaps the damn thing in two, that and splinters a hastily produced wooden spoon as well. "You geerls got anytheeng made out of hard rubber?" Which is Will Cook's introduction to the dildo. "There, thas' good. Hee's h-OK now. Le's have some fun!"

A little Latin music on the phono, and Ramon peels down to basics, gets the girls dancing, rango tango. Will Cook is still on the floor, woofin on this hard rubber tubular thing. Shape's OK, but it tastes terrible. He spits it out.

"Wha's the matter leetle man, you never seen a beeg brown brother een the raw?"

No. No. This is entirely new.

"Choc-o-lotte sandweech, geerls! Cha-cha!"

Cheryl and Joycee snuggle up with Ramon in the middle — *bump bump,* and a *rump, pump, hump, stump.*

"Come on chicito, up off thee floor, no harm done in danceeng."

Ramon presumes much too much, dance unmistakably being the work of the Devil, and since Will Cook has never seen anyone dance before, not singly, not together, not three together and not mixed race and naked, he must perforce agree with the Devil.

"Eenough!" Ramon struts up to Will Cook. "Wha's the matter, you ain' man eenough to join een?"

"I!" Will Cook tries manfully to defend himself.

"He's man enough Ramon, look, he's more man than you are!"

That's it Joycee, nothing like a little roommate baiting to get things really hot and heavy.

"You don' say, ay, well sheet on you gringo keed. I show evereebody a theeng or two. C'mon geerls, le's geet down and heavee, show heem what hee's meeseeng."

My, my — my my my, mymymy…

WARNING: THE FOLLOWING SCENE IS RAUNCH RATED TRIPLE G AND CONSISTS OF AN HISTORICAL RE-ENACTMENT THAT IS PURELY ILLUSTRATIVE OF A GENERALLY RECOGNIZED ERA OF LIBIDINAL PERMISSIVENESS. NO RECOMMENDATION NOR SANCTION OF SUCH PRACTICES ARE EITHER IMPLIED OR INTENDED. PARENTAL AVOIDANCE STRONGLY RECOMMENDED.

Joycee begins by puffing on a pipe, smoking a phenomenon Will has observed on occasion, on the bus up that morning from Motherly Love for instance. Different scent however. When she has had her fill, eyes closed, lips puckered and holding her breath, she passes the pipe to Ramon.

"I think the boy's just shy." Cheryl comments.

"Shy, sheet!" Ramon takes a heet, a beeg heet.

"But he barely knows us." Cheryl being one of those sympathetic nymphomaniac Jerseyites. "Here, try some of this." She coaxes as she passes the pipe to Will Cook. "It's good for introductions."

Will Cook sniffs at the weed, his nostrils twitch. While his religious upbringing forbids such excess, he must be polite.

"Breeathe reel deep, leetle buddee. Trust me."

COUGH COUGH-COU -COUG -COUGHCOUGHCOUGH…

"Tha's eet mon, you have to suck thees sheet een, ees good for you!"

"Ramon's right, try some more." Cheryl again offers to assist.

"NO-NO-NO…" Will Cook's protest is but a prelude to giving in — and what follows is quite predictable. Boy has heard it explained repeatedly, take one step on the slippery path to sin and the slide into the valley of damnation is steep, cheap and easy.

…HOUGH …HOUGH …HOUGH

See, second step is much easier than the first. Cheryl pounds him on the back for encouragement.

"Tha's eet, tha's eet. I theenk he's goeeng to be an OK keed."

Yes, except his usually pallid on pale complexion is turning greenish in hue. "Now, sneef some of thees bottle of brain strainer!"

"I- I don't understand what…"

"No! Sneeff eet, don't dreenk eet — *ay yiii*, ee's toxeec!"

"That a fact… Jesus! Lord of Mercy! Where did everyone go?" Poor Will Cook, that nose of his is getting him into a taste of some terrible trouble, and he doesn't see well either. But better to be momentarily blinded by his taste buds than to stare forever open-mouthed in a house with no lights — Will Cook goes into a trance. He squints and wow! — what visions doth appear: Ramon. He seems a bit distorted, a figure eight for a head, every feature elliptical, eyes like eggs, and grinning at Will Cook with a pumpkin cut up Halloween smile — wow! wow! wow! — and Cheryl here beside him suddenly sprouts ten teats like the old sow in the barn did, mama, they've swelled up like watermelons — WOOOOOW! WATCH THE SOW SOW SOME OATS, PLOW THE GOATS! WHOA! WHOA! WHOA!

"What's happening to him? Ramon, what have you done?"

"I di'n do notheeng, don' blame me, I never drank thees sheet beefore, though maybee eef the keed survives, I'll try eet."

Will Cook's head goes for a spin, his eyes start to roll.

"Ramon, if he starts foaming at the mouth again…"

"Right keed, no need to take a nose dive, much better to stay alive."

And Will Cook does overcome it, momentarily, he is instantly up and dancing with the Devil and his wives, skipping merrily unwarily down into that deep gorge from whence few return, spitting some trouble bubbles as he lopes along.

"There, you're not shy, are you?" Cheryl is cooing. "Just young and inexperienced and hung like a pile driver."

Three encumbrances easily overcome ma'am, though in the dark it's hard telling who's who and what's where and *whoops*, how do you like that? It's all a swirl anyway, globe spinning round, red hazy wolves' eyes peeling off the walls and hands grabbing at you, fingernails catch your nipples, but teeth that don't bite, tongues, teats and testicles that taste alright.

"Cheryl, Ramon, do something — PLEASE!"

Will Cook tumbles to the floor with Joycee on top of him, his legs up, stridulating, like a grasshopper does, like rapidly, but then the kid *is* a Class A fiddler, his hands holding on to the rOOmmate by her kubangas and nuzzling, suckling, better than dozens of sow's teats, feather pillows I'd like to bite into, soft on my bed and mama's hand stroking me, calming me down — I KNOW, I KNOW, IT'S AWFUL WILL, BUT IT'S ALMOST OVER FOR NOW — AND SUCH A CURSE IT IS!

But I can save myself this time mama, watch this, one flip and I'm over! "RAMON! DO SOMETHING!"

"Like what leetle seester, no whay I can top thees act?"

The boy is performing the farmyard wheelbarrow and donkey routine, holding Joycee by her ankles while he's shoveling it to her tail, and stomping and braying at the top of his lungs — "MAMA! MAMA!"

"RAMON! CHERYL!"

Joycee's doing her best to try and balance on her hands, but when Will starts to running with her, well, a girl can only pedal along so far so fast and it's *bump, dump* the pay load and roll head over heels, toppling Joycee feet first into the hopper, and who knows whose end's up top when Ramon jumps in for the thrill.

"NO MAMA! NO! NO!" Will Cook howls. "The Beasts have got hold of me!" No fangs though, no claws, but they're crawling off the walls and forcing him to do unnatural acts with the three of them, triple sin, sin cubed, and the she-wolf's engulfing him with a hot pink tongue, pillows are smothering him, whole mouthfuls, though no teeth, only tongue tips and a BILLY GOAT — and he forgot to resist — "Lordy Lord, don't desert me now!" And Will Cook does what he was taught to do when temptation is about to overcome, he starts to buck and kick, out of control, and it's Joycee still riding high on his donkey dick who starts to foam at the mouth, "CHERR-RYL! HRELP MRE!"

Gladly because Cheryl is pissed. Foursomes become threesomes, threesomes twosomes with somebody bound to get left out, though Will Cook's had plenty. He pulls out and crawls away, contentedly finishes off by licking purple gumdrops off the wallpaper while the other three retire gleefully to the waterbed for more — boy's blick sick though mercifully the effects of most inhalants, even when ingested, wear off rapidly.

SCREEEE... SCREEEE... CA-REE-REE-REEEEEEEEEEEE -EETCH!

At approximately the same moment, another deportee from the hinterland, Indiana, Iowa, someplace somewhere way out there, has arrived in the city. Name: Danny T. Specialty: 'Drummer Dynamo'. Rank: High School Senior. And the kid is tight, as in compact, a tank, a scaled down glue-it-together-yourself model, but fully equipped in authentic

"*no mama! no! no!*… The Beasts have got hold of me!"

detail with moving parts, fierce fire power, thick armor, striding straight on track, not about to stop, not for anything. Jaw set, and the veins in his neck permanently popped out, shoulders enlarged, head never veering from right to left, eyes focussed solely on forward march. His father, Walter T was a Marine, fought island to island in the Pacific during World War II and determined to raise his sons, six of them, to be tough too. He did, and Danny T is the eldest.

Kid tore through play pens as an infant, through fences, double timing it in diapers across neighborhood back yards. Every mother on the block was on the alert for him. And where was he going so young? He didn't know, he was a kid born to march to a drum beat wherever it led him. And pound that drum, pound anything, he did, he does, leads with his chin, daring you to take a swing at it, go ahead, see what you're made of jelly belly, he'll pound you.

"Wha's up bro, need a ticket t'the game?"

Danny T nods no.

"Don' wan' t'miss the Knicks while yo in town."

Danny T excelled at contact sports — JV football, wrestling, golden gloves — but he couldn't make varsity warfare because birth had deprived him of an essential element, the critical mass. Danny T is one of life's short guys, and don't think that doesn't account for much if not everything you ever need to know about the boy. Chip on the shoulder? Chip shit! Here's a shoulder smack in your gut fuck, and a crack of the head into some spare teeth. Take a big sucker down before the bell and score extra points.

"Taxi! Need a taxi?"

No, Danny T'll walk where he has to go.

Playing quarterback was his one ambition, so when he couldn't make the final cut, he passed on tournament wrestling and took to the field in his own way, he joined the drum corps. He was pissed and took it out on that drum — *tat tat / tatta-tatta tat / tat tat!* — he enjoyed that. He enjoyed the regimen despite the fact that he had to spend time with potheads and weenie wrenchers. He trotted around that field at half time and made sure everybody in the stands knew he was out there — BWOMB! BWOMB! BWOMB! BWOMB! — louder than anybody else could. Kid has arms. That was his start in music, and the freaks in the corps weren't so bad although they could stash their hash. Danny T was a clean liver, brush cut with a vengeance, scrubbed up, seams creased, spit polished, he finished high school early, honors math and science, got restless he says waiting for the rest of his class to catch up. Decided to hike into New York City meantime, see what was what. Boots, a baseball cap, the Cubs, khaki shorts, knapsack with his sticks poking out, one change of clothing, two-fisted determination and the chin to lead him cross-country.

Danny T's in taking a leak at the Port Authority after a two day non-stop bus ride out of Chicago. He's minding his own business, trying not to get splashed by the back lash when this guy, big guy, steps up to the urinal next to him. "You wanna suck my dick for a nickel kid?"

Big guy likes drinking out of the toilet — "Because here, let me flush it over your forehead again p-brain!"

Port Authority Police try to explain to Danny T that this is an everyday occurrence in New York. Place is full of the demented, so try not to take it personally, OK? "You're here to enjoy the sights and sounds of the city."

The Port Authority Bus Terminal opens out onto 8th Avenue, a quaint and charmingly untouched section of the city. Decades of exhaust grit coat the buildings in a somber gray, sidewalks are spattered with black gum droppings and pigeon shit. Aged old BO wafts out of doorways where bums without socks sleep it off. Whores and taxis stand at the ready on every corner, the pimps parked down side streets in Caddys with gold chrome. Nights are more scenic than daylight anytime, and somebody new to the city instinctively follows the hussle a dark block over 42nd Street toward Time's Square.

"I say gal, what the fuck is that headin our way?"

"Why that there's a Boy Scout hon, out on a campin trip in the city, that's what that is."

Two black girls dressed in tight mini-skirts and low'd low cut blouses, mesh stockings and high shit kickin heels, watch Danny T in his hiking shorts approach. He tries to avoid their stare, but he has never seen two street whores before, not when they're tall, leggy, black and beautiful.

"What's all the hurry little man?"

"Yah, your mama didn't teach you no manners where there's a lady concerned?" The one in the red skirt with the red bow in her hair steps directly in Danny T's path.

"Excuse me ma'am." And Danny T even doffs his Cubs cap.

"I was just tellin my friend Brenda here what a fine little fellow you seem t'be, and so polite. I bet you'd say thank you if a lady was t'reach down deep in your pocket and give you a quick treat, now wouldn't you?"

"*Ah yah, yow...* yes ma'am, I guess I would!"

"See Brenda, told you he was a little gentleman, but you're all grown up some places, aren't you?" And she slides her other hand into Danny T's other pocket.

He worries for his wallet, but she is after his jackknife instead, and boy does that spring open.

"Oooh my, he is a grown up little man, just like I suspected."

She tosses her head back and lets her tongue roll around in her mouth. Danny T's mouth is wide open too, he is taking in air, big gulps.

"You goin t'stand there gapin or you goin t'help Brenda and me out?"

She twists her hand around so she has his balls in one hand and his jackknife in her other, but money is the furthest thing from Danny T's mind as he coughs some.

Brenda, she's in the yellow skirt and matching bow, closes in on him from the behind, frisking his back pockets – Danny T's life savings are tucked securely into his boot however, so it is pocket change that is currently at risk here, that and masculine pride. After the girls are finished picking his bone, this big motha fullback type appears from around the corner: "Hey honky, leave dem girls alone, 'less you can pay, cause dey's wo'kin fo me." Bro's face is right up in Danny T's. "Yo hea's me white boy, git, 'fore I grinds yo inta da pavement." He gives Danny T a bit of a shove, and Danny T, JV footballer, decides it's best to move along, although his jaw is flexing.

Danny T weighs in at 127 and stands 5'5" which is only two inches under the national average, but those are two critical inches, and it's enough to make even a tough sucker like Danny T decide it's better sometimes to burrow in, bide his time.

A well-dressed gray-haired gentleman who has witnessed the ruse nods at him, offers his sympathy and asks if he might be a runaway, one in need of a warm place to freshen up? Danny T declines the offer, and with a well-mannered, "No thank you sir." Boy Scout is learning. The familiar sounds of the city. And Danny T hasn't even seen Wall Street yet, where they are predominantly white and dig into your socks as well as into your pockets, pick the quarters out from between your toes, plus unplug your nuts in one slick twist too.

No. He keeps on walking, hardly varies his stride. His face is young, younger than his seventeen years, and innocent looking, like a kid's.

"Gold chains. Cheap." A dude leaning against a store window offers Danny T a handful as he passes along 42nd Street.

Danny T is not innocent though, he has a reputation as a fast behind-the-line tactician back home, that is, a sneaky type who has more than once found a big guy's girlfriend neglected, squirming his way in for a quickie. The boyfriend invariably figures it out, some sense, some scent – now a big guy might tolerate one of his buddies on the team, might, but a little guy hitting on his girlfriend always bends a big guy way out of shape. And why is that? Why are big guys always suspicious of little guys? Danny T doesn't know. Life's a sport, isn't it, every man playing to win? True, but often it's the little guy who has to leave hometown Iowa or Indiana early after a couple of take-out prom night dinners got spoiled before they were ready to get buttered, and that dip-stick Danny T the culprit.

"Cameras, new… in their original boxes…"

"Not tonight, thank you."

As with any of life's major decisions, there is an accumulation of factors that spurs him outward and onward: athletic disappointment, the mounting threats of scammed lovers, his father's challenge to sign up for Paris Island, and his pals in the band daring him to do it — glums, rumbles, guns or drum rolls — it was the musical that won out.

"You lonely soldier? Need a woman's touch?"

"Not tonight, but I do appreciate the offer." As he turns the corner and catches his first glimpse of New York in all its splendor. Times Square. Lights along BROA-ODD-WAY beckoning. COCA-COLA blinking across a four story sign, JAMES BOND .007 in letters just as bold, featured at the Coronet, MY FAIR LADY at the Embassy, while MARLBORO, SONY, SEAGRAMS 7 AND CHEVROLET make nightlife into daylight, with the bad news from Vietnam winding ticker tape around the top of the Gulf and Western building.

"*Psssst* mister, I got tickets for all the shows… peep holes… anything you wants, I gots…"

Danny T has never smelt a pretzel vendor before, nor seen a nine foot naked cut-out of a lady on a theater marquee — which could be particularly intimidating to someone of the shorter perspective. The sights and sounds of the city, a jaded third world wonder to behold.

"I gots uppers, I gots downers."

People, all sorts of people coming at him from every angle, hundreds if not thousands of people criss-crossing the intersections every side of him, crowding the sidewalks in front of him, streaking yellow taxicabs cutting off all avenues of retreat!

"Postcards! Hot photos! Check it out!"

Too many unfriendlies in too tight a space, and him trapped along with them, walled in by high watt neon.

"Say fella, can you spare some change? I'm down on my lu-…"

Marauding hoards intent on robbing or pillaging or maybe more.

"You lookin for a watch friend? No? How about a diamond ring?"

No. None of these intice Danny T. He is a man on a mission whose only need at the moment is an escape route out of this confusion. Which is when he notices people scurrying into a hole in the ground. Where that hole goes, Danny T doesn't know, but he follows fast fast faster down and down, running alongside on instinct, and at the bottom, some of the crowd breaks and darts toward these turnstiles — *clink, crank, whirr* — and disappear. However, Danny T, as with so many others who neglect to buy tokens in advance, must clog to a halt and a long line-up at the cashier's booth. From this particular vantage point however, he can watch and learn where all these people are going — uptown, downtown, Queens, Brooklyn and the Bronx, on the Broadway Local, the 7th Avenue Express, the A, the

B, the D, the E, the F, even a double RR.

A badge-carrying Boy Scout could lose his sense of direction down underground, though Danny T, unlike Will Cook a few hours earlier, has heard from friends of friends that it is the East Village where he must report in order to be inducted as a musician. And there are brightly colored subway maps also, though they defy interpretation, besides he has finally reached the window of the token booth and he asks the attendant, politely, how much and which train should he take to get to the Village.

"Thirty five cents."

Thirty five cents, yes, no problem, except Danny T has no change in his pocket, no, and his jackknife is gone and his wallet with his driver's license and library card, oh no, missing-in-action and no identification — so he has to dig down deep into his boot, and why all of a sudden are the people in line behind him cursing?

"Ah c'mon!"

"Hurry up asshole!"

"Tourist!" Which is the worst taunt of all.

"What's the matter with the little bastard?"

"Shove him out of the way!"

The mob quickly becomes unruly and begins to make ugly references about his parentage. Are they going to rush him, tear him from limb to limb over thirty five cents? Danny T crouches, prepares for the worst.

"THIRTY FIVE CENTS!" The man in the booth is shouting too. For a lousy quarter and a dime, is this the end of the line? Danny T's down, fingers in his sock, and they're getting ready to trample him.

"THIRTY FIVE CENTS!"

"Here, here's a twenty!"

"HOW MANY YOU WANT?"

"One."

"ONE?"

And it's then, when they hear the twenty for one that they rise up, the multitude behind him, they raise their fists in angry dispute against him.

ONE!!!

Yea, and they shout as with one voice, but not distinctly nor in the same tongue, although their complaint is singularly clear and not at all friendly.

GET HIM! GET HIM!

For the very first time in his life, Danny T feels fright! A Boy Scout alone in New York City with an urge to flee and a need to pee — not again — because that will only take him back to the urinals where this craziness all began. But Danny T is a scrimmager, and so he learns quickly what all New Yorkers know from birth, you hold it, you suck that bladder in and you make a run for it, painful, who cares, and that's what he does, he doesn't even bother to count his change in mangled singles, he simply seizes the brass token from amidst the bills and bolts – *clink, crank, whirr* – the rabble on his heels, through tunnel after tunnel racing onward and beyond toward this ear-splitting shriek of enraged metal monsters. SCREE-EEE-YEE-YEEE-EEEECH! Mighty pythons entrapped for lifetimes in cavernous mazes. REE-REE-REE-EEEEECH! Which train? Which direction? SCRE-SCRE-SCR-SCR-SCR-SCR-SCR-SCR-SCR... In desperation Danny T flings himself onto the mercy of the first train doors he finds open, and...

"Yo man, watch wha' yo is doin, yo could go an kill a brotha jumpin at him like that!"

"Sorry."

"Sorry shit! Sorry don' mean shit!"

"Yes," and a huff and a puff, "you're right. Sor-..."

"Yo suppose t'shout 'scuse me befo yo goes an makes a su'prise move on somebody, that way yo at leas' gives'em a fightin chance t'get out the way!" SCREEEEE-YEE-YEE-YEEECH!

Danny T looks up at this tall black dude with dreadlocks, black leather jacket.

"Will yo look at all this shit the kids have gone an spray painted all ova the insides an all ova the outsides both! Can't see nothin out the windows no mo, I mean can yo believes this shit yo is readin? SOUL RUBBERS – now jus' ezactly wha' is tha' suppose t'mean, I ax yo? An this one, SANTOS 149TH, I mean who cares whea Santos lives, I don', do yo?"

"*Ah* no, not really. How do I get to the East Village?"

"East Village. Ev'rybody these days is headin down t'the East Village."

"Yes sir, that's where-..."

"Yo sho don' look like none a'them kinds t'me. Yo looks like a Connecticut kid lost in the city fo a day."

"Why? What's it like?"

"Is whea all the wei'dos go, night afta' night, they's smokin reefa – from what I ova'hea's anyway – which only gets'em goin big time, dealin in free love an such, listenin t'rock 'n' roll..."

"That's it, that's where I've got to go."

"Boy, yo ain' gots t'go nowhea if yo don't wants t' – ain' nobody gots a gun t'yo head, leas'wise not yet!"

"Wha-...?"

"Kids t'day thinkin if they travels fa enough from home they's goin t'find some place special whea they belongs, so they can be on theia own, an what is it they find when they finally gets thea, I asks yo?"

"*Ah* what?"

"Bunch a lost souls like themselves wand'rin round askin whea am I, whea do I got t'go next!"

"Yes, but which trai-..."

"Subway's full a'lost souls these days, crazy folks an drug heads, tha' wha' yo is inta?"

"What?"

"Yo one a'those subu'ban drug abusa's headin down t'the East Village t'snag some cocaine?"

"No, I'm not into drugs. I'm straight."

"Yo says that now befo yo gets thea, but I'd hate t'meet up with yo afta yo been strung out a couple a'times an dumped on the street."

"I can handle myself."

"No way, yo's jus' a squirt."

"You would be surprised what I can do once I get going, I surprised a lot of people back home, a lot of people!"

"Bet yo did, back home, but su'prise is on the otha guy's side in New Yo'k City."

"I can stay on my toes."

"Which means yo is a tenda'foot, 's that it?"

"I wrestled JV."

"Wrestled? Yo eva been in a knife fight t'save yo eyesight?"

"N-no!"

"NO SIR T'YOU RUNT!"

"No Sir."

"I didn't think yo had, an one mo bit a'advice baby brotha, is yo don' eva want t'be in no knife fight neitha — NO SIR!"

"NO SIR!"

"Yo wants t'be sma't enough t'sense the potential danga a'the situ'ation befo yo goes an gits yoself inta it, not afta it — YES SIR?"

"YES SIR!"

"Like right now, hea yo is rappin wi me like I's yo olda brotha when yo don' even knows who I's is o what crazy thing I might do next — like PULL OUT MY KNIFE HEA AN STICK IT UP NEXT YO HEAD!"

"*Yah-ya-anh-anh-anh!*"

SCREEEEEEEEEEEEEEEEEEEEEEEEEEEEEEEEEEEEEEEEEEEEEEEE!

"Yah, an yo might also notice that out a'a whole subway crowded wi people, thea ain't a one a'them even lookin this way 'cept that kid ova thea, an he ain't bout t'say nothin, not even t'his mama — NOW IS YO BEGINNIN T'SEE WHAT IT IS THIS CITY CAN TEACH YO? Yes? Sir?"

"Yes."

"Sir."

"Sir. Yes Sir."

"Su'vival, tha's wha' New Yo'k City can teach yo — now hand ova yo wallet!"

"No, no, no…"

"No Sir."

"NO SIR! NO WAY!"

"I's got a knife t'yo throat, an yo ain' goin t'hand ova a wallet, a simple shit wallet!"

"Don't have a wallet. Somebody already lifted it."

"Don' say." Dude retracts the knife. "Well, welcome to New Yo'k City anyway, too bad it couldn't a'been me."

"Sorry."

"No botha, thea's plenty a'otha wallets out thea, folks late nights like this'll doze off on the train, makes fo easy pickins, besides I ain' no man a'violence anyways."

"Could have fooled me."

"I jus' found this hea knife in a trash can up at 161st and the Grand Concou'se, somebody prob'ly had t'ditch it in a hur'y — so congratula'tions scout, yo jus' got yo fu'st awa'd in u'ban life savin, mainly yo own."

"Thank you sir."

"Yo knows how t'react fast."

"I try, sir, I try."

"An t'show my admi'ration, I is goin t' give yo this hea knife as a award."

"I- I- I couldn't accept it… I… no, no thank you sir."

"Don' be no fool, looky hea, le' me show yo how — flip open, flip close, fast — couse yo could cut the shit out a'yo own finga's if yo ain' ca'ful."

"Very nice, but I- I still couldn't… accept…"

"Then if yo don' want it as a gift, give me fifteen dolla's fo' it."

"FIFTEEN DOLLARS!"

"Hush yo mouth! Yo don' wan' the brotha's on the train hea t'know I is practic'ly givin this knife away an t'a honky t'boot, does yo?"

"*Ah?* No no."

"An a hair-trigga like yoself is definitely goin t'need a knife in the big ugly, 'specially when yo goes trav'lin on trains by yoself late in the night."

"Ten dollars?"

"FIFTEEN — an don' go tryin chislin me. I's the teacha hea, not yo!"

"Fifteen then, here you go." Danny T counts out his crumpled ones. "Now how do I get to the East Village?"

"…thu'teen, fou'teen, fifteen — that'd be the stop comin up next, jus' hike on upstaia's an yo is thea, an no extra cha'ge fo the di'rections."

"What kind of a scam- con-… artist, are you?"

"Me? I wo'k the subways, make a honest livin."

"You don't look like a train conductor or a…"

"Train hustla boy, I make my livin on the go, always trav'lin to an fro. Somethin bout bein up those staia's an outside on those streets makes me edgy, an believes yo me, yo an the rest a'the folks upstaia's don' want nobody like me up thea walkin round a'med an edgy, neva know what I might do. But down hea I fits right in."

"You must know everything there is to know about the subways."

"That an mo besides — boa'ded up tunnels, stations whea the train don' stop — livin down hea yo develops this special sense bout things, like I always seem t'know ezactly whea t'go, who t'meet up with, like yo."

"Me?"

"Tha's right, like I knows yo is goin t'be somebody mighty suc'cessful, eitha that o somebody who's goin t'get inta a whole lot a'trouble, one o the otha, I can feel it."

"No, I'm a clean kid, I play by the rules."

"Then wha's yo doin in New Yo'k? People don' come hea t'play by no rules, they come hea t'play by no rules at all."

"Can't play a fair game with no rules!"

"Yo said a mouthful thea boy, 'cept the only rule that's fair in New Yo'k is who knows who that can get yo off no matta what you've done — say, wha's yo name anyway?"

"Danny T."

"Danny T. Danny T. So what is it yo is goin t'be doin fo a livin?"

"Drummer."

"Yo don' look like no drumma, yo looks mo like a Marine recruit! Like who was it that cut up yo hair las' time?"

"My father, and he thinks his sons should look clean and mean."

"Clean — yo looks squeeky clean, but mean? Maybe naughty when yo papa's back is tu'ned, but then too yo do gots a devious smile — clean and mean, I likes that."

SCREEEEE-YEE-YEE-YEEEE-YEEECH!

"East Village. Must be somethin goin on up thea tha's wo'th all the trouble. Poke my head up some night, see what's what, might try it, might like it, yo neva' knows."

SCREEEE-SCRA-SCRA-CREEEEEEEEEEEEEEP

"This is yo stop, right up above, so ma'ch on out a'hea, an from now on yo is on yo own, yo hea me?"

"SO WHAT'S YOUR NAME IF I EVER NEED A BUCK'S WORTH OF ADVICE?"

"SALAAM SCOUT! SALAAM KAREEN KABOOM!"

SCRE-SCRE-SCREEEEEEEE-REEEEEEEEEEECH!

Meantime Will Cook has an orchesta seat for this evening's second sex act: Sky dives on the mattress, free style without parachutes. Cheryl has her legs wrapped around Ramon's shoulders while he sips at her lips, bouncing

"Then wha's yo doin in New Yo'k? People don' come hea t'play by no rules, they come hea t'play by no rules at all."

up and down on the water bed with Joycee's mouth glued to his dong, and everything / will be fine / if the three / of them can / hold a few / minutes more / before hitting ground.

But it's an act Will Cook has never seen, neither in real life nor in a movie, both being expressly prohibited in hometown PA — and to witness it done first time in his life and in this remarkably an acrobatic fashion! Well, could be traumatic.

Actually, Will Cook's reaction is more drug withdrawl paranoiac — you know, after the first feelings of free-wheeling euphoria comes the wild fibrillations and flamboyant flip-flops, what's real, what's unreal. Which is why he he must crawl closer to the rim of the water bed to watch.

"Tha's eet Joycee babee, you's makin me feel reel good!"

Yes, yes, and isn't this interesting. Horses and cows do it, though cows don't fly and flap their wings while chewing it, and horses can't hop, skip and jump while they're spewing it. Woman/Man/Woman are clearly the superior of the barnyard animals, for only they can leap and lap while they're screwing it.

"Keep eet up! Keep eet up! Keep eet up!"

Will Cook slithers around the edges, watching, sniffing, and from every possible angle, upended, down wind, floor-to-ceiling skyview, ground sore bottom — a whole head of hair rising up, eyes, big round eyes catching them as they're going at it, nose over the ledge, snorting, teeth chattering, mouth, tongue licking bubbles.

"You know, I just can't concentrate!" Joycee abruptly breaks off and wades out of bed. "This pervert here is making me self-conscious."

"But maybe he gets off on watching," Cheryl soothes, "there are voyeurs in this life, I mean I've met quite a few."

"Si, what ees eet weeth you mon! You don' like white geerls or brown boys or sometheeng? You damn neer queer or simplee prejudeeced?"

Will Cook has no idea how to respond, he loves each of God's creatures, brown white, green naked, clothed furry, smooth wings, no wings, two legs, four legs, dozens of legs, but that doesn't necessary mean he has to jump into the swamp and swim with them, does it? Can't he simply observe nature and be left alone to his private pursuits?

"Joycee pleese, don' leeve me hangeeng like thees."

But Joycee is fucking frustrated, that's what she is. She opens the window wider and calls down to a cop on his regular beat. She implores him to come up and take care of this weirdo she's found in her bedroom. Now mind you, the cop is a young ruddy cheeked Irishman appropriately named Mickey, and he's lookin, he is, square up at a lass framed in a window naked between her neck and her knees, damn-as-hell-in-distress she is, so up duty calls him. He takes the stairs three at a time and she's door wide open waiting for him, with these wonderf'ly full breasts and the soft light brown muff he's so fond of — so t'isn't long before Mickey is into it too, two girls and a Hispanic dude bein all new to him, I kid ya not.

Will Cook is back crawling on the floor and entirely engrossed in the proceedings, his mouth stretched open, his hair permanently parted, and he's making mental notes on each stage of this quadruple depravity.

Mickey, pulls up and out for a second. "Sure'n it's nothin personal, ladies and gents, I'm enjoyin meself immensely, Lord knows, but I'd be puttin it to ya sideways if I didna tell ya straight out that this guy peerin round and about the bed is makin it difficult far me to feel at me ease."

"Yah I agree," Joycee agrees, "kinda creepy. Cheryl dug him up out of the subway and he nearly savaged me."

"I'd be more'n happy to show the lad to the door, if that'd please ya ladies, and you sir as well." The Irish always deferential.

"I say wee drag heem een to eet, keeckeeng or not keekeeng, speeteeng up or sober, and finally see what hee's made of."

Cheryl votes for that one, Joycee abstains, Mickey is neutral, so with a bare majority, they rush Will Cook — and what happens next when the four jump the poor kid, it's no nice at all, no, it's wonderful. For each has her/his/their pleasure with him, take your turn, ladies first, laddies second, and even to this day Will Cook cannot say exactly what happened. He was stoned for one thing, and for another there was this vanishing image of his sainted mother, all in a blaze of color, shapes, textures, indistinguishable probes and probings, fire that snaps and sizzles but consumeth not, and when Will Cook does try to talk about it, and that's certainly not often, he goes into a state of mixed shock and ecstasy, reverse sides of the same old coin, and starts to spin — *whoop whoop* — around on the floor, spitting twittle and squeaking in tongues. See someone like Will Cook, hell like most young guys — admit it — they can boast about what they would do and lie about what they've done, but to be presented with it, all of it at once and on the same night and mattress, plus have the law of the land involved intimately into what is essentially a private act — well, it would be a brave fraternity pledge who could swallow that much swill and stay sober.

And religion? Religion makes sin sublime — flip sides, flip sides.

Whatever. It takes all four of them to carry Will Cook and his cases down the narrow steps to the street. Officer Mickey, generous to a fault, calls in a wagon to help haul Will Cook away, but where to take him is a worry. There's not much open in the middle of the night except the 3rd Precinct and St Vincent's Infirmary, but to put poor Will Cook in the tank with the Bowery Street winos seems cruel and unusual, then too the emergency room boys might ask some embarrassing questions — so what to do, what to do. Driving him round and round is starting to make Will

Cook dizzy, and Mickey, not wanting to provoke a seizure in the wagon, has the sudden unholy inspiration to drop him off at The Green Pagoda, put the boy into the mitts of the scandle-clad monks, for some religion is better than no religion, Mickey reasons, since it is 1968 and the state and the church have been such good bedfellows for so long — so so so so there's where Will Cook gets dumped — *FA KLUNK!* — baggage and all curbside, but no worse for wear, save for his reinforced leather britches which Joycee has kept as a souvenir.

 Boy's sitting there with the chills when a kindly passerby takes note — "Hey theah pahtnah, you ahright? You comin down from a bad shit trip?"

 Another stranger in the night, Will Cook reckons. Beware! Beware!

 "You huhtin anywheah rough?"

 Will Cook's inability to speak, or his reluctance, is understandable, particularly since the stranger asking the question looks himself to be coming down from whatever a bad shit trip is.

 "Been theah myself, big time, dry mouth, shivahs, shock — you might least as well move on ovah heah to the stoop."

 "I-hhh…"

 "And look at all this stuff you'h cahtin — you must be a musician."

 Will Cook manages to nod. To trust or not to trust.

 "H'yep, thought so, I'm a musician myself, play guitah and sing — you want to come upstaihs to my place, take a load off?"

 Not to trust. Will Cook begins to tremble worse.

 "Man, has somethin tehrible happened to you lately?"

 Before poor Will Cook can say no, yes, yes and no, he collapses into — well, the strangah askin all the questions introduces himself as Chippah — into Chipper's arms, and thankfully the monks of The Green Pagoda being eager early risers, as well as reluctant late nighters, rush out the heavy wooden doors of the temple to aid and abet Chipper as he drags yet another recruit in under the sanctuary of their many tiered roof.

 And so it must be purely blind fate, a nearly pure blind fate and assorted ill-wills that bring these two runaway strays in the universe together, and by the benefice of religion no less — a very peculiar sort of religion however, though more of that later — and a roof no matter how odd its shape is a roof, and the monastic routine of The Green Pagoda comes in time to suit Will Cook well, both Will and Chipper.

LOOSE NUKES

0200 hours, 01 May 68. Danny T reports for his first official tour of duty in a new city. St Mark's Place / A gypsy space. Scout commences with an inspection of the designated area, zeroing in on the indigenous population.

"Black beauties. Nickel and dime bags. Got it all. Space Juice and sweet mesc. Best selection in town." A black brother in a camouflage jacket buzzes into Danny's ear and scoots on by.

"The sex wasn't bad," a twig of a long blond haired girl informs a near look-alike, "but he had lousy drugs and his taste in music really sucked!"

Lots of loose cats hangin round.

An intense young guy with black frizzy hair and horned rimmed glasses has another guy in army fatigues pinned up against the wall, talking at him: "The role of the workers army dissolves in a socialist state as the workers return to their economic duties for the good of the revolution. There's no need for a standing army in a true socialist state, all workers are soldiers, all soldiers are workers – understand?"

"Do you sleep with boys and girls or just with girls?" A slender young fellow with green hair and a long hairpin through his eyebrow asks yet another guy in army fatigues – is some reserve company bivouacking in the area?

"I go with whoever gives the best head."

No. Reserve units would be safely bunked in their barracks at this late an hour, Danny T reassures himself as he marches straight ahead, eyes never deviating, ever looking forward, steady stride, yet his ears continue to be bombarded.

"Shit, we were at the emergency room all night waiting. We didn't know whether he was going to pull out of it or lapse into a coma. Idiot tried to jump off the freaking roof man, screaming to everybody down on the street that he could fly — everybody was screaming back up at him, 'Eddie, Eddie, don't do it!' — when he tripped over this antenna cable and gashed his head open on a vent pipe. They had to pump his stomach to get all the chemicals out of him, then they stitched him up and sedated him. Hospital scene was disgusting!"

Danny T marching along is living proof that you can see but not be swayed, hear yet ignore, smell not upchuck.

"Men suck, they're assholes, believe me I know. All they can think about are their dicks. Women are reduced to nothing but fuck holes, and I'm not going to take it any more!" A woman in army fatigues chews a toothpick and glares right at Danny T, their eyes meet, she spits it at him. Danny T keeps walking.

Stray mates / Playin safe / With loads of drugs goin down.

"As soon as they began the hormone treatments, my breasts enlarged — don't you think they're beautiful?" Two guys wearing make-up and designer military garb are staring down at a third guy's bare teats. "Doctor says in a year's time they'll be fully developed and I'll only need monthly maintenance injections, but I just love them, they're so soft and supple," he points them at Danny T and winks, "don't you?"

Danny T stumbles by that one, his mouth dry, his forehead dripping — perspiration, not sweat.

"Motha-fucka, don yo goes tellin me yo don knows 'bout the State a'EEslam! The State a'EEslam is whea it's happenin, whea Black Brothers shall unite an take ova, whea the Black Man shall rule and the White Man shall drool, whea the Black Man shall say ev'rybody be cool, whea the White Man shall play the fool." A tall bro in a dasheki, not in a uniform, is shouting at a group of bros hangin on the court, and he doesn't seem to care whether Danny T overhears him promoting subversion or not.

Danny picks up his pace, but makes a mental note of the surroundings and a brief description of the instigator, should the authorities inquire.

"My father hired this *fucking* private detective after that, tracked me down in *fucking* Baltimore, but I bit the *fucking* bastard on the hand when he tried to grab me at the *fucking* bus terminal. I had to hitch a ride east with a *fucking* trucker who dropped me off under the *fucking* West Side Highway, wanted my ass but got my knee in his *fucking* crotch instead. I've been hiding out here ever since, three *fucking* weeks now." A knock-out good looker with strawberry blond hair all curly smiles at two other girls her own age, and they giggle and they smoke their cigarettes, none of them could be more than fourteen.

"My father tried the same shit, drove into the city one night last week and found me over by the fountain in Washington Square, told me if I didn't get in the car with him and come home, he was going to beat me."

"What did you do?"

"Started screaming 'child molester' at the top of my lungs, and all the people on the sidewalk started yelling at him."

"What did he do?"

"He drove back to Greenwich without me."

"My mother and her boyfriend just upped and moved away," the third explains, "I decided to head home to Paramus for a few days because I was so strung out and I'd spent all my money, but while I was gone they had left, packed my brother, my sister, everything, and moved to Florida."

"You're lucky."

"Yeah, you're *fucking* lucky, they're gone out of your *fucking* life!"

The third one beams.

Danny T finally reaches what seems the furthestmost line of demarcation separating the villagers' enclave from the rest of society, when a cloud of smoke suddenly overcomes him. Chemical warfare and him without his infantry issue gas mask. He gags, tries not to breathe it in, but his vision's momentarily blurred, his head swims — 0230, Danny T forced into an abrupt about face — freaks, flits and sundry unfriendlies — man's surrounded. Maybe the dude in the subway was right, maybe Master Sargeant Walter T back home was right, maybe he should join the Marines, the real Marines. Paris Island couldn't be any more treacherous a terrain than that which he has just traversed.

But right then these two tall attractively slim girls, one with long black hair, the other with light, move slowly by, looking the scout up and down.

Man, real man, he drops his guard immediately.

"Do you think?" The one whispers to the other.

"No way Cheryl, not another one of your subway surprises."

And danger unbeknownst to Danny T passes him by. He steps up to a corner pizza window and buys a slice and a soda, not pop, that's out in Iowa or Indiana. Enjoys his street rations as he stands at ease.

"Hey man!" Tall kid with dirty brown hair tied back in a knot, wire rimmed glasses and the beginnings of a beard is smiling down at Danny T, a sort of normal looking guy, but skinny — short guys instinctively distrust the tall and the skinny. "New in town?"

Danny T nods, he doesn't say yes, he doesn't say no. He's chewing.

"If you need a place to crash, the Lord can provide. All you have to do is believe in Him and He will help. Also, if you leave ten bucks donation, you can get a private room, communal shower. Place is clean, no roaches, and if you're into it with guys, that's OK too." Kid finishes his pitch with a smile. "So, you into it or not?"

Danny is tired — tired tired tired tired — but he shakes his head no.

"You can't afford to believe in the Lord?"

Danny is shaking his head no, but in a way he does believe in the Lord.

"Are you into it with guys? Maybe we could split the rent."

Danny's head starts to rock around – no no no no – rocking so hard it looks as if it could come unscrewed, go rolling off on the ground.

"Catch you later then." The kid waves amiably and ambles off.

Danny fingers his new switchblade and moves away from the pizza window. From the halls of Montezu-U-ma / To the shores of TRIP-o-li.

"Pink and purple microdot. Trip out on the spot."

"Fuckin far-out man, I've been high for three weeks now and I ain't never comin down, never. I can fly man, this time I know I can. I'm gonna climb up on top of one of these buildings man, and try again. I know I can man, I know I can do it!"

"When the State a'EEslam conquers the land, the Black Man shall grow tall, the White Man shall shrink small!"

"I think he's kinda cute Joycee, and cuddly."

"No, I'm in the mood for something beefy."

Danny T is stumbling, his step faltering. Exhaustion can overcome even the most determined scout. We will fight our country's ba-A-tles / in the air on land or SEA.

A guy more like Danny T in appearance approaches him. He is bald, balder than Danny T, who has his own head shaved a bit beyond recruit length. Danny eyes him carefully. Seems a normal Marine except he is wearing a puffy oversized orange shirt, funny material, but he has regular 501s on. Danny T's not sure what to do. "You normal?" Danny T blurts out. "Or are you into religion?"

"Did you just get into town?" A normal sounding voice replies.

Danny T has to trust somebody, doesn't he? This guy's at least eye level and a shaved head is closer to a crew cut than long hair and a earring, but what about a funny orange shirt – *hunh?* – what about that? No Cubs fan would be caught dead wearing that!

"City can be a scary place."

"I guess, see I need a place to stay, but just one night. I have a knife."

"You can sleep at the Green Pagoda and you won't need your knife, and if in time you want to join, you can stay permanently."

"Join?" Danny T's head begins to pivot.

"We're monks, I'm a monk from The Green Pagoda."

"MONKS!" Scout's learning quickly to beware of religions on the street.

"But you don't have to worry, we take vows."

"Like real monks?" Danny T is skeptical, but chastity must at least mean no surprise attacks in the showers.

"Yeah, we're real monks. That's why I shave my head."

"Oh." He starts to breathe easier. Danny T was raised Sunday school religious and he needs some place to stay, besides he can defend himself, he will sleep with one eye open in case he has to, engage superior numbers in hand-to-hand combat. He will hold the line. He will dig in. He will he will, and he's so tired out that he allows himself to be led back down St Mark's Place past dopers and revolutionaries and transgenderalls to an old dilapidated theater, and above where the grand marquee used to be there is now a lone light illuminating a cut-out Oriental style dome, a green many tiered dome, a dome nailed precariously to a couple of 2x4s above the entrance to: The Green Pagoda. Health Food Restaurant. Temple of the Brotherhood. Banquets and Live Bands Every Night Except Mondays.

"You guys run a restaurant?"

"Sure do, you hungry?"

Hungry, recruit's just coming off guard duty.

"The dining room is closed, but I can get you something from the kitchen."

Danny T's stomach thinks restaurant, but his eyes see a guy who's wearing a puffy orange shirt and lives in this gook-like pagoda — "Ah- thanks, I mean it sincerely, but I- I had better keep moving."

Moving moving. Moving moving.

"Get him! Grab him!"

"I'm running as fast as I can!"

"Don't let him get away Cheryl! I've been after this one for weeks!"

Our girls are back on the streets and they're chasing this guy, beefy guy, down St Mark's Place. He's the neighborhood's star receiver, it seems, shoulders and tall as he weaves in and out with the ball and fast, but it looks like he's been injured on the play, ankle hit on the curb, and Joycee has torn half the jersey off his back.

Danny T joins the crowd lining the street. Some cheer, some jeer, some him, some her, but no matter who wins it's going to be a race for the clock.

"Is this the Italian hunk you've been so excited about?"

"Yes it's him! It's him!"

Italian hunk or not he's losing ground to these girls, because, admit it, Joycee and Cheryl are at the peak of physical condition.

"I see what you mean, he's gorgeous!"

"Yes! And look at those buns!"

Joycee is close on him, close enough to claw the rest of his shirt off, and he's a bruiser, a brused bruiser as he has to half hop, half run to stay ahead, not that he's usually runs from the women, no way, he's home grown Sicilian, but these two seem to be flush with adrenaline and no guy can take that much energy after him.

He skips out of bounds and bumps through the crowd — "Sorry, no excuse, sorry sorry" — apologies only slow him down.

"Want an assist?" This miniature packbacker asks, and despite their respective differences in height and mass, the runner replies... "Man, you throw up some interference, and I'd be mighty grateful."

"Can do." Danny T steps off the curb and tackles one — WHOOHP! — Cheryl tumbles into his arms, though he can't stop Joycee, she's nimble she is, skips by, her eye on the prize.

"Sorry, I didn't see you coming!" Danny T attempts...

"Sure."

...at least he's a gentleman about it, sets her right up. She glares at him. Girl is ambivalent about a guy her size or shorter because they're always, always always out to make a point, and ready to sharpen it on her.

"Name's Danny T."

"Fits you perfectly."

"Can I buy you a coke or... or..."

Kid doesn't realize it's those *or ors* that interest Cheryl mostly — "You new in town Danny T, I haven't seen you around before?"

"Matter of fact I am, just got in."

Have you ever.

Meantime Joycee has stradled the stallion, she's leading him limping back to her stable, past three of his street buddies who yell Score! Score! at young Roberto Tomas Aquino Bonnanza, Bubba his nickname, who's from the neighborhood, born and bred on vino and pasta, which means he's no freaky beatnik outsider, though a fling with one of these interlopers is considered fair game for a local so long as he doesn't start hanging with her funny buddies, 'specially the dudes with long hair and earrings — and there have been plenty of fights to establish the territorial boundaries, which Bubba has inadvertently invaded tonight, at least that will be his story — fact is he's been crusin chicks off limits all spring, though this one's so eager she makes him nervous. Yeah he's stud, but who else in the herd has been running with her?

Late like it is though, and a turn down a dark lettered street, what the hell, he's not scheduled to open the restaurant in the morning.

It's tread those same well-sworn steps, and tiptoe by Ramon's door because Joycee's intent on savoring this juicy meatball all by herself — and hey what's this in the dark, seems Bubba's never taken an after hours swim in a waterbed before and floating alongside, *whoa-oa no*, another couple and going at it — not the *paesano* style, though to each his own, as *slosh slosh* he's suddenly got two girls all over him and that's not so bad so long as this other dude keeps his distance — except here's a blow of smoke down your throat which is something of a religious conversion as both Danny T and he *choke choke* – stuff doesn't go down easily, but packs a wallop as Bubba and Danny T drift off to sea with two babes from Jersey.

First thing to say after you've stayed all night in an East Village walk-up is sorry, you've got to catch an early flight out because there's nothing to talk about in the morning. What you've been willing to do with strangers you don't want to discuss, and if it's more you might hanker after, you're better off with a different set altogether. So maybe some instant coffee but hold on the toast, a cigarette is harmless and here's a note with a wrong number, cause I'm out of here with not even a first name exchanged if I can avoid it, and dude, settle for a handshake, if we ever do meet up again be man enough not to say nothin, I'll do the same. Wish I could forget, but damn that was somethin else again, wasn't it!

"Listen, one question before you split."

"Yah?"

"Appreciate some help man. I know I'm way out of my league here in this city, but I can't just hop the next bus back home, not for at least a couple of weeks, my pride I suppose, but I'm lost, like turned around worse than I've ever been."

And there's something to be said about an honest question between two guys even though they'd probably be best off parting paths and never crossing the line again.

"Sanest place I've heard for any normal guy is the Green Pagoda…"

Gasp!

"…dudes who run it dress sorta strange, but I hear they keep to themselves and they serve the best lunch around."

"So you're saying it's safe and at least I can eat."

"C'mon, let's go – catch you later girls – I'll point you in the right direction. Name's Bubba by the way – can you keep your mouth shut?"

Couldn't pry Danny T's jaw open with a crowbar.

Brunch, that's what they do in New York, a breakfast buffet that runs past lunch through to supper because the city gets up late on Sundays, monks too, who practice what they preach and serve up nourishment for the body as well as for the soul, beautiful souls with beautiful bodies who file through the wide open gates of the Green Pagoda.

God knows they have their detractors, these monks, but what religion doesn't thrive on the spite of skeptics? Then too, what harm could nine young monks really do? They are for all outwardly appearances the kindly proprietors of an *au naturel* restaurant which specializes in herbal remedies and microbiotic health foods among other vaguely Oriental recipes they concoct downstairs in their steamy catacomb kitchen, toiling endlessly but without complaint, sleeping only until noon, at which time they awaken to chant tantric verses while they perform astounding ritual limbering-up exercises, contortionists *extraordinaire*, their sole common vow to take any and all pleasures whenever they can and how!

Later afternoons they creak open the double carved doors to the Pagoda — that's about four, four thirty weekdays, five thirty, six on Saturdays and Sundays, closed Mondays for R&R — and with clanging gongs they invite their converts and regular paying customers inside to a fab food fest. The monks forswear all animal flesh, alcoholic beverages, no caffeine nor nicotine, but they do allow smoking of a kind in the environs of the temple, holy smokes, with incense sticks burning as cover.

The ambience of The Green Pagoda is religiously hedonistic, the aura emanating directly from the sinewy shaved bare skinned monks themselves, swathed in their tight blue jeans and fluffy open orange shirts, beckoning their wary visitors to enter and to remove their shoes, their clothes along with whatever else of earthly encumbrance might interfere with free spiritual communing.

Once divested of all material attachments, visitors are ushered up the divided staircase of this once grand theater lobby, where they gaze in wonder uninterrupted at life size tapestries that portray the sect's many armed, ample legged, thinly veiled and heavenly endowed gods and goddesses who cavort through eternity in ingeniously inventive poses. Such is their instruction before they're led as neophytes through curtained archways into the Sanctuary Itself where crystal chandeliers give way to flickering votive candles. And if the sudden plunge into darkness causes a momentary blindness, so sporadic bursts of light from stick matches, accompanied by choke choking sounds, illuminate the scene quite clearly as the faithful sit and smoke, or recline and smoke, or sprawl out entirely after they have smoked, kicking back on the oriental rugs and up against stuffed feather pillows that have been furnished for their comfort throughout the main floor, mezzanine and overhanging balconies, all the steely folding seats having been long before removed.

The food as well as all associated services the monks provide for free, their guests asked only to donate what they have with them. Some of the kids offer a few bucks or some coins, others donate their time, some their bodies, but more of that later. Most simply contribute their presence, for they are numbered among life's larger audience, partakers in the crowd, for The Green Pagoda is a happening scene man, a happening scene, people doing their thing man, doing their thing or often enough doing each other's things. It's free love and free trade in Class C and D substances. For the monks practice a form of *laissez-faire* mercantilism with any proceeds going to support the brotherhood's charitable endeavors which remain largely unaccounted for, as with most non-profit enterprises, although rumors of a sacred trust and a behind-the-scenery foreign benefactoress are rampant. But then these are the go-go days of the 60s, and whatever financial foundation The Green Pagoda rests upon might be shaky long run, but short term there's sufficient capital to float the love boat.

"What do you think Will, think you could lay back on these pillows heah and enjoy the tastes of Heaven fah a while?"

Will Cook is conflicted. The food is certainly fine, and the company, well the company quite frankly seems unusual even for someone such as himself who saw next to no one outside his hometown Motherly Love.

"Anothah houh oah so and they staht up with the flooh show, band playin, gihls naked and dancin in a cihcle, guys too, humpin in from behind, anythin goes so long as youh pahtnah oah pahtnahs ah willin — *whoo-ee skoobeedobedobedo-ee!*"

Will Cook's eyes search for the exits, so that right after the lights dim, he can make a break for it.

Not all is hot tea with rosebuds at The Green Pagoda however. As with any suspect new religion, these monks are being routinely persecuted for their faith and ritual practices by an sanctimonious alliance of the New York City Health, Housing and Fire Departments united under the supervision of the New York City Police Department, the Controlled Substance Division, led almost singlehandedly by one zealot, Lieutenant Jepson L. Grady. Send in an Irishman to do the dirty work, you might say, but Jepson is a dark Irish, very dark, originally from Mississippi, and Jepson has no tolerance for the spiritual underpinnings of the monks' ostensibly illegal practices. Frequent and unannounced health code inspections, firemen tramping through on false alarms, narc raids, these are what have driven the monks underground, though the full force of Jepson's might has been stayed more than once by the mysterious benefactoress who lurks backstage or sometimes way up two balconies in the old projection booth. It is she, *she* they say, who smote the hand of Lt. Jepson L. Grady when armed with a bench warrant he was about to advance with his allies to smite the troublesome monks in one finely pitched advance. But stayed he was by a higher, an appellate power, which is how it should be for freedom of religion and gathering and personal choice. These rights must be protected despite the religion in question or the miraculous or not so powers that sustain it over time, the stuff of rumor, mystery and finger-pointing, for otherwise no blind faith would be required of anyone, then what — everybody'd be out of business fast, constitutional plutocracies included!

"You and me, we get a band togethah, and the monks'll let us bang around up theah on that stage instead of those dudes." Chipper points to the old theater proscenium arch, high carved gilded with plump cherubs, a deep maroon velvet curtain, stage big enough for the girlie burlesque show of its previous reincarnation, along with peep holes in the basement. Certainly the 60s with their wide-eyed open indulgence for the purient is an improvement over that closeted 50s tawdry.
"Wow!" Will Cook likes the sight of that idea. "Think we could?"
"Just got to believe in youhself and do it, make the music happen."
Doin it, that's what Will Cook's all about, makin muisc too.
For the monks are generous supporters of the arts, rock 'n' roll an essential part of their ritual, plus they're tolerant of Chipper's skepticism and his practicing full blast inexperienced late into the night, late while the monks busy themselves with their religious duties elsewhere.
So along with the prospect of a respectable gig, Chipper and now Will are allowed to bunk way high up in the old theater dressing rooms located on a narrow metal walkway above the stage, while the monks, who prefer an ascetic life, sleep it off in the caves underneath the stage. For it's dark and dank down there and conveniently located near their centrally heated Chamber of Mysteries — which would make for an interesting digression — but suffice it to say that there is a symbiosis at work between monk and musician, but with any mutually beneficial dependency, some unexpected force can intervene. Molly Dawkens is such. Though she comes later.

Up in the balcony of the Pagoda, Bubba Bonnanza, street stud, has had his Sunday brunch and settled in for the stage show. He's kicked back on some pillows and imbibin on some weed. Seems since his induction into the sins of the 60s the night before, along with Danny T, man can't get enough, and him from a good Catholic family too.
"Kinda looks like things are heatin up kid."
"Yeah, like heavy." Danny T doesn't imbibe and is reluctant to kick back, all sorts of sordid things going on around him in the dark. Twos, threes, maybe more and of which deviation he's not sure, except he's certain no other Marines are sprawled about — yeah well, catch your buddies right out of basic and see what they do for thrills.

Last light flickers out and a low moaning ensues, *oohs aahs*, zips tugs, the floor suddenly seething in bodies, surges and an undertow, catch the unwary and pull them below – even Danny T is forced to succumb – and Will Cook who couldn't make it to the emergency exit in time – you can hear him loud above the crowd, beating futilely at the waves of whatever flesh engulfs him – *blub blub blub* – but there's no escape from this escapade, whether you were brought up strictly or not, the whole known world engaging in random sexual activity at the cost of what, the collapse of civilization most assuredly – not that these kids give a good goddamn about that, world's a theater isn't it, full of live jive entertainment?

CREEEP! CREEEP! CREEEP! CREEEP! CREEEP!

"What the flyin fuck?"

Fire alarms that's what – CREEEP! CREEEP! CREEEP! – set off by the smoke, of which *cough cough* there is much and a pretext for calling in the Fire Department, like ax through the front doors guys – while the audience gropes for their clothes – without the house lights, there's only flashlights wielded by these boots in asbestos slickers who are trooping through, Lt. Jepson L. Grady at the ready to arrest them no matter what twisted positions these kids have gotten themselves into, because the practices of the Kama Sutra do not impress him, nor young girls pleading on their knees in his way as he searches for the shaved-headed perpetrators of a long list of felonies – "There goes one! Nab him!" – it's tubby Brother Luke who's not as fleet of foot as the other monks who go scurrying down a hole hidden underneath the stage, Chipper dragging Will Cook in after him – Will blathering and blubbering and followed along by one Bubba Bonnanza and right behind him and to his great relief, Danny T, who would never let himself be taken alive – come and get me copper – particularly on a morals charge, no, sin wouldn't play well back home in small town Iowa or Indiana – so down down they trundle into the basement catacombs *splash splash* all dank damp, puddles of it.

"Name's Chippah."

"Bubba."

"This heah's Will Cook."

"*Ah-* Danny T, name's Danny T."

While above – *thud thud thud thud* – the Law's got the rest of the kids under its thumb.

"Best three out of five?"

"H'yep, you'h on."

Raid's over, it's after hours, and men only behind sanctuary walls.

"Got to call out ball and pocket beforehand."

Chipper's teamed up with Will Cook shooting pool in the monks' panelled game room. Will's blinked back and he's into it, though he has a peculiar way of handling his cue. Danny T has scratched twice and this wide receiver he's got for a new partner is giving him endless grief about it.

"I say the way to approach a gihl is pretend you don't want nothin from huh, don't even ask huh name, let huh make the fuhst move and play real reluctant like. Ahways wohks fah me — yellow stripe in the side pocket."

"Nice shot!"

"Thank you, thank you."

"Suppose she walks away?"

"Then no way you wah goin to make it with huh anyway — red back heah by me."

"No way you're going to make this shot anyway."

"Step back, give me some breathin room. Ain't sayin it'll be easy."

"What if she's a real smoker?"

"'Spose you could phone huh, aftah a few days claimin you'd misplaced huh numbah."

"But you said you didn't even ask her name."

"Say hey babes, what's happenin? — Damn, missed on that one!"

"My shot."

"Here comes scratch number three."

"I'm the first to admit this isn't my game, OK? But there's more to life than hanging around the neighborhood pool hall." Danny T's about to take a shot and Bubba's sniping.

"What do you do for fun out on the farm kid, count fence posts?"

"Whoa! You two goin to bickah all night long oah shoot some pool?"

Danny is forced into a tricky bank shot, but damn if he doesn't make it. "Let's hear it for the farmboy!"

"That's a scratch fella, cause you didn't call it out fihst."

"No way! Bubba, do something!"

"Hang out with the big boys, you've got to follow their rules."

"Willy's up next — so what's youh take on the ladies? You haven't said nothin all evenin?"

Will's a little shaky still, perversion on stage and a police raid are all new to him, as is this game they're attempting to play.

"Remembah, you've got to call out youh pocket."

"Hey, no coaching!"

"My buddy heah's nevah shot pool befah."

"Mine neither."

"Blue, the blue striped ball in that pocket over there." Will Cook taps it with his stick — "There." He looks around at everybody, everybody curious at how exactly he's going to do it.

"Tough shot."

"No coaching!"

Will Cook's never even seen a pool table before, nor was he ever allowed to stand around idle with three other boys and play any game, but he's intent on learning. Simply a matter of raw physical laws, force, motion, a series of chain reactions which is the most difficult part to calculate…

"Can't wait all night."

"It's not morning yet? Does anybody here even wear a watch?"

Danny T left his at Cheryl and Joycee's and has no intention of going back and retrieving it.

"Hold on, hold on fellas, don't go makin my boy nehvous."

…except if I strike the white ball down here low off center and with just enough spin off the wrist — *craaak* — yes, I get it, it's only a matter of concentration, at which Will is expert.

"Looks like he's doing OK for himself."

Will's zeroed in on another one, he calls a hole and goes for it, solid orange in the pocket.

"Thank you very much, that's one our team won't need to bother with." Bubba stands, moves slowly around the table.

"Wait. It's still my turn, isn't it?"

"Naw, you sunk one of theih balls, we'h striped, remembah?"

"Number five, center left pocket — *whappp* — I say you have to be nice to a girl, treat her with respect, show up with flowers — three, left back corner — *whappp* — she'll cook dinner — six… six over here near me — *whappp* — then tuck you in for an all-nighter — eight in the far right — *whip-pip-pip* — shit!"

"Damn, that was close — and I say skip dinnah, cause you can ahways pick up a slice aftah somethin nice you didn't have to pay fah."

"Why bother with any preliminaries, seems like in this city all you have to do is stick out your thumb."

"Kid's got a point, lots of free love in the streets these days Chipper."

"Open season on puntah — evahrybody ready fah anothah cool one?"

"Sure."

"I'll fish some out of the coolah."

"Clean the game up for us kid, the sooner we win, the sooner we can step outside and score!"

"You're kidding, you're ready for more?"

Bubba just grins.

"What is it you two have been smilin about all evenin, act like a couple of squihrels with a secret stash all theih own."

"Mutual acquaintance."

"She a spinnah, is she?"

"Which she?"

"Hey now, we agreed we wouldn-…"

"Don't need to say no mah, my man Bubba heah sounds like he's just gone and incriminated himself — been passin some honey back and fohth between you two, that it? With oah without the flowahs?"

"My lips are sealed — one last shot's all we need."

"Whoa, don't tell me the stud heah goes in fah groupies?"

"Hey! None of that, it's against my religion."

"Then how come you'h tuhnin crimson?"

"Black, corner pocket." *Fwup fwup fwup* — Danny T does it! *Fwup fwup fwup* — followed right along behind by the cue ball… "Fuck!"

"Must be that guilty conscience you boys've got, whatevah peculiah you'h into — so what's the rule, we get the game on a scratch oah do we have to play it through?"

"Let's see you do it."

"Challenge Willy, I heah a challenge. Means it's up to me to sink it. Stand aside." WHAACK -THUNK! "That seem to do the trick?"

"Nice shot there Chipper…"

"Thank you, thank you."

"…except you forgot to call the pocket."

"Bubba?" Chipper rolls a thick joint, passes it over to Danny T who declines and hands it off to Bubba.

"Chipper?" Bubba takes a short toke, winces, and gives it to Will Cook. Man goes at it in earnest — *puffff -puffff -puffff.*

"Got a question."

"Shoot."

"Cool dude like you can't be just bluff and blustah."

"No?"

"Nope. I sense down undah that tough exteriah theah's this gentleman, like a good family man — am I right about that?"

"Hey. Guy gets older he wants a wife and kids, something dependable."

"H'yep h'yep, you've definitely got a sehrious side, romantic, some sweetheaht somewheah you haven't been tellin us about."

"Me? How about you?"

"Nevah have had a steady in my life."

"That a boast?"

"I'm not as bad-ass as you figuhe, truth is no gihl will have me…"

"I can believe that."

"…fah mah than a string of one nightahs."

"You're so full of it."

"Truth is gihls mostly go throwin themselves at me…"

"*Annh.*"

"…no no, that's why I say only way to treat a woman is ignohe huh, make huh come to you. Guy who looks despahrate's goin to stay that way."

"Attitude might work with a girl you meet casually, but one who's nice, one you kinda like, you've got to be a gentleman right from jump, otherwise she's going to pass you by."

"Hey, while we're on the subject, why is it that a girl who belongs to another guy always looks the most attractive?"

"That says a lot about you kid."

"What?"

"Don't know, Danny T might be right, guy can waste a lot of time goin aftah what he can't get."

"Dude comes sniffin out my girlfriend gonna get pounded."

"Theah you go gettin all protective, I say theah's a steady in youh life."

"If, if I had a girlfriend."

"She hot?"

"Don't start."

"Nope nope, though I 'spose she'd have to be to keep you intahrested."

"Let's drop the subject guys. Marcy's off limits."

"Mahcy! Least we got a name."

"I'm not sayin nothin more."

"She pretty? Oah one of those who ah bettah known fah pahsonality?"

"Marcy's damn good lookin, damn good lookin, has every guy in her class after her."

"Then how come you're hanging out with us tonight, not with her?"

"Parents sent her away to camp, said she was too young to go steady."

"And you'h the culprit."

"End of story."

"How young's young?"

"I'm not gettin into it. She's very mature for her age."

"Eleven?"

"No way!"

"Thirteen?"

"Fourteen. She's starting her sophomore year."

"Whoa, and you wah the senioh football hero! No wondah huh parents ah busy hustlin huh out of town."

"And in September they're sending her to an all girls boarding school in Pennyvania."

"Where in Pennsylvania?"

"Saint Heloise in someplace named Barnsburg."

"That's near where I live- lived… lived."

"So in the meantime you've got to hit the streets nights like we do?"

"For a while, I mean what's a guy supposed to do?"

"H'yep, don't want to be no introvaht, hackin off in youh sock, now do you Will? Look at you ovah theah suckin down that weed. Believe I've created a monstah."

-puffff -puffff -puffff

"So what's the endin to the stohry Bubba, ain't you and Mahcy 'sposed to live happily evahaftah?"

"Except for her brother."

"What did he do, come after you with a shotgun?"

"I should've come after him, the asshole, he's the one who started all the rumors."

"Rumahs?"

"I used to hang with him, we were on the team together, and he fell in with a go-nowhere crowd and got cut from the team senior year, wasn't my fault or nothin. But before that happened we were close, I'd be over at his house and he had this kid sister, Marsy, which is short for Maria Teresa..."

"So what happened?"

"...it was nothin really. Innocent. I'd be over there after practice and she'd be beboppin around, cute little kid, always with the wise remarks, messin... She liked to play rough, she'd come hit at me, we'd wrestle on the floor some. She had these three older brothers see, and she had to defend herself. They were always pickin on her."

"Was she mah than cute?"

"Ah man, beautiful. Soft dark hair, big bright eyes, glowin, sparklin up at you, and smilin, always smilin..."

"Fihst love."

"Didn't start out romantic, maybe a crush. She was just this kid and fun..."

"They ahways ah."

"...fun to spar with. Then one evenin after I'd stayed for dinner she was tellin me about the guys in her school always hittin on her, and I said, well that's because you're a looker and you're gonna have to learn to live with that. She says, you really think so? I say, if I was a guy in your class I'd be fightin to be first in line, and she sorta looked at me this way, and I guess... I can remember it, still feel it, I was lookin back at her the same way. It was-... it was love at first sight and I lost it, I leaned over and kissed her."

"Whoa! Romeo and Juliette."

"It was this somethin about her, somethin I'd never felt before, never felt since — and it was alright for a while, nobody noticed much and come homecoming I asked her to go with me — that's when she and me suddenly became this big deal… See, I'd been elected homecoming king so she automatically became the queen…"

"At the tendah age of fouhteen."

"…her family freaked. But they sorta had to give in, I mean what self-respecting mother is going to deny her daughter the opportunity to be homecoming queen? Only rule was I had to have her back home right after the dance, twelve thirty, one tops. Did. Shook her dad's hand. Seemed everything was goin to work out fine, except for her brother…"

"That when old envy reahed its ugly head?"

"I dunno, maybe, probably… anyway we ended up in this brawl on the street, he was goin on and on about me hittin on his kid sister, and I mean he was no piker, he caught me square on the nose, I had blood all over my clothes, but I finally decked him, dislocated his jaw and knocked out two front teeth. From then on the family was after me."

"Whoa. Feudin family, really is Romeo and Juliette. She pissed?"

"Don't think she knows what to make of it. It's not like we can sit down and talk about it. Don't even know if my letters get through. She writes, but there's this disconnect somewhere, and the brother's spreadin rumors that I'm fuckin around with every chick in the Village…"

"Along with their roommates."

"Look. We had this agreement."

"Just joking."

"Yeah, but I don't need any bad press, I've got to keep up appearances."

"Which is a lot hahdah than bein downright devoted."

"I'm a guy. What am I supposed to do, tie it in a knot?"

"Hey, you could always join a monastery!"

"Right. Any of my buddies find out I'm hangin around here with you guys and I might as well resign from the team."

"Thought you had graduated ahready?"

"You got to hang with your buddies in the neighborhood."

"You should know theah's a back entrance down an alleyway. I'll show you, cause why miss out while you'h battlin on the home front?"

"You're jaded."

"Only the best of my obvious chahractah defects."

"I'll drink to that."

"Let's do a toast… to the good Monks of the Green Pagoda!"

"Bettah get some beeh fuhst — who heah needs a refill?"

"I could use one."

"Me too."

"How about you Willy boy, oah ah you still nuhsin that wahm one you've got tucked in between youh knees?"

"I- I'm fine, really I'm-..."

"So how about you Danny T, what soht of stohry've you got?"
"Yeah kid, what's love life like in midtown USA?"
"Not much to tell."
"Like nothin to tell?"
"Like nothing like the big city has to offer." And he glances over at Bubba. Both smile.
"Just what is it you two've been up to?"
"Lips are sealed."
"Needs anothah beeh to loosin up his tongue — evahrybody up?"
"Man, am I missin somethin or didn't I just get one?"
"Yeah, I've got two sitting here in front of me."
"I'll have one, thank you."
"Will? That you talkin?"
"Yes. Thank you. I've finished drinking this one." He holds it up for everyone's inspection, and indeed the bottle is empty.
"Damn, you take to vices ahmost too eagahly."
"Are you going to roll another one of your... cigarettes?"
"Joint. That's called a joint Will, and theah's a dead one sittin ovah theah next to Bubba who had a puff off it and fahgot to pass it on."
"Sorry. This shit makes me do strange things."
Danny T laughs out loud, loud out loud.
And Bubba grins some.
"Some joke you two got between you, but that's what dope's fah, ain't it, gets you to do strange things and think even wiehdah, right Will? This stuff fuckin up youh head oah what?"
Will Cook nods agreement, and hauls in harder — *whuff -whuffff ...cough ...cough ...cough!*
Chipper claps him on the back. "Ruin youh lungs, though not as bad as tobacco, and fouh times the high — plus those dreams that come rushin out of control!"
Will Cook can agree to that. His eyes are wide and clearly gaping at some scene not of this room, some scene of another room, far off, or not so far off, merely a few blocks away on Avenue A.
"I stick to beer."
"Nothin bad about both Danny T, fact is good beeh and good smoke wah meant fah each othah, like some immutable law of natuhe, likes attractin, dislikes distractin — but heah, let me pass you the whole coolah, just in case me and Will heah drift off."
"Set it right here, because I'm waitin to hear what this kid's made of."

"I've got some stories I can tell, I don't need inducements."
"Bet you do. Somethin about the glint in youh eye."
"Does, doesn't he. Lights up like a firecracker."
"H'yep, mischief makah, what we call back home an instegatah."
"Not too much at pool."
"You going to keep bringing that up?"
"I was gettin kinda tired of carryin us both."
"Wait wait, befah you two staht in rehashin the game, remembah we ah even up, Willy Boy and I won two, you two won two, the winnahs have yet to be announced."
"Right. Besides it's story time."
"Fihsties."
"First kiss or first time?"
"Whoa! Sex is always bettah!"
"YAL!"
"You say somethin Will?"
-puff -puff -puff
"Well, summers I got sent away for six weeks to this boys camp in the woods, run by the Granary War Veterans, 2nd Regiment. We all belonged to their Junior Infantry Division…"
"Juniah boot camp?"
"No, just a regular summer camp, girls' camp was right next door…"
"Stahtin to sound intahrestin right off – right Willy Boy?"
"Right, right right… right." Will looks around.
"…on this isolated island in the middle of a lake…"
"No escape?"
"You would have to swim for it. So anyway…."
"Skip straight to the juicy paht."
"Hey, let him tell his own story. Start from the beginnin. Don't leave nothin out."
"You know Bubba, I'm beginnin to think you'h a softie down deep theah in youh gut, a lovahboy."
"Italian. What can I say?"
"I'll drink to that!"
"To the Italian!"
"In all of us!"
"OK, cut the shit. Let's hear the story."
"Wasn't a bad place, swimming, canoeing, fishing, camping…"
"Fingah fuckin in the bunks."
"…target practice on the duck pond…"
"So where were the girls?"
"There was some woods in between camps, and a fence…"

"A mind field too?"

"The HQ separated the girls' side from the boys', the commander's house in the center, the dining hall and the infirmary, the library…"

"Ahways got to be a fuckin librarhy at a summah camp."

"Like you're goin to read or somethin."

"…every morning at 0700 we had to muster for the flag raising, boys and girls…"

"Check each othah out."

"Big time, and every afternoon during drill."

"Two nevah got togethah?"

"Every Saturday evening after mess there'd be a mixer, ice cream and cokes and we had to dance…"

"Rock 'n' roll?"

"No way. Pat Boone. And we had to abide by the Junior Officers' Code."

"Which was?"

"Shoulders back, chin high, never flinch nor slouch, and button up your fly."

Will Cook nods, sagely, and puffs on that joint like a baby with a sucker.

"So at first I just swam and played baseball, caught frogs, you know, I was ten, eleven, and it was fun. I had my friends and we'd get into a little trouble when we could. Hiked off on our own once and ran up against a bear with a cub, frightened the shit out of us…"

"Theah wah beah on that island?"

"Big bear, and deer and some coyotes they were always trying to hunt down… anyway, we got brave and we'd sneak out after taps…"

"H'yep. Night time is the best time in the woods."

"The Devil's time, my mother said. She would come in and comfort me when I got spooked." Suck suck on that sucker, Will Cook.

"…at first we'd go skinny dipping in the frog pond or paddle out in a canoe in the moonlight…"

"Ow Ow Owwww!"

"Yeah, it was scary sometimes and we'd sit in the dark and tell ghost stories — got caught a couple of times, had to spend the morning doing KP — but as we got older and started to change, we'd sneak across the drill field and head through the woods…"

"Climb ovah that fence?"

"…real quiet man, we didn't want to get caught…"

"What would they have done?"

"Pack us off on the bus, first thing in the morning."

"Lots of boys get sent home eahly?"

"As we got older, there'd always be a few more, but I never got caught, well I did, but-… well anyway we'd climb over the fence and sneak real slow through the woods. One of the girls' barracks was set way back from the others, the older girls' barracks…"

"H'yep h'yep, but not like nobody planned it that way oah nothin."

"The veterans had built everything themselves, you know, back after the war, built all the buildings out of planks, and sometimes there'd be these gaps, like in the walls of the showers…"

"Convenient."

"…right, and you could crawl underneath and look up through the floorboards…"

"And what did you see?"

"Man! Everything! And they'd talk about it all the time, worse than guys, I mean they didn't hold back nothing at all and about every guy we knew, what he had for equipment, how far he'd go — it was an education!"

"Sex's got to be the best."

"Same topic night after night. We'd just lay there underneath the floorboards with the racoons and listen to them talk."

"What did they say about you?"

"Ahh- nothing special."

"Nothin special! That's wohse than bein a lonah pahvaht."

"They called me a kid, kinda cute."

"Name stuck from the beginning then?"

"Sort of. Provided me with a cover."

"You nevah got caught oah nothin? They nevah heahd you down theah breathin heavy?"

"Well, my buddies got tired. After a late-nighter you weren't much good for drill or baseball, and once we got penned under there by a family of skunks. We didn't dare move and it was almost daybreak befor-…"

"C'mon, c'mon, wheah's the juicy paht?"

"…so well, I started sneaking out on my own, I guess I was more, you know, hornier than the rest…"

"Plus you had to prove you were more than a cute kid."

"…so one night — I mean, I had been having this feeling all along, like somebody was watching me, you know how you have this feeling? Like eyes on you?"

"H'yep, suhe do."

"And I was always looking around, checking, I could feel it, I knew it, but still I kept going back."

"Wohse thing that could happen was you'd get sent home?"

"Worse than worse. You don't know my father, he was a war hero and my mother would have cried, oh my God, I didnt want that — but I couldn't help myself…"

"How about the Juniah Chiefs' Code of Honah?"

"I tried, man-o-man did I try! But it was like I couldn't control it, so one night I was under the floorboards — I knew somebody was watching, and I said to myself I'll crawl out of here, I'll sneak back to barracks and if I make it without getting caught I'll never come back here again, promise. So I slid out real slow, and quiet, didn't make a sound and just as I was clearing the porch these hands reach down and grab me by the shoulders, yank me out from under there and drag me struggling into the woods. I was so scared and it was so dark I couldn't see who it was. Threw me up against this tree and then I saw, it was this older girl, strong, a junior corporal, and I started apologizing for what I had done, I was sorry, I knew this was sick but..."

Suck, suck that smoke, Will Cook.

"...she didn't listen to a word I was saying, she had her hands on my belt and my shorts jerked down so fast I didn't know what was happening and, man, she was on me like crazy... lapping at me with this tongue, seven times, eight times man, I couldn't keep count, I couldn't think, I couldn't believe... that had to be a record... I mean all I knew it was the most wonderful feeling I had ever had in my entire life!"

"Whoa! Did you go back fah mah the next night?"

"No damn it, she didn't show for muster, and I heard later she had been sent home for crossing the line. She didn't come back next summer either."

"Sad endin."

"Wasn't so bad. Senior girls started looking at me differently after that."

"H'yep. Bet that's about when you stahted in drummin big time."

"Did as a matter of fact."

"Restless hands, that's what makes fah a musician."

"The first argument I ever had with my dad was over rock 'n' roll."

"H'yep."

"Got me so frustrated I started banging on things, out of control."

"I got serious with my guitar after Marsy left, gave me somethin to do."

"Like theah's some soht of connection between lust and music."

"Between sex 'n' drugs 'n' rock 'n' roll."

"That too."

"Seems like we all shahe a common intahrest."

"Universal."

"So what say we get togethah, play some, see how we sound?"

"I'd give it a shot, but I've got to work in my folks' restaurant evenin's 'til closin, that's Fridays and Saturdays too, Sundays off."

"Looks like it's goin to be late night reheahsals — you in Danny T?"

"This is what I came to New York to do."

"H'yep h'yep — Will?"

"*Uh -uh...*"

"Guy hasn't got much of a choice from what I can see."

"Nope, Willy's with us, fah bettah, fah wohse."

Will. Will Cook's inside that head of his, balls knocking about on a table, monks ducking into the basement, sex in the woods, girls washing their privates in public while somebody somewhere else has gotten slugged in the face, left to bleed to death on the pavement, boy's got to confess, cleanse himself entirely of sin, sex with a minor or a major leaguer is wrong, any sex at all, by yourself, seed is wasted, ground under foot, never to grow to fruition, but there seems to be so much to spare, though one drop's enough to set off a commotion, and Elder Hubert to beat you into submission, it could make a grown boy suspicious — *puff -puff -puff* on this cigarette — mama, make it all go away, but why does it stay stuck in my brain like spray painted gooey all over the walls…

"Like that stuff, don't you Willy Boy?"

"*Mmm -mufff!*"

"It suhe has saved me plenty, like from flippin out when I came of age."

"When was that?"

"You mean when I fihst stahted smokin reefah?"

"OK."

"Eleven."

"Eleven!"

"H'yep h'yep, and I haven't fried my brain up yet, noh tuhned ovah to hahdah drugs neithah. Guess I'm just a head case and nothin wohse."

"What about Will here, looks like he's hallucinating?"

"Damn — *snap* out of it boy! Only cuhe fah the panic is sugah — heah's a Sticklahs bah, chew on this."

Will does, gobbles it.

"Feel any bettah?"

Must. He's blinking, looking around at each of their faces.

"Tell us a story Will."

Story, as in storybook farmyard, cows that talk and bunny rabbits who chew lettuce up in the garden and should be executed and hung by their back legs from the porch, or pigs that you nurse from birth and play with in the pen until that dark day comes and the road leads straight from slaughterhouse to smokehouse, Bettyboo's now bacon and hamhocks.

"Heah's anothah candy bah, sometimes it takes mah than one."

Swallows it whole.

"Youh tuhn to tell evahrybody how you ended up heah in the city."

"*Uh -uh -uh…*"

"How did a religious boy like you ever learn about rock 'n' roll?"

"*Uh-* Jeremiah."

"Who?"

"Jeremiah. I had this horse named Jeremiah. He taught me."

"You had a horse that was into rock 'n' roll?"

"Jeremiah and I, we'd go out riding nights, when I was supposed to be in bed sleeping?"

"Guy growin up in the country can get mighty restless in the dahk."

"Most of the time we would ride a few miles over to Faith Junction, they had a Reformed church there and the pastor, he let me play the church organ nights, loud as I wanted."

"Good man."

"But Jeremiah didn't like the sound of church music much, he'd start in snorting and pawing the ground, kick up a real clatter."

"Nevah knew hohses had an eah fah music."

"Jeremiah did — well, one night, real late, because I had gotten carried away playing on the organ?"

"Bet."

"Jeremiah and I were galloping fast back home when this storm hit. Lightening flash spooked Jeremiah and he headed straightaway for cover, this old barn along the road… when we got there and dried off a bit, we heard this sound, coming from above, from the hay loft, and it was like something neither of us had never heard before, and Jeremiah liked it, calmed him right down, and I liked it, calmed me right down… I had to see what it was, but I was scared, I really was."

"Why's that?"

"I climbed up this ladder real slow, damn near slipped and fell a couple of times because some of the rungs were broke or missing."

"Yeah?"

"But I kept hearing this music and this moaning…"

"Moaning?"

"…I kept creeping on up there, higher and higher…"

"And?"

"…well I got up to the top rung and damned if it didn't crack, real loud, broke right out from under me."

"You slipped?"

"No I was alright, but these two folks were up in the hayloft, what with the lightening and all they were probably afraid and hiding up there under this blanket moaning…"

"Nothin like feah to set off youh hohmones."

"…they jumped up when they saw me, must have thought I was a ghost. They leapt off the hay loft, landed in this hay rack and then's when they spotted Jeremiah — and he can be a jackass when he wants to be, he started in braying and carrying on — so they took off running, right out into the rain, started up some car they had and hightailed it down the road

— they must have been strangers to our parts because nobody where I come from drives, not even tractors, since engines are the invention of industrial demons. Of course, they had scared me too, people jumping up and running off the way they did, and leaving all their clothes…"

"They left theih clothes?"

"They had them laid out on the hay to dry…"

"Right, and they had to huddle togetah to keep themselves wahm."

"…but this music was still playing, like nothing I had ever heard before, as if it was from heaven…"

"What was it?"

"There was this small black box they left on top of a post, with some funny knobs…"

"Like a transistah radio?"

"Still have it." Will Cook digs into one of his cases and pulls out a vintage late-50s Japanese Triton. "I had never seen one before and I held it right up to my ear. Startled me at first, but then I listened — *bah bah, it went, bahbipity bah bah / bahbippity bah bah* — C'mon ev'rybody / Let's *do* the twist…"

"Chubby Checkahs, that was Chubby Checkahs!"

"You know this music?"

"Hell yes, man's legend!"

"Jeremiah admired him too, started in kicking and wiggling his hind quarters."

"Rock 'n' roll can do that to a fella."

"But I shouldn't have kept it, I should have left it where I found it. It was an invention of the Devil clearly and I was stealing. I would have to admit what I had done in front of the assembly and take my punishment."

"What soht of puhishment?"

"A birch lashing across my bare backside by Elder Hubert… but I compounded the sin…"

"How's that?"

"I had never confessed that I had been out at night and playing the organ, and in the church of the anti-Christ down the road, so I hid the radio in the stable and I listened to it late at night with Jeremiah, station WHOR broadcasting the best hits from high atop the Chrysler Building in New York City, and that was my downfall, sin compounding sin, which must be why I have suffered the Lord's punishment so severely."

"Least you'h with friends heah in a monastehry."

"Oh my God, monks! Elder Hubert would whip me bloody!"

"Chubby Checkers was the first rock 'n' roll you ever heard?"

"Yes."

"Not Elvis?"

"Who?"
"Nor Buddy Holly?"
"Little Richard?"
"I have heard of him."
"Fats Domino though, he's got to be my inspihration."
"I found my thri-lll / on Blueberry Hi-lll…"
"And lingered unti-lll…"
"My-hy drea-eam came home."
BOMP-PE-TE BOMP-PE-TE BOMP-PE-TE BOMP.
"Yeah yeah!"
"Ray Charles for me. Mister Smooth."
"How about Howlin Wolf oah Mouhnful Jack Gohdon?"
"They're gods man, gods!"

And so it is that shared religious beliefs, the same faith in rock, and no money, make for friendship on St Mark's Place. Will Cook and Chipper have a room to share on the top floor of The Green Pagoda, and Danny T one of his own. Bubba is to become a frequent late night visitor, though he is unwilling to make a permanent move out of his mother's kitchen a few blocks away, where all four gather as often as they can finagle an invitation to enjoy home cooked Italian. Will Cook is the greatest beneficiary however, he has a shared room where he can watch as many unnatural acts as he wants, untouched, undisturbed in any way, since one of life's natural observers has finally struck up with one of life's naturally observed. And music shall in time overcome their differences, although tiffs over riffs and women, one Molly Dawkens, can cause a disturbance even inside the pearly gates.

"C'mon Chipper. Firsties."
"Frosties? Whole box of them in the cupboahd ovah theah."
"Sex. Everybody has to fess up before the night's over."
"Fuhsties, oah the wildest night of all?"
"Listen to the dude boast! How about the wierdest among the weirdos?"
"Don't know, but I'm suspicious I ain't the only practicin pahvaht in the place."
"Pervert."
"Somethin you two've been grinnin about all evenin."
"Firsties," Danny T suggests, "let's stick with firsties."
"First time's the best anyway."
"The wildest."
"The wierdest." Will Cook interrupts, head burrowed into his hair.

"Especially in this city."

"Hey. it was late, and this girl's been chasing me all over town for days now, two of them, Joycee and her friend there, what's her name?"

"Cheryl." Will Cook raises his chin and mumbles amidst some bubbles.

"Chehryl and Joycee — that all you two've been moanin about?"

"All? You mean we've all… all of us — not all on the same day!"

"Night, fact sounds like you all fell within three, fouh houahs of each othah. That's got to be some soht of wohld ohgy recohd way I figuhe."

Bubba looks at Danny T who glances over at Will Cook who's wide-eyed staring at nobody in particular because once you've seen it all, and on the same day and waterbed, well, there's nothing more need be said, just a blank blink at their communal comaraderie.

"Willy boy too. Proof nothin's bettah in this life than a six pack soothah on the sofa — pop'em, plop'em, toss'em ovah youh shouldah and out!"

"So what was your first encounter?"

"With the female of the species oah some otha soht of crittah?"

"Right, with an alien."

"Damn, let's see if I can remembah. Fihst smoke, fihst beeh, fihst fight… I do recall an incident when I was in fifth grade."

"Fifth grade! You were ten!"

"Twelve."

"Twelve!"

"H'yep, they'd held me back a couple of yeahs — hohny mah than ohnahry, my mothah told the teachah — see this neighbah lady of mine complained to the school principal about me and huh daughtah, Ahmada, and huh daughtah's best friend from school, Mindy oah Cindy oah Lindalee — I fahget names awful easy — we wah just messin around in Ahmada's backyahd, doctah and nuhsey in the tent, oah maybe it was shrimp divahs undah the blankies, I don't remembah which game it was fah suhe, but the principal decided since I was a yeah oah so oldah than these two gihls that I had to go see the school counselah."

"What did he say?"

"She. She was a trip. Asked me all kinds of questions about my mothah and my home life, whethah I watched TV oah hung out alone in my room, what spohts I liked to play and if I had any friends my own age at all — you suhe you want to heah all this?"

"Wouldn't miss a word."

"Wait, wait though, let me grab another beer."

"Pass me that bag of chips kid, while you're at it."

"Anybody, anything else while I'm up — Will?"

"A beer, another beer, and something to smoke."

"You know guys, you'h makin me nahvous, I was only goin to tell a shoht stohry."

"Wait wait, I've got to take a quick pee."

"Me too, I'll be right back. Don't start without me."

"Nevah thought I could genahrate this much intahrest. Will, you seem to be taken evahrythin easy."

-pufffff -puff -puff -pufffffffffffffffffff!

"Keep that up long enough and youh brain goes mush, slogs around in youh skull when you walk."

"I'll take my chances."

"Don't we all."

"OK I'm ready."

"New brews for everybody, two apiece so we won't have to get up."

"You guys about through runnin around?"

"What's wrong with Will's ears?"

Just smoke seeping out, out his nose and mouth too.

"Anyway, wheah was I – I remembah – you know how they tell you you can always trust the school counselah, you don't have to lie oah make thing's up, you should go ahead and tell huh whatevah, well I admitted when it came to friends I didn't have many if any, and fah spohts I prefahred one-on-one, but to tell you the truth lady, isn't much I enjoy bettah than fuckin around – I distinctly remembah tellin huh that."

"What was her reaction?"

"Eyes popped way out of huh head. She had me suspended from regulah school fah a while and wrote in a repoht that I was a precocious child fah my age and mahkedly sexually deviant, then she made me come see huh twice a week."

"Doesn't sound too bad."

"I thought it was wicked unfaih because I hadn't done nothin at school to begin with and my outdooh intahrests shouldn't be none of a school counselah's business, right?"

"I'd agree."

"I tried tellin my mothah why I wasn't supposed to go neah school fah a while, but she was useless, she kept repeatin ovah and ovah, you did what to the neighbah's daughtah?"

"Did they eventually let you go back to classes?"

"Nope, but they didn't hold me back neithah, fact is they promoted me mid-yeah, skipped me up two grades so I could be with students at the same level of physical development – that's what they said – but wow did I have to duke it out. Had to take on every guy in the class to prove I could hold my own, but I found out gihls a little oldah ahn't so reluctant."

"Ahmanda was the first then?"

"Technically, I suppose, but in ninth grade when it happened all ovah again, the shit really hit the fan."

"When what happened all over again?"

"Ahmada, my neighbah's daughtah? Well I should've leahned, but you know how you do with neighbahs, you try to fahgive and fahget, live togethah despite. Anyway, we took this ride out to Lunah Lake in my mothah's old Plymouth one night, rolled the suckah out of the yahd while she was asleep upstaihs — Ahmada and me and huh youngah sistah."

"Her younger sister?"

"Ronda — but it wasn't as bad as they said. I didn't do a thing with the both of them in the front and back. It was just Ahmada enjoyed it in the front like usual and huh sistah prefahhed the back — so what, I figuhed, it was all the same to me, only diffahrent, you know what I mean?"

"They burn your butt this time?"

"Hey, Maine's progressive when it comes to education, I had to repoht to the same counselah lady — see, the school district was really ruhral and they only had this budget paht-timah — well she wrote in my file that I suffahed from a chronic adolescent recuhsionary proclivity towahd sex and that I should be isolated from the othah kids in class which meant I should be thrown out of school pahmanently."

"You suffered from an adolescent what?"

"Adolescent recuhsionary proclivity — chronic."

"Re-cuh-sion-ary... recursionary?"

"That's it, right theah."

"Meaning it could happen again and again."

"H'yep — again, mah often and bettah, that became my out-of-high-school motto."

"They expelled you?"

"H'yep, went to wohk pumpin out septic tanks with Randy Hollingswood, cool dude, he'd been kicked out of school himself a couple of yeahs earliah on some rigged-up chahge he was sellin pot to minahs — hell, he was a minah himself and he could spit tobacco twenty feet, hit a beeh can on a post dead centah — anyway the counselah arranged fah me to see huh twice a week evenin's fah tutohrin. She felt sohry fah me, I s'pose, least wanted me to pass the GED."

"How did that work out?"

"Fine, we got along fine."

"And you left the little girls in the neighborhood alone."

"Soht of, but what I did do was leahn how to keep them from ahways tattlin on me."

"How'd you do that?"

"Became a rule a guy can live by. What you do is you ignohe a tattlah. You pretend you haven't got the slightest intahrest in doin anythin fun oah excitin with huh anymah, which drives huh craziah than you can imagine, fohces huh to come to you when she's hungry fah one of youh suhe fihe specials, and pahticulahly if she's gone and got huhself a steady boyfriend."

"You mean this same Armada would come back around, even after she and her mother had complained twice to the school authorities about what you had done?"

"Huh little sistah was wohse, used to cohnah me in a stohe and bluht it right out, 'You do it bettah than anybody else does it fah miles around, Chippah baby.' She'd bat huh eyes and want to get cozy. Anyway, I discovahed that if a gihl has gone and got huhself a steady boyfriend, you've got it sacked, as a mattah of speakin, cause a gihl with a steady oah a new husband don't want nobody knowin nothin bout how she spends huh free time, not huh motbah, not the school principal, not even huh best hangin buddy."

"Did you ever graduate?"

"Ahmost did, don't you know, leastwise I leahned how to write poems and stuff because this counselah made me keep this jouhnal fah her, you know, writin down all my thoughts and experiences, dreams and hot flashes and such."

"All the English teachers do that now, it's supposed to be creative and make the students feel more relaxed about expressing themselves."

"H'yep, well this counselah was definitely relaxed and creative, she wanted me to keep track of all my ohgasms fah huh."

"No way!"

"H'yep. She wanted to know. Aftah she finished thumbin through my jouhnal one evenin, she bet me she could do me one bettah than Ahmada, huh sistah oah anybody else fah that mattah — and to tell you the truth, she could and then some. I leahned all about oldah women that yeah. Oldah woman who wants it has got to be the best invention theah is fah a fumble dumb teenagah, 'specially when he's growin up fast, and school teachahs, they'h the handiest."

"You're making this up."

"Hey sweah. I told you this gal was sehrious, guidance counselahs ahways ah."

"Did she at least prepare you to take the GED?"

"Nope. She got frustrated, oldah woman with a youngah guy often does, and I figuahed I'd had enough bouts with school and hahd wintahs anyway, so I grabbed my gig bag and headed south cause fuhthah nohth was bound to be mah of the same, oah wohse. Got as fah as New Yohk, city of bright lights and not a stah in sight."

MOLLY DAWKENS

AND THE MONKS
OF THE GREEN PAGODA

"Molly? Molly Dawkens? Would you step over here please!"
"Yes S'tir. Certainly S'tir."
"Where is your sweater dear?"
"*I-hhh...* I left it in my locker S'tir."
"And why Molly?"
"I was warm S'tir, it's so hot out, and..." Poor bowed red bobbed freckle faced kid.
"Molly Molly, how many times must we have these discussions?"
"Yes S'tir, I know S'tir."
"Sometimes the Lord giveth in abundance, sometimes more than we need, more than we should justifiably have, but that is the Lord's way and we here on earth must adapt to His ways."
"Yes S'tir."
"It isn't for the sake of the other girls, it's for the sake of the janitor, poor Stelly Gomez. Stelly stares at you Molly, and although we have no idea what he is thinking, he is a man and men are licentious in nature, except for your father, naturally, and good Doctor Hornslick because he has a medical specialty, but these are the only two men in your young life who are allowed to look upon you, until of course you meet your future husband, and he only after you both have entered into the most Holy Sacrament of Matrimony. Isn't that what you have been taught Molly?"
"Yes S'tir." Molly wiggles in her blue plaid jumper, stares at her shiny oxford shoes, the pair with the taps on the heels that *click, click,* echo slick down the halls.
"But then we have spoken of these matters before, and repeatedly, haven't we Molly – look at me when I speak to you Molly!"
"Yes S'tir, we have S'tir."

"Particularly as you have grown and developed physically in size before the eyes of the Lord."

"Yes S'tir."

"And your wearing a sweater was our little compromise with the Lord's abundance, was it not?"

"Yes." *Click, click* down green and white square hopscotch tiles.

"And do you have brothers Molly?"

"Yes S'tir, two brothers."

"And are they of age?"

"Of age?"

"Have they also grown and developed physically in size before the eyes of the Lord?"

"Ye-yes S'tir, I guess S'tir." Big bruisers who beat up on me regularly, that's what size they are.

"Then you must hide your abundance from them as well, so as not to lead them nor any of their companions into lustful temptation, nor any of the other young men you may chance to meet, is that understood?"

"Yes S'tir." Do they stare, do they stare.

"And you must also be modest here at school where the other girls are concerned, for fear of inciting unwarranted interest or envy."

"Yes S'tir."

"Although Miss Slocum in gym might notice and your classmates, but only momentarily as you step from the shower."

"Yes." Miss Slocum stares.

"And Sister Claire in the infirmary if you are feeling faint, and myself if Sister Claire is feeling faint."

Sis-Sister Claire stares.

"Isn't that correct Molly?"

"Yes."

"Only yes?"

"Yes S'tir."

"That is correct, now run along like a good Catholic girl and cover yourself with your sweater."

    Scat cat! *Scit! Scit!*
    Stray cat! *Stup! Stup!*
    Scratch scratchin at the SCREEN cat
    Ain't goin to git you what you WANT at
    Scit! Scit! Stup! Stup!
    So scat fast! Trash cat!
    Stup! Stup! Scit! Scit!

SHTUNK! SHTUNK! SHTUNKA-SHTUNK!

"Ahright guys, ahright… Sounds good, but the timin's got to be bettah oah othahwise it's not goin to wohk right. Danny T little buddy, you've got to snap those brushes just a haih befah I finish that fihst line, just a haih…"

Sc't! Sc't!

"That's it. Let's take it from the top, a two, a three, and…"

> Scat cat! *Sc't! Sc't!*
> Stray cat! ***Stup! Stup!***
> Scratch scratchin at the SCREEN cat
> Ain't goin to git you wha-…

"What? What is it?"

Will Cook is shaking his head of hair. Something's wrong.

"What?"

"Bubba needs to make more of a thud, kind of a thump thump, holding the strings down tighter with his thumb like this — ***thumb-stuk thumb-stuk*** — in order to get the sound. Anyway that's how I hear it."

"Bubba?"

"Yeah OK, I can do that — ***Stuk! Stuk!***"

"Ahright and can you jump in just a haih soonah too, my man. Yeah? Ahright, let's do it! Then a two, a three…"

> Scat cat! *Sc't! Sc't!*
> Stray cat! ***Stuk! Stuk!***
> Scratch scratchin at the SCREEN cat
> Ain't goin to git you what you WANT at
> *Sc't! Sc't! **Stuk! Stuk!***
> That's a scat fast! Trash cat!
> ***Stuk! Stuk!** Sc't! Sc't!*
> SHTUNK! SHTUNK! SHTUNKA-SHTUNK! SHTUNK! SHTUNK!

"I appreciate that extra little beat you put in theah Danny Boy, theah at the end — sounds just right."

"Man's good with his feet." Bubba grins.

SHTUNK! SHTUNK! Danny T works the foot petal with some force.

"Too bad that's the only appendage he can bang with."

"And how would you know? You been sitting on my toes lately?"

"Ahright now fellas, movin along some, let's try out mah of ouh sound effects, let's do that second vahse ovah again — and by the way, how's my voice been soundin? No need to spahe me the awful truth."

"*Y'oww!*"

Hah hah hah, ho ho — RAK! RAK! RAK!

"To be perfectly honest Chipper…"

"That's ahright Will, I think I'm catchin the drift. Voice still needs some improvement."

"IMPROVEMENT!"

"That's ahright, let's… let's count now, a two, a three, and…"

> Scram rat! *Tat! Tat!*
> Fat rat! **Whap! Whap!**
> Rap rappin on the kitchen DOOH like that'll
> Get you splat flat on the lin-o-le-um FLOOH sap /
> *Tat! Tat! Whap! Whap!*
> So scram scum! / Bum brat!
> *Whap! Whap! Tat! Tat!*
> **WHUMP WHUMP! WHUMPA-WHUMPA! WHUMP! WHUMP!**

"Ahright ahright, we know you'h back theah."

WHUMP! WHUMP! WHUMP!

"Do we all agree that theah ah a few kicks too many?"

"Hey, give him a break Chipper. The boy's finally got his hands and feet coordinated!" It's Bubba baiting Danny T again.

And Danny T bites for it. "Maybe if you used your dick instead of your thumb, you could press a whole lot harder on those strings."

"Ahright ahright guys! Love and peace makes fah pahfect hahmony, ain't that the monks' motto?"

"How're you spellin piece?"

"Now don't go bad mouthin ouh benefactahs' beliefs, they got us up on this stage heah and they'h feedin us fine."

"Yeah, and what are they doing down in the basement meantime?"

SHTUNK! SHTUNK!

The trap door to which lies directly underneath where the band is standing, although God Alone knows what religious rites are practiced in the catacombs, in that vast subterranean maze where each monk has his own cave or crevice to do as he likes after lights out and without reserve or reproach, for none among them is superior in authority, nor taste, each abiding by his own rule and predilection amidst plenty of smoke and incense and much kneeling and bobbing, with a piquant BBQ sauce that leaves everyone's lips snap happy.

"*Pssst* Molly! Over here… Over here. Let's skip chapel."

"I don't know Cally, Sister Magdalena's watching out for me."

"Screw Sister Magdalena, we graduate in five weeks."

"Why do you want to skip chapel?"

Molly Dawkens is older now with rich auburn hair streaming down past her shoulders, spilling loosely into the middle of her back and her front – for Molly has developed even more fully.

"Because I've got something to tell you about Suzy Shea – meet me behind the grotto."

"What is it? Tell me now!"

"No, there's a whole story to go along with it – so come on, let's go."

They run as fast as they can in their inch heel pumps and tight navy blue skirts, their matching blazers with Saint Agnes Of The Woodsy Vale embroidered on the breast pocket.

"What is it? What is it? I'm dying to hear."

"It's what we suspected. About Suzy Shea."

"WHAT? TELL ME! TELL ME!" Molly is jumping up and down wildly as though she were still a freshman about such things.

"Let's smoke a cigarette first."

"NO! TELL ME!"

"No, not yet. Let's smoke first, we'll share one."

"Tell me! Tell me, tell me, tell me! What's happened to Suzy Shea?"

"She finally did it."

"No!"

"Yes yes yes yes yes yes —YES!"

"NO!"

"Yes and Molly, you'll never guess who with, or where."

"Who?"

"You'll never believe who."

"WHO?"

"Brad Cassidy."

"NO!" – Brad Cassidy, no.

"Yes, behind the scoreboard over at Saint Anselm's football field."

"Suzy Shea?" – Suzy Shea?

"Yes. In the back seat of his red convertible!"

"How do you know?" – In the back seat of his red convertible.

"My brother Mark saw Brad Cassidy drive into school yesterday morning with her panties flying from the antenna of his red convertible!"

"NO!"

"YES!"

"How humiliating!"

"YES!"

"And you're sure they were Suzy Shea's?" – Suzy Shea and Brad Cassidy.

"Definitely. My brother Mark and a few of the other guys on the football team went out to get in their cars after practice – they had seen her driving around the parking lot before – and they think, they're sure they saw them going at it in the back seat of his red convertible, and Brad still had his practice suit on."

"No!"

"Yes!"

"With the top down?"

"No, but the windows were open a crack."

"I don't believe it! Suzy Shea! Miss prim and proper prom queen who goes to communion every day." — Prom queen.

"Not yesterday she didn't, she didn't even come to school yesterday."

"Is she here today?"

"I don't know, we'd have to go to chapel to find out."

"You're sure it was with Brad Cassidy?" — Brad Cassidy.

"Yes. *Yuck!*"

"I'd consider giving in to Brad Cassidy."

"MOLLY! YOU WOULDN'T!"

"Yes I would! He's cute!" — He's beautiful.

"He's an ego-centered jerk, and a jock! And my brother Mark says he heard she gave in — *snap* — just like that!"

"Ohhhhhh-h!"

"YES — *SNAP* — JUST LIKE THAT!"

"With Brad Cassidy!"

"HE WAS WEARING HIS SWEATY FOOTBALL UNIFORM THE WHOLE TIME!"

"NO!"

"AND IN THE BACK SEAT OF HIS RED CONVERTIBLE!"

"NO!"

"WITH THE WINDOWS ROLLED DOWN!"

"NOOOO!"

Cally finds Molly in the halls later, after religion class.

"Molly? You OK? You look like you're about ready to throw up."

"*Uuuck-* I can't believe Father DiFuso discussed sex again, all class long. What is it with him? Don't do this, don't do that, not until after you're married! If he touches you there, it's a sin, but if he touches you here, it's only a near occasion. And if you touch yourself, you'll never get the stain off your fingers..."

"You're lucky you have him for a teacher, try Sister Immaculatta, all she talks about is devotion to the Holy Virgin."

"...the mouth is not a proper receptacle for man's seed or a boy's tongue, only the Lord's Holy Body until after you're married, otherwise you'll get germs and boys only do it to boast! You can't use contraceptives because they break God's law, rhythm is wrong and doesn't always work, and abortion, never, because you'll get hit by a bus and go straight to hell!"

"How does he know so much, he's a priest!"

"He learns it all in confession."

"But he only hears the girls' side."

"Suzy Shea's side!" Molly smiles slyly, she can be a red-headed she-devil, she can. "Do you think she told Father DiFuso what she did?"

"Bless me Father, I sinned grievously in the back seat of Brad Cassidy's red convertible." Cally begins.

"What exactly did you do my child?" Molly inquires in a deep register.

"I got tangled up in his shoulder pads Father."

"Yes, and then what happened?"

"I lost my panties on the antenna of his red convertible, *boo hoo*."

"Yes, yes and then?"

"I lost my virginity while the team watched through the windows."

"*Tsk tsk*, my child, you must sin no more. Now go in peace and say three Hail Marys — and next time be sure to roll up the windows."

Hah hah hah hah hah!

"Have you ever told him anything important in confession?"

"Never, except once — *ohhhh!*" Molly's green eyes roll top of her head.

"What?"

"I was so mortified, I thought I was going to die. I was a freshman and I didn't know any better!"

"What did you tell?"

"I told him I let Richie Maguire put his hands under my blouse."

"What did he say!"

"He asked me if anything else happened, if Richie went all the way."

"And?"

"I said no Father, just up to my collar."

Hah hah haaaaaah!

"*Shhhh!* Here comes Sister Magdalena."

They can hear the nun approach before they can see her. Sister Magdalena wears boots concealed under her long black robes, boots with thick heels, but then she is the Prioress, and she pounds with them and the hall resounds with them.

"Quick! We'll tell her we didn't go to chapel because, *uh*- because we're going to mass later, *uh*- at home, at my house, tell her some newly ordained priest with a beard and a guitar and a loaf of whole wheat bread is coming over to say mass later."

"Good morning S'tir."

"Yes and good morning to you Molly, Cally, and what's all the shush-shushing about, something you do not want Sister to overhear? Something you do not what the Lord to overhear?" She towers over the two youngsters, this W-starched up-winged bonnet attached to her head, flapping impatience.

"No, not at all, it's *uh-*... it's about -about Suz-..."

Molly steps in front of Cally. "We just stepped outside to get a breath of fresh air S'tir, after religion class, we were both so warm and-..."

"Oh you were, the both of you were?"

"I do feel so hot S'tir, like I'm going to faint S'tir, and I-... I-..." Molly does one of her practiced swoons.

"Good Heavens Molly! Here, I shall assist! I shall help you to the infirmary, and Sister Claire is faint herself today, and... and Cally?"

"Yes S'tir!"

"Run ahead and tell-..." Sister Magdalena damn near folds under Molly's weight. "...I am fine, I can manage ...simply inform Molly's next period teacher that she shall be delayed with me in the infirmary."

"Yes S'tir!" Cally curtsies and vamooses.

"And you, my poor dear Molly, this growing up is so exhausting, isn't it?" Sister Magdalena struggles down the hall with Molly's limp body, the good Sister's arms tight around the girl's waist.

Molly presses a wrist to her forehead and struggles to breathe.

"Yes, now lie down here and I will loosen your buttons – do you want me to call Doctor Hornslick?"

"NO! No S'tir, you do so much better, you really do." She sighs a sigh.

"I try Molly, the Lord knows I try."

"Ahright, let's go it again, and a two, a three..."

> Down hound! *Pound! Pound!*
> Git outta town! ***Whopf! Whopf!***
> Sniff sniffin you nose on the GROUND hog
> Fresh sprung from the lost 'n' FOUND dog
> *Pound! Pound!* ***Whopf! Whopf!***
> Down clown! / See you around!
> ***Whopf! Whopf!*** *Pound! Pound!*
> SHTUNK! SHTUNK! SHTUNKA-SHTUNK! SHTUNK! SHTUNK!

"KEEP IT CRANKIN GANG, ONE MAH TIME FROM THE TOP!"

> Scat cat! *Sc't! Sc't!*
> Spray spat! ***Stuk! Stuk!***
> Scratchin fah some snatch at the SCREEN cat...

Molly. Molly Dawkens was so much and more, for Molly Dawkens was a good Catholic girl from a good Catholic home in Morristown, New

Jersey, good Catholic horse country, and she was sent to a good, to a very good Catholic girls school, expensive, Saint Agnes Of The Woodsy Vale way out on an estate with a riding stables where she was taught to trot and to jump and to curtsy gracefully by the Sisters of the Supplicant Virgin, an order dedicated to the indoctrination of little girls into the truest faith, and the good Sisters did that well, so very well, and it was the 60s and times were changing rapidly, mostly forever in good Catholic horse country, same way they were changing everywhere else in the country. And Molly's father, Matthew T. Dawkens, Matty to his good Catholic horse country friends, was into auto insurance, big time lobbyist in Trenton, and he spent most of his time on the road traveling down to Trenton, drive drive drive and ambition, but it got him where he needed to go, for he was master over his own home and over his four adoring children, though he was particularly fond of his youngest daughter Molly — but those stories were never spoken, nor whispered, not in the confessional to good Father DiFuso, and certainly not published in the newspapers, not then, no, some things were best left folded between the pages, but Molly Dawkens was bound to learn these mysteries some way, by some teacher, if not by all those who must teach good Catholic girls that she was indeed blessed with not enormous nor gaudy gross breasts, but with ample lovely large ones, big handfuls that only the first string on the football team at Saint Anselm's could appreciate totally, or a practiced pediatrician with a teenage gynecological specialty who donated his spare time freely if not excessively to the young wards of the good sisters — breasts passing hands over time to musicians who themselves had developed a damned good sense of touch for stretched taut soft melons, and Molly learned these things from the many who had a hand in her education. And she took it upon herself to learn even more mysterious things than the good Sisters were teaching her at an impressionable age. For Molly Dawkens would on occasional late nights quietly back Matty's silver Continental out of the garage in Morristown, whether she was of age and carrying a license or whether she was not, and she would head into Manhattan, drive drive drive and obsession, but it got her into the East Village and she parked nearby St Mark's Place so she could survey a different sort of stud farm entirely, and Matty couldn't say too much because Molly might say too much too and so they had this tacit misunderstanding, plus Molly was too hot for any one man to handle anyway, and father and doctor and priest knew this, as did the good Sisters and bold coaches and feeble janitors who gaped openmouth at her in her pubescent prime, or the star football players at Saint Anselm's, though one lanky Irish kid with a red convertible did better than most athletes in her life, but she would have had to come to the city in time anyway, for as with so many other over-sexed adolescents in the early 60s, good Catholics or nay, where else could they, could she have gone, and where finally did they, did she go and graduate full bloom, but into the open arms of the shaved-headed Monks of The Green Pagoda?

> Shoo fly! *Z-zip! Z-zip!*
> So sly! *Swat! Swat!*
> Dip dive bombin outta the SKY guy
> Tryin to get some of mama's PIE fly /
> *Swat! Swat! Z-zip! Z-zip!*

Molly didn't bother to park Matty's silver Continental in one of the garages over near NYU either, the streets were plenty good for her, a few scratches, a few dents, parking tickets galore, what matter this to her, she didn't have to pay for it. A stab at the curb and she could rush to the temple for spiritual sustenance, her guidance undertaken by none other than Quentin Laurence Sparkington III, 'Sparky' for short, one of the founding fathers of the order, though none of these monks are old, nor learned nor bearded, no, these are modern day monks, young, alert, athletic, like their customers, late teens and early twenties, but shorn of all hair, carefully shaved heads, faces, arms, legs and nether places, plucked even to the eyebrows – hair considered somehow unacceptable to the cavorting gods who oversee operations. The monks are also tanned, not ascetic and pale, and well-built. They are a sight to behold with many among the faithful entering the sacred grounds merely to gawk, but such is religion, is it not, that the good works and exterior trappings are what shall attract the multitude inside the fold? And the nine monks do indeed attract a multitude, a following lined up and down St Mark's Place waiting patiently to get in, though not Molly, Molly never waits in line, she is ushered quite unceremoniously through the back alley entrance afternoons, evenings, early mornings, whenever she feels the need for Sparky's ministrations. And to be invited, as Molly has been so often, to the monks' after hours downstairs services, well, that is a distinct honor not bestowed readily on everyone, though the monks' rarefied tastes and their ingathering of elect are often baffling to outside observers, but variety is what the 60s are all about, and plenitude and variety are what The Green Pagoda is all about, particularly among those of the sex and vegetable dip conviction.

> Hey bird! *Trip! Trip!*
> Quiet down! *Chirp! Chirp!*
> Try peck peckin you way outta JAIL twerp …

Sin and the interference of the law of the land into such is a matter of ongoing constitutional debate – the use of peyote, the legality of gambling in church halls, the practice of celibacy, child seduction and polygamy –

but the belief in whatever's wild, wierd or indifferent, that's purely a matter of personal opinion and protected. In sum, you can believe in whatever you damn well please, just don't go attempting to subject the unsuspecting to the intricacies of your creed, not on the street at least, but once inside the sanctuary, what the hell goes on is nobody's business, and Molly's been raised a good Catholic, hence mum as a nun. The monks to a man are OK by her – the practices of The Green Pagoda familiar: clandestine smoking, whispers in the dark, votive candles, icons, incense, incest and a firm belief that after the hard work of establishing your church has been completed some good might even come of the effort. A light out from under a bush and a basket to lunch from. Molly has eagerly embraced the monks in both their daily and their nightly toils. She doesn't want to return to the peculiarly paternocturnal care of Matty in Morristown, not if she can help it, and she is due to graduate this very June from the clutches of the Sisters of the Supplicant Virgin. And surprisingly, despite their combined efforts, Molly has remained an idealist intactus. She can still blink and believe, a quality the young often share with those near death or unexpectedly afflicted by physical calamity. Molly is swimmingly satisfied amongst her element, and as an added ingredient there are these four unprotected musicians writhing about nights on the stage directly above her head!

> Down hound! *Pound! Pound!*
> Humpin clown! *Whopf! Whopf!*

Chipper spins around, struts butt across in front, *ee-y*-out/in, shout/spin about.

> Sniff sniffin you nose on the GROUND hog
> Out theah spreadin you scent AROUND slob
> *Pound! Pound! Whopf! Whopf!*
> Leg down! / Git outta town!
> *Whopf! Whopf! Pound! Pound!*
> SHTUNK! SHTUNK! SHTUNKA-SHTUNK! SHTUNK! SHTUNK!

"Now's when you could put in those extra beats of youhs Danny Boy!"

> *shh shh shh shh shh shh -SHTUNK! -SHTUNK! shu shu shush*
> HUNKAHUNKAHUNKA -SHTUNK! -KUNKA SHTUNK!
> SHTUNK! SHTUNK! SHTUNK! SHTUNK!

Chipper motions with his fingers for everybody to take it slow, slow, soft and low.

> *ssh ssh / shh ssh ssh-ha / sha shushu ssh-ha / sha shu ssh-ha /*
> *shu! shu-shusha-shu / sha-sha-sha /* CHAT / SCAT / SCAT CAT /
> SNAPPITY SNAP / CAT RAP / FAT SPRAT / SPLAT FAT / RAP SNAP

> SNAP / SHNAP SHNAP / SHNAP TAP / SHNAP TAP / SHNAP TAP! tap / tap / tap tap tap / tappity-tat-tat tat / scat scat / sc't sc't / sc't sc't scat scat / scat-a-tat / tat-a-tap / tap tap / tappity-tap! WHA-AAAAANG! WHA-AAANGO / WANG-WANG-WAAAAAANG!

And after Danny T finishes up, it's Will Cook on lead guitar, he lets loose and shows off what he has learned how to do, and entirely by himself way up in front of nobody in the theater.

> WHACK / WHACK / WHACH-WHACH-WHACH, WHAA-WHAA-WHAA-WHAA-WHAAAAAA-AAN-ANN-ANGGG-GGGGGG-ANG-ANG-AAAAAAANG! WANCK / WANCK / WANCK / WANCK WHAN -AN -AN-ANH / WHAN -AN -AN -ANH / WHAN- WHAN-WHAN-WHA N--AN-WHAN-AN / WHAAA-AA-AH-AAH-AAAAAAAAH!

Bubba's turn on bass, and the guy's at least got muscle:

> *stuk / stuk / stu-uck-stu-stu-uu-uck / stuk / stuk / stuk / stuka-stuka-stuka / and whap! whapwhapwhap! whap! whap!whap! hap!whap!whap! whomp! whap! whomp/ whap!whomp/whap! whomp/whap! whompwhow-ow-owww-owwww-owwwww wooooo wwwwwwoowoo -whomb!*

Scat / Cat / Stray cat! / S'cat! / Scram rat! / Stamp! / Stamp! Rat-a-tat-tat! / Down hound / Nobody wants you around / Clown! / *Tat-sc't / sc't sc't /* **Pound! Pound!** / Sweep the street / Scrub the rug / Swap twat / Sniff sniff / Stuff the muff / Spray the stray / Trail the tail / WHACK / WHACK / WHACH-A-THE-WHACK-A-THE WHACK WHACK / WHA-WHA / WHA-WHA-WHA-WHAAAAAAA-AAN-A-AAN-A-AAN-A-AAN-A-AAAA AAAAANH-AAAAAAAAAH! / *ow / oow* / Oh oh / *wo wo* / Ha ha / HANH HANH HONH HONH HAAAAAAH! / **stuk stuk** / *tat-a-tat-a-tat tat* / WHONK, WHONK-OONK-OONK-OOOOOOOO-NK-WHAP! / WHAP! WHAP! WHAP! / Yeah! Yeahh! Yeahhh! / Fast cat caught the fat rat tappin the hound dog high tail and gettin it done real go-goo-good! / *SHTUNKA-SHTUNK! SHTUNKA SHTUNKA SHTUNK SHTUNK!*

Yeah!

"Wow!"

"Is it a take, oah what?"

"Groovin!"

"Good going!"

The monks to a man emerge out of their seclusion under the stage, file out applauding, and these nine guys have never done that before, so preoccupied with the rituals of their religion…

"Whoa! Thank you fellas!"

Bands stands to take a bow.

"Pissah! Pissah pahfohmance, and not a bad audience neithah!"

No siree, not as Chipper notices that numbered among the monks is one hell of a red headed rare beauty who actually blushes as all eyes spotlight her — and how could she not be self-conscious, something of a freak to herself, but that's not what anyone else would say, just hello…

"Hey! I'm Chippah, how ah you?" And if he had a phone, he'd be handing her the number.

"Molly. Molly Dawkens. You guys are cool, really cool…"

Though some stars seek to deflect light, sparkle despite it, others burn bright on their own, no way to suppress it. They radiate while others in their orbit must simply bask in the warmth — heat, fiery red hot and the bright white meeting in space and waiting for the flash that will fill the dark void they're both drifting in.

"…incredible improvisation!"

"Th-thanks." Danny T starts to stutter and *tat-trip-tisssssshes* topples over his cymbal set trying to stand up to see her.

Will Cook's eyes are as wide as saucers. He can see her only too well as Bubba sprawls all over Chipper in an attempt to introduce himself — that's Marcy who, and where out in Pennsylvania? "Hi, I'm Bub-…"

"Jesus, pahdon me please!"

"…Bubba Bonnanza…"

"Molly. Molly Dawkens."

Do they stare or do they stare?

And Danny T who continues to *boom bang boggle* and bungle it… "D-Danny T."

"Hi! — And who's this?"

"Yahh sorry." Bubba interrupts, stepping in between. "This here is our keyboardist Will Cook." Bubba is both gracious and sly.

Though talk about stumbling! First off Will steps on his patch cord and — *SNIP* — strips it right out of its socket and — *FLOOSH* — kicks square into a not cheap monitor, and all this over an utterly ravishing red head? Yes. He does manage to make it on two feet over to the rim of the stage whereupon he trips nose first — *PLOOK PLOOK PLOOK* — hits the floor as Molly offers her hand and damned if he doesn't grasp it though — yes yes, you guessed it — Will Cook does this spiral and spin act — *WHIP WHIP WHIP -WHAP!* — besides which he's dressed all in black, something of a Pennsylvania preacher motif, black pants, black long-sleeved buttoned down shirt covering all exposed skin, bush of black hair, black dazed eyes, round and round he goes out of control, cutting a swathe clear across the stage.

Whatever Danny T hasn't knocked over of drums himself goes down now with this tornado, along with the rest of the gear — WHAM! WHAM! SLAM BAM MA'AM! — then there's the characteristic foaming about the lips.

None of the guys have seen this performance before, although Molly has, she's witnessed swoons, fits, feints, the whole gamut of infirmary ills, so when Will finally does touch ground — SWOOOMP! — she gallops on stage and does as Sister Magdalena might do.

"Don't touch his tongue."

Was anybody planning to?

"And prop his head up! Take off his clothes!" Which probably isn't what she means to say, consciously, nor a necessary remedy either, although Molly is Catholic not Freudian and doesn't notice her slip, and the guys are certainly going to oblige her whatever her request.

Will Cook in his delirium most likely thinks this is the way girls in New York do it, in groups with other guys assisting.

In all the confusion Molly at least gets to brush up next to Chipper — her freshest against his kneecaps, if you must know, and a very easy smile flashes between the two — but it is Bubba's hefty arms that suddenly surround her upper torso with a mild as mannered, "That's OK, I can handle this."

Can he? Does he? You bet!

Nor is Molly opposed to such strong arm tactics.

Two of the monks — Napta Das Ruptah and Quentin Laurence, i.e., 'Sparky' — are on the spot. Monks of all persuasions seeming to have this instinct for showing up wherever there's trouble — a bird with broken wing fallen from flight, an old lady with purse snatched in broad daylight — and they quickly take charge of the denuded Will Cook. They carry him off, splayed arms and legs and still twitching, through the trap door into the depths of their sanctuary, for who knows, some incantation, some of their cures or tortures might set him right. And with Will Cook's untimely removal from the game, the field is reduced to three, well two, Chipper backs off momentarily, dude doesn't jostle for girls, it's unseemly, besides he currently has the devotion of twin fifteen year old runaways from Larchmont to contend with, though mind you, mind you, before you chuck up a stone to throw, Chipper is only seventeen himself — so it's down to two diehards — Bubba the Bod and Danny T 'Drummer Dynamo.' Now Danny T being the cute kid brother type is worthy of a hug and a tumble on the rug, but championship play tilts inevitably Bubba's way. Six foot Italian who could have posed for The David had he been around Florence then and had he a mind to be carved up for posterity is the far away favorite over the pea shooter crewcut from Iowa or Indiana who would have been fortunate in those Renaissance days to have been allowed to sweep up the chips, and Molly may very well not even notice this variance in height. She's busy throwing her shoulders back for Bubba's benefit, which cocks her butt out and separates the cleft line neatly into perfectly congruent spheres. Nor is the girl wearing a sweater, something about sweaters Molly doesn't care for, nor bra, so when she raises her elbows to brush the hair out of her face, there is a lifting akin to two new moons arising.

"All this excitement!"

Those green eyes of hers glisten, and Bubba is plug chaw eager up to the plate, bases bloated, ready to slug a homer over that far left field wall.

SHTUNK! SHTUNK! SHTUNKA-SHTUNK!

Band practice seems to be over for the night, instruments are going to need a good fix, and while Bubba's the man to watch, a flirt's not a fuck, so nobody's yet out of luck.

"Nice meeting you guys." She waves as she disappears under the stage.

"You know, you can nevah satisfy a woman Will, nevah."

Will is writhing in his bunk. Will doesn't want to know.

"Nevah evah. Law of natuhe."

Will begins banging his head against the iron bedstead.

"Take one on a date, fah example, you got to spend a bundle."

BANG BANG BUMP BANG BUMP BUMP

"Drinks. Appetizah. Dinnah. Desseht. And do they evah offah to pay theih shahe? Nope. I mean it ain't like they'h not wohkin. They've got money, but it ahways goes fah clothes oah make-up, nevah fah tickets to the concaht oah gas – know what I'm sayin? Guy ahways has to pay."

BUMP BUMP BUMP

"You know, you'h goin to huht youself doin that – then go and try to satisfy one in the sack…"

BANG BANG

"… mean, if they'h willin, which they ahmost nevah ah, you've got to wohk half the night to get them flowin, exhaust youself…"

BONK

"…and if they ain't in the mood, you wind up wohkin youself silly, oah you hop in the cah and go aftah a little take out, except if they heah you've been out cruisin, you'h wohse off than a heap of bloody squihrel meat."

BANG BONK BUMP BANG BUMP BONK

"Sweah to God you'h goin to wind up with a powahful headache by mohnin – 'couhse if you find youself a little tigah who's hottah than a sun spot, and ahways when you'h too tihed to faht right, she'll drain all the shot you've got."

BANG BANG BANG BANG

"Don't even talk to me about how big a weddin's got to be, invite family she ain't seen fah a quahtah centuhry, diamond ring at least a cahret shoht, and the baby — she can't get huh hands on one of them suckahs soon enough, hell fihe, some of the gihls from my home town have two, three, fouh in a row, and they ain't much oldah than me."

BANG BANG BANG BANG BANG

"But that Molly Dawkens, I'm tellin you Will, she's a smokah. Gihl like that makes you wondah if one guy could evah satisfy huh. Though I'd suhe as shit like to give it a try, wouldn't you?"

BUMP BANG BANG BUMP BUMP BUMP BUMP —BONK!

"Guess it's lights out fah the night, eh buddy?"

Molly Dawkens. Like the patron saint of young men come true, like the tapestry goddess venerated in the lobby of The Green Pagoda, candles flickering at Her feet, incense wafting up toward Her ringed nostrils. She is Ducilda by name and She is the central figure woven into this elaborate landscape, complete with gold threaded auras surrounding the heads of a host of minor deities, but central to the scene is Ducilda the Virgin, not a Western style virgin, no, rather one of those Indian goddesses who indulges in everything known to woman and to man but who never loses Her zest for it, and with all these smaller figures lying prostrate at Her feet, men in embroidered clothes, adoring nymphs, animals too, the kinds of beasts that virgins love, some long necked swans, some baying hounds, a deer with one horn and bulls with two, the entire herd lying down in respectful obeisance to Her loveliness, either that or they've exhausted themselves from too many romps in the wheat field spread out in the background. Above Her head the entire universe of stars and planets circle, everything on track, and while various interpretations of the work are permissible, a close examination teaches that universal respect for life in all its forms is paramount and that while someone is respecting life, he or she might as well partake a little hereof and thereof as well.

For not only is the Virgin sublime, she is also entirely naked, standing apart in a small garden pagoda. She is curvaceous, you know, fleshy and chesty. Her lips are full. Her eyes slightly closed, meditative. She also has eight arms, none of which She is using to hide Her sacred privates from casual view, instead She seems to be motioning at everybody around Her to take a look, gape in awe if they must, although four men standing closest by Her — at least they seem to be men, they sport spun pointed moustaches but they are wearing these skirts, and they possess golden auras yet blue skin — these characters seem distracted. They are pointing upward toward the stars which are all out even though it's daytime. They are scholars no doubt, astronomers. Heavenly Bodies high out of reach interest them more than a heavenly body close by. But if the Virgin is frustrated by their lack of attention, Her face doesn't betray the slightest hint of it. In fact She seems content to stand there and be gawked at, yet ignored — women, women — still, there is a lesson to be learned from Her naked serenity as well as from the scholars' distracted study, a lesson about life and stardom and the woman. Some must seek while others are born bare bust to it.

Take Molly for instance, she was a star from birth, the object of so many men's devoted attention — too much devotion for any young girl to cope — yet because of all that early attention she will always stand out in a crowd, any crowd, among girls or guys, no matter what their sexual profession. Girls will recognize Molly because she has what every girl wants. Guys will recognize Molly because she has what every guy wants. A divine body, yes, but a mysterious force dwelling deep inside Her, an equanimity they do not have and cannot grasp, being forever Dulcilda the Unattainable, no matter how much these guys group around and grope at Her. They might as well stare up at the stars since a Goddess needs none of them, even if She has eight arms and could handle a multitude at once. Which is why these four dressed up dudes are blue while She is golden, for they must point and ponder while She merely poses and mulls Her options. The tapestry story tells all. Nothing more need be said about men and a beautiful woman — unless that is, the Goddess harbors some hidden desire in Her own heart, some inkling She doesn't dare betray, some uncontrollable yearning for a companion God who may be Himself a Star. Then, *then*, the serenity of the scene, the subdued lowing of the animals and the order of the entire galaxy, well, those things could fly out of whack fast.

...tap tap... tap tap tap tap...

Gang of three is edgily awaiting Bubba's appearance. There are rumors circulating and fevered imaginations among young guys in a band — *tap tap* — it's quarter past nine and rehearsal begins promptly at eight thirty weekday evenings, because Bubba's bussing tables.

"Maybe they had an overflow at the restaurant."

"Mah likely he's smoochin ovah in the pahk with Molly Dawkens."

...tap tap tap tap... Danny T's way up in arms, but just when he's about to begin bangin, Bubba ambles in. He waves and he's grinnin. "Hey guys, how's it hangin? Sorry to get here late, but I was up all night, never thought I'd make it out of bed this mornin and the reastaurant was gang-busters."

...tap tap tappa tappa BAM BAM BAM BAM BAM BAM BAM BAM

"What's the matter with you kid?"

Days pass and Chipper's out walking near sunset in Washington Square Park, listening to the street musicians. "Hey! Hi!" Someone calls from behind, and he turns around to notice it's Molly. "What are you doing?"

"Nothin special, how about you?"

"Great night."

"H'yep. Wheah you off to?"

"Simply enjoying the sights."

"You got nothin else to do, maybe we could go get some ice cream?"

"Sure."

"Theah's a new place ovah on Thihd Avenue. They've got these big waffle cones, hold three, fouh scoops, plus all sohts of toppin's…"

"I'm not sure I like that much ice cream."

"…hot fudge, sprinkle on some nuts – oah whatevah you want."

"Whatever you want."

"Just a place to go, maybe you'd prefah to sit somewheah quiet and have a coffee instead?"

"No, ice cream's fine."

"Slice a pizza'd do me too?"

"No. Let's go for ice cream."

"Ahright."

"So have you gotten used to the hustle of the big city?"

"Mah oah less, noise still bothahs me, nights when I'm tryin to sleep."

"Thought you worked nights, slept days?"

"Days, nights, whenevah I'm tryin to catch a few winks. Noise makes me restless, along with the crowds – seems wheahevah you go in this city theah's a crowd. Wheah I come from up nohth you can go days, nevah run into nobody."

"Is it just me, or have you noticed that even with so many people, you keep seeing the same faces over and over?"

"You mean like the guy who dresses in feathahs head to toe?"

"Orange and blue?"

"Red hat, makes him look like a day-glow roostah."

"Hangs out on Sixth Avenue by the subway entrance?"

"And the gihl with the shaved head and a tattooed diagram of huh brain, a diapah pin stuck through huh nose."

"See her a lot."

"Must've huht a bunch."

"Which, the tattoo or the diaper pin?"

"Man, eithah one."

"Crowds bother me more than the noise."

"Folks gettin in too close?"

"The way they look."
"You mean stahe at you — good lookah and guys ah goin to gawk."
"And whistle and pinch."
"That's got to be a hassle — so you seein anybody special these days?"
"You mean as in steady?"
"Sehrious, oah on the way."
"No. You?"
"Don't have time fah none of that shit."
"No?"
"Nope. Too busy with the band. Things ah stahtin to heat up, got to get ouh act togethah now that we'h gettin some attention."
"I've noticed you…"
"What?"
"I've noticed you enjoy being in the spotlight."
"Jumpin up and down in front of folks like a fool."
"Do you enjoy that?"
"Thrive on it, to be truthful."
"Center stage, every eye on you."
"Gets the juices flowin."
"Must make you nervous as well?"
"Nerves, h'yep, jumpy as a jack rabbit — nevah could stand still though, ahways been full of enahgy, evah since I was a kid."
"With people always looking at you, staring."
"Stahrin at what?"
"You. You're a sexy guy — lanky."
"Whoa, don't know, that a compliment?"
"Simply a statement of fact. You attract attention."
"Considahrin the souhce I'm takin it as a compliment."
"Why is my opinion so important?"
"Hey, people watchin you, people watchin me, togethah we could really give them somethin to stahe at — you suhe you wouldn't be up fah dinnah, candlelight at a cohnah table, bottle of Chianti?"
"Ice cream sounds fine."
"Least let's staht off with a slice."
"OK, a slice."
"Doesn't have to be low down greasy off the street neithah, they've got this gouhmet place down in SoHo, Gahmaldi's."
"I've heard about it!"
"They heap all sohts of weihd stuff on, ahtichokes and eggplant…"
"Eggplant and black olives are my favorite."
"That and they can do halves, like double cheese with a few red onions."
"I'm always up for a taste of something new."

"Ahright!"
"Wait. Look at this shop. I've never noticed it before."
"They've got all sohts of cool shit."
"Want to go inside?"
"Suhe. I'm in no rush — whatevah you've got to do."

"Neat things."
"Could use a new pipe. Ahways need screens."
"What's this?"
"Don't know. Don't want to know."
"For external use only? Caution: Keep away from pets and children."
"That about let's us out."
"Wonder what it's for?"
"You -*ah*… you'h s'posed to spray it on, you know, befah…"
"Before?"
"Befah you get it on, s'posed to keep a guy… hahdah."
"Oh!"
"H'yep."
"Does it work?"
"Whoa, don't know. Nothin I need, I can tell you that."
"This would look good on you."
"Don't do hats."
"It's a beret."
"Make me look like a French poet."
"In a way you are a poet."
"Musician's diffahrent, gets down and dihty. Ahways think of poets as ethehreal."
"Ethereal?"
"You know, nose up in the aih.."
"I guess, but Stirbee is French, isn't it? The land of poets, and lovers?"
"Paht French, what's called renegade French up wheah I come from."
"Renegade French?"
"Descendants of the huntahs and trappahs who lived in the woods and consohted with the Indians."
"A wild man."
"That's ouh reputation."
"Oh, I like this."
"What is it?"
"Nose ring."
"Like the bald gihl with the diapah pin?"
"Not at all. This would be much classier."

"People'd really stahe."
"How about on you?"
"Ain't into body piehcin, 'cept maybe a nipple ring a gihl could tug on with huh teeth."
"Ouch! How about an earring?"
"Thought about it some, but…"
"But what?"
"Tough enough just bein a musician, without goin totally weihd."
"Afraid people will think you're queer?"
"Nope, all sohts of guys ah doin it."
"I find an earring on a guy hot."
"'Spose a guy's ahready hot?"
"Makes him even hotter — I'd do it if I were you."
"Tuhn you on somethin fiehce, would it?"
"Turn all the girls on, especially on you."
"Why's that?"
"Because you're so gritty."
"Gritty?"
"You said musicians were gritty."
"Gritty."
"Earthy, maybe that was it."
"Eahthy I could live with, but gritty seems to mean somethin else, dude who doesn't bathe regulah — so, you think an eahring'd make me sexiah?"
"Definitely — do it! They do piercings."
"Who?"
"On the premises, see the sign?"
"Man, that'd huht somethin fiehce."
"No it doesn't, they numb you with ice. Needle slides right through."
"Needle!"
"Close your eyes."
"It's pahmanent. I'd be scahred fah life."
"No it's not. It'll heal over in a month if you decide you don't like it."
"Think I'll pass, don't want to ruin a decent dinnah."
"Oh come on. I thought you'd be daring."

"My eah!"
"It's cute, little gold ring."
"It's throbbin somethin fiehce."
"Keep your fingers off it. Let it heal."
"You like it?"
"Very. It's neat."

"Do I look queeh?"
"You said you didn't care what people thought?"
"Don't. Just was wondahrin."

"Try a slice of mine."
"Don't know about eggplant, looks mushy, and what's that othah slimy lookin stuff?"
"Avocado. Slides right down your throat." She takes a bite, hardly chews. "Like that!"
"Gross."
"Try some."
"Think I'll pass."
"Try some for me."
"Whoa! That some kind of dahe?"
"Take a big bite, let it slide around in your mouth."
"Damn!"
"That's it."
"Goin to gag!"
"No you're not. Swallow!"
Ulk-...
"Wasn't that bad, was it?"
"Bad enough. Let me have anothah bite."
"See. Tasty."
"It's ahright."
"More wine?"
"Suhe."
"I propose a toast. To your new earring and to- to our getting to know each other."

"So. Want to top off the night with some of that ice cream I was tellin you about eahliah?"
"I'm stuffed. I couldn't eat another thing."
"Suhe you could. Creamy spoonful'll slide right down, lot easiah than eggplant."
"Let's walk a bit, talk about it. You miss home?"
"Nothin much to miss, bein alone."
"No brothers or sisters? No friends?"
"Ahways found somebody willin to get into trouble, not much else to do in a small town."
"True."

"Ahways found somebody willin to get into trouble, not much else to do in a small town."

"Only thing I really do miss is bein able to see the stahs at night."
"The quiet."
"Somebody close."
"Who are you thinking about?"
"Nobody in pahticulah. How about you?"
"Where is this ice cream place?"
"You intahrested?"
"Why not?"
"Thihd, neah the fihe station. The Hahd Rock Candy Mountain."

"Ohdah whatevah you want. I'm payin."
"You order. I'll have a bite of yours."
"Ahright. What's youh favohrite flavoh?"
"Anything."
"Tell me. Fah futuhe refahrence."
"OK. Chocolate. Dark chocolate."
"Dahk chocolate mistah, double dip, and that maple walnut fah me."
"I can't eat that much by myself."
"We can take ouh time."
"It will melt."
"That's ahright too."

"Tastes great, hunh?"
"Delicious."
"Must be, it's runnin down youh chin."
"Do something!"
"Heah, hold on. You've got it everywheah, just like a little kid."
"Told you it would melt."
"Then let me have a lick."

As two tongues meet, a chocolate and maple walnut kiss, one then another, another lick.

"I- I've got to head home."
"No."
"Yes. I graduate from school tomorrow, and if I didn't show up, my family would be really disappointed."

Late Saturday night at The Green Pagoda. The monks pack the house in tight for the Loose Nukes' debut performance. The band is banging about on the brightly lit stage, Chipper himself is lit, gyrating out front under the spotlight and the center of everyone's attention. Including Molly Dawkens who's seated first row, next to these twins from Larchmont. Though Molly stands out in any crowd – Danny T's certainly aware of her presence – *tappity toe tap tap* – Bubba too, Will Cook despite himself, and nearly every other guy in the audience. Rest of the theater is in the dark, except for flickering candles and the glow of smoldering embers, a new shipment of Laotian hashish via the wartime CIA airlift is the house specialty for the night, a skull corroding hybrid that has affected the performers along with the audience, which is to say everyone is hot and heavy into it.

The band has nearly exhausted its list of cover numbers, and the crowd is riled up and wanting hardier fare.

"What'a you say guys, time to play some of ouh own?" Like *Getta Girl* for starters or *Scat Cat*, the extended doodly-wop version, maybe even *Maine Boy* or *Lazy Lovin*, the tender Elvis' type love ballad Chipper has recently penned. They'd better do something because Will Cook is beginning to generate vibes of a quite disturbing nature, for the boy is on the verge. So Chipper does what he has to do, he signals the band to go for it. *Lazy Lovin*, he speaks out lowly – a most appropriate first choice.

    Whoa-hoa-hoa-ho ho... HOE HOE HO HOE!

Chipper lowers his register down into the Johnny Cash range.

    Yah-hah-hah... HAAAAAAAAAAA-HH!

The kids in the audience start breathing heavily, audibly.

> I know hon I'm home late
> Been out drinkin with the GUYS
> Re'lize you've been sittin home heah alone
> Stahrin out at the SKIES

Next verse Chipper's voice turns plaintive.

> Don't need to say nothin
> Cause I can tell by youh EYES
> But 'fohe we get to fightin
> And I staht spoutin out LI-HI-HI-HIES...

The band kicks in here, Danny T with a soft thump and Will Cook with a mournful keyboard wail.

> But, ba-by, BA-AY-BY
> Let me ask you / PU-LEASE!
> How 'bout some of youh LAZY LOVIN
> Youh sweet LAZY LOVIN / TO-NIGHT?
> How 'bout some of youh LAZY LOVIN

> Youh spoonful huggin up TI-TIGHT?

There's a drum roll.

> Yah yah youh man needs youh lovin / youh LAZY LOVIN
> Cause youh LAZY LOVIN's way outta / SI-SIGHT!
> Baby / need some of youh LAZY LOVIN
> Need / Need / Need
> Some of youh LAZY LOVIN
> Youh LAZY LOVIN / you low-down CRAZY LOVIN
> TO-NIGHT / Cause that's…
> That's what makes me FEE-EEL / AH-RIGHHHT!

Bubba can't stand being left in the background, he does these muscular strums, these bass level thumps and whines with a flex and hip action that gets the place moaning for it. He also steps further forward, into the inside corner of Chipper's spotlight. Chipper's oblivious, he snaps for a quick switch to a rocker beat, chattering the words faster and faster:

> When you use those kisses baby
> You don't know what it DOES
> When I feel those kisses baby
> I get such a BUZZ
> My hands staht to shakin
> My legs staht to quakin
> Like some bumble bee nosed in a flowah real GOOD
> And ready ready / BA-AY-AY-BY
> Ready to BUH-HUH-HUH-BUHRRST!

Tempo slows way way down again.

> SO-HO-HO-HO / Please baby / PLEASE!
> Youh little boy / youh baby boy…

Chipper is down on one knee, the mic tucked in between his legs, and he is pleading with the young chicks in the front row, the fifteen year old runaways, and Molly.

> He needs some of youh LAZY LOVIN / AH-RIGHT?
> Youh boy's cravin it / cravin youh LAZY LOVIN

Something of the song must speak to her, and the visuals inherent in a live performance, Chipper center, Bubba looming over his shoulder.

> That CRAZY LOVIN only you can do so RI-HI-HIGHT!
> Youh boy needs some LAZY LOVIN / TA-NIGHT!

Backstage the star can be unruly and coarse, but up front under the bright lights he undergoes this transformation, his blond shoulder length hair and this translucent glow like a halo ring his head, though beyond that there is nothing beatific about Chipper's face — jutting chin, leathery skin and a few scars from perennial claw fights with enraged females do not an angel's countenance make — but then it's not just the face either ever, is it, it's the body, and though he might be trimmer than a running back like Bubba, Chipper is all tall muscle and it shows, through his clothes, which always look as if they are ready to leap off him, some long-standing aversion his body has for covering, even a simple t-shirt and a pair of ripped jeans — fact is they're straining at the threads right now, with Molly not unwilling to unravel them to the last stitch — sight pulls her right out of her seat, because he's pleading with her, isn't he, bleeding for every drop of understanding the girl can muster — must, she gets to bopping up and down like the cheerleader she was born to be, and she's dressed Catholic horse country girl's school, a special for tonight, plaid pleated skirt that rises on the thighs with each cheerful bounce and shirttails that have *per force* become undone — as the rhythm slows to the sappy pace of the romantic ballad.

> S'pose I could say I'm sohry
> That it won't happen AGAIN
> S'pose I could lie / try to
> Dry those sweet teahs with a GRIN

Down a third to his best baritone.

> You know fah you sake / baby
> I'd sweah off and promise most any-THIN
> But talkin won't change it / no
> Won't change my just bein a man
> A pooh weak creatuhe bohn into SIN!
> So baby / BA-AY-AY-BY!
> While the moon is so / BRI-HI-HIGHT!

Bubba can't stand back any longer, he steps center ring aside Chipper, heats the tempo up, Danny T too, pounding with excitement as only the 'Drummer Dynamo' can do it — gets Chipper charging.

> I mean I mean I mean
> Can't you just lay back and make like
> A fuhry brown puppy TA-NIGHT?
> Can't you sway back and stay back
> And sample the guppy's DE-LIGHT?
> Cause this boy / this boy / this pooh boy's
> 'Bout to take FLI-HIGH-HIGH-HIGHT!

TA-NIGH-NIGH-NIGH-NIGHT!

"YAH!" Chipper's sparkin so hard he does this leap! This straight up off the floor kind, ten feet! Startles the audience awake and out of their seats! Band too. Will Cook! Danny T! Bubba too! Why- why it's like nothing none of them, nobody has ever seen before, not on stage – nor on the level – boy's breaking new ground right there in front of them!

Yes / let's make it a long one / baby /
A long long one /

Molly is upraised as well.

Let's make it a long long LAZY LOVIN /
A HAZY LOVIN / A CRAZY LOVIN /
TA-NIGH-HIGH-HIGH-HIGH-HIGHT! ///
YEAH!
CAUSE THIS BOY NEEDS A LONG HOT LOT OF
YOUH LAZY LOVIN / GAL / YOUH LAZY LOVIN
TA-NIIIIIIIIIIIIIIIIIIIIIIIIIIIIIIIIIIIIIII-GHT!

Theater erupts with an outpouring, cheers, tears, leers – and they want more, all he can give them plus plus. And Molly? Reluctance has given way to indecency. She has her shirt open, no bra, and two pale nipples prong prone – runaways get outta the ways, let the guys in the audience gawk all they want – and appreciative, is he ever. Chipper sings the next song directly at her.

Getta Girl / Gotta Gotta
Need a girl / A lot a lotta
Gotta Gotta / Gotta getta girl

'Getta Girl' does nothing to calm the rest of the kids down either, they're up and dancing and an auditorium full of kids stoned and dancing is a life endangering form of entertainment.

"Ahright ahright, you'h askin fah it now – *Maine Boy*!"

MAINE BOY / SHAME BOY
Wheah'd you lose youh PANTS?
MAINE BOY / SHAME BOY
When you goin t'leahn t'DANCE?

Somewhere in the middle of the backwoods ditty, pants do get lost, along with shirts and skirts. Somebody douses the lights, probably Brother Sparky, along with those annoying red EXIT signs. Amplifiers might die to a whine, but do these kids take advantage of lights out? They're on the floor, on the cushions, on the rugs, and they're doing it, not so much foreplay as far in away they're screwing it — it is orgy time out-of-sight late on a Saturday night at The Green Pagoda!

In the confusion who knows who's who? But it's the 60s so put'er. there pal or gal, enough smoke 'n' rock 'n' roll 'n' I don't care who's what I'm doin! With Molly's in the middle of it — not that she panics, Molly? She's convent trained. She knows how to make the most of an emergency. She jumps the stage to escape the rabble. She's not sure who she's bumping into, and does she care? Havoc is a private schoolgirl's privilege, no matter what the damage, whether it be Chipper, self-centered unrepentant, or Bubba with the Bod, she heads for whoever where she can cause the most trouble — ship on the sea, snake in the grass, a lad with a lass — ZIP-SWIFT — somebody slips past her, short and fast, must be Danny T not knowing what he's missing, when suddenly some big hands grab hers, no doubt by mistake in the turmoil — STUMBLE AROUND TUMBLE — poor Will Cook — but she is saved amidst it all by another pair of hands, arms, very strong arms, a full field press chest to chest.

"Where can we go?" He asks, and Molly takes him by the hand, leads him way down under, down narrow stairs through to a labyrinth of passages into the catacombs!

THUMP into a low hanging pipe. "I can't see a goddamn thing!"

"You don't need to. Follow me!"

"Where are you taking me?" And him not toting any flowers.

"Somewhere where we can be alone!"

Makes sense, so quit asking, and forget the girlfriend home on break, forget the bump on the head... "*Wha-* where are we now?" He's ankle deep in water, and water underground on the Lower East Side of Manhattan is not some refreshing spring cistern.

"Right through here. Crawl!" She commands.

And crawl he does, down on all fours, murky and foul smelling but suddenly there is warmth, like heat, hot... "What?"

They've made their way to the Chamber of Mysteries and they keep crawling into the old coal bin... "Nobody will find us here."

Nor would they want to, not the monks, they wouldn't interfere. The monks know that whatever untoward may occur Molly will, with a little dusting, be almost as good as new, and good used is still OK religion, fact the sinner repented can be far more fun than the innocent undented, especially when you're talking a souped up model with a classy chassis.

"Is this place clean?" Bubba is dripping wet and with what?

"Hell, no! It's *dirty!*"

And he can see her green eyes flash fire in the dark.

Bam Bam / Bam Bam — Danny T is damn bangin mad about it — the big guy / little guy thing, the get the girl gotta gotta — it's finally gotten to the kid a lotta lotta, and it was right there up for grabs too.

Though Molly's interest in Bubba doesn't last. Molly's young, her attention easily diverted, besides which she suffers from a bad case of the hots for Chipper.

"Hey theah fella," Chipper notices a change in Bubba's playing, "what's the mattah?"

"Aw, it's nothin."

"Got to be somethin, you head's hangin off the side of you shouldah."

"Women Chipper, women — they're nothin but trouble."

"Mahcy?'

"I don't want to talk about it."

"No?" And Chipper knows who specifically.

Women remain the topic. Chipper, Will Cook and Danny T are occupied in the Men's Room Conference Center, each in their own stall, discussing their favorites, some stokin, some strokin — Will way out of sync with the other two.

"She's just playin hahd to get, that's all."

"Sparky and the gang seem to be doing OK."

"But that soht of thing don't mean nothin to a gal like huh — you've got to be willin to hold on…"

"Hold on! — *bam bam* — man, I'm getting tired of second hand!"

"Then switch."

"I'm telling you, I'm this close to losing it!"

"Don't go chokin up this close to the finish, now's when you should go fah it like a puhe bred pohkah."

"Yah! Fuck her!" Will Cook shouts out. Which provokes varied private reactions. When suddenly somebody comes breaking through the door and clambers over the walls into one of the stalls, Will Cook's — and it's Molly, seems she's intent on harnassing him, catches him pants down mid-whack and what's the poor pony to do? She mounts him bare back as he bursts out of the box, bucking like a disgorged gelding, tries throwing her off, but he's no match for a gal who's been trained to ride western. She tames him as she takes him, there on the ceramic tile floor, Chipper and Danny T peering through the cracks in amazement.

"Am I seeing things?"

"Bet both youh eyeballs you ah."

Though it must be a most satisfactory fuck since Will's only slightly lathered. Could call it love. For him it has been one hell of a race to the goal post, while for her it is merely a trial heat toward her final meet with the golden maned stallion in the winner's circle.

Bambambambambambambambam — blows the 'Drummer Dynamo' totally out of control!

But if Chipper is bummed, he pretends not to notice, and he can certainly preoccupy himself with runaways, in pairs or singles in series, since the Village is rife with them from all over Westchester County, White Plains, Scarsdale — 'spinners' Chipper calls them, so well oiled they barely squeak while he twirls them. But whatever his contentment, he has to watch for the week while Molly trails after Will Cook, constantly interrupting him in privy motion. Like Bubba, Will too falls. Breaks Will's heart, although it couldn't have lasted. Pitiful critter, here he's been eating sugar out of her hand and then suddenly it's straw in the feed bag. He will bolt back to his stall in the stable ever after, after every performance and never emerge again. Chipper can hear him in there stumping, but what can he say? "Man, loosen youh grip, tight reins on a young trottah'll nevah get him to gallop."

Even so, Will Cook does owe Molly an amount of gratitude since everyone in the band has a begrudging respect for him now. They shake their heads in wonder. The donkey must have something hanging there that none of them ever noticed. And one thing to say for Molly, by the way, is that she never tells anybody about anything about anybody else, not even later to the ingratiating investigative reporter from *Scoreboard*. She has her loyalties, this rare chestnut filly.

Late night attack of the munchies brings Chipper down into the monks' catacomb kitchen, scramble some eggs, do up some toast — and there's got to be a piece of that peach cobbler left over from dinner left in the walk-in. It's three thirty, four in the morning so he's surprised when he arrives, finds somebody's already up making breakfast.

"Whoa. Didn't expect to run into nobody."

"What! — oh, it's you… you startled me."

"Sohry… restless?"

"It's been a long night and I have to drive back to Jersey."

"You've become a regulah commutah."

"I- I found some peach cobbler in the walk-in, want some?"

"Suhe. Got this sugah cravin wicked bad."

"Well here, take this."

"You'h not goin to eat it?"

"I've had three helpings already, with whipcream."

"Dope's what does it to me, speakin of which theah's some great Maine wild bluebehry goin round — you up fah a toke?"

"I'm not into drugs."

"You'h into drugs."

"No, I don-..."

"You'h stokin on that cigahrette like a pro."

"Cigarettes are legal."

"So? They'h still addictive, nicotine's addictive, and I bet theah's othah things you'h addicted to too."

"Such as?"

"Dahk chocolate, mix the bittah with the sweet."

"Funny, isn't it, how we only see other people through our own eyes?"

"Ain't all that hahd figuhrin people out, it's gettin along with them that's the tough paht."

"You have me all figured out, do you?"

"We'h alike you and me."

"How so?"

"I like gihls, you like guys."

"That's natural."

"'Cept some get youh insides chuhnin wohse than usual."

"You're rude."

"Hey, I say it like it is, even if it pisses folks off."

"You don't know anything about me."

"Notice when you get real quiet, you staht in gnawin on youh fingahnails, like you ah now."

"And what do you do?"

"Get high, get off. In between strum my guitah."

"At least I don't flaunt myself on stage."

"Suhe caught youh attention."

"You generate a lot of energy."

"Get so jumpy I can hahdly control myself."

"You're nothing but an urge."

"What, like I don't think oah nothin? Ah you any diffahrent?"

"Girls are different. They have more to lose, more to worry about."

"Yah but they've got theih uhges too — besides we'h alike."

"You keep saying that."

"We ah. Get needy in the night. Wild child. Comes drivin into the Village, flihrtin with dangah."

"And why are we alike?"

"Cause we've both had to grow up too fast, don't have nobody we can trust that much. Vulnahrable, you and me — which only adds to the attraction."

"Notice when you get real quiet, you staht in gnawin on youh fingahnails, like you ah now."

"'Nothah toke?"

"No, I don—..."

"Blow it into youh mouth, real slow, just open youh lips — *yahhh*..." Like he's on a leash, like he's restrained, only touch lip to lip... and she's breathing in deep. "Mah?"

She closes her eyes, lays back in the dark on a blanket on the roof of the three tiered pagoda while he draws in another lung full, hollows her mouth and breathes so slowly in and out for her — the slightest touch to her wrists — *huh, huuh-huuh* — up along her arms — *huuh-huuh* — across her shoulders, strokes under her chin — *huh huh huh huh huh* — cups his fingers and brushes along her cheek bone, one finger lightly across an eyebrow — *huhhhhh!*

She's immobilized.

Nuzzles into her ear, runs his lips through her hair and down, down her neck, the nape and a kiss — so soft, soft soft kiss. Stops. Takes another long draw and starts in again.

She's naked lying back, her arms clasped up around his neck. He's palms on her breasts, lapping at one taut nipple — *huh huh huh huh* — he traces an outline on her belly drip by drip, gulping for air himself as she tightens her grip, soft head on a strong shaft through russet red hair and easily, she lifts, easily, liquid to liquid he parts her, slips in the tip — *huhhh, huhhh, huhhh* — in, in... he's panting when she locks on, twists, twitches, yanks him down flat on top of her, mouth to mouth, tongue to tongue, writhing while he floods her with life giving force.

Dawn. Past dawn. He lies bare ass on an asphalt roof, turns to pull her in close, but she's gone.

THE MOVIE BUSINESS

Bambambambam! Bumbumbumbum! Damndamndamndamn! Dumb dumbdumbdumb! Man's banging his fingers bloody. Though nobody expected Danny T would throw himself into despair over it, no, nor submit to tonsure! But unlike Chipper who has his diversions, Danny T cannot deviate. He's of the single mind set and solid conviction, Indiana, Iowa — there's only one woman out there in the universe — ***damnit! damnit!*** — Marine's been thoroughly indoctrinated in summer camp and can't stand it any other way, which may explain his sudden conversion.

"What the hell," he was heard to cry as he was swallowed whole, "if it gets me what I want, then it's worthwhile!"

Brother Sparky assured him he would never regret his decision, though once the aspirant has descended those steps, a veil of mystery shrouds what occurs next. In the haze and daze of the theater netherworld, anything can happen, does — a dose of Thai stick obliterates all remembrance, and *whew* is it dark choke smoky down under! Eyes cannot see where the blind hold sway, nor words tattle the tale, and even the bravest must grope their way.

Truly, few who have passed beyond have deigned to discuss their experiences, except to mention vague feelings of euphoria and a tingling in certain extremities lingering for days, with vivid memories for weeks, years, their entire lifetimes. Not that any have protested, as in complained to the authorities, and many a recruit has attempted to return for another crossing over these unholy waters, but the monks seem to prefer innocence over prior experience — Molly being the mighty exception to their rule.

"Danny boy, this ain't somethin you've got to do, you know."

"It feels OK, and it isn't forever."

"Don't know. You suhe youh eyebrows ah goin to grow back again?"

Thus was Danny T inducted into the Unholiest Order of the Monks of the Green Pagoda, he who had resisted so steadfastly, but life's a slippery pass at best and those in their teens seem intent on squandering it on all sorts of viscous nonsense. Every hair on his body shaved away, but his soul's OK. For the sect's creed is rather sparse, the rituals straightforward – get down and do it unto others as surely as you would have others get down and do it unto you – although some nights can be tougher than others, like when a second armada of fire trucks and police vans storm the place again, led by a defrocked monk who has a history of plea bargains, a Judas who will direct Lt. Jepson L. Grady straight to the very source of their beliefs, the coal bin Holy of Holies. Ever seen a grown fire company march into a hell hole single file? With their axes at the ready? Some of their number will never recover, tears and shakes from breathing the fumes perhaps, a medically peculiar green lung disease. Sad days after that. The Green Pagoda will be closed per order of the City Health Department, and the monks will be scattered, some upstate to Ossining, others underage to Spofford, but then religious conviction always leaves a trail of prosecution.

About the same time the band leaves on a hastily arranged tour in Danny T's VW bus where they will tarry in San Francisco. Molly will once again join them, this time as Danny T's particular appendage and back-up vocalist – though only after she has served six months time in the custody of Matty of Morristown because of her bad bad bad behavior. And after San Francisco will be sixteen months of chart climbing fame, ending with the infamous Cincinnati Summer of 69 – but that is future and way ahead of our story. Molly is the current love interest, it's still the torrid summer of 68, Danny T has embraced religion, times are good and The Green Pagoda is bustling with youthful superfluidity.

Turns out the guys have a flare for acting, musicians and monks alike. From the altar to the stage to the screen — with Chipper the easiest to cajole. Seems he has a weakness for big production numbers, and since for extra cash Molly has been making a few movies on the side, any of which are now considered classics of their genre, he decides to join with her on a project of epic proportions, cast of dozens in lurid technicolor.

"Whoa, don't know Molly. I've nevah been much of a movie buff — ain't that I'm shy oah nothin."

"You have nothing to be shy about."

"S'pose not, but… it's a romance, right?"

"Set in wartime. You're this dashing young officer who's crazy about me, and while I try to resist your advances, since I'm the wife of the general commanding the garrison, I simply can't help myself."

"So lots of love scenes, kissin and that soht of stuff?"

"It's in the script."

"What the hell. I'll give it my best shot."

The producer/director is named Svig Dryfjord, and he has a two car garage out back behind his house in Bensonhurst. Man is well known around the neighborhood and in many station houses across Brooklyn, for he has this dedication to his art that surpasses the understanding of even his most sympathetic detractors — but it's the late 60s and there's a toleration for all things long suppressed — though most of Svig's output is manufactured solely for the export market, Molly his favorite actress.

"How come they don't want a name stah?"

"The director thrives on raw talent."

The scripts are rudimentary, but they impose their demands on an aspiring young talent. Molly must often and in endless retakes perform with strange men or other women, yet Molly undertakes these assignments with gusto. She is one of life's tried and true troupers. Her method is inbred madness, an open spacy Morristown craziness for it, and memorable scenarios develop. The predictable motif of Occidental girl meet and like company of Oriental men is expanded to include a see-how-many-can-be-crammed into a golf cart as it pivots around the eighteenth hole, with the added feature of a scramble through a highly efficient auto assembly plant on the conveyor belt with hired-for-lifer non-union workers. These add-on scenes make for sure hits on the Pacific Rim.

"I figuhe I'll do fine in the looks depahtment, but when it comes to memorhizin lines and such I get nahvous. Reminds me of back when I was in fifth grade, I made a real mess out of the yeah end assembly.

"How so?"

"Well, each of us kids wah requihed to stand up and say ouh fahewell to the principal and sixth grade teachah, Mistah Jeffhahs, cause he was retihrin aftah thihty yeahs on the job…"

"Each kid in the school?"

"Theah wah only fohty of us in the whole school, all lined up. Anyway when it came my tuhn I got tongue tied as usual, bluhted out 'So long Mistah Jahkfaht', loud as I could — didn't mean to, was just what we kids used to call him behind his back. Whole auditohrium cracked up, stahted hootin, teachahs and pahrents too, totally ruined his fahewell."

"What did they do to you?"

"Had to spend the last week of school sittin in his office like ahways, ended up helpin him pack all his shit."

"He must have appreciated that."

"Nope, Jackfaht nevah liked me, not from the get go."

"The dialog in this production is mostly extemporaneous."

"Mostly what?"

"We make it up as we go along."

"Sounds a whole lot easiah, but they've got to have a speech coach on hand, don't they? I mean some folks say I've got this accent."

"Nothing worth worrying about, really."

Molly should know, she's just wrapped up an Arab white slave costume farce where she was forced to dance around in veils in a tent on a rug – and she studied for the part, took lessons with a real belly dancer from the Astoria section in Queens. There was an oil gusher number that lifted her three stories high while a lucky Texarcana drilling crew slipped and splashed in greasy money, but the camel chase scene between rival new rickety rich desert potentates going for the reddish gold of her soft pubes made this one a box-office spill-over.

"Don't have to cut my haih, do I?"

"No! Absolutely not!"

"Hahdly look like a soldiah."

"You're a British soldier, not an American one."

"Theah's a diffahrence?"

"You wouldn't believe."

"Anybody else we know goin to be paht of the show?"

"Bubba. He's cast as your rival for my affections."

"H'yep, and what happens to him?"

"He loses, you win."

"Ahright!"

"And a few of the other guys have volunteered to play extras."

"Extra what?"

Molly was there at the beginnings of the riding crop and leather strap scene, which some connoisseurs avow she invented because of her youth spent in the stables around Morristown, but its origins were no doubt much older, even ancient – still, since she thought the genre hers, she carved out a turf for herself, once again saddling up and driving for it. She even lassoed Bubba the Bod into a few flicks, and rare gems they are. Talk about a Godfather preview! Bubba can make Arab strongmen envious.

"So Bubba does OK as an actah?"

"He dives right in."

The best of Bubba's offerings was set against a pre-revolutionary Cuban backdrop. Gambling casinos, post office box banking, prostitution at wholesale prices, and virgins rolling cigars on their thighs – filmed on location in Haiti. Bubba was cast as the last Big Boss on the Strip and Molly as a pale guerrilla from the mountains. They meet on the beach outside Havana before the final small boat is about to cast off for Miami. She has a sub-machine gun and he is armed with only his dignity. It's the role reversal bit that drives Latino men mad for it. She orders him to disrobe and commences a search of his body cavities for concealed weapons –

AACH! You know the plot, it's been copied a hundred times since, but badly.

"Should I study my lines befahhand?"

"Don't bother. It's all action anyway."

"An action romance?"

"Sums it up perfectly."

This newest production however, is to be Svig Dryfjord's masterpiece. The plot is literary in origin, Rudyard Kipling. Chipper is duded up, long hair into a 19th century British naval officer's uniform with brass buttons conveniently strung down his front. All Molly requires from costume are hoops and petticoats, the step out variety. The setting is Raj Injia.

"Whoa! Take a look at me!"

Bubba reluctantly agrees to a comeback celebrity role, a conniving Raja who has been forced out of his kingdom by conquering British hordes. It's a character role. Although the Raja has been officially banished, he continues to lurk about the British Governor's wife's private chamber — he knows all the secret passageways in the palace and also happens to be an avowed disciple of the evil Ritah, goddess of tree climbing snakes. Rita is a get-even sort of bitch who recognizes in the Lady Molly a reincarnation of herself — hence Molly gets to play both roles, goddess and wayward wife, and as a bonus no other woman on the set to compete with. See, this is up-scale porn, complete with swashunbuckling adventure scenes, culminating in a sword fight between Chipper, the protagonist with blond hair and Bubba the antagonist with dark.

"To the winner shall go the spoils," in animated close-up. Claims Svig who is into *cinéma vérité*, meaning he is convinced that real underlying friction makes for better fiction. He promises that the actual winner of the staged combat gets to have at it first with the prized British Lady, though he plans that the next scene in sequence will feature the Goddess Ritah consoling the vanquished with her extended tongue, which is to say that there will be no winners nor losers in this film, only first and second runners up. To these proud young men of the movies, sloppy seconds or slurpy thirds or slippery fourths or frothy fifths are all positions worth contending for. Thus the contest is to become a real battle, which is exactly what Svig Dryfjord is instigating, each guy secretly scheming on how to prevail over the other.

But what is it driving a good boy like Bubba who should be reluctant by upbringing and temperment to expose his talents in the movies? It must be the competition of the teens, the experimentation of the times, for he certainly bears Molly no ill will over her recent rebuff, not with this opportunity to bore Molly 'til fill on her indecent bare butt — and with the camera there to record every second's worth of sweet ass revenge! Call him callous, but this episode with Molly has cost him some pride money.

Will Cook is not quite so forgiving, but neither is he vengeful. He simply spurns all offers to play the role of Lord Governor Wimpsy Wainscott who is scripted to win his wife back in the end, plus have the chance to powder and curl his shaggy mop. Nothing entices Will, though he does volunteer to watch the filming unassisted.

The monks from The Green Pagoda consent to play the bit parts, mainly as near naked native extras when needed.

Even heart-crushed Danny T agrees to appear as Kinko the Elephant Boy in brown face, though his role is as usual not explicitly defined. Svig Dryfjord can't afford to hire the elephant, so piped in jungle noises will be employed instead. It's the smallness of stature thing once again. Danny's actually the oldest by six months, possibly the wisest or wise-assed among them, but doomed by reduced physicality to play the boy.

In conception, Svig Dryfjord's *Ritah The Tree Snake Charmer* is brilliant, in execution it is to be flawed. Although the production does allow the leading lady a rare opportunity to achieve her one ambition – to be the lone center of these guys' attention and have it filmed in addition,

Thus the net is cast. With a liberal sprinking of angel dust, Act One begins: A middle of the jungle scene – *de rigueur* – the natives are writhing on the ground and making grunt sounds, the camera recording only indistinguishable fleshy parts, so that their activities are suggested rather than graphically displayed *à la la* Ricky Ryme – a slow artistic start to heat up the imagination of the audience and to prepare for the sudden appearance of Ritah, the Snake Goddess, who throws herself into the middle of the fray and is soon covered from head to toe with snakes, the monks in nothing but green slime body paint. They're squirming up her leg and fitting into her nose, intertwining about her arms and spitting in her ears, they're sliding over thighs and coming in her hair – that's until Raja Bubba appears and frightens them away with his big stick.

Ritah jumps up furious and threatens to cast him as a frog in her next film, but he replies that now is the propitious moment they have both been waiting for, to seize the palace and reclaim the throne from the barbaric British. Ritah is ripe for it. She dries and dresses quickly and rushes with Raja Bubba to the interior of the palace.

Set Change: There is no sound track by the way, no lines for Chipper to forget, with each foreign port of destination free to dub in whatever sound effects they deem appropriate for their indigenous audience.

Act Two: The English Lady is dressing or undressing herself in front of her chamber mirror when a bold blond young officer of her Naval Guard enters the room. She notices him immediately through the glass, but pretends not to be alarmed. He approaches her from behind and begins to remove a lacy camisole from off her cream sweet shoulders. Bare backed she does not resist, in fact she soon swoons, reels and finds support in his arms, from which vantage she fast awakens to begin tearing at his buttons — the authentic standard issue Foreign Service uniform being so designed as to allow rapid access — and soon both the officer and the lady are entirely undone. She falls to her knees in gratitude and purses her lips. Chipper is at rigid attention and begins with those pelvic stabs that everyone in the band thought were mere inventions of his on-stage persona — *when who should burst in upon the scene?* Not the husband and Lord, no, but Raja Bubba with the darkly veiled Goddess Ritah — a double, one of the monks disguised in drag for this rare appearance of the two women together in the same scene.

"Cut!" Svig calls. And the cameraman, a toothless old lecher who can't control his drooling, complies, along with the lighting man, a six four B-ball dribbler named Yank.

The male leads, Chipper and Bubba, and the native extras are hard into it and pull back from the edge most reluctantly — always the problem of using amateurs in an ambitious production.

Molly's a pro however. She does a quick change and reappears for the close-up of the veiled shocked Goddess, shocked not because of what the British are doing to each other with the Lord out of the room, no, she knows what they do because they have been doing it all over Injia to the Injians, Lord or no Lord in the room, and for nearly a century. Rather what it is that shocks her is the physical similarity between she, Injian Goddess, and her, English Lady. There is this silent movie back and forth from face to face sequence, and Molly obliges by stripping off one costume and donning another, without a dressing room or a seamstress, the crew and the cast nary averting their eyes, until the entire sequence is completed.

"Cut!"

Molly is inhaling and exhaling in large draws, it's a workout worthy of an Olympian, but she is young and easily exhilarated by all the attention.

Meanwhile the guys on the set are crawling with hornets. Chipper and Bubba are frame frozen in their stand off. The hunky monkeys are hungry, the camera man is slurping, Svig Dryfjord is scratching himself, and Yank in lighting is at it. And last, least anyone should forget, Danny T as Kinko the Jungle Boy. He has tightened a vice grip on himself. He glances around, yeah, there might be a line-up and he might by genetic structure be last in position, but stripped down he is proportionally as much a man as any of them, right? It's that locker room confrontation all over again, there where a shorter-than-average guy has to stand up as tall as he can among the big ones, football season on the bench, with no wonder that grunts like Danny T wrestle or play class clown, spring for early detention centers or join the Marines — the Marines, either big bruisers or little guys, either/or, no

Mister Corporal sizes in between. And why is that? Because it builds determination, that's what it does, and a willingness to learn whatever it takes to bring a big guy down.

But how is Danny T going to best these big guys? Bubba and Chipper have the lead roles. Bubba's been there before and rumor is Chipper has too, all simply a game to them, Molly their wittingly willing kickball. Danny T grits his teeth and he flexes his forearms. Sure, Molly has been with some others, a few others, so many others, but if she is to be his, and she's going to be his, then damn it she will have to surrender solely and entirely to him. Others may have unfortunately preceded, but others shall not succeed again, no way. The only question is how can he *bam bam* inch up in the line-up, next, next — NEXT!

"Stay cool little man." Sparky the head monk counsels.

Danny T nods and flips through the catalog of plays the monks have taught him in their late night pre-game strategy sessions, for they have wisely charted the many paths needed to achieve the common goal of mankind — to score and to score big — they have also devised some irregular plays here and there. And to give the monks their due, they have been infinitely patient with Danny T's education. They took him in as a rookie and they turned him around into a first draft finalist, they taught him everything they knew and many things about which they were only guessing. And Danny T 'Drummer Dynamo' endured it all, hell, what does a kid from Indiana or Iowa know about real religion? Suppose the young monks are right, and none of it felt that bad, maybe a few things at first, but the Dynamo is good to go, to face Chipper, to face Bubba, even the united brotherhood if he must, claim for himself their prize.

"You alright?"

Right! Right? Maybe. Maybe he has watched too long from the sidelines and suffers from illusions of pint-sized grandeur, because he is shaking, he is panting, he is in intense heat. Sparky notices his condition and throws a blanket over him because Danny T has advanced into a cold sweat in a very hot place, but a bucket of ice water would do him no better.

Will Cook? Will is around somewhere too. Yes, he's curled into a corner, knees up, arms crossed, eyes bulging, upper lip trembling too, and as the scene heats up, his skin begins to crawl, and his hands and feet, his instinct is to get away, and the only way out is up, up into the rafters of the garage he creeps, hand over hand over foot, hand, foot, foot, always gets those damned appendages mixed up, and the rafters aren't all that wide either, but across the top and over Svig Dryfjord's balding beaded pate he sneaks because Will's got to get a better look at the action.

"Ready on set!" Svig calls out.

The cast assembles — and does Molly herself understand any of the underlying tensions surrounding her? These stars pretend they never do, but she must have some clue if not a detailed set of notes, because when she does resume her position center stage, she flickers with her eyelashes at each one of them — Chipper the dapper undressed Naval Officer who's eager for beaver, Bubba the deposed Raja zipped up now but determined to regain what was rightfully his from the beginning, and each and every one of the muscular monks now stripped down to pecker holsters though nothing in the script dictates such a change, the frothing cameraman, Svig Dryfjord, Yank, the six four lighting master, and lastly a wink, hers, a blink, and is it involuntary, because wide-range misinterpretation is possible when a goddess is involved, wrong cue and an entire world class religious war could ensue, especially if it's directed at one dumb struck jungle boy.

A wink! Danny T starts to shivering again. "You'll get your chance to play in the game kid, just remember, stay cool." Danny T acknowledges the advice, and he churns over the many teachings of the monks' learned ways, searching for the right enlightened pathway, the dash along the ledge, the perfect uphill ploy, the best…

"Action!"

Raja Bubba finally draws his sword in order to slay the offensive officer, and British Chipper is forced to respond in kind, which he does, WHONG-G-G-G! Just as fast as that! Talk about the advantages of being a teen! Anyway, the two combatants square off and start to circle, blades upraised. Ritah rushes in between. "No," she gasps, and her hand reaches to restrain Bubba — she grabs his at the hilt is what she does, and cuts off circulation — stops the Raja in his tracks — which gives the British officer and no gentleman a certain advantage. Goddess Ritah, realizing what she has done, then rushes the British officer. He reaches out to restrain her, manfully, but it is too late, her body is the ultimate sacrifice, she is pierced, she falls upon his sword, and with loud sobbing slinks to the floor. But the scene is not over, not by a long shot. An actress the stature of Molly knows how to milk a scene. There are these death throes with Chipper on top of her, writhings and body leaps, thumping and humping — with the camera trained directly in on the central action — pull *in*, push *out*, huff 'n' puff then *shout!* There isn't a dry tongue in the studio.

"Cut!"

Molly has to clean up and change costume, while Chipper wanders about in a daze. Bubba retires to his corner, having lost in the first go-round, he's intent on winning in the second.

And Danny T? Wild man! Cold heaves have now given over to night sweats. The monks restrain him, much more fun that way.

Will Cook? He's still creak creeping above, a noncombatant out of play.

Act Three is when Lord Governor Wimpsy Wainscott is supposed to rush in, find the bloody goddess, repent for the Crown's sake and save the entire situation for the good of the subjugated empire, but with Will Cook unwilling to play the Governor, poor Svig Dryfjord must improvise. But who to do and where and exactly how? And he can't afford to quibble and so lose momentum. He signals Danny T, alias Kinko the Jungle Boy, to get ready to jump in, except that in the silence his command is misinterpreted by the crowd of native extras, poking through their holsters — and isn't that always the way, open the door of opportunity the least crack and the naked masses will rush inside entirely uninvited to spoil the ball.

DANNY T SUDDENLY FEELS LIKE THERE'S SOMETHING PSYCHO CRAWLING RIGHT ABOVE HIS HEAD! MAD MAN, ICE MAN, TAKING ALL THE HEAT!

"Are you ready to dive in there boy?" Svig Dryfjord yells at Danny T.

Yes, yes — "WHAT DO I HAVE TO DO?" Danny yells back eagerly.

"You do what we all have to do," Svig sagely replies.

Logic, no matter how convoluted, appeals to a Danny T, he understands implicitly if not explicitly. He simply has to go and do it, and do it right out there in front of everybody like everybody else is doing it — hey, he knows them all, doesn't he? Chipper, Bubba, not the director, no, but he's like a coach and these other guys his assistants, and they've all played on the same field, tossed in the same showers, he knows the monks to a man, so hell — "I'M READY WHENEVER YOU NEED ME!"

Good because the camera is already rolling on Act Four: Chipper resumes his position and advances on Bubba who is again drawn and ready more quickly than Chipper expects. What to do, well, he grabs Molly's arms — Molly is the English Lady again — using her as a shield and slipping in accidentally behind her, deep sheathing her — for a drawn blade, even if the Englishman were a gentleman, can prick somebody, and certainly if he's not artful.

Molly is kicking and screaming — MAD! Who's show is this anyway, and done in from the backside! Though her protest goes unanswered because there is no sound track, and any and all interpretations of this scene are thereby permissible in a court of law.

But Danny T hears her cries, his jaw clinches, his spine rushes alternately hot and cold — could be the angel dust.

Bubba's not unsympathetic nor empathetic, neither one, he leaps and thrusts at Molly, almost scoring, but Chipper is deft, swerving with her, parrying from side to side, while hosing her sewer wise. Bubba the Bull's enraged, he charges again, almost overthrowing both of them entirely. Chipper feints back and around, narrowly averting Bubba's lunge.

Molly is being swept about in quite the tussle, and not happy, though she is making some startling ringside noises, various naying surprises and braying challenges, some insult concerning Bubba's horns and how all three could together make motion picture history.

It's enough to make Bubba rally and drive forward once again. Chipper swerves, mad cap matador with Molly in tow, and Bubba misses again, though Molly is able to trip him as he passes. "HAH HAH!" Chipper gloats, and Bubba downed momentarily rises again and begins to circle, shoulders down, nostrils snorting fire, legs kicking, arms dangling while he inches closer. Chipper is easing in and out of Molly, goose greasing her gaily, hands on her long neck and bending her far forward. She is for once reduced to *hu-h uh huh huh-huh* sounds.

Svig Dryfjord coos encouragement. "That's it, that's it, take it slow and easy, make it last for the camera!"

Danny T is burning worse than Bubba the B, the hot lights of the playing field beckon him. He is up off the bench and raring to go. The monks are in a huddle themselves, cooking up something.

Will Cook has crept across the exposed beam, directly overhead, accompanied by ominous creakings.

Molly is roused to her insatiable best, delighting in spontaneous versatility. She shall never be bowed long however, not even by Chipper. She rears back and kicks up, cheerleader three point field goal. Bubba sees a hole and scoots through it for the tackle. Chipper falls back and lands flat on the boudoir sofa. He's on the bottom but still rumping Molly, with Bubba above and about to gore.

It's the monks who can't bear to be left out of the action any longer, and so they charge, in one of their renowned precision formations, slapping asses and rushing right by Danny T. "Hut two, grab her by the shoe, three, four, there's always room for more — seven, eight, nine in a line."

But folks, don't count Danny T out, not that much determination. He knows the monks' plays, their signals, the intricate moves they can make and just as they are about to encircle and trounce, Danny T, the pint piston, sprints forward with a time tested tactic — the slide — the short guy's ultimate weapon — glide right under the big guys and hit with a hard head up from underneath. Knock'em out of the huddle and back on their kiesters, sliding just as the they're diving and, and, and...

Hey, it would've worked Danny Boy, but like all plays that go awry at the precise split second of execution, Will Cook loses his grip, his wits and goes looping off the ceiling — WHOOP WHOOP — lands abreast of Molly and right as Bubba's about to commit a foul — WHOA-WHOA-WAIT... HE SLICES INTO WILL — by mistake, because no self-respecting Italian boy from the neighborhood would do none of that, no sir, though it's then when the monks hit from all sides, the sofa collapses in a crash, and who's caught underneath the pile-up but Danny T slipping under the host of them.

Molly is screaming mad — even a Molly's not ready for a UFO landing in her lap — FLAP SPLAT AT IT and what is it — STAB BAT AT IT she doesn't know — DAMN IT NAB IT before it spoils her show! But it's only Will Cook gal, face down poundin on you, but why is she slapping at him, he doesn't know, and what is it Bubba's doing in back of him — that's not his big toe?

Danny T heeds the poor girl's cries, he begins straining, lifting from underneath, but a twelve man mountain is more weight than a reverse bench press midwestern guy can do, Molly not helping any, squealing and squirming to Chipper's delight, Will's discomfiture and Bubba's inability to back out now — all of which leaves Danny T out of the action.

Svig Dryfjord is so excited he can only stutter and scratch. The cameraman drools and tracks in as far as he can get, yet WHAT IS IT, WHAT'S HAPPENING?

The entire man mountain looks as if it's about to erupt — Danny T, mighty mouse? NO! IT'S WILL COOK KICKING IN SPINS AGAIN! — BAH —BHOOOMB!!! — bodies go flying ev-e-ry-where! FREE FOAM AND BLATHERING! And in all the excitement, Yank the electrician trips over the portable generator cable, pulls the plug on the lights — plunging the entire set into interior darkness — camera recording shadows in the night — AND JUST AS THE ACTION WAS REACHINGGANG BANGING DECIBEL LEVELS! LORD GOD IN HEAVEN! WHAT RAW FOOTAGE IS LOST FOR POSTERITY! Though I understand there's this fellow in Canarsie, some distant near death relative of Svig's, who has a large private collection of the stars at their rip-roaring best and who has retrieved what film clips remain from the Bensonhurst estate and has painstakingly edited them anew into a reasonable facsimile of the first half original, and if he has succeeded at this, this cousin, and even if he hasn't but he is out there with the clips, please, tell him to do his bit for posterity, log on to loosenukes.com, post it on the bulletin board, because there's lots of us cult carrying card callers who'd do just about anything natural or un- to see this pistol packing 43 Double D full length feature of the band landing and lapping in their youthfestival glory!

Also, and alas theologically, for all the misery that becomes furtive sins in the dark, there's a love that bubbles to the top, a love that will endure, one that will stay hard yet pliant, that is, respectively respectful and for a hell of a long time, thus refuting at last and for all this ill-bred notion that out of sin no good can be conceived, though some have said, mostly in private, that the only good that does come, and feels good too, is out of sin so conceived. Then that could be nothing but nonsense speculation, for it's the artwork that shall endure, *Ritah The Tree Snake Charmer*, the film that could have rocketed The Loose Nukes to notorious prominence, especially in Europe which was dying at the time for raw rock 'n' roll. Yet for the misstep of Yank, a lone tall and skinny electrician — and they're a whole nother breed — the world has been left with an unrefillable void, no deposit, no return, and that in the end is the pity.

When the cast awakens, dawn and a nosy neighbor peering through the garage windows, there is Danny T like some yappy bed chamber terrier, barking away at any would-be early rising besieger, with the result that everybody gives up and wanders home — D-train Coney Island direct. Molly is stunned, and not a little disappointed, but then they've all had their fill and are gone now, so the frisky little puppy can finally pounce on her belly, lick her silly and lift her legs *hi'yup* over his fireplug, and it is dawn of the second solid day at it, but she is pleased — and that's why little guys and full size girls hit it off so well, because little guys make for the best lap size tail wagglers in the business.

No, I said, and at first I resisted, these are temptations of the flesh, aren't they, though they surround me everywhere I look, and the good Sisters warned me, no, beware, because if you're ever caught in the act by a comet, it's instant hell and it doesn't even need to be at the exact moment you're doing it, no, it can be the moment right before or right before that, whenever it was you gave into the thought of it, willingly, breathlessly for even the contemplation, the intent, the consent constitutes the sin as much as the act itself, Father DiFuso said that, so no, don't be naïve in matters of eternal damnation although it makes a girl want to stay inside and hide away from falling stars, but with all the fear of hell fire lapping up your legs, you inevitably give into it, and how can you help it when you have breasts this nice, though Margie O'Connor's are bigger and Beth Carbone shows more, then it was Doctor Hornsby first, strange the name, whispering cancer as he poked me and probed me all over, cancer, always the threat of cancer sprouting up undetected, and stand up on the little stool, my dear, he'd say, slip your clothes off, good, now sit or lie back, whichever is more comfortable, legs up and stretch apart, really *streeetch* those legs, that's it — Sister Magdalena said show due deference in the presence of authority — and I did as he checked out everything, Matty sitting patiently out in the waiting room, may be here, he would press, or here, breathe deeply, very deeply, chest out, that's right, hold that, *hmmm*, could be anywhere, it's best to keep a check, safer's better than sorry later, but no, today it looks like we're lucky, no deadly cancers yet, still we have to have our regular monthly check ups, don't we, wait, wait, before you dress completely, what's that suspicious spot, we haven't checked down there yet, have we, and oh, oh my, isn't that soft tissue prime cancer country, must be, by the way you're breathing so heavily, yes, no, is it, let me touch down there some more, lightly, yes, yes, hold still, until I bit my lip down hard and started crying, oh oh, no, must be something else entirely, now see, that's over with and it wasn't so bad, was it?

How did I know what he was probing, and when I finally got the nerve to tell Matty, he said where, that he best have a look see soft touch himself.

Some girls have to grow up early, all these threats and fears and worries, planets off course and getting pregnant and live bunny rabbit tests before booking a flight to Sweden, abortion, instant hell, and cancer, breast cancer, cervical cancer, or ovarian, doctors, fathers, but if cancer is going to be the end of me anyway, why not enjoy it while it lasts, I can always run and whisper to Father DiFuso before some comet hits me, and if that's all it takes to win votes for cheerleader and a chance to become prom queen, that's not such a high price to pay, except for the build-up and the kissing it's all over so quickly anyway, especially Brad Cassidy, he can kiss, *ohh*, but he comes so quickly because he has no idea what he's doing!

"Pull out!"

"No no!"

"Pull out!"

"No no. Not yet!"

"Pull out! PULL OUT!"

"No no — I'm not even CLOSE!"

"Yes you *are*, I can FEEL IT! I CAN TELL!"

"No, no, no no no…"

"Yes, yes, YESSSSSS!"

"*E'yow!* WHAT DID YOU GO AND DO THAT FOR?"

"I told you I could tell."

And he was sitting there cackling like a hyena, spouting all over my best school blouse, and that friend of his, Mark, Cassy's brother, he wasn't any better, dribbling down the seat while I wondered how flesh could be made out of that fluid, and they promised they wouldn't tell their buddies on the football team, but poor Suzy Shea, she had no idea what hit her, hell fire would have been easier, but I can take it better than she can and they don't seem to say anything to anyone about me, not that I've heard anyway, because I know they all want to come back for seconds is why, and they'd better keep their wise remarks about my teats to themselves, calling me all the time to invite me out for a quick date, cruise around the park, stop at the drive-in after for a hamburger and a coke, *un unh*, I tell them, no way, thank you but I'm busy tonight with somebody else, maybe tomorrow or over the weekend, and who's the lucky guy they want to know, and I say I wouldn't tell you, you'd just go and tell everybody else, and none of them care about me, just leave me hanging while I have to take care of myself and that older kid in the stables, how would he enjoy being bridled and saddled and ridden that hard, think about the poor horse for a change of pace, it's better to ride him bare back and hold onto his neck tight with your arms, bare back and hair back and nearly naked, no underwear, that's how I like to ride him, Champion, thighs tight around those powerful flanks of his, stretched out across his back, arms under his neck, galloping cross-country, leaping over the Comstocks' fence rails, and don't I have a roomful of ribbons now and trophies to boast about, thank you, can jump higher than any of them with everyone staring at me all the time, especially on Sundays after mass, gaping at me as though I was a show horse myself, a blue ribbon around my neck, and Matty proud to introduce me, this is my youngest, Molly, quite the grown up little colt, isn't she Commissioner, and the Commissioner of something with his hands all over me under the stairway in the Rotunda of the State House, asking me if I enjoyed school and did I have a steady boyfriend yet, winking, what was that supposed to mean, could he kiss me on the lips and his hands slippery wet down my shirt and rubbing under my bra for a long time, *aww*, he was just drunk, sweetie pie, don't worry about it, Matty's always understanding as if drink explains away everything, mother's always drinking but don't worry about that, Matty explains, nor her yelling about my getting fat and the kitchen a mess because I finally had to fix myself something to eat and why were you late coming home and did you take the Continental without your father's permission and why do you love him more than you love me, and Matty complaining, I'll never get to sleep with her screaming like that and you don't realize how much it upsets me, but what can I do, she's my wife until death do us part, so could you massage my forehead again and my tummy like you always do, I have a hard day's work ahead of me tomorrow and it will help me sleep, sweetie, it will, so why does helping him sleep keep me awake nights, and Sister Magdalena yapping constantly about the sweaters, ties down her own teats, Cassy says, they wrap bunting around them to make them flat like a man's, like men's dimple dots but they're just as smooth, soft skin, but so hard underneath, like monks, they're so cute, *ohh yes* they are and no hair, not a one, so careful about the way they touch me all over with their fingers and they feel my whole body up and down, everywhere, ninety finger tips at the same time, all properly coordinated, and tongues speaking different languages, I can't take it sometimes, no, the twitching, the feeling, no no, don't stop, whatever you do, don't stop, and I don't care if they need theirs done too, tastes salty, but it's OK, thicker than milk and full of tiny tadpoles, Father DiFuso says, that's why they can slide in so easily, swim upstream, and are you sure it feels OK, Molly, just say if it hurts, but what can I say, I can't speak, I can't say a word, no, yes, nothing, and they keep kissing me while they're doing it, the way they're supposed to, the way I love men to do, the way they kiss they could give lessons at it, everyone of them, but that Bubba's such a horse, can't kiss worth a damn, love his shoulders though and that body, my God, he's so strong and hairy and huge, but what an ego, thinks he's another one of God's gifts to women and the neighborhood stud, *hah*, what he has to learn and Will Cook, oh no, why did I ever do that, I must have been wrecked out of my mind, but he was so funny and cute about it and clumsy, but so intense, if only he could calm down, though his hands, *oh-hh-* he could feel me all over forever if he wanted to, I'd just lay there, lay there forever, and Danny T, where did he learn to do all that by himself and all that energy, he's better than nine monks at once, he takes his time, does the job right, and he can, he can take all the time he wants and kiss wherever, whenever, like it's going to last forever, and I feel so good I could die forever, but I can't do that, I'd definitely go straight to hell forever, wouldn't I, no no I can't, not now, can I, because I'm so young and the young shouldn't die, should they, they're just getting started, like when Ken Ryder wrapped his car around that telephone pole and killed himself and Eddie Stanton, his best friend, but everybody said they were queer anyway, always alone together and joy riding and drunk and they probably went straight to hell for that too, last day senior year after the class picnic, but Jesus never experienced any of it, not even the kissing, and that must be why he sends everyone to hell for doing it, no, I shouldn't think like that should I, no, because he must have been a good man, he was God, right, and it's just all these other people around him who are fucked-up and determined to make everybody else miserable like themselves, and Chipper, he is so beautiful and sexy and that long blond hair like a girl's I could stroke it forever and lie there and love him and lick him and lock on his lips if only he'd reach over and touch me, touch me again... but who does he think he is anyway, JESUS CHRIST, no no no no, don't say that, no, but he's worse a flirt than any girl could ever be, playing all those games, head games, hide and seek, do you really want me, then you have to crawl if you do, prove it, beg on your hands and knees, he's a cock tease... what do you want from me anyway, to burn in hell for you, no no, big beautiful breasts and a blow job's not good enough for you, it's good enough for any other guy, but oh my God, I would do anything, anything, *oh-h*, I would, I... would... do... anything, anything, if only you would touch me, no, I would, I mean it, it's the truth, anything, anything, *oh-h oh-h*, I would, I shouldn't, but I would... *no oh, ohh* I would, *ohh, ohhh* I would, I would do anything! Anything! If only you would touch me – touch me – touch me!

TIME'S UP

...THE EIGHTEEN MONTHS BEFORE WEMBLEY

"Betsy, babydoll, wake up! We've got to head out!"
-wha-wha wher-*rr*?
"The eahth's goin to be passin through the von Patton Belt tonight."
The von Patton Belt?
"It'll be anotheh fifty yeahs befah we'll get to see a meateoh showah this awesome. Let's hike up Eagle Roost and watch from ouh front row seats."
-rr rowl, it's May chum, thirty degrees, and you want to do an overnighter on top of a rock?
"Quit youh complainin, we ain't nevah goin to get this chance again."
What, to freeze our tailbones off?
"They'h predictin a meteohrite a minute, so what'll we take along – jug of my premium dahk to wahd off the cold, couple of fat juicy buds… got my pipe on me heah somewheah, lightah… that oughta do…"
What about *food! food!*
"Food, right, how about some baloney and mustahd sandwiches?"
That's it, go gourmet.
"Got a fresh bag of these roasted gahlic and vinegah chips you like…"
Curl your tongue on one of those.
"…bowl fah you… you want me to lug watah oah will a slug of my homebrew do?"
Well, if it's a special occasion, I might indulge – have any pale ale?
"Still got some of that cranbehry ambah you wah pahtial to at New Yeah's – so get up, we've got to get movin."
Betsy lifts herself off the rug in front of the wood stove, stretches.
"Seem to be missin somethin…"
Your mind, don't forget to pack that.
"…*whoa*, I know – shrooms. Can't fahget those. Special night, might as well blow ouh brains out altogethah."

-roh no, not that foul tasting fungus you grow.

"Glad you reminded me." Chipper slides a pallet out from under his bed and plucks a few round firm heads, heads black as the night soil they're planted in. "Puhe mooseshit mushrooms, that'll send us soahrin."

As in floating a few feet above ground.

"Should've stahted munchin on these a lot soonah. Show'll be half ovah befah they kick in — want a bite?"

You're on your own with those chum, I need my wits about me if I'm going rock climbing in the dark.

"Anythin else majah I'm fahgettin?"

-rrah -rrah -rash -ri-ri...

"Bug spray? Theah won't be any mosquitoes this eahly in the season."

-roh! -rrah-rash- r-right.

"Flashlight, right! See if I've got one that wohks… let's see…nope, this suckah's cohroded."

They stumble out of the dugout into a full moon.

"Pahfect weathah. Crisp, cleah, not a cloud in sight."

-brrrrrr

"Look, theah goes one, shootin right ovah head!"

Betsy must have blinked because she misses it.

"And look at the stahs, like a cosmic fihewohks display." They start hiking through the woods, Chipper in the lead. "Did you know that hidden behind some fah away twinklah, theah's a whole othah galaxy with as many stahs and planets as ouh own Milky Way."

-rrraw! Betsy yawns. She's been yawning a lot lately. Could be advanced age, she is nearly eleven, or boredom — Saturday night and all Chipper can find to do is sit on top of a rock in nowhere northernmost Maine and gaze over distances.

"And that stah you'h lookin at fah fah out theah, that's only the tailin's off a gallaxy racin away billions of light yeahs beyond ouh reach — *y'ouch!*"

What's the matter?

"Cracked my big toe on somethin — and we fahgot the flashlight."

If you'd pull that fool head of yours out of the stars and watch where you're going! *-roh* I can tell, this is going to be one of those nights.

"Look, ovah to the left, theah goes anothah meteohrite!"

Betsy catches this one.

"They'll be blazin at us from evahry dihrection — *damn!*" A tree root this time. "You'd bettah take the lead gihl."

Which she does. Betsy's hiked to the bald top of Eagle Roost so often she could do it blindfolded. It's the highest outcrop in the vicinity with an unobstructed view of the entire St John's river valley, and the exclusive redoubt of one Chipper Stirbee, who's busy whoofing down shrooms.

"We should've gotten a *chomp chomp* eahliah staht."

Early, late, Betsy's hiked this path through rain, through blinding sleet, over snow packed three, four feet or deeper, and during hot humid summers with squadrons of mosquitoes on the attack, and always always late at night when Chipper gets really restless.

"Damn!" Man smacks into a branch this time, swallows a cap whole. "Fuckin waste." Besides he's choking on the thing. "Got to chew evahry mohsel real slow, absohb the essence — suhe you don't want a bite?"

What, so we can both trip along on moose shit?

"Pissah light show!"

You said it chum, worth a night on a cold rock any time.

"Nevah seen so many meteohrites in my life — look ovah theah! Man that's got the longest tail yet. And theah goes anothah — anothah! *Whoa!*"

Betsy's impressed. She has easily seen a hundred, maybe more, some in groups of ten or four, and speeding from every direction, left, right, front, back, high overhead. Like nothing she's ever seen before.

Chipper covers her back side with his blanket. "Suhe you don't want to chew on some shroom, puts you right in the groove."

No thanks. The girl's actually feeling a bit dizzy, and being anchored to something solid is very reassuring.

"How about anothah bowl of that cranbehry ambah then?"

Maybe a smidge.

"You can undahstand why the ancients figuhed the eahth was stationahry and the sun and the stahs went cihclin round them."

No surprise there, only old men would be convinced they're the center of the universe.

"Awesome. Entihe gallaxy in fast fahwahd!"

Betsy laps at the amber to steady her nerves.

"Kicked back, takin in the whole show — I mean you've got to admit it's downright inspihrin."

Betsy goes belly to the ground, though she's eyes wide and watching.

"Makes you wondah wheah we came from, wheah we'h headin…"

Not far, not tonight.

"…stahry nights, flashin lights, sky spihralin round on top of us!" Chipper suddenly bolts straight up, whips the blanket off — "*whoo ee…*"

What's this?

"…feel the chill! Moon ripe, yankin at the tides. Eahth into a spin, axis tiltin, 'bout ready to catch some spring rays with stahs shootin off evahry which way!" Sight sends him into a spin, he grabs at his knees and pivots on his butt. "Can you heah the music baby doll, can you? That's the sound of the spheahs pahfectly tuned to the hahmonic commotion!"

Betsy hears nothing of the sort, but she can recognize a psilocybin fit when she sees one.

"It's like I'm caught inside this gigantic pinwheel, silvah spahks flickin off the sides as we go glidin through space at a million miles pah second."

I'm fine where I'm at, thank you, but -*how rowrow* many of those things did you gobble?

"Night of nights, full of frights, see the sights!" Boy jackknifes out of the fetal and is about to take a running dive off the edge — when Betsy throws a body block that sends him sprawling face flat on the rock.

"Damn!" Blood red about the nose, but no more spinning pinwheels.

Sorry.

"Was like a vision gihl, fah a split second, the entihe univehse closin into this cyclone spout, swihlin fastah and fastah around us..."

Never mind that Galileo disproved the homeocentricity of the universe four hundred years ago.

"...and pullin us way away out theah into it!"

Bet. Whole bag would have probably launched you clear to Jupiter.

"Man's got to break his chains, shed his skin, sprout wings and soah!"

Except his take-off's bound to be bumpy.

"Vision like nothin I've evah seen!"

Nor will again, at least when you're sober.

You *ro-ro-ove-rr* your early spring madness?

Must be, he's nosed into his blanket, chewing.

Surely you're not eating more of those dreadful things?

"Baloney and mustuhd, want some?"

Hold on the mustard.

"You know, theah's one thing that's still got me stumped. Just can't quite figuhe how in the hell I'm evah goin to get up theah, up theah among those stahs — you know what I'm sayin?"

Betsy knows what Chipper is saying. Betsy has sat on this same rock a hundred times, a hundred times a hundred. She has stared up at those same stars a hundred times, a hundred times a hundred, and if not her then her mother has sat here with Chipper and her mother before that and her mother before that, generations of nondescript half Lab/half Dobbie black hound dogs who have sniffed along behind generations of nondescript half French/half Norse blond Stirbees, and none of them, not a one of them, not black hound dogs nor blond Stirbees has ever wondered how they were going to get up there to those stars. Fact is that up until now hound dogs and Stirbees have both known instinctively to leave those stars alone, because there's enough of them up there, God knows, and those stars will do just fine, a long time, without one more among them, and without a Stirbee among them a lot longer than that.

"I know you'h snickahrin to youhself. I can ahways tell when you'h snickahrin and sayin this jokah's nevah goin to get nowheah neah those stahs. Well I'm tellin you gihl, I'm goin to do it. As suhe as we'h sittin heah on this rock watchin this showah, I'm goin to figuah a way."

Betsy's not snickering, nor does she snore, yet she is accused of both regularly. It's her stomach that gurgles, usually after a bowl of those tasteless corn pellets Chipper's been buying for her over at the Grand Northern, buck fifty for a ten pound bag.

"Time's about ready fah us to make a move, can feel it in my bones."

Cold, that's what you feel, and at least one more blizzard predicted.

"See, you and me, we've got to do somethin, somethin big, make a change — oppohtunity's due to pass us by."

What is this you and me bit?

"We've got to reach out to those stahs, latch onto the futuah. Animals too. You've got to raih up on youh hind legs and howl, chase aftah the bastahds who buhnt that hole through the ozone layah, all those extra fluohrohcahbons causin the ice caps to melt and disruptin ouh nohmal weathah pattahns, that's why we've been havin all the floods and why the wintahs ah so wahm now — we don't act fast and we might nevah have any mah blizzahds."

There's a cause. Save our blizzards.

"Sun'll buhn right through that hide of youhs, cook youh ohgans. We'll all have to move indoohs, buhrow in duhrin the day, travel round nights like raccoons."

Those scavengers — but then it wouldn't change your routine any, I mean, you're not exactly what they call a morning person.

"Tropics will disappeah into desehrts, cities along the coast flood ovah, folks will be fohced to move into the hills heah, crowd in with us."

Convert the woodshed into a year-round rental.

"Two degree hike in avahrage tempahratuhe, and you've got youhself a global catastrophe, ihrahvahsible — can't go patchin it ovah by launchin tankahs full of ozone neithah, only solution is to stop people from pumpin exhaust out theih tailpipes."

Sounds reasonable.

"Once you undahstand the repuhcussions from a calamity like this, you've got to do somethin. Can't just sit back on youh duff and stew."

What can I do?

"I don't mean only you. I mean me, evahrybody. We've got to unite!"

But what voice does a pup have? Nobody in their right mind talks to dogs, let alone bothers to ask our opinions. Can never bark back. Go, come, that's all most folks have to say to a dog. And if you fuss too much, it's pack you off to the vet for a sex-change operation.

"Time's now. Spring's ahmost heah, change of season, I can feel it, feel like climbin clean cleah out of my skin."

I'm a bit restless myself.

"You can smell it, smell the eathah hangin heavy in the aih…"

Low pressure pocket pushing ahead of that storm from the Great Lakes.

"…we've got to struggle, got to fight if we'h evah goin to win this battle ovah the futuhe of ouh own planet."

At least rattle the sabers.

"I'm tellin you, somethin's up…" Chipper's up. Wobbily legs and all.

-roh no! Not another run for the edge!

"…can you heah the constellations shiftin position? Can you?"

No. Nothing. Not even a pine cone drop.

"That pack of stahs ovah theah especially, can you feel the draw?"

Which where?

"Ohrion, the Huntah, see, he's layin low on the westahn horizon, about to go undah. And right behind him Sihrius, the Dog Stah…"

Dog Star?

"…can't miss the Dog Stah, he's the brightest stah in ouh sky…"

I'm not surprised.

"…faithful companion to Ohrion, follows close on his heels as he travels across the heavens…"

Dog's lot, isn't it, always forced to tag along.

"…ahright now, trace a line to the right of Sihrius and down slightly, see those three stahs in a row theah? That's Ohrion's belt, and right below, kinda hangin in between his legs, that's the Ohrion nebula… M 42 they call it officially…"

Catchy.

"…you could see it bettah if the moon wasn't so bright — but inside theah's this massive blast fuhnace wheah new stahs ah bein bohn this very second, thousands of them in the midst of creation, young hot white and ready to buhst upon the scene, staht spawnin little planets of theih own, maybe one like ouhs."

My my.

"And that's wheah we've got to go Betsy, you and me, got to get ouh butts up theah and in on the action."

Nova superstud.

"They say it's sixteen hundred light yeahs away, that's about ten thousand trillion miles oah so."

Quite a jump.

"Univahse is a big place, galaxies aftah galaxies strung out as fah as we can see a pinpoint of light, and fuhthuh, out wheah we only heah faint radio signals. Why theah's mah stahs in space than people who've evah lived on this planet, which has got to make you stop and wondah wheah exactly two individuals like you and me fit into the grand scheme."

Scheme, as in a plot?

"The infinitesimal has got to be lots mah tehrifyin to contemplate than the infinite, like what can one speck of a man be wohth in the immensity of this univahse? Oah a dog? Oah this whole goddamn planet? One among the countless millions of billions, one stinkin little atom in a cosmic reaction that's been goin on since time began — that's all we ah gihl, bits of mattah and enahgy in some identifiable fohm, nothin mah, but to listen to us brag about ouhselves, you'd think we wah the Titans who fohged it all. Nope. We'h the peons of space, wookah bees busy buzzin round one lousy hive, tryin to suhvive — suhvive, that's the only job we qualify fah. And that's what you and me have got to do, stahtin from tonight."

You and me, something about the sound of that makes me nervous.

"Tonight." Chipper has to crawl backunder his blanket. "Thought about how small we ah can be mighty sobahrin…"

Betsy lays back herself. Tonight's sky does look slightly overwhelming.

"…'specially if you'h feelin alone, but togethah Betsy, you and me, we could tackle it, make the futuhe ouh own."

Tackle. You mean as in getting trampled under foot?

"And we've got to do it, shake folks up, get them wohkin ovahtime to save the one spot in all these galaxies we can safely call home. It's eithah that oah just plain fahget it, go rushin naked through the woods towahd the bonfihe and embrace it."

Though the thought of this heretofore undefined, yet enormous undertaking momentarily silences Chipper. To Betsy's relief. Not that she minds a discussion on matters astrophysical, philosophical and such, no, it's just that the Recovery Channel is usually much more enlightening on these topics than one of Chipper's impassioned monologues, particularly when he's been indulging in multiple substances.

"Folks fahget too easy." As he lights up more of his homegrown. "They think some govahnment agency is takin cahe of the envihronment fah them, but the govahnment takes cahe of itself fihst, punchin the clock and issuin paychecks, passin the papahwohk on to the next administration."

Mercifully his ramblings will be a blur by morning. First thing he'll do is wake up asking what it was they were discussing the night before. He figures it must have been important because he went to bed with his boots on. Then he spends half the day attempting to salvage the wreckage in his head, line his thoughts back on straight while he huffs and he puffs on more of his homegrown, which sends him off on some other sidetrack entirely — not that Chipper's a bad lot, no way, he does for a dog what a human's supposed to do, he lets her inside out of the rain, doesn't bother her none when she chases squirrels, and he can scratch her head for her, up top where a paw can't conveniently reach. He doesn't seem to mind too much when she snuggles up under the blankets on a cold night, though in return she does have to listen to him talk. Dogs do. They have to play attentive — *yaw-aw-awn* — can't scratch at themselves nor snip at ticks, can't clean out their tail pipes, nope, not while their master's yapping.

"You remembah back when I was a kid and you wah just a pup?" Chipper wraps his arm around Betsy, tucks her in close.

-rr right, except that was my great grandmother Lady Kate, but no matter, we black hounds all look alike and thank these heavens I wasn't around then to have my ears pinched or my eyes poked. Missed out on most of that childhood crap. Kids, they're the worst, and a dog has to tolerate it too, because if we put up one growl of protest, it's a boot out the back door. People and their kids — whap those brats with a tail across the backside once in a while and the world would be a better place for it.

"We'd sit up heah and we'd discuss the futuhe of the planet. I promised myself, you can beah me witness, I said Chippuh, some day you'h goin to be up theah among those stahs, no lie, you ah, you'h goin to shine way high in the fihmament…"

-rr firmament? Fermented — that's what you mean, as in inebriated?

"…you'h goin to shine as bright as any of them, brightah."

Soused on your homebrew. Slug that stuff down and you go totally gonzo, have to prove yourself with acts of physical prowess. Like standing on your hands or running a steep roof, walking that skinny pine pole across Otter's Ledge, a trick every teenager in town has to try once, drunk, and you regularly. Dunk fifteen feet into that icy water and when you haul yourself out, the same question — 'Damn, what did I go and do that fah?'

"Need anothah toke Betsy, because I've got to see this vision in my brain mah cleahly."

Homebrew, homegrown, mooseshit mushrooms all mixed up together, *roh roh*, going to be a long walk home again tonight.

He puffs contentedly away.

Had better watch which way you're blowing smoke because a few more sniffs of that and a girl could forget the path back herself.

"I know you think I'm crazy, evahrybody around heah does…"

Around here! Every place you've ever been, and a lot more places that have only heard mention of your name.

"…but I sweah, those stahs ah closah to us than we can evah imagine, like time sliced thin and slid in so slick we can ahmost touch them."

Swallow another lung full chum, and those men-from-Mars friends of yours will be advising you on your right to remain silent.

"Can feel this enahgy wellin up from deep inside me, it's gut. Now's the propitious moment, now's when it's finally goin to happen."

-*prropri*-what? And deep feelings welling up where — spare me! The only deep feelings you have are unprintable, even in Swedish. The things I have had to witness — if I weren't black I'd be blushing — and what a story I could write if only I could get my paws on a word processor.

"I don't know why I talk to you about my dreams and aspihrations, you hahdly listen to a wohd I say."

So -*grroan*, say something I haven't heard a hundred times before, a hundred times a hun-…

"Millions of yeahs ago this univahse was fohmed out of a couple of specks of neahly nothin that crossed paths. They got this spahk passin between them and POW! Biggest jump staht evah! Stuff explodin, gasses whihlin, convolutin, minglin with each othah, chunks collectin and slowly coolin down, gettin hahd, hahd as rocks but spinnin round in theih own little ohbits — *whoop whoop whoop* — then befah long othah stuff stahted growin on those rocks, moss and bacteria and crab like creatuhes's creepin all ovah and fuckin each othah…"

Story must inevitably reach this chapter.

"…creatuhes fuckin othah creatuhes because they knew that fuckin was good and that it'd spread life around fastah. Soon the eahth was completely ovahgrown with life — suhe, some creatuhes wah eatin up on othahs, and some species got gobbled up entihely, but most things suhvived in some fohm and ah still heah with us, fuckin to this day…"

Heavens, is that all you really do have on the brain?

"…eatin and drinkin and havin a kick ass good time. Then what? Man gets to fencin off fields and drivin crittahs out of theih natuhral habitats, mowin down trees, inventin machines to plow, plant and pick evahrythin in sight, pissin and shittin and pollutin the watah, pumpin smoke into the aih, chokin the bihds and dumpin theih leftovah sludge into the rivahs, killin the fish, the tuhtles, the ottahs, th-…"

Good. Nothing but troublemakers, those otters.

"…bihrthin billions mah babies than we've got diapahs to wipe theih asses with — whole planet about ready to go into toxic shock, devolve back into solid rock, swimmin in gases with nothin able to breathe oah drink oah do nothin fah fun — and that ain't right Betsy, ain't right at all!"

-*rr* what, what's not right? I must have dozed off.

"That's why we've got to do somethin befah the Last Calamity, I mean, what's that day goin to be like when we finally wake up and realize theah's nothin left we can eat oah fuck with? What ah we goin to do then?"

-roh? You mean no squirrels to chase? Old Golden Maximillian gone?

"Too late to do nothin but stahe stoned into space!"

You're right, that wouldn't be nice. Squirrels and Maximilian are what keep a hound like me going, that and a sniff once in a while of that homegrown you're exhaling – *rr woe woe* – if things are really that bleak, you might as well blow a puff more my way.

"Got to do somethin Betsy, got to. Ain't doin nobody no good just sittin heah wohryin about it. Wohryin about somethin ain't no way to get nothin done. Which is why we've got to do somethin, do somethin fast!"

We? We? We? I don't know, I mean these pea brain schemes of yours always get us both into so much trouble – like the night you decided the world was short on love, rememb-*rrr*? So what did you do, stoned on your homegrown, you go trotting into that bar outside Fort Kent, nobody says hello, nobody nods nor grunts, nobody even shouts get that damn dog out of here. I could tell it was a rough place right from the get go, no pretzels, no dancing, just slam down drinking, but what do you do, you propose that free love is the only answer to the world's problems, and to who – the bartender's girlfriend! 'You know ma'am, if we all got down and screwed each othah a real good one, people would stop screwin each othah so many bad ones.' *-roh -roh!* Do I remember those prophetic words! What was the bartender's name, Sledge? That was it. And his girl friend? Maggie. Maggie's sitting there sipping White Russians and I can hear her still – 'You think? You really think? I don't know, what do you think Sledge? Maybe I should have anothah shoht one?' Well, Maggie had been belting down plenty of short ones before you walked up, and you had to repeat yourself a few times before she understood exactly what it was you were preaching – and she was trying to listen, she was staring at the lit end of her cigarette, and once she did catch on she shouted it out, 'Great! Let's get goin at it handsome – flooh heah good enough fah you?' Started with a striptease, remember, while she talked everyone of the regulars on the stools into working on a joint solution to world peace. That's until Sledge decided to take the issue on single handily. Talk about a brawl! I can see it like yesterday. Sledge was over that bar so fast I thought you were going to be a rolled roadside possum. BIG! UGLY! Guy was part brown bear. And if I hadn't been there beside you, hadn't taken a lunge for the bruiser's testicles, you wouldn't be sitting here today foretelling the world's bleak future – and then, then… if the worst in life can only get worse, that damn Subaru of yours wouldn't start! With Sledge's hand clamped on the door handle, the door that nobody could ever get to open, not even with a crowbar? Except damned if Sledge didn't open it, open it right up, me sitting on the seat next to him, staring into his snake pit eyes! *-yii! -yii! -yii!* Finally the Subaru cranks and we floor it out of the parking lot, leave him standing there holding the door, hinges and all, you steering, me working the pedals, and we've never been back to that place since, Sidewater Sam's, unless you have and didn't have the gumption to tell me about it.

"You about through with youh bellyachin?"

Pity you humans never listen to us creatures. We could save you so much trouble.

"Past is past Betsy, way fah behind us. Futuah is as eahly as the next second. That's why we've got to do somethin quick — and I'm goin to need youh help." Chipper wraps his arm tighter around her neck.

When you start in with the hugs, I become very suspicious.

"Can't do it all alone anymah because I don't have the enahgy I used to when I was a young dude."

Mercifully. Talk about trouble, the law threatening to kick in the door!

"I admit I'm gettin oldah, and it's true what they say — while an oldah fella knows what's got to be done, it takes a youngah man with some spunk to do it. So what we've got to do is ohganize the kids, roll up ouh sleeves and get aftah them to do somethin spectaculah."

With all due respect to your taller cranium, you're wrong about old men. Old men think they know what needs to be done and they're always coaching the school kids, sending them off to battle some rival team across the planet. I mean look at those has-beens in Peking or in the Senate, the sooner that generation retires, graciously or not, the better everything is going to be.

"Kids ah smaht these days gihl, don't go undahestimatin them."

Kids — *har-rar-rowlrowl* — born simply to waste time on trifles, drinking and screwing around like you, play stations instead of homework. No. You want something earth-shaking done chum, you had better plan on doing it yourself.

"You'h skeptical, I can tell, you ahways ah…"

Skeptical!

"…and it's just because you run around on fouh legs instead of two, got that nose of youhs dug in too close to the ground…"

I sense an insult.

"…which is why you think you know evahrythin theah is to know too, suhe, at diht level, but let me tell you pooch, it's because man can stand up heah highah in the sky that he can see fuhthah. I can see a valley green as green can be and a stream crystal cleah and meadows and fohrests and quaint towns with chuhch steeples, children playin happily with theih mothahs, and theih fathahs standin close by, proud and protective, families ahm-in-ahm, smilin pleased at what they can achieve!"

-hruff-hruff-hruff-hruff! That's a cloud of smoke you're up there breathing, and save the quaint New England calendar prints for the hard

currency folks in Connecticut. This is rural Maine, we're still reeling from the Great Depression of seventy five years ago.

"How come I've got to be the lone optimist in times like these? Ain't nobody else out theah who sees it like I do?"

Could be. Lots of odd people believe in lots of odd things.

"The bleakness suhrounds me, evahrywheah I step, shit's seepin undah the dooh. I tell you, man's got to believe in somethin beyond his paycheck — like ouh futuah as eahth dwellahs? Not all of us can move into self-containment units on the moon."

What precisely are you proposing we do? I hear about the bellyache, but what's the cure?

"Fihst off we've got to gaze openly out at the stahs…"

Might as well examine the steaming entrails of a squirrel.

"…those stahs ah spahklin theah to remind us we ah paht of them, paht of time, paht of the futuhe, and that soonah oah latah we ah goin to buhn up in a flash just like they have to."

That's it, preach hellfire and damnation to warm your audience up for the sales pitch.

"But that don't mean we have to drive hell bent fah destruction befah that time comes. No sih, let's get togethah and clean the place up, because fah most of us, if not fah all of us, it's the only place in space we've got. Life evahaftah might be right heah — least you can see these trees with youh own eyes — but no mattah what you believe about some heahaftah, we've got to keep this pahty rockin meantime, cause we lose this and we and all ouh grandchildren ah goin to pehrish fah suhe."

Lead on master, I'll play Trusty the Mascot and traipse along behind you into the vague unknown, because even if I had some place else to go, I probably wouldn't. Life with you is at least interesting — except let's get this straight from the outset, we hit the campaign trail and it's you who have to stand up tall and do all the howling.

Howling? You haven't heard howling Betsy, not until you've heard the likes of Molly Dawkens down on her hindquarters — *ow-ow-oooooooow!*

Tide's up. Moon's full. Venus ascendant.

And on the Staten Island sub-continent across the waters from downtown Manhattan, there's a bitch in heat. She's squatting on her haunches and baying at the moon. It's way past midnight, that time of the month and Molly Dawkens has unbuttoned her gown, exposed her abundant bosom. She's standing out on the balcony of her old hilltop sea captain's house with her tail raised, and the lady's going to let somebody know about it — *ow -wow woooooow!*

Howl seems to reverberate throughout the heavens — anyway knocks some stars around — not that Molly much notices, she's too intent on her own disturbance. Besides, Danny T is away on an all-night gig in Atlantic City, so Molly has the house to herself and no neighbors nearby. "O Mother Moon, help me! I have these horrible urges back, I'm burning!"

It's every woman on her own potion, and Molly does what she has to do in the dark, late and in the open before the Great Goddess Luna, who tends to treat Molly fondly.

Strange though, the images racing through Molly's mind tonight, an image of Chipper Stirbee. Why him, why now? "Tell me Mistress of Night Love, is the man of my daydreams ready to reappear?"

The moon whole unblinking stares down. The pressure inside Molly surges close to breaking — since she is at one with nature, she needs nothing to regulate her, every twenty seven days with the tides, the upward swell, the undertow. She separates herself, the dry becomes moist: "CHIP-PER! CHIP-PER!" Her tongue sticks to her teeth tips, then gives, speaks his name boldly over water, loudly across land mass: "CHIP-PER! CHIP-PER!" Sweet salubrious salivary sluice slips off her lushly lubricated lips. "CHIP-PER! CHIP-PER!"

"You heah somethin, somethin strange?"
Woodsy noises, owl hoots and bat flaps, peepers squeeking in the bog.
"Don't know. Sounds mah wounded human to me."

"*Ohhhhh!* You must do something — LUNA! I CAN'T STAND IT, NOT ONE SECOND LONGER!"
Moonlight cast on the water doesn't dimple the surface.
"I SAID I CAN'T STAND IT! DO SOMETHING — *PLEASE!*"
Must be the magic word. For Luna takes pity on her, tugs at the tides for her, stirs the Breeze above the waters for her — '*Alo!* '*Alo!*

"Whoa, should nevah have stood up that fast, not with the whole univahse in a spin."
Predictable.
"You'd bettah take point, let me guahd the reah."
Homegrown and magical mushrooms, not a good mix, and we're what, a half hour's hike through the State Wilderness Preserve, unmarked trail and like I can see in the dark or something..
"I'm dizziah than a humminbihd on an azalea bush."

Strange what people expect from a dog. Presume we come equipped with night vision — anyway watch your step here — *root root* — you could take a terrible tumble.

"Take it slow — ahmost fell and broke my neck on that tree stump!"

Wonder what I'd do if you did trip. Have to play Lassie, I guess, run to the nearest pay phone — what is it, 911 for medical emergency? Except what would I say — *hur-rr-rrrr-i-hrup* — and hope they work late, because there's no way I could drag your carcass home by myself, I'm too old for that routine — *sniff? snifff?* — you smell that? Something rotten in our path?

"Watch out, you neahly tripped me ovah!"

-*hush.*

"What is it?"

Something's fishy.

"You want to run up ahead and see what it is?"

-*grrripes!* Send me in, dog's expendable.

"I'll wait right heah fah you."

Best to take it real slow, sink way low to the ground, crawl along, ears up, listening, listening… footsteps? Little ones. Running. Two legs, not four or more. Human. Little human footsteps — they're the worst — and coming straight this way. Better sneak under a bush — *ee-y'ouch!* — patch of brambles, wouldn't you know!

"Heah doggie doggie."

Nowhere to hide.

"Betsy? Is that you, oah is it that fat badgah I've been gunnin fah?"

-*roh*, a tot toting a 22. Thought there was a ban on kids with weapons.

"Come out oah I'll shoot!"

Alright alright, I give up.

"It's me Lloyd, Lloyd Duchamps."

Trouble with a big crossed T and armed, wonder what he's doing out here alone in the dark?

"I got to find Chippuh fast."

-*rrr-rrrr!* First I'll send a shiver up your backside.

"Heah, hold on! Nice doggie, good doggie."

Don't try sweet talking me, you precocious pest, I'll scare the shit out of you — *RAW! RAW! RAW!*

"Don't go bahrin youh teeth at me! I'm comin to wahn Chippuh. Rangah Dohbs is up to the house with Hugh Fahmah to avenge the honah of his wife, and he brought my old man with him, seems he's gone stompin mad cause Chippuh's been doin my sistahs one right aftah the othah as they've growed up. You'd bettah take me to him and fast."

-*row r'all* right, and what are you angling for, a bounty, you scrawny backwoods whelp.

"Betsy, what's all the racket? You caught somethin?"

You dolthead, you should have stayed behind!

"Chippuh, is that you?"

"Who's askin?"

"It's me, Lloyd Duchamps, you'h about to step into a trap!"

"What kind of trap?"

"Law! Rangah Dohbs and his brothahs, Hugh Fahmah and my pa too, they'h all hidin out by youh place waitin, and they'h maddah than a bunch of skunks cohnahed in the woodshed, tails up and ready aimed to fihe."

"Damn!"

"They'h sayin it's high time to put youh kind out of business, like pahmanently."

"Why'h you out heah wahnin me?"

My question precisely.

"Cause when you head fah the bohdah until this blows ovah, you'll need somebody you can trust to watch aftah youh cash crop, besides…"

"Besides what?"

"…Belinda told pa you'd done no wohse to huh than I'd been doin."

"Whoa! What did youh pa say to that?"

"Somethin 'bout puttin my peckah out of sahvice too, says he's the only one allowed to do fah huh befah she's propahly run off, but I wasn't 'bout to ahgue that the whole county's been slammin through ouh back dooh all along — and that's why I ran on up heah to wahn you."

"How come you ain't plannin to run away and save youh own skin?"

"Cause aftah pa cools down, he'll remembah I saw old lady Fahmah shovelin pa's potatoes down huh root cellah."

"So why don't you go and tell that to Rangah Dohbs and his bastahd brothahs, save us both a lot of grief?"

"I can't go tell the law on my pa! What kind of a kid do you think I am?"

-rr rut rot riff raff.

"Shush gihl, ain't right to call somebody helpin you out a filthy name."

-rrrr…

"You want me to take cahe of Betsy while you'h away?"

-ro!

"Nope, Betsy goes wheahevah I go."

Those are my alternatives! This kid's mitts or on the lam with you? But then I can't run off to the woods and follow the caribou north for the winter, not during their spring return — so let's hit the road chum, I'd hoof it to the border before I'd bunk with this runt!

"Not suhe I'll be leavin anyway. Dohbs clan and Hugh Fahmah don't pose much of a threat."

"I heahd Shahriff Dohbs say somethin 'bout them havin a wahrant from some judge named Straints?"

"Brickyahd Straints, that's what the inmates call him — well maybe I will head south fah a few months needed vacation."

"Ah you goin to show me wheah you grow youh dope, oah not?"

"Prefah to let it go to weed rathah than hand it ovah to the likes of you."

"Yeah well, you'h goin to need youh Subahru and youh guitah to flee the state, unless you and Betsy want to hitchhike to Vahmont."

"How ah you goin to help me get my Subahru and my guitah?"

"I've ahready gone and pahked youh cah in an old fahmyahd, with a change of clothin, but I ain't goin to hand ovah the keys unless you show me youh patch of golden."

Maximum security wouldn't be enough for this kid, he would scam his way out with the warden skipping a step ahead to unlock the gates.

"Could shake you upside down and take those keys right off you."

"Ain't on me. Belinda's got them tucked in huh pocket."

"Belinda?"

"She's packed and ready to go too."

"She's a minah."

"Says when she's with you she feels real grown up."

"Ain't a question how it feels, it's the facts of life that mattah."

"Belinda don't know much 'bout those, she just likes doin it."

"Well no use goin and tellin huh difahrent, that'd only confuse huh. Innocence is hahd enough to come by these days, don't you know."

"That mean you'h goin to take huh with you?"

"Why'h you so anxious to get rid of Belinda?"

"Don't want huh tellin pa I've been makin money off the Dohbs brothahs since she came into season."

"Dohbs brothahs! That's wheah she's pickin up those cheap tricks!"

"What'h you want, amateuh class?"

"You'h somethin else, you really ah."

"Hey, sometimes in life you need a pahtnah Chippuh, what can I say? Ain't nevah done you no real hahm, and I've always been willin to shahe my sistahs."

"That's true, plus it don't seem like I've got much fah options."

"Suhe you do, you could go live at Thomaston State fah ten yeahs to life aftah my sistahs line up fah witnesses at youh trial."

"What if they tuhn and snitch on you?"

"I'm theih brothah, nobody in this state's goin to convict a family membah snowed in fah the wintah."

"You drive a hahd bahgain Lloyd Duchamps."

"Bettah me than Useless Dohbs."

"That son-of-a-bitch, watch out fah him."

"Hey, sometimes in life you need a pahtnah Chippuh, what can I say?"

"Don't wohry, caught him goosin my little brothah in the ravine back behind the school house last Septembah."

"Sounds like you've got all youh bases covahed."

"You bet, been wohkin on closin this deal fah bettah paht of a yeah."

"Makes me wondah who put Hugh Fahmah and the othahs on my trail in the fihst place?"

"Can't hold me responsible fah nobody else's actions 'cept my own."

Kid should run for president, black tar paper shack leads easily to Pennsylvania Avenue, the woods to the swamps, plus he knows who does who and ends up on top.

"OHHH! MOTHER MOON! I CAN'T CONTAIN IT!" Pitcher is filled to the brim and overpouring. "Golden Orb In The Sky, Light Unto The Darkness, guide me." Seems Molly has aged rather gracelessly over the decades since Cincinnati Summer of 69, the year of Chipper's earthly disappearance, for now she must placate herself by braying openly outdoors. "BRING ME WHAT I DESERVE AFTER THESE YEARS OF FAITHFUL DEVOTION!"

Mother Moon doesn't blink.

"NO NO, YOU'RE NOT GOING TO IGNORE ME!"

Moon might, but the Breeze deep in the bay hears.

Molly pounds her breast, struts across her balcony. "Something's up. I can feel it!" She grips the railing, she begins screeching like a diva! "O MAMA MAMA, HELP ME, I'M READY TO BURST!"

On command, the very stars begin to rotate which prompts Molly to unveil herself to the natural elements.

Perks the Breeze right up — *'Alo!* He surfaces on the water. *'Alo! Little mama! Miss me?*

She opens her robe to receive him.

Been down south carousin with El Niño's crowd, an oo-ee can they party! Had to head home, take time t'dry out.

Molly's beside herself and could care less.

See you're on one a'your periodic nocturnals, an complainin loud 'bout it as usual!

"My time has come Luna. I have waited patiently long enough — I WANT ACTION!" Molly making threats? The Night Mistress overhead isn't paying any attention, but Molly's not one to be ignored, not by anybody, no matter how high they rank in the cosmic realm.

Breeze is there by her side in a gust.

She waves the creep away and seats herself sideways on a chaise.

He blows here, he blows there, lettin it be known he's around.

Molly's intent on her business. She begins to remove her many bracelets, her necklaces, the demon's head ring with amethyst eyes, an emerald from her deceased mother and without pause, her worn wedding band. For one must approach the Night Mistress supplicant and naked.

Slow strip, tha's the part a'the show I enjoy most.

Seems Molly has had to content her middle years with collecting — exotic trinkets and jewelry, ancient amulets, rare crystals, coins and precious stones. She has learned yoga and walked barefoot on burning coals. She meditates and levitates, listening to hours of repetitive one note musical compositions on the stereo. She exists by eating figs and dates, asparagus and avocados, purple plums, chocolate Moldavian truffles and Belgian endive, spurning any flesh — though there's something of a hankering inside her tonight — 'Alo! 'Alo! — some insatiable craving. For a romance frustrated in its prime never surrenders. "One would expect you above anyone, O Patroness of Forbidden Love, to understand…"

Moon's unmoved by Molly's petulance, but not Breeze — *Moody mama. Looks like I've got to sit tight 'til the time's ripe to do me some snatchin.*

"…but no, I am clearly mistaken. I must face the uncertainty entirely on my own." To which task Molly lights a candle and places it center on a small table. She delicately opens an onyx box with her enameled nails, a box with a cameo carved on top, an aristocratic lady in relief, hair in piled ringlets. Molly's own hair falls likewise in ringlets. "I'M GOING TO FIND OUT WHAT'S GOING ON, YOU HEAR ME!" She removes a deck of cards from the box, but not just any deck, no no, these are the Tarot, an ancient and elaborate set of twenty two face cards in addition to the common four suits, a study to which Molly has devoted herself these many years after graduating St Agnes of the Woodsy Vale — well, the images are religious in a way and certainly no more mysterious than anything else she was taught.

Sassy lady, she's into a mood an gettin ready t'tempt Fate.

Molly feels assured she has penetrated the mysteries of the Tarot and can foretell the future, bits and pieces at least, and as she shuffles she speaks something of a prophecy to herself, "This is the beginning of something big, I can tell… but how is Chipper Stirbee a player?"

There's no answer from the heavens, just the sleazy old Breeze lapping at her toes. *Hold on now, no need to go both'rin yourself none 'bout that clown, not when you've got the Breeze here to please you.*

"Damn it, leave me alone!" She stamps at him with her foot. "Can't you see that I'm busy!"

Tha's a'right. I can wait my chance. No need t'hurry on my account.

"I SHALL CALL UPON THE COSMOS! I SHALL CONSULT THE COUNCIL OF INTERPLANETARY POWERS!"

Still no response from that mother moon.

Such a delight t'the sight watchin you beatin about, workin yourself into a lather — an believe me I bleed, I do, way down deep inside for your sorry predicament.

"I shall deal the Pentangle — you hear me, the Pentangle! That will satisfy my curiosity."

Betsy with the boys in tow proceeds cross country through the brambles — *ooh ahh ee-y'ouch!* — blue jeans simply not as effective for protecting the shins as a good coat of dog hide, but they can't exactly go tramping main trail into an ambush, now can they?

Betsy pauses, cocks her ears!!

"What is it you heah baby doll?"

Nothing, which means something's definitely up. Not a sound, no tree owl hooting, no skunks rustling, and no suspicious looking characters either — and it might as well be noon, with the outline of everything bathed in bright moonlight.

"Damn full moon. Got the whole town up in ahms."

The dense pine woods do provide cover for the three of them however, woods that grow right up to Chipper's front hatch cover down cellah.

"Wheah'h the bastahds hidin?" When Chipper notices the glow of a cigarette behind a clump of evergreens. "H'yep, theah they ah, luhkin behind the blue spruce."

"Looks like Useless Dohbs and Hugh Fahmah ovah by the woodshed."

"H'yep, Useless, can ahways tell him by his ovahsized head."

"They'h waitin fah you to drive up in youh Subahru aftah a night of drinkin, then's when they plan to nab you by the balls."

-y'ulp! Though at least Lloyd doesn't embellish.

"Nevah figuahed I'd have to hide out from my own neighbahs."

"You'h lucky Cohkah hasn't showed up yet with his pack of dogs."

That riff-raff!

"Why'd Cohkah take a tuhn against me? I've nevah done him no hahm, hahdly wave hello."

"Just it. He thinks you'h uppity, you bein a fohmah rockstah and all."

"Still am a rockstah, simply enjoyin some well-desahved seclusion."

"Not with a five state bulletin aftah you."

The three watch the watchers, then pass on.

"Pretty scahry seein a vigilante pahty pahked outside youh own home. Could suhe use a blow of good dope about now, calm my nahves. Fact I'm goin to need a supply of my homegrown to take with me fah the trip."

-roh noh, Betsy objects, that's the one thing in the world you don't need to take with you.

"Heah you go. Roll some of this." Lloyd proffers some dust in a bag.

"Thank you Lloyd, this comes unexpected."

"Ain't nothin. It's youhs anyway."

"How'd you get some of mine?"

"You traded it to me fihst night you hooked up with Belinda, 'membah? Said take a bundle cause you might need some covah down the road."

"Don't remembah sayin nothin of the soht. You've been filchin buds off me long as I've known you."

"Proves you can trust me Chippuh."

"How so?"

"Cause I nevah take mah than I need, so little you've hahdly been missin it."

He's been mssing it more than you think squirt, though the truth is he rarely fires on all cylinders and never in sequence.

"Thought a patnah was supposed to be somebody you could trust one hundred pahcent?"

"Pahtnah's somebody you can trust 'til the goin gets good and theah's somethin wohth grabbin. You ought to know that by youh age Chippuh. Besides, you don't show me wheah you've got youh grove hidden, whole plot's goin to tuhn to weed, and neithah of us'll own nothin."

"Kept the location top secret all these yeahs."

"Know. Been seahchin fah it fah months myself, evah since I got sprung from the county youth fahm."

"That wheah you disappeahed to? Nobody told me."

"Don't you read the Foht Kent Gazette, page one, son-of-a-bitch Buck Dohbs nabbed me in the aisle ovah at the Sumo Maht aftah houhs, pulled his patrol cah up in the dahk so I wouldn't notice."

"What wah you attemptin to do, they've got a lock safe in the flooh?"

"Was tryin to come down from a high so I could see to drive home, didn't want to run nobody ovah on the road and needed a cold soda, plus a pack of them chocolate cream filled Tinkah Bell cupcakes I like. Dooh was locked so I was helpin myself."

"What'd the judge say?"

"Six months in, six months on."

"Hahsh."

"Said I had a long recohd of petty thievahry. I thought my recohd was supposed to be sealed since I was a minah."

You'll be a juvenile until they bury you.

"Youh life's an open book at that couhthouse, plus they see you about weekly, don't they?"

"Still ain't faih. Breakin and entry was nothin compahed to what I'd done befah I tuhned fouhteen."

"Law's a mystahry to me."

"Seems they know you pretty well too Chippuh. Kept sayin I lived in a notohriously bad neighbahhood, mentioned youh name among othahs."

"Who'd be the othahs?"

"Hugh Fahmah fah one, heahd they've hauled him in a couple of times fah threatenin his wife with a deadly weapon."

"What, his dick?"

"Nah, one of those assault rifles he keeps in his collection, and old man Cohkah's no saint neithah."

"How come?"

"Animal abuse."

Doesn't surprise me, that's no kennel, that's a junkyard.

"What kind of animal abuse?"

"They didn't say, just looked the othah way."

"Somethin they don't even want to joke about, but theah ain't an ounce of fun in the whole bunch at the couhthouse anyway."

"You can say that again. Judge Straints theah, he nevah cracks a smile."

"Nevah did. Known him since I was a kid. Didn't like me then, don't like me now."

Your reputation with the law, one could say, is fairly well established.

"You and me got to stick togethah Chippuh, we'h like in-laws."

Outlaw in-laws.

"Ahright, you win. 'Spect you'h the only friend I've got these pahts, so I'll show you my grove, but you've got to promise me you'll tend it with tandah lovin cahe."

"Whatevah."

"Theah's a trick oah two wohth knowin about prize plants, 'specially when you clip the buds, it's just like with a young gihl…"

"I know, pick'em right when they'h ripe and juicy, don't want them too dry oah too greasy, otahwise you've got a sticky mess on youh hands and nothin to show fah profit — you've told me that a thousand times befah."

"H'yep well, you'll probably do ahright at it then."

I bet he will. These boys from Northern Maine are naturals at all the farmyard tricks — *ranh ranh ranh ranh.*

"Hush up Betsy, and show the boy the way to the ganje grove."

-*rr* step aside brat, follow me, and may the state troopers descend upon you as you stand some sunny afternoon right up to your chin in it!

"Remembah not to get greedy with pluckin buds neithah, just like with the gihls, you can take them easy, but only when they'h willin, plus if you stroke'em nice they'll keep springin back fah mah."

"I know, and watah them only when they'h belly achin dry fah it."

"Nope, bettah to keep them moist to the touch."

See. Every farmyard trick — passed from father to son, or neighbor to neighbor's son or to cousin to complete stranger hiking through the woods unawares, and that's why everybody up here is relation, even among the domestic herds.

"Up ahead's the hollow neah the spring, see how soggy the ground is?"
"H'yep."
"Well this rise is the only dry path you've got to the centah…"
"THE CENTAH OF THE HOLLOW! YOU'VE GOT TO BE JOKIN ON ME!"
"H'yep, wicked clevah, don't you know."
"I've been lookin evahrywheah and nevah would've thought of the hollow! I'm impressed Chippuh Stuhbee, damned impressed!"

Kids his age are so impressionable, and sneaky.

"If you'h really as savvy as you say you ah, you'll keep the wheahabouts of this grove stricty confidential, nevah say nothin to nobody, 'specially to youh family, just get youhself a smaht hound dog."
"Like Betsy."

Don't try buttering me up at this late date kiddo, I'm wise to your wiles.

"We've got to jump from rock to rock along heah and walk a tree limb, can you handle the acrobatics?"
"Went to the same school you did Chippuh."
"Don't go gettin disrespectful, you don't own the grove yet."

Slosh slup splack splunk!

"What's Betsy doin?"
"She don't much like climbin, prefahs to wade through the muddy watah instead."
"Must come out smellin like dead fish."

One woman's cologne is another woman's stench, and me, I prefer to stink terribly, drives my boyfriends to distraction.

"Don't go thinkin I won't be back by the way, to claim what's rightfully mine — that's aftah folks calm down and I can cleah my name."
"I'll be waitin right heah fah you pahtnah, you can count on it — want to shake?" Lloyd offers an unwashed hand.
"We've got to get up and ovah this tree limb fihst, and you bein the lightest, you'd bettah go on ahead."
"Why me?"
"Bein heaviah I don't want to buhden the limb none, might dunk you in the swamp and nevah notice. Need a hand climbin on up theah?"

-rr how about a shove?

"Naw, can take cahe of myself, but I can't see nothin in front of me."

Myopic squirt, I'm surprised you ever learned how to crawl.

"Just head on across like you'h doin. When you get to the othah side, give a hollah fah me to follow."
"Can't see fah shit."

"Betsy?"

-rr-rut?

"Should I wahn him about the quicksand, oah save that fah latah?"

-ra rah

"What's that you'h sayin Chippuh?"

"I was askin if you wah suhe you packed my best guitah, my vintage Fendahbendah?"

"Is that the black and whi-... goddamn, this log's covahed with slippahry gunk and somethin fuzzy runnin undah my fingahs!"

"Tree suckahs. They'h hahmless unless one gets to the tip of youh peckah."

Y'OUCH!

Don't ask.

"So tell me, that guitah you packed, is that the black and white one with my initials cahved on it?"

"H'yep, that's the one I packed – damn, you've got to be some monkey to get across this tree limb!"

"Take youh time. See you kids today, you'h always in too much of a huhry. You haven't leahned yet that the real oppohtunities in life take time, so go slow, hand ovah hand, don't rush it."

"Ahright ahright, choke on the advice."

"How about my acoustic guitah, the one packed in the case covahed with spahe the envihronment decals?"

"I didn't have time to pack evahrythin, not with the law comin up the road, just what I considahed essential, like a spahe paih of jeans and a case of youh gold label homebrew."

"H'yep, the gold label, might be muhky dahk in coloh, but that batch is a gut raisah with a strong flavah of roasted hops."

"Made suhe theah was anothah case of it left fah me."

"Fah you?"

"H'yep, you don't mind me movin into youh basement digs fah a while, do you? Somebody's got to keep the pipes from freezin."

"Summah's comin."

"That don't mean nothin up heahabouts."

"Nope, 'spose not, besides you've got eveahythin else of mine in youh pocket – how about my amplifiah geah?"

"That was shoved behind the cab seat ahready."

"Right right – how'd you know that?"

"Been seahchin youh truck fah smoke all along, know evahry inch of it by touch."

"Ahways thought that was the raccoons at night."

"Been both of us. They don't bothah me, I don't bothah them, we just happen to be huntin fah diffahrent things."

"Bet you fahgot my drivin glasses."

"Didn't know you wohe no glasses."

"Can bahely see the road in front of me in the dahk without them." Chipper shakes the tree limb some.

"Hey! What'h you doin, I might fall in?"

"Sohry, thought you'd made it across by now."

"I'll hollah."

"Bet you will."

"What? What'h you sayin?"

"Watch out fah the snappin tuhtles."

"You didn't say nothin 'bout no snappin tuhtles!"

"Quit wohryin and huhry it up. Theah's lots I've got to show you befah I take off — don't want you messin up on me."

"Quit wohryin youhself. Ain't nothin to tendin a few plants."

"Say that now when you've got me around to ask — and wheah did you pahk my damn Subahru anyway?"

"Now that we'h full pahtnahs, I 'spect I can tell you. Inside Hahve Clayton's old bahn, nobody'd think to look theah."

"Good thinkin, nobody would, not since he moved back to Boston — those Hahvahd fellas, fuck you ovah so quick they hahdly unzip theih fly."

"You know I'm a hell of a lot smahtah than people give me credit fah, 'specially those teachahs in school, except fah my guidance counselah, she appreciates what a guy like me can do."

"Is that Miss Goodwill still? She was counselah back in my time. She's somethin else altogethah, ain't she?"

"I'll say, woman's got a tongue as slimy as a frog's."

"H'yep, that she does — you makin any progress cross that limb?"

"Can't tell nothin fah suhe, feels like I'm a wicked hell of a ways out in the middle of nowheah."

"You ah, just keep crawlin — and don't go fallin off into the quicksand neithah."

"What? What'd you just say?"

"I said if a guy wants somethin bad enough he's got to be willin to bend some."

"I'll remembah that Chippuh."

Kid almost sounds respectful.

"Ahright. Let's scramble Betsy, make fah Hahve Clayton's old bahn."

"Chippuh? — CHIPPUH! — YOU AIN'T PLANNIN ON DESAHTIN ME OUT HEAH IN THE MIDDLE OF NOWHEAH, AH YOU?"

"'Fraid so Lloyd, but let me leave you with one last wohd of advice, and that's that life's a lot like an unchahted swamp in the night, and when you find youhself crawlin through it, you've got to be caheful you don't trip and fall in because if you do you'll end up smellin like a too eagah she-beavah in heat!"

"CHIPPUH, WAIT! YOU CAN'T GO DESAHTIN ME! WE'H PAHTNAHS!"

"THAT'S RIGHT, AND DAMNED IF THAT'S NOT WHAT PAHTNAHS UP NEW ENGLAND WAY DO FAH ONE ANOTHAH — CATCH YOU LATAH!"

-*hrr roh roh,* mite of a spider like him would get stuck in a web of his own making — bye byes Lloyd, won't ever forget you.

"Lead the way Betsy, and fast, you nevah know, that kid could sprout up squahe in the middle of ouh path again. Them Duchamps ah fiehce suhvivahs. Figuhe most we've got on him is twenty minutes, unless he rushes it and falls in…"

SUH-PLASH!

"…whoa, no need to push now gal, kid'll be at least an houh behind us, time he gets through squihmin out of that quicksand, that's if he can withstand the snappin tuhtles…"

OUCH! OUCH!

"And why is it neighbahs ah ahways so ready to tuhn on you?"

-*whroo hros?*

"'Bout the only thing that family was evah any good fah was screwin."

Molly meanwhile is deep into her divinations, she shuffles though the twenty two trump. "I shall throw the Pentacle and call upon the Four Powers!"

Pentacle, oo ooh, that's a fast track t'disaster.

Bold move indeed. A dark cloud in an otherwise clear sky passes over the face of the moon, earth trembles and a rogue wave rolls from the depths. Even the Breeze shivers.

Doesn't deter Molly one bit. She draws a five pointed star in one continuous motion with her lipstick — much more humane than the blood of a rat or a newborn infant. At each point and at each depression she places a card face down, ten of them, then adds an eleventh, her ascendant influence, in the center. The rules for this arrangement are simple. She may turn the center card at any time, to identify which force shall prevail, but she must proceed from the topmost point of the star to the left if she needs to unravel the past or to the right if she desires to foretell her future.

The Breeze sidles up next to her. *Let's see, let's see. Pentacle is so excitin!*

She taps at the middle card with her enameled fingernail — Molly's not much for patience, so she quick flips it over — "Mother Moon!"

Is she relieved or what, for Luna, the Moon Goddess Herself has been Molly's lifelong companion, accomplice, whatever. Portrayed in this esoteric deck as Diana the Huntress, a quiver of arrows and a long bow slung across her shoulders, she holds two fierce dogs at bay. A cello leans against a chair where the lady can straddle the instrument and have at it, for Luna is both mistress of passion and fearless warrior, to entrap or intimately intimidate, either way she captures her prey.

"O Mighty Warrioress, console me!" Molly most assuredly needs it, for who can control the wild urges this time of the month and late nights in particular — hell, afternoons are no better which must explain why she attacked the electrician earlier, backing him into a corner as he waved snapshots of the wife and children in a last ditch effort to ward her off, but to no avail, man lost his grounding and got zip-zapped pants down around his knees and Molly overworking his circuits — "Luna, Luna please!" Molly's up from her chaise, arms raised. "O Tamer of Wild Beasts who stalk the shadows, Eye Unto Darkness, the Force of Tides, of monthly return and renewal!" Renewal, yes, refreshingly liquid delight. "Help me in my moment of need!"

And Breeze he's instantly roused and down there sniff whiffing every sweet droplet. WHAP! Molly snaps the spigot shut, leaves him tongue hung out to dry mouth.

Tha-tha-that's a'right, a'right, I'll revive. Though don't ever count a devoted syrup sipper out, un unh, he'll be back and pantin for more.

Molly settles back to her table and stares at the card at the uppermost point of the Pentacle. She has no choice so she turns that one over.

Wheel a'Fortune. O that's ominous right off the bat, ain't it? Means somethin major's 'bout t'happen an wont ever let go.

Molly can appreciate that fact for herself, thank you.

Picture is an organ grinder, a monkey in a short red jacket and gold braid, cap to match, cranking the handle mischievously, while nearby on a leash a crocodile smiles, a sphynx is affixed to the top of the box and a waterfall cascades in the background. The trip to this zoo could turn threatening however. Imp's head is cocked and laughing out at Molly, like he knows something she doesn't, but keep dancing you creep, the thing significant about this card is a signal that life's ready to take a new spin.

Motion's commotion and streamin your way.

Stars are still shooting every which way above her head.

"We'll see, we'll see." Molly sets the candlestick on top of the monkey's conniving face.

Now comes the interestin part. Breeze rustles her robe as he squeezes in closer. *See who's who and what's what, which way you're goin t'get churned.*

Molly must reflect a bit, a move counter-clockwise on the Pentacle means a re-examination of the past, which she knows all too well, where a move clockwise and she can decipher what's to come. Choice is easy,

Molly's a future kind of gal.
All the way, that's what I say, even if it leaves you breathless.
"Will you buzz off!"
By golly Miss Molly, you're sure a hard woman t'satisfy!
Card to the right turns up The Fool.
"Nice!" Molly recognizes him immediately. The smiling face, the eager eyes, sturdy stride…
That joker's one a'life's true amateurs.
Might be, but a handsome young man is he, pictured here as out backpacking in the mountains. A large black dog nips at his heels, playfully or not so is a matter for interpretation, but the dog is The Fool's sole companion on what is to be his grand journey through life. While the road will twist and turn rugged, at this juncture the young man is carefree, cavorting along a narrow high path, though slipping dangerously close to the edge. His backpack bulges with gold and he carries a six stringed lute. He is a student perhaps, an apprentice, a novice, and yes, innocence incarnate, yet so zealous to learn the ways of the world that in the end he shall pay dearly for his education, not hundreds of thousands in guaranteed loans, no, he shall surrender that entire bag of gold before he finds his way back home. "Poor boy, poor poor boy," Molly sighs, for we all know the inevitable ending, with this picture the mere beginning of his travels, his travails, while he wanders unaware of what dangers await him, displaying the silly pride of youth upon his face, fearless. Much too soon he shall stumble and tumble into the ravine below, but then the pleasures that accompany his downfall shall surely be more than worth the trip.
An a way way we go, bare pleasures a'the flesh an comin up quick!
"Yes!" Molly kisses this card, for she has always held The Fool fondly. She was once young, and these adventurous, reckless handsome fellows are but bait for the taking by some worldly wise she-beast who lies in wait with teeth, and Molly assures herself that she'll be the one who'll best whoever this boy is, you betcha!
Why bother with a child when you've got a man here beside you? The Breeze gets to messin with her buttons.
"*Huhh!* Keep those cold hands to yourself!"
Hold-hold on, I'll warm them right up here in my lap for you.
The prospect of a tryst with yet another shiftless young man does have its drawbacks however. "Is this all I can expect during my mature years? The Brotherhood of Electricians!" Feelings so fleeting and illusory as well. "Have you nothing better to offer me Madame Moon? Why not a young relationship that can endure!" The thought leaves Molly distraught. She buries her face upon the table and weeps.
Why are you wo'ryin your pretty little head about this shit, when you've

got me nearby t'gratify you?" The Breeze caresses her hair.

"NO, NO NO NO, THERE'S ONLY ONE WHO CAN FULFILL ME!"

Who? That prancin has-been musician!

Him. He. "Tell me where he is this very second? Luna, you who see through the darkness, is he asleep by chance, somewhere in repose and dreaming of me?"

If he ain't out humpin some strumpet, I'd be mighty surprised!

But Molly's too busy for regrets, she has more cards to play, one next in order will do — *snap* — Maid Temperance!

Restraint? Abstinence? Denial! Is this the moon's idea of a joke? Molly squints at the card which depicts the epitome of balance and harmony in nature, of fresh life, a maiden with long golden locks piled in braids upon her head and a blue cinched gown, a flute lies to one side on a flowering bush. She pours pure water from one pitcher to another, silver to golden and daintily, not a drop lost, her bare toe cautiously touching the pool of life at her feet, although a couple of gargoyles, one shaped like a lion and another like an eagle sip from the same source, an unpleasant reminder that one slip and Temperance would be but bait for the craven.

Molly eyes the bitch coolly. "Whoever else you are, you simp, you're not me. Everybody knows I'm no timid virgin!"

Got that right sister, you're the one havin all the fun. Breeze snuggles back up tight.

Truly typecast Molly is, always to play the troublesome other woman. Ah well, at least she doesn't have to study the script. "Temperance!" Molly's still incensed, and her temperature rises accordingly. She flicks the prude aside and turns another card — uncovers to her surprise the Evening Star, Venus, earth's twin and the closest planet, represented here as all woman, the reverse of Maid Temperance. The Evening Star plays the slide trombone and lustily, she wades naked into the stream of life, heaving bountiful breasts, thighs spread full frontal and wantonly pouring from the same gold and silver pitchers Maid Temperance filled so protectively — life feral and fertile surrounding her, fields of green, herds of cattle grazing nearby, maybe satyrs — earth, air, water, fire combined to create life.

Molly clasps the card to her own breasts and lies back on the chaise — *'Alo! 'Alo!* — Breeze begins by caressing her ankles, smoothly soothing along her legs while kissing at her thighs, lifting, lapping, separating with his tongue, lips to lips, slips in — Molly bleating like a spring stuck ewe.

"Hi theah Chippuh, I've been wohried you'd nevah get heah."

"Belinda?"

"Been sittin in this old bahn fah ovah an houh, what took you so long?"

In the dark it's hard to see, but that's her sure enough, sittin on the hood of his much modified 82 Subaru.

"It was *uh-* Lloyd… Lloyd was…"

"I bet, he's such a slow poke, nevah comes on time. Gihl can get so bohed just waitin fah him."

"So Belinda, Lloyd said you've got the keys to my Subahru?"

"Don't have no keys. Lloyd had to hotwihe this damn truck to get it stahted, but I did find me an address book while I was seahchin through youh sock drawah."

"That's old and out of date."

"Suhe listed lots of othah gihls' numbahs."

"Friends, acquaintances…"

"Dates, times and crude comments, lot like a diahry."

"Give me that. That's pahsonal."

"No, not 'til you promise to take me with you wheahevah it is you'h plannin on runnin to. I'll teah one page out fah each mile we go and throw it out the window."

-urrulp!

"Brought some of my things along in an old suitcase ma had up in the attic and some spahe cash my pa had hidden away in a tobacco tin in the chimney, fohty five dollahs, in case we need any money fah an emahgency." She hands the tin to Chipper. "It's all I've got in this wohld so fah Chippuh, but I trust you to love, chehrish and take cahe of me."

"Then give me back my address book, best I put my past behind me."

"Don't trust no man that much. You go dumpin me fah one of these hussies, and what's a young gihl like me goin to do, alone in a big ugly city with no one to tuhn to?"

I'm sure-*rr* you would do just fine.

"This is youh pa's money, *hunh*?"

"Couldn't find wheah Lloyd stashes his, looked half the evenin, don't you know, most of it was my eahnin's anyway."

"Mighty obliged Belinda. You'h such a nice gihl and cute as a ladybug."

-no no, don't compliment her, that'll play right into her wiles. Just dump the punkster and let's scram. That brother of hers will be swinging down out of the tree tops any second now, and he's not going to take kindly to being cut out of your cash crop — RIGHT? RIGHT? RIGHT?

"Quiet down Betsy! I can handle my own affaihs — Belinda, honey lips, theah's a problem heah, with you bein undah age and all, you know what I'm sayin?"

"But I'm willin Chippuh, willin as all hell."

"I know you ah, and the good Lohd knows I appreciate that fact, but in a couht of law, see, willin oah unwillin ain't the issue, and besides I'm goin to be crossin state lines in a huhry, and while takin unfaih advantage of a local gihl might land a Mainah in minimum secuhrity oah a local mental facility fah a spell, kidnappin, well, that's a whole diffahrent mattah, constitutes fedahral intahfehrence with an individual's state of rights."

"Evahrybody says I look oldah fah my age, and you ahways said I acted matuhe enough to please you."

"You do, you cahtainly do, you can do a lot fah a gihl youh age."

"Most of which I leahned from you."

"Now don't go givin me credit fah what I don't desahve, youh brothah got you stahted with the basics… and a few of the Dohbs brothahs too."

"But I ain't goin to tell no judge on Lloyd. Wouldn't be right rattin on my own brothah. I'm goin to tell the judge you undid me and made me bleed and then broke my heaht aftah you wah done pleasuhrin youhself."

"But honey lips, that'd be lyin."

"You ahways said lyin ain't wrong if it's fah a good reason, and besides that's why you'h goin to take me with you wheahvah you go, to keep me from fahgettin myself and sayin somethin tehrible to some judge."

-roh woe, Betsy buries her head between her paws, and didn't I try to tell him, try, I stuck my nose in where it didn't belong many times. I would crawl up on top of them, bounce a ball on their beanies, yawn in their faces, fart, sprawl out in the middle of the bed, drool, barf, anything I could think of, because I could see this doubletaker stalking up the road, I mean you don't need a schnozz the size of mine to snort out a lying pack of neighbors – one sniff of that Duchamps bunch would ward off a champion Spottower sales team. But that's nothing now, how are you going to wiggle out of this pickle, you *-rr rogue?*

"Hush up Betsy, I said I can handle this."

"CHIPPUH! WHAT AH YOU DOIN? PUT ME DOWN! PUT ME DOWN OAH I'LL SCREAM, I WILL! I'LL TELL EVERYBODY YOU WAH MANHANDLIN ME ROUGHLY IN HAHVE CLAYTON'S SMELLY OLD BAHN!"

"Honey lips, quit youh kickin and get youh sweet ass off my truck, you'h just makin this situation wohse fah the both of us."

"PUT ME DOWN!"

"Heah you go, now run on home and be a good little gihl and wait fah me to come fetch you latah, when you'h at least a yeah oah two oldah and I'm settled some place comfohtable so I can take cahe of you propahly. Othahwise I'm goin to plumb fahget about you, honest I will, and you know if I do that you'll have lost any chance you evah had fah a cahreah as a famous singah cause I'll tell evahrybody in New Yawk you haven't got an ounce wohth of talent in you."

"You wouldn't."

"I would. I'd say the best thing that gihl could do is spend a lifetime up in the Maine woods sehrenadin the chipmunks, and they'd believe me in New Yawk, they would, cause I'm a stah."

"How could you go and say that aftah all the nice things you said, about what beautiful lungs I had and my mouth, a puhe delight, you said my mouth was a puhe delight."

You-*rr* making this up, aren't you? She's making this up, isn't she?

"Betsy, I can handle this — Belinda, listen, don't fohce me to just leave heah and fahget you, tell folks I nevah even heahd of you, might've seen you once oah twice in passin, that's it."

"No!"

"H'yep, stah like me has got to protect himself and his reputation."

"You'h a hahd man Chippuh Stuhbee."

"Got to be hahd because life is hahd, neighbohs layin in wait, ready to snahe you evahry step you take, but you know I've got a soft spot in my heaht fah you."

"You'h just sayin that to please me."

This script borders on the utterly disgusting.

"No suh, I mean evahry wohd, and the minute you tuhn sixteen I'll be back up heah to nab you and take you down to New Yawk with me, oah maybe out to Hollywood wheah I'll introduce you to evahrybody impahtant, promise."

"How do I know you'll keep youh promise?"

"Cause you know deep down inside I love you honey lips, how may times have I told you that, hunh?"

"Oh Chippuh! You can be so sweet when you want to be…"

"How could you evah mistrust me?"

-*rr ret/ ret/ ret/*

"I guess I'm just a pooh weak creatuhe — then too I do have youh little black book."

"If you really loved me back, you'd give me back that book."

ret/ ret/

"What's wrong with that dog of youhs?"

"Probably's got somethin stuck in huh throat — you know you ah so young and beautiful Belinda, and you've been my comfoht. I could nevah fahget you, you and youh sistahs, I could nevah have suhvived the wintahs without you folks."

"I guess if you say you need me like that, with conviction and all, and if you promise you'h goin to come fetch me, I'll head on home to be with my family to tough out ouh sepahration."

"It's hahd on me too, but it'd be fah the best."

"If it's what you want, I'll make the sacrifice, but I'm goin to miss you awfully much — *boo, boohoohoohoo…*"

"Aw Belinda, don't cry fah me like that."

ret/ ret/ -ch retch/ rolph/ rawlllllll!

"Youh dog just up-chucked all ovah my best shoes!"

"Damn Betsy! That's most of youh lunch and all youh suppah!"

"What am I goin to do?"

"It'll wash off soon as you get youhself home — and you've got to trust me, you really do. I'll be back befah you realize I've even gone. Now give me a great big hug good-bye — YEAHH! — and meantime you've got to do youh utmost to cleah my name, make suhe no nasty rumahs go lingahrin."

"I will, I'll do evahrythin I possibly can."

"Fah stahtahs why don't you just hand ovah that address book."

"Don't wohry youhself none Chippuh, you know I'm real good at keepin secrets, 'specially what goes on between two lovahs."

"Secrets ah one thing, hahd evidence anothah."

"A heahtbroke gihl has got to have some keepsake, besides I done hid it fah away from pryin eyes."

"Let me have a look in that suitcase of youhs."

"Chippuh! You keep youh hands off my pahsoanl belongin's."

"Ain't youhs, it's mine!" Couple of quick clicks and what does he find rolled in her underwear, not the family bible. "*Whew!* What a relief!"

"Couldn't read youh scrawlin anyway." Belinda's got a pout on her mug, arms crossed and she's stamping her foot.

"It's all in shohthand, cause I don't need the long ahm of the law snoopin into my private affaihs."

"Didn't see my name anywheah, just my sistahs Annie Lynn and Faith."

"I was goin to put youh's in, I'm just behind on my entries."

"You suhe?"

"Promise peaches, do it fihst thing in the mohnin befah I buhn it, and you've got to promise me you won't go makin no statements nah signin nothin on papah, and nevah nothin in front of that Judge Straints fella."

What are you doing, handing her the *-rr*-rope to string you up with.

"It'll be all I can do to sit home pinin fah you-..."

Here — *hrr-roop/ oop/ throo oop* — I'll hurry this tender love scene along.

"...*yuck!* — that dog of youhs puked on my leg! You had bettah take huh to a doctah, she's ahways throwin up, mostly when we ah togethah."

"Betsy's got a delicate stomach."

"If she wahn't ahways woofin down vahmin, she'd feel a lot bettah..."

Should be woofin down neighbor children, we'd all feel a lot better.

"...and I promise I'll keep everythin out of the newspapahs Chippuh, I will, because neithah of us wants the wohld to shahe ouh intimate secrets, do we, not fah money oah fah nothin else, like fame and a candid best-sellin autobiography, and no way I'd want my pictuhe pasted on the front page of evahry issue of the Weekly Scohe in the grocahry stohe, with my pitiful sad eyes and a detailed stohry of how I was wronged real young and tendahly at the hands of a neighbah man fouh times my age who I thought I could trust — but I ain't like those othah gihls you've got listed in that book of youhs who you know would step fahwahd in ohdah to cash in."

"Right Belinda, a story like that could ruin youh reputation fahevah."

"And youhs too Chippuh, so I'll tell you what you've got to do to make things right between us."

"What's that child?"

"You've got to call me long distance from wheahevah you ah, twice, no three times a day, mohnin's to wake me up, noon time to cheeh me and late nights to tuck me in, that way I'd be cahtain you wahn't with anothah gihl and you wah propahly pinin fah me."

"You'h my oahphan baby Belinda…"

"And you'h my Daddy Wahtbugs." Hug. Hug.

"That's right, and I'd call you, I would, every houh on the houh, but youh folks haven't got a phone."

This is too too touching, I can't hold back the tears a minute longer — *ro ro ro ro -rr… runnn!*

"Shush Betsy — but that's huh special way of tellin me we've got to be hittin the road, make some tracks fah the bohdah."

"I undahstand Chippuh, you got to do what you got to do."

"That's right, simple natuhe of the law."

"And I got to do what I got to do too, same simple principle."

"Now don't go and alienate my affections."

"I won't, I won't, not when I know you'h at least goin to be sendin me a pictuhe postcahd everyday, ain't you, with youh name and some kisses signed on the bottom?"

"Everyday, wouldn't want you fahgettin how to spell Chippuh, now would I?"

"Nah Stuhbee, like in Mrs."

"H'yep — jump on in Betsy. Betsy?"

"She's ahready in the cab Chippuh, sittin ovah theah in the drivah's seat. Looks to me like she's tryin to hotwihe the ignition."

Must be a trick to it, something you have to press with your thumb while you're busy splicing wires together — too bad I don't have a thumb.

"I guess it's latah Belinda, and make suhe you tell Lloyd to concentrate his seahch on that bog."

"What bog?"

"Any bog…"

VROOOM! VROOOM! VARROOOOOOOM!

"…so long! Love and kisses!"

"I undahstand Chippuh, you got to do what you got to do… and I got to do what I got to do too…"

"Those great big scrumptious kinds!"

-*roh -roh*, that was a cinch!

"Betsy, have you plumb lost youh senses? Move ovah and let me drive, this ain't some soht of practice run."

No. Nor a B-grade movie either, I mean that love scene was pathetic.

But that's past as they get to gunning it, spinning out of the barnyard and down the yellow brickbat and splice spiked road, leaving the remains of Maine rustic life as far and as fast behind them as possible. With Belinda waving them on.

"You bettah hold on tight Betsy, even those Dohbs ain't dumb enough to sit and wait fah us 'til mohnin — and don't go sayin one wohd, not one, cause when I want advice from a dog, I'll ask fah it."

Advice from a dog, -*rr rog rog rog*...

"Hush up. Takes all I can mustah to concentrate on the road. Wouldn't have done so many shrooms had I thought we'd be packed up and headin out of state — have a look undah the seat theah gihl, see if you can spot my specs fah me."

-*hmm* let me see — rolling papers, matches, good supply of condoms — your keys! — but no, no pair of glasses.

"You keep youh eyes peeled on the road behind and I'll keep mine on the road ahead."

Betsy peels her eyes out through the back slider window, sees a whole swarm of state vehicles coming up fast behind them.

Floo-*rr-roar* it!

"Clunkah could've used a spring tunin. About how many you reckon we've got aftah us?"

Let's see, two with flashing blue lights, must be the Dorbs who are law men, Leon the state trooper and Buck the deputy sheriff, then another with a whirling yellow light, that'd be Eustus the Forestry Ranger — so -*ro-ree!*

"Don't fahget they'h arhmed and a dangah to the state."

KA-FLUNG! As a shot goes winging by.

Betsy ducks under the seat.

"That'd be Hugh Fahmah's prize thuhty aught six. He's just tryin to scahe us."

KA-FLUNG! -FLING! Clips off Chipper's side mirror.

"Damn, he's usin us fah tahget practice."

KA-FLUNG! -CRACK! Back slider window shatters, glass goes flying all over the cab.

"Whoa! We'd bettah head cross-country, see if that loafah can hold a rifle steady down a rutted road — HANG ON GIHL!" As Chipper turns sharply and rumbles down a gravel obstacle course cut through the woods.

FLUKE! FLUKE! Of course the militiaman can't hold anything steady as he blasts away at the treetops.

They're tearing down this service road some Canadian electrical crew uses to maintain a row of high intensity power towers, and thumpy bumpy — "*Whoo-ee*, let's watch while Hugh Fahmah dislocates his shouldah!"

FLUNK... which he must do or nearly so, because the shooting stops as suddenly as it started.

Is it safe? Betsy crawls back up on the seat, spies out the open slider.

"How'h we doin?"

The Subaru with its trussed up suspension and super shocks can hold its own against the low slung squad cars any day, but Useless has a 4x4, big Cram Dodger, though mercifully he's been issued no gun.

"You'h fahgettin some fool Congressman went and ahmed the fohrest rangahs a while back, case they got caught in a shoot-out with a tehrohrist touhrist bus."

Even armed Useless wouldn't know which way to fire, man can barely scratch his crotch and walk straight at the same time, but with Hugh Fahmah as his gunner watch out!

"Whoa! Don't know wheah this road goes." Which is the problem with a service sort of road, doesn't go anywhere you want, even though it goes everywhere the Canadians want all along East Coast backyards — well they've got spare Hydro-Quebec electricity to sell, that's after they went and flooded half of the St Edmund's countryside to produce it, in the process destroying thousands of acres of wildlife habitat — but what's the big Yankee beef? Canadians are signatories to the International Whale Oil Agreement and they officially protest the destruction of the rain forests in Brazil, like every other conscientious *Norte Americano*, but money doesn't grow on trees, don't you know, and buck for buck water power's best, and if the provincials had to waste the environment to save it, it's a hell of a better deal than additional nuclear reactors. Besides, drowning the critters is much more humane than burning out their intestines.

"JESUS BETSY! Quit stahrin up at those towahs and watch the road, will you? Can't see much of nothin cleahly — like ah they still behind us, oah did we outrun them?"

-*rr* right right, let's see, can't see with these high beams shining directly into my eyeballs — *Yip! Yipes!* — it's Useless Dorbs tight on our tail and gaining, fact he's fastened on to our ass end — RUM-RUM, RUMP BUMP-BUMP-BUMP-BUMP! — attempting that bumper stumper intimidation tactic back woodsy woodies do.

Chipper tries an evasive weaving action because Useless' full size pick-up can't maneuver the ruts in the road as well as Chipper's nimbler

Subaru, especially since Chipper installed the Monster Tires — *stump! thump!* — it's the sound Useless makes as he scrapes the rise in the middle, though what's a leak in an oil pan to a real man.

"How'h we holdin gihl?"

-reff! -reff! -reff!

"swing left? look left? which is it?"

-rook!

Sure enough, Useless has seized the high ground in a clearing between two towers and he's ram gunning straight at Chipper from the left, out to score on a broadside, Hugh Fahmaharmed and ready.

"Nevah know when to quit, do they? 'Spose I'm just goin to have to tuhn this baby around and go hohn to hohn with the suckahs!" Subaru's frame is wider than the cab sitting on it, gives Chipper a extra measure of stability as he turns on a dime, sets headlight to headlights and stomps on it! "chick' chick' chick'... c'mon and get me coppah!"

-g/ -g/ -g/ -g/ -g/...

"Don't go gag bahfin on me now Betsy, who knows when we'h goin to have time to stop fah mah grub." And speaking of cookie tossing time! "*Whoa-ah oh-woe-ho* — hold on!"

Does does she does, does she!

-room -room -room -room... It's Useless who flinches in a stare down, bangs a hard right — well he'd have to explain the after hours damage to a board of state investigators — but is he even looking where he's heading, most likely not because most people don't go full throttle at the concrete base of a power tower, not unless they want to crunchinto chunksofmangled4x4 — but Useless won't have to worry about explaining all that, no, not as Hugh Farmer accidentally empties his magazine aloft, snaps off enough high intensity to light a city — clack cracklingatthestatestarcrackerjack — fries both their assholes silly.

"Whoa! Get a load of the fihewohks!"

Betsy is awestruck — sparks, zaps, flashes akin to lightening bolts with accompanying sound effects, and as a finale this *boom-ba-boom!* billowing mushroom of a red and yellow gasoline explosion!

Chipper stops, he's honor bound to pay his last respects to a worthy adversary, but then that's the price one has to pay to play off-road games for keeps — Chipper's paid a price too, as he backs out of that old rutted road, he notices his alignment is screwy skewed up like permanently. Dude's got to yank on the wheel full right rudder to keep the Suburu heading straight ahead and out of the Maine wilderness forever.

You would think Chipper would head for the Canadian border, which is only a few feet away, a splash and a dash across the mud flats of the St John's River, a climb over some slippery rocks, and a slide home free. There's even some Stirbees that side of the river, though they'll have none of him either. Seems the Province of New Brunswick has a warrant out for his arrest, same as Aroostook County Maine, some vague allegations about him and an underaged Edmundston girl and her two school chums in knickers, and he's no better off in Quebec, his northernmost excursions being quite well documented. And when a guy's wanted in one state and two provinces, the smartest thing he can do is head south, fast as he can, and New York City's not a bad choice for a fugitive, easy to get lost in the crowd, plus Manhattan temp agencies are always looking for seasoned lifers to do hazardous duty in investment banking.

Thus Chipper and Betsy barrel along sort of southerly to safety via the back roads with one headlight flickering, and no taillights, a plate from another state, another era, 50s Vermont, and a registration duly recorded in the name of one Edna Lightcomb of Stewartstown, recently deceased — any of which infractions could draw some unwanted attention on a major highway. Besides, Chipper has no license. "Nevah did have one, if the truth wah told, nevah had a propah bihth cahtificate neithah, somethin scrawled on the back of a motel matchbook, the one they say my mothah used when she buhnt my official cahtificate up in some squabble with my papa ovah whose baby I was oah wasn't oah couldn't possibly be no mattah how tight she was hangin with the accused fathah."

Betsy hasn't any sort of license or dogtag either. Neither she nor Chipper have ever been vaccinated against anything contagious, though they are both quite susceptible to any plague that can befall man or beast, not that the two of them seem concerned, no, with the steady THUMP THUMP rhythm of the miles passing by, they lumber into night drive oblivion, responding only to occasional onrushes of headlights and startled deer.

"You've got to leahn to fahget life's losses Betsy, the neah misses."

-roh?

"H'yep, keep youh eye on the futuhe, cause life's an adventuhe fah those who can take it. The rest fall by the wayside of routine and fat retihement accounts."

-roh.

"And you and me will get along fine so long as I've got my guitah to play fah ready cash and the old Subaru keeps runnin" — CLUNKY CLUNK CLUNK — beating a steady rhythm of its own as they drive along — THUMP THUMP / THUMP THUMP / THUMP THUMPITY CLUNK CLUNK — but Betsy's up for the adventure, she's sitting up front, head up, watching the woods flash by. Although she's never seen New York City personally, she has read about it in magazines and looked at pictures of the skyline. Sort of surreal but almost any move upward and out of a dug-out basement has got to be an improvement, she *grr*-rumbles to herself, and leaving those Duchamps brats behind, Belinda and Lloyd and the rest of the pack of nameless bathless wonderkins, always trying to ride her like she was their pony. Dump them off when nobody was looking, down the rocky ravine. Some new generation growing up this is! Each fresh litter of pups worse than the last, eyes pinched closed and yapping me first, me first. Maybe folks up Maine way need to introduce a fresh bloodline.

"Haven't been away from home fah yeahs now, it'll be good to see how the rest of the wohld is makin it."

-*mmm*... In Maine Betsy's been noticing there are fewer and fewer dogs around, fewer and fewer animals around period, migratory birds in particular, though the squirrel herds seem ample. But are the moose and the brown bear all fleeing somewhere and haven't told her? Or are they hiding out with the other endangered species until it's over – until what's over? That atmospheric disaster Chipper keeps forecasting? Things seem relatively stable to her, but then she's a nose-to-the-ground sort of hound who leaves such speculation to others. The extent of the universe and the course of the future are nothing one lone dog can figure out, no matter how often she's up pacing in the night – so might as well sit in front, shut up and stare out the windshield, face whatever's coming, stick her nose out the window for a breath of fresh air and enjoy the show.

"Whoa! Look up ahead theah Betsy! Suhe sign of ouh delivahrance!"

Welcome to New Hampshire – and *Bienvenue* to you too.

"We've made it gihl, we've made it!"

Betsy does a quick glance out the back to doublecheck, and no, nobody tracking them – ROO! ROO! ROO!

"We'h launched babydoll, blastin out through dahk endless spaces, on to the bright lights of New Yahk City and anothah shot at stahdom!"

Right, onward to one of life's rare second chances.

"Let's celebrate. How 'bout a medley of ouh outlaw hits – staht off with *Loosie Anna*?"

-*rawl* right – hit it!

> Loosie Anna / Loosie Anna / O why O why O?
> Loosie Anna / Loosie Anna / O tell me it ain't so
> Loosie Anna / Loosie Anna / O no no no OOO!
> They'h shoutin about you all ovah the bayou

Catch it on the downbeat gihl

> CHUCK IT TA YUH / CHUCK IT TA YUH
> CHUCK IT TA YUH / CHUCK IT TA YUH

Betsy's going at it with unclipped claws across the metal speaker grate on the dashboard, wild down home Zydeco style.

> Whoa! Whoa! WHOA!
> -rrow! -rrow! -RROW!
> CHUCK IT TA YUH / CHUCK IT TA YUH
> O no no NOO!
> CHUCK IT TA YUH / CHUCK IT TA YUH
> Not my Loosie-yanny Anna!
> Cause I been countin on you gal…
> CHUCK IT TA YUH / CHUCK IT TA YUH
> Woe! Woe! WOE!
> -roh! -roh! -ROH!
> O tell me it ain't so
> Loosie Anna / Loosie Anna
> CHUCK IT TA YUH / CHUCK IT TA YUH

Take it real slow

> CHUCKA CHUCKA / CHUCKA CHUCKA
> Loosie Anna / Loosie Anna / O why O why O?
> Loosie Anna / Loosie Anna / O tell me it ain't so
> Loosie Anna / Loosie Anna / O no no no OOO!
> Open huh up now
> CHUCK IT TA YUH / CHUCK IT TA YUH
> Loosie Anna / Loosie Anna
> They'h shoutin the news all ovah the bayou!
> Loosie Anna Anna Anna Anna
> They'h sayin you just run off
> With some othah fel-low
> CHUCK IT TA YUH / CHUCK IT TA YUH
>
> O no no / no no no / no no NOO!
> -roh! -roh! -ROH!
> Loosie Anna / Loosie Anna
> How could you have done me so cal-low?
> CHUCK IT TA YUH / CHUCK IT TA YUH

Take huh home gihl!

> CHUCKA CHUCKA CHUCKA CHUCKA / CHUCK YOU!
> Big ol' fingah stuffah uppah full of it!
> -ranh!

Breeze has got Molly clicking her heels in the air, and he's going at it at a gallop — *Su-weet sweet mama!* — when out of nowhere she swift kicks him in the jaw, he reels back in time for her to toe the cad in the gonads — *so-HOK!*

"I'VE HAD ABOUT ENOUGH OF THIS SHIT!"

Guess so, as Breeze beats a retreat to a corner.

Molly rises from the chaise and rinses herself with sweat from her own body, she is cleansed by her nighttime revels and renewed — reborn as it were — she combs her fingers through her hair and wraps her robe around tight, coldly eyeing the cards on the table — the candle is burnt to a stub, wax spattered all over the imp monkey's laughing face.

Once the wheel gets spun, there's nowhere to run. Breeze hobbles over.

Molly turns her sixth card out of the eleven, a pivotal position, and uncovers The Magician. He's the prime power in the Tarot, the first face the young initiate encounters. Portrayed here as a young man in carnival costume. Already entertaining you with a beguiling smile, he juggles clubs, cups, coins, swords in infinite succession above his head, and more — brass, woodwinds, strings and percussion — for he is the consummate musician, the master of illusion, a facileness you could easily come to distrust, for behind the curtain where he performs lurks a myriad of adversaries as well as allies, whoever's interest you might momentarily serve.

Future's collusion, what more did you suspect?

Molly can do without the play-by-play commentary, thank you very much. She sits on the edge of her couch and assesses what's face up before her. "Let me see. Let me see." There seems to be a cosmic conflict in the making, with The Moon and The Evening Star surprisingly allied on the same side, one for passion, the other the creative urge. Then there's Maid Temperance in opposition, reserved and tidy tight — which emboldens Molly as the Earth Mother to battle for her birthright. Though now there's this Magician, impulsive, unpredictable, while he may not take sides openly, he will constantly interfere behind the scenes. Molly stares into his eyes, something about The Magician reminds her of the monkey cranking the Wheel of Fortune, and if there's one sort of creature a robust sort of woman like Molly can't trust, it's a jerky little guy with a curl to his tail.

LATE NIGHT RE-ENTRY

"Look.Theah's still some straglahs left ovah from the meteoh showah."
Keep your eyes on the road chum, we've got a long night's haul ahead.
"Theah goes anothah – damn…"
-*rroh*. Betsy covers her eyes.
"…ain't like no othah stah show I've evah seen."
Will you stay this side of the double yellow line! She reaches out a paw.
"Whole galaxies spin, did you know that, and spihral and wahrp."
As in all over the road?
"Come a time, lot soonah than we expect, and they'h goin to launch a probe to explohe deep space – they'll be fohced to seahch the most remote cohnahs of the univahse to find a fresh oxygen souhce and some potable watah. We'll have contaminated whatevah's left of ouh own by then."
Now that you mention it, I have noticed an acid taste to our well water.
"And once they'h way way out theah, they'h goin to leahn that the shohtest distance between two points in deep space not only ain't a straight line but's a full cihcle. See, space wraps, and you know why that is?"
Haven't a clue.
"Ain't cause each planet rotates in its own eccentric ohbit, like you might suspect, it's cause whole galaxies spin as they propel fahward, like giant frisbees sailin off, pushin at the vehry fringes of space as they go, same time deflectin back, cuhlin undahneath."
Giant frisbees?
"Some of the great galaxies spihral, up and down like spinnin tops, but most ah flat disks. And in the centah theah's this bulge wheah the thehmonucleah genahrath's located, blasts of gas and stahdust that fuel the fuhry, probably with an immense dense black hole anchohrin it like the hub of a wheel while the whole contraption whips round and round."
Why a girl could get dizzy just trying to imagine it – will you slow

down some on those curves chum!

"'Couhse it takes millions of yeahs to complete a cycle, but by the time that probe we sent approaches its destination, it will have bent around slowly, impahceptibly, wahrpin, foldin undah, until *whooof* — it emahges somewheah else entihely — that and if the probe does suhvive the crash landin, the trip back's no snap neithah."

An adventure not unlike Chipper and Betsy's. They're heading from an immense space way far away in Northern Maine down toward New York City, a place that surely rotates in its own eccentric orbit, and they're not following a straight line nor anything resembling a straight line, in fact they are deliberately zig-zagging all over the map to avoid highway patrols, which if they should collide would no doubt send them back fast where they began, though under heavy guard. And why are they undertaking this far out journey anyway? It's not a quest for fresh air, they abandoned abundant supplies of that back home, along with entire lakes and fresh flowing streams, no, they're seeking something even more essential for their survival, a refuge from justice and the law protecting willing minors.

"Awesome, ain't it?"

As in overpowering.

"Whoa — what's up ahead? Someone in distress?"

A guy is standing along the roadside, there in the middle of nowhere, no town, no house, no lights — Betsy can hardly make his figure out in the dark. Probably needs a lift somewhere, poor fellow, though perhaps best to leave him be — the wary Dobbie in her talking.

"H'yep. Somebody needin somethin." No way Chipper's going to speed by, he's not that kind of guy. "How you doin strangah?"

Betsy rolls down her window so Chipper can holler over.

"Alright. You?"

They both take their time talking. Down Easters are like that, particularly when they first meet one another or when someone from out of state stops and confounds them by asking for directions, but catch them at home and Mainers are chatterheads like anybody anywhere.

"You broke down oah ah you just lost?"

"Certainly appreciate your stopping and asking. Took a tumble on my bike and I'm tryin to hitch a ride into the next town open."

Which can be a ways backcountry.

"You huhtin any?"

"Nope. Scratch or two at most."

A middle of the night hitchhiker makes Betsy mighty suspicious as she sticks that muzzle of hers out the window and straight into the guy's face. Turns out he's a ruddy cheeked young fellow, innocent enough looking, but then so are most serial killers.

"What kind of bike?"
"Old S90 BMW."
"Shaft driven?"
"Yep, and air cooled."
"Classic."
"Restored it myself."
Except where is it — *hrunh?* — where's this old bike?
"Had to stash it in a culvert, it'll be safe there until I get back…"
-*rr* right, likely story.
"…how far are you going?"
"New Yahk."
"Can you give me a lift down the road?"
"Suhe."
"Really appreciate the ride. Not much traffic this time of night. State cruiser stopped to warn me of a manhunt along the border."
"Which side, New Hampshihe oah Maine?"
"Both I guess. He was out looking for some kind of sex fiend from what I could gather. He was fairly tight-lipped about the particulars."
"Officah have a soht of lahge squahe head?"
"Matter of fact he did."
"H'yep, anothah one of the Dohbs brothahs, probably Edgah, he'd be in on anythin suspicious."
"I didn't catch which flavor this jailbird favors, but *uh*- makes you sort of nervous when you're stranded by yourself and off the main highway."
Each looks the other over, who knows who could be what underneath their respective belt buckles. Fellow doesn't appear life threatening however, suspendered sort, plaid shirt, furry face and sporting a Red Sox cap — how fearsome can those league losers be?
"I could sit in the bed in back."
And how disingenuous?
"Nah, no reason. I'll put the dog in back, she likes the fresh aih blowin cross huh noggin."
I don't mind something soft to sit on either.
"Jump down gihl, got to be hospitable to strangahs."
-*rowlll*, you go freeze in the back then. Enjoy the wind blowing across your noggin.
"You sure? Nice dog. She looks mighty comfortable where she's at."
-*rr* right, listen to him — and thank you for the compliment stranger.
"She'll be fine. Sometimes she fahgets she's a dog. Hop in."
Fellow tosses his saddle bags in the back while Betsy troops around. A dog? A dog? Like I'm some sort of wild animal, not the compassionate creature who crawled into the cave with mankind, kept guard while he

slept, warned him about fire or a savage intruder, licked his wounds, disposed of his garbage, herded his goats, watched over his kids, in a word befriended the ungrateful rogue when nobody else from the primeval savannah would, except cats, but when did a cat ever earn its keep? Catch a mouse now and then. Go try and fry that up for dinner mister. Never have known a cat to chase down a rabbit for you or swim after a duck — thankless, that's what you humans are — don't deserve the loyalty of a longtime companion.

"How come you wahn't ridin youh bike ovah on the main highway?"

"Prefer back roads."

Prefer back roads, sure pal, wonder what kind of a lumberjack you really are? Betsy sticks her nose through the hole of the slider window, listens in, has to figure this character out.

"Back road is usually more scenic…"

In the dark, right.

"…and no eighteen wheelers to knock you from lane to lane or those drivers who don't even glance back — cut you off and leave you skidding toward the shoulder."

Is it a knife you carry, you seem like a knife type — well let me tell you, Chipper hasn't anything worth stealing and I can be one tough cookie to contend with — like take a look at me when I smile -*rrlllllll!*

Fellow catches her poking through the rear window at him, big jaw full of exposed canines. "You certain your dog enjoys riding in back?"

"Betsy can be mighty protective."

"Most folks think the roads are swarming with perverts or they're going to get robbed by a hitchhiker at knife point. People don't trust one another anymore, you notice that?"

"Feah only breeds mah feah."

You can never be too careful, Betsy murmurs as she noses in further to inspect the nape of the guy's neck. She samples a whiff and takes a lick. No men's cologne, can't be too perverted, and *blick*, he's had a bath in the past twenty four hours! She continues to taste her tongue, mulling the flavor over in her mouth. Definitely French, local variety, young yet, needs aging, probably middle to late twenties, full bodied, but not aromatic, though neither fruity nor bitter, a solid vintage best served with beef or venison.

"You from somewheah around heah?"

"Orono. How about you?"

"Lived most of my life in Ottah's Ledge — know wheah that is?"

"Up near Fort Kent."

"H'yep, 'bout as fah away from people as I can get and still collect my disability — got agent ohranged in Nam, suffah pahmanent memohry loss."

"Have an uncle like that, loses track of his thoughts mid-sentence."

"Spend my spahe time mostly strummin guitah and writin songs."
"Poet?"
"Nope. What I've got to say is mah basic."
"Most good poetry is."
"What ah you into?"
"Study philosophy, when I can afford to."
"H'yep. Lots to be philosophical about these days, don't you know."
"Keeps me sane, that and hiking outdoors."
"You look like an eagah backpackah to me strangah."

A mite too early for an Appalachian trail blazer though. Maybe he's one of those protestors who go around driving spikes into trees ahead of the deforestation crews.

"Any of your songs been recorded?"
"Few. Why me and Betsy have been doin a medley, what we call ouh late night specials. Want to join in?"
-*roh* no, the forbidden list!
"I'm pretty near tone deaf."
"So hold the rhythm fah us – how 'bout the ballad of *Cindy Sue* fah stahtahs. I use that to wahm up the crowd at one of my bahroom gigs."

Betsy simply sighs.

"See Cindy Sue, she lives way out theah in those deep dahk nohthuhn woods we all know so well, alone with huh mohtah and kid sistah, house set back in the prickly pines… and some nights late, well…"

> Cindy Sue she gets huhself a yeahnin
> 'Specially when the moon is full
> Huh insides they staht in chuhnin
> Satuhday nights when TV is dull
>
> Gal hikes out to the roadside
> Thumbs the fihst lone truckah down
> Climbs right up and sits beside him
> Befah long she's doin the clown
>
> Cindy Sue / Cindy Sue
> She does fah Stan / She'll do fah you
> Cindy Sue / Cindy Sue
> Gal's bettah than pay-pah-view

"Ain't no reason evahrybody can't sing along on the chohrus."

> Cindy Sue / Cindy Sue
> She does fah Stan / She'll do fah you
> Cindy Sue / Cindy Sue

Gal's bettah than pay-pah-view

Truckah he gets plumb tuckahed
Pulls his bob tail into a rest stop
Idles while Cindy Sue's busy revvin up
Befah long she's out prowlin the lot

Cindy Sue / Cindy Sue
She does fah Stan / She'll do fah you
Cindy Sue / Cindy Sue
Lot lizahd's bettah than pay-pah-view

"Got this cool guitah lick I put in aftah the chohrus."

Plum dumba bumpta bumma / -pew -pew
Pip piddily pit stop / pop pop diddily whop

Truckah he rides on fah days now
With Cindy Sue theah in his cab
Gal has so many ways down
He just mahks them on huh tab

Cindy Sue / Cindy Sue
She does fah Stan / She'll do fah you
Cindy Sue / Cindy Sue
She's hottah than pay-pah-view

But come a Monday mohnin eahly
With Cindy Sue so fah from home
Ridin up front theah gettin sulky
Why'd she evah staht to roam

Gal you've got to quit youh whinin
Woman travels with huh man
But if you find eighteen wheelahs tihrin
You can ahways thumb down a van

Cindy Sue / Cindy Sue
She does fah Stan / She'll do fah you
Cindy Sue / Cindy Sue
She's cheapah than pay-pah-view

"One last time fah remindahs! Evahrybody!"

Cindy Sue / Cindy Sue
She does fah Stan / She'll do fah you

Cindy Sue / Cindy Sue
Gal's bettah than pay-pah-view

Pip pip pa-didilly plop / and do do do

"That's it, that's the ballad of Cindy Sue."
"Remarkable!"
"Guahanteed to get the whole bahroom kicked back, gals too."

Betsy doesn't join in the frivolity. She has never approved of the ballad of *Cindy Sue,* a lonely girl's worn torrid tale, one all too familiar and not in need of repeating, particularly in a bar full of rowdies. Not that Betsy is puritanical, no way, Betsy is a hound dog and she can sniff around with the best of them, she's curled her tail for many a pleasant go at it. Still, too much is made of such an activity to suit her sensibilities, and one thing she has learned is that dogs simply do it, they don't sing about it or worse crow, but humans, men in particular, they talk about nothing else, yet do much less of it than they let on. And she has been there, she has observed close up. Chipper for all his reputation spends many a night with his hand attached to a beer bottle only to wail out this same song over and over until rosy fingered dawn bends down and takes him on.

"You know Cindy Sue personally, do you Chipper?"
"To tell the truth strangah, I've known lots of Cindy Sues."

Stranger nods. Seems he has too.

"So you were front line in Nam?"
"Ahmy aihbohn, jumpin into ambushes age nineteen. Talk about wakin up quick. Nevah had to wohry much about sleep aftah that."
"My generation missed out on the war."
"You ahmost sound regretful. Best to be thankful. Soldiah nevah wins. Nightmahes if he's lucky, planted cross if he's not. Theah's no glohry — oh a careeh type likes to boast, get himself pumped up, but a regulah, he wants out fast as he can. Suhvival, that's what the Ahmy teaches you, respect fah life, youh own fah stahtahs, but nothin useful, cahtainly not a job."
"Was self-survival the only lesson you learned from Vietnam?"
"Nam was the wah that ended all wahs, least fah the US militahry. Evahrythin since then's been tahget practice. Enemy who can't shoot back ain't goin to scratch youh fancy new hahdwahe, that's until the Chinese get theih own Stah Wahs set launched — window of oppohtunity, that what they call it? Scoop up on it befah it comes crashin down on youh fingahs."
"You see war as inevitable?"
"Like huhricanes and head-on collisions, you nevah know which oah when — makes slow death by old age a real luxuhry."
"In between wars there can be a truce…"
"Convenient time fah an all-out economic attack, free trade in guns

and guidance systems, make the wohld safe fah tankahs of oil, each side geahrin up fah the inevitable Ahmageddon. And that day'll come, I predict it, cause greed rules, and theah's ahways a bunch of young fools who can be convinced to go off and fight."

"History is marked by its major conflicts."

"H'yep, wahs fought by the pooh to benefit the rich."

"Is that why you retreated to Otter's Ledge?"

"Travelin round gets mighty tirin, and bein on youh own's a tough way to leahn."

Stranger nods. Seems he's already had his share of scrapes.

"Don't get me wrong. Life's been ahright. Besides I got to retihe to povahty eahly, didn't have to wait fah sixty seven and Social Secuhrity."

"No regrets?"

"Scrappy suhvivah's bettah off than a resentful lifah any day. Suhe, I've had to struggle, but a joinah don't get the time to make a life fah himself, dab of pay and nothin of his own wohk to show fah it. Spends his life locked in a bungalow full of possessions he's got to guahd, won't throw a thing out, 'til one day he up and dies. They caht him off, dump most of his shit in the trash. But his biggest buhden is he's been stuck livin with himself, no one else. Kids scoot out on him soon as they'h out of school. Wife occupies huhself gossipin on the phone with huh chuhch cihcle. Friend he despises is probably the only friend he's got, and his enemies know his credit cahd numbah backwahds and fahwahds cause he's handed it ovah to them thousands of times no questions asked. So he sits theah sullen and contents himself with the game on TV. Easiah to watch than to play. Discusses nothin mah contravahsial than the weathah othahwise his neighbahs will avoid him if he mumbles one wohd of dissent oah cuts a faht at the seniah centah. He's leahned it's best to keep politics and religion to himself, like sex, but he can drink himself doughty so long as he doesn't pass out in the lobby. Waxes his cah and plays golf, life's only a hobby. Doin anythin else would be contrahry, like that long-haihed 60s fellah down the road who won't listen to populah propogandah on the radio."

"Dissenter ends up a loner."

"Live long enough, no mattah who you ah, you end up a lonah. It's just some of us staht in eahly. Take the most impohtant events in a guy's life — bihth, death, school, goin off to wah, oah mahriage and the job — what say has he got? Gettin bohn, well that's the choice of whoevah youh mothah happens to be and what kind of bihth control she fahgot to use, huh and whoevah she claims was the fathah."

"Did you know your father?"

"My mothah was faihly mum about who fathahed who, knew my granpappy though. He was a chahractah — but we wah talkin about life's majah decisions."

"Well, school, you're young and education is mandated by the state."

"Teachahs ah like preachahs, pat answahs to questions nobody's askin."

"War's certainly not an individual choice."

"Maybe it should be. Maybe any kind of death should be. Bill of Rights could be extended. Come a wah, let's toss the two toughest genahrals in the pit, let them slug it out, eithah that oah mahch whoevah stands to profit most to the front line."

"How can you include marriage? It's the one choice your parents and the state can't dictate."

"Mahriage is when the gal decides it's time to cohnah you, when she gets pregnant and takes advantage of youh fathahly instincts. She eithah tells you she's goin to put youh only flesh and bloody child up fah adoption oah have a wicked messy abohtion you'h s'posed to pay fah. But if neithah of those pahsuades you, she announces she's goin ahead and havin it anyway, keep it at home fah huh mothah to take cahe of, plus let the whole town know what you've done and ain't man enough to own up to. Those ah youh options. Might appeah you've got some say in the mattah, some free choices, like you could deny the child, try and besmihch the gal's reputation, tell evahrybody huh favohrite uncle did it to huh aftah Thanksgivin dinnah, and you'h a handy covah up, but nowadays they've got blood tests, so you bettah just mahry huh – oah run away and try to avoid child suppoht until some state prosecutah posts youh face on the top twenty most haunted list – but whatevah the truth is, in the end the decision to get mahried ain't up to you, it's up to some gal and huh baby."

-*row* revolting! That is the most convoluted logic I have ever heard!

"But a critic might ask who made her pregnant in the first place?"

"Guy's got no control ovah his dick gettin hahd, he's just groovin along like guys do, screwin evahry chance he can get – and damned if a gal doesn't use his weakness against him."

Talk about a tirade against women! Have you no decency?

"She's the one intent on makin a baby, she knows whethah she's ripe oah not, plus she's been pinin about gettin mahried since she was five yeahs old. She buys bride magazines and daydreams about the cehremony, how she's goin to look in huh fluffy white dress, who will be in the weddin pahty, who on the groom's side is definitely goin to get left off the guest list. But the guy, he's not wohryin 'bout none of that crap, he just wants to get laid on a regulah basis."

"But that's still a decision, isn't it?"

"Necessity don't breed freedom of choice, besides youh dick's the fuhthest thing from youh head, physically speakin, 'cept fah youh knees oah youh toes and those don't get most guys in trouble."

This discussion is pathetic, all this misplaced concern for men and their aberrant hormones! Castration might be the only solution. Like when they did in poor Maximillian — except he was no good for anything after that, hung around outside and moaned, easily distracted, couldn't even wag his tail right — although marriage is no sweetheart deal for the bride either, let me tell you. Sure she might yearn for a nice church wedding, but can you blame her? One day in a lifetime she feels like a queen, otherwise she's doomed to be a servant, washing, cleaning, cooking — that's no decision she makes freely, that's a misfortune she has to face daily — and babies, you two try being a nursemaid to a dozen pups when you only have ten milk spigots, see how much you enjoy being chewed on. Mother's day is never done. Father's day is spent lying in the sun.

"And wohk, this careah shit guidance counselahs talk about only adds to a man's sohdid othah misfohtunes — pooh suckah's got some job he doesn't want no paht of, and that's a drag, not a decision. Back in Maine you eithah wohk fah the state guahdin the fohrests oah you wohk fah the lumbah companies cuttin down the fohrests, though some folks wohk fah both and make a shit load of money playin the one off the othah. That's called a trade-off, makin the best out of a bad situation gettin wohse, and nobody can nevah call that free choice. Then theah's death, not a topic most folks enjoy discussin except fah muhdahs oah gohry cah accidents, but most times death's out of youh hands entihely, though not always, man can attempt the rope and stool trick, hope it wohks and he doesn't end strung up on feedin tubes fah a quartah centuhry listenin to some rehab jahk badgahrin him to count his fingahs."

"What's an example of free choice then Chipper?"

"Gettin up one mohnin, stokin on a bone and promisin youhself you'h goin to get the hell out, head some place wheah nobody has a hand in youh pocket — that's a sample of free choice."

"In the final analysis then, you don't believe man has free will?"

"Problem is man hasn't got that much time fah free will, life flies by too fast fah him to reflect on what he's doin, best he can manage is to steeh cleah, hang on fah the ride."

"Sounds to me as though you're a determinist Chipper, view man as having little control over his own destiny."

"That's nice you say that. Most folks up nohth call me peculiah, those with a philosophical tuhn of mind."

Anybody I've heard calls you a no account backwoods crazyman if not an outright sociopath.

"I've been accused of evahry crime imaginable, just cause I choose to to tell it like it is, live deep in the woods by myself, tryin to keep the neighbahs at bay, which ain't easy no mattah how fah out of town you move."

Not when you're regularly raiding their chicken coops.

"Then let's not fahget old age — folks think adolescence was rough, try walkin backwahds into the grave — time's wohth nothin 'til it stahts to run out. Then's when you've got to scramble. But *whoops*, don't stumble, you'h none too nimble, plus you've nevah stood up fah nothin befah, 'cept to sing the national anthem. Covah youh heaht hell, covah youh eyes, plug youh eahs, cause theah's things out theah you cleahly don't want to heah, and nobody can hit the high notes anyway. 'But wait, wait now, don't count me out, somebody's on the phone takin a poll. They'h askin what's my view on the critical issues of the day? Well I agree mostly with the majohity, like what's the eighty pahcentahs oah bettah got to say? I'll put my money on the winnah of the next wah, OK? And son, befah you hang up, can you explain to me exactly what it is we'h ovah theah fightin fah? Ah we still against communism and laboh unions, oah is it this new Ahrab tehrorhist thing, cause the only wah I recollect we've won in the past fifty yeahs was ovah gasoline prices.'"

"What say we sing anothah song?"
"OK."
"Bet you've heahd this one befah strangah. Wrote it back when I about was youh age. It's called *Getta Gihl* — refrain goes like this."

> Getta gihl / Gotta gotta
> Spot a gihl / hotta hotta…

"Wait. You wrote *Getta Girl*?"
"H'yep."
"You-you're Chipper Stirbee?"
"Can't deny it."
"Awesome! My father said you were the best ever."
"We held ouh own among the front runnahs, fah a while anyway."
"Claimed you were still alive somewhere back in the woods."
If you can call living in the backwoods alive.
"And two weeks ago this dude from New York gave me a lift home, told me he was out searching for you."
"Lou Stahcrave?"
"That was his name. Did he ever find you?"
"Man's tryin to put togethah some soht of revival of ouh old band."
"Is that why you're heading down to New York?"
"Sohta…"

-*humph* — which goes right back to that discussion you two were having about free will.

"…though sometimes it's somethin else you don't suspect that gets you up and movin."

-rohk! -rohk! -rohk! Betsy has snuggled her way back into the cab, resting her head on the young stranger's lap, as he strokes her velvet ears.

"You got somethin to say babydoll, spit it right out."

I would if I could.

"Betsy heah is a chronic complainah."

Try listening to him from noon to sun up seven days a week, and see if your eardrums don't roll. Why if dogs barked as much as you folks talk, none of us would ever get any rest.

"Anyway, I've got this philosophical question fah you strangah."

"What's that?"

"Is what you do what you ah? Oah is what you ah what you do?"

Come again?

"Is what you do what you ah? Oah is what you ah what you do?"

"A metaphysical question."

As in circular, wher-*rr* the one statement simply repeats the other.

"Now don't go tryin to answah that until you'h propahly prepahed — need a hit of my own preminum homegrown fuhst."

"Oh!" Stranger lights up at the suggestion.

"Theah's a fresh bag stashed in the dooh linah ovah on youh side — that's it, take a whiff."

"Wow! Skunky!"

"That sappy oah what? Won the Golden Bud Awahd last Septembah at the Aroostook County Growah's Fahm Festival."

"Bet that's some contest."

Talk about humans making total fools of themselves.

"Way it wohks is openin night we pass round some samplin's. Judges take a few tokes of each, and whoevah's weed knocks the majohity on theih butts wins the awahd — wheah's my pipe Betsy, you sittin on it as usual?"

I'm probably sittting on all sorts of things, it's not like I have a lot of room here.

"Betsy's ahways hidin my stash on me oah my favohrite pipe. She gets real squeamish when I smoke and drive, and lately she's been speakin huh mind out about it, about lots of things — evah since she's become a dues payin membah of NAAG, the mail ohdah National Association of Animal Gripes? Been houndin me like crazy ovah one thing oah anothah, pahticulahly my attitude towahd fouh legged crittahs…"

I'm hardly a nag. I merely point out the obvious.

"…she figuhes if I'm smokin while I'm drivin, I might hit a raccoon oah run down a skunk — what she doesn't undahstand is I'm much mah attuned to natuhe when I'm totally wrecked out of my mind."

You mean when you see double, swerve to avoid one and hit the other.
"No pipe?"
-*roh* let me check under the seat — *scratch scratch scratch.*
"While you'h down theah gihl, grab me a pack of papahs — you any good at rollin strangah?"
"No, not really."
"Then let me show you my famous one-handed trick. Took yeahs of practice behind the whee-... KEERIPES! What's that up ahead?"
"Where?"
"In the middle of the road theah! *Whoa-ho* hold on!" As the Subaru dips into a ditch then tracks back up on the roadway, some possum trying to waddle across to the other side.
"*Whew-ee,* just missed the pitiful creatuhe."
Betsy pokes her nose out the hole in the back to make certain — could be a mother with pups home in the den or someone's life-long companion, victims of untold misery one thoughtless act can cause.
"Close call — what was it I was doin... oh, rollin a bone..."
You watch your driving, I'll do the rolling.
"It almost seems as though this dog talks."
"Ahways on my case is what she is — hey! What the fuck ah you doin with my prize pickin's!"
Betsy uses her claw to scrape some ganje out on a paper, she spills not a speck, spreads it evenly with the tip of her nose, then laps the sucker up, rolls it around on her tongue and lets it hang off her lip. Might be a bit to the moist, but take a hit chum, the spit'll burn off as soon as it's lit.
"Damn! Packed pahfect!"
Thank you. Thank you.
"Wheah'd you evah leahn how to do that?"
Night after night with nothing to do except watch you — want to see some *bow-wow*-ser card tricks?
"One smart dog you've got here."
"H'yep. Brains of a Dobahman mixed in with the loyalty of a Lab, plus a dose of the pesky pahsistent."
Pesky?
"Only jokin gihl." He strokes her ruffled coat.
-*humph!*
"Fihe that suckah up strangah."
-*huh-huh-huh -huuuuuuuuup!*
"Fihst hit of this shit's the kickah — best cuhe is to haul down anothah."
-*huuuuuuuuuuuuuup -hup*... HACK HACK HACK HACK!
Chipper pounds the stranger on the back. "Theah you go, you'h on youh way to some sehrious damage now — so gulp down a chasah."

-huuh -huuh -huuh...
Sad to see another good soul sent packing along the road to ruin.
HACK HACK HACK HACK HACK HACK!
-rah well, Betsy settles in for more of a nonsense discussion, sniffs a bit of the ambient air herself.
"So, what was the question?"
"Is what we do what we ah? Oah is what we ah what we do?"

And way off the map altogether, Molly Dawkens is still sitting on her porch, sweating it out. Breeze flaps around, trying to cool her down, but she's still fuming. It's the feud between her kind and that Temperance Woman — "Yeah well, I've got the moon on my side bitch, wait and see, that young stud's going to end up suckling his thumb in my lap!"
You tell her little mama, you tell her where she can go an how fast she can ride on that broomstick she's got t'get there.
"Luna! Listen to me! Who's it going to be, me or her?" — Molly's been at these divinations most of the night and she's not at all happy with what she's been dealt. "I want an answer!" For which forthwith she prepares herself, she bares her breasts — *'Alo!* — they sizzle as she anoints each fiery tip with lavender oil, cups under and offers them up, still smooth, still firm, still magnificent.
'Alo! 'Alo!
Clouds shadow the moon's face, the sight of such shamelessness must embarrass even the likes of Luna, but Breeze reaches over.
Molly whaps his hands.
Chee-ripes!
For the gesture is merely symbolic, she doesn't have time nor patience for elaborate ritual, not this late at night. Moon's on the wane and... and Molly senses some intense interplanetary force circling closer and closer, some old sorcerer perhaps, some young charmer. So she makes her next move — SNAP! — it's an old game this lady plays.
Breeze is breathless in anticipation.
Card is The Cosmos at the instant of creation — a sunburst and in the center of all the commotion this voluptuous woman emerging — "Yes! There's my answer!" The constellations swirl about her, a full symphonic orchestra — Aries, Taurus, Leo, the twelve powers of nocturnal inspiration, while she, this Eve, this Creatrix embraces a giant dragon with a python-like tail who entwines himself between her naked thighs. A Single Eye encased in a translucent pyramid observes from on high as she writhes about with this slithery suitor.
"Ohh-..." Molly fresh fluid in response slumps back on her chaise, and

Breeze… he can be such a snake or such a charmer, whatever it takes to please her

Breeze, he's on her in an instant though she's hardly resistant — he can be such a snake or such a charmer, whatever it takes to please her.

"OHH- OHHHH- OHHHHHHHH!" She squirms, she relents, she beats with her fists since she's about had enough of this slip sliding frontside — *'Alo! 'Alo!* — seems she wants it flipped over backassward!

O'h'h'h'h'… tight in and as sassy as ever!

"Why did you ever give up your musical career Chipper, if you don't mind my asking…"

Betsy gulps, way down that long stretched neck of hers.

"…was celebrity too high a price to pay for your privacy?"

"'Spose you could say that, then theah was Cincinnati Summah of 69."

"Cincinnati Summer of 69?"

"Times wah diffahrent way back then, times wahn't ready fah my soht of music."

-ro, they were ready for you alright, they had a noose, they had a mob.

"Was this one pahticulah judge in Cincinnati — seems he objected to the lyrics of this song I wrote…"

"How about free speech?"

"H'yep well, we nevah got to ahgue the constitutional issue."

-rr-roak -roak -roak

"You tell the stohry Miss Know-It-All, 'cept you wahn't even bohn yet."

No but my great-great grandmother was, and we Lab/Dobie mixes have a long tradition of oral history.

Chipper ignores her, hums a little tune — *dut dutta / doop ta dooda do.*

"You were telling me about Cincinnati Summer of 69."

"*Dut dutta…* right, I was. See, we'd been invited to pahticipate at Woodstock, so we had to cancel some stops in ouh regulah summah touh and head upstate New Yahk. Ouh last stop was Cincinnati. See Ohio, down in the southahn paht of the state theah, well they'h faihly consahvative, don't you know, Bible Belt consahvative, which means not libahral, not at all, and this judge didn't happen to cahe much fah rock 'n' roll — white trash singin colohed boy's music, oah so he said. That and we wah intrudin on his tuhf — we'd have been off scot-free in Cleveland oah Columbus oah anywheah else fuhthuh nohth — but theah we wah in town fah a couple of concahts. Sold out. Fihst night they kept callin us back fah mah cuhtain calls so we, I — was a mattah of some dispute among us who actally made the suggestion — but I had this new song I'd been wohkin on. Will Cook had the melody down mostly. I was still dabblin with the lyrics. Anyway band was playin and I was out front dancin around like usual and this gihl in the front row, she shouted she'd trade me huh bra fah my t-shiht. I said suhe and tossed mine ovah. Friend next to huh decided to go huh one bettah, suggested an exchange of undahweah…"

"You didn't."

"Tell the truth, these two wah real smokahs, I'd had my eye on both all along… and I didn't expose myself like they said — oh a little moonin — flung mine right back at huh. Suddenly I was bein bombahded, whole place strippin down. Wasn't much mah I could lose 'cept my jeans…"

"Did they arrest you?"

"See times wah way difahrent then, Beatles wah still pahfohmin in coat and tie, and me bein a casual kind of guy… then too the hall was full of smoke, this dude offahed me a joint, though I was mostly blown out ahready on some of my own, but the whole scene sohta got out of hand and next thing I knew the police wah up on the stage handcuffin me, Bubba, Danny T, evahrybody in the band. Was a hohrah show, fans screamin, rushin the stage, throwin shoes at the police — we wah lucky to get out of theah with ouh hides."

"Were there reporters handy, photographers to witness all this?"

"Unfohtunately."

"Oh, I understand."

You're -rr-only beginning to understand.

"Besides…"

"There's more?"

You have no idea. Once trouble starts, this guy dives in.

"…see, I nevah figuhed folks listened to the wohds of a song all that close — then too a few of the kids wah makin cassette recohdins which I guess got confiscated… Upshot. Next mohnin I was hauled in front of the judge. Guess he'd decided to single me out, well I wasn't about to go bluhbbahrin on like Bubba about his motah's honah, and Will Cook had pulled a nutty in the cell — they sent him right off to a mental facility — which only left me and Danny T to face the music. He copped a plea, told the judge he was guilty as hell, but a good Christian undahneath, promised he'd repent and got off with a reprimand, but me… well the judge was pitched back itchin to throw the book at somebody, me soht of stubbohn standin theah in front of him…"

You? Stubborn?

"…and if theah's one thing authohity can't abide it's defiance — so fihst off he issues this injunction against the distribution of all ouh recohdin's in his district until theah was a full heahrin on the mehrits. 'Couhse the damage was ahready done, radio stations cross the country immediately jehked us off the aih — ain't many populah tunes that can suhvive close scrutiny of the lyrics."

"Lot of counts against you."

"H'yep h'yep…"

And you haven't heard the last half of the story yet.

"I ahways say, life ain't bad, not until it gets wohse."

Worse? Try degenerate!

"What did the film coverage show?"

"Some pahts wah definitely ovahexposed, but hey evahrythin's open to intahpretation, least that's what we wah ahguin – looked like we wah makin progress until the judge called a recess fah lunch."

"Then what?"

Tell the man.

"That revehred great grandmothah of youhs wasn't theah neithah, she got all huh infohmation second hand."

Then let's hear a full account of your side of the story once and for all.

"Way this dog looks at me, I don't know why I put up with huh."

Why you put up with me – give me a *brr*-eak!

"Anyhow, I didn't know who this gihl was fah suhe, didn't even have time to ask huh name. She was just motionin at me to follow aftah huh, and she was young, good lookah and then some, so I skipped lunch and went straight fah the dessaht tray. Helped myself to a buttahscotch sundae with a chehry to pop, took my mind right off the proceedin's when out of nowheah the judge comes slammin through the dooh!"

So far the same version I heard, although condensed some.

"The door to where?"

"No way in hell I knew I was humpin on his leathah chambah sofa."

-*hmm*, here there is a divergence, with some pertinent details missing.

"Ahright. Gihl was his daughtah and she was just tuhnin sixteen that day, guess I was huh bihthday present to huhself."

"Wha- what happened?"

"It was eithah five to ten oah dismissal on a technicality, that's if I'd agree to banishment and keep my mouth shut."

"What technicality? Wasn't it statutory?"

"Southahn states have a funny notion about undahage, despite theih religious convictions, fifteen was ahright in Texas if I recall cohrectly, and Alabama was even mah lenient, Mississippi, Louisiana too, but Missouhri was tough – anyway sixteen was bingo in Ohio, since half the state was soht of progressive – and the fact that it was huh bihthday wasn't in dispute, but seems she hadn't been bohn until latah in the night, and this bein right aftah lunch, judge wasn't goin to give in easy – fathahs and theih daughtahs, I mean some dude somewheah along the line is goin to have the distinct pleasuhe of relievin huh of huh ch-…"

"You didn't argue that point, did you?"

"Nope, recohd company lawyah told me to shut up and keep my eyes

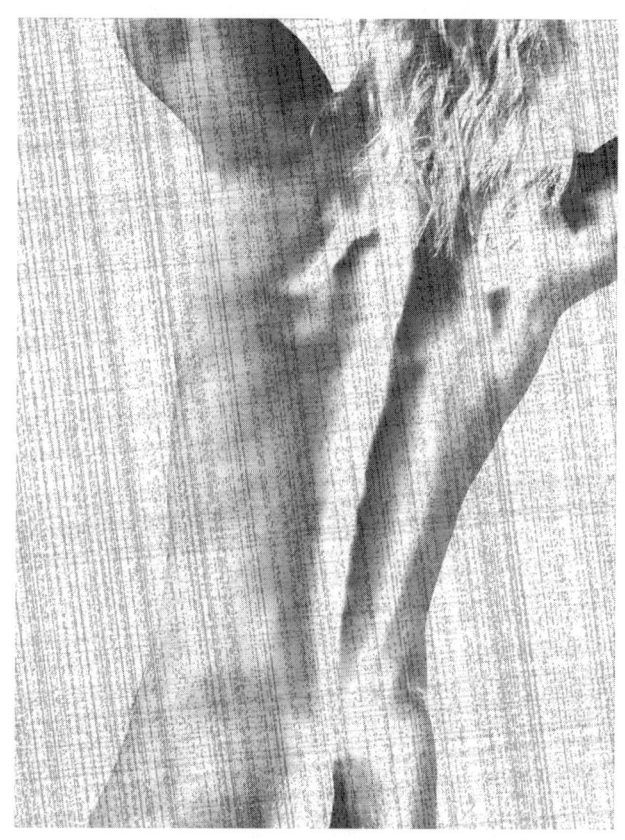

"H'yep, front page news cross the country, luhrid photographs though so grainy you could nevah have proved they wah me on the flooh if I didn't want to do jail time — judge, when he got ovah his sputtahrin decided to cut a deal."

"So you got away unscathed?"

"Not altogethah. Judge made his injunction pahmanent, fined me my life savin's right to the dime, then ohdahed me run out of town. I went straight from the couhthouse to the aihpoht, but on the delicate subject of his daughtah, he did back down, seems he was aftah some appointment to the Couht of Appeals and in those days a dude in his position didn't want no diht on his family made paht of the public recohd."

"Close call."

"H'yep, front page news cross the country, luhrid photographs though so grainy you could nevah have proved they wah me, editahs agreein I was the wohst example of a bad breed of new musicians. Meant the instant end of the Loose Nukes and fah me pahmanent exile — but wahn't we discussin somethin else strangah, befah we got off on this sideline, somethin about the inherent conflict between man's natuhe and his right to wohk?"

"How does the song go, I don't think I've ever heard it?"

"Only vahsion was a studio take, song's mostly lost to postehrity."

Posterity! And lost? Buried is more like it!

Chipper clears his throat. "Don't sing it too much myself, well you know, bittah memohries, but once in a while when I get edgy I'll hum the tune — *dut dutta / doop ta dooda do.*"

"You don't remember the words?"

Don't abet him!

"Do. Remembah evahry syllable as distinct as if it was yestahday. It's called *Love Baby* — 'couhse it'd sound bettah with instrumental back-up — think you could handle the rhythm paht fah me strangah?"

"Try. What do I have to do?"

"Basic beat — *dut dutta* — pause — *doop ta dooda do* — keeps repeatin ovah and ovah."

"*Dut dutta / doop ta dooda do?*"

"You've got it, just stay in the groove no mattah what I do, ahright?"

"*Dut dutta / doop ta dooda do.*"

"Yah yah yah yah…" Chipper's voice takes on a soft plaintive edge.

> Love Baby / You'h MINE so fine
> Love Baby / Let's have a TASTY time
> *Dut dutta / doop ta dooda do*

Why it's the tenderest of love ballads, yes, almost a lullaby.

> Love Baby / Come KISS youh daddy

There's a sudden drop as the last phrase descends into a deeper register, much as Elvis would have done, had he lived to sing this ditty.

> Love Baby / Just don't TELL nobody
> *Dut dutta / doop ta dooda do*

> Love Baby / Come sit HEAH by me
> Love Baby / Shahe a BITE fah free
> *Dut dutta / doop ta dooda do*

Betsy scrunches way down low, covers her ears with her paws.

> Love Baby / It'd suhe FEEL nice
> Love Baby / Cut me ANOTHAH… big ol' slice

"Keep the beat fah me strangah – *dut dutta / doop ta dooda do // dut dutta / doop ta dooda do* – can't you just heah a soft jazzy brush off a snahe about now?"

> Love Baby / Skin so SMOOTH and soft
> Love Baby / Please… help youh DADDY get off

-*rr-rr*-reprobate!

> *Dut dutta / doop ta dooda do*
> *Dut dutta / doop ta dooda do*
> Love Baby / Don't that FEELgood
> Love Baby / Like you KNEW it would

In the studio rendition this verse was followed by a soaring Will Cook keyboard solo, splendid in its intricacy, in its eccentricity, with a shifting return to a heart-wrenching E-flat minor.

> Love Baby / Hold youh BREATH a minute
> Love Baby / Ain't you GLAD you did it

"Wait now, theah's mah."
As with such depravity there must inevitably be.

> *Dut dutta / doop ta dooda do*
> *Dut dutta / doop ta dooda do*
> Love Baby / Got to keep this SECRET all ouhs
> Love Baby / Othahwise… they'll put DADDY behind bahs

Dut dut-…

AND THEY SHOULD HAVE APPOINTED THAT JUDGE IN CINCINNATI TO THE SUPREME COURT! BY NATIONAL ACCLAMATION! -RR-ROOT! -ROOT!

"Do-... do you believe in an all-forgiving God Chipper?"

"You mean sin and that soht of thing?"

"Yes, I guess..."

"Well, I did have this religious epehrience once when I was young – at the Last Call Cathedral?"

"Where?"

"Some smaht aleck kid in my Sunday School class named it that – well the congregation was tryin theih best to stay sobah. See folks in Maine get real tihed of plowin snow and choppin wood, don't you know, 'specially along the nohthun bohdah wheah they could only get the one TV channel, and that was on a cleah night. Social life was the local bah and grill, fahget the grill, it closed by five. Oldah kids had a table resehved in the back neah the jukebox wheah we could dance and drink pitchahs of beeh. Nobody checked IDs so long as you least acted oldah and had some cash on you. Best place to hit on the gihls too, though stumblin home drunk could result in some mighty suhprisin combinations. Woke up a couple of times to find some wounded pride on the triggah end of a shotgun. 'Nothin happened' was about all you could think to say, oah if the dude was pahsistent, 'I was too drunk to get it up, sohry' – somethin about belittlin youhself befah an enraged boyfriend oah fathah oah husband could usually get you off the hook – but then if you did get caught in the act, youh only recouhse was to hide behind huh and pray he wouldn't shoot through his steady piece just to prove how manly he was. Had to scramble out the dooh into a snowstohm buck naked once to save myself from extinction – anyway we wah discussin religion..."

"Uh-..."

You'll learn chum, never ask Chipper an open-ended question. Joker will fill you in on every dirty detail.

"...religion was like juniah high fah me, I passed through but none of it stuck. Then my mama was nevah much of a chuhch goah neithah, but when I came of age, she figuhed I needed to be reined in somehow – well I was a hell raisah of sohts. Not that I was opposed to religion oah nothin, I was a cuhrious kid, except gettin up eahly was a pain. Had this Sunday School teachah, Miss Heavins, she was the preachah's spinstah sistah. Woman had these huge teats which would staht in heavin whenevah she got huhself wohked up about THE LOHD JESUS! She would shout out, and huh teats would heave up and down. HE WILL SAVE YOU! Though from what oah fah what, I nevah got cleah. Sex. She would talk a lot about sex and encouhrage us kids to get baptized in this great big glass fish tank they had attached to the chuhch. 'Couhse befah people could dive into the tank and be saved, they'd have to kneel down in front of the congregation and confess theih sins, which was the most intahrestin paht of the sehvice, fah a kid. Anyway, Miss Heavin's wanted me to get baptized in the wohst way. She'd take me aside, she'd look me in the eye and say, 'Chippuh, you'h old fah youh yeahs. I know you've got some mighty sins to confess – don't you?' I'd stuttah and I'd think, 'spose I do but I ain't about to broadcast them to the whole chuhch. She told me I was bein recalcitrant – remembah the wohd – that my day'd soon come. So this one sweaty Sunday aftahnoon, seems evahrybody was gettin doused and I didn't think folks would evah run out of sins to confess – how they swohe at home oah lost theih tempahs, how they got drunk and gambled away theih paycheck oah went out cahrousin – though they nevah got too particulah about what they did when they went out cahrousin. Most of us kids knew who was doin who anyway, small town, and we knew nobody was doin Miss Heavins which seemed like such a waste of good teat – when who should stand up but Miss Heavins huhself. Whole congregation hushed up quick, evahrybody, even the babies, nobody wanted to miss a wohd of this woman's sinnin. 'FAHGIVE ME LOHD!' She yells real loud right theah in front of huh ministah brothah, man's eyes bulgin – 'BECAUSE I HAVE SINNED MIGHTILY,. AND RIGHT IN YOUH FACE!' Like I say, this woman had some powahful lungs and a big flowahed dress on, teats a'heavin like all hell. 'I HAVE TRIED TO SUHPRESS IT LOHD! BUT I AM A POOH WEAK CREATUHE LIKE EVAHRYBODY ELSE IN THIS WOHLD, AND I REPENT THE LUST I HAVE FELT IN MY HEAHT… TOWAHD LITTLE CHIPPUH!'"

-hmm, I've never heard this story before.

"Me? I damn neah slipped off the bench! I was only fouhteen and growin up fast as I could, but I hahdly knew what lust was, though I cahtainly had some late night inklin's."

"What happened?"

"Predictable. Evahrybody tuhned around to stahe. My mothah's jaw dropped open, you know how folks do when they go into shock, and I was squihmin in my seat. I must be to blame, right? Victim's ahways provokin folks, and I must've provoked Miss Heavins wicked bad because she was down on huh knees and cryin to the Lohd fah mehcy when without wahnin she ups and takes a dive fah the tank – *SUPLASH!* – flowahed dress and all, sunk straight to the bottom then came bobbin up spoutin about how clean she felt and that if little Chippuh was evah to have a chance at salvation they had bettah douse him fast – man, did I teah out of theah. Ran. Nevah glanced back."

"Were there repercussions?"

"Well I began wohryin that theah must be somethin wrong with me, young as I was I had the damndest women feelin these powahful uhges. And my mothah, when she got home, she was real upset."

"How so?"

Betsy's all ears — kid stories, they're the best — other kids'stories though, never your own.

"She said she just couldn't believe nobody could get chased out of a chuhch fah just bein lusted aftah. I must've been up to somethin no good as usual. But like I say, nobody's got no use fah a victim, I mean even my own mothah didn't believe me — fact she was 'bout ready to hand me ovah to the preachah, bound hand and foot. He said he'd dunk me by the heels 'til I tuhned blue if I didn't confess."

"What did you do?"

"Ran away, fihst time in my life. Took Betsy heah's great great grandmothah with me, Lady Kate, hid out in a Indian cave we had discovahed up neah the Canadian bohdah…"

Know the cave, never knew the history.

"…when I finally did come back, hungry as a tad goat, my grandpappy took me aside, out back of the woodshed and he said, 'Son, you'h a Stuhbee through and through, and I can tell that dick of youhs is goin to get you into nothin but trouble, you and ouh whole family too.' I stuttahed back, 'I 'spect it will pappy.' I had to answah the truth. So he says, 'But don't evah let a little trouble get in the way of youh havin fun' — and those ah the wohds I still live by today. Figuah if the Great Lohd had wanted man to abstain oah save himself fah anothah lifetime, he would nevah have given him a peckah, but since he did, I say let God wohry about savin people because that's the way he chooses to run his business, and I'll wohry about the trouble my peckah causes me because that's my business — anyway that's what I leahned young about sin and ohganized religion — you leahn anythin much diffahrent in youh Sunday School?"

Ma Ma LOON! Ma Ma LOON!

Breeze is beating his bongos about the porch, bragging *bossa nova*!

Ma Ma loo-oo-oo-OON!

Molly ignores him, clasps her robe up under her chin. She has five cards left and is anxious to play them, for she is certainly assured the title role of Earth Mother in what's to become a stellar performance — *la la la / la la la* — she practices trills in a husky contralto.

That's right sister, hit it! Breeze himself plays saxaphone.

But Molly's concerned about her public image. While her lusty side has been generously fulfilled, she seeks reassurance that history shall not underrate her as some untoward cosmic slut — "Luna, please! I'm concerned about my public image, how will I be remembered?"

Maybe so, but the next card is The Hermit. "Him!" Dressed in hooded monk's robes and hoisting a lantern, he carries along a hollow wood bassoon. Man's thin and myopic, eyes to the ground as he studies roots and fungus in order to concoct various remedies — perhaps a love potion? No, he's far too ethereal for that, studies science not sin, some gloomy traveler peddling philosophy and doom. What would he know of the profundity of the cosmos, its raw energy and fecundity? Unlike Molly who is gushing bountifully beautifully!

Don't much want t'wither under his scrutiny, now do you?

She views the ascetic Hermit allied with the prudish and quickly shoves him aside, turns the next card — "Now we're getting somewhere!" — it's The Chariot thundering through the skies, billows of stardust in its wake, a he-man Centurion in leather straps driving the rig, big, brawny, bald, a drummer, huge hands harnassing a great winged pterodactyl with two heads, one with a hawk beak, the other with serpent fangs, claws for feet and a bifurcated tail — manly or beastial, Molly knows not which — is he rushing to rescue her, or kidnap and drag her back to his lair!

Hot damn, you've got one fevered imagination!

Oh what do you know? No man can appreciate the delicacy of the woman's situation. She has but one stake in life, her reputation, and if she gambles it away too freely, well, let the chips fall where they may. On the other hand, if she's shrewd, places her bets just right, she can have her man and eat him too. It's a delicate dilemma she faces: Play loose, and she'll never be a wife. Play tight, he won't come home at night.

Then take a bite a'both, little sister.

No no, you don't understand. Lovers, they come and go, but husbands, they never leave! The thought of which distresses Molly, like the great pterodactyl she is being torn in twain, there's the new, the tender youth so terribly tasty, then the familiar lover who's no more appetizing than a slice of cold meatloaf off the back shelf of the refrigerator.

Hungry? Here, chew on this — only snack you're goin t'get delivered this late at night!

"What do you know about love, you lech!" Molly is incensed. "I've about had enough of your sick remarks!" And she tears after the Breeze with a broom she's got handy, swats, sweeps him right off her porch.

Breeze dodges around the corner of the house.

"I'll play these cards any way I want — hear me!" She announces to the moon, and to a family of skunks scavenging below through the trash.

"Could suhe go fah a frosty cool one about now — Betsy, reach in the coolah theah and snag a couple of homebrews fah me and the strangah."

-rr right, right. Betsy noses around for a treasure buried deep in the ice — *scrap scrap* — no twist off cap, and you can bet I'm not going to crack one of my teeth over it. You do that trick, humans don't use their bone crushers for much else anymore.

"Thank you gihl, appreciate it." CRUNCH! — *thpip... thpip...*

That's it, spit out the glass.

"*Hmm* tasty. Thank you."

CRUNCH! — *thpip* again.

Phenomenal.

"Think nothin of it. Enjoyin the company on a night like this — say, wahn't we supposed to be lettin you off somewheah along the way?"

"Wouldn't miss this ride for anything Chipper, not often I get the opportunity to talk with a rock 'n' roll legend."

"Man cruisin towahd his destiny — me and my babydoll heah." He gives Betsy a much needed pet. "You up fah a round of youh favohrite song gihl? Strangah you can join in — ready? A one, two, three and fouh…"

> Go sow, sow, sow youh oats, down the valleys green,
> *rr-ow r-ow r-ow rrr-roroats, grr-grown ro-riitiis grr-rreem*

"Strangah!"

> Go sow, sow, sow your oats, down the valleys green,
> Wahrily, wahrily, wahrily, life's nothin like a dream!
> *rr-rare-ri rare-ri rare-ri, rife-ruff ruff ru- ream!*
> Go sow, sow, sow youh oats, down the valleys green,
> Warily, warily, warily, life's nothin like a dream!
> *rr-ow r-ow r-ow rrr-roroats, grr-grown ro-riitiis grr-rreem*
> Wahrily, wahrily, wahrily, life's nothin like a dream!
> Go sow, sow, sow your oats, down the valleys green,
> *rr-rare-ri rare-ri rare-ri, rife-ruff ruff ru- ream!*
> Wahrily, wahrily, wahrily, life's nothin like a dream!

"One mah time…"

> Go sow, sow, sow youh oats, down the valleys green,
> *rr-ow r-ow r-ow rrr-rowt, grr-ri grown grr-rreem*
> Go sow, sow, sow your oats, down the valleys green,
> Wahrily, wahrily, wahrily, life's nothin like a…

REE-O-REE-O RIP! RIP! RIP! / REE-O-REE-O RIP! RIP! RIP!
-roh oh!.

"Damn, stash that open beeh undah the seat!"

Chipper eases his ersatz Subaru over into the breakdown lane.

Flashing blue lights, and a bruiser from the Vermont State Patrol walking towards them. It's the first glimpse any officer of the law outside Maine has had of Chipper's customized roadster — and recall Edna Lightcomb's antique license plates, the lack of tail lights, the smashed glass rear slider window, things not meant to endear a driver to a trooper.

"What's this thing?" State comes directly to the point.

Chipper sticks his dazed head out the window, nods a greeting.

"You wouldn't happen to have a registration and a license, would you?" Big man, big voice.

Chipper hands him Edna Lightcomb's registration and her driver's license, which has not only expired back before they put pictures on such things, but states clearly that her date of birth is June 11, 1917, also that she's four feet two, dark eyes and dark hair."

"This you in a former life, or what?"

"No, cahtainly not, that's my pooh deceased auntie, and I'm tryin despahrately to get huh cah down to New Yawk in time fah the funahral — suhprised the damn thing still runs, had a wicked lot of trouble stahtin it."

"You wouldn't happen to have insurance on this junker, would you?"

"Don't know if she kept it up oah not, she got pretty fahgetful neah the end, don't you know."

"You think you could walk a straight line for me down the middle of the road here?"

"Damn, not suhe if I can even stand up, grief's just eatin on me somethin fiehce."

"Grief?"

"The wohst. See Auntie Edna was the last in a long li—…"

"What's in that plastic bag there on the seat next to you?"

"This? No mah than a couple ounces, but you'h welcome to it."

"Bale in the back? That why you're traveling county roads in the middle of the night?" Trooper points his flashlight on the tool box built across the bed, lifts the lid. "What the flying fuck have you got in here?"

It's Betsy huddled inside, four legs sticking up and nary a twitch.

"That's- that's Auntie Edna, that's who that is. Rigah mahtis has twisted huh up tehrible, don't think anybody'll evah get huh stretched out flat."

"You are transporting a dead body in this truck!" Lid slams back.

"Is theah some law against that in Vahmont? We do it all the time up in Nohthun Maine."

"We're a bit more civilized down this way — now I want you to step out of the vehicle, hands clasped on top of your head… slowly, step outside where I can see you while I examine the contents of that tool box."

"Yes sih, anythin you say sih."

And where did the strange hitchhiker disappear to?

Betsy is past master at playing dead, retracted, contorted, and when the trooper sticks his head under the lid for a closer inspection, it's her ass end he gets and a face full of compressed dog fart which causes him to jolt back — KABAM! — bangs his head on the lid, which is no late model molded plastic, but old fashioned crimped metal instead — man staggers back — and whether it's the gas attack, the shriveled-up corpse turned black furry moldy, or the bonk on the beanie — he swoons, passes out on the asphalt.

"Look what you've done Betsy, scahed the pooh fellah half to death!"

Wasn't that the plan?

Apparently not. Chipper is immediately transformed into roadside medic, taking the fallen Marine's pulse, listening for a heartbeat.

-RR RUN! RUN!

"Can't go and leave a man huhtin gihl, wouldn't be right, pahticulaly a fella whose done us no hahm."

Not yet, -yep -yep!

"Help me get him back on his feet."

Betsy reluctantly plays nurse, applies moist warm compresses about the forehead and mouth, with her ever handy tongue — and something about a dog's tongue in a human mouth that brings back the near dead instantly.

"Wha-wha-wha-..."

"Bettah not to talk when you've sustained an injuhry to the head, and don't try gettin up, not quite yet."

"Ar-are... you-..."

"Can you move youh fingahs? Good. Now signal to me by a wave of the hand: Is youh vision foggy? Yes? Do you heah a ringin? Yes? How about youh toes, ah they tinglin?"

-rr roes?

"Happens. You've cleahly nevah been knocked out cold."

-rrue

"I -mu, I'm-mu-mu..."

"See Betsy, sluhred speech. You've seen that symptom befah."

"...g-go-gong..."

"No, you'h not, you'll pull through, believe me, I've taken so many blows to the head I've lost count."

"...ta-ta half have ta-ta-take yu-yu-yu-..."

"In?" Chipper prompts. "Well, maybe you will, maybe you won't, but whatevah you do, you'h goin to have to lay heah and rest up a bit fuhst."

And why is it Chipper doesn't run? Deserted road? Darkness of night? Ask Betsy, she'll tell you — it's because he's just not that kind of guy. He wishes nobody any harm, unless they've really sprung up and coming straight for him, then's when he really gets pissed and goes for a fist.

"Wh-who are you?" The trooper is still lying prone, his mouth dry, tongue glued to the roof of his mouth, but he's got to know. "I know- know you, I-I've seen your f-face some-somewhere?" His mind no doubt flipping though countless file photos, where a quite recent fax notice would do. "Y-you have a fam-famil-familiar face."

Blurred vision pal, you've been out way past the bell.

"Are you one of those ra-radical so-so-socialists…'

"Don't go blamin me fah nothin. I haven't voted fah thuhty yeahs."

"…who ch-chained themselves to the fence at Boo-boo-Booth Bay Atomic last week?"

Chipper shakes his head, no, of course not, he might be anarchist by inclination, but he has never chained anybody to anything, never would, unless of course they wanted to really get kinky.

"What are you then, a mu-musician or something worse? Is that why you've bleached your hair and wear an earring?"

"This is my natuhral colah and I ain't piehced nowheah wohse."

"Then who are you?"

"Got to level with you friend, my real name's Chippuh Stuhbee and…"

And is it near extradition time or what, transportation back to Maine in those chains previously bespoke, and for life with no hope of parole?

"…and I just need to get Betsy, my hound dog heah and me down to New Yawk and fast, seems we've got this date with destiny…"

"Chip-Chipper Stirbee! …and the Loose Nukes?"

"Same. You've heahd of us?"

"Way back, way way back when… *Little Red Rooster*?"

"Nope, that was the Stones' covah of an old Howlin Wolf tune, ouhs was *Getta Gihl*, released about the same time. Folks get the two mixed up."

"Right right." There's some saliva seeping back in the trooper's mouth. "Gotta poppa / A lot alotta."

"That's it, you remembah!"

"Could never forget that line, love-loved it when I was a kid, but I reckoned you were dead and buried or stuck away in a mental institution."

Almost. You have no idea how close.

"Nope, just hidin out in the woods, waitin fah the best time to make a comeback, which is about now — besides they've done closed all the mental institutions up Maine way and damn neah evahrywheah else I heah — legislatuhe declahed the insane cuhred, and next they'h plannin on doin the same fah the brain dead. It's some budget trick they can do fah relievin the middle class of all theih health cahe heahaches — but to my way of thinkin it's a bonafide mihracle."

"I heard about that too. Some messiah from the south is going to spread the cure across the nation."

"H'yep, then they'll fihe the police and release all the prisonahs, let them run wild, probably one been relocated to youh home town ahready."

"More than that in my town, in fact I've got a whole family of them right next door."

"Me too, least three oah fouh."

"Chipper, Chipper Stirbee." Trooper raises himself up on one arm, blinks, eyes Betsy whose sniffing his chin, pets her right where she likes it — which is dangerous, subverts Iron Rule No. 1 of the *Universal Trooper Code:* Thou Shalt Not Fraternize With Thine Public Enemy. But the man's not certain what he should do, not when the enemy's a celebrity. Arrest him and make headlines, let him go and get his autograph.

"It's nothing personal Chipper, but I think you got screwed back there in Cincinnati Summer of 69." And that's the State of Vermont's final comment on the matter.

Chipper shakes his head h'yep, he can agree with that. He gives the trooper a hand. Man struggles up, dusts himself off.

"Tell you what I can do."

"H'yep?"

"I can escort you to the New York border, but after that you're on your own." Trooper hands Chipper back Edna Lightcomb's registration and license. "You might need these." And naturally asks him for his autograph.

Chipper obliges by signing the packet cover off his rolling papers — they both nod, star celebrity and state trooper, the way folks do when they want to get out of each other's path as rapidly as possible, trooper back to a coffee mug and nursing a headache in an all night diner, Chipper forward to meet this destiny.

Molly breathes deeply in an attempt to regain her composure. She has but two cards remaining, two cards that will seal her fate, maybe forever. She's been humbled however. She raises her face toward Luna, bathes in the glow, then bows eyes down in supplication. She even crosses herself for the Most Holy Trinity, because if one religion won't work, always try another, three or more might do the trick or dangle a chicken head on a stick — whatever it takes. *Thump!* Next card is the High Priest!

Did she expect less?

Seated on a throne, stern gaze, a triple crowned mitre upon his head, he holds a scepter, for he rules the world of the Unknown. One foot rests firmly upon a closed book while his other crushes the serpent of ancient superstitions. Arrayed behind him a mighty cathedral pipe organ and legions of winged creatures awaiting his command. He represents a spiritual force, one to be reckoned with.

Must. Breeze has disappeared.

Leaves Molly stumped on the significance of this one — "High Priest must be in league with The Hermit and that nun Temperance, celibate, not an ounce of fun in any of them… maybe music, there's an organ and doesn't every man have his secret weakness?"

But that's the trouble with the Tarot, it needs interpretation and if the High Priest is enigmatic to Molly, wait until she flips the final card of the Pentangle – The Tower – "Oh my God!" The scene is gothic, a fortress on a cliff with a tall tower overlooking the ocean, but a crack in the sky and lightening strikes the turret, down tumble two discernible figures, The Fool and The Magician, and behind them an entire pantheon while the fortress itself is reduced to rubble. It is cosmic chaos, reason in ruin along with passion – the result of pride, of presumption, for who is man that he seeks to build such a tower, reach for the heavens?

Molly is beside herself, the forces of repression are arrayed against the powers of creation in roughly equal number, and what of closure – how can she have scaled the heights and fallen to the depths in the spate of one evening's reading?

Which is when Breeze blows back in and brushes what's left off the table. *Never again tempt Fate with the blood red Pentangle.*

"You bastard! One more turn and I could have found my salvation!"

It's over sister, that was the 'leventh an last, you've played your hand and lost – big time!

"No. No no no! This is unacceptable!" Molly's down on her knees, she bleats, she begs, she crawls from card to card – "Where am I in all this mess?"– frantically searching for a happier ending.

Your fortune's like everybody else's, nothin much clear and what you do uncover is disappointin!

"Here I am." Molly lifts a card, raises it to the moon – it is the likeness of Empress Wisdom, the female force who can subdue even the excesses of the moon – for this is She who personifies domestic order and tranquility, She who is reasonable, She who is seated at the spinet, playing chords of well-tempered harmony.

That's you a'right, in your gauzy early mornin daydreams.

Indeed. The face Molly actually meets is that of the mature woman, old age her future, a hag staring back through a looking glass. Molly shudders. For the late fifties are the worst on a woman, watching the hair gray year by year, then the sixties and a woman's chance of remarriage expired, what's hanging in the closet is what she has to wear, seventies she might as well order in, and by eighty she will be confined to a walker. Ninety she has shriveled to a housecoat, no appetite once so ever, oh some jello, some lightly buttered toast with tepid tea to wash down the pills.

So sadly Molly must acknowledge that youth has passed and with it dashed hopes of a first love regained, no trump left to play. She lifts her head and stares into the vast indifferent distance and at a cold hearted Breeze who in a tantrum scatters the Tarot to the four winds, then deserts her to the darkness, such that even Molly, the temptress of the tempest, crumples on the floor, forced to contemplate the futility of these silly things and more.

"Guess it's you and me Betsy, like usual, two creatuhes drawn by the same stahs, pahtakin in the same free spihrit." Chipper reaches over and pulls her closer. Natural combination these two, she snaps at mosquitoes for him and he pulls ticks off her fur, they share the same mangy mattress, same dinner dishes, he gets first licks, she gets seconds. "Wondah whatevah happened to the hitchhikin strangah?"

Took off on a moon lit cross-country run.

"Must have some soht of wahrant aftah him too."

Either that or he can't take the company of an aging dope-smoking rockstar whose primary pasttime is defiling our nation's youth.

"Just don't know fah suhe what it is about me that upsets folks so."

-*roh no?*

"Must be what I've got to say. But whatevah, man's got to keep pedal to the flooh and nevah stop haulin along his own peculiah road."

Welcome to New York looms large on a sign along the roadside, as Vermont hands them off with a let her RIP-O-RIP and a flash on his high beams. Chipper waves, pulls behind the sign to take a whizz, Betsy squatting beside him. Traffic is picking up, tractor-trailers trying to beat the early morning rush into the city. "Hope we can make it befah dawn. Don't need no mah troopahs snoopin round the Subahru."

-*hmmp* Betsy must surely agree, but something about these eighteen wheelers zipping by them at ninety or better unnerves her.

"Don't know, this mixtuhe of homegrown, homebrew and mooseshit mushrooms suddenly's gettin to me. Guess I just don't have the resistance I used to, though if you'h comin down, best thing is to fihe up anothah bowl." Which he does once he's in the driver's seat, stuffs his pipe with a pinch off the end of his last full bud, torches it — *fwoof fwoof fwooooooof... ahhhhh!* Slaps him right back. "Whoa-hoh! Heah we go! Prepahe fah blast off!" He gooses it and careens out into the middle of the high rollers — WONK WONK — as a two trailer rig swerves quick into the left lane to avoid flattening the Subaru out altogether. "Successful launch into ouh comeback careeah!"

Dut dutta / doop ta dooda do — Chipper's excited, bouncing around...

Got that little ditty on the brain, do you?

...*bam bam bam bam* — pounding the sides of the seat — *whippity whap*

/ whap whap whap — up against the dash.

-hmm? Telltale signs of the initial manic phase of a full blown mushroom relapse.

"Flash of lights! Wohld in a spin! Meteoh showah blastin along side us on the highway — *whap whap whap whap!*"

Indeed they are, eighteen-wheelers passing both sides, left lane and right, with another bumper to bumper behind, and noise?

WONK! WONK! WONK! WONK!

Chipper's all over the road and trying to keep up. "Got to keep this pod heah from buhnin up as we draw in closah to the eahth's atmospheah!" Which is all fine until he begins to experience a bout of weightlessness, mild euphoria in the head that fans out across lungs and limbs as he goes floating up and around the cab — *Dut dutta / doop ta dooda do* — with the speedometer locked in on ninety.

The manic gives way to the panic. Means that Betsy must resort to emergency measures, first anchoring Chipper into the rider's seat — "Fasten youh belts fah set-down!" — while she settles in front of the controls. OK let me see, driving can't be all that difficult, sixteen-year-olds and senile old men can do it, though not very well. Hands would be helpful, but my paws are better coordinated than most people's mitts, and I notice nobody uses their teeth for anything — *ah,* steering while shifting — though I can barely reach the pedals.

"*Whoa-ho!* Is this pissah, oah what!"

Pisser it is, as Chipper dozes and Betsy sets the blinker off, manages to ease to a stop in the breakdown lane.

"Ah we theah?" Chipper bolts up. "Have we made it all the way home from the othah side of the moon?"

Not really, no, just trying to get a feel for the stick shift — let's see…

He lapses back into his snooze.

…first is up, second down, third, fourth… is there a fifth? Pity the war-torn Subaru isn't automatic with just one gear, one pedal, one stomp down and go, but despite a par five handicap Betsy's off, chug-sputtering forward in whatever gear is handy because the clutch is a hard whore to handle even for the steady customer — *roh oh,* she almost goes sliding off the seat after the pedals, but once she's firmly in gear she can keep up a steady race, though why's all that black crap spouting out the tailpipe? Maybe fifty in first isn't the best selection. That means another shift and so she stretches — *clank krrr-rank!* — but she makes it, though second doesn't stanch the gook in the back, so *ho* it's another try for thir-… hell no, scrap that and go straight for fourth, fifth, how ever many gears this carriage's got — but no, don't jam it into reverse, not going this fast because *clank crank crunch* — third will have to do. Simply go slower on the miles per hour, though what's that dial doing up in the red zone? Driving much more complicated than she ever imagined except she's rolling along, so what's to worry with a little steam escaping off the hood when she's streaming along quite nicely?

WONK! WONK! WONK! WONK! WONK! WONK!

Betsy hoists an elbow out her window, signalling a universally misunderstood up and down motion.

WONK! WONK! Trucker returns the gesture.

When she accidentally triggers cruise control. Instantly makes her job easier. She can settle back and WONK! WONK! along with the best of them.

In time, Betsy comes upon a sight she has never seen before — bright city lights in the distance, the unearthly glow, and up front the George Washington Bridge spanning the entrance to this, one of the seven wonders of the modern world, the Manhattan skyline.

"Behold the City of God!" Chipper mutters in his sleep.

Mammon, Betsy moans.

Depends which neighborhood you roam in, and — REE-O-REE-O RIP! RIP! RIP! // REE-O-REE-O RIP! RIP! RIP! — another patrol cruiser rides right up behind her — RIP! RIP! RIP! — she edges over toward the breakdown lane — REE-O-REE-O... Remembrances of near misses past puts Betsy into a panic! Cars everywhere surrounding her, more cars than she's ever seen, but this close to the goal, she's not going to be taken dead or alive either — merge left, some sign says, but Betsy's not about to and SLAM! BAM! — well then get out of my way ma'am! If you can't stand a dent, then go hide inside your garage!

ZROOOM ZROOOM — a couple of motorcycles whip by her. Yeah, and what's holding us up ahead there anyway? REE-O-REE-O... Pipe down, will you. I'm doing the best I can to get out of this jam. But traffic has slowed to a crawl on the approach to the bridge, and some semi's throwing a tissy fit to her right — WONK! WONK! — lots of compressed air, tires squeaking, and mouth making contortions. Betsy tries her best to grin and wave back, but he's motioning at her — WONK! WONK! — move over.

-roh sorry. She's been meandering over into his lane, but as she corrects herself she cuts somebody off to the left — scrrrrrrrrrew WRENCH! A pushy Mercedes bumps into a delivery van — anh, Jersey drivers!

REE-O-REE-O RIP! RIP! RIP! Same trooper's showing his teeth in her rearview and gesticulating. She gesticulates back. Hold your horses, and what's with these toll booths? Like I have a quarter in my pocket. Give me a break, I've got no pockets to begin with, so pay you next time I'm in the vicinity. She gives the Subaru some gas and slams through.

Will you look up at the cables, the towers, it's the tallest suspension bridge she's ever seen and with such a wide river running fast underneath, a clear view of the city lights down stream — we're getting somewhere now

— though where exactly? It's hard to enjoy the sights and simultaneously read the road signs overhead because Betsy has to go word for word with her paw, pronounce each syllable out loud: Hen-ry. Hud-son. Pkwy. Who's he and what's a pkwy? 186th and Broad-way. Must be the place every aspiring actress wants to land — and Next. Exit. The Bronx. Which doesn't sound too terribly promising.

Of course, while she's parked on the roadway reading, a two, a four, a six or eight SKID- SCRAPE- SCRAP- SCRUNCH- piles up behind her! But hey, they shouldn't have been following that close to a pooch to begin with.

REE-O! REE-O! Him again! REE-LY! RIP-SHIT! When behold, the traffic in front conveniently separates, opens up an express lane where before there was none — REE-O-REE-O — it's been fun playing bumper cars friends, but I've got to get down to business. Betsy elbows her blinker and exits the off-ramp, curving much, much too fast, gaining an uncertain momentum as she whips around — *roh-oh!* — she spins the wheel while attempting to brake, but damn she slips off the seat again! With barely enough time to scramble up off the floor, she's face-to-face with a retaining wall — *wrulp!* — jerk of the wheel and the Subaru goes careening onto 186th Street, except what's that dead ahead, a red light?

REE-O-REE-O-RIP! -CLIP! -FLIP! Port Authority Patrol can't take curves as easily as Betsy, collides sideways into the concrete barrier. Tough luck but he was outside his jurisdiction to begin with, and that's not Betsy's concern, not as she jams but misses the brakes and runs the red light — SCREEE-SCREEE — bursts onto Broadway and bounces BUMP! off a bus — but does he even notice? — as she skims along the opposite side of the street, sideswiping a long line of taxis before bashing into a fire hydrant — WHOMP! POP! SPIGOT'S OFF! — with kids instantly dancing in the water.

-*rah* well, at least we've landed safely sort of, though a tumble around the cab fails to wake Chipper — *slumpslumpslumbersunk*… Hence Betsy has to hop out and assess the damage herself. Monster Tires point in different directions, front end's maligned, side panel's a sight. It's what a smart-ass insurance adjuster would call a total. Though Betsy has seen Chipper resurrect worse.

REE-O-REE-O RIP! RIP! RIP!
Them again.
REE-O-REE-O RIP! RIP! RIP!
More than one.
REE-O-REE-O RIP! RIP! RIP!

They're converging from all sides. Quick! She pulls Chipper out of the wreckage by his collar, drags him through the water spout, deposits him curbside. There's just enough time to retrieve his gig bag when the first NYPD squad car arrives. Betsy settles in to watch for her favorite character, the cute red haired guy who's always so sensitive to women's issues, but this must be the off-camera eleven-to-seven shift because they're gruff, talk in grunts. "Who was driving this heap? Some country yokel?"

I'm not sure I appreciate your attitude pal.

"Any of you good citizens witness the incident?" Bus driver was off-duty and is long gone. Cabbies are gypsies and want no problemos, and the kids who shouldn't even be allowed out this late, that's at five in the morning, they answer no — saw it all but witnessed nothing — and the bum in the gutter with the dog's too blotto to talk. One cop even pats Betsy on the noggin. "You deserve better than hanging on the street with this deadbeat."

Maybe, though you guys aren't all that cuddly either.

Scene ends as the NYDP call in a wrecker.

C'mon Chipper, you've got to wake *up! up! up! up!*

"Wha- what's happenin? Wheah ah we?"

-*Roo-Roo-Rork!*

Then's when he notices the wrecker hauling off the remains of his customized Subaru.

"Betsy! What the fuck did you do to the truck?"

Me? I-... she doesn't have to explain anything!

Meanwhile Chipper's up, he's about to rush over and complain when Betsy trips him, sends him sprawling on the sidewalk, and the cops laugh as the last drive off.

"What did you go and do that fah — BAD DOG!"

Ba-baa-bad dog! Betsy is stunned. Her tail goes silent. Bad dog? She hasn't been called that in ages, not since she was a frisky pup and didn't know any better about where she had to tinkle and do number two. Besides, this is Betsy, loyal to her master, Betsy, Chipper's closest hanging buddy, Betsy, his sole companion through the ages, Betsy, who's never harmed anybody ever, Betsy, slumping to the pavement, Betsy, lowering her chin, Betsy, eyes closed, Betsy, offended.

"Sohry gihl, I didn't mean t-..."

She turns her head away.

"Just I don't know how I'm 'sposed to get through tomohrow without any reefah."

I don't know either, but you had better start rehearsing your withdrawls now chum, because the sun's coming up — take a look. Those stars of yours are blinking out one by one.

NEW YORK

Man's down on his luck / Out scroungin a buck /
And that's no joke…

"'Scuse me ma'am — can you spahe some change fah the subway?"
Woman stalks right on by.

"'Scuse me, 'scuse me sih, ma'am," Chipper passes a paper cup under a his and her pair of noses, "need some change fah the subway."

Betsy takes in the flow. A few stop, flip Chipper a nickle or a dime, though most pass by without even glancing.

"Costs two bucks fah the train nowadays gihl. I remembah when it was a quahtah — let's see, one seventy one, seventy two, three, fouh, five… maybe we can pass you off as a seein eye dog, that way I can get a cup of coffee and we can both ride fah free." Which is when an elderly lady with a walker tosses in that last quarter. "Two bucks babydoll, let's book."

You've got nothin to lose / Long as you sleep in youh shoes
On a Union Squahe bench…

He walks her to this fenced off hole in the sidewalk, sign says IRT, a flight of stairs reaches down into the dark. Betsy balks.

"We'll head out to Brooklyn and bunk with Will Cook fah a few days."

Stairs lead into this vast underground cavern, lined with green and yellow tiles like a bath house, and the stench — *whoff?* — *s*tale urine?

SCREEE-SCREEE- SCREEECH! SCREEEEEEEECH!

Screams from levels below! Ear chiseling. Betsy refuses to budge.

"Damn gihl, theah's no othah way we can get theah."

Where are we anyway, in the city sewer?

Leaks, streaks of brakish brown drips from the ceiling, drab grey concrete on a floor bespattered with dried chewing gum pellets.

SCREE-REE-REE-REACH!

People running all around them, a few lucky ones escaping up the stairs, but the rest, old, young, school children in neatly pressed uniforms rushing frantically to whatever doom awaits them deeper down.

SCREECH! SCREECH! SCREECH!

"No way we can walk, and we haven't got the cash to spring fah a taxi."

A small girl stops to pet Betsy — *Perrito! Perrito!* — she proffers her hand. Betsy licks at it, peers deeply into the child's eyes, poor thing, what have you done to deserve this?

FREEEK! FREEEK!

"¡Avanza! No toques ese perro!" A mother claps her hands. "Core que vas a llegar tarde pa' la escuela!" Child scampers after her schoolmates.

Betsy stares up at Chipper, wanly.

"It's just a train, nothin wohse, runs through tunnels undahground."

SCREEEEEEEEEEEEEEEEEEEEEEEEEEEEEEEEEEEEEEEEEECH!

He tugs on her collar, has to slide her toward the token booth on her toenails. "Now let me do the talkin while you duck undah the tuhnstyle."

"You got a disability pass sir? ...SIR?"

"Beg pahdon, is somebody speakin to me?" Chipper is suddenly shuffling along, with his eyes squinted closed and waving his hands back and forth in front of him.

"I asked to see your pass."

"H'yep, it's pinned heah on my shiht."

"I don't see anything pinned on your shirt."

"No? Must've fahgotten it at home."

"Then you have to pay."

"Last two bucks I've got on me."

"Complain to your case worker. I don't make the rules."

"But you enfohce them?"

"That's right. Two dollars. And what's that with you, a seeing-eye dog?"

"You bet, Betsy's got me out of mah scrapes than you'd evah imagine."

"And you're legally blind, right?"

"You can definitely say I'm not seein things too cleahly this mohnin."

"Rule says only dogs allowed on a train are seeing-eye."

"Well, you suhe don't want me trippin in front of some train, do you, konkin out on the thihd rail?"

Woman inside this glass cage looks Chipper up and down, then starts in on Betsy. Betsy nudges Chipper forward. Whatever it is you've got to do chum, you had better do it now.

"Two dollahs?"

"Two dollars or you can audition this trick dog act for the cross-Bronx bus driver upstairs."

"Heah you go."
SKREEEE-YEE-YEE...
"New Yohkahs, they'h one tough breed gihl."
Betsy needs no convincing.

If you can fake it heah, you can fake it anywheah…

...YEE-YEE-YEEEEEEEEEEEEEEEEEEEEEEEEEEEEEECH!
"That's ouh train, Numbah 2 Express. Huhry up, and watch out fah the slidin dooh." Which are banging open and shut, open and shut — some blue uniform conductor shouting. "Clear the doors! Clear the doors!"
"Go to gihl, jump!"
Jump?
"Jump!" And just in time because — SCREE-SCREE-SCREE-CHHHHHH — train's already pulling out of the station.
"Damn! That was a close call."
Car is packed. People hanging on to these ceiling straps with one hand, reading the paper with the other. More people sit in a row along the sides, and all of them sway as the train picks up speed into a curve. Betsy, she has nothing to hold on to, she slips one way, another, bumping up against this leg and that until Chipper clasps her by the collar and makes his way in deeper. "'Scuse us folks, sohry… sohry… 'scuse us."
"Ezcuse yo is right, an sor'y? Pitiful's mo like it."
Chipper nods. "We've traveled a long way to get heah my man."
"Bet yo has, an wha's this animal yo gots with yo? They don' us'u'ly allow no dogs t'ride on this hea subway."
"Betsy? She thinks she's human."
"Maybe she do, but no moto'man's goin t'agree with that assessment, not with fangs like she's spo'tin."
Don't like fangs? Then how about one of my handy howdy-do smiles — ROWLLL! — incisors, bone-crushers and then some!
"Hold on now! Don' need t'cop no at'itude at me doggy-do, not this ea'ly in the mo'nin. I's only mentionin the possibility a'some unfo'tunate misunda'standin — if yo wants t'ride, tha's a'right by me."
You're the one getting jumpy pal, and what is it? Chipper flashes a grin and everyone takes to him, I show my pearlies and folks go rabid?
"Betsy heah's as gentle as a lamb, though I appreciate the advice."
"Tha' so? Well yo can thank me with a dolla contribution."
"A dollah? I was about to ask if you could spahe one youhself."
"No bro, yo gots it wrong, see I's the subway hustla an yo is-… 'spect yo is some down-on-his-luck musician judgin from that beat-up guita case yo is luggin."
"You know, theah's somethin about you that I-…"

"Now don' go takin no offense, I's jus' makin conva'sation."
Something about him I don't care much for either.
"…h'yep, undah that grey beahd and haih theah, I recognize someone I used to know named Salaam, Salaam Kareen-Kaboo-…"

-KREEE-KREEE-KAREEK!

"Who's askin?"
"Whoa! Take a closah look old man!"
"No. No way. I don' believe in no ghosts!" Man's aghast. "Chippa, Chippa Stu'bee — that jive-ass honky from nowhea somewhea up no'th?"
"In the flesh."
"I heard yo was dead!"
"Not quite."
"Damn bro, yo is a sight fo so'ry eyes!"
"You ain't lookin too good youhself."
"Damn! Damn! Damn!" And the two of them are doing this bizarre sort of hand shake, and hugging each other, bear hugs and tears — can't barfing believe it — tears! And who is this blowhard anyway?
"Neva in a thousand yea's thought I'd run inta the likes a'yo, neva."
"Just got into the city. Intend to make a new staht."
"Hope yo gets a betta shake than yo did las' time round. A fat'ality a'the sixies ment'ality if eva thea was one."
"H'yep, times about did me in."
"Yo desa'ved betta. Yo's a livin mir'acle when it comes to showmanship — don' know 'bout musicianship."
"I'm new and improved."
"Practice don' make fo pa'fect with yo white boys, neva quites get the rhythm down. Yo can rock but yo can't roll — t'roll yo gots t'slide the finga's round smooth, like a lady's thigh, strum ha softly, make ha beg fo ma'cy."
"Cryin out in the middle of the night fah mah."
"Yo least gots the concept down bro."
"H'yep. They've been playin the old songs on the radio, and theah's talk of a stage revival."
"They's been diggin up graves stagin revivals. Broadway's nothin but."
"Wohth a try, old guys like us don't have loads of options — say, by the way, this heah's my main pooch — Betsy, shake hands with the one and the only Salaam Kareen-Kaboo-…"

-REACH-REACH

Didn't catch the last name, but any friend of Chipper certainly makes me suspicious.
"Same goes fo me doggy-do."

-REAAAAAAAAAACH!

"Yo gots t'excuse me fo a second — 125TH STREET! 125TH! CHANGE HEA

FO THE LOCO! — I a'ways helps the conducto out when I can — STEP LIVELY NOW! AN WATCH OUT FO THEM CLOSIN DOO'S!"

-SCR-RUNSCH Woman's bag is inside. She's outside. And her hand's caught in the middle. Doors reopen. She walks off in a huff.

"So what have you been doin all these yeahs Salaam?"

...SCR ...SCR ...SCR ...SCRRRSCRRRSCRRRSCRRRSCRRR

"Same scam as a'ways, assistin passenga's on an off, shoppin the stations fo all the best ba'gains..."

"Still sellin reefah, cause I'm fresh out?"

"No sa, don't do no drugs no mo, not since the kids've got so heavy inta it. Thea's this epidemic out thea bro, an nobody doin nothin t'stop it."

"Gone clean on us, have you Salaam?"

"Gone establishment. Only panhandle the very best neighbahoods nowadays, been investin my ea'nin's in the ma'ket like ev'rybody else."

Betsy stares up at this Afro-dude, grayed wooly, beard, and a big beaded bag slung over one shoulder.

"You into mutual funds?"

"Wha' yo take me fo, some amat'ua? I's gots me a private account with a broka uptown. Wheneva I gets a hot tip, I'm on the phone and placin a oa'da fo a few sha'es — best eva's been QuotLink Inc. I got in at the bottom."

"QuotLink Inc?"

"Yo ain' neva hea'd a'them? Whea yo been, hidin out in the woods?"

Well yes actually.

"They's got t'be the hottest item t'eva hit Wall Street, betta than Microscoff o ICBM any day, made millionai's out a'lots a'folks."

"You'h a millionaihe!"

"So damn close sometimes I could feel my asshole pinch up tight at tax time, but..."

"But what?"

"...le's step back inta my private club ca, don' want t'go discussin my financial situa'tion in public, if yo catches my drift?"

Drift? You mean draft, as in somebody left your mouth open on a hot summer day.

Chipper signals Betsy to follow as the three troop car-to-car through sliding steel doors, metal tred under foot, chain link to hold onto, except you don't dare hold onto anything not only because you don't have hands but also because you're jumping the couplings, a practice any New York ten-year-old learns quickly, but Betsy's from the country — she's walked logs, she's climbed cliffs, swam rapids, but — RUMBLE RUMBLE RUMBLE RUMBLE — stepping over sparking rails and rolling steel wheels, that's new.

SCREE-ree -ree-REEEEEEEEEEEEEEEEEEEEEEEEEEEE...

Especially while the train is careening through the dark.

SCREEEE- SCREEEE- SCREEEE-

Not that she's totally freaked or anything, but when they finally do reach the nearly empty caboose, she's definitely relieved — piddles on a paper someone's conveniently discarded on the floor, which obliterates the most newsworthy account of the day.

<u>Shake, Rattle And Roll</u>

Quadlink Inc Adds Askantics Label To Its Growing Presence In Recording Industry
----

Record Distribution Now Reduced From Three to Two Major Players
----

Friendly Justice Department Not Expected to Lodge Anti-Trust Complaint
----

By HOLLY DAYLY
Staff Reporter of The Wall Street Journal

NEW YORK – With what appears to be an insatiable appetite for recording company takeovers, record-breaking QuotLink Inc has agreed to pay $850 million in stock for venerable Askantics Records of Los Angeles. This adds to the list of recent acquisitions, which now includes Spangle and Peptic, the former CRONY subsidiaries, as well as Slapdisc, the specialty techno label recently purchased from the German publishing giant Gobblesmann AG for an undisclosed sum.

Askantics is one of the last independents to fall victim to a takeover, but what makes the company a desirable target is its rare archival collection of such legendary rock artists of the 60s as The Tar Hills Billy Band, the Superettes, and the late Chipper Stirbee of Loose Nukes' fame.

Sid Nebberstoff, the 88 year old Chairman who founded Askantics back in the heyday of the 60s, said there was unfortunately little he could do to halt the sale by discontented members of his family.

Butyl E. Neebgard, the usually reclusive Executive Liaison for QuadLink Inc's Entire Northern

Hemispheric Region, explained in a telephone interview from his London office yesterday that the company's acquisition of Askantics is the final piece needed to complete their long-term goal of controlling the rights to all the significant rock 'n' roll recordings from the seminal 60s era.

Industry observers when pressed to comment on why the staid corporation seeks a dominant position among the so-called 'Woodstock Generation' of musicians point to rumors on the street that the mega-communications division may be readying itself to open a 60s theme park on a 10,000 acre ranch outside Waco, Texas which they leased recently from the Right Reverend Jimmy Clappert's Church of the Ascendant Majority. One close source who asked to remain anonymous jokingly referred to the acquisition of Askantics as the closest thing Mr. Neebgard could possibly have to a love affair. High executive officers at QuotLink Inc reportedly take a vow of celibacy so that personal emotions do not interfere with corporate

Please turn to Page A6, Column 1

"Can't be too ca'ful when yo gets rich. Relatives callin on the phone, old friends lined up at yo doo, begga's followin wheaeva yo goes. Best thin t'do is dress down, keep yo hands buried in yo pockets. Put on any ai's an yo'll get bashed in yo head o se'ved with papa's by the motha a'some kid yo neva knew yo had — but between yo an me, I's semi-reti'ed, livin off IRAs an my dividends, a'couse I been supplementin my pension with what I can bum off folks down heah unda'ground."

"Lucky we ran into you."

"I limits myself t'a mo'nin ride on the Broadway Loco down t'Wall Street, cause tha's whea I picks up my hot tips. Like back in May a'87 I was ridin along, mostly mindin my own bus'ness when I ova'hea's these two suits talkin 'bout a fou fo one stock split comin up. I cock my ea's on that bit. They don' wan' nobody knowin they is discussin it, so they looks round, sees thea ain' nobody else besides this subway bum listenin in, an they goes back to theia discussion…"

Against all SEC rules and regulations.

"…they keeps sayin, buy QuotLink Inc any price, but make su'a t'get yoself a strong position, then holds on t'yo hat cause the company's ready t'raise the roof. Soon as the ca doo's open, I's phonin my broka. Bet as much as I could beg, bo'row o steal on QuotLink Inc t'win, an did it eva. Only slowed down once, late 80s when they wouldn't reelect Ronnie Reagan to a thihd term, but since then stock's been blastin higha an higha."

"So you one of those rich street people we read about, sleeps on a pahk bench nights but has half a million stashed in a savin's account?"

"Wish. Wish I'd'a held on, but cocaine got the betta a'me durin the slump. Sold off ev'ry sha I had fo peanuts t'sniff at the snow white bitch. Then woke up one moa'nin, swoa off drugs, an I stand befo yo the man I am today, clean, clean in the extreme."

And an ex-millionaire.

"Minute I got my hands on some mo cash, I jumped back inta QuotLink Inc, had to buy high, but damn if they didn' soa mo! Ain' livin on the Eas' Side jus' yet, but I's comfo'table in a condo on West 95th, gots me a regula lady friend who comes inta cook."

"Good fah you."

"Yo bets, an if yo eva needs cash t'finance this comeback careea a'yo's, give me a call. Hea's my ca'd."

"Madame Ibis Fogiére. Sees All. Tells All…"

"Tha's ha."

"…Divinations, Cuhses Guahranteed, Spells To Wake The Dead."

"All's yo gots t'do is call ha up at the numba listed on the bottom, any time night o day, an she'll be su'a t'get me the message."

"She's like youh answahin sahvice?"

"Mo than a answ'rin sa'vice, Ibis can see inta the futua."

"Not so suhe I'd want to know. Take the fun out of tryin to trick it."

"Besides, the woman's crazy bout me."

Woman's crazy, enough said.

SCREEE-*yee-yee-yeeeeeeeeeeeeeeeeeks!*

"14th Street Chippa, got to switch to the loco."

"Man, it was good seein you."

"Be seein yo too, yo an yo attack dog."

"I might take you up on youh offah fah some financial backin."

"Offa's sincea. It'd be a shrewd investment. Yo been thea befa, yo can get thea again. Fo a few bucks t'day, I can collect plenty fo tomo'row."

"Thanks fah the vote of confidence."

"Jus' don' go wastin anymo a'yo life waitin fo Lady Luck t'discova yo. Sea'ch ha out, chase afta ha — an by the way, will a couple a'hundred get yo sta'ted on the road t'recov'ry?"

"Whoa. Don't know if I can take that much!"

Take it, *rr*-will you!

"Proud man's one who stumbles when he's just sta'tin t'pull out a'the pack finally pulls out a'the pack — humble man ba'ly makes it off the line."

Take it! Take it!

"Ahright, appreciate it. Promise you I'll give this ventuhe my best shot."

"Ezpect yo is goin t'have to, ain' much fun wand'rin the streets a'this city broke. And if yo needs a secluded place t'get away, I's gots some give-away tou packages t'this unspoiled island in the Caribbean."

"Whoa! Could use some sun."

"Yo calls me, hea? When yo is ready, yo leaves Madame Ibis a message."

"I will Salaam, I will."

*-scree-heep-heep-*HEEEEEEEECH*!*

> Easy to break up / In a city
> That nevah wakes up / It's a pity
> You evah left home… / Now that you'h livin alone /
> In one of the outah bohroughs.

Grand Army Plaza. Brooklyn. Betsy b-lines it up the stairs and out onto the sidewalk. Chipper's two steps at a time, hurrying behind. "Caheful! Caheful gihl! Watch out fah traffic!"

Traffic can watch out for her! Girl has to take a mighty whizz, but where? There's no convenient grassy patches, so I suppose the sidewalk is going to have to do. Wonder where they hide the parks in this city? Whoops, guess I've got to poop-a-do too.

"Look at that Emma!"

"I can see for myself Myra. It's disgusting!"

An ancient two headed hydra is looking on, a pair of aged sisters perhaps? Or a mother and and her daughter? A monster and her whelp? Whatever, the duo stop to watch Betsy finish doing her thing – and Betsy doesn't particularly like to be gaped at while she's taking a dump, who does? Dog is vulnerable to an assault from behind about that time, some city jackel could tackle her mid-plop and she'd never know what hit her, though the sisters soon turn their attention on Chipper.

"You better have a pooper-scooper!"

"Or a flip-notch sandwich bag because there's a law in this city!"

"That's right, you can't leave that pile of steaming doggie stew in the middle of the sidewalk!" These two matched heads are screaming advice.

"You have to clean it up!"

"Put it in your pocket!"

"Take it home with you and flush it!"

Emma points at a sign which alludes to curbings and $100 fines.

Old crones, Betsy moans, ought to be a law about sticking your noses in other people's business.

"There's a leash law too!"

A leash! Put you two on a leash, although you'd probably enjoy it, guide you on and off the bus tours, make sure neither of you gets lost in between lunch and hot cocoa, which is what you should be doing this very second — vamoose, it must be time for your mid-morning nap. *Rough! Rough!*

The blue-haired twins who seem joined at the elbows barely flinch.

And Chipper is confused. True, he hasn't had his morning toke, but he is honestly attempting to comprehend the enormity of the situation.

Pay them no mind pal, and you had better hear me out on this. I didn't paddle along behind you all the way to New York City to wear a leash, and that's my last word on the subject!

A small crowd has gathered around the mound. They point and speak in multiple tongues. They shake their heads and stare in dismay, at the culprit, at the crap, but mostly at Chipper.

"Look what you've done gihl, stihrin up all this commotion," Chipper attempts to shift the blame, shakes his finger at Betsy's nose.

Don't go scolding me. Only thing I did was answer nature's call. Besides you're the one they expect to bend down and pick it up, and that ought to be a hoot to watch.

"Some people are born irresponsible Emma."

"That's true Myra, plain ignorance, no respect for the rights of others."

"They should be fined."

"Fixed."

"Forced to take courses in community etiquette."

"No, they should be imprisoned. Throw away the key."

"Yes, and the dog impounded."

"C'mon Betsy, looks like we'd bettah head befah they reinstitute the death penalty fah poopin in public."

"Hey you, what about the mess you left on the sidewalk!"

"Yeah, you can't just walk away and leave it!"

"What do you think you're doing mister!"

"You're some sort of menace!"

Betsy and Chipper rush across streets, dodge cars, take a quick turn down an alleyway, which turns out to be a dead end, so it's back again, and the crowd has grown, raised fists and shouting.

"Heah, quick, President Street — 83 — and will you take a look at this, Will Cook's definitely gone middle class on us."

Middle class? To Betsy a five story brownstone appears a mansion.

Chipper knocks on the big oak door, peers through the leaded glass window. "You see a bell oah anythin?" Chipper goes to knock again and the door swings wide open on its own. "Hello?" No response from within.

You're su-*rr* this is the right place?

"Says -*Cook* heah on the mailbox. Anybody home? Will? The little missus?" Chipper nudges the door further, ever so gently. He steps in, ever so gingerly. "Will?" Everything seems fine, except… except there is nothing inside the house — bare walls and floors. "Place looks desahted."

Betsy's nose is twitching, something is definitely amiss. There's no scents to the place, none at all, no dirt nor dust — is it habitable?

"WILL?"   WALL?
"HELLO!"   HOLLOW!

So clean, yet so empty.

"Strange, don't you think?"

-*sniff*? -*sniff*? Something tells me we had better take a look upstairs.

"Betsy, you can't just go roamin through somebody else's hou-…"

She's up the stairs in an instinct.

"Betsy?"

Her tail disappears around the second floor banister.

"BETSY!" Chipper's forced to follow. Up he tramps, footsteps echoing through the rooms. Second floor is empty too, no furniture, nothing on the walls, nothing in the closets, not even discarded hangers.

"BETSY? WHEAH'D YOU GO?" Up another floor, more bedrooms and entirely empty, except one small rag doll has been left on a window sill, a Raggety Andy doll, left alone with no Raggety Ann.

"BETSY? BETSY?" Up she goes to the top floor landing, and another door, closed, locked tight, Betsy's snorting furtively under the crack.

-*rr rook -rr rook,* she orders, and Chipper knocks, tries the knob, but it's locked from within.

ROOK! ROOK! ROOK! She is insistent. ROOKROOKROOK ROOK ROOK ROOK! Betsy is beyond impatient.

"Ahright gihl." Chipper does this rush, shoulder first — WHUMP! -y'ouch! CRUNCH! "Whoa! Will you take a look at all this stuff!"

Will has constructed a state-of-the-art recording studio in his upstair garret, keyboards and synthesizers, an old Hammond B-3, a couple of Korgs, a Kurzweil, a grand piano, guitars, drums and all the electronic gear imaginable, a two tiered master console, a computer workstation, digtal array and DAT recorder, mics, amps, mega monitors…

-*rr room,* Betsy scratches at the bottom of another door, also locked. Chipper gives that one a jolt — inside a small bathroom and draped around the bowl a body, long and lanky and not moving a nostril.

Betsy has fortunately had rescue training and a man drowned in a toilet is textbook, a fast whack of her tail across the victim's backside brings forth a wretching sound, the body contorting and rising a nose above the blue tide line in order to barf — Betsy immediately alongside to take a stomach sample — *mmm,* sour mesh, at least the man has taste, with a trace of some sort of -*thip-thip* soporific.

"Suicide attempt?"

Afraid so-*roh.*

"Will he make it?"

Hard to tell. Betsy licks poor Will's eyes, his ears and lips, smacks at her own as well — fool's tried to drown his sorrows, that's obvious.

Holp-holp-... Wait, where there's movement there's-... *hollllllllllp...* Gobs of it. And Betsy helping him out with each scrumptious drop.

"'Spose we should lay him out flat." Chipper hoists Will's head out of the toilet and drags him to the middle of the studio. "Which way does it go? Head up fah someone passed out, oah feet up? I can nevah remembah."

Feet up. You want the blood to rush back to his head, and get some blankets while you're at it, boy has the chills.

Whap! Whap! Chipper's trying to bring Will out of it.

Massage his temples pal, don't slap him around. You've been watching too many late night gangster movies. Whatever the remedy Will's breathing easier, although he's still tinted blue. Betsy's on the telephone pawing out 911, but she contacts the weather service instead... 56 the current temperature, with sunny skies lasting through the afternoon, cool tonight in the low 40s...

"Will, speak to me, tell me you'h ahright?"

"Ship-..." Will's mouth barely moves. "Ship-per?"

"H'yep, it's me Will, youh old rock 'n' roll buddy heah beside you, and just in the nick of time it looks like too."

"Ship-per."

"So what wah you plannin on doin, slippin out on us? Oah was it somethin you didn't cook long enough befah you ate it fah suppah?"

"Ship-per?"

"Should we call an ambulance, oah ah you goin to stick around long enough fah the reunion?"

"Ship-per. You-... you've-... you've come-come back?"

Betsy deposits an empty bottle of Zaptrapz™ at Chipper's feet.

"Whoa! You wah sherious!"

"Shipper, she-... she-... Shipper, she-..." Whatever it is Will is trying to say seems to stick in his throat, he starts sobbing instead — Chipper has his arms around his old buddy's shoulders. "She, she left me, Shipper... she's gone... she took-took-took my life away!" And the poor fellow heaves, heaves from his heart, tears, he heaves and he heaves, Betsy's there lapping up after him, and Will is grateful, he raises his hand, chucks her under the chin. Something about a pup and some sympathetic eyes when you're desperate, Will seems to improve in color — yes, he's quickly coming back to his normal pasty white — *hulp* HULP! *hulp* HULP! *hulp* HULP!

-*roh* no, dry heaves. They're the worst.

"*Sun, SUN/sun… -sunnnn -sunnnn…*"

Will's pulse, his breathing have returned to normal, but the guy needs some serious sleep. Chipper's been sitting on the cot next to him tuning. He's twisting pegs on his Fenderbender, his ear damn near resting on the frets. "*…sun -sum -SUM/hummm…* gettin theah."

There where? Betsy's convinced Chipper sings off-key simply to irritate her, though he swears he's a devotee of some ancient pantonic mode, that his natural voice is as old as man itself.

Can't convince me chum, you're tone deaf and too proud to admit it.

-*plung -plungg -plunk!* "Whoa, touch too much." -*plunggg!* "Pahfect!"

He'll spend entire evenings at this impossible task, matching strings to fit his homebred harmonics, somehow convinced that if he cannot leave the world a memorable tune, he can at least foist a unique new scale upon them. But if it's more discord the world needs, Betsy can offer some moans of her own — *roe -roe/ROLL -rrhone…*

"Go ahead, mock me all you want, but I'm on to somethin impohtant heah, you just can't appreciate it, that's all."

-*roh*, I appreciate it OK, don't you notice the fur along my spine standing in line?

"I could suhe use a breathah. You think we could leave Will heah by himself and hike up to the roof deck fah awhile? Might be able to see the lights of the city ovah the treetops."

-*mm*, Will's sleeping as peacefully as a newborn, so they hike up a narrow staircase to the roof.

"Whoa, take a look at the view, now that's got to be impressive!"

Take a look at the sheer five story drop, that's even more impressive.

"Don't go stickin youh nose ovah the edge. Then's when you'll fall. Bettah when you'h high up to keep youh eyes dead ahead."

And trip over the edge.

"Amazin, ain't it, how these ah the same stahs we can see right outside ouh doohstep in Maine? Makes you feel kind of cozy, don't it, that you ahways know exactly wheah you ah in all time and space."

Amazing the rooftops are deserted, not one dog baying at the moon.

"Buildin's and people, lots of people, some real charachtahs, but mostly nameless faces in the crowd. Makes New Yahk's the pahfect place to hide out, blend in."

You're a character pal, a real one, like a throwback to another era.

"The public, that's what they call us if they need to know what we think We've only got opinions, not convictions. Oah we'h the electohrate when they'h tellin us how to vote, the masses if we evah decided to revolt, but mostly we'h consumahs they can segment into mahkets by type and taste. I like strawbehry while you'h suhe to vote plain vanilla, and in a two pahty system, theah's no room fah dahk chocolate on the ticket."

Not to mention that dogs are entirely disenfranchised.

"Mass mahket means mediocrity, unifohmity, so evahry package looks and sounds the same. Folks dressin alike, talkin alike, listenin to the same tihed songs ovah and ovah again on the radio. Nobody'll listen to nothin new unless it's got some authohity's seal of approval stamped all ovah it, like a man's got no taste of his own. He's a dangah to the state if he thinks fah himself, some anti-social eccentric. I mean if they don't sell it at Sprawlmaht then by God you don't need to buy it. Which is why a guy like me's got to attempt somethin way fah out, blaze a new trail, set a couhse fah a distant stah."

New, as in bizarre?

"Futuhe. Futuhe is oppohtunity, no mattah how old you get. Futuhe's ahways theah fah those who dahe."

Are you going through one of those mid-life crises?

"Get nowheah if you pay attention to the critics cahpin at youh heels, cynics like youhself."

Me? Cynical?

"You ah, you'h downright cynical."

Maybe because dogs are born that way. Somebody has to yowl like hell. Doesn't do much good to play cat and mouse, wait idly by to pounce or be contstantly on the run. Dog's a doer, though naturally she will pause, rest while she ponders her next move, hunker down if she's stumped, but eventually she gets up and barks along with the best of them.

"Cynical and souh."

You'd be sour too if people were always out to fence you in, tie you up, keep you in a cage. Dogs were born to run, give chase, not to be leashed, fettered in chains like a common criminal. What have we done to deserve this? Freedom is all we ask for, what's so foreign about that? Strangers on the planet are what we've become, no place left to roam, like aliens from space instead of natural born inhabitants of the land.

"I realize what's really bothahrin you — it's this leash bit. But it's only fah show, keeps these civic-minded snoops off ouh backs, plus we won't lose each othah in the crowd. Leash fohges this soht of bond between us."

Then wrap it around your neck and hand me the lead.

"See, we'h unique, you and me, that's why we've got to band togethah, protect ouh individuality. Cause evahry creatuhe's got an undeniable right to be himself, to create himself in whatevah image he pleases. He can dress odd, talk to himself about anythin he wants and pass right by without sayin hello. Ain't no rule he's got to tip his hat, eat roasted oats oah buy some huckstah's brand of soap. Fact is he don't even have to take a bath."

I doubt those were the rights the Founding Fathers were espousing.

"Point is we've got to safeguahd the principle of the individual, up against a majohity demandin confohmity."

Thought you wanted to hide out, blend in.

Chipper wraps his arm tight around Betsy, pulls her close. "Nope, it ain't easy bein two lonahs in the univahse."

"Late like this I suhe get itchy twitchy, about ready to crawl out of my skin – could suhe use a hahd hit of reefah."

-mmph -mmph

"Sweah, some day I've got to lay off the shit..."

Heard you say that before.

"...'specially when I'm fresh out – you smell somethin?"

Exhaust fumes.

"Somethin's out theah, I know it, I can smell it." Chipper's up sniffing.

-rr rotch rout!

"Heah you gihl, but I'm catchin a familiah odah downwind, somethin mighty fine – eahly bud, like a young vihgin in huh fihst spring heat..."

No no, this isn't northern Maine where a jury might consider leniency, this is New York and Attica's definitely not Thompson State.

"Wondah what that glow is ovah theah on that roof?"

Which what! Over where?

"Sweah, theah's somethin ovah theah wohth jumpin up and down about." At which Chipper begins this springboard action – with this ten foot chasm separating one roof from its neighbor, and he's back-tracking, he's gunning, he's running, he's jumping and – *whoffff* – Betsy can't watch, well she is watching, it's more that she doesn't believe her eyes until she sees him land safely on the other side, and *-roh* no her turn, for where he leads she's bound to follow, that's what dogs do – blindly leaping because she's not about to open her eyes on this one, and *thud*, she makes it, but where, why, what's worth the risk of just another roof top? But there goes Chipper disappearing over another ledge, though this one's a drop not a gorge, he's hanging by his finger tips, he's letting go, a twelve foot drop straight down, with Betsy bounding blindly behind.

"Betsy! Ovah heah. You've got to see this!" Chipper's staring down into a brightly lit skylight.

What a time for tom-peeping, though it must be a hell of a good show because damn if the stupid fucker doesn't trip over the rim face first through the glass – SMASH, CRASH and then SPLASH – splash? Betsy rushes to see what that could be.

"Whoa!" Chipper's paddling amidst a hydroponic field of grass — a towering overgrowth of wonderous buds WHEN ALL OF A SUDDEN:

BOOM! BOOM!

Betsy's ears perk

BOOM! BOOM!

There it goes again.

STAND BACK!

Pardon?

BOOM! BOOM! / STAND BACK! / STAN MAAX! / BOOM! BOOM!

Hold on the kick-drum, will you pal? Who's what?

STAND BACK! / STAN MAAX! / AD MAN! / BOOM! BOOM! That's who. A 400 at-the-least pound Tyrannosaurus Rex of a man, slick skinned, shaved bald and BOOM! BOOM! positively PO'd — "WHO THE FUCK ARE YOU, AND WHAT ARE YOU DOING IN THE MIDDLE OF MY GARDEN?"

"Please excuse the intrusion, but look at all this beautiful weed! Whoevah planted this batch is a goddamn genius!"

Which is a compliment in a way from one connoisseur to another, sincerely expressed, even from the lips of a poacher. And STAND BACK! / STAN MAAX can be flattered, particularly as the hippo wades in to get a closer look — and what is it that STAN MAAX sees? "*An angel!*" — man is transfixed — "an angel of the Lord with platinum blond hair has descended to pay me a *visit!*"

-*roh*, another religious nut!

Yes, but of a far older, more primitive cult. And STAN MAAX is not all fat and flubber no, STAN MAAX keeps in humongous good shape with daily workouts at the West Village Fitness and Disco Center. He also has this booming voice, as befits his body mass — "What a *delight!* And are you *alright?* Did you bruise or break anything?"

ROOF! ROOF! Betsy pokes her snout through the hole in the skylight.

"AAAACK! WHAT ARE YOU? THE ACCOMPLICE FROM HELL? — THOSE FANGS! THAT BREATH! — BACK! BACK!"

-*rowl?*

"WHAT DO YOU DO, SNORT FIRE FOR AN ENCORE?"

Betsy muzzles it — is her breath really that bad? What to do, what to do? Gargling might help or more regular brushings.

"AN ANGEL AND A GARGOYLE! *BEAUTE ET LE BÊTE NOIRE*! You two must be from the church around the corner — those silly old Episcopal queens, what will they conjure up *next!*" STAN MAAX offers Chipper a sizable hand. "Here dear, let me help you out, why you're all wet and in need of a warm towel, some dry clothes perhaps or a twirl in the *jacuuzzi*, and if you're good I could whip up a candlelight *supper!*"

-rwow! That'd be nice.

"Who invited you frowzy face, three's such a *crowd!*"

-roh¡

"Oh I suppose I could find an old bone in the fridge, but let me take care of my *heavenly* visitor first — so tell me, have you journeyed *far?*"

"Nope, but I think I sprained my tailbone, it's awful sohe." Chipper wiggles his butt some.

"Not to worry! Backsides are the house specialty — and truly I was about to sit down to some homemade pasta *al dente* with an eggplant, mushroom and fresh basil sauce and a house salad with a *lucious,* simply *luscious* avocado dressing, see I'm vegetarian in what I devour, but a meat lover in every *other* respect!"

"Suhe am hungry and mighty appreciative of youh offah, but *-uh,* you think I might be able to sample some pickin's from youh gahden befah the fihst couhse?"

"Love the *accent!* Like a Kennedy cousin with a *head cold!*"

"I'm from Ottah's Ledge, Maine."

"No, I don't believe it, a regular rustic, and fallen from amidst the stars, along with a trusty canine companion. It's positively *mystic!* All you need is a bag of gold, and I'll bet you have a couple of those hidden somewhere — *heavens to Betsy!*"

Ru-ru-ruck-ruckus!

"Did I say the magic word? Do I collect an extra hundred *dollars?*"

"H'yep, this is my evah-lovin loyal companion Betsy!"

At the mere mention of her name, Betsy betakes the plunge herself and down she falls, landing atop STAN MAAX! / BOOM! BOOM! / flattens the AD MAN on his back!

"Are you a friendly beast or *foe?*"

Friendly unless I learn better, she riposts as Chipper indulges in a round of water sports while awash in these Elysian Fields of Golden!

"Thank your lucky star Chipper. You've dropped into the right shop, my name is legend in the marketing and promotion business, *legend*! I am renowned the world over as the AD MAN! / BOOM! BOOM!"

-wholp -wholp, Betsy covers her ears.

"Sorry dear, I'll turn down the *volume!*" STAN MAAX stands before a massive fireplace, a fire roaring behind him — seems it's unseasonably cool tonight — he grips a snifter of cognac, a Napoleon. Chipper is sprawled across a couch, sucking on a yard long bong and struggling to be attentive. Betsy's on a fur rug, lapping out of Chipper's snifter and drifting.

"You give me some useless, nameless product, some piece of *crap* you can manufacture cheaply in your own backyard, and in six months time I can make that crap a recognized brand name worth millions of dollars, an item no household in America can do without!"

-hmmm, millions you say? Why it just so happens I've been making a product like that in my backyard for some time, brought the secret formula with me to New York, costs me next to nothing to manufacture, but it must be worth something to somebody – tell me more AD MAN.

"I wasn't talking to you!" STAN MAAX sniffs, more cognac, and he paces. Seems the giant at seven feet eight is constantly in motion, yet as nimble as a Saturday morning wrestling hulk – which he resembles even down to the black silk robe he's wearing, Betsy notes, with a fancy S&M embroidered on the back.

"Give me some *tramp* off the streets, with no voice, no acting ability, just a pair of good sized *teats*, and I'll have her in her own striptease TV series by next *season!*"

I happen to own five pairs of teats myself, but no one has ever expressed any appreciation for my acting ability.

"A good salesman can sell anything, as long as he can gain entré to the right customer – find his *niche*."

Park his cart on the busiest street corner.

"Marketing is mainly a matter of research – consumer profiling we call it in the trade – which simply means we target some unsuspecting segment of the population and study their every move…"

Stick your nose in their private affairs, do you?

"…what do they *want*, what do they *need* – and I don't mean basic necessities here such as foodstuffs and deodorants where the mark-up is not insignificant – I mean *luxuries*, some substance they can't live without and will pay plenty for by the *ounce!* Because that's where you can punch up those margins *baby!*"

But how about a guy like Chipper who grows his own?

"*Weakness!* Show me a man's weakness, the illicit, the indecent, the utterly degenerate he secretly craves, and I'll make you those *millions!*"

Chipper has access to freebies next door, doesn't shell out a nickel.

"What can you *tempt* a guy with? What will he *salivate* over?"

A good thick hambone will usually do me.

"Watch the drool on the bearskin *sweetie!*"

-roolp! Sorry. I hadn't noticed.

"Take Ricky Rime Fragrances for example. Joe at home could care less if he stinks, but later when he's got an urge, an animal instinct to get out and rub close-up…"

Essence of dead fish drives my boyfriends wild, a clump under my chin.

"…then's when we sock him with the goods on home TV – here

jockstrap, catch a load of *this!* 30 second spot is all it takes, spooled top of each hour from nine to midnight…"

"I remembah those ads."

"…ostensibly innocent, but subliminally *kinky!*"

"All I know is they wah hot!"

"Some motherhood movement from the suburbs was upset, but everyone else in the country *gaped!* No dialog, because one word interrupts the urge where a steady backbeat fuels the flames, lots of bodies, plenty of *attitude!*"

"I wanted to jump right in theah with them."

"Wearing nothing but your *Ricky Rime!*"

"I bought some, thihty bucks wohth, but the gals wah all ovah me, thought my undahweah was snazzy too."

"Piss sells by the millions of ounces…"

-*hmm*, another animal by-product I could readily supply.

"…with returns in the billions — more cognac?"

Don't mind if I do.

"Whoa, no."

"Have a *smidge!*"

"It'd be a waste."

Just a taste, thank you.

"Think you could sell a rockstah like me?"

"You'd be easy. The basic premise is the tease. Say little to nothing, build suspense. A flash, a dab to wet their appetite is all your audience deserves, and you never want to overexpose yourself. No, hold back, play coy, hard to get, rely on surprise — remember celebrity is a *mystery!* To be doled out in small doses. The scarcer the supply, the greater the demand. That's the essence of stardom. Otherwise you're no more interesting than the jerk next door, or Mr Reliable coming home every evening at six. Public wants a love affair with you, not a new dish washer installed."

"Whoa! I figuhed folks would prefah me to be myself."

"*Wrong!* People live long and prosperous lifetimes entirely inside their imaginations. Virtual reality is more than sufficient, *thank you!* There's the evening news if they feel they must, and come a night when they're really hungry for raw meat, they can always drive down an unsavory street to sample some street vendor's wares, when what they really want is a meaty burrito with a blast of *hot sauce!*"

"This cahreah thing is goin to be mah difficult than I evah expected."

"Simply leave the promo to me. All you have to do is work out, write songs and do what you're told."

"Got to wahn you up front, I've got nothin on me fah money, little ovah a hundred that's got to last me through the month."

"Pleasure is all *mine!*"
-roh?

"These papahs wah stuck in the dooh fah you Will, want me to open them up and read them to you? That a yes, oah do you still got a chill?"
Man merely blinks.
"Ahright let's see. Notice of Intent to File Fah Divohce… no suhpprise theah. Petitionah, Cloe Bhramsley Houselandah-Cook. Respondent, Willbahfohce Rhinehaht Cook — whoa, no wondah you settled fah just plain Will — anyway you ahready know that, let me see if I can skip to the who-gets-what paht… Wheahas. Wheahas. Wheahas. Says heah you've been mahried fah twenty seven yeahs! That's got to be a recohd in this day and age… *oh oh*, what's this… wheahas you've been 'mentally cruel' and 'emotionally abusive' — nevah would've figuhed you fah a wife-beatah Will, what've you got to say fah youhself…"
Groan.
"…got to do bettah than that at the heahrin — wheahas you've 'acted as an impediment to said pahty's puhsual of an independent and gainful careeh' and damn, 'squandahed the family's meagah savin's on dubiously financial musical adventuhes' — Will, you'h neahly a criminal, though theah's nothin nowheah about any philandahrin, least you stayed zippahed up those twenty seven yeahs…"
Mere mention sets Will's teeth to chattering.
"…heah we go, the wheahfohes. She's wants sole custody of the kids, claims you'h 'unfit to assume the responsibility of a pahrent in any capacity once so evah' — woman's definitely on youh case. Looks like she gets the fouh-wheelah, since you don't drive anyway, and the summah cottage on the lake, you'h allahgic to the trees. She wants the brownstone too, its 'entihe contents' and you and youh equipment 'removed fohthwith' which means tomohrow if not soonah — don't look like she intends to leave you much of nothin 'cept 'the tools of youh trade' — concahnin which she has appended a list, and heah's a handwritten note at the bottom, says it's eithah accept huh tehms oah face a full exposuhe — full exposuhe of what she doesn't mention."
Will's chattering spreads rapidly from his head to his toes.
"Looks like you'h goin to have to fight huh in couht."
Spasms.
"You've got to. Othahwise she's goin to wipe you out entihely."
Convulsions.
"Betsy, quick! Fetch him a stick!"

"Elli! How you doin gal… No, don't go and hang up on me again, it's Chippuh Stuhbee, from way back when… yah gal… how you doin?"

Chipper's on a pay phone outside the train station at Grand Army Plaza, and Betsy's on guard duty. No sign of the two-headed sisters, but lots of other sideshow folks, more people a minute than this girl has seen in a lifetime along with dogs on exhibit, each neatly attached to a leash and parked curbside to take a leak.

"…damn neah fohty yeahs, I know it… whole lifetime's gone by…"

Poor poodle, look at the little thing quake, glance around. Could get run down by a truck while she's squatting.

"…h'yep, just got in yestahday mohnin eahly, been bunkin with Will Cook ovah in Pahk Slope…"

Everyone gawking at her.

"…he's doin fine, you know Willy Boy, hasn't changed all that much ovah the yeahs, 'cept his wife up and left a couple of days ago… h'yep, cleaned the house out, took off with the kids to Kansas I think he said – he's pretty mum on the details…"

And look, that bitch she's got for a mistress is tugging on her, trying to hurry her along!

"…thanks fah the offah, but we'h comfohtable, plenty of room… We? Theah's Betsy, my hound dog and me… right… right… no problem… I undahstand, you've got cats, though I appreciate the offah…"

RAP! RAP! RAP! RAP!

"Betsy! Quiet down! I'm on the phone!"

RAP! RAP! Betsy's after the woman, telling her a thing or two about the proper care of a loyal household pet.

"Damn gihl! Get back heah! You can't go attackin pedestrians!"

Guess not, woman's dragging the pooch down the block while she's in the middle of taking a plop.

"Stay right heah by my side, otahwise we've got to get you a leash."

Beg pardon?

"…sorry… no, just a little incident in the street – Betsy can get indignant, she's sohta headstrong… right… right… you've got cats…"

Egad cats! Worse vermin than squirrels and nowhere near as tasty.

"…anyway, I haven't been able to get a hold of Lou, and his answahrin machine's full up too… h'yep…"

Here comes another one, an Afghan, nose in the air and prancing. Let's see how she handles the traffic.

"…stressed out, doesn't want to talk to nobody no mattah – doesn't sound much like Lou, he's nohmally pretty gregahrious – must be in the middle of some mid-life crisis…"

-rrue, and who are you Miss Snoot? Not even a curious wag of the tail?

"No! No way! Not Bubba! I don't believe it... when did it happen?"

"Daphne, heel!"

In your face too, you prissy purebred.

"Whoa, when youh friends staht dyin off on you definitely means you'h gettin old."

-rowlf -rowlf

"Betsy, mind youh mannahs — so when's the funahral?"

-rowlf -rowlf -rowlf

"Daphne, I said heel! Heel!"

-rrr I'll show you a thing or two — **rough! roughtoughandtrouble!**

"Would you please restrain your dog!"

"Damn, got to run Elli. I'm soht of caught in the middle of a dog fight.... ahright.... ahrigh... we'll do dinnah... h'yep, just the two of us. Bye. — BETSY!"

-tumbleroverroveruntilshegetshumble!

"Daphne! Daphne! O my God, somebody do something!"

"Get a grip gihl!" Chipper nabs her by the collar.

"That dog should be on a leash!"

"Yes ma'am, I undahstand." Lady's a looker, so Chipper tries a prize-winning smile.

"There are laws to protect society from mongrels..."

Except there's no need for charm when the struggle's clearly over class.

"...and their irresponsible owners."

Lady shows no restraint with the insults, so Chipper lets go of Betsy — we'll soon see who gets the better of who or whom.

-rrrolldaphnerightoverandgoforhergut.

Nothing like a sidewalk brawl to draw spectators, and police, they're on the scene in a flash — "Betsy. You've made youh point, let's head."

-runh? Why stop when I'm on top?

"Police babydoll. Gas chambah, remembah?"

-rr right right, which way to run?

Good question, they're surrounded. And Betsy with her back turned gets nipped on the hind quarter by the Afghan, that's just as the police intervene. While there can be an endless discussion about who jumped who first, no leash and loss of leash, lady's dog certainly appears the aggressor, plus Betsy's missing a hunk of hair — that and the woman attacks Chipper *ad hominem*. He however responds in a more courtly Maine manner. "Got to be hahd fah a little lady like youhself to control such a lahge dog, don't you know, but maybe a couhse oah two at obedience school would do."

Her calling him condescending and a chauvinist pig doesn't enhance her credibility with the cops. They side with the guy — invariably, Betsy sighs, although in this case her own principles are divided if not entirely compromised.

"Better get a leash mister. Next time it'll be the pound."

Chipper's deferential, apologizes for the inconvenience. Betsy trots off with a *humph* of her tail. It's not her hide, it's her pride that's been assaulted. Another minute and she could have wiped the street with that bitch's bloody entrails, though for now she walks, free to take another pee when and wherever she pleases.

"Don't know Will, you've got to have a suit in heah somewheah?"

Closet is full of black, black pants, black jackets, black sweaters, turtleneck, the kind you can duck your head under.

"'Spose we could just hang around outside the chuhch in blue jeans."

Besides which Will has the quakes, like itchy twitchy at the very thought of a crowd, or a funeral?

"You one of those who gets himself all wohked up ovah death?"

Must, his eyes bulge as his neck stretches.

"Inevitable's the way I look at it, no mattah how much inshuhrance you've been talked into."

Now his head's looping side-to-side.

"And bein high on mohphine ain't goin to make that last scene any easiah, mah of a nightmahe than if you just choked on a spoon."

And starting to revolve full circle.

"I'd prefah to huhl myself off a bridge and drown instead of waitin around fah somebody to pull the plug. Though most folks don't evah want to talk about it, bettah to believe in a last minute reprieve, angel by youh bedside offahrin you a free ride."

Will crumples to the ground.

"You know you could stay home. I'm suhe Betsy wouldn't mind watchin you"

Speaking of black Molly's swathed in it, velvet by the yard cinched tight at the waist and covering her head a lace mantilla. Her hair hangs loose in ringlets underneath, the auburn rinse subdued. Her complexion is sallow as befits the occasion, pale with grief and no glow to her cheeks. She does apply mascara to her lashes however to accentuate her eyes, and her lips mauve, the slightest hint of the sensuous.

As Molly dabbles in front of her mirror, she reflects on the years, first Chipper, now Bubba, memories long past. Perhaps a slight tint to her eyelids. Bubba, so broad-shouldered, so manly. Chipper, so boyish. Men. Lovers in her life. So many, yet never enough — then love is ephemeral. She ponders as she powders.

The dread of seeing him laid out in his casket, such a barbaric custom, such a cosmetic marvel, a *trompe l'œil* before he's sealed away from sight forever. She shivers and next accesorizes. Mauve scarf tucked into the collar and plain silver earrings, a brooch on her breast — no, not the goddess — instead a simple cross dangling on a chain. Much appropriately Catholic. Rings. Here she indulges, though no bracelets, none — the amethyst, the scrolled silver set and a diamond, the five carat twenty fifth anniversery.

And if someone were to recognize her, a reporter for instance, ask her to reflect — how should she respon?. An old friend, an old lover, past, gone, vanished into the night. No. He was a wonderfully warm man, whom I shall dearly miss — though we haven't spoken for decades.

What is the worth of it all, she wonders and stands full length, every inch the lover's widow herself.Tasteless yet not graceless.

"…guess Lou won't be goin to the funahral then… no, I undahstand Elli, ain't easy fah any of us to face, besides he's medicated…"

Chipper's back on the pay phone, seems the little lady disconnected Will's, and this time he's got a firm grip on Betsy — via a leash.

Betsy's subdued, as in pissed, and glowering at the crowd passing.

"…you don't see him much anymah… h'yep, those old wah wounds neveh do heal, but how about you gal, thought maybe we could all get togethah at McSohley's fah a beeh oah two aftahwahds like old times…"

A boxer noses in for a sniff, bow-legged bowser, but he' still got his balls intact. Maybe I'll indulge, here have a whiff.

"Brutus! Bad dog!"

Who invited you to intrude buster?

"Behave yourself!"

He is behaving himself. See that pink prickly rise, he's all animal.

"Brutus!"

He gets led off, on a chain no less. Betsy squats back down on her hiney — *drr-rats* — because what fun is there if you can't chase after it?

"…nope, don't blame you, too many memohries, but if you do heah from Lou, tell him I'm ovah at Will's, ahright babes, that I'd appreciate heahrin from him… if you by chance talk to him… h'yep… see you soon."

Chipper hangs up but Betsy won't even look up at him. "It's fah youh own good, so don't go blamin me, I didn't make up the rules."

-humph!

"I've just got to pick up a few things at the stohe, then we'll head back, ahright? But I don't know what we'h goin to do if we can't hook up with Lou. He's the man with the connections – unless I call Salaam. Salaam's the man and Stan, 'spose togethah those two could get us up and rockin."

"So what do I do to get stahted on this second careeh of mine?"
Chipper's back at Stan's for his evening fix.
"I've been giving that some thought actually. What we need is a gimmick, some stunt that grabs people's attention, puts your name back in lights in an *instant!*"
"Used to be talent and good looks wah enough to make it in the music business."
"Where have you been hiding out the past few decades? The music business is show business, you want to listen to musicians you buy tickets to the symphony."
"That's sad to heah. We had Jimi Hendrix back then, Rogah Daltry, Pete Townshend, Jehry Gahcia, Jimmy Page, Robbie Robahtson, Pink Floyd – I mean *Dahk Side of the Moon* still sells big time and evahryone of those dudes wah tremendous musicians."
"And showmen, each with his own special hook."
"'Spose you could look at it from that angle, but…"
"But you've had the good fortune to drop in on THE GIMMICK MAN!"
As in BAM! BAM! / STAND-UP STAN!
"This dog of yours is a lippy *bitch!*"
Those who know and appreciate me say I have a biting wit.
"So let me see, a hook… nevah could dazzle a crowd with guitah licks, that's fah suhe, and my voice has ahways had this raspy edge…"
Raspy? Gaspy, as in no lungs left to hold onto a pitch!
"…but I can juggle pretty well."
"No no, we need headlines, some show stopper people can't help but *notice!* Because you don't have time to drag along the comeback trail. Too bad you can't *fly,* a dive off the Chrysler Building would bring out the camera crews."
"Don't know about divin, but I could suhe climb the suckah."
"*Yesss!* In a Ricky Rime jock sock!"
That'd be a sight, this bambylegged rooster with his bare ass in the air – *rawl rawl* – but whatever you two decide, let's not forget Cincinnati, summer of *-rx-ree-rine!*
"What's that dog mouthing about now?"
"*Uh-…* it'd probably be best if I kept my pants on this time around. I mean I've got my chahms, but I'm hahdly a stud centahfold."
"They can touch up the photographs pixel by pixel – the point is you

need a *gimmick!*"

Take more than a gimmick to sell this character, he's going to need a full-blown *-rr-*rouse.

"I was figuhin at my age I'd finally be appreciated as a sehrious ahtist."

"You want an alcove in the Hall of Fame or center stage at Madison Square Garden?"

"A little stahlight would wahm these old bones."

"Then sex is what sells, along with a salacious *scandal!*"

Chipper could easily provide both of those key ingredients.

"And why sex you might ask?"

"I know, I know, cause it's the one thing folks, 'specially the guys can nevah get enough of."

"Instinctual, irresistible, insatiable. Sex brings out the beast in the species — he'll drink it, he'll drive it, he'll smoke it, aim and shoot it, stand in line to take a peek at it! It's the most delicious addiction imaginable. Whatever its cost he willingly spends, he'll risk his life, piss off the wife, gamble his reputation — and isn't sex the best if it's under duress, dark of night and the chilly thrill of a possible arrest?"

"Whoa! Don't you know!"

"Thursday night, Friday night, he's restless, but by Saturday night, the urge is stressing him out, as in *intense!* He worries, he paces — should I or shouldn't I? Am I impossibly romantic or simply neurotic? Does the mustache attract or repel? Does the gut show? Will a phone call get me in trouble, even diseased? Do I dare get kinky, wear something frilly, be hung up by my heels, stroked or poked, my photo posted on the internet, indecently exposed doing what I enjoy most — the fear, the build up, when *bam!* — some sex junky steps in and finishes him off, a blast past Jupiter and it's mercifully *over!* He might wander off in a daze, feeling a mite guilty, but he's relieved, urge is past and he can go back to work come Monday morning."

"Hohmones. They'h to blame fah all mankind's woes, but it's rock 'n' roll that gets the bad rep fah drivin guys to it."

"Well-deserved, well-rehearsed, and you the High Priest, the masses dancing naked at your feet while you gyrate to a rock solid drum beat — sing about whatever you want as long as you stir their *loins!*"

"You make it sound like a concaht's some soht of pagan ritual."

"Primitive in its appeal, enhanced with drugs, flashing lights, mind-numbing rhythms, dancers entranced, following wherever you lead."

"Too much powah fah a pooh country boy to wield, eithah fah good oah fah evil."

"To yield the maximum return on each dollar invested, but whatever your goal, we need to kick-off the campaign with a bang — more cognac?"

Pou-*rr* away pal, this swill's a lot better than bee-*rr*.
"Your dog is a souse."
"To heah huh talk, you'd think she was a teetotalah."
"When she finishes dipping into your glass, she heads after mine."
"Pahsonally I'd prefah anothah hit of youh prime."
"Help yourself to a bundle."
"Appreciate it – oh and besides jugglin I can walk on my hands."
"Could you juggle with your feet while walking upside down on one of the cables across the Brooklyn Bridge?"
"Usually it's one oah the othah…"
Now comes the time when the jester shall reign.
"…though I 'spose I could spruce up my act a little."
Though one man's fool is another man's dunce – *hiccup*…
"Too bad you can't walk on water or cure the blind."
No feat's too difficult for a true troubador and his trusty mutt – *hup hup / hup hup*…
"Is this dog of yours feeling OK?"
"Just drunk as a skunk got into the mash pile."
Begging your pardon. I can stand on my hind legs like any human.
"How about hackysack, I'm a past mastah at that?"
"Who?"
"You see the school kids jumpin around bouncin a bean bag off theih knees and elbows and such?"
"So that's what they're doing. I presumed they were in the final throes of narcotic withdrawal – no, we need a stunt with dramatic appeal."
-rook! -rook! I can walk while balancing a snifter of cognac on my nose!
"Betsy, be caheful!"
"That's my Louie Bonapart 77 she's playing with!"
I'll be the tacky dog part of the performance!
"Well! If anyone can get in on the act, then watch *this!*" And **BOOM! BOOM!** / clear the room / **STAN MAAX** demonstrates how he can double as back-up disco dancer – "You want'a touch'a touch'a touch me *baby!*" – he bellows, and have you ever seen a whale prancing about on dorsel toes? "Munch'a munch'a munch on me like *crazy!*" – the sight's enough to bring the house down – **HAM! SLAM! BAM! WHAM!** – **MAN** trips Betsy over, although her recovery is phenomenol, a forward somersault that a gymnast would envy, without spilling a drop off the snifter – but the **AD MAN** comes crashing mid-pirouette, topples with a mighty splash into his water garden, breech beached, mouth open and spouting out lung fulls of *laughter!*
"Whoa! Whoa! Both you headlinahs ah hihed!"

Chipper and Betsy and a very unsteady Will Cook get off the subway at West 4th and dash in the rain along MacDougal, passed dark shops, empty cafes, the narrow street deserted until they approach Bleeker – and on the corner Ristorante Bonnanza where a huge crowd of black umbrellas huddles outside. The restaurant is gated, the curtains drawn tight.

È terrible, someone moans.

They mingle with the crowd as it grows thicker, as it floods into puddles in the street – Will though averse to both people and water, like some bolt of human flesh might suddenly strike him down.

"Why don't you lead him by the leash gihl, while I try and find out what's happenin."

Will's amenable, he clutches onto his end for dear life.

"'Scuse me sih, 'scuse me, sohry to bothah, but wheah's the procession stahtin oah endin?" Chipper inquires of an old timer in a dark wool sailor's cap, who's nearly toothless in his reply.

"He wassa sucha good boy, sucha good boy."

"Bubba? Bubba Bonnanza?"

"The best, and is wonda'ful to see, ev'ry'body from the neighba'hood turn out, they closa uppa the shops, they comma out in the rain."

Bubablubblub's the mumble, amid much misery and tears when these large double doors to the mortuary across from where they stand are abruptly thrown open. A dozen men, with not a few boys, big boys, struggle to shoulder this enormous coffin into the dense crowd.

And a brass band begins to play – *brr* RASH! RASH! *and a –ranh –ranh –rum –drr-rum drum* – muffled drums, trumpets, tubas and striking cymbals.

"He made ussa all proud, the whole neighba'hood wassa proud."

RANH! RANH! *–rumm -rumm*

The band, the many pallbearers stand to as flags are furled, Old Glory, Holy Mother Church, Saint Anthony's Shrine, the striped green, white and orange of the Republic.

–brraa –brraa –brraa -brr-rash BRASH!

"He wassa bigga sta, a bigga bigga sta, the besta evva, except maybe fa Frankie or Dino."

*–bubbubba –bumpbum…*CRASH! CRASH! CRASH!

The priest proceeds in long gold embroidered robes, his white surplice servers, incense swirls and holy water, the raised cross of the stripped silent sufferer, as the sea of black umbrellas splits and the cortege slowly rounds the corner down Bleeker.

"He wassa gooda boy, no matta whatta nobody says about whatta happened away aback along ago."

"Folks down heah still remembah all that?"

"Nobody saysa much a'nothin, betta sucha stuff neva gets spoken, but it wasna him, notta Bubba, he wassa innocent, it wassa that otha fella witha the hair, he wassa the culprit."

"The blond fellah out front, he's ahways to blame."

"Thassa right, he wasna from the neighba'hood, he wassa fromma somma place else."

The men, the boys, strain under the weight, the bronze coffin so wide it scrapes the lamp posts alongside. Chipper, the old man have to duck, and Will Cook's backed up against a wall, alongside Betsy who's bravely holding up her end of the bargain.

–brr rush BRUSH! BRUSH!

"So you still remembah the Loose Nukes?"

"Mosta people faget, not me. My jobba ista rememba. I standa on this co'na ev'a'ry day, I keep a watch out fa trouble. Mosta people faget the past, they only rememba yesta'day, the day befa that, maybe…"

"No one who knew Bubba could evah fahget him."

"…they faget whe'a they comma from issa whe'a they agonna go back…"

Maria Teresa, the widow, passes, grieving in black, a long dark veil covering her face and beside her, his hand steady on her arm, a son, a dutiful son — Chipper startles like he's seen a ghost — it's Bubba! Anyway the kids looks like Bubba, looks exactly like Bubba used to look when he was young!

Kid looks straight at Chipper, eyes in a crowd, that instant of recognition, something somehow somewhere out there, two of the same spirit among the billions of other.

"Issa shock, he no wassa old, I mean, looka me, I'mma old, he wassa justa big, bigga big, in fact he wassa too big, thassa what it was, he wassa too big…"

BRASS! BRASS! *–brumma* BRUM! *–brum –brumbummabumm…*

Chipper, Will, Betsy, the old man join the procession — *slosh slosh* across gutters.

CRASH! CRASH! The coffin tilts to one side, nearly slides. Strong arms reach to steady it.

"…too bigga, too bigga boy, thassa alla the'a wassa to it, he wassa justa too big…"

"How did it happen?"

"He wassa eatin — this issa what I hear, I wassa no the'a — he wassa eatin hissa suppa, spaghet witha thick reda meat sauce anda homa'made sausage, mama's own special, cooka all day 'til they wassa real fat anda juicy — you know the kinda I mean, they poppa in you mouth — and thassa what done him in…"

"A sausage?"

"…he wassa eatin hissa suppa anda he eatta a wonna sausage too many, like I'mma tellin you, he wassa bigga boy, bigga bigga, he popped a wonna too many, he go to swallow, he canna no swallow, canna no wash it down, canna no do nothin, so they try slappin himma on the back, do the Heimlicha hold, but nothin awork. It wassa too late, he starta to gag, he turnna the blue, you know, he busta hissa buttons…"

"Busted his buttons?"

"…wonna too many, he blew hissa guts alla ovva the table, biggassa mess you evva did see, thassa what they say, took'emma two days to cleanna everythin up, Ristorante Bonanza, family owned, they alla worka the'a togetha, the mama, the kids, they clossa it up fa at leasta five days, maybe longa."

The procession inches its way toward Saint Anthony's Shrine, the high green tiled copulas in the distance. They pass a black crepe memorial with two photographs of Bubba prominently displayed, one tinted in deep pastels like an icon, a young stud *straordinario*, dark curly hair, big eyes, bright white teeth, probably a plump cherub when he was a baby, but now broad shoulders with muscles, trim waist, and pinned next a more recent instamatic, grayed curls, same eyes, but adrift in a sea of face, no chin, no neck, only the wide open maw of a baby whale.

The procession stalls as it approaches the steps of Saint Anthony's, the tall white granite church where Bubba and generations of Bonnanzas, including his own brood of eleven were baptized, where he and Maria Teresa were married, around the corner from where the two went to Catholic school, down Spring Street where they lived their entire lives, their forty years in wedded bliss, and now where he shall lie in state.

Except they're having a problem getting the coffin up the steep steps from the street and through the doors, like using it as a battering ram won't work, the solid oak frame won't budge, so they have to tilt it at a diagonal, and a thud as the body slides to one side, but they can wedge it through, some crawling with the weight on their backs, others stretched over the top, long arms guiding and the shouting, watch it, watch it – the priest in his mitre safe in the sanctuary, the widow watching in horror from without – watch it! OK alright alright alright, it's through!

Among the bystanders at the steps a woman with a mature figure stands alone in the rain, wrapped in a plain gray trench coat, a scarf tied close around her head, mauve, and oversize dark glasses, hunched under a black umbrella like everyone else.

"Think we've seen enough guys and gals, I mean, we've paid ouh final respects, haven't we, besides theah's no need fah me to go bahrelin in theah and remindin the family of some tihrd old scandal."

Will's agreed, like where's the nearest exit, and Betsy's sopped wet nose to toe.

"H'yep, let's head ovah to McSohley's and have a few beehs. Best you can do at a time like this is drink down youh grief."

And so it is that Chipper, Will Cook too, turn from the path that would have taken them directly past the woman standing at the church door, Molly Dawkens, that age old siren who taunted them, tempted them, young virgins all, and whose final costume selection proves much less conspicuous.

Late that night Chipper's draped over Stan's sofa, a cloud of smoke hovering above his head. AD MAN stands back to the fireplace in a gallant pose, and Betsy's on the bear rug snoozing.

"You know, I don't mean to boast, but what I can do best is jump."

"Been done, that blond chunk in the 80s."

"No, I can jump real high."

"How high?"

"Well I've been out of trainin some time now, but I've gotten up to fouhty, fifty feet when I'm in decent shape."

"Like you can leap over tall buildings in a *flash?*"

"Ovah, no, but hop on top, that's a cinch."

"You're kidding me?"

"Sweah. I was bohn with this soht of abnohmality — lots of abnohmalities my mothah ahways said — anyway when I was youngah I could do a standin high, no assist, a good thihty feet and I set a recohd runnin vahtical at fifty seven feet, nine inches. Nobody else has evah come close, least not up Maine way. Betsy's a pro too, she can do triple huh length to snag a frisbee mid aih, but no way she can compete with me."

-hrulp? Did I doze off?

"Why didn't you mention this particular talent right away?"

"Nevah took it too sehriously. Aroostook regional's the only school district in the nation that recognizes the free leap as a competition spoht. Team got bohed havin meets among ouhselves — you know, why keep tryin if you'h nevah goin to get a shot at state-wide oah the nationals?"

Notice he has neglected to mention the many near misses as well, the multiple fractures to the skull he has sustained, but if he wants to risk life and limb in this silly sport again, I am powerless to prevent it. He is of age, almost, and does what he wants. Only thing I can do is survey the damage and drag home the pieces.

"*My my!* The possibilities are endless — a bounding leap from one

Boeing 777 warming up for take-off to another, no net underneath, or a spring through a fiery hoop suspended fifty feet off the ground with a beefy New York City pumper crew standing by…"

"Try my best, goin to have to limbah up some, cut back on the beehs and the smoke."

That would be a feat in itself.

"*Yesss!* I'll line up my contacts with the all-news networks while you hit the gym."

"Ahright, I agree, reluctantly…"

"*Reluctantly?*"

"Don't know, gotten old, wohryin 'bout the envihronment and such — I mean I don't want none of these high jinx intahfehrin with my main message caus-…"

"*Message!* What *message?* You haven't mentioned a *message!* You don't need a *message!* You don't want a *message!*"

"I've got to make the wohld awahe of what they'h doin to the atmospheah, ouh watah resouhces and fohrests…"

Wildlife! Biodiversity!

"…tell it to them dihrect, see if the kids today will band togethah and do somethin about it befah some majah disastah occuhs, like the mohnin the migratohry bihds come floppin out of the sky because of unchecked auto emissions…"

"My dear Chipper, *no no no!* Message and media do not mix. If you want to be a success in show business, you appeal to the mid-section, and I don't mean the *intestines!* Maybe the heart on occasion with some simpy romantic ballad, but never the *brain!* Not even the geek will listen to you, and the rest of his classmates can't read, they only dimly comprehend what's flickering in front of them on *MTV!*"

"You go and undahestimate youh audience and you'll lose them. Kids today ah much mah media savvy than we evah wah, and if you look close you can see through a lot of the shit they broadcast at you."

"*Chipper!* The 60s are *gone!* Along with protests and mass movements. Kids in the 2000s can't get a free fuck anymore, CD's cost fifteen bucks, and as for a cause you're entirely out of *luck!*"

"But I didn't travel all the way back heah just to entahtain the troops, that's what they've got Hollywood fah — I've got my message to get out…"

Have we forgotten the long arm of the law?

"…plus I'm too old to play games."

"OK OK a message, you want a message… you could rant on about America the beautiful, voracious skies and patriotism — those old charms still sell — but the *environment!* It would be easier to go for Jesus, and much more *profitable!*"

"They've been crankin out those old song and dance routines fahevah."

"Yes but Jesus makes more sense than the environment, he might be altogether mysterious, but the environment is this intractable problem that would cost twice the military budget to barely *dent!* A massive cleanup would be prohibitive, probably socialistic, and they will never grant you air time, not even on *PBS!* They rely on corporate sponsors anyway and a membership who wants its news intake strictly limited to one hour so they can settle in and watch costume dramas from cocktails until bedtime."

"That bad?"

"Bad! Try *horrendous!* I meet with these media midgets on a regular basis where they sit and discuss their mansions in the Hamptons and what deal's finally going to build them their very own heliport – it's message or money, not both – not even Bill Clinton could pull that act off, and that guy was good, *real good!* Money honey, gold that glitters and 30 year treasuries – get a load of that first, then devote yourself to charity work."

"Ain't got time to wait on fohtune, need fame to fan the flames a lot soonah than that."

-sniff?

"Music's your profession, not *prophecy.* Song, not *philosophy!* So show off what's left of the pecs, pad your bulge and wail your heart out, expose yourself if you have to, but whatever you do, swallow the message…"

-sniff? -sniff?

"…because it's way past prime time for the both of us."

-sniff? -sniff? -sniff? -sniff?

"Somethin wrong gihl, you got to go outside?"

While Betsy's the first to get a whiff of it, STAND BACK / STAN MAAX – he catches a dose too, then Chipper's nose starts to twitch – smoke?

Yes, and where there's more there's *FIRE!*

WHANG! WHANG! WHANG! outside alerts them to a three alarmer. Sends the AD MAN on a quick search of his duplex, but signals to Betsy it'd be best to take a look from the *-roof! -roof? -roof!*

Chipper performs one of his aforementioned fifteen foot champion verticals out through the hole in the skylight, Stan and Betsy perforce use the stairs, and as they arrive Chipper has already leapt one roof and is sprinting toward the next because it's all five stories owned jointly by the Houselander-Cooks that are ablaze, with the sole remaining occupant passed out from grief and too many beers on a cot inside.

Those aforementioned firefighters are up their ladder trucks with hoses, dousing the house and the abutters as well. A crowd of onlookers has assembled, and a searchlight illuminates the scene, but no one, not a one is prepared for the sight of this aged Maine varsity jumper bounding across rooftops and diving straight into the flames.

-*rrolp!* But there's nothing Betsy can do, nor STAND BACK STAN, the crowd on the street and a circling news helicopter…

Wait.

When who carrying whom should emerge, stagger to the edge of the burning building and leap again — my God in Heaven! — fifteen feet over to the neighbor's and safety, then one, two more bravura hurdles — the entire sequence caught on camera from the air, luckily, since Chipper himself has now been rescued from any number of STAN MAAX'S proposed circus stunts, and publicity? You want publicity? Try the same sixty second tape looped over and over again on countless newscasts, celebrity showcases, Kerry Clannerdy's exclusive hour-long interview broadcast live coast-to-coast, from Puget Sound to Bar Harbor — *hrulp!* — you said it girl, for an officer of the court with a warrant plus a grudge is like a parched slug stuck under your armpit and sucking blood, justice without mercy applying for a timely extradition — instant celebrity? Sex and salacious scandals in the making? Successfully launches Chipper on his comeback career!

ÎLE DE SAINTE CÉCILE

"OK yo two, listen up. Wha' yo gots t'do is pop yoselves in tha' rowboat at the end a'the pier thea an go."

"You expectin us to row all the way to the Cahribbean Salaam?"

"No no, yo jus' gots t'row on out t'tha' freighta ancho'd in the ha'bo – an keep yo voices low, yo don' want t'be attractin nobody's attention."

"Which freightah ah you pointin at?"

"The real da'k one off t'the left, named the *Charon*…"

"*Sharon?*"

"*Charon.* No way yo's goin t'miss it."

"Don't know, freightah suhe ain't my idea of a leisuhely cruise to a sun splashed island."

"Spa'e me the attitude bro. Yo's the one who ain' got no passpo't – besides yo wants this dog a'yo's caged in qua'antine fo thi'ty days o'mo?"

Quar-*rar-rar*-antine, that's as good as jail!

"So gets in tha' boat thea an row!"

"You ain' goin with us?"

"Ain' nothin bout the sea appeals t'me. I prefa's t'flies the friendly skies."

"Ahright ahright… jump aboahd Betsy…"

Aboard this sinker?

"…and stay centah. Don't go rockin around none. You've got to help me keep pooh Will sittin upright."

Betsy balances in the bow as Chipper and Salaam lower Will Cook down by his armpits. Boy's hardly twitching.

"Have a safe trip. I'll be down t'give yo a grand tou'a a'the island."

Good God, what a *murr*-ky night, no moon and what's that stench, a burnt-out oil slick?

"Watch out gihl, Will's stahtin to tottah."

-row -row, I'll handle the zombie.

swoosh swoosh swoosh swoosh
"Lot fuhthuh out heah than it looked from shohe."
-rohl, what do I know. I lose all sense of direction on the water.
swoosh swoosh swoosh swoosh
"You'h the retrievah in the family."
Don't usually go duck hunting off the Atlantic coast.
swoosh swoosh swoosh swoosh
"Boat ovah theah looks like the one Salaam was pointin at — AHOY!"
Thought you were supposed to keep quiet, not make any noise?
"AHOY! AHOY! — I've got to attract theih attention somehow."
swoosh swoosh —SWUNK!
A little knock alongside, that should attract their attention.
"Can you read those lettahs up theah on the hull? Ch-... Chaih-..."
-Char... Charon.
"Must be Russian oah somethin."
Wonder when they last painted this rust bucket, 1917?
"AHOY! AHOY THEAH!"
"Ahoy yerself. Who ye be down thar doin all the hollarin?"
"Salaam sent us... SALAAM SENT US!"
"Aye, he did did he?" A lantern rises from high on the prow. "And did he give ya any farthar ward o'advice matey?"
"MATTAH OF FACT HE DID, HE SAID DON'T SAY A WOHD!"
"Then why don't ye heed his advice and shut yar gob?"
-roh, told you so.
"I'll drop a line. Ye can haul yar own arse abard."
"I've got my hound dog with me and anothah fella not feelin so good."
The lantern lowers a little. "Thar's what I need, a rail tendar and a sea dog t'crap all ovar me fresh swabbed decks."
At no extra cha-*rrg.*

The crew's called into action with a boom, and slowly the three are raised away high up in a thick rope net and swung centerhold, unloaded with a thud. Chipper nods a thank you, but Betsy's immediately complaining about a jolt to her tailbone, and Will Cook, Will's oblivious.

The Captain stumps over. He's straight out of *Treasure Island,* peg leg, black patch, one eye that drills clear through you.

-grrr-row-row-rowll

"I'll be tolaratin none o'yar garf mutty, not abard me ship." He booms as he looms above her.

-wulp! Simply swallow my tongue, duration of the voyage.

"Me name's Blight, Hosiah Blight out o'New Bedford and Captain o'this har freightar. Ya'll be quartar'd in the First Mate's cabin — been empty evar since the bastard jumped ship in Vlora right befar we got undarway with a cargo o'fugitive Albanians bound far Trieste…"

"Chippuh, Chippuh Stuhbee's the name, and this heah's my dog Betsy."

"…had t'tarn back, Italians got wind we war undar way – but I couldn't find the traitar anywhar along the coast, hard he fled into the interiar."

"Must be tough keepin good crew these days?"

"Whar's a Chinie goin t'find wark in Albania, ya tell me?"

"Eagah hands ahways make do, that's what my granny used t-…"

"What be this ya'r cartin with ya, a body war supposed t'sling ovarbard with no ceramony at sea?"

"Nope, this heah's Will Cook, pooh fella's been undah the weathah evah since his wife up and left him, took the cah, the kids, everythin he had."

"He should be chin up dancin far joy. Not a woman alive warth a pennyweight o'any man's tears."

-ro?

"Plus Will doesn't much like watah."

"Can drown himself in a cask o'whisky far all I care. Stash him ovar thar in the cargo bay, and lash him down, case we encountar starmy weathar."

THUMP!

"Easy matey. 'Til war 200 miles out, ya had bettar make yarself scarce."

"Won't say a wohd, won't talk to the crew."

"Talk t'them all ya like, but unless ya speak Cantonese they won't undarstand a ward ya say – and keep the dog out o'sight or she'll end up a pot o'soup on the stove."

"She'll be at my side the entihe time, ahways is."

True, don't think I'll stray far this voyage.

"Rule abard this vessel is simple, ya don't make no troubles far me, I don't make no troubles far ye – questions?"

"Nope. Fresh out."

"Keep it that way. Questions interrupt me concentration, and ye don't want me losin track o'me bearin's on open ocean."

"We just want to get theah, like everybody else." Chipper glances at the crew, nods. They simply stare back, eye Will Cook suspiciously.

"Don't assume whar this scarvy bunch might want t'go, cause the only port that'll have 'em gladly is Hell!"

"H'yep h'yep, sunniest spot in the wohld so they say."

"Ye won't like it at farst go, but aftar a while ye sink into the routine."

"H'yep h'y-…"

The crossing is stormy of course, some out of season hurricane, one of those with no name. And the ship tosses, waves break forty feet or more over the bow, kick as hard against the stern. Captain's at the wheel in an oiled slicker, his mug stained brown with coffee grounds.

"Rough." Is how Chipper greets him, Betsy glued to his leg.

"Seen bettar. Seen warse."

"Must be a blessin all these new satellite instruments they've got fah navigation nowadays – takes out the guesswohk."

"I go by sight meself, with me trusty astrolabe."

Astrolabe?

"Compass cracked on me last crossin t'Calcutta while sailin through the treacharous Bay o'Bengal. Thar war currents and crosswinds gangin up on me, drivin rain, couldn't see beyond me thumb in any direction. Crew had barred themselves below. Was up to me and me mate who I had chained to the wheel while I handled lookout, belly down in the prow – got me a good eye in a starm, and a nose far sniffin any shifts in the wind."

"No radah?"

"Caught a stiff whiff off rocks dead ahead – hard t'lee, I hollared back, and we skirted barely by, nary a scrape, when I smelt some mar rocks off t'port. T'was one nar disastar aftar anothar 'til I sighted this break in the reef and a quiet cove beyond, guided har through to calmar watars whar we tossed anchar and rode out the starm like a babe rockin in har cradle."

"Bet you've got lots of haih-raisin stohries you can tell."

"Sailar's got t'trust his instincts at sea. Charts and instruments are good as far as they go, but them newfangled electronic devices could go bust on ya, cause ya t'get lost so far out ya'r nevar hard from again."

"H'yep, but we haven't seen the sun fah days now to take any readin's, nah the stahs much neithah."

"Fog's the real ball-bustar matey, little rain's marely a test o'me talents."

"So wheah do you figuhe we ah about now?"

"Atlantic."

"He doggy doggy, he he."

Hee hee yourself chum. I can see the cleaver you've got hidden between your shoulder blades.

"Yo wan din din?"

Don't want to be anybody's din din, thank you.

"Go spessal on menu."

Like a plucked duck.

"Vewy vewy spessal" – *heeeave...* HO! HO! HO!

Southern sword style, is it? Well here's a low lying northern trick I was taught – slither like a cobra, snap like a crocodile, nip a nut...

-*YIII* -*YIII*

…and away he runs to save the other.
-*YIII* -*YIII* -*YIII* -*YIII* -*YIII*
-*mmm* tangy. Touch of hot sauce and *munch munch*, quite tender.

"Will, snap out of it. Can't brood ovah a lost love fahevah."
…*huh* …*huh* …*huh*
"Still got the shivahs? You keep this up and you'h goin to be pahmanently palsy."
…*huh* …*huh* …*huh* …*huh* …*huh*
"We've got nothin to do 'cept have some fun in the sun, I mean heah we ah on ouh way to an all-expense paid vacay in the Caribbean, with sand and suhf, native gihls with no tops, plenty of ganje — what mah could a guy want? Besides you've nevah been on a cruise befah."
…*huh* …*huh* "…once, once before…"
"When was that?"
"…on my honeymoo- *moo- moo- moo-*…"
"Whoa! Why did I bring it up?"
moo- moo-…
"Will. Get a grip. Staht lookin at life squahe on, like how about all the hot sex on the beach you can do in a day, I mean man, you'h free!"
-*huh*/*huh* -*huh*/*huh* *huh*/*huh* -*huh*/*huh*…

"Betsy, *shh-*… ovah heah."
What's up, chum?
"You figuhe ouh lives ah in any dangah?"
Not yours, you're too bony, but mine! I've got a pirate missing one eyeball on search for a course and a cook missing one screwball on a hunt for my carcass.
"So maybe we should plan out some sohta emahgency proceduhe."
As in where to -*rr*-run? Clearly not the kitchen!
"I'll try and locate an inconspicuous lifeboat somewheah, just in case we've got to do a quick dive ovahboahd."
Guess I've been a bit more vigilant than you, because lifeboats are quite conspicuous by their absence, like none, not a one. Seems everybody on this tub's a lifer.
"Once I've wohked out an escape plan, I'll get back to you."
Do, do, and in the meantime I'll keep sharpening my incisors on this leftover boot I found — *flackflackflackflackflack*

Creep creepcreep creep creep creepcreepcreepcreep creep
-mm, bare feet on the gangway... four or more...
Creep creep creep —craaaack through the hatch.
Never sleep, never worry.
Leeeeep — PO! PO! PO! PO! PO! PO!
That's it, pound on the bag I was sleeping in — what are there, two of you this time?
"Wha? Wha?"
*-sur-*prise! Just Blight's old boot inside, while I'm crouched back here behind you and ready to SPRING!
"Wha..." -ACK! -ACK!
A bite off the butt out of the both of you.
YIP YIP YIP...
And back down the hatch you run.
YIP YIP YIP YIP YIP YIP
Better give it up guys, or there'll be nothing left of you worth nibbling.

Though lo, when the clouds seem their dense bleakest, the sun suddenly breaks through to tweek us, and what should Chipper and Betsy awaken to, not the doom of shipwreck nor the centerpiece of the crew's mess, but canoes filled with savages surrounding the steamer in droves — all feathers and skins which they did not buy bargain at an off-island Wal-Mart, no, no, they had to hunt and kill for their colorful spring ensembles — and cosmetics must have accounted for most of the cash sales because these folks are painted from forehead to ankles, and the noise they're making could chill the dead.

Though yonder comes a motored runabout with a uniformed colonial representative, flying a familiar flag of a European semipower, though whose tri-color is it? Italian? Couldn't be, Columbus sold out to Spain long before he sailed. The Germans? No, there weren't any U-boats around in the seventeenth century. Dutch is a remote possibility, or French... *mais oui!* Deliciously decadent with overtones of strong-arm police tactics.

"WEL'COME! WEL'COME TA DI IS'LAND A'FUN..."
And a British boarding school accent.
"...WHEA YA CAN PLAYS ALL DI DAYS TA YA HEART'S CON'TENT WID DI CHILD'REN A DI SUN." This voice from the runabout shouts out a megaphone, a voice not officious nor malicious, not in the least, nor a voice very deep with authority either. "AN DID YA FOLKS HAP'PEN TA RE'MEM'BA TA BRING A'LONG PLEN'TY A'YA YANKEE DOL'LA'S?"

Though if the fellow in his faded colonial duds seems high-pitched friendly, then what's with these savages whooping it up in the canoes?

"GOT A WHOLE POCKETFUL!" Chipper cups his hands and shouts back. "THA'S MUSIC TA MI EARS MON. WEL'COME! WEL'COME!"

Must be the local station they're tuned into because damned if the savages don't straightaway strip off their feathers and hides, down to their naked breasts — breasts? — as they break into song... It's a... It's a...

>It's a Sat'u'day night an time fo CA'NI'VAL
>So get ya la'dy an ya mon an SING DIS SONG
>Got ta get out ta'night an raise a LIT'TLE HELL
>Been wo'kin in di fields MUCH TOO LONG

>I say, I say...

>It's a Sat'u'day night an time fo CA'NI'VAL
>So get ya la'dy an ya mon an SING DIS SONG
>Got ta get out ta'night an raise a LIT'TLE HELL
>Been wo'kin in di fields MUCH TOO LONG

The Île de Sainte Cécile is named for a martyred Roman virgin of the Second Century who was beatified the patroness of musicians. It is said that her voice was so divinely inspired that after her head had been severed from her torso her tongue continued to sing well over an hour for the greater glory of God and also for the edification of her executioner. At the cessation of which he knelt and bore witness to his faith in the one true God and was thereupon executed himself without uttering a note.

The island itself is the tiniest, rarest gem of an atoll, the coral reef keeping the Gulf Stream waves at bay except for one spectacular breach of a surfing beach, untouched it appears, with only a few native villages scattered along the coast, the remainder covered in lush tropical overgrowth, though poked up center is a massive, largely inactive volcano surrounded by a sapphire blue lagoon. The Île de Sainte Cécile remains an uncharted paradise, lying slightly east of the colorful Grenadines and slightly north of the foibled Reagan Republic of Grenada.

>Now, ma'ma don' ya go an SCOLD YA SON /
>No, pa'pa can't lock ya daught'a IN HA ROOM /
>It's time ta blow some dope an SIP SOME RUM /
>Time ta dance a'round na'ked in DI FULL MOON

>O ya'self, now...

>It's a Sat'u'day night an time fo CA'NI'VAL
>So get ya la'dy an ya mon an SING DIS SONG
>Got ta get out ta'night an raise a LIT'TLE HELL
>Been wo'kin in di fields MUCH TOO LONG

Betsy's beating her tail to the catchy calypso while the runabout with the official cheerleader coasts up to the steamer.

"Hal'lo Cap'i'tan. Con'sul Gen'ral Sé'bas'ti'en down hea, will ya an ya crew be stayin fo din'na?"

"None o'me scarvy crew'll be debarkin, only these payin passengars, so ya might as well call off the welcomin party, it's a waste o'yar money."

"Not ta wor'ry Cap'i'tan, dey's got no'thin else ta do all di day long 'cept sing an play fo free in di sun."

And as with any big production number, there's more than one costume change scripted in, as the fierce natives let their hair down, peel down to bare essentials and up the volume.

> It's a Sat'u'day night an time fo CA'NI'VAL
> So get ya la'dy an ya mon an SING DIS SONG
> Got ta get out ta'night an raise a LIT'TLE HELL
> Been wo'kin dese streets MUCH TOO LONG

Except they are anything but fierce warriors out there warbling in their canoes, they are all young girls in nothing but flowered bikinis of the bottoms up only variety.

> It's a Sat'u'day night an time fo CA'NI'VAL
> So get ya la'dy an ya mon an sin-...

BOOM!!!

The *Charon* lets go with a fusillade, brings the curtain down with a shower of lead drops — runabout turns about and runs.

"Deplarable display o'yar wares, ye harlots and ye parveyars!"

Captain Blight has a long Puritanical streak. He orders his crew below deck and the passengers to debark as rapidly as possible — for whose convenience he drops a line over the side, Will Cook up and about now. Though Betsy may have a hard time shimmying down a rope, her being digitally challenged and all, but Chipper's ready to dive off if he has to, with the native girls in the canoes giggling and waving up at him — seems they're not as easily frightened off as the colonial official. Fact they paddle closer to the *Charon* and reach to assist as Chipper pauses in his descent to capture the Kodak moment — never again to view such a scene, a cast of thousand island girls, arms raised in utterly uplifting surrender! Man clings to the lifeline as his breath catches up.

The Captain's impatient however. "Lowar away!"

Chipper's foot touches bottom and twenty arms envelope him. He succumbs without a struggle.

Betsy's next, and ever try to step from a dangling rope end with your carry-ons into a tipsy canoe? NO! She slips, but they catch her first bounce, thanks much.

Another canoe maneuvers into place for Will Cook, and he is nervous nervous, poker can't swim and the mere motion of the water makes him nauseous. But Blight's had about enough of dalliance in a pagan land. He orders the poor soul to walk the plank. Although where there's a Will there's a way to get wet, and with each step he must stare down and face it. The canoe full of giggling girls backs a bit, then pulls forward while he tips on his toes for balance, but to no avail because it's about then when he loses it — THA-THWIP — over he goes — SPLAT! BWA-WOB BLOB-BLOB — it only takes a cupful if you swallow.

Though these girls aren't about to lose a paying tourist. A few dive in while the rest leisurely lean over to scoop him up, two canoe loads of them as a matter of fact, forty soft brown arms — NO NO, GOOD GOD, DON'T TOUCH THAT DROWNING MAN! Like a fish caught fast in a net they toss him aboard, where naturally he begins flailing about like violently, so what do they do, they sit on him, and twenty tender thighs which would make any man alive or half so give in — except Will Cook, for whatever it is about the touch of the female, gentle on the cradle or a hard rockin mama, he rolls that canoe over and out with all of them into the water, giggling and jostling to save him, arms around his neck, a leg, an arm, whatever extremity's handy — WHOOSH! — lifts out of the water like a huge blue in fright for its life — which only brings a hundred other merry maidens paddling over to aid and abet.

Charon steams off in a huff. There's only so much the old Yankee Captain can watch, besides there's his crew to consider and much in them of mutiny.

Customs is a flash of the bankroll, as two sparkling officials in short white skirts with matching teeth bow to let Chipper pass, one even stoops to pat Betsy on the noggin.

Then there's the usual souvenir shops for duty free liquor and perfume, a t-shirt pushcart dealer, fine island arts displayed on a blanket, including a batch of shrunken heads attached to sticks by an elastic, which as Betsy is to learn is a specialty craft of the locals, a goat ride along the picturesque though not lengthy Boulevard de la Republique, urchins trailing along with palms up for pennies, the village tobacconist specializing in warped grass roof native blends — all the excitement and the bright sunshine send Betsy scurrying from vendor to vendor in search of a pair of Ray-Bans with rhinestone frames — because it's a... it's a...

> It's a Sat'u'day night an time fo CA'NI'VAL
> So get ya la'dy an ya mon an SING DIS SONG
> Got ta get out ta'night an raise a LIT'TLE HELL
> Been wo'kin in di fields a MITE TOO LONG

A traveler can't but join in the carnival spirit, particularly when the party is being thrown solely for him — seems nobody else touristry is out or about — but then maybe they're still in bed sleeping off the prior evening's festivities. Not the native girls however, a bevy of the tropical beauties has Chipper surrounded...

"Hel'lo han'some, I'm Mango." And she bites at him.

"I'm Tangle." All arms and some pearlies too.

"Tam'a'rind." Who needs a peel to get tasty.

"We show ya a'round di is'land."

"First ya might be wantin a cool bath ta relax ya from ya jou'ney."

"An afta dat a hot oil rub'down." It's long-limbed Tamarind who's the masseuse.

"Yes, le's show him ta his ho'tel room right'a'way."

And they dance him mer'rily outta town an up di only hill a'round.

Betsy follows behind some, ears on alert with her inbred Dobbie suspicion. French, is it? Whole island full of Duchamps, she fears, although this Caribbean branch of the family is made up entirely of nubile native girls and a few old women in outmoded nanny garb with toddlers and babies in hammocks, but none of those bratty adolescent boys, the kind who yank on your tail and throw sticks at you, no men whatsoever, except for the one duded-up official — plus the mangiest low life canines she's ever laid eyes on. So how is it, she wonders, can old women and young children account for a thriving cultural life in face of the low growth economic forecast for the region generally? But... but...

> It's a Sat'u'day night an time fo CA'NI'VAL /
> So get ya la'dy an ya mon an-...

Cut! Betsy wails. I caught the jingle on the opening comm-*rrr*-cial!

"Wheah'h you gihls takin me?"

"Ta get a taste a'hea'ven."

"With you three babes, I wouldn't mind a sip of hell."

"Dat comes lat'a, afta you've had ya sup'pa."

"Whoa! What did you say youh names wah again?"

Mango's her name and blushing beauty's her game. Then there's Tangle if you're man enough to take her on, and Tamarind, bitter tasting on the

Mango, Tangle and Tamarind… tasty tropical island treats

outside, but succulent su-weet on the in. The three lead Chipper along a dusty path up to the island's only hotel, perched high on a bluff overlooking the lagoon.

"What a view!"

Takes your breath away — *pant pant pant* — doesn't it?

The hotel is grand in the grand old tradition of grand old hotels, OLD! The structure itself is turn of the century and built entirely of grayed ship's planking removed from the hundreds of wrecks on the reef ringing the island, with a triple mansard roof and a covered gingerbread veranda stretching across the front and around the side facing the lagoon. The plank steps do sag some, the steps that are not missing entirely, and the roof has caved in here and there. Some of the louvered shutters are flapping in the breeze as is the frayed tricolor from atop a peeling flag pole. Grounds are largely unattended except by a small crew of chickens, but the hotel has survived gracefully over the ages and perhaps its guests shall too.

The girls relieve Chipper of his bags and go skipping giddily barefoot around him up the steps, disappearing through the screen door.

"This is somethin else, ain't it?"

Couldn't have put it better myself. Betsy dutifully follows inside.

"Wel'come, wel'come mi friends ta di Île de Sainte Cécile an ta di wo'ld fam'ous Hô'tel Par'a'di'so!" It's the colonial officer from the runabout speaking, only on closer inspection he looks mostly like a bellhop. Must be the square French Legion cap, the short fitted coat with the epaulets and the buffed white sneakers. "Mi name is Sé'bas'ti'en an I'll be ya host dur'in ya stay."

"We'h musicians heah fah a holiday."

"Ya don say, an what kind a'in'stru'ment does di dog'gy play?"

Bones buster.

"This fella from New Yahk sent us, named Salaam Kareen Kaboom, said he'd be pickin up the tab."

"We all know a'bout Mis'ta Sa'laam, he's no strang'a ta di is'land."

"He said we'd be livin in luxuhry, but he didn't say which centuhry."

"Di Hô'tel Par'a'di'so's been hea al'mos fo'eva."

The lobby is another era indeed. A grand four story atrium with central staircase, all ironwork in loops around a many tiered chandelier and leading upward along two sides, carpeted in remnants of a once lush red.

"Must've been somethin in its day."

"On'ly di best a'people came ta stay."

The burnished mahogany front desk sits off to one side, and directly above their heads instead of a fan there's a tapestry sort of affair wafting back and forth to cool the lobby, a labored, rope-driven Injia raj-style device.

"How's that wohk?"

"Can't tell, it's one a'di ho'tel's bes kept se'crets."

Of which there are many mo-*rr*, no doubt.

The chandelier is missing nearly all of its crystals, and the overstuffed chairs have been shredded, perhaps by the goat tethered to the desk, who this moment is munching on what must be the leather-bound guest book.

"Shoo shoo, ya nin'ny."

Betsy's nose twitches, since she's not normally partial to goats. First off there's the stench! Get it on your coat and you might as well take yourself straight to the dry cleaners, and while she doesn't like to generalize, goats are known for their atrocious table manners, and back stabbers, can't trust a one.

"Would ya be wantin two sing'les o will a dou'ble bed do fo di bot a'ya ta'day?"

"O my God!" Chipper turns white as a ghost. "I fohgot Will Cook!"

"Beg'gin ya pa'don?"

"My lifelong friend! He fell off the boat into the hahbah!"

"No need ta wo'ry yo'self mon. I'm cer'tain he's in safe hands. Di girls, dey'll bring him back good as new — if he was in any dan'ga a'drownin dey'd'a called out di bri'gade by now. I'd'a had ta change mi hat an go."

"But you don't undahstand, Will's allahrgic to the female touch."

"Why didn' ya jus say he was spe'cial, I'll send mi nephew off ta fetch him right a'way — Lu'ci'en!"

"Oui on'cle?" A kid darts out from somewhere, he has an over-eager-to-please face same as Sébastien and a matching uniform, though the shoulders of his jacket sag way low and the arms have to be rolled way up.

"Get ya'self down in'ta town an find dis man's trav'e'lin com'pan'ion." Sébastien claps his hands and the boy runs off.

"Thank you, I apprecia-..."

"Not ta wor'ry, Lu'ci'en's one a'dose cu'ri'ous boys his'self. He knows jus what ta do wit dese del'i'cate cases."

Mango and Tangle come rushing down the grand staircase, they bow and they giggle, then go running upstairs again.

"O dese young'sta's ta'day, dey know no re'straints, dey play an dey play, but what can we say?"

"*Ah* listen... Sébastien..."

"At ya sa'vice."

"Tell me, what's the age limit, you know, heah on the island?"

"Age limit?"

Good God I don't believe it, first words out of his mouth!

"You know, fah gihls and guys to *ah-... ah-...* get it rockin?"

"Beg'gin ya pa'don?"

He couldn't ask the bellhop in the privacy of his room while he passes him a fiver, no, he has to blurt it out at the front desk.

"*Ah*, you know, fah gettin down dihty and doin it?" To which Chipper adds a graphic gesture.

"I got ya."

"H'yep?"

"Ain' no limits I know not'tin a'bout on dis is'land, an I should know cause I'm di actin gov'na-gen'ral."

"Whoa! Two rooms, no, make that three, that way evahrybody can have theih privacy — wheah do I registah?"

"So'ry ta say, I have only di two rooms wid a shared bath in be'tween — but whea did mi book dis'ap'pea ta?"

-*roke roke roke roke*... that goat's a joke!

"Wha'd'ya doin now, chewin on di pages? Some'times I won'da whea'da he gots good sense — hea ya go, sign right unda di last guest's sig'na'tu."

"Herr Rudolf Schmidt und Frau Huelga, Bremerhaven, August 14, 1945 — so what, ah you full up?"

"No, di rest a'di rooms have un'fot'u'nate'ly fallen in'ta mis'use."

-*oh?* Betsy reckons. More than the nephew is curious around here, and what is the story with this goat? He's busy chomping on what looks like it might be Sébastien's safety brigade helmet, but that's no concern of hers. Goat does what goats do. Law of the jungle is simple, eat grass if that's what you're into, swing from the trees, but let each and every other kind be, unless of course some poacher gets a hankering for your children, then tear after him with bared tusk.

BAMBANGBUMPBUMP —DUMP! A dozen young maidens led by lone Lucien come rushing into the lobby with a body as stiff as a board.

"Don go get'tin sand on di or'i'entals wid dose filt'y feet child'ren, an put him ova der on di sofa — gent'ly gent'ly — looks like he's breathin heavy an his eye'balls done gone pop out a'his sock'ets!"

Chipper insists they call a doctor. They look at him quizzically, whisper among themselves. "We've got to get a doctah."

"On'ly doc'ta we know a'bout, he's a fou hou flight from di Gre'na'da mail-od'a med'i'cal school by di bi'plane, which comes buzzin ova once ev'ry two months. But we can call on Big Ma'ma Ma'Gee, she's a wiz'ad when it comes ta cases like dese."

-*rulp!*

"She knows all di time tes'ted rem'e'dies."

No, no no you don't, roots and lizard gizzards simply won't do, let me through! Betsy begins by licking Will's forehead — *s*light fever and -*rruk*

salty! What did you folks do, try pickling him in brine?
"Will, ol' buddy. Speak to me."
"He be di best." One sweet young thing coos.
"Mon'o'mon an den some." Comments another, sweeter.
"Even bet'ta…"
"Bigga!"
"…dan Gran'daddy Cash!"
The rest of the island maidens nod vigorously.
In defense Will Cook can only moan, low but constant.

Whatever his constitution or his constituency, he is in need of immediate attention. So nurse Betsy barks in his ears. He blinks – *mmm* – from which she deduces his condition's not critical. He simply needs a cool bath, a long rest, and he'll be his regular flipped-out self by morning.

Chipper's not convinced, but Betsy has pulled him through on many similar occasions, so he does as she says. He grabs Will Cook's shoulders, Lucien his feet, and they follow behind Sébastien and the goat

"Be'lieve ya me, if ya leaves dis crit'te a'lone fo a sing'le se'cond, he's goin ta tear di whole place up" – up, up the grand old staircase they ascend to the fourth floor luxury suites.

The lift, I presume, is temporarily out-of-service, sniffs Betsy?

Hey, it's top floor, any which way you have to climb to get there. For despite the paucity of private baths, the rooms are spacious, each opening out through double doors *sans* glass onto a balcony *sans* railing, where the view of the lagoon is breathtaking.

"Whoa! That's about as blue as blue is evah goin to get, and what's the mountain top in the middle?"

"We call him El Snorro, he's ou own special vol'ca'no."

"Volcano?"

"Don' wo'ry ya'self none, he snoozes all di day."

"And at night?"

"Oh some'times he wakes up in a bad mood, spews an spits a lit'tle, but den he rolls back ova an falls a'sleep fo a'notha hun'dred yea's o so."

"When was the last time he woke up with acid indigestion?"

"'Bout a hun'dred an some yea's ago."

"So he's due."

Overdue.

"He's a grouch, dat old El Snorro, dat's why di Spanish left so soon afta dey dis'cov'ed him, an di Dutch. But di French dey know bet'ta. Dey say leave him be. Ev'ry child on di is'land is schooled e'nough ta know ne'va ta sneak up an dis'tub El Snorro, not while he's rest'in."

The furnishings in each room are antique as well. Bedstead is iron and the springs squeak. The feather mattress envelopes you, and there are buckets stylishly placed throughout the room should the roof take to leaking in an afternoon rain. Above each bed is a raj-style hand cranked fan like the one in the lobby, cranked by hands hidden away some place else however — in the attic or in the walls, though these fans could be of a more advanced colonial invention with central handcranking located somewhere in the basement. The French were expert in the design of out-of-sight labor slaving devices.

"S'pose that volcano erupts? What do we do then?"

"Jus don pa'nic, take a deep breath an den run fo ya life ta'wa'd di cool wa'ta's a'di sea."

"Dive in?"

"Pre'cise'ly."

In each room there is a sole bare light bulb stuck on the ceiling with a chain dangling down, also a gas jet on a sconce on the wall, and a good supply of candles on a table, evidence of the hotel's continuous adaptation to the marvels of new technology.

"Ya has ta be pre'pa'ed fo any e'ma'gen'cy on di Île de Sainte Cécile, cept dere's no nat'ral gas, ne'va was."

-ro?

"An we'a' prob'ly di bet'ta off wid'out it be'cause a'di ex'ten'sive hur'i'cane sea'son. Don wan no'thin ta go explo'din."

"Whoa! How extensive a season you got?"

"Le's jus say we've passed tru di wo'se an leave it at dat."

"You folks got electricity?" Chipper dares ask.

"Some'time."

And what did he expect for an answer?

Betsy bunks with Will Cook the first night. Sure he snores, sort of a gurgling sound that typically ends with a sharp snort. But during the night he might need attention, and she certainly couldn't abide the bed springing antics Chipper and Mango and Tangle and Tamarind are engaging in, nice girls, but don't they require sleep?

Daybreak and Betsy has to get out for her morning constitutional, a sniff around, see what's what and who's been spraying the bushes. -*hmm*? That's a fresh trace, wonder if he left it for me? Girl can never tell for certain, some of the young studs do giftwrap, others are entirely indiscriminate, but might as well follow the path, see where it leads, yes, yes, getting stronger every step, through some bushes, over by a tree, warm, he can't be too far ahead, through these brambles -*ooch* -*ouch* -*ahh*, an open meadow and what is it we see… -*rrach!* I must be out of my senses? It's that mangy billygoat!

Betsy's a poor sight as she backs out of the brambles, head humbled. First sign of dotage, she sighs, I'll be wandering in circles soon, mad after my own tail. Ah well, I'll meander into town, nothing much else I can do until the master rises, which won't be much before sunset, I gua-*rr*-antee.

The walk into town is easy, all down hill. Before long Betsy's hoofing it amongst the locals who pay her no mind. Being a dog she blends easily into the indigenous population — *aanh,* one or two of her kind greet her with a growl or get pissy, but mostly she's left to wander where she pleases.

Town's made up of mat huts, some situated high on poles, others at ground level, most folks engaged in some form of cottage industry. No doors, so she pokes her nose into lots of different people's business, here a seamstress, there a basket weaver, bark canoes and tourist crafts — *hmm* that's the vat where they shrink the heads for the island's most curious curio — and what's this? 'Big Mama Ma'Gee's Home Remedies,' reads a sign — might as well have a look-see in here.

"…she neva lis'tens ta me, but dat don stop me from speakin mi mind. I tell ha she ain goin ta have no money left fo ha re'ti'ment lest she sta'ts put'tin some a'side ta'day…"

Betsy settles into a corner to watch the old woman, give a listen.

"I ain got noth'in ta feed ya doggie, a'ready give what I had a'way."

Betsy's fine, she doesn't usually do breakfast.

"…but if she don sta't wor'ryin bout ha'self, who's goin ta? Not dat man she's mar'ried ta, dat Ca'l'ton, he's a wo'th'less no-a'count who's been livin off a'ha from befa di wed'din…"

Seems Big Mama Ma'Gee doesn't mind discussing family matters, even if there's no one to listen, unless you count the baby gurgling in the hammock or Betsy — I mean, simply because we dogs can't talk, people presume we don't listen. We do. Although we tend to ignore most of what's said as so much *blah blah.*

"…run'nin round New Yo'k City wid di fan'cy girls…"

That's until the story gets meaty.

"…lyin ta her dat he's workin late nights at di ho'tel when ev'ry'bo'dy knows di truth bout dat…"

What could we do with the information anyway? Nobody trusts the word of a dog. No, best to lie here and look disinterested, scratch an ear, wait for the story to get jucier and jucier.

"…what he ain out spendin on di girl'friends, he's gamb'lin a'way at di ra'ces like he was a mil'lion'aire when he's no'tin bet'ta dan any a'di rest a'us havin ta mi'grate ta di main'land ta find wo'k an' den sendin some bit a'nothin home ta sup'pot di fam'ly, like it's easy on us reti'ed old nan'nies ta take care a'all der child'ren fo dem, an she's no bet'ta."

-*mm*, so that's the reason why you see only old women and children in the village, except what have you done with your sons?

"Dings dey've got'ten a lit'tle bet'ta since di Quot'Links got di boys wo'kin ova on di lava slide, but dey ain payin dem no'thin fo wages…"

Then why not prime the local economy, build up a thriving tourist industry, I mean, you've got the white sand beaches, virgin forests, nubile young ladies as a steady source of non-unionized labor?

"…it's all be'cause a'dat ir'ra'table vol'ca'no…an di French…"

French. Say no more. Why we had a settlement of them up our way, the Duchamps, and let me tell you-…

"…dey a'ways doin dat nu'cle'a testin, dat's wha trig'ga'd di e'rup'tion. Migh'ty Lo'd in Hea'ven, wiped out di whole east'an half a'di is'land, not a tree left standin, an we wid'out no UN dis'as'ta re'lief funds set aside…"

A salient fact the guidebook neglects to mention.

"…di French, dey packed up an left be'cause a'di po'ten'tial lia'bilities, so no wonda all di young folks had ta move ta New Yo'k City ta clean up in di hos'pi'tals, drive di taxis an wash di dishes in di ho'tel kitch'ins, o like me, mind di white lad'ies' ba'bies on Pa'k Av'e'nue til I gets too old – an dey won pay no soc'i'al se'cu'i'ty be'ne'fits fo fo'eign nan'nies, only had what I'd saved up ta come home ta mi is'land…"

Her plight would make for a great PBS special, except the producer probably has Mama Ma'Gee's sister watching her brats afternoons, that's after the morning's cleaning finished and before she has to make supper.

"…not dat I'm com'plain'in bout no'thin, no, I have mi two great gran'daught'as ta be lookin afta an a long life a'plea'sant me'ma'ries. All in all I con'sid'a mi'self one a'di Lad'ies a'Fo'tune…"

Then why is Mama Ma'Gee sobbing so silently, Betsy wonders.

"…it's a great life, dat's wha mi ma'ma said ta me, it's a great life long as ya don weak'en…"

Betsy watches while Mama Ma'Gee rises slowly from her seat as only a 300+ size woman can, with a load of effort. "No time fa tears, time's fa makin ya fu'ture." She rocks the baby in the cradle and she reaches for a small wooden box off the shelf. "Goin ta trow Seven in a Cir'cle be'fa di sun gets too high an mighty in di sky, goin ta see what's whea an who's movin bout di is'land." She empties out a deck of cards on her table, face cards with all sorts of colorful characters.

Peaks Betsy's interest.

"Got ta first get rea'dy fa comp'ny." Big Mama dusts her seat, she dusts round her table, she dusts the cupboard with a carved handled whisk and she chants to herself while she does it.

> Come di spir'its a'mo'nin / Put a'side ya wo'kin
> Come di spir'its a'noon / None a'ya nap'pin

Betsy scoots under the table.

> Come di cen'ti'pedes / Come out a'ya hi'din

Betsy's bugeyed. The floor is instantly aswarm with them.

> Come di ma'caws / Come wit'ness di pro'ceed'ins

rawk rawk rawk rawk rawk rawk — a flock settles across an old clothes line in back of the hut.

> Come di fie'ce da'k clouds / Come di light'nin

Big billowy thundercaps roll out of nowhere, blow, send the whole village scampering for cover.

> Come di Devil His'self / Da's if He dares

Betsy cowers, paws over her eyes. Girl can't abide thunder and lightning. And there's a rumble — *That him? That him?* Dark clouds blot out the sun... though there's no flash, not even a sparkle. Sound and plenty of fury, but no, not the devil.

-phew! Guess he decided to pass on the invitation.

> Come di La'dies a'Fo'tune / Come whea ya bid'den
> I's di Queen a'di Cups / An' ya pre'sence is re'quest'ed

Neighbors is it?

> Out a'di ground / Fire from di sky
> Wind tru di trees / In di dep'ts a'di ocean
> Come sit ya'selves down / Come pou out some tea

Tea?

The kettle is whistling, when suddenly there's this rustling a'bustling through the door — **krrr-klump an der klunk** — lots of banging about though nothing corporeal.

Betsy ducks down while the sound of skirts rustles over.

"Seat ya'selves any'whea looks com'fo'ta'ble." As Mama Ma'Gee sits with a thump and begins to shuffle.

Der bump a'di rump — breezy bunch follows suit, chairs scoot, cups rattle, though nobody's in the room except Big Mama, the babe and Betsy! Voices, if you count those, all gad'din bout gos'sip.

"Shush, shush up now, we goin ta be'gin."

Spirits go silent.

She deals out seven cards in a circle. "Tu'n each ca'd face up one af'ta a'no'ta… le's see, le's see… fi'st one's, o me – di Prince wi di Coins, all 'leven a'dem."

Betsy has to stretch her neck up over the edge of the table to see.

"He's luck'y wi di mon'ey, dis fan'cy man, but un'luck'y in love, con'stan'ly gam'blin way his fo'tune – jus like dat no-a'count Ca'lton."

Jack of Diamonds, Betsy perceives.

"Prince a'Coins means der's lots a'mo'ney in'volved."

The Ladies around clatter agreement.

"Now come di se'cond ca'd… he be… di High Priest."

Women round the table don't utter a sound.

"Got t'watch ou ev'ry move when he comes snoopin round."

Though he looks benign enough to Betsy, long leopard robes and a high headdress, face painted a bit to the severe, with eyes that stare.

"Got t'keep ou secrets to ou'selves."

The women quietly agree.

"Wha's next, wha's it goin ta be… di Final Judgment!"

An audible gasp.

An angel with a trumpet hovers over a graveyard as both the sun and the moon rise from behind. The various costumed characters of the deck overturn their headstones and emerge into the unearthly light.

"Means some'tin dire's bout ta hap'pen, we all gots ta keep a look'out."

"Wha's next, we gots ta see… Ten Dag'gas Drawn!"

Ten of Spades. *Mumble mumble.* As Betsy's ears twitch. She glances from side to side, hears much, sees nobody – ten fierce warriors with shields and spears circling around.

"Dat's ten dag'gas loose in di shad'ows! We gots ta be extra vig'i'lant dis ev'nin. Lock up di young'stas an di goats in di shed wi di chick'ens."

Guests get to rustling again. Betsy can't understand what they're saying, not distinctly, but something about doom and devestation.

"Shush up. We got ta see who's be'hind dis ca'tas'tro'phe…"

Ma'ma Ma'Gee, her fingers quake, but she's quick, she flips the card and look… looks like it's goin ta be di Devil His'self!"

Gr-rumble gr-runt an der ravin – new card certainly stirs the spirit world up as they face Satan.

"Ol Mon's not wel'come in mi house, no sir! Why jus look at dat smirk on his face! His ma'ma should'a slapped him up'side di head cause he's a'ways up ta no good an laughin bout it as us'ul."

Betsy peeks over Mama Ma'Gee's shoulder -*hmm,* fellow's half naked human, the other half furry animal, at least in the hindquarters. But what kind? Bull maybe, goat? Tail, horns and hooves, that's for certain.

"Don like it Lad'ies, don like it when Sa'tan tu'ns up at ou tea pa'ty."

Ghosts rattle around the place, seem to agree.

"La'dies, La'dies, keep ya pla'ces if ya please. Le's see wha we gots so fa, five ca'ds. Der's decent mo'ney on di ta'ble, but drawn dag'gas by di hand'ful. Der's dis sus'pi'cious Priest an di angel a'God a'nouncin di Final Judgment wi di ol' Devil Hisself in attendance…"

Doesn't sound good to Betsy, nor to the forces surrounding her.

"…who's ta come next, vic'tim o van'quished – two ma ca'ds will tell."

Everyone's breathless as Big Mama turns the next card face up.

"O would'n ya know, di Cou't Jesta?"

The mood in the room relaxes in a sigh of relief.

"Jus di way'far'in young man? Wha's he doin mix'in wi dis mis'rable com'pan'y, I'd like ta know?"

Picture of a smooth cheek lad out travelling on his own, clothed as the joker of the deck. He's hiking along a mountain path with his pooch – black dog who looks a lot like *moi* – makes you wonder what's up?

"A'ways wi di smile on his face, like he's up'ta some so't a'mis'chief his'self, a'ways care'free…"

-*hmm?* Fellow's attitude looks very familiar. Wonder if there is something to this mumbo-jumbo.

"…an dat man'gy dog's a'long wid him as us'ul."

Mangy? I beg to differ. Loyal companion clearly suffering through the rigors of wildlife, without the convenience of a hot shower.

"Walk'in di edge he is, walk'in di edge an whist'lin, not watch'in whea he's goin, see, he's bout read'y ta trip an go tum'blin down dat ra'vine."

Clearly one reads into these pictures whatever one pleases.

"Haven't seen any fool boy'scouts round des parts fo a while now, not since di ban come a'long on di hi'kin an di camp'in in di woods."

Sleeping outdoors isn't my idea of any fun either.

"Las card Lad'ies! A' ya read'y?"

Tension is palpable.

"Le's hope fa di best."

A pin could drop.

"Ma'ci'ful Heav'ens! Di wo'st I could fea – di Hanged Man!"

Other elements around the table murmur and concur.

Who? Betsy's back over Mama's shoulder. Same young man as before, only this time he's been undone, strung up a tree by his toes, backpack gone and where's his trusty bowser?

"Poo boy, poo poo boy, nough ta make ya cry."

Seems OK to me, a little tarnished, but still some twinkle to his eye.

"Don take a gen'ius ta read dis set, some poo moth'a's son goin ta be sac'ri'ficed, hope'ful'ly fo di sake a'di othas, one gone but di rest su'vive."

A gloom descends upon the room.

Is there something I've missed, I mean, whatever happened to the

Hollywood story with the predictable happy ending?

"Could be di end a'di wo'ld, ea'ly as ta'night."

Why? Betsy stares at the card. What's so dire?

"Got ta get ta mo'vin Good La'dies a'Fo'tune, got ta save ou daugh'tas an who'evas left a'ou sons."

Room begins a whirlwind — *rum a'dum dum end'a'd'fun* — upsetting table and chairs as the furies flee, disappear as quickly as they came, while overhead the afternoon's thundershower, a crack of white lightening — *KA-WHACK!* Looks like it might have landed smack on top of the mountain.

Big Mama shoos Betsy out. "Nex time if der be a nex time — been good ta see ya."

Outside the village is in a flurry, winds rage as darkness prevails, and high atop El Snorro there's a smolder.

Will Cook hardly notices the abrupt change in the weather. He's found an ancient upright in the saloon and he's tuning it — *do re mi fa so... so... so...* — much to Sébastien's delight.

"We haven't had mu'sic in di place since di end a'di wa."

"Which war?"

"Was so long a'go I can't re'mem'ba."

...so la ...so la ...so la

Sound of music brings Chipper and the native girls down the grand staircase, Mango and Tangle and Tamarind and Lucien — Lucien? He's traipsing behind, wrapped to his chin in a red feather boa.

"Wha do ya tink ya doin child, dressin up like a tramp! Ya leave di payin guests ta der own pu'ri'ent pur'suits."

"O on'cle, ya a'ways spoilin mi fun."

"Don go sas'sin me none, git on wid ya du'ties, feed di goat — an take dat wrap off, red's not ya co'la."

"Baa!"

"If I told dat boy once, I told him a tou'sand times, he looks his best in yel'low, but does he lis'ten ta me? Ne'va."

...ti ...ti ...ti ...ti ...ti

"So Will, I've got this idea fah a song, this sohta modahn day love ballad, you know, somethin socially relevant that'll send us rocketin back to the top of the chahts — you ready?"

"OK...?"

-roh no, when our boy gets creative, it's time to duck.

"It's got a snappy 50s beat, Little Richahd style — *bumpa bumpa bumpa*

bumpa / bumpa bumpa bumpa bumpa — kind that nevah lets up — I mean, don't stop fah nothin."

"Anything you say."

"Three chohds — B, D-flat, F — nothin complicated."

Will sounds it out on the upright.

"Ahright, that's good, let's give it a try — a two, a three, a fouh…"

> We'h talkin bout a newfangled woman
> Newfangled woman
> Newfangled woman's got a hold on me
> Newfangled woman / Newfangled woman
> She's got to be free
> Newfangled woman / Newfangled woman
> Makin it all on huh own.
>
> H'yep, this newfangled woman / Newfangled woman
> She's got the family
> Not just one / She's got to have two oah three
> Newfangled woman / Newfangled woman
> And she's eahnin lots mah than you oah me!
>
> Newfangled woman / Newfangled woman
> She's on huh cell phone
> Newfangled woman /Newfangled woman
> She's pushin financial advice
> To newfangled women / To newfangled women
> At a hefty price.
>
> Cause she's a newfangled woman / Newfangled woman/
> Yes she is.
> Newfangled woman / Newfangled woman
> Makin trades on huh own account.

"This is wheah you can break out, strut youh stuff.

> *Plink'a plank plank a'plunka / Plank plank a'plunka*
> *Plink plank a'plunka / Plunk! Plunk! Plunk!*
>
> Newfangled woman / Newfangled woman
> She's got a hold on me
> Newfangled woman / Newfangled woman
> She's detahmined to be free.
> *Plink plank a'plunka /Plink plank a'plunka*

"Love that acoustic effect Willy Boy!"

Newfangled woman / Newfangled woman
Makin it all on huh own.

"Keep up the beat now, see me straight through to the end."

We're talkin bout my newfangled woman
Newfangled woman / Newfangled woman
She's up and she's at it one eahly mohn
Cashin out of huh stocks and bonds
Newfangled woman
Cleahs out huh closet full of clothes
Newfangled woman
Pins a note on my old Fohd.

Cause she's a newfangled woman
Plank a'plank a'planka
And a newfangled woman's got to be free.

Newfangled woman / Newfangled woman
She's left the moh'gage payment on the flooh
Plinka plank!
Stashed the kids with huh mothah in Iowa
Plunk! Plunk! Plunk!
This newfangled woman
Says she'll call collect sometime from Flohida.

Newfangled woman / Newfangled woman
Goin to make it all on huh own.
This newfangled woman
She don't need a man no mah
Plink plank a'plunka
Why's that?
Plank! Plank!
Cause she's bought huh own fouh-by-fouh.

"Bring huh home Willy Boy."

Plink plink a'plank a'planka
Plank plank ka- ka- plunka
No not this newfangled woman
She's dropped huh hold on me
Newfangled woman / She's got to be free

Newfangled woman / Newfangled woman
Goin to make it all on huh own
Plank! Plank!

Newfangled woman…
She's done found huhself alone.
Plink plank a'plunka
Newfangled woman
Plink plank a'plunka
She's got no hold on me
No, this newfangled woman
She's set huhself free.
Plank plank plank / plunka … KA-PLUNK!

There's a thud on the piano, Will's collapsed, forehead in his hands.
Now-*ow-ow*, look what you've done.
"But they say if you can put youh misahry to music, you've as good as fahgotten about it."

"Think theah's somethin strange about this place gihl?"
Ceiling fans cranking on every time you go to get into bed, no switch, no warning, or the bathtub that mysteriously fills up with steaming salt water exactly when you feel the need to soak.
"I've got Sébastien oah that Lucien kid followin me around evahrywheah I go like I was some dotty old fool."
Well?
"And sweah I've been heahin things…"
The isle is full of noises, that entertain but hurt not.
"…rumblin sounds somewheah in the vicinity of that volcano."
Like look out the window!
"You think that suckah's gettin ready to blow?"
And just whose path are we conveniently situated on?
"Life on the edge Betsy, 'spose it makes each day mah intahrestin."

Later comes an eerie stillness, wakes Chipper up. Girls' night off as he flails around in bed. Bothers Betsy who has him shoved way over into one corner of the springy mattress, with the *flap flap* of the inscrutable raj fan above and her stretched out four legged square in the middle underneath it, enjoying every flap of the breeze for herself.
"You know you'h a goddamn bed hog, that's what you ah." He pushes her off center and down some.
And she's indignant! *-grr-umble mumble…* She pries one eyelid open slightly, laps her lips, resumes her snoozing.
Now that Chipper's awake he wanders over and opens the balcony shutters. He peers out at El Snorro, fire blazing on top and the start of a

spiraling thin plume.

"Feelin restless Betsy. We ought to do some explohrin on ouh own."

-right right right... perfect time for a moonlit stroll.

"New moon."

New moon probably why I've been chasing after that skanky old goat.

"Got to find out what's goin on round this island, can't be all fuckin fun in the sun." Chipper leans way over the rickety balcony rail. "Like to know what's up with that volcano fah stahtahs."

Somethings in life you don't need to know about, *nope*, like volcanoes.

"C'mon Betsy, let's head."

You're serious, aren't you?

Must be, Chipper pulls on a dark jumpsuit.

Going incognito?

"You comin, you stayin?"

Yaw-awn, she gets up, stretches — no way I can let you go trouble dipping on your own — she follows along the hall, down the staircase. He's creeping tip toes, so she tries the same — *clip clip clip clip clip* — toenails that need some serious filing, down and past Sébastien who's asleep in a once upholstered chair in the lobby with the billy goat tucked under his arm — WHEW-EE! I'd bag it alone if I were you pal.

Goat doesn't hear them sneak by either — *croa-oak-r-oak* — one of the dilapidated steps on the porch.

"Let's head along the ridge, see how fah we can see."

The moon is indeed bright and the path clear, mostly clear.

"Will you look at the view!"

Magnificent, she must agree. Ocean on one side, white caps breaking out against the reef, smooth lagoon on the other side — that foul mouthed volcano sputtering — whereupon El Snorro spits up, heaves a red stream over the lip.

"Whoa!"

-rr think maybe we should flee to the sea?

"We could row ovah oah swim, can't be that fah."

Sure swim, swim toward an active volcano. Why not be the first on the island to feel the hot lava rush.

"Sight like this comes once in a lifetime!" Chipper shouts as he charges down the ridge to the edge of the lagoon. Shoreline's high reeds and soft slime up to the ankles.

"Hope theah's none of those blood suckahs floatin in the watah."

Blood-sucker what?

"Y'ouch!"

Piranha or leech?

"Goddamn leech-like ugly fish with a couple of hundred shahp teeth!"

Which Chipper picks *hoh* so carefully off his leg and tosses.

-mm, marine specimen you can live without... *sniff sniff*, what's this? Somebody's dropped a something here, electronic. Japanese. See, proof positive they are dumping their trade surpluses at ground level prices.

"What've you got theah gihl, looks like a two-way radio. Maybe we can bohrow it fah awhile, might come in handy if we got lost."

Handy? As in how handily it fits into your back pocket?

Chipper borrows one of the native dug-out canoes as casually as he does the electronics, some personal code of ethics he holds about found objects in nature. "Goin to be a trick maneuvahrin one of these things, they don't seem pahticulahly stable."

Borrowed or brand new, a canoe's a canoe, one false move and it's roll over.

"You ride up front and I'll paddle." Chipper pushes off, and after a shaky start, they glide noiselessly across the lagoon.

"Look at the size of that monstah!"

They soon reach the shadow of the volcano wall where all is darkness with Betsy yapping – *rook rook* – rocks, lots, jutting out of the water.

"H'yep, we'd bettah take it slow. You slip to the back and let me climb up front." He starts crawling toward the bow while Betsy switches to the stern, she steps right over him, and naturally the damn canoe starts in pitching – *o whow whow* – are we going down for the big one?

No. They make the exchange without incident. Chipper lays low in the front, paddling with one hand and pushing his way through the rocks with the other. Betsy keeps a lookout from the back.

Unawares, they pass over a sensor pod, one that emits a peep, one that in turn alerts a QuotLink cruiser patrol which is instantly skimming across the water towards them. Simultaneously the two-way in Chipper's back pocket squawks. He can't make out much of what is said, but both he and Betsy here the word INTRUDER clearly enough.

Chipper squeezes the canoe in between two large outcroppings, narrowly missing another sensor pod, and he waits, waits and listens.

Betsy's feels something bouncing off her skull and off the rocks around her. Unnerves her. It's all she can do to resist an urge to howl, not Chipper, he's thick, doesn't feel the slightest ping.

The QuotLink patrol zeroes in, and talk about the urge to howl, all QuotLink security personnel come factory equipped with sonar transducers embedded in their frontal lobes and night vision scanner rods inserted directly into their pupils, patented devices not generally available on the commercial market, although the alert shopper, the shopper who wants to stay on the alert, can purchase a do-it-to-yourself mail order kit through a small ad placed in the back pages of *Munitions Monthly* magazine from a spy supply house buried deep in Idaho. Not that Betsy has any idea what's zapping at her, but feel it, does she ever — *zing-zong* city between the ears and more than a match for extra strength Tabvul.

"Quiet gihl, don't move a muscle."

Chipper has his own set of sensors. He watches the QuotLink cruiser pass, two darkened figures in grease paint and camouflage standing and pinging the rocks.

"Wondah what those dudes ah out heah protectin?"

Nothing that needs concern us.

"Whatevah it is, we'd bettah be extra caheful from heah on in."

Betsy's eyes by now are doing jackpot twirls, not that she's disoriented and feeling wobbly on her feet, no not at all, she simply loses her balance and falls over, and with her of course goes the canoe — WHIP TIP / FLIP DIP — both take a bath, and a spare knee taps another pod — *peep peep peep peep* — freeging thing goes off like an alarm clock.

"Heah, ovah heah, behind these rocks!"

Betsy dog-paddles over, nose, eyes out of the water watching, when Chipper's hip radio starts up — bells, buzzers and whistles — two unidentifiable creatures floating in the lagoon. INTRUDERS! INTRUDERS! They can hear the patrol boat circling back.

"Theah's only one way out of this mess."

Which is!

"Up!" He points. Up the magma cliffs to the top of the volcano.

-roh no! Betsy's preference would be to pad around in the water, attempt some innocent explanation, bat her curly lashes, but cliffs and climbing, best to leave that to the osprey.

"Let's climb out of sight."

The head lamp of the patrol boat is bearing directly down upon them.

"C'mon gihl, ain't like we've got that many options."

The logic is irrefutable, and besides Chipper's a Maine boy, thrill of the climb, pay no mind that this is sheer rock wall, as Chipper boosts Betsy up — "I'll be right heah behind you, evahry step of the way!"

Betsy's fairly adept at chimney straddling, and this being a crevice, she's paw up with a back leg push, paw up with another back leg push!

"Wondah what it's like up top?"

RUMBLE! RUMBLE! RUMBLE! RUMBLE!

That's what it's like up top, and down below the patrol has discovered the capsized canoe. QuotLinks play their light on the cliff, while Betsy and Chipper huddle tight inside the crevice. Light crosses by, one way, then another. Finding nothing the QuotLinks switch their attention to the water, pan among the rocks, they cannot swim, let alone dive, not with all the electronics they pack, including a plasma-powered radio transmitter which has been installed in their left inner-ear cavities. They simply lock their jaws and rotate their corneal dishes, thereby channeling neural impulses directly to central processors at HQ – more convenient than the handheld device in Chipper back pocket, the one buzzing – INTRUDERS ON THE ROCKS! INTRUDERS ON THE ROCKS!

So what do they want, intruders with a splash and a twist?

The light flashes back along the crevice. The possibility of anyone scaling the western face of El Sorro is slight, not only is the wall sheer smooth, but near the summit there's a lip that protrudes another thirty or forty feet further out over the water – still, as a precaution the QuotLinks issue an order – UNLEASH THE CATS! UNLEASH THE CATS!

Cats! Betsy has to hear that! Talk about raising her hackles, and what kind of a cat would hang out on these rocks anyway?

Panther cats, that's what kind Betsy, an imported bad ass variety with oily black fur and squinty yellow eyes. But they're for later, current calamities take precedence.

The QuotLinks take one last look – INTRUDERS PRESUMED DROWNED – and they speed off.

DROWNED – Betsy sighs.

"That was close."

They could at least call off the cats.

"Climb this steep is goin to be a real challenge."

You're telling me pal, as Betsy stares up at easily five hundred feet, no paw holds she can see, and the two of them without picks or pitons or ropes, just claws and padded feet.

"Guess I'm goin to have to go freehand. You bettah ride on my back and cling like a monkey – watch out with those nails of youhs!"

Betsy's nails have been this constant sore point between them. They'll get to wrestling, gloves off, and damned if Chipper won't start in griping about some scratch he's sustained, complain about it for days. Whatever. Betsy plays backpack and Chipper does this finger hold and raw toe act, free climb it is and no doubt about it the guy is phenomenal, a plenty legged spider couldn't do any better – although what's this, no toes – he's clinging by his fingertips, not only that, he's lifting his body weight, and hers, entirely by finger power – easy, easy *heee's* up to this ledge, he is – Betsy's got her eyes closed, she's trying not to slobber down his neck, and when she looks, she sees they are standing there, well he is, she's still clinging – "Will you watch with those claws!"

Sorry.

"That's skin I've got on, not cowhide."

Sorry. Sorry.

"Was wohried fah a second." As he flexes his fingers. "Wasn't suhe I could make it."

Some feat. Got to say that, and with only another four hundred and ninety feet of the same treacherous terrain to go.

That and those panthers alluded to previously? The dripping black drooling ones? They're padding back and forth at the crest, hungrily awaiting dinner to be delivered.

"We've bit off a mouthful this time gihl, but can you imagine the view of the stahs once we'h up theah?" And he reaches out for another finger hold.

They luck into a slim vertical shaft, the width of a body, where Chipper and Betsy separate, wedge in and do some more chimney straddling — paw in the crevice with a back leg push, paw in the crevice with a back leg *push push push push...* good for an additional fifty feet.

All the closer to bared saliva tinctured teeth, my sweets.

There's more finger and toe climbing to go, so Betsy is back clutching to her master's shoulders, tongue hanging out — such a distressed damsel is she — but she's the one who has a head up and notices a sizable ledge off to the right. *-grr-ripe-ripe,* she pipes into his ear.

"What wheah?"

-ripe!

"Right?"

-ripe!

"H'yep, I see it... but how ah we evah goin to get ovah to it?"

Hey, I spotted it spiderman, you handle the logistics.

Ledge is located a mere twenty feet across, across rock so smooth it shines like a mirror, no handholds, no toeholds.

"If we can get up, h'yep... if we can just get... get up up, h'yep... up a little highah heah... highah... highah, highah, h'yep, highah than the ledge ovah theah, h'yep, now... now you know what we can do?"

No?

"We can leap!"

Nooooooo!

"H'yep! We can LEAP FROM HEAH   OVAH TO HEAH!"

Chipper does one of his fabulous leaps, straight across the face! And the boy lands on his feet.

"Now how's that fah some fancy footwohk?"

Betsy would normally pause in admiration, at the boldness in conception, the gracefulness in execution, but she has momentarily swallowed her tongue. Though with a small cough, some retching...

"Damn gihl, you've got my neck all wet!"

Thlorry, thlorry, juth a thlip of the thlongue, thlo to thpleak.

"Bet you theah ah even bettah thrills ahead."

A motht comflothing thlought.

This ledge at least allows them to walk on their own two, four feet, spiral up and around, take them within a hundred and fifty feet of what must be the summit, except who can tell with the lip jutting so far outward — that's out over the water — out over the rocks — a three hundred and fifty foot drop — which means that not only do they have to continue the climb upwards, but do it while suspended outwards and downwards!

"My granpappy used to say mountain climbin was like life…"

The family philosopher in his moments of sobriety.

"…once you've stahted you've got to keep headin, because the othah way is back down flat wheah you began."

And we don't want to do that.

"Stuhbees always finish what they stahted."

Wise words to l-l-live by young Chipper, and equally wise words to d-d-die by.

"Stop lookin down, only makes mattahs wohse."

True. The drop. The rocks. The water.

"And suck in that tongue!"

Yes Sir! Teeth clinched! Eyes forward!

Chipper ducks beneath the overhang and proceeds on hands and knees, groping with both palms at the underside of the promintory.

"Feels like a giant teat."

How comforting.

What catches his attention is a thin vein of a cleft extending the entire length to the tip, about the width of his hand.

"Don't know gihl, this is beginnin to look difficult!"

And this from a veteran who even in his most hacked out handbook-in-hand mountain climber's daydreams has never imagined a situation quite like this. Though daring times demand timely dares. Chipper pries his clenched fists into the extended crack in the rock and with a fist-over-fist fissure pressure makes his way — FIST/FEET FIST/FEET FIST/FEET — fishtailing with his legs — FIST/FEAT.

Betsy is strapped to his back and this time watching wide-eyed. Strange, she reflects, when you actually do face the end, the exact moment thereof, you watch, probably because you can't believe this is it, with no time left to do anything else but, not even blink, no, not when it's staring full face in front of you — full face in front — full — face — and finally he reaches the end of the crevice, the protruding tip of the lip and away out over the water and away down to the boulders below…

-thwulpp! There goes her tongue again.

…because the tip presents a problem admitting of no expert solution. Hands swollen, feet dangling, jaw clinched, and nothing above the tip for him to grasp onto!

Soooo, Chipper does what he can do, he executes a one arm pull up of the muscle popping, tendon stretching, excruciating pain type, sort of a show off competition stunt, and he is flexed there in animated suspension while he slaps above his head with his other hand, the right one, blindly groping for any small chink in the rock. But there is none within reach — one of course, and that slightly out of reach.

Chipper has to lower himself for a second's breather, and things don't look good for the Eagle Scout as he hangs one fist from the promontory. But he pulls himself up again, gritting and groaning, muscle straining, and slapping around... up... there... around up there because there's got... got to be... "Betsy, bet you, theah's got to be somethin I can latch onto!"

Yeah right, there's got to be something, and Betsy being a head up on him, she extends that long neck of hers to see what she can see and *-ROOT! -ROOT!* What she sees she snaps onto, onto this twig growing in a shallow, and she hopes to high heaven it's got a long sucker tap root because — CLOMP! — she's got her teeth gritted tightly and tendons in her neck popping too! She holds on for dear life, dear dear life! And suddenly it's Chipper's turn to clutch onto her back — as he pulls, pulls himself — *hup pup, h'yup up and over* — elbows then knees onto this steep slope on the top of the outcropping, a slope that'd be an easy slide right back off with Betsy doing no better as the root gives and she's forced to take a big chomp into the only thing handy — *yi-yi-yi-yipes!* — CHIPPER'S BUTT! And he's scareaming about it! But does he scamper up that slippery rock slope faster than a jack rabbit with Betsy clasped to his ass? SCRAP-SCRATCH SCRAM SCRABBLE-FAST he does!

"Betsy? Betsy gihl?"

-unh?

"We'h ahright now. We'h at the top now."

-un hunh?

"So, so you've got to let go."

Whoops! Sorry. I'll open wide. Is that any better?

"Ohhh..."

She licks her lips. You've got a sweet tasting bum chum.

"...about the only good thing you can say about pain is it's bettah when it's ovah."

True!

And it is over, they're over, over the top, and the two of them can finally plop themselves down and heave heavy breaths they can, so loudly they don't hear two slanty eyed cats sauntering up either side of them.

"Will you take a look at those stahs!"

Betsy's too busy breathing to look.

"Can't believe how close they feel!"

Yaaaaaaaaaaaaaaaaaaaaaaaaaaanh!

Breathing stops. What was that?

The slight gloating hiss two cats make as they close in on their prey — a distinctive sort of sound that rolls Chipper over on all fours — best stance the human can take when confronted with a fierce jungle creature, domesticated canine to. Betsy's up, on eye-to-eye level… Four yellow cat's eyes in the bush, stepping slowly, elongated sleek slime seeping creep peeping creatures — CRACK! — a give-a-way signaling a pounce attack, and at that the cats SPRRRR-ING!

AND IT'S THE YELLOW OF THEIR EYES CHIPPER AND BETSY SEE FIRST — TIGER TIGER BURNING BRIGHT — EYES THAT ALIGHT FROM DARK SHADOWS — FOUR HUNDRED PLUS POUNDS OF MUSCLE AND FUR EACH — and not a few fangs — DIVING TOWARD THEM — and for some inexplicable reason Chipper and Betsy duck… duck?

BAM CRACK — CATS ATTACK — SPAT SLAP STAB SCRATCH! The two damn things smash smack into one another and tear, tear their entrails inside out, and it's only a matter of seconds before the both of them are shredded — which must mean it was some sort of domestic squabble to begin with.

Whatever. Betsy and Chipper do them the last honors of rolling their ravished remains off the rim — SPLASH! SPLASH! — 500 feet below.

The noise instantly alerting the QuotLink cruiser.

But time can be measured in lapses between crises, brief moments when two ol' buddies can huddle and stare up at the stars.

"Don't they just spahkle from way up high like this?" His arm wrapped around her stretched neck, her snout tucked in under his chin, snout and chin cocked upwards, beast and her man locked together.

And Betsy has to agree with him — *grr-rr-roar-ri-ous!*

RUMRUMRUM -RUMBA -RUMBA

"Whoa? What was that?"

Ground's trembling, that's what.

BUMBUMBUM -BUMPA -BUMPA

Rocks tumbling, accompanied by FIRE and SMOKE and NOISE and good God, what a STENCH!

"*Phew-ee* Betsy, this ain't no ohdinahry tremoh!"

I'd say not, not with this big sucker bonfire burning up behind us!

Intense, glowing red, vapors rising, vapors that sear leaves off trees, and ash, light, dry, hot, floating dense clouds of it. Seems El Snorro's awakening from his slumber and has brought a nightmare back along with him.

GRUMBLEGRUMBLE — TROUBLE AND STRIFE!

"Nevah seen an active volcano up close befah."

No and who wants to, although Betsy follows the fool over the edge. Though this close, a girl's got to have a look for herself too.

"Whoa!"

They approach the rim and stare down the chasm into another world, the primordial stuff that created the very ground on which they stand, stuff that will in due course wipe that ground right out from under them.

RUMBLERUMBLE — RUN FOR YOUR LIVES!

Betsy approaches with fear and trembling, and with her nose twitching. Rotten eggs? Chipper too is cautious, he sinks low to the quaking underfoot, almost to his knees. Both are speechless before such a sight.

"Nasty, nasty... goin t'cause a heap a'trouble befo it bu'ns itself off."
"Salaam?"
"Hey, how yo two doin? Looks like yo made yo way."
"How'd you get up heah?"
"Took the elevata."
"Elevatah, who'd install an elevatah up a volcano?"
"QuotLinks, tha's who, they ain' about t'scale the cliff ev'rytime they gots t'do theia bus'ness."
"Volcano's a business these days?"
"Big time, an profitable. Why yo could supply the enti'e planet with ee'lectricity if yo could ha'ness one tenth the powa this little baby gots."
"Little!"
"El Snorro ain' nowhea the size a'Mount Etna o Colima which makes it a prime candidate fo tappin — an tha's ezactly wha' QuotLink Inc Geo-Tha'mal Division intends t'do."
"QuotLink Inc?"
"Tha's right, they owns the min'ral rights t'the island, had t'pay off some mighty impo'tant fo'ces t'get control a'ev'rythin unda'ground."

Which may explain why surface resources such as tourism and native craft industries have never been developed.

"A'cou'se the whole island's slated fo co'mercial exploita'tion – project's hush hush, propri'etary rights and industrial secrets, fea's a'co'porate espionage an such, fo'eign gove'ment inte'vention, specially the French who could still lay an old colonial claim — but I'll give yo two the grand tou' so yo can see fo yoself."

FWOOOM! FWOOOM!

Better be quick about it. Doesn't look like El Snorro's commercial potential has been tapped quite yet.

"How come you know so much about these cohporate secrets Salaam?"

"I's a insida on account a'my bi'th. My fatha's from Bed Sty, but my motha's a islanda, Big Mama MaGee, woman's a fo'ce t'be reckoned with on this hea island…"

Women seem to be the only force on the island.

"…I keeps comin back regula'ly t'visit – an check on my invest'ments."

Which makes you the brother-in-law of that no-account Carlton.

"Must've mentioned befo, I's gots ev'ry cent a'my savin's tied up in sha'es a'QuotLink Inc – HO OH! Get down! Quick!"

"What is it?"

"QuotLink patrol – they gots o'da's t'shoot intruda's on sight."

"Thought you wah a majoh shaheholdah?"

"They'd soon as shoot me too."

That what they do with prickly shareholders these days?

QuotLink patrol STOMPSTOMPSTOMPS on by.

"Man, tha' was close. We gots t'stay on the lookout each step we go."

"What's wohth the risk of seein Salaam?"

"Don' ask bro, but befo we'a through, yo an yo pooch hea is goin t'have PhDs in ee'conomic re'al'ity – believes yo me. Besides it's a long hike back down by foot."

"'Spose it's bettah to know than not to know."

"An know yo will."

RUM RUM DUMBER BALL – DON'T SWALLOW THE HYPE!

"OK now, le's move out. Keep low." Salaam takes point, Chipper next, with Betsy bringing up the rear. "Yo spot a patrol, give out a whistle."

-wh-whi-whith-whith… Girl never could manage a whistle.

"Don't quite undahstand why these QuotLinks ah puttin so much effoht into guahdin hot rocks?"

"Right off it's clea' yo don' know nothin bout runnin a giant inte'national co'poration, cause the first lesson yo learns is that t'make the big money yo gots t'hide yo assets in some otha country, an tha's jus' what QuotLink Inc's done did."

What's molten lava trading at on today's market?

"Island this remote's the last place on ea'th anybody's eva goin t'look. Uncha'ted. Undeveloped. Unspoiled. No taxman, no spy plane's eva goin t'come snoopin, none a'them envi'onmental groupies neitha."

"Got a lot to hide, these QuotLinks?"

"Ev'rythin buried right hea unda'neath ou feet."

SQUISH SQUISH

"Yo's walkin cross a'trillion dolla empire."

Ground under their feet is riddled with running rivlets and steaming geysers.

"What ah they cookin up down theah?"

"Depends whea yo steps. Defense Depa'tment's right unda hea — palmsize rocket launcha's, clusta fuck bombs, those plastic explosives the te'rorists use t'day, tons a'deadly viruses an nasty gasses — whateva's been banned by the Geneva Convention they gots stocked on the shelves."

"Whoa!" Chipper steps lightly.

"Hey. Saves yo av'rage demo'cracy the embar'assment a'producin the stuff on theia own."

Along with the convenience of one-stop shopping.

"'Cou'se they's manufactu'in a full line a peacetime products too, medical mi'racles like fresh grown o'ganic replacement pa'ts in the Bio-Med Division ova thea unda'neath those rocks — company this size's gots t'diva'sify. Then they's big inta off-shore bankin, numba'd accounts no ISR's eva goin t'crack, not that they's goin t'come lookin anyway."

"This wheah you bank Salaam?"

"Yo gots t'be jokin. Takes twenty million minimum t'open up a account — yo should see the size a'theia vault!"

SQUISH SQUISH — must be what they mean by liquid assets.

"How about illegal drugs?"

"They ain' got time fo that shit. They's legit. Afta the devestation a'the last e'ruption, they's had t'-…"

"When was this last eruption?"

"Yea ago bout now."

"A yeah ago!"

"El Sno'ro seems t'have got it all out a'his system."

"Don't recall readin about a volcano eruptin down these pahts."

"They keeps events in the Caribbean pretty much unda wraps, why go an get folks in the States upset bout much a'nothin — besides, QuotLink Inc's done replaced catastrophe wi ingenuity, along wi buildin hundreds a'billions in sha-holda value."

"This hot mud's up to my knees Salaam."

Betsy's swimming in it.

"Who ah these QuotLinks anyway?"

"Yo mean the o'rig'nal models?"

"I 'spose."

"The Elda's, the COs, they's priv'leged, an a whole dif'rent breed from the ground grunts who've been chasin round afta us. The Elda's fo'med this secret society way back afta the wa — gen'rals an diplomats, industrialists, financee's, a see'lection from ev'ry side…"

"Which wa'?"

"…Wo'ld Wa One. Then's when they decided t'go co'porate, spread theia assets out ova the globe. That way whetha theia own country won o lost wouldn' matta much, they'd have a stake in whoeva su'vived."

"Smaht."

"Nobody accuses the Council a'Elda's a'bein stupid."

"But they'd be a hundred yeahs oah oldah by now!"

"Goddamn mi'racles, ev'ry one."

"What about these othah kind of QuotLinks?"

"Military types, they's built solely fo durabil'ity."

"Built?"

"They's gots ev'ry body pa't imaginable sto'ed in theia ea'thquake-proof bunka righ' beneath ou feet, an a brand new stainless steel assembly plant comin on stream within a month."

"You mean these QuotLinks ah bein put togethah from scratch?"

"Toe t'head an most a'what goes on in between."

"How do they manage that?"

"They sta't out wi a stump a'somebody, implant this, transplant that, an grind out a whole line a'combat infantry t'spec, a'long wi theia non-coms."

"No way?"

"Yah they do, an wi the way medical technology's advancin, they soon won't need t'rely on new live recruits fo nothin."

"Wheah do they get theih supply of anatomicals?"

"Battlefield salvage back in the beginnin — a'ways been plenty a'that layin round the playgounds a'Europe — 'cept when tha' sou'ce dried up, they had t'sta't impo'tin theia spare pa'ts from Asia — they gots themselves on some fast track trade pact with China. Whole boatloads a'prisona's been arrivin on a daily basis."

That's how Captain Blight and the mutinous crew of the *Charon* fit in.

"Prisonahs! Ain't right!"

"Chippa, yo done gots a cause fo ev'rythin. Wo'ld's a'bout business, globalization, not humanitarian issues — ain' yo lea'nt that lesson yet?"

So it wasn't simply soup on board the *Charon*, I was being earmarked for some rich bitch poodle's hip replacement.

"Cahvin up prisonahs has got to be illegal even on open ocean."

"Hey, don' know, don' ask. Basic principle a'free trade. Whateva I can't buy locally o legally, some fo'eigna's goin t'have t'su'ply fo the lowest price possible — besides, theys gots nothin but people ova thea, an fresh — freshness is ev'rythin in the body pa'ts business."

"How about theih private pahts?"

"Have some decency bro. I don' go askin no pa'sonal questions — though I hea'd ruma's QuotLinks pass on those."

"No balls?"

That's it, spade them, makes them as docile and obedient as pups.

"QuotLinks mo'n make up fo whateva they lacks in raw ambition."

"So these Eldahs, they must've traded in damn neah evahry ohgan and bone they wah bohn with by now?"

"Yo betta believes it, they's got a whole new lease on life, full fact'ry reconditionin, lifetime wa'ranty on most movin pa'ts — why they could live fo'eva theo'retic'ly."

Only way to live forever is theoretically.

"And these othah, these lessah than elite QuotLinks, they wah stitched togethah from the staht out of off-the-shelf pahts?"

"Yo gots it."

"Means none of them ah any longah human."

"Some so'ta is, some so'ta ain't."

"Sohta?"

-*mm*, new hybrid, sort-of-humans.

"It's simply a'matta a'te'minology. Le's say fo ezample yo heart gets busted. Yo tellin me yo wouldn't go straight out an buy yoself a new one?"

"Maybe. It's no mah than a fuel pump really."

"Right, an tha' don' make yo no less human."

"I've heahd stories about transplant folks havin eerie feelin's theih donoh's still livin inside."

Which would explain a sudden craving for Szechwan.

"Yo still gots yo own stomach an kidneys, an miles a'ol' intestines."

"True."

"So yo is still yo."

Intestines make the man.

"Don't know though if I'd evah want to go walkin around in somebody else's body."

Particularly without a set of goldens.

"Yo breaks down some night side-a'the road, yo'd go hoppin in fo a ride wi a'most any strangah."

"But 'spose you no longah look like you, ah you really still you?"

"Question ain' philosophical, question is whetha o'not yo can affo'd the full physical make-ova."

"But what would it be like stahrin in the mihror evahry mohnin at somebody else?"

"Then go piecemeal, jus' sta't redecoratin the interio."

"Somewheah along the line you'h no longah you, you'h somethin entihely diffahrent."

No soul, no sense of self.

"O don' go quib'lin wi me. Point is QuotLink Inc's in a primo position t'co'na the wo'ld ma'ket on life!"

At a premium price!

"Why is it folks is a'ways resis'tant t'change? Some scientist finds a cure fo the common cold, an he's hailed as a hero. Some comp'ny designs a wo'k-around on death, and they's criticized fo bein greedy."

"'Spose some add-on piece becomes obsolete?"

"So spring fo the premium package, locks yo onto a free upgrade path, somethin goes wrong all's yo gots t'do is telephone technical suppo't."

What about *-brr-rr-rains?*

"Wha's tha' dog moanin bout now?"

"Brains. What do these chahractahs do fah brains?"

"Tha's the best invention yet. Brains is made t'orda, no obsolete o'ganic pa'ts, jus' ee'lectronic gizmos wi state'a-the-art computa chips — gots t'live with a coolin fan buzzin in yo ear, but tha's a small price t'pay fo the convenience of a 50,000 gig RAID array."

"What about youh past, youh misty coloahed memohries?"

"They's all downloaded. Yo can rearrange them any which way, touch up the snapshots, trash whateva haunts yo."

"That's impressive."

"It's the ee'lectronic age, mankind's been finally reinvented t'meet the challenges a'the Twenty Fu'st Centu'ry — bout the only thin they ain' got right yet is eyeballs, those is 100% recycled human — means a QuotLink'll go blind befo he goes batty — but otha'wise they'll su'vive beyond the next millennium."

"Sounds like they've got life pretty much sacked."

"Patented."

"Unless they hang out alongside that pohtable nucleah reactah too long."

"Yo keeps ha'pin on bout nothin. One, they gots teflon-coatin fo skin. Two, that handy-andy reacto yo is knockin happens t'powa all theia assembly lines an refrigera'tion units, the lights in the mines an down a'long the hallways in He-…"

"Mines? What mines?"

"Lava mines. They gots the island kids wo'kin shifts round the clock, excavatin caves so's they can open up theia new unda'ground industrial pa'k on schedule."

"Ain't that exploitation of minahs?"

"Thea yo goes again, talkin humanitar'ianism when we should be thankful fo the extra dolla's flowin into the loco economy — plus we no longa gots t'cope wi petty street crime o'break-ins, no fleecin the tou'ists — these kids is payin theia own way wi a little ha'd wo'k an no time left ova fo any a'that adolescent rebel'ion — proof positive, yo primes the economic pump an yo drains the bottom out a'yo social problems."

"What about child laboh laws?"

"Island's an independent colony these days, QuotLink Inc makes its own rules."

"How young do the kids staht in?"

"Leven, twelve, wheneva they's big enough t'lift a shovel — see these mines, they ain' as bad as they used t'be. Kids get out fo air least three times a day."

"How long's a shift?"

"Twelve hou's. An the pay's goin rate fo day labo in the Ca'ribbean."

Which is?

"Two fifty a hou plus lifetime dusty lung benefits."

Sounds sort-of-humane.

"Don't know Salaam, somethin about all this don't sound right to me, like these QuotLinks, they just don't sound nohmal."

"They ain't no'mal. An yo neva wants t'get nvolved in no bu'ness dealin's wi them neitha. They can out think yo ev'ry move — why wi the Slog 2010 central processo tha' comes standa'd equipment, they can calculate the bucks fasta than a Big Two accountin firm."

"Hey. I'm just a Maine boy, play guitah, sing songs, don't evah intend to meet up with any of these creatuhes, not if I can help it."

"Yo neva knows when yo might bump up against one. They's been designed t'blend in wi the indigenous population."

"So how can you tell them apaht from the rest of us?"

"Theia heads is way bigga, way way bigga. See they throws away theia ol' heads cause the regula issue cranium is much too small fo them t'cram in all theia advanced equipment."

-roh, that's who's been supplying the native industry with skulls to shrink.

"Lots of folks I've met have big heads, so how would I recognize one if I saw one?"

"The eyes. They neva seem t'get the eyes aligned right, somethin bout the way they look straight through yo, this greedy stare an no remo'se, not a blink's wo'th, an bad breath, choke yo up comin an goin. Got so I don' botha t'even say hello, dispense wi any a'the pleasantries — an neva go askin mo questions than yo needs t'know. Questions make QuotLinks suspicious."

"Tell me squahe Salaam, they plannin on takin ovah the wohld?"

"Le's jus' say tha' once they gets this new plant they's buildin up t'speed, ain' no end a'how many a'themselves they can roll out in a twenty-fou' hou' wo'kday."

PLUME! PLUME! Through the flues.

"So what's with this sneakin around Salaam, thought you wah all buddy buddy with some of these QuotLinks?"

"Ain' nobody on a fi'st name basis with a QuotLink Chippa, they tolerates me cause I knows who's who on the island, otha'wise they don' botha wi no introductions."

"No?"

"It's all code numba's an' titles wi them, yes sa, no sa, escuse me fo livin sa — see it ain' like thea's some holy vision leadin this crowd, no mission statement neitha, no common bond o'cam'raderie, only int'rest they share is maintainin the cash flow."

"Sounds mighty uninspihrin to me, but then who cohpohrate can you trust?"

INTRUDERS! INTRUDERS NEAR THE REACTOR!

"Duck!"

STOMP STOMP STOMP STOMP STOMP

"Damn! You'h right about theih eyes!"

A squad of QuotLink irregulars passes close by.

Piercing.

"Wondah if they evah sleep?"

No dreams I'd want to watch.

"Ain' tha' much fu'tha we gots t'go. We'll grab a quick look at Limbo Village, then we begins ou descent."

"Limbo Village?"

Our descent?

"Step right up on this rise hea an have a look fo yoself."

-*rulp!*

"Damn!"

The devastation runs down the mountainside clear to the coastline — no fauna, no flora, not even a stick — no monkeys, no parrots, no lizards nor frogs — here and there an intrepid centipede.

-*hmm*, the newly paved lava slide Big Mama MaGee mentioned.

"Le's hike out a bit so's yo two can get the full pictu'e."

The entire eastern side of the island is terraced in new red tiled villas, all whitewashed and gleaming in the glow of halogen lights set up for round-the-clock earth mover machinery and construction crews, nothing over two story except for a massive cathedral in the center.

"Behold! I gives yo Limbo Village!"

-*wholp!*

"Whoa!"

"Yo is lookin at the fo'most model in a planned retia'ment community wi some half million units when the plan is ultimately completed, condos, managed ca'e…"

"Looks desahted."

"They's jus' about gea'd up fo the grand openin, Then yo watch, those baby booma's flush wi cash a goin t'invade, live out theia golden yea's wi ev'ry convenience imaginable: five 36 hole pro go'f cou'ses, deep basin marina, showboat casino featurin 50s musicals, duty-free liqua on ev'ry street co'na, fresh fudge outdoo' cafe, discount fact'ry outlets… it'll put Palm Beach an Boca Raton on the auction block."

The marina at the base is already active, boats unloading containers of cargo. Betsy spies the Gambler's Riverboat with a gaudy marquee anchored there permanently, and off in the distance the blinking lights of an airport.

"Impressive!"

"Rivals anythin the Saudis own on the Riviera."

"But bahe rock ain't my idea of an island paradise."

"Well it's goin t'take some time fo the trees t'grow back, but Limbo Village's got the one amenity no place in Flo'ida can match…"

"Somethin bettah than Wondah Wohld?"

"…QuotLink Inc's Miracle Medical Centa, smack dab theah in the middle…"

The basilica with the golden dome?

"…whea these rich ol' folks can get a quick fix along wi the promise a'life eva'lastin."

-roh!

"One mo prime ezample a'how that costly military resea'ch can be put t'peace time comma'cial use, lift the economy right out a'the doldrums."

"Don't know, but it looks to me like you guys had bettah cut El Snohro in on a fat piece of the action."

"QuotLink Inc's got its own set a'powa'ful financial pa'tna's."

"Secretive Swiss banka's?"

"Mo powa'ful than that."

"The New Democrats?"

"Yo ain' goin t'believe me, not 'til yo sees it fo yoself."

"Least give me a hint."

INTRUDERS! INTRUDERS!

Betsy's ears spring up.

INTRUDERS ON THE RIM!

"Oops, sounds like we'd betta be movin the tou' bus along."

"This new medical technology they've got…"

"Gots t'walk fast, talk fasta."

"…this goin to be available eventually fah us folks left behind on Minicahe?"

"No bro, only a millionai'a can affo'd the complete make-ova."

"So the rest of us ah scheduled to croak as usual?"

"Tha's the way the numba's seem t'crunch."

And dogs? *-wha rr-ra-ra rub-rout rrogs?*

"Ain' cost effective doggy-do, not when the pound's full a'cheap puppy substitutes, besides no pets allowed in Limbo Village, no nasty children neitha."

-humph! Perfectly planned community for the daft and the clueless.

INTRUDERS! INTRUDERS SIGHTED IN THE VICINITY OF LIMBO VILLAGE!

"Damn. Le's ci'cle round back. QuotLinks'd neva suspect us t'do that."

Route back takes them along the far perimeter of the volcano's rim. Ground under their feet is firmer, but a thin fiery rivlet of red rushes alongside their path.

"What's that up ahead, pahked neah the cratah, a giant cement mixah?"

"That big tracto-traila?"

"H'yep."

"Tha's one a QuotLink Inc's most ingenious inventions yet — a po'table nuclea reacto."

"A pohtable what!"

"Nuclea reacto. They's usin it t'keep all theia ente'prises crankin."

I thought they were trying to tap geo-thermal?

"Why would they evah pahk a reactah theah?"

"Easia t'chuck the waste inta the volcano than t'shipit t'Nevada."

Vapor plumes flare up near the trailered container.

"Le's hope it don' go explodin, not while we is passin by."

"You mean you'h not wohried about the effects of a melt-down scattahrin contaminated pahticals all across the Cahribbean?"

"Hey, QuotLinks is flush, they gots cash t'pay fo any unfo'tunate catas'trophe."

FWOOOM go the plumes! *FWOOOM! FWOOOM!*

"Will yo two hu'ry along, this ain' some kind a'movie thrilla."

"Wheah exactly ah we headin Salaam?"

"Hea, slip unda the brush…"

Brush nothing, prickly briars!

"…hush up… round those rocks…"

-hoo -haw -hee -hoh, hot rocks, as in sizzling.

"…an ova the edge into the crata…"

"Into the cratah!"

"Jus' go! They ain' about t'follow us down hea. QuotLinks can't tolerate extreme changes in temp'eture."

What, like we can *-hoh -hoh?*

"Whoa, ground's gone wobbily soft!"

And what are these puddles of bubbly goo?

INTRUDERS! INTRUDERS! INTRUDERS IN THE LAVA BOG!

Lava bog?

"Watch whea yo step. We make it through this mine field, we can fin'ly proceed wi ou descent in peace — down whea nobody goes, down whea nobody knows."

"Down fuhthuh into this fuhnace?"

The three have to leap from rock to rock, leap over rivlets of red.

"Yo a'ways said yo wanted t'see a active volcano up close."

"Up close, not inside!"

"Stick wi me Chippa, I's goin t'show yo mo than a volcano...."

Betsy's pads are fuming.

"...I's goin t'show yo the greatest wonda a'the wo'ld, an at no extra cha'ge — no siree, oppo'tunity like this don' happen ev'ryday."

Thankfully.

"What oppohtunity ah you talkin about?"

"We gots an open vent clea t'the ea'th's co'e."

-corr?

"Ain' no deepa yo can go."

"No way we can withstand this heat Salaam."

And sulfur and brimstone aren't much good for the delicate tissues of the lungs either.

Still they proceed, the three — black dog, black man and white — surrounded by flames, the kind that burneth but consumeth not, rock burbling into froth, geysers shooting like roman candles into the night sky.

INTRUDERS! INTRUDERS HAVE ENTERED HELL!

"Hell?"

Hell!

"Will yo two jus' walk, spa'e me the talk!"

THE DESCENT

"Damn Salaam, can't see shit wheah I'm headin." Betsy nose to his cuff.
"Ain' nothin t'see — not yet anyways."
cough! cough! Smoke so thick they can barely breathe, and — *e'youch!* — hot hot on dainty bare pads, though more like a sauna than a furnace.
"Hold up, we'a hea."
"Heah wheah?"
"Day a'Judgment, Day a'Doom! O Lo'dy Lo'dy, save us some room!"
"Say what?"
With which incantation the haze lifts like a curtain. Eyes and mouths gape down, for they are standing on the rim of a canyon, vast, round, paved smooth like the concrete spillway off a gigantic dam, then plummeting fathoms further layer upon layer of jagged rock, lava streams overflowing and at bottom a violent white violet boil.
"Jesus H!" Chipper adjusts the dark wire rim spectacles he's been sporting and stares full face into the inferno.
"Yo is lookin inta the very depths a'Hell."
So this is how it ends — as was foretold. Betsy hangs her neck over the edge, sniffs. Brimstone.
"Fi'a bu'ns, consumes whateva remains til ev'rythin in creation's tu'ned ta ash, wa'mth recedes ta cold, the light ta da'kness, life unta death."
The sight, the sounds, cries far off. Betsy growls.
"What is it gihl, somethin suspicious?" Chipper squints. "Is it my eyes playin tricks on me, oah ah theah fools down theah climbin the walls?"
Indeed. Bodies piling upon bodies, hundreds of legs upon shoulders and arms reaching up, this pyramid of limbs building toward the top of the spillway, one, this intense little dude within arm's length. Chipper reaches down, grabs a hand and yanks him up and over.
Dude dusts himself off, nods, darts away.

"Wheah's he goin in such a huhry?"

"Sumo Ma't's just up the road."

"Sumo Maht! You mean they've got convenience stohes down heah?"

"Hell yes! Friend a'mine owns the rimside franchise, rakes it in — slices, chips, ice cream on a stick, six pack a'cold beea when the shift's ova."

"You mean that man's on a packy run?"

"Folks get a little stir crazy night afta night, same old routine, so they scrapes up theia spa'e change an sends a runna off fo cigarettes."

"Cigahrettes! People still smokin in Hell?"

"Ha'd habit ta kick, 'specially down hea, I mean, the'a ain't ezactly much in the way a'positive reinfo'cements."

"Thought Hell was supposed to be hahsh, etahnity of hahd labah?"

"Jus an endless thu'd shift with an occasional break fo a cigarette."

"S'pose that's punishment enough."

"Besides Slug Rites is sellin fo seven fifty a pack."

"Seven fifty! That's highway rob'hry!"

"Depends which side a'the road yo walks on. Doin time ain' about crime, an thou shalt not steal don' say nothin bout price gougin."

Dude comes racing back by, flip pack of Slug Rites in one hand, six pack in the other. He waves, vaults the rim and goes sliding down the spillway.

"Whoa!" Chipper watches as he disappears fast from view. "Anybody evah try and escape?"

"Thea ain' no escapin Hell, besides afta mo'n one attempt, theys gets really pissed an kicks yo butt down a level o two, an the only thing wo'se than the graveya'd shift's the graveya'd itself."

INTRUDERS! INTRUDERS IN HELL!

"Betta keep movin. Ain' got time ta jus stand hea an gawk."

"We ain't plannin on headin down into that pit, ah we?"

"Got ta see what ya can see bro, only got one lifetime t'look. And thea's nine levels below with two mo cu'rently unda construction."

"Mean they'h still buildin Hell?"

"La'gest ea'th-movin project eva attempted, billion ya'ds a'molten magma an enough concrete an reba ta extend the great wall a'China ta the No'th Pole. Quotlink Inc's Engineerin Division's the prime contracta though lots a'locals have snagged theia share a'the proceeds."

"Figuahed they would've planned ahead, way back from the beginnin."

"Nobody done planned on that post wa Baby Boom, wo'ld population doublin what, ev'ry thu'ty yea's o so? Ev'rybody elbowin ev'rybody else, wa, mo wa, ethnic cleansins, tribe afta tribe, religion afta religion, estimated hundred million refugees wo'ld-wide, ter'ra tactics comin at yo from all sides, sma't bombs, dumb bombs, a'med satellites zappin out a'the skies, not enough schools o hospitals, food, wata sho'tages, pova'ty whea'eva yo look, children sta'vin in theia mama's a'ms, an no betta down hea — chronic ovacrowded conditions, ne'a riots, why they's got people sleepin on top a'one anotha, an not fo no fun neitha…"

"People still get it on in Hell?"

"Cou'se they still gets it on — told yo thea ain' that much t'do down hea — still get it on — yo white guys a'ways askin the dumbest questions."

True, white guys do ask dumb questions, whereas we dogs are more intuitive, plus we like to get it on ourselves, that's if we still have our innards intact. Wag the tail, hello hello, mind if I sniff around, back down and underneath here some, bit of a lick, remember the thrills of my girlhood years. Even still, Betsy's surprised by some things she's seen, and she's a black dog too, but then color, gender, sex, never mind genus or specie, bottom line no one gives a hoot if it interferes with their making a buck. Take mammals for example, hunt them to extinction, then herd what's left into barns or drive through zoos, biodiversity or outright perveristy whichever way you turn, mankind has the exclusive — really makes you wonder aloud whether or not *-rr-rare rare-ro-rogs row rear?*

"Swea bro, this dog sounds like she's talkin."

"She's just wondahrin if thea's any dogs down heah in Hell?"

"No dog's neva done no ha'm that'd wind him up in a place like this!"

Her — and true, true — Hell's surely a human invention.

INTRUDERS! INTRUDERS IN HELL!

"Quick, this way, befa they unleash them blood-thu'sty hounds on us."

Thought you said there were no dogs down here?

"Any resemblance between the Hounds a'Hell an yo av'rage domestic canine is pu'ely coincidental – duck down this da'k alley. We'll blend in."

One dark alley after another, passed rows of dark brick tenements, and they're blending in except for Chipper whose hair is glowing white like it's been recently radiated.

"Is it just me, oah do you guys have this funny feelin in yuh bones?"

Betsy has a funny feeling of her own, a tingle here, a tingle there as she cautiously marks their trail.

"I heah somethin up ahead."

Like a noise, like music, like a brass band, like slightly out of tune, and lights and bright carnival colors and people. The closer the three get, the thicker the crowd, folks of all ages and sex, the younger among them almost if not entirely naked and prancing in the street masked. Elaborate floats pass by, bedecked with beauty queens in beads and feathers and varied genders waving and tossing kisses, tiny packets too — the crowd desperately shoving and grabbing for them, samples it seems of class C and D substances — each float sponsored by a main line pharmaceutical firm. There are balloons too with corporate logos and confetti streaming down from wrought iron balconies. Betsy's ears curl in the commotion.

"What's this, Mahdi Gras?"

"Last dance befo doom."

No matter, as Chipper dives directly into the center, these two young beauties bumping and grinding him right into the rush. "*Whoa-hoa!* Let's rock'n'roll!" Which they do. "Eithah of you sweetheahts got a name oah speak English?"

No and no, though one's tall and broad shouldered Nordic with ample bare boobs. Or how about her friend here who's Asiatic, petite and has a neckline that plunges way down her back to the crack of her ass?

Chipper's impressed and dispenses with mere formalities himself, sheds his jumpsuit, and since he eschews underwear, he's stark raving naked except for his sneakers. Gets the two beauties grinding harder. Though on closer inspection the blond's pale on pale, a bit bluish under thick layers of foundation with a scar that jags clear across her throat. Not that any of this slows her down, she yanks a vial out of her purse, takes a snort and hands it off to her friend who is thinner than thin, veins popped and terribly excitable. She lingers over the vial longingly, lovingly, then lifts her pretty little head, all sweet ringlets and a smile, pupils behind a rhinestone mask dilated the size of quarters. She offers the vial to Chipper. Hey, he's not one to offend and since neither of them fell into a swoon, damn fool takes a sniff. Something chemical sets his nostrils twitching as he inhales even deeper. Heart thumping, head banging, he's ready for the next round, tiny orange tabs out of a tossed packet that set each of them into gyration. In an instant the three are the focus of attention, Chipper bouncing up and down, six, eight, ten feet or better. Draws a crowd, a reggae band for accompaniment and hoots and hollers urging him on.

Betsy retires to the sidelines with a sigh, she might have been quite the party animal in her younger years, but age has taken its toll and keeping an eye on Chipper in this ghoulish crowd is going to occupy her every minute.

The parade, with Chipper bounding high up and low down, extends a mile's length along the main thoroughfare, which is a cut out replica of Bourbon Street – as fabricated by the designers of Quotlink Inc's highly successful amusement park subsidiary – each block featuring its own unique theme. There's the Pirates's Cove next to the captured Spanish galleon, though the sailors seem to be mixing quite freely with the local ladies. There's the French Quarter with mademoiselles lurking luridly in doorways, young monsieurs too for the overseas kink trade. Casinos cater to various tastes, slots in neon arcades, craps down alleyways, black jack stalls, and roulette in tiered chandelliered halls. China Town features cushy opium dens though none too quiet with firecrackers popping off by the pound — *pang pang pang pang pang pang pang* — along with a forty footed undulating dragon. Caribs from the many islands are the best and less dressed, but the contingent from Rio takes the grand prize for sheer beauty and pageantry, Jamaican steel bands and West African drummers, hard rock on the bed of a truck, plus country, punk, fusion and disco along with a regiment of marching Scots pipers. There are drag queens and motorcycle babes, cowboys from Texas, Aussies, East Enders, denizens of Key West alongside swells off the Côte d'Azur. Count no one out: barristers, bankers, brokers, barbers, busboys, blokes, bruisers and broads from the world over, some authentic though most mere observers who like Chipper fit in anywhere there's a crowd, good music and an open bar.

Chipper gets stuck at one such curbside counter, downing pints of Belfast Trigger Ale with the two Miss Global runner-ups, so Betsy saunters over, one smile with fangs from a black bitch is all it takes to scare the two bimbos away. She hops up on the barstool next to Chipper.

"Theah yuh ah gihl, wohried yu'd gotten lost in the crowd." As he tosses down his pint. "Damn! Is this a pahty oah what? Free booze, gohgious gals galoah and ev'rybody gettin down and dihrty in full public view."

Betsy hangs out her tongue and thumps her tail.

"Right — 'scuse me suh, what've you got on tap fah the little lady?"

"Smack, crack, coke, crystal meth or pharmaceutical grade morphine. Fixings are extra and clean."

"Whoa, no reefah?"

"Man, what are you, overage?"

"'Spose anothah draw a'Triggah Dahk'll have to do."

Betsy pounds with the tail. *-rr, did you forget someone?*

"Damn, sohry — 'scuse me? The little lady heah needs a drink too."

"Fresh out of Shirley Temples."

How did he know?

"Bottled watah will do."

"That costs."

Chipper goes to search his pockets, but discovers that next to his golden nuggets, he's fresh out of change. "Wheah's my clothes?"

Ball wadded up in Betsy's mouth is where.

"Nevah leave the house without a few bucks on me."

-rr-row about the twenty you have stuffed in your shoe?

"Done spent that. This dude in a top hat had some dynamite Extra X."

Then I'll have what he's having, thanks. She reaches over and takes a puff off one of the girls' smoldering cigarello.

"Nevah expected Hell to be such a rousah pahty, did you?"

Makes sense, if you think about it — Betsy slurps at her beer, dark yuk, where a fine pilsner would be preferable — they would have to provide some venue for people to purge themselves before being forced to face the trials of eternal damnation.

Etahrnal damnation. The very thought gives Chipper the chills.

Then zip up the jumpsuit stud, that is, if you're through flaunting yourself for the evening.

"Damn." He steps into it. "Got to give some sehrious considahration to givin up on the sauce, you know, befah it gets me in some tehrible trouble."

Terrible trouble. You even sniff at a bottle of beer and you're in trouble — not to mention all that other stuff you've been sampling.

"Whoa! Suddenly got the spins wicked fiehce."

"Spins?" Fellow on the stool otherside of Betsy leans over. "Chew on one of these." He offers Chipper an open tin.

"What ah they?"

"Basically bicarbonate of soda laced with codine, will cure the dry heaves just as effectively."

"Appreciate the offah." Chipper pops two.

Do you ever stop to consider what you are so casually introducing into your system?

"Nice!" He smiles, and add in the hair glow, he almost looks beatific.

"Manufacture them myself." Fellow hands Chipper his card. "Here's my cell phone in case you need a speedy delivery. Tin costs $25, two for $45."

"Wohth evahry penny."

"Whatever it takes to keep the party going."

"I'll drink to that!" And Chipper does, slugs down what remains of his beer and orders another.

"You new?"

"'Spose I'd have to say yes."

"Everybody's in denial when they first arrive, can't believe it could happen to them, convinced they always had it under control, deserved better than the riffraff next door."

Them!

"Place ain't so bad considahrin."

"Starts to get to you night after night, could use the peace and quiet."

"Don't know, been pahtyin since I was thihteen, we get stahted eahly up nohth wheah I come from."

I can certainly attest to that.

"Any wife or kids?"

"None I'd admit to, snuck out on my couht ohdahed DNA test."

Through a fourth story skylight no less.

"Only suhe cuhe fah the hohrnies is the threat of a patahnity suit."

"Lost mine to tequila and cheap Tijuana whores, then switched to crack cocaine in LA, graduated fast to mainlining heroin in Beverley Hills."

"Whoa!"

"Man giving up's not a pretty sight."

"Finally fohced to refohm?"

"Reform. One program after another, two stints in the slammer. Wasn't back on the street more than half a day before I was at it again. OD'd in a fifteen buck a night motel room in Vegas on Christmas Eve, choking on my own barf — the instant I came up with the formula for these tablets."

"So *ah-, ah-* have you been remanded to etahnal dam- dam–…"

Damnation.

"…on account of yuh add- add-…"

Addictions.

"…cause of what was puhpohtedly found on youh possession?"

"Damnation? I suppose you could call a life out-of-control damnation. Living hell is how I'd describe it, nothing but a waste. And punishment? Sitting on a barstool rehashing events with any fool who wanders in."

"Sohry. Didn't mean to pry."

"No matter. Give a call when you start into the spins. We're all in this together, same masks strung out along the same street night after night, because no matter how you dress it up it's the same parade, the damned and their user buddies hanging on to one another for what's left of a life."

The fellow who looks to all the world as sober — buttoned down shirt, blue blazer, bow tie, clipped hair and a neat pencil mustache — climbs off his stool and wanders off into the crowd.

Chipper's one glum stare. "You don't think I'm that bad off, do you?"

Well, he did say there's an initial period of denial…

"I've nevah let myself go that fah."

…followed by what, a momentary realization of…

"Theah have been times, howevah."

…profound loss, a slide back into self-pity along with stronger dosages.

"Wintahs ah the wohst, waitin fah that damn spring thaw."

Blaming anything, anyone else except yourself.

"Finally some sunshine stahts to break through."

With a fresh crop of fuzzy buds.

"Nevah have done no hahd drugs."

But enough beer and reefer to permanently dull your senses.

"Ain't goin to end up heah, no way. Got to refohm — bah tendah, fresh round fah me and the little lady — got to do some sehrious thinkin."

Fresh round of denial.

"So thea yo a bro, been sea'chin ev'rywhea, should've known yo'd be tryin out the loco microbrew… what the… steady now!" Salaam catches Chipper just before he does this backflip off his stool.

Deep pangs of remorse no doubt setting in.

"Hold on now, hold on, ain' nothin we ain' been through befo — an we can grab a mug a'strong coffee at the Sumo Ma't, maybe a jelly donut, soba yo up befo we gets on with the toua."

That's it, add the caffeine shakes to the alcohol tremors, a shot of sugar — guaranteed to keep our boy off balance for the rest of the descent.

The three — Salaam who knows too well the fault lines that underlie each step, Betsy who has roamed the surface of this earth agelessly, and Chipper with his head cocked slightly upward toward the heavens — these three travel fearlessly forward, for life holds no mystery to those willing to open their eyes, hear the cries of the anguished and gaze undazed at the fate lurking ahead.

"OK now, you've got to explain, wheah have we been and wheah ah we headin. I need to know." Chipper has a 64 oz insulated mug of coffee in his hand, a mug with a lime green sumo wrestler stenciled on it, the kind the Sumo Mart gives away free to repeat customers, and he's walking toe to heel along as straight a line as he can.

Betsy's munching on the donut included in the $2.69 special, honey glazed chocolate with pink and yellow sprinkles.

"Ain' nothin that unfamilia' bout Hell, nothin yo ain' seen befo."

"Free booze."

"Tha's only cause this was a Monday night, rest a'the week yo pays premium price an no floo' show, jus pound'em down with the regula's."

"Same old same old."

"An why's that yo is prob'ly askin? Cause people's the same whea'eva they goes, 'cept hea they ain' goin no fu'tha. Soona than lata they gets trapped inta one a'the nine rings a'Hell."

Following the classical tradition.

"We goin to get to see all nine rings?"

"Try ou best — it's pa't o'the package — may even get a glance at the two new ultra-modu'n rings they's gettin ready fa the grand openin."

Eleven rings, that would be a fairly recent innovation.

"So Bouhbon Street, that was the fihst ring, right?"

"Excess. Excess used t'be a whole lot wo'se, but tha's the fu'st ring they done renovated, gave it a whole new look an feel, an nothin co'po'real."

"Cohpohreal?"

"Yo knows, physical punishment, straight jackets, isolation wa'ds, shock treatments an such, clap yo inta a padded cell fo lookin at'em crosseyed."

Like a nineteeth century asylum.

"They was still doin that shit all the ways up t'the 60s, befo they sta'ted handin out pills in street co'na clinics."

And releasing everyone back into the community.

"It's called consciousness raisin, talkin it through, with sensitivity sessions instead a'doin ha'd time."

All the while addicting people to tranquilizers and mood stabilizers.

"Excess t'day's mo like a holdin tank, yo knows, so'ta a detox centa whea yo stays jus so long, until yo gets yoself acclimated ta unfamilia su'roundins. Afta a time yo eitha soba's up some an sta'ts the descent on yo own o one night afta closin they figu'a yo's incor'igible an jus rolls yo drunk ova the rim. Whicheva way yo goes, yo soon sinks ta yo own level."

"Anybody jusy try and hang on in theah?"

"Month o two a'endless pa'tyin gets ta the best a'them — an the reason thea's some leeway hea is cause excess in itself ain' the wo'se a'the evils, not even close, the evil's the grief yo causes otha's."

Isn't evil always the grief you cause others, and sin the sense of shame or remorse you feel?

"Yo knows, yo listen long enough an yo can damn nea hea through this dog's accent."

My accent!

"Ahright now, let's say you decide to go seahchin these nine rings out on youh own. How do you know fah suhe when you reach the exact one?"

"Yo knows it the second yo gets thea bro, yo fits right in."

Not everyone condemned to Hell, however, suffers from excess.

"Tha's true, though most do. See excess is that cravin that grabs hold a'yo, strangles yo — could be drugs, could be money, sex o havin powa ova somebody else — excess seva's the fragile bond connectin yo ta otha folks yo should be carin 'bout instead a'usin o abusin."

But some souls are coldly calculating, couldn't be bothered with excess.

"They's esco'ted directly ta theia appropriate level."

"Whichevah way they get theah," Chipper tries a sip of the scalding hot coffee, "what's the punishment they've got to enduhe fah- fah-…"

Eternity.

"Kind fits the crime."

"Does it huht much?"

"Ain' like no Med'i'eval to'tua chamba, if tha's what yo thinkin."

So no one's being roasted alive or hung, drawn and quartered?

"Do they use youh body fah chemical expehrimentations oah sex?"

"None a'that fah out shit bro, tha's what I'm tryin t'tell yo. Hell's much mo lib'ral t'day, they plays with yo head instead."

Chipper takes another hot sip.

"Yo'll see. Devil, he's sly. He jus sits back an smirks, lets each individual stew in hu o his own natu'ly nasty acids…"

Gulp.

"…don't even botha ta stir, no sir…"

"Sounds somehow wohse."

"…an fo'eva an eva amen."

Hence the reason for giving us this extended preview.

"Gua'ranteed t'soba yo up quicka'n that green mug a'coffee yo is totin."

Their eyes slowly adjust to the darkness, glowing red embers underfoot, an occasional spark, only sound the crunch of their steps, though once in a while a far off cry, the silence forcing them to speak in whispers.

"So wheah's this place called Puhgatory, same soht of punishments I was told, but you've ahways got some hope of parole?"

"QuotLinks sold tha' franchise off t'some A'gentineans who run a string a'fitness centa's on the mainland. Yo wants ta wash yo sins away t'day, yo gots ta run the treadmills in place an sweat'em off like ev'rybody else."

"How did the QuotLinks gain so much control?"

"Some backroom deal they cooked up durin the last Republican administration. Contract was up fo bid, an QuotLink Inc had connections cause they'd been managin a string a'fo profit prisons down south. Ta nobody's su'prise they slid in with the lowest offa."

"So these QuotLinks ah ev'rywheah, an nobody suspectin?"

"One day soon they's goin ta own it all. Ev'rybody'll be wo'kin low wage in a QuotLink shop. Story a'history, new masta's, same slaves."

"But what about the Devil and his minions? They still a fohce?"

"A'cou'se the Devil's still a fo'ce fo no good, but most a'His minions bolted fo mo lucrative careea's on Wall Street decades ago."

"Leavin the QuotLinks to guahd the inmates down heah."

"Guests, they's called guests nowadays, pa'manent guests – QuotLink Inc fancies itself a sa'vice provida – see, sellin sa'vices ta the educated consuma's mo profitable bottom line than plain ol' exto'tion a'the masses."

"You mean not all people in Hell ah treated equal?"

"Yo know white boy, yo naïvete is sta'tin ta get on my nu'ves. Whea'd yo grow up anyway, some cave in the woods?"

If only you knew.

"Man ain' created equal an he don' treat nobody equal, women neitha. They's both out fo themselves in a wo'ld whea winna's take it all an mostly thea's losa's. Cold ha'd cash is what gets yo by in the unda'wo'ld too, contrary ta what they taught yo in Sunday school…"

Oh no, don't mention Sunday school!

"…an yo *can* take it with yo beyond the grave."

"I thought that was law numbah one against it."

"Not at all, yo jus' gots t'bank it conveniently in a Misa'Ca'd account befo yo croaks. Cash is available twenty fou' houa's a day in ova 1500 handy QuotCity ATMs in the environs a'Hell alone."

"Hell ain't nothin like I evah imagined!"

"That's cause yo is relyin on what that Sunday school teacha told yo back when yo was some wide-eyed impressionable kid, ain' that so?"

"Miss Heavins, she said I'd get my nuts buhnt off if I didn't sit still and behave, stop lookin up the little gihls' skihrts."

"An devils with pitchfo'ks sneakin up from behind an goosin yo."

"Mah oah less."

"Yah well, this Miss Heavins was way out-a-date back then, taday she'd be liable fo misleadin mino's. Hell's Hell, ain' tellin yo no dif'rent, but mo discomfo't than real pain, that's if yo can pay fo relief – but howeva they've redeco'rated, it still ain' no deluxe cruise ship waftin off inta outa space…"

"That's Heaven, right?"

-rr right?

"Damn! The both a'yo – an I's 'specially su'prised at yo doggie-do, yo seems like yo gots mo sense."

But these are mysteries, revealed only to true believers, no?

"Ain' no way a multi-billion dolla enta'prise can calculate retu'ns on investment by relyin on no myst'ries. Yo gots ta project yo futu'a based on cur'ent ma'ket conditions."

If you begin with the premiss that the economic model has a certain predictive reliability, then yes.

"Cause we's talkin bucks hea, big bucks, investment decisions that impact on yo an ev'rybody else's old age, health an secu'rity, decisions that yo hopes involve minimal risk – Mysteries! Might make sense ta oua primitive ancestas runnin round in animal hides – meanin no offense – but t'day solid appreciation on investment's the name a'the game, pua' profit, an biotechnology's has ema'ged as the key ta eva'lastin life, not old time religion no Oprah no ten million dolla lota'ry."

So?

"So, bottom line. The sma't money's investin in Hell cause tha's whea all them Baby Booma's a movin ta next, along with theia bulked up bank accounts. Only way ta keep on earnin the supa'bucks in taday's economy is ta keep on tappin those brats' reti'ement funds. Only pool a'liquidity left. An QuotLink Inc's got this hea afta-ma'ket sewed up – infa'nel damnation might not be much fun, but at least t'day it's mo tola'able – if yo can affo'd the price. Now yo tells me if QuotLink Inc ain' got a hellified business plan, one that analysts agree takes co'po'rot syna'gies t'a whole new dimension."

Ingenious.

"Betta believe. An it ain' no big mystery neitha, jus the final frontie'a fo the Co'po'rot Welfa'e State ta go — cradle ta the grave an beyond."

But what about Heaven?

"Ain' no money t'be made in that."

"You sayin theah ain't no Heaven Salaam?"

"Best t'make heaven whea yo finds it bro. Folks yo enjoy keepin company with, presu'vin the ea'th so gena'rations afta yo can live on. So don' go squand'rin yo chips on cheap thrills o buy inta some broka's come-ons, o no cheatin, stealin, lyin, jus' ta get a'step ahead a'yo neighbo."

But there must be something else, something bet-...

INTRUDERS IN HELL! INTRUDERS IN HELL!

"Too much talkin friends, we gots ta keep movin."

INTRUDERS IN HELL! RELEASE THE HOUNDS!

-rr, did I hear what I thought I heard?

RELEASE THE HOUNDS!

"Damn! They's closin in. We gots ta hot foot it out'a hea!"

GROUGHGROUGHGROUGHGROUGHGROUGHGROUGHGROUGH

Betsy can smell them, the acrid breath of those that feed on their own, which surely marks them as a separate genotype entirely.

"Le's take the back path, it's a little rocky but mo scenic. Dates all the way t'antiquity, though thea's not much fo roadside sa'vices"

Is it even a single degree cooler? Because Betsy's sizzled tip of the tail to her whispy whiskers.

GROUGHGROUGHGROUGHGROUGHGROUGHGROUGHGROUGHGROUGH

Back path it is, as Betsy lifts a leg to mark the entrance. Unaware they pass underneath an ancient archway with an inscription chiseled in the stone — Abandon Hope All Ye Who Enter Here — but writ in some cryptic script that few can readily decipher.

Salaam grasps a torch out of an iron socket, lights it and leads the way deeper into a blackened cave. "Watch these steps, way's narrow an they's get slipp'ry with ice — yo can take a nasty spill."

Ice feels nice on twenty roasted toes.

The path spirals steeply around this massive iced stalagnite, Salaam leading along single file with the torch, casting their shadows high against the cave wall. After a time Salaam's, next Chipper's and finally Betsy's shadow disappears. Each realizes they are crossing a catwalk high above a cavern, the breadth and the depth of which none of them can fathom in the darkness. Betsy's the most sure-footed and she's damn near apoplectic. Salaam's shadow reappears, though on the opposite wall, then Chipper's, then hers — *whew!* — her breathing gets easier.

In time they come upon a clearing with these mounds of rags piled here and there among the rocks. As they weave their way through, they notice the mounds are shivering in the cold — *roh?* — seems the mounds are people, sitting with backs to one another and brooding mute. Not a head turns as the strangers pass.

Chipper, being irrepressible by nature, squats in front of one bundle and smiles — which is returned by a narrowing of the eyes and an icy stare.

Betsy sniffs at another. The bundle snorts in response.

"This level's the resentful, them an the jus plain spiteful."

Neither have much to say. Not until Chipper trips over one.

"What do you want?"

"Nothin, sohry — sohry ma'am. Nothin at all."

A crone gets up in his face. "Knew somebody like you when I was a youngster, all smiley and happy!"

"Nice fella?"

"Blond hair, rosy cheeks, thought he was the life of the party. Well we showed him, dipped him in the ice pond until he turned blue."

"You must've been a regulah sweetheaht back then."

"I kept to my own."

"Bet. Othah beady-eyed moles like youhself."

"Yeah, we had one like that in our school." An old geezer sticks his nose in. "Got good grades in math. Once said he'd help me with my homework, so I turned him in. Principal expelled him for cheating."

And another has two cents worth to toss. "Girl we knew was real snooty, just because she was pretty. We took care of her in the woods, tickled her ass plenty."

"How about the class goody-goody?" One among them shouts.

"Those who could sing or dressed nice?"

"Or the big hero who catches the winning pass at homecoming?"

"Cheerleaders!"

"CHASE'EM AWAY! CHASE'EM AWAY! CHASE'EM AWAY WITH STICKS!"

Mob of bundles has suddenly become unruly, could turn ugly.

-rr think we ought to make a break for it chums?

Which they do fast, across this pile of loose shale that's about as fast as running in place, but the resentful choose not to pursue.

"Whoa! That clan was nasty."

"They's only gets nastia the lowa we go."

-roh?

"What exactly was theih problem?"

"The resentful? They's just full a envy. Snatch yo plate right out from unda yo fo'k, neva pick up the tab, neva leave a tip. Spend theia lives wantin what ev'rybody else's got — a'ways shoulda'rin some grudge, ready t'slap a lawsuit on yo fo lookin at'em cross-eyed."

"So what's theih pahticulah punishment anyway?"

"Wo'se imaginable…"

Betsy imagines a plague of tropical weight mosquitoes.

"…bein locked up with theia own kind fo'eva — an tell me that ain't equal ta the mis'ry they've done caused ev'rybody else?"

"Taste of theih own medicine."

Swallow a whole mouthful.

"But I don't quite undahstand Salaam, did they do away with hellfihe too? It's freezin cold along heah."

"Cold's sometimes wo'se punishment than fia' could eva be."

"Even so, it ain't nowheah neah what my Sunday school preachah used to rail about."

"He eva say he actually done visited?"

"Nope, noh did he intend to if I remembah cohrectly."

"Big change in the 60s, like I've been tellin yo. The wa'dens decided psychological abuse was wo'se than physical. Then's when they fin'ly gave up dunkin heretics by theia toes in boilin oil."

"What do they do with them now?"

"Let'em run wild from level t'level, spoutin all so'ts a'nonsense — an yo should see the brand spankin new rolla coasta they built fo lia's, swindla's an cheats, rides'em round an round, upside down, day in, day out — they neva knows which way they's goin t'go spinnin."

"How about adultahahs, fohnicatohs, pahvahts of evahry pahsuasion?"

"They's mostly gettin by with leniency these days, few houa's a'community sa'vice — they's the ones keepin the campgrounds so tidy."

"Thought along with mobstahs and mass murda'ahs they wah damned from the get-go?"

"Only repeat sex offenda's, they's fo'ced ta wea ankle bracelets, sounds an ala'm in case one comes chagin afta yo. But if yo's inta'rested in seein all the sideshow crim'nals that made histo'ry's headlines, yo gots ta plan anotha day jus' ta visit the zoo."

"They'h kept sepahrate?"

"It's the quiet sneaky types we'a goin ta see, the ones who kept theia crimes private, whole multitude mo a'those than the ones unlucky enough ta get caught up in pre-trial publicity."

"So wheah'h we headed next?"

"On the trail a'Wickedness and Deceipt — so watch yo wallets, anythin yo gots is fai'a game fo the taka's comin up next. They's slick sick, steal from theia own motha's if they eva got half a chance."

"Any relation to the folks we just met?"

"Fu'st cousins in depravity."

The damned are inbred, are they?

"They's done changed these roads round, all this new construction, le's duck inta this tunnel hea an tries a sho'tcut — keep yo heads low."

Shaft is fresh hewn, timbers shore up the ceilings and loose rubble falls on occasion from overhead.

"They's been reo'ganizin on a massive scale, movin people hea an thea, got some masta plan they won' publicly discuss — Big Dig, they calls it, but don' seem like they's eva goin ta get the job done."

They emerge upon a wide, flat plateau, the landscape unremittingly gray and dusty, loads of mine trailings in makeshift mounds drop fast off the edge into an enormous sink hole. And everywhere surrounding there are lanterns lit and small fires. Plateau is densely populated, looks like a refugee camp, wagons and trailers and trunks, luggage in all shapes and sizes, plastic bags, some heaped on rusty shopping carts.

"Thought you couldn't take nothin with you to the grave?"

"Not these creeps, these'a the greedy, they knows how ta smuggle things through, hold on ta pennies with theia bony tight finga's."

Bony for sure, skeletal with jutting jaws and big teeth, grabby long arms and eyes that don't blink, sprawled around ready for a graveyard feast. They send up a clatter as the newcomers pass.

"Want your palm read?" Demands one wearing a raggy black wig and arms lined with bracelets. "Learn your fate?"

"Prefah not to know, but thank you fah askin."

"How about life insurance, backdated variable annuity or fixed? Consider the family. Give you the best rates available." Fellow seems friendly at first, but something about the shift to his eyes.

"Nope. Betsy heah's my next of kin, and she can suhvive on huh own."

"Grow hair on an egg with this miracle potient." Comes some bald guy with a gimmick.

"Still got all mine if you didn't bothah to notice?"

"How about friends and relatives, could set you up in a business of your own, telephone from the comfort of your home, enroll steady customers as marketing reps and take in ten percent of their gross, earn six figures within weeks — others have, why not you?"

"What's the initial puhchase?"

"One grand in product up front, and that includes my premium line of natural vitamins as advertised on nighttime TV, including gel capsules of pulverized boar's tusk that will give you a hard-on for a guaranteed five days straight or your money back, no questions asked…"

"Whoa! Let me take a look?"

"Chippa Chippa, yo don' need none a'that."

"'Couhse not, stud like me, but you don't casually pass it by neithah."

"Come on, keep walkin. Thea'a mo scams pa squa'e inch round hea than on a Fou'teenth Street sidewalk."

"Hello handsome, you man enough to invest in derivatives on the commodities exchange? Pork bellies, soy beans, oil futures? Ten thousand initial, plus fees, could net you forty on a good day in the market…"

"I can be a gamblah babes, but I can't affohd youh ante."

"Give me a figure, something I can work with."

"Let me see, I've still got five bucks left on me and a hundred oah two in travellah's checks back at the hotel…"

"C'mon bro, neva knew yo was such a sucka fo a deal."

If you only knew how many hair restorers he doesn't need in his medicine cabinet — and ground boar's tusk? Pack that beside the bottles of shark nectar and freeze-dried ram's testicles.

"Don't go lettin out all my secrets gihl. Man's got to protect his private intahrests fuhst and fohemost."

"Protect yoself is right, from these poacha's."

"*Pssst!* Vote for me friend, next election. Promise you everything imaginable plus a no-show job in my state house office."

The three travelers are surrounded, for indeed the greedy are legion.

"Any way out of this mess Salaam?"

"Man on the make's a ha'd man t'shake."

And loud, close-up hawking their wares, a lot of somethings made out of nothings but packaged with elaborate four color brochures, hardware and software promotions, fly cheap with nothing to eat and take a peek at these bopeeps, or quick, order a zircon the size of a golfball to flit on your finger and receive a pair of matching earrings for free — downscale mass or up-bred market, we've got just the thing for you in our pocket.

"Walk fast, don' act like yo is the least bit inta'rested. If yo totally igno'es them yo gots a chance they'll go away, 'til they sta'ts in cold-callin anyway."

The three focus on their footsteps.

"Tha's it, come eye-ta-eye an yo could end up like them, sell sell sell," sung like a mantra, whateva yo can buy cheap an foist on the unsuspectin."

"Step right up, which shell hides the bean? Bet a dollar, win ten!"

The stupid, it seems, have little recourse.

"Read the book Wall Street never wanted published. How to sell short and win in a down market. Your's for just $39.99."

"Only justice in this pa't a'Hell is they gots ta listen ta each otha's pitches throughout eta'nity."

"No escape?"

"Holidays they gets ta mingle with the resentful upstaia's."

"The two get along togethah?"

"Resentful wants, greedy gots, but neitha side bites. That way they can frustrate one anotha 'til Hell totally freezes ova."

They walk fast, where to they don't know, go sliding off the edge of the plateau, down the mine tailings, down until they bump into the remains of an old growth forest, fossilized tree stalks with prickly undergrowth when *BOOM!* — what was that a land mine? No. A rocket flies overhead, lands close by with another *BOOM!* Followed by scattered shooting in the vicinity, someone screams and yet another rocket is launched.

"Whoa! Wheah ah we now?"

BOOM!

"Wa zone. Valley a'the Vengeful."

"The vengeful?"

"Yo knows, broken truces, blood feuds, ethnic cleansin — aim at yo neighbo an shoot him dead, rape his wife, bulldoze his house, bu'n his fields, foul his wata, o'phan his kids — daily routine."

"Wait one damn minute, me and Betsy didn't bahgain fah this!"

"Most people don', they jus' wakes up one mo'nin in the middle a'somebody else's battle, an befo they knows it they's up ta theia ea'lobes."

Four men in black berets rush the path in front of them, disappear into the bush, then a child comes wandering out crying, a mother quick lifts her up and goes running. There are more shots, and the child quits crying.

"She get killed?"

"Univa'sal rule they's all abide by, yo only gots ta die once in a lifetime."

But you can be terrorized repeatedly.

Yaaanh! Child's still crying.

"What about us, we'h still livin?"

"Fo'ces yo ta consida each step yo takes, now don' it?"

Indeed, quick steps and slunkered down.

"Don't know Salaam, don't know."

"Don' know neitha, vengeance is baff'lin cause in the end nobody wins, they jus' keeps battlin."

And the man who kills another wounds himself mortally.

"So who's fightin who heah?"

"Could be anybody, one a'those wa's a'liba'ration tha' goes on fo gena'rations, Irish against Scots Irish, when both should be battlin the British ta retake the Highlands, o Israelis against the Arabs su'roundin them on all sides, Kurds got ta be batt'lin least fou' bo'da'line countries, then thea's Indians against Pakistanis, Sa'bs against Albanians against Croats against Bosnians, Macedonians, Greeks takin on the Tu'ks, it's endless who hates who the most — then thea's those tribes coast ta coast a'Africa inta nothin less than total annihilation."

"You mean they'h all down heah still fightin?"

"Yo espects any a'them ta call it quits afta they's done put theia lives on the line fo the cause? Hell, they even gots a few Spanish su'viva's from the

A'mada wa'rin with drunkin British sailo's, French revolutiona'ries strugglin amongst factions a'theia own, an religious crusada's from ova seven centuries afta any Ottoman they spot — good Lo'd! The vengeful, they neva stop…"

-ii-eeeeee!

"…not 'til they drop, and tha's why they gots this whole level a'Hell all ta themselves — plenty a'room fo ta'get practice."

DOOM! DOOM! DOOM! DOOM! DOOM!

"Those ah mohtah shells! Duck!" Three are face on the ground where a squad of some sort of Partisans discovers them. "Whose side are you on?"

"Liba'ration tried an true!"

"Check! Let's head!" Squad jogs off.

"How'd you know to say that?"

"Loyalist fohces would've shot us without even askin the question."

Betsy dusts herself off, finds some relief behind a tree.

"Salaam, theah's got to be bettah way…"

"An I ain' even mentioned the schoolya'd bullies, the rival street gang memba's, inta'national drug ca'tels an those fat ass country cracka's! Shee'a numba confined ta this region is stagg'rin."

"I'm sympathetic, but-…"

"Don' say that too loud, yo neva knows how that could be inta'preted."

"…but theah's got to be some othah way around all this."

"Solution ain' been found yet! US bombs don' wo'k, no none a'them UN peacekeepin missions, aid fo the hungry gets diva'ted ta wa'lo'ds an even those who succeed in drivin theia neighba's out can't get enough peace an quiet t'enjoy a full night's sleep."

"No no, some way out of this valley, got to get ouh butts out of heah!"

"How? Ain' like we can go tu'nin back."

"What do you mean? Nothin we went through the last two levels would've gotten us killed."

"Physical danga ain' a hell of a lot wo'se than bein ta'gets a'the greedy — they'll bleed yo jus' as fast — an don' go fogettin that lynch mob mentality among the begrudged. Let them loose an they'll stone yo ta a bloody pulp."

And even you couldn't party hardy enough with the excessive.

"Tha's the point a the toua bro, one step jus' leads t'anotha, man shootin sta'ted out resentful an from envy graduated ta greedy."

"Don't need no lectuhe on mohrals right now, I want to know how we can get ouhselves out of this battlefield, you mumblin runt, and fast!"

"Don' go callin me no names, yo backassed woodsman!"

"Why I should break you up into kindlin sticks just fah gettin me and Betsy into the line of fihe!"

"Like ta see yo try, yo wimp wristed honky tonk motha fucka!"

"Stuff that loud jig mouth of youhs up pahmanently."
"Here boy, shoot the jive bastard with this."
"Thank you kindly friend, don't mind if I do!"

An ally along the road hands Chipper an automatic. Seems Chipper and Salaam's dispute has drawn a supportive crowd, whole mix of unfriendlies has climbed out of the darkness. Most are dressed in jungle fatigues, but also Russian mafioso in modish black leather, others in bright red coats and long white socks, even a few in full suits of armor.

"Jus' jokin Chippa ol' buddy ol' pal — yo can put that gun down now."
"Oh my God, what was I about to do? Salaam, fahgive me!"
"No sweat bro, heat a'passion, jus' so long as yo don' pull no trigga."
"You mean you're not going to shoot the sucker?"
"Nope nope, on second thought I'd soht of miss the suckah."
"Then give me back my automatic."
"Suhe suhe, heah you go."
"We've got a real war going on, none of your pathetic video imitations."
"H'yep, we'h simply down heah scoutin out locations fah the next action packed episode."

Crowd of onlookers hears that and melts into the bush.

Betsy's *pant pant* — was that a close call or what?

"I didn' mean nothin I said Chippa, 'bout yo-... yo bein a bleached out white asshole."
"Me neithah Salaam. You'h not that much of a monkey runt."

-roh go ahead then, kiss and make up.

"No need to go that fah…"
"Nah, simple truce plus a handshake'll do jus' fine."

DOOM! DOOM! DOOM! DOOM! DOOM!

"Run!"
"Which way wheah?"
"Don' know, jus' go!"

"Damn!" Chipper comes crawling out of the underbrush on his elbows. Shooting continues in the distance. "You ahright gihl? Gihl? — BETSY!"

Fine fine fine, nev-*rr* bett-*rr*, ears ringing a bit, slight disorientation, possible diarrhea — no, on second sniff, I'm holding solid.

"SALAAM?"

That's it, shout in my ear.

"SALAAM?"

I can take it. I'm only animal.

"Wondah wheah he's disappeahed to?"

Maybe he mistook the royalist party for the socialist, or he possibly took offense at your threat and abandoned you to your own misfortune.

"Salaam ain't somebody who'd hold a grudge, not fah long. He and I have had ouh shahe of squabbles ovah the yeahs and suhvived."

On your own.

"You suhe can be distrustful."

Man who talks non-stop has too much to say.

"Down!"

Why, what's up?

"Stay down! Theah's somebody keepin a lookout ovah theah on top of that ridge, see him?"

-*hmm*, but why the long robes? Some monk who's pulled guard duty?

"Seems hahmless whoevah he is."

Seeming can be deceiving, I advise we approach with extreme caution,

Not Chipper. "'Scuse me suh, me and my pooch heah seem to have gotten lost…'scuse me? 'Scuse me, suh?"

Monk listens not, simply stares off into distances, though from his vantage point, the view of the charred valley is vast, but breathtakingly beautiful it is not, nor from him any response.

"We must have taken a wrong tuhn oah somethin, seems we'h way off the trail in the middle of nowheah in Hell, got sepahrated from ouh trusty guide in the Valley of the Vengeful an-…"

"I am not here. I see nothing. I know less."

"H'yep, how about anybody else from these pahts, figuhe theah is anybody we could trust to point us in the right dihrection?"

"You travel forward at your peril."

"Seems so."

"Beware, any who passes through here is lost."

"Right, but I'm only booked fah a shoht stopovah."

"Mostly there is darkness, then comes a slow dawn. The more you understand your wayward life, the more you can see a glimmer of light."

"Mind me askin what you'h in heah fah strangah?"

"I turned away from those in need, looked aside, ignored their pleas."

"Well, lots of beggahs out theah lookin fah handouts these days, evahry city street cohnah crowded with them."

"Now I see no one." Fellow turns in the direction of Chipper's voice.

"Whoa!"

His eyes are gouged out, gaping dark bloody sockets.

"Better not to see than to look aside."

ROH! ROH! ROH! ROH!

"Back off, Betsy, no need to bahk at everythin you don't undahstand."

So what's with the colored mantel and the squared off cap he's wearing?

"Who did this to you fella, oah why?"

"We do it to ourselves, and worse, we do it to others unsuspecting."

"You didn't notice what was goin on, right? Can't be all youh fault?"

"Didn't look, didn't care. Easily turned away, so caught up with my own interests, I was oblivious to suffering. The world full of greed, each to his own interests, no concern for the rest. For such I am damned, decades I have stood on this precipice, fearful to see, fearful to take another step."

"Probably could guide you somewheah, just don't know my way around heahabouts."

"Everywhere is the same, everyone lost in his own concerns, trapped in his own preoccupations, his own advancement. We have no vision, we wander blind."

"Bet, but still theah's no reason fah you to be stuck out heah by youhself. Least I can do is get you across the road."

"No, you do not understand, I am damned to everlasting isolation, though I thank you for your offer. You seem sincere."

"S'pose, s'pose I am — what do you think Betsy?"

Sincere, well yes I guess — a trifle misguided perhaps, trifle, that's an understatement, but sincere, you mean well, you're good hearted…

"Damned by faint praise, eh?"

-*rr* no, I've simply never considered the question.

"What did you do friend, you know, in youh prioh life?"

"Professor Emeritus, Dean of my Peers, I rewrote history, rejected the truth, sought enlightenment in causes, sought grants from monied interests and glossed over the obvious."

"That doesn't sound all bad, how'd you evah end up down heah?"

"I lapsed into the self-serving and the pride of the academic elect, I grew intolerant of those whom I considered ignorant. I pursued privilege and in time wealth from investments in impoverished continents."

"You didn't give youh ill-gotten gains away to the pooh right befohe you croaked?"

"I endowed universities for the education of my own kind, libraries, and museums."

-*roh*

"Beware of the scholar's words, the wisdom of the sage. Solely by his actions shall you know him. Discourse alone is no salvation, the issues of the day transparent. The mind is tricked by convenient answers, common opinion our conviction, the brain useful for scant more than to rationalize our own actions. We delude ourselves and our children, hear merely what pleases us, ignore the rest."

"Pretty glum assessment of scholahship you got theah."

"And do you yourself know of any better?"

"Man can be mighty rotten, 'specially the ones who claim they'h not."

"Those who do speak the truth, those who can see beyond prejudice and self-serving are ignored, doomed as the prophets of old. They foretell and only destruction follows. We dismiss, we deride them, worry that the economy might collapse, our retirement funds along with it. Better to believe the lie, the politician's promise, while inside our guts wrench at every mention of the unthinkable."

"You sound like a prophet youhself."

"To be forgotten on a precipice without eyes, only my hearing intact and my soul as hollow as the space between rocks."

"Wheah you figuhe we ah gihl?"

Seems the further we go, the more obscure it gets.

"Place is eerily quiet."

Better than somebody shooting.

"Tough justice when a univahsity professoh gets tossed into solitahry."

Spent his life merely talking to himself.

"Makes sense if it's youh addictions oah stealin oah breakin somebody's bones, but nevah figuhed wohds could huht you."

He had the power to enlighten and wasted it indulging his wit.

"But most teachahs I've evah known ah hahmless."

Harmlessness is no virtue.

"Betsy. We've got to get ouhselves out of heah, bust out if we have to."

How do you propose we do that pal? Tunnels lead out of one hole into another, walking only takes us deeper, and neither of our species has yet mastered flight.

"And wheah did Salaam disappeah to?"

Ditched us in the fiery underbrush.

"Maybe theah's a lesson in this, some soht of test — whoa, you ahmost tripped me ovah?"

Quiet. Somebody's ranting and raving up ahead.

"Suhe as shit. I can heah it."

Gets louder as the two move closer, and whoever it is stands astride the path waving his arms about like a madman.

"Ain't nobody around to listen."

Just us.

"'Scuse me theah fellah, could I bothah you with a question?"

"Brother be saved. Amen."

"I could do with some salvation, and some dihrections…"

"Repent and thou shalt be saved. Confess thy sins and be cleansed."

"Ain't got time fah all them right now, got to keep movin ahead."

"Believe in the Lord, for only through Him shalt thou walk the path of self-righteousness."

"Righteousness is ahright as fah as it goes, but when you'h lost you fuhst got to get back to the main highway…"

"Wide and welcoming, an easy ride."

"…some shohtcut, even a duhty detouh will do…"

"Yea, they who seek the easy way shall soon encounter obstacles."

"Obstacles man, road blocks…"

"The path rocky, the slope slippery."

"…streets with no names, folks who've nevah traveled much beyond theih own neighbahoods…"

"False prophets abound, and many among you misguided, no one to trust save the Lord Alleluia."

"The Lohd Alleluia. So which way is out?"

"For those not baptized, the only way is surely down for they are lost to their sin and understand not the errancy of their ways."

"Me to a T, but could you at least point us towahd the dooh?"

"Straight ahead until you come to a fork in the road, right is the Miseries of Centuries, left Promises of Uncertainty. It is your choice, for man must travel the final steps on his own."

"Bettah alone than with somebody else who thinks he can lead you."

"The Lord is thine constant companion."

"H'yep, and I thank you kindly fah the dihrections."

Directions turn out to be a bum steer as Betsy and Chipper become lost in a cactus patch, sounds of snakes in the grass and some type of buzzard keeping tabs overhead.

"Whoa, you got the feelin we'h really lost this time?"

Talk to me, and every which way you look the terrain is the same, bleak grey and smoldering.

"Notice everybody we meet's got an angle they'h playin."

-hook!

"Can't see beyond theih own eyelids, and if they listen to you at all, they only heah what they want."

Something's lurking behind that rock.

"Ah hah!"

"Whoa!"

"Gotcha!"

"Guess you do."

"You new friend?"

"Sohta."

"Well you've come to the right place. Step in."

Pudgy fellow, greased-back hair – for not all denizens of Hell are gaunt and sallow, with the fat spit roasted off them – he motions Chipper to a niche in the stone. Seats himself opposite. Above his head a scroll work degree from somewhere unfamiliar is framed on the wall.

"Could get you out of here eventually – five to seven minimum, if you're willing to cop a plea."

"Hey, we'h just visitin!"

"They all say that. First defense is denial, couldn't be me, followed by a slow and painful realization that wait a minute, this is like no place I've ever been before."

"Haven't."

"Accompanied often enough by a giddy sense this must be a dream."

"Nightmahe – so you tellin me this is it?"

"Apparently."

"But I nevah saw it comin."

"Few do."

"Wasn't prepahed."

"Who is? Death sneaks up, and wham, most people die intestate."

"What ah you implyin about my goldens?"

"Whatever was of value to you, the key question is who is listed as beneficiary, or even more importantly who might lay claim? The best answer always is to have a will."

"A will? Who evah thinks of that?"

"My point exactly."

"Betsy, I would've left all my valuables to you if I had thought of it."

Never had a hankering for your goldens.

"Generous offer my friend, except for any animal you would need to establish a trust, name an executor."

"We'h talkin all my eahthly belongin's, my Fendahbendah, my sound equipment, my fields of ganje, my fresh brew collection…"

I have made provision for my own future, a treasury of buried bones.

"…the rights to my songs…"

"All of which shall fall into the possession of the state, unless some distant cousin files a timely challenge."

"Them wohthless bastahds, bettah the state."

"Down here however, we have a saying – nothing is ever too late."

"Funny, I'd've figuhed you'd say the opposite."

"Amazing things can be done when you have connections."

"I nevah had any connections in my life, except maybe Salaam."

Salaam, as in salaam the door, sucker, smack in your puss.

"Don't go bad mouthin pooh Salaam Betsy. He's probably goin crazy seahchin fah us this very minute."

Crazy, I'll agree with that assessment.

"A friend only goes so far in the end."

True. No sense flinging yourself weeping on the pyre.

"Which is where I come in."

-ow?

"First, how much did you leave behind in your bank accounts? I have family on the outside who could forward us the money, for a fee of course."

I get it. You're a jailhouse lawyer.

"Listen, it's not what you think. I'm still alive, heah feel, theah's flesh on these tihed old bones."

"Mine too. Comes from eating well in Hell."

Though the bags under the eyes suggest you're not sleeping so good.

"No no, I just wandahed down heah by mistake…"

"Yes yes, however you got into this fix, fact is you're never going to get back out. Not on your own, not unless you're lucky enough to hire someone such as me, and my rates aren't as bad as others in the vicinity."

Perhaps we should shop around.

"Naturally there are no guarantees, depends which judge gets rotated your way, his mood in the morning, the larger issues of the day."

"Hey, I'm innocent. Just a down-on-my-luck travelin musician."

"Everybody's innocent here. Best thing to do is admit to a lesser offense, then claim you were a victim of circumstance. Always blame it on others, bad neighborhood, dysfunctional family, beatings by your mother's boyfriend, never enough welfare, and if none of the above seems to be convincing, claim you got molested by the third shift supervisor at Blister Burger, scarred you for the rest of your adult life."

"Sehriously?"

"Got that accurate my friend. Facing life in the mineshaft is no fun."

"I'm just down heah on a visit — wheah's Salaam — SALAAM! SALAAM!"

-ow -ow -owoowoo!

"Please don't wail. Rocks resound. Soon everybody'll be off the walls and howling."

"Just can't figuhe what happened, Salaam was a step behind me…"

"Only thing I see is a big black dog."

"H'yep, this heah's Betsy by the way, I'm Chippuh."

"Not for long my friend, but I do admit the dog bit is unusual."

"Theah's a chance?"

"Longshot. Normally pets aren't allowed. Unless she was part of the act, a trademark character perhaps, something generally recognized as associated with your personna? Are you two by chance inseparable?"

"Betsy, pooh Betsy, I've always taken you fah granted, nevah have given you the recognition you so richly desahve."

What's this, a deathbed confession?

"Deathbed confession isn't worth the breath it's whispered on. This is a parole state, everything contained within the four corners of the page."

"I should nevah have drug pooh Betsy into this."

"Acquitting her as an accomplice after the fact, that's a possibility. Jury can be swayed by loyal companionship gone awry."

"Pooh pooh gihl, come to papa."

None of the dogs at home would believe this!

"We prove she was forced to act, did so unwittingly."

"Aftah yeahs of selfless loyalty, I go and walk you straight into Hell."

Don't bother yourself with this blubbering, I followed along by my own free will. Life with you has always been an adventure, although I never expected we would end up here together, and forever?

"A few tears could get you off for time served."

"We just got to get out of heah Betsy, follow that nose of youhs."

"No hound my friend, is going to lead you out of Hell, be she seeing eye or simply scamming."

Don't go underestimating my abilities bud, I've been marking the trail as I've gone along.

"Paths only lead downward. Best thing you can do is park here where you're at and set up camp, believe me, you don't want to dig any deeper."

You mean I've been pissing in vain! But we dogs have never done anything to deserve this, oh an occasional rottweiler pulls a postal, attacks a neighborhood brat, but the majority of us are loyal tail waggers.

"Fault of a dog is whom he befriends."

She, she befriends, and it's not as though we have much choice in this life, do we? It's not you folks who are impounded for us to pick and choose from — look how cute that human is and cuddly, see how she comes directly to me — *ro-ro* no — we're the ones who have to nibble from your fingers, either that or wait for the grim reaper to come clean out the cages, make room for a newly hatched brood.

"I'm only trying to help here, but I do cost money."

My pouch happens to be empty.

"No *pro bono* in the pits, although everybody in Hell eventually ends up a charity case. Relatives on the outside use up what cash is left in the estate — well, what more does the old bastard need, some headstone to commemorate how upstanding he once was, while down here he's left shuffling among the rubble. Ancestor worship might work in Asia, but nobody in the West gives a damn. Died, dead, done with it, whose name's on the accounts or do we have to await probate."

-rr-oll's lost.

"We could make a case you wandered in accidentally, plead ignorance."

Dumb dog act. I've played that many times to my advantage — *roof-doof-foof-foof* — roll over, shake my paw.

"Perhaps you have an uncle who could set the dog up in a trust?"

"Grandfathah who hides his money undah the mattress, that do?"

"Maybe maybe. I'm simply thinking out loud."

Better than not thinking at all.

"Your case is unique, which could work to our advantage. I've never seen any dogs hereabouts, although they say Satan keeps hounds, but He's a few levels below and nobody you would want to visit."

Humans with horns are at all times to be avoided.

"But I require an advance. I've got filing fees and a typist to pay."

Well, if you have to pay to walk in this old world, I'll see what I can scrounge, meantime hope you don't mind if I sniff around on my own.

"Suit yourself."

May take your advice, establish base camp here, plan an ascent for later.

"Ledge to the left is empty. Fellow who was there got up in the middle of the night to take a whizz, dropped off and was never seen again."

Don't much care for heights myself, but don't see the need to nose down any deeper either.

"What about me? You got huh off easy, what ah my chances?"

"Your case is lost my friend, no contest."

"I've got rights to a faih trial, judge and juhry…"

"Everyone incarcerated converts to a staunch defender of the Bill of Rights, something they never accorded anyone else on the outside."

"…twelve honohrable men…"

"Won't muster them easily, men in Hell can be mighty resentful, and as for judges, they're not serving time down here for exemplary behavior on the bench."

"About how many judges you got down heah anyway?"

"Depends on whether they were appointed or elected?"

"Which is wohse?"

"Appointed. At least with elected you've got a chance in Hell of getting rid of one."

"Whoa! Doesn't sound good!"

"Not here at the trial court level anyway. Deep down in Appellate, there are more justices than claimants."

"HELP! HELP! GET ME OUTTA HELL!"

OUT! OUT! Betsy joins in too, and the rest of the inmates in their caves and caverns, level upon level chiming in, a lost cacophony with chorale, Betsy mezzo and beltin it out with the best of them!

GET ME OUTTA HELL!   -HELL!   HELL!

Bunch of demons, giant bird-like creatures hear the howling and come swooping through the air, Chipper's along on all fours with Betsy and scrambling down this narrow ravine, the flutter of wings rushing them as they go slip sliding, shin kicking into rocks in the dark, no moonlight, no starlight, no lights at all.

"Whoa- whoa- whoa-..."

Trying not to fall when eventually the howling stops, an end to the hot breath on their backs and the two hear an iron gate slam shut behind them, the telltale sound of a key in a lock.

-*rrolk?* Are we locked in or locked out?

No way of knowing for certain, though they both sense instinctively there's no going back that craggy path — *clackclackclatterclap* — at the bottom of the ravine comes pebbles and what feels underfoot like grass. Can't see in the darkness, "Wheah do you s'pose we ah?"

Betsy's nose to the ground and hasn't a clue.

"Don't know about you, but I'm close to roastin."

Indeed, the temperature has risen significantly. Humidity, and Betsy's tongue is hanging long out her mouth.

"Could suhe go fah a tall frosty Belfast Triggah Ale, how about you?"

The mere mention of moisture is unbearable to Betsy, except what's this — *splash splash* — mud and weeds and whoops she's suddenly out of her depth, afloat and being pulled way out into a current fast and furious. She barks Chipper back. Too late. He's knees, hips and over his head too. "Hang on babydoll, I'll save you!"

No time for heroics chum, at least one of us has to survive — in order to warn the others.

"Wahn the othahs about what?"

The pitfalls of mankind — the lure of soporifics, envy, cunning and greed, general genocide, the dearth of truth, the intolerance of religion, the rule of law for the few who can afford it, -*roh* and that laughable bit about economics is best when everyone's grubbing for his own special interest.

"Nevah need fah despaih, no mattah how despahrate it gets!" Like now with Chipper treading water and furiously trying to find her. "Hang on! Cause this can't be the end, not aftah all we've been through togethah — flushed down some whihlpool in Hell!"

-*blub-blub-blub*

"AHOY?"

-*blub?*

"Who thar be raftin the rapids at this ungodly hou'ar?"

A familiar voice, not friendly, and a lantern is struck high on the prow of a rat ridden vessel.

"Woman ovahboahd! Toss out a line!" Chipper responds bravely.

"What's that, a lass in distress?"

Betsy's beating fast against an undertow. She's a strong swimmer but she could be drug under.

"Har ye go, though it's narmally a rule o'mine not t'parmit women abard the *Charon*, no mattar how dire thar situation."

Groan no, the *Charon*. Betsy would nearly prefer a watery grave to that floating shipwreck. Still, her instinct is to survival and she locks hold of this *blick* tarred thick rope some swaby has thrown and endures the indignity of being fished out of the drink by her canines.

"Who'ere she be, she looks mar like a wrung out mutt than a rare beauty!" Captain Hosiah Blight stands at his station as his coolies wind the wench up, haul her haunches over the rail.

Betsy's deposited a clump on the deck while one boot and the stump make their way over to inspect.

"Shar I remembar this bitch from somewhar." He snorts as he leans in close with the lantern. "Those fangs she's got far teeth."

And how prettily she curls her upper lip for him as he draws near.

"Reeks like a dog."

Talk about a scent pal, you'd flunk the first grade whiff test handily.

Indeed, the Captain doesn't believe in bathing, holding sway over his crew by rank odor alone.

Light exposes the lady to those standing around.

Soup. The crew drools, and Betsy so tuckered out she could go for a hot bath, though she'll pass on the onions and carrots sloshing in with her.

"Whoa!" Chipper shouts as he clambers aboard on his own. "That's my best buddy Betsy you'h about to cahve up."

Carve? Nobody's as yet mentioned a knife! Dagger stares and surely a cleaver hidden under an apron, swords drawn immediately as the Captain recognizes Chipper.

"Ye scum, is it? Considared me and me men wa rid o'ye."

Not so and where are we anchored, in your subterranean hideout?

"Name youh price to get us out of heah."

"Last time I noticed ye war all balls and no cash."

"H'yep, back befah I found the map to the buhried treasuhe."

"Ye say treasare?"

What treasure?

"Treasuhe, you know, pieces of eight, gold plate?"

-ro right right, that treasure.

"TRAYSOH!" Crew gasps in unison. Don't forget traitors are among the players on this here holiday cruise.

"Ye attemptin t'sow mutiny among me men?" Hosiah Blight stomps up to Chipper, pokes his scowl directly under Chipper's chin.

"Enough to make everyone of us rich beyond ouh wildest dreams."

Don't goad him, Betsy warns, you don't want to know this man's wildest dreams.

"Whar's thar a map matey, a bit o'proof might well do t'spare yar hide."

A map, Betsy moans, how are you going to produce one of those?

"Stowed in my nose."

"Whar?" Blight is staring directly up such.

"Nose fah gold."

"Ye'r puttin it t'me?"

Hasn't even started.

"Map got washed away in the cuhrent."

"Nevar much liked the look o'yar lowar lip."

"Any supahficial appeahrances to the contrahry, I've got a scent fah bullion, coins and chests full of jewels."

"Wharabouts be this nose o'yars leadin ye?"

"An island."

Treasure island, of course — no need for the author to be brilliant, merely consistent with a time-tested story line.

"Only one island down har in Hell, Devil's Island."

Unbelievable, he's swallowed the bait!

"So that's why the two o'ye landed out har in the middle o'nowhar — buried treasare. Makin music war only a ruse."

As good as a ruse gets.

"We've got to make ouh way to the old graveyahd."

"Island be covared with graves, mausoleums sinkin intar the slime."

-roh? Betsy gets wet mop off the floor and wrings herself out all over the crew. *Ho sooo...* Backs the limeys off quickly, something about dog sog that sends most people scrambling.

"Graveyahd somewheah neah the centah on a rise, theah's this unmahked grave of a great sea captain like youhself, his treashuh buhried with his bones undah a heaped pile of rocks."

"Great sea captain, ye say? Might be warth explarin since wa'r down har waitin far fresh cargo anyhoo."

Fresh cargo from Hell? What exactly would they be exporting, something the world needs less of no doubt.

"Got to go in undah covah of dahkness, means we'd bettah move fast befah daybreak."

"No harry on that account, thar hasn't been a beam o'light down undar since the flash o'creation."

Oh, you a believer in the big bang or the big bump?

"What I larned young was stay out o'the heat no mattar how foolproof the plot."

True pragmatism. Not even an opinion.

"Ye shar ye know what ye be talkin about?"

-*pssst!* Be vague about details. Say it's a puzzle and the most you have are a few missing pieces.

"Mighty puzzlin what I ovahheahed on the exact wheahabouts of this grave, but they wah suhe cleah on one essential detail…"

"Ay matey, and what was that?"

"…twenty tons of puhe gold bullion from some Spanish galleon that sunk within sight of these vehry shoahs."

"That'd be the El Garbanzo out o'Asumpçion th'ar refarrin to, sunk off the eastarly side o'Sainty Cecily in 1747 in a mighty starm with all hands lost and a king's ransom abard."

"Now that you mention it, they did talk about some old Spanish galleon and this legendahry privateeah whose name I didn't quite catch."

"That'd be the Captain Hobart Quill tha'r refarin to, out of Nantucket, and as wily a sailor as evars sailed these treach'rous seas."

"Must be the one."

Of course it is, when overburdened with reality, we must necessarily resort to the whims of imagination.

"Nevar dar'd step foot on Devil's Island, all's swamp an stunted tree stumps, those mad with hatred runnin riot…"

-*roh oh*

"Maybe we bettah call this misadventuhe off, tryin to find a dead body in a swamp's not much fun."

"…and mammoth tartles I've been told about but nevar seen, huge gargoyle hawks who crap all ovar me decks, blarsted bards have carried off dozens o'me crew in the many yars I've been tradin in these parts."

"These hawks ah big enough to cahry off a grown man?"

"Screamin and kickin. But they'd have a fight with a man tough as me."

Hosiah's not tall, not at all, he's squat, but dense like a lead cannon ball and so grizzled that even a giant hawk would find him too rough to gnaw.

"So you've nevah actually dropped anchoh and gone ashohe?"

"Take me far a fool, do ye?"

"Whoa no!"

"Can't take a chance with these swabies, they'd disappar int'the undargrowth in the blink o'an eye," of which Blight has only the one. "nevar come back."

Take their chances among the mad, these prehistoric turtles and birds, any monstrosity rather than you.

"Suhprisin, 'specially when you considah the genehrous fringe benefits you must be providin."

"Nevar satisfied, these Chinie crews, give'em anythin, and they only want mar."

"Ain't that the unfohtunate cuhse of the wohkin man?"

"Hold back a crust o'bread and they'll rush t'do yar biddin, but nevar trust'em, nary a one."

"No. None?"

Captain Blight glances over at his slanty brow crew. "Take a good long look at 'em."

They seem deferential, nodding and shuffling, not comprehending any of what is being spoken in their own prosecution.

"See what you mean."

"Believe ye me, these bastards'll be takin ovar the warld yet."

"How's that?"

"Breedin. Ovarpopulatin. Thar'll be tharty billion o'them t'ev'ry one o'us in no time soon."

"Which means we've got to stick togethah, you and me, make suhe they don't cahry out theih nefahrious plan."

"Ye'r catchin on. We'll rely on'em far the assault, then cut'em down from the rear aftar the prize be taken."

"Excellent strategy, but why risk it if theah's so much dangah?"

"Then you and me can duel it out between us on the beach."

"Whoa! Upfront!"

"In yar face. Far what makes ye think I'd trust the likes o'ye anymar than I'd trust the likes o'them?"

"Best not to trust anybody in this life, family oah friend."

"Not if thar be riches within reach, and even without any loot ye got t'take propar precautions."

"Appreciate what you'h sayin – and you'h still sehrious about raidin this Devil's Island?"

"Why, ye be gettin cold feet – ar ye be lyin through yar nose about this har gold?"

Heap of both.

"Cause if ye be lyin, I'll sevar yar tongue from yar pallet." And to emphasize his point, there's this glint of a spark uncinched off Blight's belt, and a blade at Chipper's throat.

"Hell no, I'm damn neah dyin to go, but- but-…"

"But, but, sputtar what?"

"…it's just… well… you wouldn't happen to have a spahe fireahm handy, oah somethin I could use to help protect ouh mutual intahrests from swaby oah some prehistohric beast?"

"Keep the only one abard holstared closely at me side." Blight pats his pocket. "This har flintlock and a trusty blundarbuss in me cabin, fill it with buckshot and watch'em scattar."

"Looks like you've got youh bases covahed."

"What makes me a mastar o'men — assume yar stations, ye blightars! Start engines!"

Boat groans as the crankshaft turns, that and a rough rattlin on deck.

"Ready undarway?"

Lots of yesses and sirs and salutes.

"Powar har up! 180 right ruddar!"

Betsy's worried, for they'll soon be drawn into deeper waters, and off in the distance, she hears a faint cry of what must be the totally tormented.

"Best I could do on the spot gihl, but any plot's bettah than none."

Particularly one that can backfire — a blunderbuss, no less.

"Lick youhself ovah, get ready fah a landin…"

On a swamp island inhabited by the damn mad, overgrown snapping turtles and war hardened hawks.

"…cause theah's no tuhnin back now."

Charon comes about slowly, sets course.

Never has been, Betsy bleats, not much of a puppyhood and it's been a run with the pack ever since. And behind her the sound of a wood foot.

"W'ar goin t'have t'anchar dangerously close and wade the crew ashare, thar's but one lifeboat abard, belongs t'me."

"Any spahe inflatables?"

"We'll fling what we've got far lifevests ovarbard and the crew aftar that, ye with me?"

Better than being against ye, Betsy nods vigorously.

"I'll fire a round with me blunderbuss, and in the confusion ye two hoist who ye can by his suspendars and heave him ovarbard, spar not a one. Them without a vest will be farced t'swim, if they make it they make it, if not they'll drown."

"Hahsh."

"Way at sea matey. Can't leave'em behind, they'd sail off with me ship and thar's only so much room in a lifeboat, unless ya'r some sart o'champion yarself and prefar t'dive in?"

"That's ahright. We'll ride — Betsy heah to sniff out old bones."

"Gold's what we'ar aftar! Thar'd be plenty mar baried down har, all them big swindlars and cheats who've checked in parmanently."

The best of the worst, is it?

"Gold's been me lifelong quest."

"Undah this loose pile of stones on a rise, dead centah of the island — they kept repeatin that."

This story grows more implausible with each chug of steam.

"Who be these gents ye ovarhard talkin matey?" Blight has that pointy knife at Chipper's throat again.

"Quo- QuotLinks... although admittedly I didn't get a good look at theih faces... except fah theih shifty eyes."

"QuotLinks, now they be a diffarent stary altagethar. Tha'r gold diggars themselves, and good at it, but not as good as me — why didn't ye mention thar identities befar?"

"Sohry, slit- slip- slipped my mind entihely..."

Nothing's been slipping your mind today pal. I'm impressed. Maybe we can attribute that to the fact you've been missing your hourly doses of premium grasses?

"...see, my memohry ain't what it used to be."

"Age'll do that t'the weakar man, but not t'me matey, I'm oldar than most but I nevar farget the man who's done me damage — nevar farget duplicity nar the darty doublecross."

"A grudge, they say, is always the last to let go."

"Ye doubledeed me and yar nose'll get flung ovar farst, followed by all yar othar appendages." Blight slides the knife away, sheathes it.

"Come to, ye swabies!"

Old boat abruptly shifts into reverse — CRANKCRANKCRANK —CLUNK! — and floats forward into the sandy shoals off Devil's Island.

"Prepar t'drop anchar!"

SLINKSLINKSLINSLINKSLINK —SANK —SUNK!

As the crew scurries to obey orders, Captain Blight fires the old blunderbuss, throws them into total panic. On cue Chipper and Betsy hurl what there are of lifevests overboard, straw not styrofoam and wrapped loosely in gunny sack, though they balk at heaving off men, except Betsy trips up the cook.

Ho he yo yo. Imp goes splashing overboard.

If you can't stomach the soup, then don't go dishing it out, Betsy barks.

Captain Blight's not so squeamish and with a *thud thud thud* one hapless sailor after another is flung overboard.

"Lowar me lifeboat!" He calls as he settles himself mid-board with his blunderbuss across his knees. With picks and shovels and a collection of brass oil lanterns, his looming presence leaves scant room for much else.

Chipper handles the crank. Betsy watches over the gunnel — *srow, srow, srow...*

"Harry it up, they'll get thar befar we do!"

-rr raster! raster!

If any get there at all, straw is for pillows and separates on the surface as the stronger swim off. The cries of the weaker go unanswered.

The lifeboat hits with a splash, immediately begins taking in water.

"Scramble abard!"

Chipper and Betsy hesitate.

"Pinhole leaks be all, otharwise she's parfectly seawarthy."

They have little choice. Chipper climbs down the ladder, Betsy wrapped around his shoulders. There's a rustling about as each assumes a position. Betsy goes on lookout with a lantern clinched in her jaw, Chipper is center and rowing, Blight's on the tiller and guiding the lifeboat through the slackers who can't swim. "Off ye heathen, we are goin far gold!" He jabs at them with his peg leg.

Betsy and Chipper stare forward, heedless of the carnage.

"Curses! Devil's Island's been right har undar me nose all along and I nevar suspected thar'd be treasare."

Nor we.

"Sure be the wark o'ol' Cap'n Quill, sly seadog, only he'd'av thunk t'stash his horde in the last uninhabited haven o'Hell."

Betsy chances a glance back at Chipper. He's intent on his rowing.

"I might be o'a mind t'spare ye two iffin we find this har grave mound with its treasare."

"We'h gettin any closah?"

BUNK, they are, they hit bottom and have to wade the rest of the way through murk and mud. Blight, a lantern in one hand, his blunderbuss in the other, hurries to round up the remains of his force. Chipper taps Betsy on the noggin and motions her to follow in the opposite direction.

Are you *su-rrr* this is a good idea?

"Prefah prehistohric beasts oah howlin souls to a one-eyed swindlah."

Betsy has to agree, although the fluttering of giant wings above in the darkness makes her terribly nervous.

Devil's Island's all marsh, Betsy up to her belly sloshing through, the handle of the lantern clinched in her jaw and something fishy with teeth nipping at her ankles.

WHOW-HOW! HO-HO-HO... WOE-O-WOE!

"What the fuck was that?"

"Perhaps we should backtrack to the boat and row off.

WOE-O-WOE! Some such something goes whithering ground up and whirls around them.

HO-HO-HO-HO-HO-HO-HO...

More of whatever pop up like vapors out of the muck, encircle them.

WOE! WOE! WOE!

Betsy and Chipper twist and turn, casting light in every direction. Even in the intense glow of the oil lanterns, these swamp gasses are barely visible, but what features the two can discern are encrusted in mud, ragged in bones and wild-eyed, mouths open and hooting.

WOE! WOE! WOE! WOE! WOE! WOE! WOE! WOE! WOE!
"We'h friendly, whoevah you ah. We come in peace."
And whatever you do, don't take us to your leader.
WOE-OH-OH-OH!
One's right up in Chipper's face. His, its hair long and bedraggled, deep wrinkles like woodgrain line its face, a syrupy venom seeps from its lips. It attempts to speak but can only sputter, then fades as quickly as it appeared.

Everywhere they step Betsy and Chipper disturb more.
WOE! WOE! WOE! WOE! WOE! WHO! WHO ARE YOU?
"Did you hear that?"

A voice, a voice crying out in the wildness, but where — there! Look! This wretch drags through the swamp and comes straight at them. Betsy and Chipper shine their lights right at… her! It's a she, definitely a she, and more corporeal, rusted chains hung loosely from her shoulders. "I am guilty as charged!" The sight of the lights doesn't stop her. "Worse!"

Something about that face, Betsy remembers seeing it somewhere.

"I knew what I was doing! I did it anyway!"

She's face-on-face with Chipper and ranting. "Feigned insane so they'd lock me up in solitary. I had nothing to say to them, nothing to say to you, nothing at all!"

"Got to say gal, you've got the mad act down. Convinces me. I wouldn't come within fifty feet, not willin'ly."

"They deserved what they got, those damn bawling brats! Tried to chase them away — *LEAVE ME ALONE!*"

"Hey, I get that way myself, moody moody, 'specially afta a long night on my own homebrew."

"*LEAVE ME ALO-O-O-NE!*"

"Could be the weathah though, wheah I come from it'll get dahk soonah and cold. Long wintahs and no light, that can get to a sensitive soht of guy like me."

"*ALO-O-O-O-O-O-NE! ON MY OWN!*"

"Figuhe she wants us out of heah Betsy?"

How perceptive. Must be that sensitivity of yours kicking in.

They turn to run except they encounter another one — two, there's two, a team, a he and a she, they're chained together.

"They claimed we acted together."
"Thought alike."
"Exactly the same."
"We did."
"We do."
"They're right."
"H'yep, married couples mostly get that way, don't you know, they even

staht to dress alike, his and huh wohk-out suits, same shoht haih cuts, stuffed guts, hahd to tell who's who."

"We're mother and son."

"Damn. Even hahdah to tell who's who."

"Wherever we go…"

"Whatever we do…"

"TOGETHER! WE DO IT TOGETHER!" They're insistent. "WHATEVER! AS LONG AS WE'RE TOGETHER!"

"Don't want to know what they do togethah, do you gihl?"

No way, and I'm a beast, remember?

"TOGETHER! TOGETHER! FOREVER! TOGETHER!"

"Swamp gas, it'll tuhn you crazy if you breathe in enough on an empty stomach."

These folks we're crazy long before they discovered swamp gas.

"STOP!" Another one, a younger one, in a restraint jacket strapped tight around his chest.

"We'h not heah to distuhb anyone."

No, as a matter of fact, we're trying our damndest to get out of here.

"Help me please."

"Suhe, anything we can do."

"I have to find her."

"Who, youh mothah?"

"No. My wife. Last time I saw her I was standing top of the cellar stairs."

"And?"

"That's all I remember… except…"

"Except?"

"…she was lying at the bottom…"

-roh?

"…her head all bloody. And I must have panicked, that must be why I ran, not because I was guilty…"

"Did you explain this to the juhry?"

"…yes, I admit it, I had sawed the top step in half, I admit to that, I was planning on replacing it. She was just so fat — *fat! fat! fat!* — and she was yapping at me — *yap! yap! yap!* — saying something nasty, how stupid I was, how clumsy, how I started things and never finished — but who was she to talk, she'd lay on the couch all day in front of the TV and stuff her mouth with cheezy tidbits and yap — *yap! yap! yap!* — and spit tidbits at me — *thap! thap! thap!*"

And that's why you pushed her.

"I didn't push her, she fell! I was standing there, watching as she fell, she took one fat step while she was yapping at me, and the board snapped — *snap! snap! snap!* — one right after another, and she fell flat splat on her fat face stuffed with cheezy tidbits, spitting up teeth and blood!"

"So you got life instead of the gas chambah?"

"Because the week before she set fire to my bed!"

"*Ah-*, you two have some soht of histohry of domestic violence?"

"But I won! I won! She split her head wide open on the cellar floor!"

"Did you evah even considah a divohce?"

"It's against my religion!"

And murder one isn't?

"They kept asking me why I waited all day before I dialed 911."

"Why did you?"

"I had to make sure she was dead!"

So she lingered?

"Hours and hours, yapping and spitting, calling me names!"

Such as?

"A twerp and worse, that I had a pencil stub for a dick and no balls!"

"Man, that's abuse, did you cop an insanity plea?"

"They claimed everything I did was premeditated, but look at me, I'm not as bad as the rest of them around here — like her." He motions with his chin over at Miss Alone. "She drowned her own children in the bathtub — *blub! blub! blub!* — three little babies in a tub!"

Thought her face looked familiar.

"And those two, the mother and the son team — they hacked a dozen young women he brought home for dinner to death — *hack! hack! hack!* — whacked them to death, buried their corpses among the tomatoes."

That was front page in the grocery store tabloids for months.

"And there's worse — mass murderers, cannibals, child molesters, radio talk show hosts…"

"You mean to tell me that even aftah you've sahved time up above, you still got mah to go down below?"

"I never begged for mercy."

Hence, you never showed remorse, never accepted the consequences of your own actions?

"She deserved it, that fat yappy bitch. She's dead!"

But then so are you.

"She's down here somewhere, I know it. I just need help finding her."

"Because it's nevah too late to repent, that's what the preachah told me long ago, even fah somethin you've done that's totally disgustin."

"And when I find her, I'm telling you, when I do I'll grab her by the throat and I'll bat that last gasp of breath right out of her — *bat! bat! bat!* — I will! I will!" And he's jumping up and down in this straight jacket, stamping his feet in the muck, disturbing the roots of more mad souls who rise in a ring and chant alongside him.

woe! woe! woe! woe! woe! woe! woe! woe! woe! woe! woe! woe!

Chipper gets spattered, so does Betsy. "Damn, you see any high ground anywheah at all?"

She points the way toward some thick trunks of trees in a grove and — *rook!* — a turtle standing in their path, about half the height of Betsy.

"So much fah the myth of the mammoth tuhtles."

Maybe so, but those giant hawks flying overhead are real. Betsy can feel the flap of their wings like a small squall.

Chipper slogs over among the tree stumps and points his lantern directly at the turtle, a high peaked dark red ribbed shell, a characteristic beak, with the only feature distinct from any species he's ever seen a razor back ridge along the spine. "Theah's a mahrine biologist's wet dream."

The turtle's immobilized by the first light it's probably ever encountered in its life, that and the sight of an erect two legged creature akin to a shore bird but without feathers or wings, possibly harmless, though equipped with one hell of an enormous glowing yellow eyeball.

It's a scene from another era as man discovers the incredible in dank dark nature when suddenly — SUDDENLY! — the forest stumps surrounding begin to move — Betsy flashes her own glowing yellow eyeball upwards in time to see an enormous beak the size of an elephant's tusk come crunching down on Chipper!

But he's quick, that boy, he leaps atop the mama mammoth's shell, has to step lively among her own snazzy set of razor back blades, while Betsy hightails it further underneath mom's armored belly. Unfortunately in the shock Betsy's jaw drops and her lantern gets crunched in one sturdy step.

Well, that's what you get when you violate rule number one of the jungle, don't mess with no mother's baby.

"You ahright gihl?" Chipper has to shout because the ruckus has brought a flock of pterodactyl size dive bombers at him. The razored spine grove offers him momentary protection from the birds, that's until the forest picks up momentum, mama lumbering off somewhere.

"BETSY!"

She's too busy underneath to respond, doing a fancy fourstep to avoid being squished, and in total darkness no less.

"BETSY!"

Something about this screeching single glow-eyed parasite the monster has on her back irritates her, so she turns instinctively, heads off toward water, for a bath will surely rid her of the pest.

Betsy's left on the shore as she watches Chipper carried out to sea, the glow of his lamp growing dimmer and dimmer. ROH? Is this how their lifelong adventure is to end, she left to wonder, stranded alone in a dark swamp in the very depths of Hell with mad souls howling about and these bitsy barracudas sniping at her undercarriage. It is the world of Hieronymus Bosch despite what that blowhard Salaam piously reassured her — Hell has modernized with the times — Up Yours! — she barks defiantly into the thick density abounding.

Though lo, when all at sea seems a loss, who should come lapping to shore but Chipper. For some among us are undaunted, though weary, wary and winded. "Betsy!" He whispers weakly.

She laps at his mouth, bores the seaweed out of his ears.

"I've got these tiny bites all ovah me."

What is it with these damn things? She paws furiously at the water.

"We've got to keep movin, othahwise they'll nibble us to death."

So they go, man and his dog slogging blindly toward the heart of the darkness.

"Who ye be thar?"

The light of an oil lantern makes its way at them.

"Stand by and make ready far the fight o'yar life!"

"Captain Blight, that you?"

"Who from these parts acknowledges me name?"

"It's Chippuh, Chippuh Stuhbee and Betsy, and thank goodness we've found you, must've gotten sepahrated at the beach."

No way even this imbecile is going to fall for that script again! Let's run, run for our lives!

"Back t'claim yar share o'the trasure, are ye, well ye can farget that unless ye'r man enough t'take me down!"

"You- you found the gold?"

"Nowhar nar as much as yar pals war boastin, but four right heavy bags o'Spanish doubloons undar a pile o'stones on the only rise me and me men found in this infested swamp."

"Unbelievable!"

As in incredible.

"Evarywhar we stepped these ghosts sproutin up and screechin thar lungs out and monstar tartles who hacked up all me coolies, the ones who warn't carried off by them infarnal gargoyles."

"This must be the real Hell."

"Maybe, maybe not. Nothin's evar what ye suspect in this har undarwarld though all's gone accardin t'plan 'til now dag'nabbit, me longboat's eithar been taken by these banshees ar drifted off."

No no, Betsy's boggled, the thought of being stranded in a bog among prehistoric beasts, unrepentent souls and Blight — this would be punsihment beyond what any sin of hers could warrant.

"What can we do to help?" Chipper must be of the same mind.
"Sarch far and fast. Think this dang dog could sniff out me skiff?"
"Betsy, suhe, fah a few pieces of youh take."
That's it, put my nose on the line.
"Deal, though it barns me to do it, but I'm a man of me ward when I'm put to it."
"Shake?"
"Keep me hand t'meself, thank ye. Me ward's enough far the scarvy likes o'yar kind."
Man so smelly so picky — *whuff* — dog rolled in dead fish is a whiff better than you.
"Lead on poochie befar those damnable bards come swoopin."
"Need help with those bags you'h heftin?"
"Buzz off, thar mine."
Betsy tracks and backtracks on a search for firm footing. While marshlands might be ideal refuge for most wildlife, web feet or a set of meaty froglegs would do better than paws.
"Hold steady. Thar's somethin nippin at me good leg."
"Been havin at us all along."
"It's them damn gargantuas, plague o'these parts, half demon, half piranha, tiny teeth and bullwhip tails."
Tell me about it.
"Blast from me blunderbuss'll scare the nightlice off'em!"
KA-BLOOF!
Nibblers scatter.
"Loads mar whar those come from, so ye bettar pick up on the scent."
Scent, boat, right — but what does a longboat smell like? *-sniff? -sniff?* Like a peb-legged captain who hasn't bathed since Spain laid claim to Cuba. Stench that ripe shouldn't be hard to find on a moonless night, like right, right, no left some… possibly through these cattails…
"Whar's that damn dog o'yars disappar'd to?"
BONK! Head's up! Longboat's over *her-rr-rr*, half sunk in the shallows.
"Guess we'h goin to have to bail watah."
Except the gargantuas are back in division strength this time, and a second blast with the blunderbuss doesn't phase them. They attack by leaping with mouths open, spiked teeth — and no fair because Blight and Chipper are bent over bailing.
"*Y'ouch!*" Fiendish blood-suckers have Chipper covered, he tries brushing them off, but not until he bites back does he gain any advantage, *blick* though, they taste so… gamey? It'd take a lot of Louisiana hot sauce to cover their ferocious flavor, yet who's feeding on who or whom anyway, guest or dinner, for in those days, woe, beasts shall feast on one another.

"I'll show ye varmin!" Blight's at them with a fork he conveniently carries in his breast pocket. "Best weapon thar be against rodents." And can he ever, once he's free of them, he picks more off Chipper, flicks them a furlong away. "Inta the longboat, our only safety's at sea!"

"Damn, nevah expected you'd be the one savin me!"

"Don't make too much o'it matey, simply need ye far crew while I guard me bags o'gold." Blight's easy astern, tiller in hand, hollarin out ordars. Chipper hunched over haulin on the oars.

"Confound it, whar be me ship?"

Certainly not where you left it.

"I'm not a man t'lose me bearin's. Must be the scurvy Chinie, one o'mar sarvived and set off without me!"

That's it, when things go awry blame the masses.

Blame somebody as the sea begins to churn, the waves rise and rush over the skiff, nearly sweep away Betsy who's furthest front and taking hits fast and furious.

"How long could a stohm like this last?" Chipper's back to it, waves lashing him.

"Hard t'say, o'whar it's drivin us."

"Theah any way out to open ocean?"

"Narrow channel, but trecharous it be, even in the best o'conditions."

RUE! RUE! Betsy gets booted with a barrel of water, then another as the sea begins to swirl round and round, then down and down — they're swept into a funnel. Blight's hard on the tiller, peg leg stomped squarely on his bags of gold. Betsy's wavering in the breeze, a fuzzy pennant with her claws locked on the prow. Chipper's forced to give up on the rowing, though he holds on to the oars, for they shall surely be lost if he loses those.

"Should I not sarvive mateys, make cartain ye tell the history books I went undar with a cargo o'the purest Spanish bullion from Hell!" With that said there's a snap of the tiller, a wash as Captain Blight is swept over, though not with his gold.

His abrupt departure leaves Betsy and Chipper at the mercy of the water spout pulling them deeper.

"Whoa!"

WOE!

Is the only escape from one tragedy to yet another?

"Hang on babydoll!"

Seems not, for from above a mighty wave claps over them, plunges away any last hope of salvation as they are sucked low to the blackest bottom in the darkness.

THE DEVIL HISSELF

The surf laps at the toes of two castaways wantonly tossed upon a smooth stone landing — two bags of gold tumbled ashore along with them — and when they awake there's a glow, torches, polished marble steps rising from the sea.

"Wheah ah we?"

Betsy's soaked and groggy, but her eye surveys a portico constructed of rows of graceful Corinthian columns.

"What've we, finally reached Heaven's gate?"

Same scent of sulfur, however. Betsy wrings herself out, looks around. Gone indeed is the hellfire, even the damnation, instead a lost temple beneath the lowest ocean — my guess is we've simply sunk deeper into Hell.

In point of fact she is correct, they are a layer above the earth's molten core, as low to the center as any creature dare go without being consumed.

"Hottah than blazes!"

Yet — *clip-clip-clip* — her nails click — the marble provides a cool relief.

"Feel the breeze?"

Drafty.

"Why ah you ahways so damn skeptical?"

Must be the company I keep.

"Wheahevah we ah, we'h definitely someplace else."

They mount the stairs and tread through chamber after empty chamber, eventually into a lofty rotunda,

"What's that up theah?"

A frieze atop the columns depicts some richly robed monarch on horseback, a tyrant no doubt, the way he's riding roughshod over serfs or slaves, while off to the side merchants offer him their wares, farmers their grain, maidens rush with cups brimming over, soldiers lay down their arms and nobles kneel, priests and astrologers as well.

"Satan?"

Some devil.

Beneath the frieze stands an altar, an altar bereft of candles or flowers, bare except for a large golden disk propped upright.

"Don't suppose we'h trespassin, do you?"

As in forgive us if we are?

They approach as close to the altar as they dare. Embossed upon the disk is the profile of an emperor or god, youthful, long locks tossed, his chin raised in adolescent disdain.

"Must be some soht of shrine?"

More tomb than shrine.

"May I help you?" Voice out of nowhere. A figure enters from an archway, certainly not a priest for he wears no robes, rather a dark three piece pinstripe suit with regimental tie, grayed tall and erect, stride measured as he approaches directly — "I say, may I help you?"

"We wah just admihrin youh gold disk."

"Yes, the largest coin ever minted, Alexander's Drachma. It lay buried for centuries until it was accidentally discovered by grave robbers in Alexandria, who were forthwith beheaded along with their secret while this resplendent prize was brought here to be displayed."

"Suckah glows."

"As does only the purest of gold — tell me, are you an earthly celebrity perhaps, judging by your casual attire and bleached straggly hair?"

"Once hahdly, not much since."

"No? Then you have most unfortunately descended far beneath your station."

"Say what?"

Who are you to judge others by mere appearances, besides you priss, the hair is premium platinum.

"And pray tell what is this?"

"This heah's Betsy."

"Really now? We do not permit livestock in the hall."

"Hey, neithah of us evah want to be wheah we'h not welcome, so show us the revolvin dooh and we'll gladly disappeah."

"Not easily done, I fear, nor do we usually suffer such intrusion. You must have been sent here for a reason."

"Damn bad luck's what I reckon."

"We prefer to consider our presence at this stratum the result of good fortune and careful estate planning, an invitation to spend eternity among the finest of families."

"That cahtainly leaves me out. Betsy's got ancestry, though no best of show, and my family's descended from Nohth Amehrican ohriginals."

"We accept those from inherited wealth as well as successful entrepreneurs."

Whoever has clawed their way to the top, in other words.

"We do not discriminate. Membership is open to anyone with the means to pay entrance fees." He glowers down his nose, especially at Betsy.

Betsy glowers back. When it comes to snouts hers is almost as big as his.

"She's with me, and do you think these bags of Spanish doubloons heah could get us in among the elite?"

CLUNK? CLUNK?

"Gold prices have rallied recently."

"How about greenbacks, I've got at least five bucks on me somewheah."

"No matter. Dollars remain roughly on par with the Euro. We prefer Swiss interbank notes when trading for our own account."

"Looks like gold's all I got."

"These relics would appeal to certain collectors, hence we could proceed with the intake interview, discuss your final investment options."

"Got nothin in the way of a retihement fund."

"Shall we begin with a closer inspection of the contents of the bag you are carrying?" Inspect the prig does, snout and all, sticks his head way deep in. After a snort he seems satisfied. "I shall be pleased to put this to your account, with any final decision contingent upon an assessment of the precise weight and worth."

"That mean we'h in?"

"Temporarily."

"Tempohrary's time enough."

"Have you other valuables to declare? For this is the Last Universal Bank of Settlements where you must divest yourself entirely of all your worldly possessions — that which was dearest to you above must be handed over for safekeeping below."

"Most I got on me is my Timex, band's broke, and Betsy's spohtin a brass name tag on huh collah, nothin much else."

You failed to mention your goldens.

"Pittance. One does wonder how you two have made it this far in a tight economy — home equity loan, was it?"

There's a racket, almost as lucrative as managed health care.

"I shant ask how you came into possession of this gold, I shall merely assume it was nefarious, though no matter, gold is gold, whether one dug, earned, found or stole it."

"Ouhs was salvaged from the sea."

"Nautical law carries its own set of precedents."

"What ah you goin to do with it?"

"We put your money to work for you — equities mainly, T-bills, a smaller percentage in real estate — and we credit your cash account accordingly. While your net worth may fluctuate, over the past two decades we have averaged over 30% appreciation for every dollar invested. "Only the best brokerages manage our funds, mainly because we have so many of their former partners on our Board of Associates."

"Damn! I could walk out of heah a wealthy man!"

"Perhaps you were ill-informed at the processing center, but no one has ever been known to leave the confines of Hell."

"Yeah well, we came in the back way, see, on a guided touah…"

"Pray tell who was this guide? Not that old fraud Æneas?"

"No, ouh guide's name is Salaam — Salaam Kareen Kaboom, you've probably heahd of him?"

"You allowed an infidel to lead you without any resistance into Hell?"

"I'm not suhe what Salaam believes in…"

Sometimes he goes on and on like a tent show revivalist.

"…but he's an all-around decent fellow."

"Decency has little currency in this hall."

"The mah I see down heah, the mah that looks to be the case, but why? Don't folks basically want to trust one anothah? Doesn't that make life eventually easiah on evahryone?"

"Trust? Our trust department relies wholly on advisers with proven track records, otherwise we switch firms. With the expertise assembled on our own board, we can provide an oversight on investment second to none, save perhaps Harvard's Endowment Fund."

-*pssst* pal, I don't think you two are on the same wavelength.

"Don't mean you still can't try and communicate gihl."

"Beg pardon?"

"Sohry, sometimes I've got to stop and try to reassuhe Betsy heah, she's become so distrustful of strangahs."

This high priest of finance stares down at her.

Nor does she blink back.

"Name's Chippuh Stuhbee." Chipper steps up a step, extends a hand.

"We prefer numbered accounts, and a verbal more than suffices."

-*surr*, but can we trust a man who won't shake?

Close up this modern day priest's face is drawn, his complexion sallow, his eyes deep and recessed back to tiny pin points in his skull.

"Wheah exactly do you fit into the pictuhe?"

"I sir, am the Comptroller of Hell. Prior to this position I was the Undersecretary for South American Economic Affairs with the IMF."

"They some soht of credit cahd company?"

"In essence. A lender of last resort to despots tottering close to default."

"I could suhe use a loan to tide me ovah."

The Devil Hisself

"What pray tell is your average annual income?"

"Got the promise of a successful second careeh ahead of me, if only I could scohe a recohd breakin hit."

"Intangibles do not qualify."

"Been a musician most of my life, eahned what I could honestly…"

"Honesty is notoriously suspect in these quarters?"

"…nevah stole nothin – oh filch a little weed heah oah theah, bohrow a wrench, sometimes fahget to retuhn it…"

"Common thievery is not acceptable here. We cater to big money interests, those who have proven themselves capable of accumulating millions if not billions."

"They say, behind evahry great fohtune theah's some soht of fraud."

"Good heavens, don't bore me with a recitation on the exploitation of the masses, that theory has been thoroughly discredited. Free trade, particularly in investment capital, demonstrably works the best. Globalization as a pursuable policy raises prices, creates excess capacity, floats takeovers, enhances established monopolies, supercharges the stock market and in the process brings organized labor to its knees."

"Don't seem to be nobody wohshippin heah in youh temple?"

"Our congregation is far too preoccupied for religion! Not that we object so long as they regularly mail in their contributions."

"No Friday night buffet suppahs fah the homeless?"

"Hardly – and was it not Jesus Christ Himself who said, 'The poor thou shalt always have with you?'"

"That and somethin about the rich tryin to steeh theih way cleah around the eye of a needle."

"Passages in that opus are clearly open to various interpretations. Surely the only thing that matters in the end is how well we are loaded."

"Ahright ahright, let me get this straight. The folks we met upstaihs, even among the greedy theah, they wah numbahed among the pooh and unfohtunate?"

"Or the mere middle class."

"So Hell's got a whole diffahrent level fah the rich and famous?"

"Most assuredly. Along with prepaid advance reservation. Walk-in trade is greatly discouraged. Would you have expected otherwise?"

"Nope, now that you mention it."

"I, for example, was an investment wizard. I thrived during the go-go 60s and survived the panic of the late 70s. The Reagan tax cut netted me millions and the Clinton bull market, the longest on record, brought me to the threshold of being a billionaire. Even during the Great Correction that inevitably followed, I wallowed in treasury bills and never felt the slightest shock nor repercussion. I died a decidedly wealthy man."

"Whoa! What was youh secret?"

"My lips are sealed forever — although it was rumored at the time of my passing that I had access to advance information and a reliable Luxembourg banker."

"That kind of like insidah tradin?"

"Ugly word to describe the routine occupation of Wall Street."

"Meanin nobody makes money just dumbly playin the mahket?"

"Hardly. One does not work his way up by entrusting his fortune to a gambler's luck."

"Right. Odds ah with you only if you can pick the winnahs befahhand."

"Precisely."

"Any suggestions I could wagah on if I do succeed in pullin myself out of this jam?"

"The chances of that are slim to nil, hence I could indulge you — QuotLink Inc, buy at any price."

Those thieves.

"I heah they've even got deals with you guys."

"Lowest management has granted them a ninety-nine year lease on mineral disposal rights and a limited security agreement in exchange for a percentage share on biotechnological patents they have accumulated, with all long term proprietary rights reverting to us upon termination."

"We've seen the site of theih new biotech fabrication plant."

"A lucrative once-in-an-eon opportunity in which we have a solid minority share. Additionally, we have hired their heavy construction division to tunnel out new chasms in the limestone layers for the overflow Baby Boomers we anticipate will be joining our ranks quite soon."

"So rumah's true, you ah runnin out of room?"

"Let me say, off the record of course, that we failed to anticipate the financial opportunities associated with a population increase of this magnitude and a new class of billionaires who would tolerate nothing less than the best in afterlife accommodations."

"So QuotLink Inc's a majah paht of youh investment strategy?"

"We recognized their potential early on, which is why we provided them with most of their start-up capital — as a matter of fact, and I say this to you in the strictest of confidence…" Man bends close and hisses.

Is this what they call a hot tip?

"…there is talk of more than a partnership on certain pet projects — there's the possibility, nay the probability of an announcement soon of a full-scale merger that would benefit both parties immeasurably."

"Whoa! QuotLink Inc would be in league with the Devil Himself?"

"Quite."

"I'll have to remembah to phone my brokah soon as I get myself out of heah. What's theih tickah symbol?"

"QQLI — but you shall never 'get yourself out of here,' not you and not your mouthy little mutt either!" Man in the pinstripe suit turns abruptly unpleasant as men in high position are wont to do, especially when wheedled out of free financial advice. He starts stamping about in his fancy Italian shoes, frightens the nightlights out of Betsy who dashes for the door of the open vault, Chipper not far behind — *click click and whirr* — as the tumblers lock into place — and bright choice it is because through that very gate lies the gold glowing staircase to the deepest depository of Hell.

One gold brick stairwell leads to another, the walls rose marble, the ceilings Byzantine mosaic, like the Kremlin stop on the Moscow line, but dusty to neglected and here and there a leak, though golden as in a rich yellow vein.

"See Betsy, prospehrity does trickle down."

Not nearly enough and makes a mess on the floor.

"They might not be budgetin much fah maintenance these days, but in its prime this place must've been mighty impressive."

At least it's lit, dry and temperate, plus the signs point in the same direction, downward.

"Remembah the Double A membahship motto: You can't staht climbin back up 'til you've skidded to rocky bottom." Which happens, tunnel dead ends against a rough hewn wall. There is a heavy double oak door, brass devil's head knocker, no name plate — "Whoa! Don't know!"

Do I discern a note of hesitation?

Luckily there's an oak bench alongside — a bench with a bum curled up asleep on it.

"'Scuse me suh, sohry to bothah, bu-…"

"Botha? No botha bro, jus' waitin on a friend, tha's all." Dude doesn't pry open an eyelid.

Bro? *-hmm* mighty suspicious — *Bark! Bark! Bark!*

"Betsy, mind youh mannahs!"

"Who what? Chippa, tha' yo?"

"Salaam?"

"Damn man, wha' took yo so long? Tia'd me out jus' waitin."

"Tihed you out? How about Betsy and me — and wheah'd you disappeah to back theah in the Valley of the Vengeful?"

"So'ry 'bout that, but I's played toua guide once too often, an crawlin through that firin range was wearin on my nu'ves. Betta I said t'myself, let yo two ezplo'a the countryside on yo own while I wanda's ova t'get a looksee at what the QuatLinks was upta. Besides, the goin got easia the fu'thu down yo went, right? Intellectual crime and white colla pilf'rin don't usually lead t'no attacks on pu'son."

Easier! Betsy seriously considers a lunge at Salaam's bloated Adam's apple.

"Down gihl, down. Leastwise we'h heah now, safe and sound – sohta."

"Soona o'lata yo was bound t'reach up with me, road don' go nowhea else but."

"We could've been killed oah wohse, trapped some place with weihdos suhroundin us evahaftah – that Devil's Island was the closest call of all."

And those toothy gargantuas.

"How'd yo eva arrange a layova on Devil's Island?"

A layov-*rr-rr*! Betsy has to be restrained.

"Ain' neva been thea myself, too dang'rous I been told, an way off the beaten path. No wonda it took yo two so long t'catch up."

-RR-RAWRAW-ROAR*!*

"Betsy! Get a grip!"

I'm trying, I'm trying, tight around his neck!

"What's happened ta make ha tu'n so mean? I know bros an dogs got this long his'try a'mistrust, but I figu'd yo an me done patched that misunda'standin up."

"Betsy babydoll." Chipper is down at her level, attempting to reason with her. "This grudge ain't goin to get none of us nowheah."

-*grr-rudge!* What, are you defending him?

"Nope, but sometimes a familiah face is the only one you can rely on."

"We bout ova the grumpin an growlin?"

Betsy snarls.

"H'yep, ahways bettah to let bygones be – least some of us have got to keep tryin to get along togethah."

"Tha's right, don' wan' t'end up down hea like the resentful, stabbin each otha in the back."

"Oah the vengeful, shootin at one anothah, too thick to call a truce."

"Seemed the lowah we went Salaam, the smahtah they got."

"Those wa the deceitful. They's educated a'right, licensed, ca'tified memba's a'the pro'fess'nal elite. Ambitious an smug 'bout it too, convinced they is priv'leged, desa've nothin but the best an all the rest yo might as well sign ova t'them too – but bro, yo ain' seen nothin yet. Yo still gots one las' level ta go – the high rolla's an big time scamma's, they makes a street pimp look like a prince."

"Wait! Wait a minute. Befah you drag us any deepah, we've got to get a few things straight."

"Lay it on me bro."

"All these levels… I'm confused. Now pride, that's still the root of all evil, right?"

"No way, envy is. Envy's the fu'st a'the Seven Deadliest Sins. Envy breeds resentment an greed, afta that vengeance — tha's when yo wants what somebody else's got so bad yo'd kill fo it."

"Venegful I undahstood, what happened aftah that?""

"Deceit — whole 'notha stage a'development."

They're slicker, they didn't seem as prone to resort to physical violence.

"Don' make'em any nica. Can' trust nothin they say. They cheat, they lie, they steal, shift blame off t'somebody else, a'ways instigatin. Cowa'ds is what they a', hidin behind the letta a'the law."

"So what's comin up next?"

"Treach'ry, then a'rogance — the las' two an the deadliest sins a'all."

"Treachahry?"

"Treach'ry's when nobody can trust yo, not even yo own kind, when yo is totally out fo yoself, a'ways on the prowl — predato'ry — man who holds no values knows no rest, a'ways gots t'sleep with one eye propped open."

"And ahrogance is the same as pride, right?"

"Ev'rythin builds ta pride. Envy begins it, a'rogance ends it."

The mad souls on Devil's Island, they were treacherous, they killed their own, and they were arrogant, they showed no remorse.

"The denizens a'Devil's Island, they's so hateful, they's done gone way off the cha'ts — tha's why they is kept in theia own isolated ring."

Similar to those suffering from excess?

"Excess, we is talkin 'bout folks who is lost, wand'rin round in a daze."

"Let me see if I've got this right. Each level down heah cohresponds to one of these seven deadly sins — envy, resentment, greed, vengeance — and what wah the othahs?"

Deceit, treachery and arrogance, but not excess — that's somehow less an offense these days, and the hateful are simply out of their minds.

"Yo gots the basic idea, but thea's this otha dimensin yo is missin…"

Not to mention there are nine rings of Hell and only seven deadly sins.

"Unda'lyin each level's the same evils, only mo intense as yo plunges deepa. See, one evil's rooted in anotha, and it ain' like yo gets condemned fo jus' one. As yo goes through life, yo gets stuck in yo ways, yo gets entangled in one mess afta anotha. An whea yo ends up, tha's whea yo is stuck — this ring o'that, dependin on how low down mean an nasty yo has finally sunk."

"Each man his own misahry?"

"Ezactly, he's struggled ha'd t'earn it, so he def'nitely desa'ves it, but envy's the sou'ce, man's inbo'n selfishness."

Hence you equate envy with being self-centered?

"Yo can see envy sta't in a child, crabby grabby by age three, wants what that otha kid's got, wants it a lot, resentful a'that otha kid jus' fo havin it. An if a fist poundin tantrum don' get it fo him, he ups an grabs it — boda'line vengeful. Don' take long befo he's olda an reso'ted ta deceit, learns easily how t'outsma't the gullible an good-natu'ed, snatch it away from them without them even catchin on, graduates from gramma school with one clea lesson — he can get away with most any treacha'ry, 'long as he don' get caught. Leaves him as a'rogant as all Hell rest o'his life."

True, pups can be playful until they develop their canines.

"But ain't all kids bohn innocent?"

"Not t'a wolf pack fo parents."

-rr wait, wait a second. Wolves are first cousins of mine. They have suffered lots of bad press historically, when all they've been attempting to do is survive extinction.

"Ezcuse my ref'rence, I means hyenas, nobody claims kinship with those scavenga's."

Nor have they been lobbying Congress with much success either — although again the hyena is somewhat akin to us dogs.

"Yo ain' raisin the question a'orig'nal sin, is yo?"

Nature or nurture? Sure bet or wager?

"I mean, I agree ev'ry baby's bo'n with the capacity ta be gen'rous, each lovin bundle — but who's holdin that bundle, o'not holdin that bundle? Who's gone off an left that infant t'fend fo hisself? Like motha like son, like fatha, like daughta, kid don' a'ways have no place t'tu'n fo guidance. Befo long he's done grown up from bein self-centa'd t'full-blown defiant, resentful t'a'rogant, vengeful t'a mean streak runnin the length a'his spine."

And no tail to wag for the fun of it.

"Kid's done moved off the playground an onta Main Street, whea life's nothin but a gamble, an high stakes rolla's can win big playin with otha people's money."

Or lose it and wipe out everyone's savings.

"Hey, maybe if I sings yo a song I wrote, show yo some moves, yo can pull it togetha."

Never thought of you as a song and dance man.

"I's full a'su'prises hot diggidy dog."

Guess so.

"Song's called *Insatiable* an goes somethin like this…"

> Lust is loveliest
> The loneliest afta'noon
> Some so't a'self-indulgence
> Tempts me ta swoon

"Whoa! 40s big band style!"

And basically baritone.

> What matta's if I'm envious
> Delightfully devious
> Peevish o'pitiless
> Resentful some too?
> My simply insatiable me

"Man can croon!"

"Thank yo, thank yo. Now if yo two'll hum a few ba's fo me, I'll do some soft shoe." And he does, he taps himself silly up and down the slick marble staircase — *clickityclickclick clickityclick clickityclickity click…*

> It's undeniable
> I'm so unreliable / See
> Kinda entitled / That's me
> Fo what's yo's is mostly liable
> T'end up mine / Ova time

Betsy's on the beat with her tail.

> So come let me put my a'ms
> All ova yo
> Fondle while fleecin yo
> Tempt yo while teasin yo / Fo
> Man can't do without greed
> No not my terribly
> Incomparably insatiable me

-clickity clickity click
-clippity clipin' it. Betsy jumps in. She's a hoofer.
-click click
-*clip clip*
-clickity click
-*clippity clip*
-clickityclickityclickity click
-*clippityclippityclippity clip*

The two of them slap happy dueling it.

> So what if I'm a'rogant
> Who's that yo starin at
> Craven's acceptable
> Evasion's respectable
> Nothin's disgraceful these days

-clip clip -clip clip

Why try denyin it
When I'm a guy gettin by with it
Lyin in spite of it
Too deceitfully
Me / me me me meee
That simply insatiable me

-*clickity click click*
-***clippity clip quit.***
"Thank yo ma'am!"
My pleasure, I'm sure.

"'Bout time, time fo the fool t'learn who's who, time t'pee'a inta the da'kness, see what evil lurks deep in the hearts a'men."

It's going to get worse, I can tell.

"Behind these doo's lies the Lowest Chamba a'Hell."

"And we'h just goin to bust right in?"

"Supreme Cou't a'Final Appeals. Yo gots t'wo'k a lifetime t'get yo case hea'd in hea."

"'Spect it ain't small claims oah paltry misdemeanahs."

"U'sully some high tail son-of-a-bitch gettin his honky white ass kicked…"

Which could prove interesting.

"…bent ova beggin fo ma'cy o one las' chance t'redeem hisself fo'eva."

"Do any of them evah succeed?"

"Ha'dly neva."

"That's what I want to see, justice done with a dash of evahlastin retribution."

"Did I mention thea's a definite downside t'be consida'd befa we enta?"

-*rowl*-ways is.

"This ain' the fun house yo knows, this is the depths a'To'ment an Abuse, the sou'ce a'man's misa'ries an woes from centu'ry unta centu'ry — an no place fo no amateu's neitha."

Only professionals.

"These ain' robba's prowlin round in the night. These thieves do what they do with lights blazin, the cam'ras rollin, whole slew a'newspapa repo'ta's standin by askin them nothin but polite questions."

-*roh?*

"Can' let'em fool yo none. Smooth don' make them nice, no way, this bunch'll rob yo a'ev'rythin yo owns an in full view — real legal like — then bury yo mostly wo'thless remains in a unma'ked hole!"

"But we'h just innocent bystandahs?"

"Nobody snoopin down this deep's innocent. Yo gets too close t'the fi'a an yo's goin t'get yo finga's singed — so yo two gots to be su'a yo wants t'tangle with these lifa's?"

"'Spose if we've come this fah… and like my grandpappy used to say, only places wohth nosin into anyway ah dahk, dank and foul smellin."

I can vouch for that.

"A'right. Jus' don' go blamin me lata, sayin I didn' wa'n yo o'nothin."

Are there any more prehistoric beasts?

"Jus' humans who'll do a lot mo damage befo they's become eztinct."

Met up with their kind before.

"Folks inside hea is treach'rous treach'rous, an we gots t'be downright sneaky ou'selves."

Betsy instinctively hunkers down on her belly.

"Fu'st, we gots t'open this hea doo'…"

"How about the fihe alahm?"

"Ain' no fi'a ala'ms in Hell bro!"

-KROAK

"Now go real slow an quiet like."

-KROAK-RR-ROAK

"Sticks yo head right on in thea doggie-do, make su'a the way is clea."

Me? Surely you jest?

"Chippa quick, see what yo can see."

"You suhe theah's no monstah guahdin the gate?"

"That ol' crocodile head's stationed ova at the main entrance these days, besides he ain' nowhea nea as frightenin as he's been po'trayed."

-KROAK-KROAK-KROAK

"Poke yo heads in!"

-*umm*, why don't you take the lead chum. I've never minded being one of life's cheerful followers.

"All I see is a dahk passageway."

"We's goin through a fo'gotten passageway, one they'd only use t'flee in case a'some ema'gency. Le's scoot on through."

Which they do.

"You tellin me these folks can use this fihe escape from Hell any time they want?"

"Su'a'nough! Wha' yo think, sma't basta'ds like these is goin t'lock themselves in? No siree, a'ways gots t'allow yoself some wiggle room."

"Wheah you figuah they'd go aftah they left heah?"

"These devils? They'd eitha blow south t'Rio o'straight up the coast t'Miami."

Assumed they had bought up the beach front there already.

"Think they'h plannin on makin a run any time soon?"

"This is yo miscreant elite Chippa, an between me an yo, they ain' leavin hea 'less they'a fo'ced ta. They likes whea they's at, they's associatin with theia kind a'people in the only place eta'nally int'restin t'be."

"And they don't mind if we stand theah and gawk?"

"Only a damn fool would attempt the stunt we'h pullin."

Says something about us, doesn't it?

"This crowd's got t'be the most a'rogant eva assembled, like in self-satisfied, man'o'man, convinced! They figu'a they is aristocrats, ev'ry one, whetha bo'n ta it o'bought inta it, each betta than the next an entitled — they's above any law, any po'wa on ea'th o anywhea else fo that matta."

"Ah they?"

"'Cept fo a few mino inconven'ences hea an thea, they's pretty much had theia own way. Hist'ry might be unkind t'theia mem'ry fo awhile, but hey they won big an theia descendants is still reapin the rewa'ds…"

SLAM! SLAM!

"What in hell is that?"

"Quiet! We's gettin close. Gots t'go on tippytoes from hea on in."

-clip-clip-clip-clip…

"Tippytoes!"

Sorry, but that's about as tippy as my toes go… *-clip… -clip… clip…* I probably should have stayed behind, played the trusty mutt guarding the gate — *clip* — but there are somethings in life you simply can't believe, not until you have seen for yourself — and the last judgment has got to be one… *-clip… -clip… -clip… -clip…*

SLAM! SLAM!

"Halt! Shush!"

-hulp! -hulp!

The dull thud of wood upon wood resounds from inside the hall.

"We is no mo than three o fou' steps away from ent'rin the Main Cou't — who's that quakin in theia boots back thea?"

Only m-me. For there are places in this world where even a ferocious Dobbie fears to tread.

"What's we gots t'do hea is pry open this loose panel a crack, so's I can take a pee-…"

-pee? As in a quick one now before I dribble down my leg?

"…-peek."

-oh!

"We don' want t'jus' go ba'gin in!"

Absolutely not, never dream of it. Pee- peek, long as you like.

-KRAAAAAACK

"Tha's it, tha's enough, le me look — *hmmmm* — they's in ezecutive session — this is goin t'be mighty in'trestin…"

Executive session?

"…fact is, they's in between sessions — yo can tell — they gets as noisy as grackles befo the spring migration."

Good. Wouldn't want them as quiet as hawks on a lone wintry hunt.

"An too busy as usu'l t'notice us way up hea in the uppa upstaia's balcony. So crouch down low, low as yo can go, an don' make no noise, don' say nothin — yo hea's me?"

Loud and clea-*rr*.

"Ready? Le's go — an be real ca'eful not t'go stickin yo head up ova the balcony rail, yo might jus' gets it shot off."

-KRA-RAA-RAA-RAAAAAAACK   -RACK! -RACK! -RACK!

Chipper and Salaam crawl along old theater seating bolted to the floor, Betsy dragging behind on her belly. They go from aisle to aisle until they bump up against the balcony railing.

"Wheah ah we exactly?"

"The old visito's gall'ry, but since they put a stop t'regula toua's a'Hell, it's been abandoned."

"When was that?"

"Back in the 70s when most folks gave up on religion — fea a'Hell fell t'an all-time popula low."

"How come you know about this secret panel?"

"Used t'sneak down hea when I was a kid with some a'the hood, a'cou'se then we had no idea what it was we wa watchin, seemed downright borin t'us."

"And you nevah got caught?"

"These cha'racta's keeps theia eyes glued t'the main floo, don' wan' t'miss a move. Cou'troom drama's bout the only fo'm a'enta'tainment they gots left, that an watchin the poo souls above slip off the rocks an tumble down kickin an screamin inta that caldron a'blue bubblin at the bottom."

"Safe to take a look?"

"Long as it's yo head bro, not mine."

"Whoa!" Chipper peers over.

What? Betsy's ears and eyes over too.

"What ah they doin down theah Salaam?"

"Will yo jus' take a look at the woodwo'k, hand ca'ved, an the Tuscan ma'ble linin the walls. This place was built t'last 'til the end a'time."

Cool.

"They fin'ly broke down an installed ai'a-conditionin back in the 80s. Befo that it was hotta than Hades."

Place is a cross between a senate chamber and a huge antique Viennese opera house, ornate, with velvet draped private boxes and balustrade balconies tiered high, crowded to capacity, people in their finest evening dress, all murmuring, all intent on the proceedings below.

"That's what they do? Stand around on the flooh and talk?"

"Ain' jus' talk, no siree, they's busy makin deals."

The players on the main floor are robed in black with wigs and move from the defense to the prosecution tables with an easy camaraderie. The court has taken a short recess, and a single throne behind the bench is momentarily unoccupied. There is no jury box, and the prisoner's dock stands by itself on a platform and center for all to watch.

"Couhtroom's no bettah than a tohtuhe chambah." Which Chipper should know since he's seen the inner workings of so many.

"See that box ova thea, the one draped in red, white an blue?"

"Next to the one done up in the Union Jack?"

"Tha's resa'ved ezclusively fo presidents a'the United States."

"Damn!"

"Seven thus fa has ended up down hea fo one reason o'anotha, fou' a'them from the twentieth centu'ry alone."

I can believe it. Those guys didn't get to the top by being nice. What you wonder is how the rest got off so easy?

"What about the otha boxes?"

"Kings an Queens, mighty Pharaohs, invincible Empa'o's with the Gen'rals a'theia a'mies, Prime Ministas's, theia Financeea's an Profiteea's, an Military Dictato's too, the petty ones along with the completely ruthless."

"That Napoleon with the three cohnah hat?"

"Right next t'Mussolini. Been told they's become soulmates."

"So mostly politicians?"

"Politicians along with wa'lords, a'ms ma'chants, opposition pa'ty leada's who neva raised a'wo'd in protest — whole section a'the mezzanine's been resa'ved fo those who betrayed theia country, yo know, led them inta wa o' bilked them out a'theia life savin's by manipulatin the ma'kets."

"So theah is some justice in the aftahlife?"

"Yo'll see, yo'll see — that tier ove'thea is dedicated t'monopoly winna's from the times a'Babylon t'the present."

"Lots of histohry doin time togethah. How about industrial pollutahs?

"I hea's rumo's they's slavin in the fu'nace room, shovelin coal, but I couldn't get close enough t'see it fo myself — QuotLinks've thrown up a razo-wire fence round that opa'ration."

I'm sure they could hire the less fortunate to do the shoveling for them.

"Main floo' is what yo came t'see Chippa, sight should wa'm the cockles a'yo soul."

"Why's that?"

"Tha's all those lawya's yo been wond'rin bout, not all that has eva ezisted, hell, Hell itself couldn't hold all a'them."

"Still, that's a fat pack of lawyahs."

"These is the select, the ones who wa so a'rogant they dispensed with the spirit a'the law an bent the letta jus' so they could get theia rich buddies off with minimum sentences."

In other words, the successful ones.

"Who'h the ones among them weahrin the scahlet robes? They seem mah impohtant than the rest."

"Them's the judges, political cronies appointed fo life, high cou't an low, ones without a drop a'equity in theia veins."

-*mm*, they do look terribly pale and somber, like unhappy faces with the ends of their mouths turned down.

"They done sold out justice in theia back chamba's t'la'ge law firms fo sur'eptitious donations t'theia fav'rite political causes, an endo'sements fo advancement on the bench – tha's if they didn't wan' t'seem unseemly by grabbin at ha'd cash passed 'cross theia desks."

"They suhe have made my life misahrable."

"Man who presumes t'sit in judgment ova his fellow man had betta have his hands clean, be humble, but not these self-righteous prunes, they had the powa t'restrain kings, but used it t'punish the peasants instead."

"What exactly is goin on right now?"

"Usu'ly someone who's been recently condemned appealin the decision that sent him t'Hell. This is it, high as high can go low, las' chance in the univa'se t'get yo conviction set aside, all decisions final."

"They can't appeal to Heaven, beg fah fahgiveness and mahcy?"

"Heaven ain' goin ta conca'n itself with this crim'nal element, besides they's got t'contend with ova'capacity these days too."

"Can't see how standin around a couhtroom all day talkin is much of a punishment, not fah whole careeahs spent practicin nothin but licensed extohtion?"

"Tha's ezactly the point – how the kind fits the crime – see nothin eva gets resolved inside these chamba walls. Lawya's gots t'argue theia cases ova an ova an ova with endless delays an opposition motions, agonizin eons 'til the judge fin'ly gets round t'writin a decision, which ain' neva goin t'go in yo favo, an no chance t'ova'tu'n nothin nohow."

SLAM! SLAM! SLAM! SLAM! SLAM! SLAM!

Order! Order! This Court shall come to order! All rise! His Majesty Lord Lucifer enters the Hall!

Nary a cough nor a rustle, not even a breath as all eyes follow He Who Has The Power To Decide who shall rest in peace, who shall live in infamy.

"Must be a big case if Ol' Lux Hisself is goin t'be presidin."

SLAM! SLAM! SLAM! SLAM! SLAM! SLAM! SLAM! SLAM! SLAM! SLAM!

Tall, massive creature, enlarged head and ears, dressed in ermine robes enters the chamber slowly, almost painfully, and behind him a train of scarlet drags along the floor.

"Is it me seein things, oah is that long cloak covahrin a tail?"

"He's one a the o'riginals."

"So that's Lucifer!"

"No no, tha's Colón, Lucifa's Wa'den."

Others, one more deformed than the next, but dressed in regal apparel parade in, look side to side while everyone stands rigidly at attention. Last in line a trim figure, dressed in a black velvet shirt and tight leather pants, with a flat hat like a star flamenco follows last. The tension's tangible when without warning he cracks this whip!

"That his tail?"

"Slap yo down so fast yo neva knowed what hit yo!"

"Whoa!"

"Yo betta believes, nobody messes with Ol' Lux."

Much younger than I would have expected — and *sniff sniff* musky — quite handsome in a dark mysterious way.

"He got claws fah fingahs?"

"No, no horns neitha like most folks imagine."

"Mah human than beast."

No surprise there.

"Lookie see what he's packin out front. Yo thinks yo can top that act!"

"Big pokah."

"Look close if yo dare. Tha's two big poka's he's got, pair a'poka prongs, bend yo ova front an back, take His pleasua!"

Does he eschew dogmeat?

"Don' go temptin the devil, 'specially Lucifa Rex, the Hon'rable Chief Justice a'All Hell!"

"C'mon. Everybody's got to have a lightah side?"

"What makes him laugh, most folks don' find funny."

SLAM! SLAM! "My Lord!" Colón intones as the dignitaries take positions around the throne. "The appeal of Billy Roy Bopps concerning the Judgment of Damnation found against him."

"Wait a second! Billy Roy Bopps — he's the President!"

"Claims he's been set up, that Congress has gone too fa this time."

"Accohdin to the polls he's the most populah president evah."

"Plannin on havin his profile chiseled inta Mount Rushmo."

"Besides, he ain't even dead yet!"

"Some folks is so impo'tant, they tries t'wo'k out a deal befo'hand."

"What've they got on him they don't on any othah recent president?"

"Some scuttlebutt. Le's watch an see. Defense team's goin t'present a sho't film commentary on his life an ambitions."

A screen's furled. The lights in the High Chamber dim.

President Billy Roy Bopps grew up dirt poor in South Texas with seven brothers and sisters, of which he was the youngest, his roustabout father having deserted the children when Billy Roy was a mere four months old. He mainly skipped school until that fateful day when company surveyors discovered a vast oil reserve underneath the family's flat eighty acres. Money was what radically changed the boy's motivation.

The Assembly nods approvingly.

Young Billy Roy began his political career as a Dixie Democrat, switched to Republican during the fat years, back to the Democrats during the lean, although he made an independent run around both for the presidency. Won. Man's fiscally conservative, big on defense, all out for free trade, deaf to strident union demands, and slick slick, went to law school as did most recent presidents at Yale. Yet Billy Roy remembers poverty and what poverty does to an individual's self-esteem. He makes certain that any country club he joins hires colors to tend the greens. He's a man of the people, he shares their concerns, eats and shits grits, and his four sons have been brought up to make millions on their own – founding a chain of walk-in Mediache clinics for the region's poor, largely Spanish-speaking population. Billy Roy is committed to maintaining good relations with our nearest southern neighbor, he hires only wetbacks to thin sugar beats and to harvest cantaloupes seasonally on his own irrigated farmlands. He considers working bent over all day in the hot sun a character-building exercise, taking time even while senior senator from the Lone Star State to supervise the entire operation, which may explain his permanent saddle leather tan.

Billy Roy Bopps is the man nobody really wanted elected president, but after his recent predecessors who can be choosy when it comes to large party offerings, particularly when he's one of America's very own prairie cowboys. He believes in cowpoke diplomacy, rustle whatever you want from the neighbors and brand it before they catch you at it. And if there's anything left in the Treasury when he and his cabinet buddies get through horsing around, you can bet the cash will be spent on huge farm subsidies, that paid-up protection plan they've got for billion dollar agribusinesses.

"Let those dirty cities up North there rot," Billy Roy has said for attribution, "cause that's where all our Negroes run off to anyway."

The Assembly votes with their hands, long and loudly, Billy Roy Bopps is their kind of man.
SLAM! SLAM! SLAN! SLAM! SLAM! SLAM! SLAM! SLAM!

Despite Billy Roy Bopps' fortnightly excursions across the border to Ciudad Juárez, he has remained faithful to his fifth wife Belle, who explained their apparent wedded bliss to a late night caller on Harvey Hovenclop's talk show thusly: "Honey, you get ya man squeelin like a stuck pig nights and he ain't goin to be runnin round ruttin on ya none."

Belle, like everybody else on the campaign train, has been mum however about the string of Ethics Committee investigations trailing behind Billy Roy from his twelve years served as the blow-dried Majority Leader in the Yewnited Snakes Syndicate. But whatever the accusations, the man has fought hard for a social agenda. He supports women's rights, particularly pro-life female fetuses who might develop into frisky little fillies later on, and minorities, well, he wants to help them out of the grip of affirmative action, and gays, why they can screw anybody they want so long as it's within the confines of an abandoned Nevada testing site.

His appointments to the federal judiciary include his chauffeur's daughter and a house-broke mule. His idea of foreign policy is fuck the oil-producing countries, fuck them real good, and on the environment, spare the Christmas trees and cover over the coal mines, rely on clean spleen nuclear power, and we'll figure out how to hide the spent fuel rods later – long after Billy Roy's term has come and gone. Education policy is every kid for himself, and

'Ol Lux… always watching, finger to his lips, and listening intently

universal health care, no way, the old folks have got money squirreled away for a rainy day and the poor are going to die off no matter who pays for it.

Billy Roy's not typical neo-political, not at all, he can use a knife and fork when required, although his jaw does jut out in an eat-you, eat-anybody attitude, and the low sneaky brow is not necessarily a sign of lesser intelligence as his friendships with Hollywood movie moguls and used Treasury Bond salesmen demonstrate. The man has some culture.

Besides it looks as if his re-election is secure, he's this life-long believer in the One, the True and the Invisible Hand that does slight side-show tricks to balance market forces while stock prices jump through high hoops – one slip and beware though, because it will be all over for everybody everywhere, and yet the President's most recent comment on the economy seems to ring solid: "I can't predict the future my friends, don't seem like nobody else can neither, but this constant bad-mouthin bout Merica's prosperity is beginnin to wear a little thin on my nerves, how about yers?"

At which the Assembly breaks into spontaneous applause.
SLAM! SLAM! SLAM! SLAM! SLAM! SLAM! SLAM! SLAM! SLAM! SLAM!
Ol' Lux, He sits, He's watching when the lights come back on. Always watching, finger to his lips, and listening intently to whatever is said, His face immobile. Nor does His Honor often ask for clarifications. Lets His minions keep order. Only His eyes betray His disposition, flash fire destruction augured in every glance. Best strategy for a litigant is self-effacement, gaze cast down, accept his fate with not the slightest protest nor word in explanation, pray for mercy – except some do, some have to stand up there and *yak yak* at Him, think they're so important – but not before Lucifer Rex who has seen it all, seen it from time in the beginning until time never ending.

"Your Honor, I must say in my defense, I only did what I had to do."

Lucifer glowers at Billy Roy.

"I admit to takin a few interest free loans from friends and cash here or there from ingratiating Taiwanese industrialists, but in general I bought my own elections, and not one penny in corporate contributions ever influenced my decisions. I would have ruled in their favor anyway."

Lucifer smiles, raises an eyebrow – clearly He enjoys this display of bare ass self-incrimination.

"I've been no worse than a politician can be. That's the heart of my defense, man should only do what the electorate expects of him, no more. Raising people's hopes only makes them hungry for more handouts."

His Honor snorts, puff of smoke.

"If the people want ideals they should elect a philosopher king. Meantime I stand for popular democracy, no disclosure of campaign donors and winner-takes-all in the presidential sweepstakes — because if you win in this world, it doesn't matter how you did it. That's the rule I've lived by, and anybody who wants to change things had better not go fomenting a revolution because I'll put that down with all the force at my command, which is not inconsiderable. Laws get passed in back room sessions by bartering with special interest lobbyists, and anybody who thinks things should be done differently ought to move to China."

Lucifer clears his throat, with a blowtorch from His intestines.

Whole chamber gags.

"And What About Those Who Have No Cash To Bring To The Negotiating Table." Lucifer inquires. "What About Their Interests?"

"To be honest, your Honor…"

"Please Do."

"…only the rich are part of the political process, that was enshrined centuries ago in our Constitution, and funny money has been ruled protected speech."

"I See. Then You Have Acquitted Your Office Admirably."

"Thank you your Honor, I apprecia-…"

Lucifer rises, towering mightily over all in the hall, his prong pointers vibrating at a furious pitch as He renders His verdict in a voice lowdown low. "The Only Place Worthy Of Your Company Is Here, With Your Fellow Believers. Welcome Mister President. Forever And Ever!"

AMEN! resounds throughout the hall.

That said Ol' Lux lets go with a tongue lashing, braises Billy Roy with a third degree sunburn, sends him yelping back to his seat.

"And As For You Three Whispering In The Uppermost Balcony!" Head snaps rapidly about, eyes fastened on Salaam, Chipper and Betsy, eyes that ignite, tongue that does worse. "I've Had Enough Of Your Inspection. Get Out Of Hell! And Don't Come Back Unless You Can Handle The Action!"

"Motha a'ma'cy, le's clea out a'hea!"

Betsy doesn't hesitate, she's out the crack in the panel and up the passageway in a flash. Salaam and Chipper crash into one another attempting to go seconds, Salaam rebounds first, Chipper behind. Ol' Lux's tail comes zappin fast up the hatch after them, stings Chipper by the heels.

"Whoa!"

And about how fast can three chattering monkeys go racing up a two mile vent to the top of El Snorro? Plenty fast. Betsy scampers in the lead, and *right-fright* behind her, Chipper and Salaam. Though once they have safely escaped, they've got to *pant pant* slow the pace some.

"Hold on, hold on a minute, damn, I've got to take a breathah. I'm just gettin too old fah a long jog up hill."

The three squat down on the dark steps. Only light is a glow from puddles of liquid blue collected here and there. Betsy braves a sniff but foregoes a taste.

"That Lucifah, he's fiehce!"

"Told yo so bro."

"How long you figuah he knew we wah up theah watchin?"

"Prob'ly from jump. Basta'd QuotLinks must've repo'ted ou presence. They gots t'have instant access ta His inna sanctum by now."

"Why'd he let us watch as long as he did then?"

"Hell hath no fu'ry o'fright, less some'v'us su'vives t'bring it t'light."

True, but who would listen to a one of us?

"Still, some things ah naggin at me. like Billy Roy Bopps theah. Suhe, he's all out fo himself, but when you'h way up in public office, you'h bound to make biggah mistakes than some low down pushah off the streets."

"So?"

"So how come he gets condemned to the lowest level of Hell while the pushah's up catchin excess rays on the roof?"

"Ol' Lux ain' inclined t'spend no eta'nity with common riffraff off the streets, he prefa's the company a'big pricks like Hisself."

"But Billy Roy, he's not the wohst."

"He ain' the best neitha — besides bro, yo is missin the point, I mean like completely."

"What point's that?"

"The meanin a'modu'n day hellfi'a. See it ain' a'ways what yo did tha' gets yo inta deep shit, it's what yo didn' do…"

Sins of omission.

"…an Billy Roy, man's in a position t'get somethin done fo the benefit a'ev'rybody the wo'ld ova — global wa'min, ethnic wa'fare, infants sta'vin in theia motha's arms — but instead he's jus' out thea scoopin fo hisself. Tha's the crime tha' condemns him."

Lordly disdain coupled with his own petty greed.

"Now, he claims in his defense that he ain' no wo'se than nobody else, but we've seen tha's true a'ev'rybody at ev'ry level we done visited. Hence, that ezcuse jus' won' hold up."

Free him, and they would have to free everyone.

"Ezactly. All Hell'd break loose."

"But Billy Roy Bopps is ahguably the most powahful man on eahth."

"Don' matta, heart a'democracy's the rule a'law, means they's at least gots t'keep up the pretense, no matta how high above the law they is."

"Sounds about right, but we wahn't taught none of this as kids."

"Means as adults yo gots t'keep studyin."

"So how exactly did some peon like you evah figuhe this all out?"

"Well, let me ezplain it t'yo in detail. See, when yo only gets the oppo'tunity t'look at life from the bottomside up, yo begins noticin who's got what, who's callin the shots. Life ain' no puttin green, approach fo some folks is full a'potholes an occasional drive-by shootin's, no fancy home facin the fai'ways, jus' blocks afta blocks a'tenements with letta's an no numba's, no wata, no heat. Fo'ces yo ea'ly t'look at the dispa'rity. See, pova'ty's a crime, not a condition. Reason one man's got nothin's because the man next doo's got mo than he needs. Fo'ces the poo' man t'poke his head up, look round, try an find out who's t'blame. Yesta'day's Wall Street Jou'nal out a'the trash offa's a few clues."

ROAR-ER OAR! OAR!

Heads -rr-rup!

This glowing acid blue sluice comes rushing down the passageway, hits knee high and passes by, leaves fresh puddles at the travelers' feet.

SPLISHSPLISHSPLISH

"What sohta crud is this?"

Crud it is. Betsy's drenched in it.

"QuotLinks could be releasin some a theia waste wata down this old vent hole."

The blue glows brightly, especially on Betsy.

"Won't this eventually seep into the Assembly Hall?"

"Yo bet, i'ritate the shit out a'Ol' Lux."

"What'll he do?"

"Fine 'em."

"That's all?"

"Thea's lots a vent holes round an active volcano. QuotLinks'll claim they picked the wrong one, simple human err'a."

But they aren't human.

"Same as human, a'rogant, full a'deceit, an so fa out a'theia minds they'll reso't ta any ezcuse ta cova theia crimes."

Much as the mad howlers on Devil's Island.

"Tha's it doggie-do, a'rogance an treach'ry ultimately leads t'delusion, delusions a'powa, mixed in with deep down par'anoia."

And that's how madness fits as the last step in your theory of the seven deadliest sins.

"Ain' no theo'ry, i's fact! Paranoia fo'ces the QuotLinks ta ova'react, dig in theia heels an push theia evil pu'suits even futh'a."

"What if folks knew and wah to oppose them?"

"They'd go bullshit, reso't ta mo treach'ry an mo treach'ry afta that."

Like mass murderers.

"Tha's right. They knows no bounds. QuotLinks is out t'take it all, make slaves a'the rest a'us. An free trade, the strong dolla extends theia reach wo'ldwide. Soon they's goin t'own ev'rythin. Tha's why they's got t'be stopped."

Exiled to Devil's Island?

"Not a bad idea fo sta'tas, isolate'em in the middle a'Hell whea the wo'st they can do is haunt each otha 'til they slowly goes out a'theia minds, evapo'rate inta the swamp."

Kind fits the crime.

"Ezactly. Dog. Ezactly."

ROAR-ER-OAR MORE! MORE!

Another wave comes rolling down, high crest, washes over the heads of all three this time.

"Whoa!"

Stuff sparkles.

"This is the same shit we saw bottom of the pit when we fuhst looked ovah the rim."

"An notice how it's radiatin."

Who knows the curies, but Betsy can feel a tingle in her spine.

"Tried my dam'nest t'get up close t'that bottom new ring they've been constructin — while's yo guys wa takin the scenic toua — jus' had t'see, but they've gots secu'rity tied up so tight yo'd need a bulldoza ta bore through, an I wasn't about ta take a high dive off the top."

"So what do you figuah they'h up to?"

"Who knows, some so't a'new damnation, but pushed t'the wall I'd have t'say they's prob'ly goin t'sto'a all that nuclea waste they's been accumulatin the wo'ld ova, that enriched uranium and that spent plutonium, that's what they'a prob'ly pumpin down hea."

"Why heah, what's wrong with Yucca Mountain out in the middle of the Nevada desaht?"

"Ain' safe thea neitha, not fo the ten thousand yea's it'd take fo that crap t'cool down."

"Just a time bomb tickin."

"Besides, this spot's the closest shot they gots t'the inna co'a a'the planet whea reactions a'reacto-size magnitude a an hou'aly occu'rence."

Sounds reasonable. Incinerate the stuff. What's the problem with that?

"QuotLinks, they's shrewd at business, ma'ketin, advu'tisin theia wares, and best a'all at finance, but when it comes t'basic scientific resea'ch, they ain't ezactly Nobel prize winna's."

"You mean they'h not suhe about the technology they'h usin?"

"Hell no, 'specially at calculatin the intensity a'atomic reactions. All they knows is if the concept'll sell ta institutional investo's, they'll push it on the Street, an at a premium price."

-rogues!

"I'm tellin yo bro, QuotLinks is gamblin with ou futu'a fo no mo than a buck o two pa share."

And no force in the universe can stop them.

"How about Lucifah, he's sittin right theah at ground zero?"

"Looks like He's done missed a bet on this one — I'm tellin yo, these QuotLinks, they's shrewd, they'd ca'rve up yo grandma an sell hu back t'yo fo roast beef Sunday dinna."

"We've got to wahn folks."

"Fate nobody wants t'hea."

"Still got to try."

"Fate's fate, knowin's not goin t'change nothin nohow."

"Ahways bettah to know than not to know."

-rr-right! And Betsy nipnaps at Salaam's heels.

"Know what? What they've known all along, only this time doomsday's lurkin round the next cona?"

Conditions of uncertainty bordering on the chaotic.

"'Splain that ta yo av'rage consuma. OK folks, we's not only got the capacity t'endanga ou very existence, we gots the audacity!"

"Ignohrance is no answah neithah."

"Can't send the whole planet inta panic, ev'rybody'd line up t'book flights t'the moon. What good'll that do?"

And what about wildlife?

"Besides, nobody neva believes in what no prophet comes ragin at'em about. They's got a hundred TV channels t'chill'em out, glib ancha'man's wo'ds t'soothe'em."

"I can't believe that mankind, womankind, youh kind too Betsy — that evahrybody's goin to stand still and watch some dumb company dump nucleah waste down an active volcano!"

"Ain' no su'prise bro, not iffin yo thinks about it. We lives in a wo'ld whea it's ev'ry man out fo hisself, tha's his basic natu'a. Evidence we've seen seems incontrova'tible."

"But folks have the capacity to reason, to considah what the impact of theih decisions ah on the futuhe, on genahrations to come."

"Man only uses his mind fo rationalizin, makin up ezcuses t'justify his nasty behavio'a."

"Hahsh assessment you'h makin about the whole human race. You suhe you haven't been lookin at things from the bottom up too long?"

What about the human's claim to intellectual superiority, moral integrity?

"Man's only mo'ral is his mouth."

"Maybe you'h right, my grandpappy used to say if you can't eat it, fuck it oah put it in youh pocket, what good is it."

"Wise man. He still kickin?"

Scratching.

"Mankind don' care nothin bout no futu'a, they's too busy grubbin hou'a by hou'a, hand t'mouth."

"Mankind's still got to get up eahly and try, that's deep inside his natuhe too."

So sin you would say lies more in its consequence than in its intent or in the very action itself?

"Yo gots t'judge evil by the devastation it leaves behind. Who cares how some con man tries t'justify his manipulations."

Distinctions, -*ral*-ways distinctions.

Salaam and Betsy go canine to canine.

"Let me gives yo an ezample, doggie-do, keep the discussion simple — man lyin in the gutta with his throat slashed ain' got no mo life t'go."

-*roh-k*.

"Now tha's a consequence starin yo right in the face. Some basta'd's done taken away this man's futu'a an run — yo with me so fa?"

Blood in the street's a tough rap to beat.

"But an act tha's a long time happenin o travels long distance, thea's whea a consida'ration a'the consequences is crucial. Ezample. Child sta'vin in the Sub-Sahara while the gov'ment pays fa'ma's in the States not t'plant grain. Bit ha'd fo the kid t'point his bony little finga at the culprit, but who half way 'round the globe is accountable?"

Price of grain plunges on the commodities market, who goes broke?

"Kid sta'vin in Africa is definit'ly wo'se off than a Chicago trada losin out on some pocket change, plus fahma's get gova'ment suppo't whetha they plant o'not."

-*hmm*

"Take chemicals in the ai'a destroyin the ozone lay'a, thea's some smokestack somewhea responsible fo that. Gots t'find that factory, close it down befo it poisons yo own backya'd veg'table ga'den."

True.

"Gena'ratin plant in Singa'po put folks in the fact'ries t'wo'k, but the toxic emissions results in ha'm in ru'al Indonesian fo'rests."

Intent in such a case could conceivably be for the common good.

"Intent don' cut it. Damage is done. An somebody's made that decision.

He's one o the ones ultimately responsible."

Despite his good intentions.

"Majo envi'ronmental disasta's i'reversible, like whala's in Japan wipin out one enti'a species an sailin onta the next."

"What about cah emissions Salaam? They'h just as bad as smokestacks on the greenhouse effect. Youh avahrage automobile belches out its weight in cahbon dioxide evahry yeah, and the whole country's out theah drivin."

And the problem with prosecuting cases of environmental pollution is that there aren't laws broad enough nor courts high enough to accuse the likes of multinational corporations or foreign governments, let alone an entire nation of drivers with gross negligence. A focus on consequences would necessitate a significant shift in the practice of international law.

"What? Yo two gangin up on me? Take a look at the way the Chinese figu'a it — somebody's a'ways responsible, a'ways, an they goes fact by fact 'til they finds him."

Until they reach too high into the gerontocracy.

"Va'dict in the end gots t'be what some sucka's done t'cause so much mis'ry."

Sounds like a long trial to me.

"Pollution's the greatest crime in the hist'ry a'humanity, fa wo'se than any wa, cause it'll eventua'ly destroy life itself."

"I agree. Wohst crime is crime against the planet."

And man will be to blame, not some astroid or God.

"An yo can't jus' sit round patiently waitin fo the old boa'd memba's t'die off. New gena'ration a'self-servin middle agers ain' goin' t'be no betta. So yo gots t'get t'the sou'ce a'pollution long befo it gets t'yo."

Man thus has a moral imperative to act in order to avoid certain otherwise unavoidable consequences.

"Bet. We gots t 'set up a High Co'mission Fo Crimes Against Ea'th, drag these ezecutives an politicians, entie'a nations if we gots to befo the ba a'justice — wait an it's goin t'be too late."

"What about youh avahrage dude? He's definitely paht of the problem — then too what can he do? He doesn't see the envihronment as his obligation. Individual ahways blames the govahnment fuhst."

"Fact is he's got a vote, he's got a mouth, he can rally. Decision's got t'be made t'day. An if he don't, he's got t'accept the consequences a'his lack a'action. He's bought hisself an ezpensive share a'the final catastrophe, catastrophe that'll hova ova his great grandchildrens' graves inta infamy."

"Still, sohta hahsh, don't you think, askin some pooh dude to stand up on his own and rail against the wohld?"

"Man who knows don' speak up, who else's goin to?"

And a barking dog is thought a nuisance no matter what she has to say.

"You'h right, theah's too much at stake this time around."

"An the fo'ces against us is legion. Take the greedy an the resentful yo met along the way, it ain' like they goes off t'brood an leaves the rest a'us in peace. No, they's a'ways up in yo face tryin to take yo fo somethin. An the vengeful, 'memba them? They's out thea layin traps t'esnare anybody who happens t'be walkin down the wrong road, innocent bystanda, blood enemy, don' make no dif'rence — fact they'll tu'n on one anotha with the same venom — an neva care nothin bout no consequences, jus' one mo enemy co'pse tossed up top a'the heap."

People in excess have simply blinked off. The deceitful feed off strangers wholesale. The mad roam in the darkness alone. Which leaves the treacherous and the arrogant to run the show.

"Precisely. An these QuotLinks in cha'ge is a whole new breed, made up a'the nastiest pieces an pa'ts all these wa's done disca'ded. They's got resentment an ruthlessness packed inta theia skulls."

"Grim."

"Besides which they's got theia allies, flesh an blood politicians an lobbyists, agency regulata's an pitchmen, presidents like Billy Roy Bopps, ready t'sell out theia countrymen fo a slice a'the action."

ROAR! ROAR! HERE COMES LOADS MORE!

"Jesus H! Ah we goin to get out of heah alive?"

-*splush-splush-splush-splush* — first Chipper, then Betsy come sloshing out the top of the vent hole, both drenched in sparkling blue. They collapse on a flat hot rock — *huhhhhhhhhhhhh!* — to try and dry off. Volcano sputtering nearby is a comfort compared to the fiery circus scene below.

"Least we can say we've been to the depths gihl."

-*humph*. Betsy's too pooped to wring herself out.

"We've watched ouh fate fohged in the vehry heat of creation." Chipper lounges lazily beside her. "And tell me those stahs up theah don't look mighty cool and comfohtin aftah all we've been through?"

RUMBLE RUMBLE

"And you know someday, someday soon, I'm goin to be up theah shinin right alongside, I know I am."

You already have a glow on chum.

"Bound to be a supahstah, I can feel it. It's just this somethin I've got pumpin in my blood."

You mean as in incurable?

"This fohce couhsin through me, inchin through my veins inta my brain, chahgin me up."

Betsy can feel it too, only she's too tired to try and scratch at it.

"I know if I try hahd enough, I can reach up theah, reach way up theah and tickle those stahs 'til they tingle!"

"On'cle! On'cle!"
Lucien comes running into the hotel lobby.
"Wha-wha-wha's goin on…"
Wakes up Sébastien with a start, and di billygoat too.
"…it's di mid'dle a'di night boy!"
"Big Ma'ma Ma'Gee, she says it's di end a'di wo'ld, saw it in ha dream."
"Go back ta ya bed, di ol ladies o'Fo'tune, dey gets lone'ly in di da'k an dey wo'k dem'selves up ova not much a'no'thin."
"She says she saw di Gyp'sy Fool his'self a'tee'terin on di cliff a'long di bluffs in di wind, wi all di child'ren on di is'land fol'low'in a'long."
"What Gyp'sy Fool?"
"Di one wi di long white hair an di big black dog."
"He's a pay'in guest!"
"Pay o'no pay, Big Ma'ma Ma'Gee says when di Gyp'sy Fool trips an falls off di ledge, it means di end a'di wo'ld."
"Da's a whole lot a'nonsense. Be'sides we need di Gyp'sy Fool's dol'las."
"But onc'le, di sky's gone yel'low."
"How yel'low?"
"Bright as day, an di rooste's a'crowin' in di mid'dle a'di night."
RUMBLE RUMBLE RUMBLE RUMBLE
Ground starts to tremble, shakes Sébastien right out of his armchair, goat along with him.
"Get me ma bri'gade hel'met, dis def'i'ni'tly looks like trou'ble."
"Big Ma'ma Ma'Gee is countin out di corn an stewin up di chick'en's feet in di pot wid di pig's eye."
"Good. Dat'll keep ha bu'sy while we get ev'ry'bo'dy ta high ground. Ya knows di rou'tine. Sound di bell an warn di othe' payin guest."
Will Cook? Will Cook needs no warning. He's up. Been up teeth chattering and knees knocking for hours.

INTRUDERS!
Betsy and Chipper are curled up for a snooze on the flat rock.
INTRUDERS! STAND!
-*whoof?*
STAND!
Ten QuotLink operational units have them surrounded, and not the newer high tech models either, these are leftover world war vintage, half-

stitched mixed-matched muscle-bound units who could stomp our heroes half to death if they were not restrained in their impulses by an explicit instruction set programmed into their recorder boxes by a Higher Authority, namely some contract programmer in Silicon Valley.

INTRUDER! STAND! Accompanied by a low blow boot to the backside.

"Wha-...!"

STAND!

Chipper jumps up, and the grim demeanor these security types sport does not inspire much confidence in authority, not at all, nor do they look like State Troopers who'd be amenable to some spare cash in exchange for a warning, no no, these hulks are clomping their hooves, entire squad ready to kick ass.

Betsy assumes her maximum defense posture, crunch crotch crouch, considering a desperate lunge at the lead creep's sacred tumblers — Betsy not aware that there is a lively debate among technically minded observers in obscure physiology journals about whether or not the soft tissue parts in question have been discarded in the rehab of QuotLink clones for the sake of streamlined efficiency, and docility, since everyone knows that it's not the eunuchs of this life who are the movers and the shakers, and why's that? Because there's no need to make moves if you're thusly deprived, and shaking it would be simply a useless gesture.

MOVE!

With the limited speech capacity of the 00907 chip, these QuotLinks can only mouth syllables and motion the way.

"We'h outnumbahed gihl, isn't much else we can do except suhrendah — and remembah undah the rules of the Geneva Conventions you'h only obliged to give them name, rank and sehrial numbah."

A couple of barks will have to do as Chipper and Betsy follow their captors — but where is Salaam? Gone. That's where he's usually at.

Though they're not force-marched far, a steel door set in a rock and down a ladder to the lobby of the QuotLink Body Parts Field Laboratory where an officer at a desk in a black QSS uniform stares most inhospitably.

Stone floor of the field lab is cold despite the intense heat of the blast furnace outside, lab in fact is air-conditioned to the max to maintain the remains of these QuotLink security forces in some degree of comfort, the same who on closer inspection under the flourescents have been assembled with no eye for pleasing line or comely detail. While aesthetics is truly in the eye of the beholder, these models have a definably stodgy 50s look about them, then when only hugeness of size counted for much, with hands that don't match, a leg or an arm shorter, longer, limping, dragging, but uniformly broad beamed tail assemblages like law enforcers everywhere, and why is that?

The QSS Specialist is clearly of a more advanced design with GQ features and green x-ray eyes which immediately scan the irises of the prisoners for conclusive identification.

"Half breed human and mixed-pedigree dog. Names?" His speech is completely intelligible, but then Chipper does notice a small decal stamped on his forehead – *Sentinel Inside*.

"Chippuh Stuhbee, civilain, no pahmanent address."

-ruff! -ruff!

"What are you two doing here, spying? Who sent you? – I said, what are you two doing here? Who sent you?"

Chipper stands at attention, eyes forward, refusing to answer.

"*Hoah hoah hoah* – play time." One of the lowtech security units laughs and moves menacingly towards them – now a QuotLink laugh is a strange sound to hear, imagine a crow clutched to a live power line in a lightening storm – but the unit's levity is short lived when a much more distinguished QuotLink in a Savoy Row suit enters the room, QuotLinks having a marked affectation for all things British. It is a diplomat, it is the Executive Liaison for the Entire Northern Hemispheric Region in fact, on a routine inspection of the so so profitable Caribbean operations, and he circles Chipper and Betsy with a frown. He has conducted many an investigation himself, being practiced in the fine art of sub-dermal interrogatory procedures from his days of service with the Chilean Military Protectorate.

"CIA?" His voice is that dry emotionless drone of a QuotLink deprived of salivary glands, of all glands actually, any liquid that might short out electronic circuits which in turn causes the accumulated toxins of the body to seep freely through the corpus and poison vital organs – liver failure often the earliest detectable malfunction, thus necessitating regular monthly check-ups and 25,000 mile replacements of most moving parts. "No, too clever a disguise for them, and a dog? An intriguing accessory."

-mm thanks, I'll consider that a compliment.

"We have been monitoring their activities for most of the night your Eminence." The QSS Specialist informs the diplomat.

"Indeed. Giving them ample opportunity to complete their mission before apprehending them, you *shrinkfastspasticcolon!*" The Liaison's eyes are particularly beady. He examies Chipper from head to toe. "A most unusual specimen, throwback 60s. What is your purpose?"

"Chippuh Stuhbee, civilain, no pahmanent address."

-ruff! -ruff!

"*Hakhak-clickityclack!* I love the pretense of a Down East accent which means that you are definitely M15, for only an Englishman would think it necessary to mimic a Down Easter so thoroughly! Yes? Am I getting warmer?" There is a certain admiration in the Executive Liaison's voice, as he steps directly into Chipper's face — and talk about a dose of bad breath and puppies — "Identify yourself, your real name along with the purpose of this intrusion? And spare me the aggravation of lies! Spare yourself the agony of an exquisite incision deep down where YOUR BALLS USED TO BE!"

Talk about intimidation, and for emphasis the Liaison grabs Chipper by the nubiles, and thus has something even more to admire about the man, except admiration in a lessor inevitably turns to envy of the superior, and this QuotLink, not equipped with any such himsel, turns green with it, then pissy yellow and finally an enraged red — "YOUR NAME JIZZBALL!"

Chipper has not a little to lose, the vaunted manhood he has grown accustomed to lo these many years.

"Chippuh Stuhbee, civilain, no pahmanent address."

-*ruff! -ruff!*

"Don't trifle with me, you- you-..." There's an unexpected flash of confusion in the Liaison's enzyme operated central processor. "Chip- Chap- Chompers..." He sputters, while his teeth rattle and his pupils restrict, a sign that hard core memory is kicking into gear with the only read-out making any sense a recent entry entitled, Stirbee, Chipper, no known middle initial. "STIRBEE?" He outputs in apparent confusion.

"Chippah Stuhbee, like I said and this is my trusty hound dog Betsy."

"PROFESSION?"

"I seek to do no mah hahm to my fellow man than to entahtain him with song."

"CHIP- CHIP-... AND THE LOOSE NUKES?"

"You mean you've heahd of us?" Does music perchance penetrate even the most scavenged war-torn skull?

The Liaison's eyes do not revive as rapidly as usual. No, there's this swirling pattern about his corneas and slight plumes of white smoke smoldering from his ears. Is he hot and bothered about something? A recent unfriendly take-over by chance?

"ASS- ASS- ASKANTIKS RECORDS..."

"Damn, Salaam told us you folks own the music business."

-*roh*nly name, rank and serial number, remember?

"Salaam? Who is this man and where do I find him?"

"Salaam Kareen-Kaboom — majoh QuotLink Inc stockholdah?"

"You dare trifle with me, you *retrograderockster*, I'll turn you over to our lab technicians who can disassemble you into a dry ice chest full of useful body organs in less than twenty minutes!"

"Hahsh. You mean you've nevah heahd of Salaam?"

"Never!"

No su-*rr*-prise there.

"He suhe knew a lot about you folks and the backstaihs passageway down to Hell and back…"

"YOU MEAN YOU- YOU- YOU- YOU-…"

Disk death. A stuttering in the most advanced diplomatic design is not a good omen, suggesting a data overload, and what amount of information could possibly overload a miniaturized Mitsizoto 2.2 Billion Tetraflop?

"…YOU- YOU- YOU- YOU-…"

The Liaison's stutter alarms the Specialist, who immediately telephones to bring the resident genius running.

"…YOU- YOU- YOU- YOU-…"

"Jezuz, not again!" This creature climbs down a spiral iron ladder, agonizingly. "I leave you alone vor more zan ten zecondz, un vhat happenz, you popz your zircuitz…"

-*rolf rawl -ruffruffruff…* something overcomes Betsy, she instinctively attacks this stumped-over clam on the half-shell.

"Back! Back! Vho vaz talkink to you?"

-*ohh?* Sorry.

"Vhat iz it vitz dogz anyvay? Zey alvayz come at me vitz zuch verozity?"

It's an impulse sort of thing, comes on me in a flash, something I've had to learn to live with over the years.

"I've never harmed an animal in my live, but humanz, boy-o-boy zat's a divverent ztory. Hacked lotz ov zoze up into bite-zized piezez – un vat'z ziz? Tall, blond – a little older zan I prever – but ztill zo vell-preserved!"

"Chippuh Stuhbee."

"Zat'z az bad a name az mine, Queezac, no virzt, no lazt, only ze vone. Zey zay my motzer took vone look at me in my crib un ran, zcreamink down ze ztreet, repeatink my name over un over."

"…YOU- YOU- YOU- YOU-…"

"Voopz, vorgotz myzelv az uzual. Ze Liaizon'z zputterink nonzenze again. Iz zimple to vix really, juzt reach up behind ze back levt ear lobe un turn down ze voltage, by lowerink ze inpulze to ze powver zupply, ve lower ze janze ov an incapazitatink overload – zere, all betzer?"

"This- this- despicable human has presumably been given a detailed inspection of our entire plant by some operative using a code-name Salaad something something!"

"Salaam Kareen-Kaboom. That's what he's ahways called himself."

"Your Eminence. Sir." The Specialist dares interrupt. "Not by way of excuse, for our lack of diligence is unquestionably deplorable, but by way of explanation…"

"Yes?"

"…we at QSS have information concerning a certain half-native/half US national who was reported to have returned to the island for reasons we cannot as yet ascertain. He is said to be quite familiar with the terrain, having spent time here as a child. Despite our best efforts to isolate and positively identify him, he has eluded capture."

"So, it is possible that this Salaam character has led this fool and his dog here on a tour without their appreciation of the circumstances?"

"Yes sir, it is possible."

"And why were tourists permitted on the island in the first place?"

"Their arrival was entirely unexpected. As nearly as we can ascertain, they came as paying passengers aboard a freighter named the *Charon*."

"Hosiah Blight! I might have known. That sanctimonious *shakerof stalesaltpeter*, up to his old rum-running tricks, is he!"

-*mm*, at least this eminence guy and I can agree on one thing.

"Additionally sir! There is another undercover agent accompanying these two, a Will Cook by name, who lists himself also as a musicia-…"

"I see, an accomplice." The Executive Liaison circles Chipper and Betsy. "Conveniently left behind to inform your superiors should you not return by the expected hour. Apprehend this Will Cook at once!"

"Sir, yes sir, but…"

"But what?"

"…up to this point sir, his capture has been difficult. Since their arrival both men have used the company of native girls as cover, making isolation and apprehension difficult."

"Clever, very clever."

"Had our counter-espionage units not kept tripping over the antiquated fan and water controls inside the walls of the hotel, we would have arrested all three of them sooner…"

Not the ghosts of slaves past then.

"…we nearly entrapped the dog however, by using our specially cloned goat staked out in a meadow."

It wasn't love? Quit. You're b-*rr*-eaking my heart.

"You mean Sébastien and Lucien ah QuotLink clones too?"

"Hardly!"

"Zat vould be a jallenge, mimickink zeir jaunty native demeanor, but zen vhy botzer, zeze Caribz are qvite harmlezz already."

"Harmless! Harmless translates into useless, useless translates into unnecessary, and someone unnecessary can stumble dumbly in the way of progress, which is why we must ever endeavor to stick to plan, overrunning the globe with our own kind in every position of power – Queezac!"

"Eminenze?"

"Tomorrow you shall undertake to design a more suitable French version of a colonial official."

"Jezuz! Not Vrench! A Britizh vone maybe, vone vitzout ze uppitzy attitude un zat impozzible language to pronounze…"

"Whichever — Aide!"

"Sir!"

"This breach of security is intolerable!"

"Yes sir. Sir, I take full responsi-…"

"For your incompetence you shall be completely reprogrammed."

The QSS Specialist pales.

"Eminenze, pleaze reconzider. Iv we zap hiz harddrive, ve have to ztartz all over again vrom zcratj un zat vould take hourz iv not dayz to inztall all zoze exztenzionz un driverz."

"THESE INTRUDERS HAVE HAD A COMPLETE TOUR OF HELL!"

"Zo vhat? Who can zey tell? Nobody'z ever goink to believe a vord zey zay! Zey'll lock zem up vitz ze lulus in a padded zell un tzrow avay ze keyz!"

"YOU TOO DARE QUESTION MY AUTHORITY, YOUCRASSINSUBORDINATE CRAWDAD, WHILE I'LL- I'LL- I'LL- I'LL- I'LL-…"

"Comink up — lezz voltz yet!" Quuezac reaches behind the Liaison's left earlobe and cranks down the volume. "Eminenze, you've gotz to keep your vluid prezzure under control. Ziz muj ztrezz iz no good vor your vintage dezign, no ziree bob, zomeday zoon you're goink to tzrow a vit vhen I'm not around un it'll be Humpzy-Dumpzy, gumz un gutz all over ze vall."

"Some- some- day Queezac," His Eminence regains his composure, "some wonderful day I shall have the pleasure of encasing your pitiful remains in concrete and lobbing them into the depths of this volcano."

"I ztrongly doubt you're goink to outlive me Eminenze, not vitz all zeze temper tantrumz you keep pullink."

"Scat!" The Liaison stamps his foot. "Get out! You're no longer needed."

"Can I takez ze blond hunk vitz me?"

"NO! GO!"

"Zorry Jibber, ve could've had zo muj fun togetzer — zome otzer time?"

"GO! — Aide! Prepare surgeries for both of these specimens!"

"Yes Sir!"

-roh-roh, Betsy has been through flea baths before, and Chipper is always burning ticks off her coat with a lit cigarette, but surgery, that's not her idea of an evening of summer fun.

RUMBLE RUMBLE

"This way, you two!" And he's not as nice as he looks, this black uniformed green-eyed QSS officer, he's pushy.

"*Youtwoidioticeavesdroppers*, we'll see what you are made out of soon enough…"

RUMBLE RUMBLE — THINGS START TO TUMBLE!

"…what's this? Why is the floor quaking…"

CRUMBLE CRUMBLE — TO TUMBLE AND FALL!

"…and the walls cracking…"

RUBBLE RUBBLE — BESTREWING THE HALL!

"Run you duztballz, ve gotz to vamooze! Zave yourzelves, zertainly nobody elze iz goink to!"

"Run? Why?"

BLEAK!BLEAK!BLEAK!BLEAK!BLEAK!BLEAK!

"Zat'z a Red Zix Alert!"

"Red Six?"

"Az on ze Richzter zcale — ziz volcanoz about to blow uz all to Hell!"

"Why, why now? What has provoked this?"

"All zoze nuclear leftoverz you've been dumpink down zat vent hole, like I varned you, it vould zomeday come exzplodink back in your faze!"

BLEAK!BLEAK!BLEAK!BLEAK!BLEAK!BLEAK!BLEAK!

"Alert'z up to zeven!"

"Where do we run?"

"To ze helicopter pad Eminenze — vhat do you vant, to ztick around un zee yorzelv inzinerated?"

"But all our work! Decades of preparation! Our plans for the imminent overthrow of humanity!"

"Zat'z inevitable anyvay. Ve zimply have to pack up un zetz our operationz up zomevhere elze unzuzpectink."

"It will take time to replicate what we have constructed here!"

"Zo? Vitz my brainz un your nazty dizpozition, ve can zuczeed anyvhere anytime — Belgrade, Calcutta, Zingapore, LA — meanvhile zere'z no need vor uz to go down vitz a zinkink zhip. Bezidez, my demize iz not adequately compenzated vor in my contract."

"How can you be so cavalier about all we have worked to achieve!"

"Vill you getz a move-on un leave ze heroicz to ze zero zero nine zero zeven unitz, vhile ve getz our more advanced azzez outz ov here!"

And they do, the Executive Liaison, the QSS Specialist and Queezac run — Queezac run? You bet he does, rolls right along like a rockslide.

STUMBLE STUMBLE — ONE MISSTEP AND YOU'RE STUBBLE!

BLEAK!BLEAK!BLEAK!BLEAK!BLEAK!BLEAK!BLEAK!BLEAK!BLEAK!

"Up to nine now Betsy."

And something tells me they're not planning on taking us with them.

"Quick! Up the staihs — nine point means this suckah's about to erupt!"

How perceptive.

"We've got to do something, and fast!"

Like *-rrrrrr-run* for our lives!

"If all that blue sludge goes explodin out of the cohe, radioactive ash will blanket the entihe region, go floatin off on the jet stream and come rainin down all ovah the planet."

The Devil Hisself

Yes, and what exactly can we two do to prevent it?

"Don't know what we can do gihl, no idea, but we've got to try. We'h paht of the eahth. It's ouh responsibility."

O my God! Stung by our own moral imperative!

They stand together, ground zero and around them fiery cracks and gushing flame geysers.

"Chippa! Chippa! I brung help, all the islanda boys from the mines. We gots t'do somethin fast!"

"Salaam!"

"So'ry t'scram out on yo two, but roundin up a crew a'teenage kids ain' ezactly the easiest trick."

"Bet. Let's… let's dive in and do somethin!"

Dive in!

RUMBLE! RUMBLE! CAN'T BUNGLE IT NOW GALS AND GUYS! FUMBLE OR STUMBLE, IT'S KIDS AND DOGS WHO'LL SHARE OUR FRIGHTFUL FATE!

"A'right, a'right now…" Sébastien has his brigade helmet on. "Don no'body need ta panic! An watch di or'i'en'tals wid dose dir'ty feet an di chick'ens. Dere's room fa ev'ry'body in di Hôtel Par'a'di'so, highest ground on di is'land – Lu'ci'en?"

"Oui onc'le."

"Show folks where dey can go."

"Where's ev'ry'bo'dy goin ta fit onc'le? Di whole place is crowd'ed wid di babies an di nan'nies an di pigs an di goats."

"How 'bout ou payin guest? He com'fo't'able?"

"Di girls, dey's up di stairs in his room tryin ta calm him down."

"Da's good. Dey know not ta touch him no'whea on his pri'vate per'son?"

"What ya sayin onc'le? I be too young ta unde'stand much a'nothin."

"Ya un'de'stands mo dan ya wants ta pre'tend Lu'ci'en."

Back! …back back back – baaaaaaaaaaaaaaaaaaack!

Lucien listens from the bottom of the circular staircase. "Sounds like we be too late ta do much good fo di payin guest onc'le."

But… But…

> It's a Sat'u'day night an time fo di VOL'CA'NO
> So get di lead out a'ya tail an RUN A'LONG
> When di top goes boom an di skies GO YEL'LOW
> Ra'di'o'act'ive ash'll spew all OVA DI GROUND!
>
> Ev'ry'bo'dy sing a'long now… I say, I say…

It's a Sat'u'day night an time fo…
GRUMBLE GRUMBLE
Not much fun for El Snorro either. Dude hasn't had a decent night's sleep for days now, stomach in an uproar, belching blue smoke, then the dry heaves with hot ash flying everywhere, mama mama, he hangs his head over the rim and lets go with a flow, first trickle runs right alongside the portable nuclear reactor, then the lava stream pools into a waterfall, *plip plop* over the rocks and drips into the sapphire lagoon. Won't be long before that fills up and then it's straightaway for the Hôtel Paradiso.

"Ahright! Ahright! What we've got to do fuhst is push that reactah ovah the cliff into the lagoon."

-rr, that's push what *wher-rr?*

"But it's less an envihronmental disastah to pollute the watah in a self-contained lake than havin it slip into the volcano and buhn up in smoke."

"Poison the wata o poison the ai'a, that's a ha'd call bro."

"Eithah of you two got a bettah solution?"

A question? How exactly are you and I, Salaam and a bunch of little kids going to push an oversize tractor-trailer on a hot mudslide over a cliff?

"Goin to be a tough to impossible feat, but we've got to be prepahed fah that — mighty times call fah mighty effoht."

CALL IT A GAMBLE, CALL IT A GOOF — BETTER HOPE ALL YOUR TROUBLE DOESN'T BURN UP IN SOOT!

El Snorro's not making it any easier either, latest belch tips the reactor closer yet to the rim.

"You kids ready to try youh luck at walkin on hot coals?"

They line up single file behind him. Such impetuous youthfulness.

"Let's head!"

Fool and his fool dog lead these fool children along the edge, what there is of an edge, squishy slippery slide down one side into a fiery gorge or tricky trip down the other off sheer rock into the lagoon. Yet up they follow, up, up until they reach the upended reactor trailer where they get every which way they can around it, underneath it lifting, alongside shoving, on top yelling — all to no avail.

"Can't drive it nowheah neithah?"

Betsy's trying, she goes through the gears, but the wheels do nothing except spin in the molten mud.

Kids look to Chipper, well, he's white and it's the bwana bit, they've seen the pre-PC jungle movies too, and nobody teaches fluid mechanics in the primary schools anymore, nor the dry as a bone brand either — though the lever principle isn't too difficult to grasp, except you're going to need more weight than this crew can muster to tip a massive truck upside over.

TO TEETER THEN TOTTER — WILL TAKE MORE MUSCLE TO MUSTER!

When suddenly, out of nowhere – an even greater white hope! Bigger! Which must necessarily mean Better! As in STAND BACK! // BOOM! BOOM! // STAN MAAX! // STAND BACK! // STAN MAAX! // AD MAN! // BOOM! BOOM!

Kids have never seen a Madison Avenue advertising executive before, let alone a STAN MAAX! – this huge laughing giant in full leather regalia, like from some heavily offbeat fairy tale, and arriving in a helicopter, a sturdy old Sea King. Kids break into a cheer!

STAN THE MAN acknowledges the acolade with a dismissive wave. Seems he was flying down to the Île de Ste Cécile with a Japanese film crew in order to catch Chipper on the first leg of his comeback tour, and he hitched a ride with the U.S. Navy – naturally – who have been on maneuvers near Granada. They spotted the smoke and went in for a closer inspection.

Media coverage. Raises another cheer!

"Heah! Ovah heah!" Chipper's waving his arms, this lone thin silouette dancing on the rim of an exploding volcano with a big black dog, both back lit with red plumes. Man's determined to get some attention.

-rr-here use this, and Betsy hands him the pocketed cellular device.

"Help!" Chipper hollers into it.

No, you have to press the send button while you holler.

"Ahright ahright – HELP, YOU'VE GOT TO HELP US LIFT THIS POHTABLE REACTAH OFF THE RIM BEFAH WE ALL GET CREMATED!"

Chipper has to repeat the message a few times before the pilot fully comprehends the situation. Understandably. Because what's a nuclear reactor doing on a deserted island on the rim of a purportedly inactive volcano in the first place? A good question from the field, and then there's the chain of command to consider, something about high level confirmation required before undertaking a potentially life-threatening rescue operation, which to the Navy's credit comes back an expedited, "Hell yes sailor, anything you need to do to save humanity!'

With cameras recording every harrowing moment of it, the Sea King drops a tow line, kids hook it to the trailer hitch and lift! …lift! …lift!

Sucker won't budge, lava around the back axle has solidified.

"Oh hell, just drop me off somewhere down there, will you?" STAN'S a man who can't stand still. But the helicopter can maneuver in only so close. "Anywhere's fine. Watch out below!" STAN takes a leap and BOOM! BOOM! Lands in a hot bed of smoke!

"*Hoh hoh heeheehee hoh* – that's hot!" And sticky itchy, good thing the AD MAN has his chaps and boots on, otherwise he'd be a sole stoker for the rest of his life. "All I asked for was the facial!"

Kids are wide eyed. Whatever they expected from their storybook tales, this giant exceeds as he plods out of the mud hole. And talk about the mountain coming to you! Awesome!

"It's nothing kiddos, eat enough soggy corn flakes in the mornings and you can be as big as any drag queen — Hi hon!" He pecks Chipper on both cheeks, wherewith Salaam ducks. Betsy offers a furry paw. "And what sort of trouble are you two into at the moment?"

WHOOMPF! A mushroom shaped from behind reminds them of the unthinkable.

Chipper points at the reactor, then the rock ledge, shrugs his shoulders.

"Hon, that's easy." With hot ash raining down on his shaved bald head, STAN slogs toward the trailer-tractor. STAND BACK! One hand, that's a mere five fingers, and STAN MAAX! // HE MAN! lifts it hovering over his head. "Where is it you want this sucker?"

Chipper shouts "LEFT, LEFT — TOSS IT OVER THE EDGE!"

You mean right, his right, not your left!

STAN THE MAN's confused. He glances to his left, sees the idyllic lagoon, then to his right, this raging volcano. "What's this?" He wonders aloud. "Script didn't mention pyrotechnics!"

"RIGHT! RIGHT! OVER THE EDGE!"

Right over the edge, which he does, slams it smack center of the volcano. BOOM! BOOM! The reactor plunges down some 2000 feet, and as a compliment to QuotLink Inc's Heavy Engineering and Shipyard Division in Oslo, the core container does not crack, not as it bounces off the jagged rock edges nor as it plunges square into El Snorro's monstrous maw.

BLULP!

There's this respite as El Snorro spits and sputters, rolls the eighteen wheeler around in his throat — BULK! BULK! — he seethes some, attempts to swallow, but the reactor's stuck. Only thing the old buzzard can do is gulp. Reactor sinks from view into a pool of acid blue.

BULP- BULP-

A hiccup or two sends the kids running off the rim, fast as kids can, with Salaam, Betsy, Chipper and STAN lagging behind — *runrunrunrun* — the fearless Japanese film crew catching every desperate second.

BULP- BULP- BULP- BULP-

El Snorro in acute gastric distress…

BUL-BLU-BLU-BLOOOOOOOOOOM!

…bursts his guts out the flue, waves over the rim and down the cliff side, flows through the lagoon, over land and into the sea, wiping out the remaining western side of the island entirely. Only thing left standing, high on a hill, the Hôtel Paradiso with all the nannies, the goats and the babes tucked safely inside, Will Cook too, except he's experiencing an implosive sort of turmoil, and all di lit'tle girls too — when there's this aftershocker…

BLA- BLA- BLAHBLOOM!

…it's Ol' Lux and his club buddies hightailing it out of Hell, like a rocket heading straight for the Florida coast, Eleventh Federal Circuit had better be prepared for the onslaught.

Fleet of Sea Kings ferry out the survivors from the hotel roof, Will Cook strapped into a stretcher in ear-piercing fright, Big Ol' Ma'ma Ma'Gee — Mango, Tangle and Tamarind too — while Sébastien chooses to remain, along with Lucien, some old-fashioned faith that someday the tall echoing lobby of the Hôtel Paradiso will again resound with genteel guests seeking safe haven amidst the turmoil of life's worries and woes.
I say... I say...

> It's a Sat'u'day night an time fo di GRAND MASK BALL /
> Wid di ghosts an di gob'lins FILLIN DI HALL //
> Be di last on di pla'net ta SING DIS SONG /
> Neva know fo su what REAL'LY WENT WRONG

But until nature takes recourse, the U.S. Government, as the dominant political force in the Americas, must determine where to warehouse the survivors. Detention camps at Guantanamo Bay are filled to the barbed wire brim, and are these kids truly political refugees or merely economic ones anyway? Some fine distinction the State Department must ponder, and for some reason Florida doesn't want any more poor little brown brothers and sisters within their borders. Since President Billy Roy Bopps is particularly sensitive to the wishes of this key electoral constituency, the decision gets bounced to the usually pliant Department of Immigration and Naturalization which decides to ship them north to the Bronx, the ultimate Southern solution, but at least there they can be reunited with their families, and there too the authorities trust that an enlightened and yet again newly reorganized New York City Board of Education can make model citizens out of them, teach them survival skills like Knife Fighting 101 in the hallways and Shooting Up 232 in the lavatories, those lifetime high school credits these kids are going to need for the trendy 2000s.

Takes three weeks for the smoke to lift over the Îsle de Ste Cécile. A Navy scout scours the charred countryside for stragglers. A tree here, a chimp there, but where would a hundred kids, an old subway codger, a has-been rocker, his dog and STAN MAAX! // AD MAN! be stranded? Pentagon wants to know.
"Hur'ry!"
-*rurry*
A head pokes out of a hole, two heads, Betsy's and some kid's named

Coco, he's as eager as she is. "Gots ta see di he'li'copter!"

Reconnaisance craft catches it on film, a hundred little kids crawling single file out of a spout in the spill, then Chipper and- and- STAN MAAX!

"God damn it! I'm stuck!" AD MAN's caught tight, right about belly line.

"Whoa!" Chipper has to give him a yank. *An- an- an- BAM!* STAN's out and after him Betsy, Salaam… "Salaam?"

"I's fine Chippa, fine — nice a'yo t'ask — but yo can run along now, takes yo bows, an please, be su'a an leave my name off the list a'credits."

"Why, what'h you plannin on doin, stayin heah?"

"Maybe fo awhile, see I don' need no press, don' want none a'them hot little mamas out thea seein my face on TVs Most Hunted Hubbies."

"Theah somethin in youh past you don't want nobody knowin?"

"Damn right. How 'bout yo's?"

"Mine's an open book."

"Well, I prefa's t'keep mine shut tight — but don' you go worryin none, I'll be poppin up in yo life sometime when yo least espects it."

-hmm, that's reassuring.

"So long poochie, gots t'admit, yo is some trip."

Which Betsy can certainly say ditto about Salaam.

What follows is non-stop media coverage, the almost total devastation the island has suffered, the nearly worldwide environmental catastrophe as atomic clouds waft across international borders. Then there's the personal tragedies along with the home-boy heroics, the stuff that makes up the birth of a superstar — enough footage for The Celebrity Channel to feature Chipper's exploits over and over again for months, not to mention the front covers of *Spunk*, *Newspeak* and *The Weatherman's Weekly* — and will he be available for talk-show interviews? Just try and shut the man up!

STAN MAAX has the Loose Nukes remastered CD on the shelves within twenty four hours, on a QuotLink label no less — for why bother with a grudge when there's plenty of bucks to throw around.

Except, STAN cautions Chipper, read the fine print. When QuotLink Inc bought out Askantics Records, they inherited his 60s contract too.

"So?"

"So they still own you. Outright."

"Damn! If it ain't one thing, it's a mothah."

Mildred agrees to yet another televised interview, and she's not the Holy Virgin with child kind of mother either. "He's not bad as much as ohnahry, and all that trouble he got into back in middle school? It's simply not true — those little girls have only themselves to blame."

"Whoa! Blow the covah cleah off that pot boilah!"

Indeed. One Belinda Duchamps is camped on the doorstep of a New York publisher with a handwritten biography, and the facsimile of a phonebook with tell-all marginal notations and copies of court records.

"*Hakhak* — we have to hack that boy's balls off as soon as we can."

"Gotz to catch up vitz him virzt Eminenze."

"I had him exactly where I wanted him," the Liaison steps up to the tee, "but couldn't locate his name in my drive directories rapidly enough."

"Alvayz program data bazez in Java, Vindowz 2010 is uzelezz."

"Another twenty minutes and zip, I would have had microscopic slices for close observation."

Queezac recommends a two wood, but the Liaison insists on a new type weighted composite.

"Un ve could've cloned him vor ze teenage market, put on live zhowz in multiple zitiez acrozz ze country zimultaneouzly."

Liaison allows himself a practice shot.

"Ztay on your toes, don't plant your heelz — vhy he could have pervormed live vor zenturiez, or ve could have ztored him avay in a deep vreeze vor anotzer vivty yearz, vheeled him out vor periodic boxed zet TV commerzialz, but oh no, you ver determined to ruzh ze job, un botch it up did you ever, let ze chicken trot right ov ze butjer block."

"We might have another chance, sooner than you think — at Wembley."

"Butz he'z zurrounded by groupiez mornink, noon un all tzrough ze nightz."

"QSS has a plan."

"QZZ haz notzink but planz. I'd truzt ze Boy Zcoutz bevore I'd tzrow in zoze clownz."

"We will be better prepared this time." Liaison readies his swing.

"Viz you in jarge, I vouldn't countz on it."

"When I need your advice, *youbarnacleencrustedcrab*, I'll press the buzzer on your cage — *yak yak yak* — take that!"

Strong drive with the composite launches Queezac in a high arc a respectable 230 yards, but a rightward hook lands him in a sand trap way short of the green. Queezac burrows in quickly. For a few bad hacks with a nine iron could leave him with a backache for days.

There's the requisite ticker tape parade down Wall Street and up Fifth Avenue in *dumb diddily fun / New Yahk / New Yahhhhk!*

STAN MAAX rides in the open limousine with our hero, Chipper's arm slung around the neck of his heroine, Betsy beaming — the event covered live world-wide — then on to the awards banquet at the White House.

"My fellow 'Mericans, I am proud to present this nation's highest honor, the Steely Eagle, awarded for meritorious action to a civilian during wartime (or during any limited objective military excursion with or without the prior consent of Congress) to Mister Chipper Stirbee, popular musical entertainer, for his valiant efforts to save the children of the Caribbean from a natural disaster of unimaginable proportions…"

CLAPCLAPCLAPCLAPCLAPCLAPCLAPCLAPCLAPCLAPCLAPCLAP!

"…and I'd also like to welcome to the White House on this auspicious occasion Mister Stirbee's corporate sponsor — for QuotLink Inc, His Eminence, the Executive Liaison for the Entire Northern Hemisphere…"

CLAP!

"We meet yet again, His Eminence mentions in greeting — *hack hack!*"

-rrowl!

Then there's an off-the-record meeting of the parties behind closed doors. "My friends," Billy Roy throws one arm around Chipper's shoulders, his other around the Liaison, "you'll be glad to hear the eruption wasn't a total wash. QuotLink Inc and I are about ready to close on a deal, the eastern half of the island gets privately developed as condominiums and the western half the Air Force boys will lease back as a base should we ever need to intervene in one of those confounded coups in Central America — seems things never really change much down there in chico land, do they?"

"Happy to heah you two made good off othah folks' misahry."

"*Hah hah,* this boy's got some sense of humor, doesn't he Eminence? And I'm advised you are bound for even greater musical success."

"H'yep, got new tunes QuotLink heah's goin to agree to release…"

"That remains to be seen Stirbee."

"…and a wohld concaht series in the makin."

"We shall see."

"Wait. Gentlemen, please, let's not leave matters among us unsettled. We each have our own set of priorities. Your Eminence doesn't want a UN investigation of QuotLink Inc's near world-wide environmental disaster, and Chipper here, I understand, has a few outstanding warrants issuing out of the Maine courts, so we each have to compromise."

"You drive a hahd bahgain Mistah President."

"That's why I'm the Chief Executive. So do we have a deal, your Eminence? Chipper? A few songs traded for some peace and quiet?"

"*Hack hack…*"

"Sounds like yes to me — Chipper?"

"Only thing mah I need is a passpoht."

"That's do-able, and call me Billy Roy, everybody does — by the way, I have a distinct impression that you and I have met somewhere before?"

"Maybe in an altahed state."

"*Hah hah hah hah* — this boy does have a sense of humor."

Chipper's audience with the Pope is predictably brief. "Youh Holiness," Chipper nods as the Pope enters the tapestried chapel in the Vatican. STAN MAAX, standing back, has advised Chipper not to offer to shake the Pope's hand nor shout gimme five. Although His Holiness is the first all-American Pope, a winner of the Heisman Trophy, He is restrained by centuries of protocol and speaks in the measured cadences of a near saint.

"You have caused quite the sensation around the globe Mister Stirbee, a songster and a bard, a military hero, a champion of the environment." At the close of which brief speech, His Holiness does extend His hand.

Chipper grasps it by the fingy tips. "Thank you Sih." And he does this boyish grin he does and takes a bow, something Chipper's been doing a lot of in these latter days of greater fame. "I'm just tryin to do my thing."

"As are We all, and We can assure you the environment is a cause that is dear to Our own heart as well. We must protect God's creation and tend it as Our own special vineyard. And your influence among the young, your ability to reach them with your song add urgency to the dilemma of our times. These gifts you possess are quite remarkable."

"Thank you."

"Use them wisely and always for the benefit of others."

"I'll try. I know I've been a sinful man in the past..."

"As have We all, but these rumors, these allegations of your past remain simply that in Our eyes. In Our Lord's own words, 'Go and sin no more.'"

"I'll try that out too."

"Excellent, for you see sincere intent to refrain along with sincere confession of the sin suffice for forgiveness. Our belief: Love the sinner, hate the sin." The Pope raises His hands in benediction.

"Like love the liahs, hate the lies?"

"Yes, by extension, that would no doubt hold true..."

"But lovin them don't mean we've got to vote fah them, does it?"

"No, I presume not, that wouldn't necessarily hold, but... you have Our wholehearted support in all your endeavors, and We unfortunately have much of holy other matters to which We must attend..."

"H'yep. End of discussion."

And so it goes, sad news and glad — Bubba Bonnanza's unexpected demise, though Lou bounces back from psychosis to neurosis, and Bubba's youngest son Bubba Two, the spit and lick image of his famous father, steps up into his shoes. All the while Chipper travels the globe, he and Betsy, along with a reluctant Will Cook, who in truth has no place else to bunk. They sing new songs, of which *If I Had Wings* takes to the top of the charts, followed closely by *Newfangled Woman*.

But a reunion with the Loose Nukes seems remote, despite Chipper's new found fame. His sell-out shows in Amsterdam, Berlin, Stockholm, Prague, Rome don't seem enough to convince Danny T and Molly to join with him — well, Molly, she'd be willing to join with him…

STAN MAAX! // AD MAN! // has flown ahead to London to plan a final concert for the tour, and as a cap, he has negotiated with every major world religious leader to gather by satellite simulcast and join in singing a closing paean to environmental unity — dependent of course, on Chipper's ability to restrain himself off stage and on with those of the underage proclivity. "I can hold on fah a while gihl, three weeks, fouh most, but then on a dusky moonlit evenin I'll get to feelin like I'm about ready to buhst. Got to go stohmin at somebody who ain't too peculiah, noh too pahticulah neithah."

Don't go looking for any sympathy from me pal, I've got tail-raising yearnings of my own.

Chipper spends the last days before his final concert hiking in the Australian Outback alone with Betsy, but since he is a social creature by nature, he engages the company of an elderly Aborigine shaman as a guide, a fellow who has this soul-searing wild root he chews, and Betsy grows fond of the man's weather-beaten dingo. Hence, the lasting sunset of Chipper's rebirth is spent on the plain, wrapped in a blanket with his pooch, admiring the clear night sky from Down Under.

"Some day gihl, some day real soon, I'm goin to be up theah…"

-grr-roan

"…I know it, I can feel it gnawin deep inside me. Befah it's ovah I'm goin to be way way up theah glowin among those stahs."

FIGHTIN

A portion of the auto park immediately adjacent to the stadium at Wembley has been fenced off as a backlot staging area — band crew, construction crew, sound, light and video crews, each with their own distinctive jackets and caps — and fans, some fortunate youngster few who have been specially selected from the multitude who converged outside the gates hours before show time and begged admittance, offering whatever was theirs in exchange for the rarest of a lifetime opportunity, that of being let through to the inside.

"Let's queue up ladies — ladies? That's it, keep it nice and orderly." A portly old guard London Bobby is trying to keep the youngsters in line.

"Queue up me arse Abby, I've got'ta git meself in there."
"Righ'. Befa all the res'ta these tarts beat us to'im."
"Is the chance a'a lifetime an I got me 'eart set on seein'im up close."
"Righ'."
"Touch'im."
"Oo righ', righ'."
"Is not like 'e shows up ev'ry day a'the week, u know…"
"One at a time now. No need to push."
"…an tha' bloke there's standin in me way."
"Whole bunch a blokes standin in the way Lucy."
"I don' care, I've got'ta git through tha' bleedin gate."
"Only those with passes will be allowed through."
"Passes. Ev'rybody 'ere's got a pass."
"'Cept us."
"Please now. Keep your passes handy."
"Wha' a we goin ta do?"
"'Ere, I know…"
"Wha?"

"…lift up ur shirt."
"Me shirt?"
"Show the bloody blokes ur teats."
"Me teats?"
"Ur teats! Jus' show the bloke ur teats an run righ through!"
"Hey! Hey you two, hold on there!"
"Runnnn!"
"Hey! Hey! Stop those two! Stop them!"
"Run Abby, runnnn!"

A particularly resourceful QuotNet remote team has occupied a crow's nest up a light pole, whence to roost and video the swarming terrain below — and there's lots of action for the roving eye to behold. Crisis after crisis, crews scurrying to cope and scrumptious clumps of teeny fans standing anywhere in the way they can. The contours are colorful, they can be mapped, pools and eddies in a continuous flow, a sea of life, larvae infested, with the focus mostly on the aerobe hatchlings who if exposed to direct sunlight, as in daylight, would evaporate, but who at night in this viscous element burgeon to do the one thing they do do so well.

CHIP- CHIP- CHIP- CHIP- CHIP- CHIP-

It would be a picture of quiet calamity and bliss were it not for the presence of QuotLink Security patrols, whose numbers continue to be augmented as well.

"'E's got ta be back 'ere somewhere Lucy, we jus' got ta keep lookin til we find 'im."
"I know 'e's close, I can feel 'is presence."
"'Is wha'?"
"You know, like when u wake up in the da'k all sweaty an wet, an u feel some zippa jerk off the street co'na standin in the room beside u."
"Righ'. Breathin 'eavy?"
"An lookin down at u lyin naked in ur bed."
"Like 'e's abou' ready ta crawl in on top a'u."
"An u so tucka'd out u can 'adly resist 'is advances."

CHIPPER!

That's their mating call. Those. Them. The adolescent shrill shriekers who have been tagged for easy identification by the gatekeepers with luminous orange day-glo passes pinned to their budding breasts. Yet despite tight controls at the gate, they have swollen in number, pulsing with excitement, back behind equipment trucks, underneath sound towers, at costume, at catering, sneaking around barriers, cramming the walkways to the dressing room trailers — all to catch a glimpse of a star.

CHIPPER! CHIPPER!

It's a creative chaos. The exhilaration, the noise, the incessant moaning that gives Chipper the energy he needs to inspire himself to greatness.

CHIP- CHIP-

It's a security nightmare. Even the strong armed QSS SQWAT squads are no match for wandering hordes of heaving teenagers, particularly when the borders backstage are so fluid.

CHIPPER!

"'Scuse , 'scuse me gihls, comin through heah."

"Wha'?"

"Sohry. Got to get through heah." Crew member in a yellow band jacket and a bike helmet is trying to push a specialty chrome and white Harley through the mob.

"'Scuse me."

"'Scuse u."

"No, 'scuse me."

"Naw a'all. 'Scuse me firs'."

"Whatevah you say miss."

"An since we'a bein so poli'e an all mate, can I ask u a bloody question?"

"Suhe."

"'Ave u seen 'im anywhere around back 'ere?"

"Who?"

"U know 'oo. Is 'e back 'ere like they say 'e is or isn' 'e?"

"Righ'. Is 'e 'idin away some place?"

"Who, who ah you lookin fah?"

"Chippa Stabee, 'oo else?"

"Him? H'yep, he's got to be back heah somewheah. Wouldn't just up and disappeah off the face of the planet, now would he?"

"'E's so slip'ry, 'at one is, 'e could wind up a'most any place."

"Like righ' 'ere in me lap, 'e could. I'd go fa 'at jus' dandy."

"You know, u'r a slut Lucy, 'at's wha' u a."

"I'm naw'a slut, I jus' like me men long an blond an sexy, 'at's all."

"I kinda got the 'ots fa tha' Bubba Two. 'E's so da'k an 'airy wi muscles."

"'Ow abou' Will Cook then, 'e's da'k an 'airy?"

"Bu 'e's so bony an moody lookin Lucy."

"Kind'a kinky if u ask me."

"'At's true, tie 'im up an get 'im jumpin in 'is trousas."

"Do wha'eva u wan' wi any a'them, jus' leave Chippa ta me. 'E's the man a'me dreams, 'e is. I'd do'im up an down wi me tongue, 'ead ta toe I would, an a lick a'ev'rythin else in between."

"'At's disgustin."

"I wouldn' let up on 'im neitha, I'd lick 'im 'til he cried ou' fa ma'cy."

"Naw, jus' grab onta'im an' go straight ta business, plop uself down an ride 'im abou' like a pony. Besides I 'ear 'e' likes it like 'at."

"Whoa, lucky dude!"
"Mite luckia'n u mate."
"I'd say."
"'Oo a u anyway, pa't'a 'is crew?"
"Soht of."
"Tha's lucky."
"You get so you hahdly notice."
"Na'me, I couldn' keep me eyes off'a 'im, naw fa a second."
"Is i' true 'e goes wi a dif'rent gi'l ev'ry ev'nin?"
"Rumah is… can't say too much, you know, loyalty of the crew, but…"
"Bu' wha'?"
"…rumah is he takes whatevah he can get…"
"Wha'?"
"…same as you and me."
"Some 'ow I don' like wha' u'a insinua'in."
"Don' go a'guin wi the wonka Lucy."
"'E's insinua'in I'm some sor'a'slut."
"We're all only human."
"So jus' wha' a u insinua'in?"
"Le' off 'im Lucy, we've got'ta find Chippa an fast, find'im befa some tart back 'ere makes off wi 'im."
"So where is 'e righ' now, Mista Know-i'-all, righ' this very second?"
"Tell you the truth — they lock him up in a cage behind the stage, guahd him in between sets so gihls like you two can't get at him."
"Wha'?"
"U'a playin wi me 'ead, 'at's wha' u'a doin."
"No it's true, he's a cahtified sexual menace."
"Na'way."
"Wohse, he preys on unsuspectin young women like youhself, eats them up whole, one, two at a go, fouh oah mah evahry night."
"U'a makin 'is up."
"An 'oo asked u anyway? C'mon Abby, why waste time talkin ta some stupid roadie in a yellow jacke', le's go ask 'oo'seva in cha'ge around 'ere."
"Righ'! Zippa jerk!"
"Double 'eaded zippa jerk!"
"Le's go ask those two blokes ova 'ere in the blue unifo'ms, 'ey look like 'eir in cha'ge."
"Righ'."
"'Ey mista, u in cha'ge back 'ere?"
"I am QuotLink Security. I am in charge."
"'Scuse me fellas, 'scuse me, got to get through heah."
"Zippa jerk."

"Clear a path. Allow the attendant with the machine to pass."
"Thanks fellas."
"You seek information?"
"Righ', like where a u blokes 'idin me Chippa?"
"We QuotLinks hide no one. Our orders are to protect those who comply with the rules, contain those who do not."
"Tha's not wha' we've been told."
"No. We 'ear u've got 'im locked up in a cage be'ind the stage?"
"This rumor is false. We search for him ourselves."
"U mean 'e's ou' roamin loose 'ere somewhere? 'E's naw in 'is cage!"
"We regret the momentary lapse in security. But you can rest assured we shall find him."
"Did u 'ear 'at Lucy?"
"Make certain you civilians contact us if you should sight him."
"Righ' – did u 'ear tha' Lucy? 'E's loose."
"An 'e ain' all tha' choosy if 'e goes wi fou dif'rent gi'ls ev'ry ev'nin."
"Righ', an tha' wonka said 'e's a cer'ified sexu'l menace."
"Love ta meet up wi 'im in a da'k alley, wouldn' u?"
"No tellin wha' 'e'd fo'ce u ta do in oada ta please 'im."
"I'm ready ta wet meself jus' thinkin abou' it."
"Means we betta 'urry."
"Snatch'im up befa some 'uffy stree' tart does."

While on the giant screens inside the stadium and on home TV:

PARENTAL ADVISORY #11

Scruffy young dude shows up on the doorstep of a nice young girl's house. Father opens the door and he's not happy. He's got two teenage daughters and the fourteen year old is starting to get interested in what he's been assured by professionals in the field wouldn't occur until junior prom night.

Daughter claims this date's different, though the kid smells of musk and alcohol, and that's got to be one of his team buddies out there behind the wheel. Poor sop attempts one last argument – "O Daddy! Daddy! How can you be so cruel?" – daughter's out the door, into the car with the buddy driving away crazily.

But hey, kid ditches his buddy, gets her parked back of the A&P

dumpster, and it isn't the beer, the cigarettes or the promise of a love life hereafter, it's the hormones unassisted, while a cool breeze over naked bodies makes first time flubbing the most satisfying ever.

A paid parental reminder: Preach condoms and consequences, and better the boy next door than the delinquent across town, because you got to forget it pop, old taboo says it can never be you, and who wants the honors going to a roadside copper?

THIS MESSAGE SPONSORED BY THE WHITE HOUSE SELECT COMMITTEE ON YOUTHFUL INDISCRETION.

"OK alright, lets keep rolling with the payload, and what's up backstage — anybody got an inkling?" Cub McCluff's flipping frantically from monitor to monitor. "What's the delay? Why aren't the Loose Nukes setting up on stage — and goddamn it where's Chipper?" Cub has readicams everywhere, out back, out front, he has crowd scenes and candids of celebrities, yet not one shot of the star. "Where's that bastard hiding?"

Lou Starcrave's not hiding, not yet, he's crimped about the mid-section in the swivel chair next to Cub. Cub? Man's shifting from panic to manic and running out of commercials. But we can't afford to get rattled, now can we? Can't *SNAP!*

Bottom of the ninth, bases loaded, two batters out. Call is three and two and you step back up to the plate. What is it you and the sweaty mitt on the mound have in common?

Spit.

That's it.

Dark and syrupy native North Carolina's finest — *Chaw'd Taw*® — a plug of which nestles neatly in your lower jaw.

He spits.

So do you.

And there's the pitch, low curve and fast, you swing, you connect — it's a ground ball past pitcher, past short stop and well on its way to center field, man's on it but one run goes in, two, while you take a dive and slide into second. Crowd is out of their seats and roaring. So what do you do for an encore?

Spit again.

Chaw'd Taw®. North Carolina's finest.

[Warning: The Surgeon General cautions that throat cancer may be linked clinically to continued use of this and other tobacco products.]

And another thing.

Ever wonder what happened to Pan Am or Eastern, Polar Cap or Transcontinental? Along with their fleets of aged D3s and nifty turboprops? They've been deep sixed by deregulation, but we're still flyin — **Vintage Air!** We can get you anywhere — on the cheap: San Diego to DesMoines, $189 round trip.* Salt Lake City to Baton Rouge $204.* Providence to Ottawa $211.* And that's only a sampling. Plus kids or a small stranger can ride for free so long as they sit on your lap. 600,000 sky miles will get you half way to our hub in Louisville from virtually any North American city. And if you can lug it on, we'll stuff it in an overhead. Our motto is: **We care less!** But bring your own pillow and a bag lunch. Variable arrivals and doubtful departures, six hour delays on the tarmac without water are routine, though you can smoke or smooch in the lav, no problemo. We offer all the conveniences of a Trailways bus without the hustlers and the fuss. So welcome aboard — next flight might be canceled, but there's plenty of floor space at the gate to sprawl on.

So if you value your wallet more than your personal safety, call us direct and speak to one of our automated reservationists.

* 120 day advance reservations required. Fares not refundable under any conditions. Federal and local taxes, taxiing charges and flight crew gratuities not included. As for complaints fax your Congressman and see what she/he will do for you.

Though in between adverts and teens, roving video teams and QuotLinks on the prowl, it will be two men with machines that'll battle 'til the death throttle in the trenches tonight. For over in the darkest corner of the auto park sits a shadow astride a black camouflaged attack cycle — one Colonel L.L. Peckler — the new man in charge of corporate forces on the ground since the Executive Liaison's unanticipated retirement.

"'Scuse me. Got to get through heah."

The Colonel watches he does and he chews, on a plug of Chaw'd Taw®. Man can reconnoiter for himself, his eyes concealed behind mirrored aviator glasses, a shiny domed helmet set squarely upon his low brow, spit polished hip boots, short army jacket with many ribbons and glinty medals attached, and in his hand a riding crop with which to whip his own ass into a gallop.

"'Scuse me, 'scuse me please."

He has his orders. Mission is covert with a limited objective, the capture of one Chipper Stirbee. Alive. L.L. is to pursue. BUT WHATEVER THE TACTICAL ADVANTAGE OF THE MOMENT, EMPLOY RESTRAINT, BE SENSITIVE TO THE DELICACY OF THE FESTIVAL SITUATION AS WELL AS THE CONGESTION. These precautions and more dash across the screen installed recently in the frontal lobe of the old soldier's chrome-plated skull.

"*Uhmm'plh.*"

PRIORITY ALERT: ABOVE ALL AVOID ANY CONTACT WITH THE MEDIA. ABORT MISSION IMMEDIATELY UPON SIGHTING A CAMERA WITHIN RANGE.

"*Kluk'glu'flunkup!*"

ASSAULT MUST APPEAR ROUTINE. ISOLATE TARGET. MINIMIZE INVOLVEMENT WITH SURROUNDING POPULATION. ZERO CASUALTIES WILL BE TOLERATED, THOUGH LEAVE NO WITNESSES EITHER.

"*'U'gunk'kumpfs!*"

The QuotLink Executive Committee transmitting from the blimp is far from sanguine about entrusting an assignment with such potentially dire repercussions into the hands of this rehabed world war tank commander, but then they've attempted diplomacy all evening to no successful effect.

The Colonel is nonplused, he's spine erect, fixed and fit for any assignment, even the amateur adventure this prissy desk set is suggesting.

REPEAT: SHOULD YOU ENCOUNTER A VIDEO TEAM, YOU MUST ABORT OPERATION AT ONCE. AVOID DETECTION BY POPULAR MEDIA AT ALL COSTS.

"*Humpfh!*" Being read a riot act by one's nominal superiors is odious enough, but the background briefing by what looks to be a hard shell crab is downright irksome — "*Urk'!*"

"Yez vell, ziz iz no B-grade zhootz-'em-up you're undertakink, no ziree-bob. Ziz mizzion requirez carevul timink un prezize pozitionink, no margin vor error iz pozzible. Ve have ziz one janz un zat'z zat."

"*Olpfh?*"

"You muzt nonjalantly ride up alongzide Jibber Ztirbee un zen qvik az a vlash grab him."

"*Gyez!*"

"Un at ze exact zame zecond you muzt subztitute ziz Irizh look-a-like

I've rezently rezuzitated vitzout anyvone ever zuzpectink."

"*Glok?*"

"You muzt underztand, ze zvitj-er-roo iz az cruzial az nabbink ze zuper-ztar in ze virzt plaze." That said, Queezac unveils his invention. "Behold! I give you JibberKlon!"

"*Wholp!*"

The Irish look-a-like is amazingly that. He stands tall and lanky like he's secured only at the shoulders. His head flops to one side at an aw shucks angle, and the rest of him, especially the hips are so loose that he dances around like a puppet on strings, limbs bouncing up and down all rubber.

"He'z a little wobbly on hiz feetz at ze moment, butz vhen ze drugz vear ovv, he'll be az jumpy az a horny toad. He'z our mozt advanced zecret veapon, un ve muzt pozition him zureptiziouzly behind enemy linez vhere he can do lotz ov damage – zough I muzt zay I am very hezitant to plaze a dizign ziz zovhizticated into ze handz ov ze regular army."

Peckler glowers down at the craggily creature crouched about knee height, he clears his throat, spats – "*Huk!*" – whatever it is, it's impertinent.

Whereupon follows a brief instructional demo: "Ziz patent pendink devize haz mozt ov ze built-in veaturez ov ze original model."

"*Gno-zhlik?*"

"Zere'z a vull zet ov zampled zound bitez, zomezink vizeazz to zay vor every occazion. Litzen." *H'yep. Whoa! Nope. Ahright! Hey guys and gals, how'h you hangin tonight? Could you go fah a tune oah two about now?* "Zoundz exzactly like him, doezn't it?"

The Colonel is speechless.

"Ze faze, ze hair, zat deviant attitude un cockzure arroganze – don't tzink duplicatink all zat vaz eazy. My creation haz to pazz cloze-up zcruitiny, un I vaz vorever gettink ze cadenzes right, but he'z a jip ovv ze old block now un exztremely pliable, controlled by vone eazy-to-uze remote. Zee, ziz button getz him zinkink – *Cindy Sue / Cindy Sue / She does fah Stan / She'll do fah you* – vhile togglink back un vortz vitz ziz lever getz him jumpkickink."

WONGG- WONGG- whacks smack up against the Colonel's helmet.

"*Glaskole!*"

"He'z an exzact replica, down to ze most intimate detailz – zee, he can expoze himzelv in public."

"*Huuunk!*" Old soldier is truly dumb struck, nor could he speak if he wanted to, having shouted his larynx out during the Great Gulp War, to the relief of the General Staff who considered him insolent if not downright insubordinate, although his remaining repertoire of low-throat gutturals expresses his personal preferences quite explicitly – "*Pfluck'klu!*"

Wherewith and underneath the stern gaze of the QuotLink Elders in the blimp, Queezac must reluctantly hand over his prize possession to the safekeeping of L.L.

"Ve'll juzt zecure him to ze back ov your zycle vitz zeze all-purpoze bungy cordz — zere, he'z all zet."

WACK WACK WACK WACK
Set he is, snapping at Peckler's back.

"I'll mizz you JibberKlon."

Peckler won't, he unsnaps the bungie cords and slings the robot over his shoulder, sort of salutes and roars off on his attack cycle to head up the troops — leaves Queezac coughing in the exhaust.

Once out of eyeshot Peckler makes a pit stop, heaves JibberKlon into the trash heap of discarded policies from his pussy predecessor, then speeds on. If you're going to war, sack the cute covert activities and open up straight into the enemy's faces, one round hot after another.

SCOOT? SCOOT? "Lou?" Cub rolls around on his swivel chair. "Come out, come out from wherever you are."

Lou's disappeared from view.

HUNCH! Bear climbs off. *SCRUNCH!* Squats down on the floor. *GRUNTS!* "Ahh, there you are!"

Lou's huddled underneath his matching chair, with fuzzy bear's face glowering in at him.

"Haul out from under there, we've got to talk shop."

Lou won't budge, so Cub has to poke around some, snag him by the collar, drag him out kicking — *FLUNK!* — plops him back in his seat. "Here, have a cigarette. It'll clear your head." Cub lights one up for himself as well. "Way I'm looking at it, if we scratch *Cyclin For Her Love* off the playlist, we save an easy ten to fifteen minutes, maybe more."

"Fightin…"

"What's that?"

"Fightin. *Fightin For Her Luv*."

"Then we reduce this medley of old Loose Nuke hits to half, that's two songs running six minutes tops, saves us enough time to set up for the Finale — you making mental notes Lou? Because somebody's got to hightail it backstage and inform Chipper."

"*Fightin's* a classic, his fans wou-…"

"O come off it! How in the hell would you define a classic on a planet spinning this fast?"

"Time proven, a hit that's been long associated with a particular group, an identifying theme, an overall image reminder, a signifi-…"

"Cut the crap. I'm not interested in a lecture on pop culture, I want to know which songs you two are going to ax?"

"We can't cut *Fightin Fah Huh Luv*. The fans would be inconsolable."

"And we can't have that, can we? Better to leave the world's religious leaders hanging until daybreak rather than have the fans inconsolable."

Lou notices Cub has two smokes going at once, one in each paw.

"Cub, I'm sympa—…"

"Speak up. I can't hear you."

"…sympathetic, but this is the Loose Nukes' reunion and a benefit for the environment, not a made-for-TV special. You can't cram history into a fifteen minute video segment, the kids won't have it, they'll riot."

Not a word anybody at Wembley wants to hear, not Cub, not his QuotLink superiors — man burns at the mere mention of it.

"He's the only one who can calm this crowd — and they didn't come to see the Pope make a TV appearance, they came to listen to Chipper."

Bear takes a puff, first one fist then the other, stares through Lou.

"He speaks their language, soothes their fears, raises their hopes, he might even be able to spark a much needed spiritual renewal in an age soured with cynicism, shackled with hesitation, hobbled by doub-…"

"Spark a what?" *Puff? Puff?*

"A spiritual renewal — see Cub, there's this reluctance in our time to commit to a cause, one with a universal appeal, but a concerted effort against an impending environmental disaster would be precisely-…"

"Stop. Think. You're talking about Chipper Stirbee here."

"You saw for yourself how he touched their hearts, how they sang along with him, how they danced, jumped up and dow-…"

"I'll say they jumped up and down. Thought for a second the roof was going to cave in on this new newfangled stadium, crush everyone of us into the ground."

"Chipper's the consummate communicator, that's his special talent. He can reach the kids, tell it like it is, and despite the odds against any definable success they could see in their own lifetimes, he could inspire them to go for greatness — the salvation of the very planet!"

"Inspire what? Are we talking about the same guy here, mister headline news with his passport lifted for indecent exposure?"

"He was having a spiritual encounter in the desert!"

"He was out of his mind on some native drug in the Outback and dancing in front of our affiliate QuotNet news crew. I have seen the footage personally, and there's nothing spiritual about wagging your male membership card in front of a camera!"

"He was on a high, he had just come off a few weeks' fast with an elderly Aborigine shaman."

"You're telling me his jig was a religious experience?"

Lou squirms some. "In a way, they say food deprivation in the hot sun can leave you feeling ecstatic…"

"Ecstatic?"

"…infused with new insight, a revived faith."

"What, belief in the almighty weed?"

"The sort of faith I- we-… there was no evidence of any illegal substance… and everyone of us has to believe in something worthwhile or as a race we shall degenerate into the primal slugfest we crawled out of."

"Yeah right, degenerate, there's a word that sums this discussion up, Chipper emerging from the desert wagging the only thing he believes in."

"You must acknowledge that these new songs he's written are inspired."

"I'd say so. He's top of the charts and still climbing, but let's not go mixing faith up with royalties. This guy's all show, no guru. Childish. Impulsive. Self-centered. I've watched a whole slew like him from my swivel chair over the past forty five years — and benefits? I've televised hundreds. These characters come trotting across the stage, spout on and on about whatever cause comes to mind, play some tired old number from their collected hits, then dash for the limo. The only thing they're committed to is a Platinum Pop-Off Award and new cash from residuals."

"I'm stunned how jaded you've become Cub. You see sincerity in a man like this, yet you believe in nothing he says. You even question his motives."

"I can't believe you're sitting here defending Chipper Stirbee after a lifetime devoted to the moronic — but none of this talk is getting us anywhere." Cub pauses — *puff puff puff puff* — Big Bear's really smoking tonight. "Look Lou, the guys and I are tired, really tired, we've been trapped inside an airless control trailer for over twenty four hours — twenty four hours! So we've got to finish this gig and get the fuck out of here before we spontaneously combust! ARE YOU LISTENING TO ME?"

Lou's not sure how to respond, plus he has this smoldering brush in his face. While on air…

Scene is a pre-school, toddlers running riot with no clothes on. Miss Krumple can't believe it, Miss Lipscold's opposed to physical controls, and there's not enough of Miss Hardkick to go around. Youngsters have torn up their coloring books, trashed potties and covered the walls with graffiti, plus the cookies and fruity cups have all been eaten. 911's an option, but then there's what to say on the evening news and parents alarmed with lawsuits. Can't three mommies make a decent living out of a garage daycare any more?

Yes they can, and quite handsomely, with **Nippim**™ — two flavorful gel tablets a day, morning on waking and noon after lunch, by bedtime the precious is guaranteed groggy for eight to ten hours of solid parental relief.

Phone your local school nurse for she can legally write a prescription without an MD's intervention, and the only known contraindication is a life of continuous addiction. But if **Nippim**™ can control world-wide infantile rage, then it's worth any price.

Product of QuotLink Pharmaceuticals. Great Neck, Long Island.

"I understand your time constraints, I really do, but you have to understand that Chipper Stirbee is a phenomenon Cub, a phenomenon!"
"When you start in with all the PR, I get suspicious — so come on, level with me. What can the guys and I do to prepare for your next trick?"
"Trick? There are no tricks!"
"Mirrors, fades, fakes and disappearing acts, this joker's been juggling with our heads for the past sixteen months!"
"You've got him wrong, it's his music, his message that drives hi-…"
"He's a magician, not a musician!"
"Chipper's one of a kind, he's unique, the sort of individual who only comes around once in a lifetime, once every hundred years or so."
"Like a burnt-out comet?"
"Like a sunburst, like a new universe, and that's what you're not seeing, not comprehending. This boy's hot, ready to burst, explode!"
"I know, I know he is, and that's why we're prepared if he pulls another one of his surprise striptease acts…"
"No no, you don't understand. He's a phenomenon!"
"You keep saying that."
"He's unique!"
"What, like a freak?"
"No no no…"
"Yes yes yes…"
"No. You don't see."
"And you don't listen!"
"All I can say Cub, is that something incredible is happening before your very eyes and you're missing it!"
"I'm shouting in your ear and you're not listening. You can't hear anything beyond your own hype!"
"I hea-…"

"Lou! No more surprises! Mark my words, if he rips his pants off and goes diving into The Pit with the teeny-screechers tonight, I'll pull the plug. I will. Nobody's going to expose themselves on one of my satellite hook-ups, you hear me? I have canned footage from his other concerts I can substitute — SO I'M WARNING YOU ONE LAST TIME!" And papa bear rises out of his chair, rises high above Lou, his great paws outstretched, his face in flames. "WE HAVE TO STICK TO SCHEDULE! YOU AND YOUR BOY CHIPPER HAVE TO STICK TO SCHEDULE — ARE YOU LISTENING TO ME?"

Lou is, it's just that his jaw is locked open, a physical phenomenon that in the hard-of-listening often enhances their ability to hear.

"We're down to the end zone, the guys and me, minutes to go, we've finally arrived at this ridiculous finale — I mean whoever dreamt this act up? Some hundred and thirty performers linked together electronically for a sing-along, plus the world's major religious leaders — do you have any idea what it takes to link three stadiums and twelve capitol cities spread over five continents so they can lip-synch along, no delays in the relays?"

Lou doesn't know, hasn't a clue.

"It takes thirty three simultaneous satellite downlinks — thirty three simultaneous satellite downlinks..." Growls the fact into Lou's ear. "...and timed to a millisecond — A MILLISECOND!"

"It is an electronic marvel and a compliment to your ingenui-..."

"Which means we can't afford to have you and your boy Chipper screwing up on us again!"

"I understand, I really do. I am confident that at this very moment he's patiently standing in the wings, awaiting his cue."

"Somehow I'm not convinced, no, I sense that you're in league with him and you're not listening to a word I say."

Of course he is, Lou's trapped he is, listening to every word and to every threat implied therein. "But Chipper is Chipper..."

"Don't start in on me with meaningless tautologies, you have to make this boy understand I won't tolerate any more of his antics, or I'll cut him off at the waist..."

Lou moves his mouth, but there's no sound.

"You can't talk? You have nothing more to say?"

Lou tries to speak. His lips are moving, quivering actually, his tongue tumbling around slowly in his mouth.

"I can't hear you!"

"...you you..."

"Yeah?"

"...you can't stop... can't stop... Chipper..."

"Is that a threat?"

"...no, no, it's just that nobody can stop Chipper, I can't, you can't-..."

"Yes I can, and you know how?"

Lou shakes his head, up-down yes, side-to-side no, he doesn't know?

"By showing the world what a fool Chipper Stirbee really is, and I can do that. I have all the clips I need stored right here beside me in my archives. Instant hard copy biography. Just give me another twenty minute break in the broadcast and I'll expose him cavorting on countless home videos with hundreds of parents' underaged daughters — I'll turn Wembley from a revival to a show trial, complete with an on-stage execution!"

"You would-would-wouldn't…"

"Yes I would, not only because I don't approve of his behavior — nor do most God-fearing, tax-paying citizens — but I'm tired Lou, the boys and I are tired of all this nonsense, we've had it up to here with your boy Chipper." Cub does a cut at the neck.

"You couldn't."

"I can. I will. I make the news here inside my windowless trailer. I decide what people see — what's said, what side, what footage, even down to the least flattering camera angle." This is the nasty side of the bad news bear, the grizzly giant corporate creature the public never sees. "I can make that boy or I can break that boy — I CAN BREAK YOU!" Cub's up again, Cub's plunging down, he yanks Lou out of his swivel chair, by Lou's upraised throat, Lou's throat in Cub's big hairy hands — BWAP BWAP BWAP BWAP — a few bangs against the back of the chair for starters, then comes the squeeze as he cuts off air down the esophagus, restricts blood up to the brain — BWAP BWAP BWAP again.

And the techie crew's too tired to notice, busy, they're configuring transponders — Teheran, Tibet, not easy places to reach even by satellite.

"I- I- I-…"

"You- you- you-… you're right!" Cub drops Lou back into his seat, but he doesn't let go, no, he squeezes the harder. Lou is defenseless, besides he's choking. "You never listen!"

Lou listens, damn it, he hears. And he watches, warily, but he watches and he can see even if he can't comprehend all the forces that swirl around him in a cyclone fierce frenzy.

"So let me say it one more time — LOUDLY, SO YOU CAN HEAR!"

Lou chitters, he chatters.

And Cub leans down, blasts flames right in his face. "YOU BETTER HUSTLE BACKSTAGE AND YOU BETTER WARN THAT PUNTFUCK THAT I'LL GLADLY MAKE HIM LOOK THE FAKER HE IS ON WORLD-WIDE TELEVISION — WARN HIM THAT I WILL BUST HIS BUBBLE LOU STARCRAVE, YOU HEAR ME? I WILL BUST HIS BUBBLE REAL GOOD!"

Nod. Nod yes. Agree to anything, so long as the bully bear lets go.

Which Cub does, he relents, and Lou staggers to the door, staggers out into the crowd, he's got to catch a breath, stretch his neck — *strrrretch* — next he's got to get to Chipper, how he doesn't know, not with every avenue backstage blocked by a contingent of QuotLink Security, but he's got to somehow, he's got to warn Chipper that the show's still far from over.

"You suppose that old timer knew Chipper Stirbee back when?"
Two longhairs watch while Lou spazzes by.
"When?"
"You know, back when, whenever, 50s, 60s, back when it all began."
"Back when what all began?"
"Rock 'n' roll — where have you been?"
"Dunno man, history sucks, besides all that shit went down long before I was born."

Lou's in fact in a fog — well the entire stadium floor is clouded over with this smoky substance which makes thinking along with walking a chore, and crowded, like Lou's got to squeeze through...

> All eyes / All eyes
> Midriffs and thighs
> Out on a nighttime prowl together
> Survival of the fit and the fast
> Feast on the fat
> Try not to fall prey to the predators

...Lou stumbles forward toward the stage, all light but no illumination, and how's he going to get through the crush up front or past the teenies in The Pit?

A convoy of troop carriers arrives outside the stadium at that very second, additional QuotLink units being deployed to various check points backstage, with Colonel L.L. Peckler, 'Old Chrome Dome' himself, parked on the spot, spit sputtering and in command.

Most of the newly reconditioned recruits are dressed in the QuotLink uniform dark blue blazers with two-ways and cattle-prods, but others are outfitted in black and tan fatigues with 9 mm automatics holstered on their hips. It's the latter who take positions outside the stadium in full confrontational view of the masses in the street.

QuotLink irregulars are disguised as concert goers in faded jeans and various rainbow colored t-shirts, their orders to look inconspicuous and infiltrate the audience, although their mechanical swagger and pushy-ass manner are dead giveaways of their paramilitary origins.

Forward these diverse forces march, under one banner — GET CHIPPER!

An opposing force, younger, more diverse, has reached critical mass in front of Wembley. The protestors now numbering nearly four million strong are converging on the site from all over London and the continent beyond, arriving by rail, by car, by foot, they have the stadium surrounded, and though they might be quiet for the moment, it wouldn't take much to spark a conflagration.

Speaking of sparks a gang of large biker lasses is mingling among them — how to get in, how to get in, and once in how to get at Chipper? They caucus to devise a strategy — CRANKCRANKCRANKCRANK — QuotLinks might have the kids at the gates momentarily intimidated, and Lou entirely confounded, but not Cissy Coombs gang, they've been battle-tested in the Midlands

While on broadcast there's a spot especially sensitive to ecological concerns, a luxury Swedish motor car that exceeds the most rigorous standards of pollution control by running on pure popcorn oil:

The Bolvol... crackling with power on a rugged mountainside roadway... accelerating from a standing start to a lid-raising 95 miles per hour in fewer than .7 seconds... the all new Bolvol... a marvel of old-world ingenuity that is 100 per cent environmentally safe and zesty... there's a steady climb up a steep incline without a sputter or pop...

The unaffordable Bolvol four door family wagon... contemporary styling excellence tossed rapidly together with advanced engineering brilliance... $68,095.00 f.o.b. with factory rebate included... delivery and service charges, local taxes, salt and hot melted butter additional where applicable...

More in pocket change than one gal has on her, sitting there backstage, tail still, watchful, ears back, nose twitching. It's Betsy and she sniffs trouble in the crowd, a mixed bag of young girls and uniforms, two things to which she does not as a rule take kindly.

"The's so many blokes Lucy, 'ow a we eva goin ta find Chippa?"

"I's 'is 'air, 'at's wha' gives 'im away, 'at shiny blond straw."

"Righ'. Na'way ta disguise 'at, is the'?"

"Bu' whe do we sta't lookin? So many people, i's so confusin."

Betsy can't tell who's who either, partly the dialects, but mostly the sheer number. Crowd's a crowd in her view, everybody working it from a different angle, and not a one among them a country girl can trust — *rr ruff* — which is when she spies a bright yellow helmeted stagehand rolling Chipper's specialty Harley out of the back lot — ROLLING CHIPPER'S SPECIALTY HARLEY OUT OF THE BACK LOT!

-ro ray, as she gets up and running, though on a circuitous route. It's the Dobie in her, smart, protective, she knows that making a b-line for her baby would only alert the authorities.

Cub McCluff's on the trail too, scouring the monitors on the racks in front of him for some clue to Chipper's whereabouts. Cub has two dozen readicam teams backstage, and one of them — "Come on guys, let's get a move on! *Snap! Snap!*" — one of them is bound to catch sight of the star.

Guess again Cub. Your boys are mired fast in the swamps. The team on the pole, for instance, has swooped down on a covey of freshly hatched chicks, poking their heads up and fluffing their feathers, while another team has a young starlet pinned against a wall. They're interviewing her against her will, asking questions about her sexual proclivities.

"So you like guys?"

"Of course."

"How about guys plural?"

"Why not?"

"Other women?"

"Might. For a thrill."

Well then, how about me and my drooling soundman here Mik?

Another remote is tagging along behind a SQWAT squad, scouting for the first installment of a new TV action-adventure series, when there in the corner of the screen Cub spies a furry speck — Betsy — *snap snap* — "Track that black dog — PT 10 — that's Chipper's mutt, keep after him!"

Her Cub, her, although Betsy does have a he-man disposition. And ever see a camera team try and chase a Dobie-retriever mix through a mob? A dodge to the right, a feint to the left, lift a leg — this girl's not into squatting — a nosedive under an idling tractor-trailer. Betsy's gained fifty yards in a single pass. Video team? Back at the scrimmage line attempting to focus.

"Idiots, you missed her! Who's up on that pole — PT 13? — cut the cutsy crap and find me that dog, *snappity snap!*" A chase is all it takes to get Cub's adrenaline rising, and what does a mighty media weight do when he needs a lift? He downs another Copa Cola, one gulp, two, no need to chew.

Betsy wiggles around underneath the truck, impatient, watchful... *hmm...* a clump of thick black boots over that-a-way... maybe if she could sidewind along the sandals and sneakers, she could make it without getting spotted... one thing's certain, avoid the high heels, a shriek from one of those bimbos and the hunt would be ov-*rr*.

STUMP STUMP STUMP STUMP STUMP

Betsy ducks as a QuotLink patrol marches by, sniffs at an old ball cap somebody's dropped. A diguise? Might help, she decides, and plops it over her ears, then pokes her head up, stealthily in the best black dog tradition, and sprints — *fwoof* — slips in among the sandals and sneakers who are mostly in motion, and crawling across a dance floor on all fours is a feat unto itself, whilst staying on the alert for the least trace of her master.

"'Scuse me."

Her ears spike.

"'Scuse me..."

It's him. That breathless rasp he has for a voice.

"...'scuse me, got to get through heah."

Then's when she spots him a few feet off. She does a quick glance left to right, coast's clear so she goes charging — lands in the midst of some thick booted bikers — bikers? But these aren't the usual shaggy kind with missing teeth and flabby beerbelly buttonholes, why no they're...

"Yoo!"

-*ro-o, roo!*

"Whir's that roody looser yoo'r usually coodlin with?"

Chipp-*er*, you must mean Chipp-*er*?

"Don't try doopin me, yoo mangy muut, I'll yank yoor toonails oot woon by woon til yoo talk."

-*rah*, you and how many of these oversized tire tubs you're toting?

Whoa! And is Cissy Coombs sensitive to the mere mention of her plus plus sized figure — bong goes the bell and so begins round two!

R-O-W-L!

Toenails? Take ten on your ample side rolls sis.

Yes, but teeth, Cissy's are implants deep into her vicegrip jawbones and clamped on Betsy's ear — which is why they clip most Dobie pups to begin with — though not Betsy's whose tail's intact too and a whip across the bitch's backside sends Cissy plunging butt up face down on the asphalt, not that a scraped nose is about to stop a north country girl.

"Yoo gott the best oof me once, boot yoo won't doo it again!"

-*ro no?*

stump stump stump — QuotLinks rush to see what's the ruckus. Betsy backs off, and Cissy stands, dusting herself off.

"Took a bad tuumble oof me bike mates. Sooory foor the coomotion."

QuotLinks might be suspicious, a factory installed trait, but they have too much to attend to and so they move on — which is what Betsy attempts to do as well when she notices she's surrounded by row upon row of solid black boots. The Sisterhood *en masse*.

"We're throo bein nice doog. It's talk oor we stomp yoo too a bloody poodle oof puulp."

What's there to say, especially when you can't speak.

"I'm oonly askin oonce. Whir's that uuseless scuumbag aboot new?"

About now? He'd be wheeling his way out of here, but maybe if I tap it out on the ground you could comprehend. Betsy paws some, then she pads about, tail up, does a turn or two.

"Whit's all this shit spoosed too mean?"

Betsy's forced to repeat herself, only this time she reverses direction.

Cissy and her girls are losing patience. One takes a menacing step forward, and another, breaks ranks, which is rule number one of the front line don't-dos — leave a breach and you're bound to get broached — as Betsy goes boring through the boots, bowling a few of the bruisers offside and just as they join in stomping non-stop on sisterly toes, and who says solidarity among the fair sex is a given?

stomp stomp stomp stomp stomp — bash attracts the attention of both QuotLinks and readicams, Cub in his truck — man splashes half a can of cola on his pants. "*Snap* — PT 13! PT 13! GET ON HIM!"

Her. Cub. Team on the pole narrows in on Betsy as she hightails it out of there, and no mistaking it, she's trailing directly after a crew guy in a bright yellow jacket pushing a bike.

-rrip-per! -rrip-per!

"That's got to be Chipper! Don't let him out of your sights — he's going for the great escape — *snap snap snap*…"

Snapped! Something happens to the feed from the flag pole. Seems the team climbed too far out and fell off flat into the hatchery.

"OK alright then, get me access to the camera in the blimp!"

No no Cub, don't! Alerting QuotLink Aerial Command will blow Chipper's cover. Though Cub has never concerned himself much with the ethical implications of fast breaking news coverage. He has airtime to fill — that's the gaps in between commercials — and so what if the newsman's involvement has an injurious impact on the outcome of what he's covering? Feed the newborns to the jackals, his job is raw footage.

Cub's request to the high command is immediately rerouted to the Colonel. "*Holk!*" L.L. gloats, almost swallows his plug whole and signals his

Betsy… pokes her head up, stealthily in the best black dog tradition, and sprints — *fwoof*

squadron into immediate pursuit.

-rr-rr-rip-per!

"Betsy baby, is that you?"

-rr-rr-rare-rarr-rou-rou-row-rrin?

"Truth is pooch, I've got to get out of heah fah a breath of fresh aih, got to try and cleah my head a few seconds befah that finale…"

It'd take more than a few seconds to accomplish that feat my friend, with all you have been tokin.

"…you know how I hate feelin confined, plus I owe my fans outside in the pahkin lot a visit, they've been up-in-ahms all evenin."

-rrrr

"Won't do you no good tryin to talk me out of it – so you might as well climb on back fah the ride."

-ROH-OH! Betsy doesn't much care for bikes, not since a nasty spill across a gravel road when she was but a pup.

"Ahright have it youh way and stay."

-roh-roh-rip-per!

Ripper? Some pothead standing close by is expert at deciphering dog talk. "Chipper?" Cry goes up like wildfire.

CHIPPER! CHIPPER!

Lucy and Abby heed the call, notice the troops and the cameras making toward a narrow gate to the auto park.

"Somethin's up Abby!"

"Righ?"

"They must've spotted me Chippa!"

"We've got ta get ta'im befa they do."

And they're off: the two girls at their long-legged best, Cissy Coombs, battered but not beaten, with Peckler racing to overtake them both, and the press never too far behind.

"Blast it!" Chipper's trying to kickstart his Harley – *fwooof-foof.*

-rr try switching on the ignition chum.

-FWOOM -FWOOOOOOM! "Now we'h smokin! Hop up babydoll and hang on tight, know you wouldn't want to miss out on any of the action!"

-rohrohroh

But which of the converging forces has the best chance of funneling through the tiny gate first? QuotLinks riding along the sides slightly ahead of the camera crews, Lucy and Abby muscling into the muddle in the middle, Cissy Coombs hauling from behind or Chipper driving dizzily all over the field? Is the solution purely physical or merely statistical? Two girls are hot and have a distinct high-heeled advantage, Peckler's already up to speed, news today is nearly instantaneous, Cissy's got her cause, but then Chipper and Betsy *are* riding a Harley.

-rulp!

Rule must follow that whoever has the most to lose wins despite their respective angle of incidence, because it's Lucy and Abby who reach the gate first, except the gatekeepers have locked arms to prevent them.

"O'no u don't." Lucy takes a bite out of the nearest strong arm restraining her — "Barf! Wha's 'e got fa blood, mota oil?"

More akin to brake fluid, but whatever its distinct chemical characteristics the QuotLink is gushing green all over the ground and in the confusion the two girls make a break for it, when — *GUNRUNRUN -RUN-RUN-RUNNNNNNNNNN* — Chipper rips through the gears and comes heading straight at them.

"Tha' can' be me Chippa!"

"Na way, tha's tha' zippa jerk we met up wi befa!"

"He wasn' the man a'me dreams."

"Naw'up close he wasn'."

Closer and closer and dream or no dream it's him. The girls scatter as he tears past them and blasts out the back gate, Betsy's paws wrapped around his waist, ears flapping and holding on for dear life.

ZOOOOOOOOOOOOOOOOOOOOOM! — something else mechanical goes shooting past. Peckler. And after him — *ZOOM! ZOOM! ZOOM! ZOOM! ZOOM! ZOOM! ZOOM! ZOOM! ZOOM! ZOOM! ZOOM!* — a dirty dozen from the QuotLink Mounted Motor Division.

Not far behind Cissy Coombs and her gang of muscle bikes.

Lucy and Abby are still in the race, but the press is a distant fifth and easily restrained by the leaky QuotLink remainders who slam shut the gate.

In the sky above, the QuotLink blimp blacks out its brightly lit marquee — *QUOT • LINK • INC • • PRE • SENTS • • CHIP • PER • DISSTIR • B* — and assumes a battlefield command position.

"Whoa! Will you take a look at this!" As Chipper goes charging into the parking lot.

-rwow!

It's a carnival camp, a troupe of painted bodies and multi-colored vans, roadsters parked beside bimmers with plenty of hybrid sub-compacts in between, board scrapers, bros, goths, surfers, jocks with suburban chicks, geeks, greasers, hips on trips and kids not in any cliques, flesh and metal commingling, tailgating, all brands of Americans fraternizing with as many varieties of Euro and duded-up East Enders — shaved heads, illustrated leather jackets, tattoos, pierced eyebrows, nipples and tongues —

they're sharing hits, slogging down brew, dunk dancing to old Loose Nukes tunes on their boomboxes. Why it must be the greatest threat to Western Civilization since Woodstock in 69, although the crowd's mellow mellow about the damage they're doing — no shirts, see-through skirts, flirts and openly groping. Tie-dyed peddlers are selling t's, posters and pirated CDs, inflatable dolphins and some seeds from trees felled in the Amazon along with the Chipper puppets that have become so popular, each lovingly handcrafted from sour apples and dried corn stalks by cottage Mainers. There's cold drinks and chips from coal burners, bags and vials and candy whams stashed in the back of vans — a taste for whatever ails you — when from everywhere at once a cry arises…

CHIPPER!

Flashing by on a bike and waving.

CHIP- CHIP- CHIP- CHIP-

He weaves in and out of parked cars, close by crafts and pedestrians, doing a sharp angled U'y and passing back by again.

CHIPPER! CHIPPER! CHIPPER! CHIPPER! CHIPPER! CHIPPER!

The kids jump up and down while Chipper obliges with a display of biker gymnastics. On a straightaway he kicks up off the pedals and does a handstand off the handlebars, clicking his heels in the air — such a feat from a low slung Harley — bitchin man, bitchin!

Next it's Betsy's turn. She climbs high on Chipper's shoulders, stands on her back legs, then he stands on the seat, both with barely a wobble.

SISTER! SISTER!

You bet. Betsy's no ordinary pooch, nor is the Harley an ordinary machine — Harley slows, slows down to a complete stop, holds, while the two balance atop — *whoa whoa, whoa baby go!* — Harley starts up again on cue and rides them round the ring.

Try that trick with one of those cheap Asian imports.

MACHINE!

And the audience is mightily appreciative, they hoot and they holler, for these are the kids who couldn't get inside even if they tried, the ones who never arrive on time and wouldn't stand in line if they could afford the price of a ticket, but crash the gate, that they're expert at — h'yep, these are among Chipper's most devoted.

He finds a vacant spot on the lot and wheels around in a circle, foot down and touches ground. The fans instantly enclose.

"Say hey, how'h you folks holdin up out heah?"

CHIPPER!

"Whoa! Go easy guys and gals!" Man's mobbed as they reach out to touch him, shake his hand, slap him on the back, one girl prostrate on the ground kisses his foot. And although he must officially protest, the dude loves it, bathes in it. Someone hands him a beer, another a toke, somebody else something to snort — *gulp, puff, sniff* in rapid succession — "Damn, what was that shit?" — a buzz through the brain is what with momentary optical distortion. "Can't believe you cats, this is wheah the real pahty's at!"

Certainly not overhead. A quiet surge of the rotary prop and the QuotLink blimp is hovering directly above the parking lot, casting a dark shadow over the evening's festivities. A heat-sensitive photocell scrutinizes the scene below, locking in on its target, on the freewheeling Harley and on the rings of human bodies clustered around it. The blimp plots the coordinates and instantly updates the Colonel.

Peckler's chrome helmet jiggles with the signal as he eagerly drives into action to survey the scene for himself, scout for some chink in the wall of gyrating youth flesh — "*Skunkspunk!*" — the gypsy encampment having been hands off to QuotLink patrols all day, pursuant to official policy that deemed it best not to provoke the slightest disturbance, a policy Peckler is about to debunk when he goes after that prize bull's eye in the center.

And on the issue of civilian casualties, Peckler's hard line — life's a lot like war, serious serious, and these kids might look innocent, all puppies and free love, but they ain't. Pack of spoiled brats who think the world's easy pickins — yeah, well throw those throats open, boys and girls, you're about to get a nasty dose of reality *zoo-zoo-zoo-zoon!*

Fact two kids tossing a frisbee nearby recognize him, if not him personally, then what he stands for — Peckler the man commanding the picked pack of unprincipled peckerheads arrayed against them.

L.L. could care less. Kids today aren't about to admire him nor respect any authority, so if it's contempt toward the forces of his kind of liberty, so be it. He'll play the spoiler tonight.

One kid flashes 'Old Chrome Dome' the finger.

"*Hunh?*" L.L. makes a mental note, run that puny poker down on his way to get Chipper.

"Zmitzy, qvick qvick, help me vitz hiz Eminenze." Queezac has lugged the Executive Liaison's remains into the emergency room set up in the basement of the home team's locker room.

Smitty, Queezac's equally evil assistant is about the same size and sight as Queezac, a white coated lab rat with bristly whiskers. The two must struggle to lift the bucket of Liaison up over their heads and empty it onto a gurney — "Be carevul, ve don't vant to zpill his gutz all over ze vloor!"

Smitty can barely conceal his glee at the prospect of diving sleeves first into the murky work of reinflating the shrunken diplomat.

"Iv ve hurry, ve've got a zlight jance, otzervize he'z a goner."

Slight is an exaggeration, as Smitty is assigned the delicate task of reassembling the fragments of bone. He climbs on the table and begins stuffing each piece back into the Executive Liaison's shark skin suit.

Queezac handles the innards and goes at the task like a madman possessed, for this is his Liaison, his alter ego and then some. He spoons each ounce of his Eminence's precious fluids into a jar, and surely the electronics are salvageable, simply dip them into a handy acid bath — *zip zip*, watch how they sizzle — and there in the midst of the puddle floats the Liaison's most prized possession, his gleaming new white dentures. Queezac's quick to retrieve them, packs them into his vest pocket.

"Want to shake your hand dude."
"Shake youhs back."
"Friends back home will never believe I really met up with you."
"Belief's a hahd commodity to come by these days."
And next in line.
"Hi!"
"How's it goin?"
"My mother says she saw you perform in the late 60s."
"That makes youh mom an old lady."
"But why not you?"
"'Spose what they say is true? Goodness like beauty nevah ages."
-brarr-rar-rarf
"Nobody asked youh opinion Betsy."
"'At's 'im Lucy, I told 'u so."
"The roadie wi the bike! It's unbelievable!"
"'E looks so dif'rent now."
"'E's jus' got a glow on, 'at's all."
"How'h you two gihls doin?"
"We met up wi u befa."
"I remembah. You called me a zippah jahk."
"Did'n mean it."
"How about all those othah things you wah sayin, 'spose you didn't mean any of them neithah?"
"Like wha'?"
"All those things you said you'd do if you caught me alone in the dahk."
"'At's jus' gi'l talk, 'at's all 'at is."
"Relieved to heah that. I was wohried about my pahsonal safety."
"So go ahead an ask'im Lucy."

"Naw, i's too embar'assin."
"Naw i'ain', i's ur big chance!"
"Abby! Leave it be!"
"Then I'll do it fa u. Chippa?"
"H'yep?"
"Would u give Lucy 'ere somethin she's a'ways wanted?"
"Depends."
"She's a'ways sayin 'at u a the man 'a 'er dreams."
"Abby!"
"U do, don' go fibbin abou' it now.
"I'm jus' so embar'assed."
"Woul' u give 'er ur autograph?"
"That's easy."
"Jus' pu' it 'ere righ' on me thigh?" As she rips up her skirt.
"Whoa! Got a felt-tip pen?"
"U naw really a ce'tified sexu'l menace, a u?"
"Nope. Wohse."
-*rr* worse than worse.

"Shush gihl, you keep stickin youh nose in wheah it doesn't belong, and I'm goin to send you home in a doggie carriah. We've got to keep up appeahrances, 'specially when we'h out heah meetin the fans."

Sure sure, anything you say to keep the dusty myth alive.

"How's that suit youh fancy?"
"Feels good, i' does! I won' wash it away eva."
"Now 'ow abou' one fa me, righ' 'ere across me chest?"
"Sohry, got to draw the line somewheah, leastwise while we'h out heah in public."
"Hey man!"
"Hey!"
"Me and my buddies really appreciate your music."
"Thank you."
"Yeah, you tell it like it is."
"H'yep. Least I can do. You fellas do the same, heah?"
"Will do."
"Promise. Got to promise. Othahwise we'h only addin constahnation to the confusion."

A girl with an exposed belly ring sidles her way up. "My daddy says you don't believe in anything other than sex, drugs and rock 'n' roll."

"What's youh daddy believe in?"

"Those old time values, prayer before meals, mandatory military conscription and a return to the gold standard."

"And what keeps youh pretty little head a'buzzin?"

"You." She slithers across the Harley face fronting him. "Mostly."

Chipper traces the outline of her belly with his finger, tugs on the ring.

"You have any advice for young people today?"

"Probably nothin you haven't heahd ahready."

"Must be something?" She reaches around Chipper's neck, plays with his pony tail.

"If you don't go and try things out, you'h nevah goin to know."

"Know what?"

"Know that with most things theah's this point of no retuhn, this point when things get so fah out of control theah's simply no tuhnin back."

"You mean like when you have no choice except to give in?"

Her father is right, there's not a drop of decency in you.

"Nope, the point when you've got to resist with evahrythin you've got. See, theah's no law in natuhe that says just cause things ah bad, you've got to throw youh hands up in the aih and let them get wohse."

"But I don't want to resist you."

He's tracing a downy fine line from the ring to her zipper.

"Got to resist whoevah's goin to take youh hehritage away from you babydoll, like the only planet you'll evah call home…"

She wraps her arms around his neck and presses her chest against his.

"…cause- cause if you and youh genahration don't staht fightin them now, the battle's ahready lost."

"Them? Who's them?"

"Them makin the most money destroyin youh envihronment."

"Like my daddy?" She's heaving little breasts and kisses, probably not taking in a word he's saying.

"Who's youh daddy?"

"He's *press-press* president of the Atmospheric Disposal Corporation, ever hear of them?"

"ADCRAP! They'h the ones who'h plannin on shootin nucleah waste aboahd rusty Chinese rockets out towahd Mahs?"

She momentarily disengages. "Daddy says it's safe and economical, and the only permanent solution to seepage from land-based waste dumps."

"What's he plannin on doin when one of those loads comes blowin back in his face?"

"He tells me and my mom not to worry, that we'll survive as a family OK if only world currencies are tied to a solid standard we can count on."

"H'yep?"

"Then all our treasury bonds in the safe deposit box wouldn't get devalued too terribly."

"Damn…"

"Failing that, he says we're going to have to depend on the military."

"...no wondah youh daddy prays fah grace befah he eats his suppah."

Circling him there's a mass in motion, primordial, approaching a flash point as bodies swirl round and round in concentric circles, packed so fast they create a heat far in excess of their numbers, spinning in time to the revolutions per second per second of the Harley and radiating an energy at their core so hot it charges Chipper as he's never been charged before.

Peckler too, he's sparking atop six cylinders. For this could turn out to be the greatest battle of his career and an excellent chance to set history back at least half a century — isn't that what warfare's for anyway? Besides the Colonel's a defiant cuss, he revs the baby between his legs — *zo-zo-zoon* — his ass hotter'n a grenade launcher, while the QuotLink Elders in the blimp debate. Should they? Shouldn't they? Is it too late for further negotiations, some way to salvage the situation on the ground without resort to a military solution? There is world opinion to consider and class action suits should anything go terribly wrong.

But a pull-back this far into the assault would surely test the limits of the old soldier's endurance. For on the issue of a commander's autonomy in the field, the Colonel has a set opinion: He didn't create this mess, although he's the one who's got to mop it up. It's those politicians, they're to blame. For once diplomacy fails, the military has to be ready to step in. Containment, *bullshit!* Don't constrain it, *squash it!* L.L. doesn't spit his tobaccy, he gulps it.

So while the Council of Elders vacillates, L.L. decides to take matters into his own hands. He pulls ahead and signals his cycle squads into formation. *zooooom!* He's off — riding astride his Scrapskawa Scavenger, a stripped-down attack version of the popular 669 roadster series, a highway hazard if ever there was one, entirely un-American in manufacture and slung so low to the ground that L.L. has to squint through his kneecaps to see the road in front, his butt set to a slow burn directly on top of the pistol-bored slant-shafted titanium alloy engine, fired with a fierce fuel injection and twin cataclysmic afterburners. Only a real man would have what it takes to ride a whore this hot — the Colonel being such and meat-eater meaner than most. He can tuck his under his balls and up the back crack, fuck himself silly while he charges full throttle into battle — *zoom! zoom! zoom! zoom! zoom! zoom! zoom! zoom! zoom! zoom! zoom!* — with his squadron stoking right in line behind him.

Some friendlies on the fringe see the riders coming. They rush in to warn the others.

CHIPPER! CHIPPER!

But Chipper and Betsy are busy grandstanding again, he's stomach on the seat of his Harley, legs and arms outstretched and steering with his nose. Betsy's doing a headstand off his back.

The kids are ecstatic, laughing and clapping, egging them on.

As Peckler's cycle squads reach the periphery of the circle, they hesitate, blinded momentarily by the dazzling display of colors, the writhing bodies, the shrieking laughter, the easy exchange of trinkets, glances, smiles and embraces — it's the last in particular, the sense of touch that sets these grafted together guardians' filed teeth on edge, cause their pupils to constrict into night vision preparedness, pump their body armor into bulky profusion — *hoo-ah hoo-ah hoo-ah* — for these are seasoned volunteers, the real veteran parts of foreign wars, retrofitted with the latest in wartime bio-electronic technology, sonar sensors implanted at the temples, transmitter cells incised at the calyx of the cranium, whence they constantly emit and receive commands of migraine intensity which drive them to ravage and mangle mankind without mercy.

"Hey! Watch it!" Some straggler stands up to defy them. "Who do you think you're shovin around, you bio-bastards?"

"Yeah, up yours!" His buddy joins in.

Hoo- hah hah — if these kids only knew — see QuotLink Cycle Squads have been further adapted, form welded to function, with the riders permanently attached to their machines, butts bolted to the carburetors, an entirely internalized combustion, their intestines intermingled with the exhaust systems — though not Colonel Peckler, he's the exception. He's aged human and has an altogether different device for controlling his toxic emissions — *stunka stunka* — man can torque his own shaft more snugly than a farmboy's corncob stuffer.

ZOOM! ZOOM! ZOOM! — the QuotLinks separate into squads of three, with Peckler and two companions continuing to circle the periphery — he'll wait, he will, until he has a clear shot at Chipper — while he sends in the others. They easily penetrate the outer, less tightly woven rings. Kids can offer scant resistance, most hop out of the way — hey, they're here to have a good time, supine, arms upraised in supplicant v-v-v's, swaying wildly, straying idly, submissive to the music, the light, the energy — though ZOOM! ZOOM! ZOOM! tranquillity soon turns to tragedy as a few get caught in the onslaught and the taste of blood emboldens the riders — red blood, the type that circulates through human veins.

CHIPPER! CHIPPER! CHIPPER! CHIPPER!

Cries rise in decibels as the cycles cut a swath through the thickly populated middle rings, using what is termed a pliers-and-prod maneuver: Two of the three cycles in a squad are equipped with sharp bladed rims

"'Av a fistfull a'nails fa knuckles, u pa'va'ts."
"Yeah, an a chain cross the face fa some dimples."

which they use to bear down on either side of their prey, forcing him or whomever to fall back into the path of the third, the prod, lagging slightly behind and ready to gorge the victim with its tough protruding tusks.

CHIP- CHIP-

One squad attempting to funnel a couple of East End punkers into the path of their prod, but these are streetwise kids who are alert to danger and have seen the casualties of modern urban warfare in their very own neighborhoods. As the two attack cycles shear along the sides quite close to them, the kids spring into action.

"'Av a fistfull a'nails fa knuckles, u pa'va'ts."

"Yeah, an a chain cross the face fa some dimples."

Takes the two blades right out, and the prod's suddenly forced to brake, rider's flung forward and gorges himself – *ha-hoofff!* – at tusk force speed into his own handlebars.

HEY HEY! Nothing like a first casualty to slow down an armored infantry assault, and with off-the-shelf corner hardware. Hence there's a lesson to be learnt here soldier, don't mess with an East End crowd, nor with those kids visiting from Connecticut either, the former travel with chains and blades, the latter with mouths and more than their baby teeth intact. Though ultimately what are the chances of slightly armed civilians up against a motorized division of non-humans?

CHIPPER!

"Whoa-oa?" Can't see them, not yet, but he can smell them, stiff whiffs of refuse crankcase grease. "HEADS UP GUYS AND GIHLS!" Chipper shouts above the crowd. "LOOKS LIKE THESE SUCKAHS AH SEHRIOUS!" He waves for the crowd to clear a path – *ROOOOOOOM!* – figures if he can scoot out of target range, he can divert attention away from the kids to himself. He bends down, pats the underside of his Harley and gives her some gas.

"Hold on to youh seat gihl, this is the big one we've been waitin fah!"

-ROW!

Sea of bodies splits miraculously in twain to let him pass – *FA-FA-WOOOOOOOOOOOM!* – Chipper bursts out of the center with the force of a newborn star, a molten gold streak shooting clear across the auto park.

Video team huddled among bundles on top a hippy van catches it on tape, and Peckler, who's out there circling, he sees it too, might be lightening fast, but it's his chance to take Chipper one-on-one.

On a rise another pair of eyes is watching the scene intently – "Doon knew." It's Cissy Coombs, she hauls off her bike to have a closer look – "Soomthin's gooin oon doown thir, can't make it oot, but it's noo right."

Noo right at all. L.L.'s got his sights set on Chipper, and the QuotLink mounted goons are beating on the fans without mercy. While men against men isn't Cissy's sort of battle, innocent women and children are involved.

"We've goot too doo soomthin Sistoors, even oop the fight."

Video team stays on it — this is the award-winning PT 13 — they've been sending a feed back to the control trailer the entire time. Cub's been monitoring it. But it's one of those ethical dilemmas he prefers not to deal with, whether the reporter has an obligation to broadcast all the news or merely that which he determines relevant? Wait and see is a handy expediency, who knows, in the meantime the dilemma might go away.

"Cub! Take a look at PT 7!"

"OK alright, what are we looking at, *snap snap*? I see nothing but arms and legs waving? What's PT 7 doing with his nose in the gravel?"

It's the thick soled boot planted at the nape of PT 7's neck that Cub McCluff and the techies can't see on the monitor, nor hear, because some other lug's slugged the soundman. Although another such thud is audible to everyone in the control trailer, and a readicam flipped over and filming the snarl on a SQWAT security thug's mug close-up until *swack*, the lens shatters. Then's when Cub gets the full picture. Various other remotes black out for reasons unknown, though terrified voices in the background provide the commentary — there's a massacre of the press going on outside in the auto park, and an enemy intent on leaving no witnesses.

Big Bear broods. A lone team — PT 13 — is still bundled on top of that van and transmitting. Cub doesn't like it, but he's being forced to one of those make-it-or-break-it career decisions, and his life-time buddies in the trailer are all turned and staring at him while he does it.

Hey. There's always freelance work and directing commercials

"OK ALRIGHT GENTLEMEN, BROADCAST IT! THIS IS WHAT WE IN THE BUSINESS CALL SWEET-ASS REVENGE!" — and the sight's not pretty, cops bashing newsmen and kids never are, nor are the sounds, not like Hollywood special effects, nor the stench — *whew-eeeee!* — did somebody cut one or what?

No. Somebody left the rear door to the control trailer open, or it's blown open, or it's been thrown op-... OR WHAT IN THE HELL ARE THOSE?

A detachment of QSS Intelligence clones has stormed the control trailer and they're issuing orders. "Douse the picture on the broadcast monitor McCluff!" The effect is chilling. "This is a high priority military mission, and we're ordering a total news blackout."

"But- but-..." Cub attempts, as he squeezes himself out of his swivel chair in an effort to rise.

No need to stand, extend a hand nor speak McCluff, only to listen and to be spoken to. "You have your orders. And call off the news hounds while you're at it. QuotNet can ill afford dozens more in disability claims."

Some sympathetic would say Cub is forced to, it's *halitosis ferociosis* in his face, plus he has no idea what to say, seems he's torn, there is the newsman's instinct somewhere deep in his extended gut, but then he's got this stomach too, and a Porsche to support, so Cub does what he does, looks aside, coughs twice – *snip! snip!* – pulls the plug, goes blank screen with over six billion watching.

"You must have some commercial filler." The QSS Specialist suggests. Seems QuotLinks understand the media business intimately. They should. They own it.

So while Cub's own men are being clubbed down outside, home viewers sit staring at a crusty fry pan.

It's Reb Dixon himself... shrunken headed chicken farmer in a faded baseball cap... extolling a Border State creed that promises the salvation of the broiler and fryer industry... my "feathery little friends" he calls'em... and vows in a choked-up warbler necked voice that he allows his chickens to run wild for forty days and forty nights... feasting on mixed whole grains and berries... before they get served up for your family's dining pleasure in a painless stainless steel procedure...

Lest you or anyone else across the nation doubt his sincerity, there's a documentary sure enough... scrawny chickens scrambling all over a barnyard, frolicking in their freedom and gobbling their fill... when suddenly, forty days, forty nights, time is up – WHATTHEFWOOKFWOOKFWOOKWASTHATWHACK – down comes a cleaver, a three second bloody spurt and the worst is over...

Reb's "feathery little friends" get plucked, get skinned and quickly dismembered as they ride along on a shiny metal conveyor... soon they'll be sizzling in a fry pan with assorted veggies... while a mixed race family, a father of color, a liberated Asiatic mother, a college-bound Hispanic son and an indiscriminately blondy daughter are gathered around the TV kitchen table and chomping some... for sturdy energy... for good health and fun...

FORTY DAY POULTRY — FRESH DAILY AT YOUR NEAREST NATURAL FOODS GROCER

A few frames of rough footage, however, is all it takes to put the kids in the bleachers on guard. For this is the TV generation and they are *muy media savvy* — could it be that their hero's in danger?

CHIPPER?

Sends a shudder to the highest levels of — QUOT • LINK • INC — should the slaughter of innocents become widely known, the tide could turn in favor of this resurgent wave of isolationist rock 'n' rollers.

Quick flash on the big screen turns Lou in his tracks, sends him racing back to the control trailer.

News leak means nothing to Peckler, he's busy attempting to draw a bead on the streaking superstar — FWOOOOOSH! — first he's here — FWOOSH! FWOOSH! — then he's there. *"Glugpfluck!"* Coward's sneaking away.

Could be one explanation Colonel — FWOOOOOOOOOSH! — or maybe it's a specialty Harley running circles around you — FWOO-FWOO-FWOO

Anyway, L.L. is not amused. He constricts the old sphincter muscle around the head of his piston and grunts — ZOOM! — pump starts himself off in hot pursuit, along with the squad of slice cycles either side of him.

-rook! -rook!

"I see them gihl, and we both know who they'h aftah — about how many you figuhe?"

-rr rroo-rroo rree!

"Ain't a man among them who could take me on by himself."

Though Peckler's willing. He slides in behind his accomplices, flips his handlebars over into a set of spiked horns. He'll play the prod, finish Chipper off after the other two dice him in pieces.

-rulp!

Chipper's cool. Harley can outrun a pack of Scrapskawa Scavengers any day except a hung-over Sunday, and this being an early Saturday all-nighter, he's got time to spare as he leisurely picks up speed.

Though Betsy's not as sanguine, something about knife sharp hubcaps — and what's with the forked sorethroat in between!

Chipper moseys out into the open, does a lazy ∞, baits the bastards — come and get me you croppers.

While on home television it's commercial after commercial.

This one's something about bad breath and body odor, flakes of dandruff as big as corn flakes and protracted acne — youngsters can't cope, either they smell terrible or they're disintegrating slowly — can't today's science engineer a breakthrough?

An all-star tan volleyball team slams their ball down on a Monterey beachside and stares accusingly at the camera. Though no need for

concern girls and guys, indeed science can, plus wash your t-shirts like new and freshen your toilet bowls too.

Introducing CYCLOPS 1. The miracle cleaner. Scopes in on dirt, dust, grease and fungus wherever it finds it, internal or ex, natural or un — and how, how can new CYCLOPS 1 do it? Because CYCLOPS 1 is not a soap, not at all, not a harsh detergent nor a scratchy cleanser nor anything chemical. CYCLOPS 1 is entirely organic, as in cultivated microbes that will eat nasty grime off whatever they're exposed to Athlete's foot? Finished before the game's begun. Bug guts on your windshield? Swabs them off in a single swipe. Puppy-poo on the carpet? Gobbles it. Inadvertent oil spill in the harbor? Vanished before the shorebirds skid in for breakfast.

Teen team at the beach can resume play confident that CYCLOPS 1 is watching protectively. Green fiend will clean anything.

CYCLOPS 1. Proven effective as well as eco-friendly.
CYCLOPS 1. Comes in a bucket. You can spray, dunk or gargle with it.

Except where do the microscopic vermin disappear to after they've had their fill? Peckler could care, so long as they're not eating on him, and maybe a cooked up concentrate will rid him of the bloody aftermath he's leaving in his wake.

—

Queezac meanwhile is toiling in the basement under a bare light bulb, attempting the impossible. His trusted assistant Smitzy is simply pathetic, assisting at this senseless attempt without the least protest.

"Eminenze, look vhat zey've done to you. You're vorze ovv zan a can ov Cramvull'z jicken noodle zoup! Un didn't I alvayz varn you zoze stuck-up mucky-muckz in ze blimp could never be truzted. Ve zhould have zhot zem down vhen ve had ze janze back zere in 45 bevor ze Ruzkiez liberated Belgrade. Vone vell planted explozive devize un ve could've blown zem to zmiztzereenz, but no no you argued zey vould have aczezz to capital reservez ve could tap. Yez vell vhat good vaz zat, ve zupplied ze ideaz un zey ended up rij becauze zey owned ze patentz. Now you're a mezz un zay've ztolen my prize creation, zat beautivul Irizh hunk I vaz zavink vor my retirement amuzement." Still Queezac labors against the odds, barely pausing to wipe his brows. "But how can I zkold you, altzough you did abuze me zo horribly, you'd at leazt lizten to my schemez. Un ve've had our zhare ov zoze, haven't ve, un laughz – all ze dirtzy deedz ve've done – I'm goink to mizz you old vriend, live'z lonely in ziz zorry vorld, ezpezially vhen you're gnarled un pitivul."

Zmitzy attempts to comfort poor Queezac, who's weeping profusely into the pool the Executive Liaison's become, and Queezac seems grateful, he nods his head and in the nodding some notion, an inspiration perhaps, a full blown solution! He bounces back to his former miserable self – "Zmitzy!" – and the erstwhile technician smiles with this slightest of recognition, only to glance up and see a scalpel plunging down toward his maximal arterial vesicle – "Yez! Vhy didn't I ztink ov ziz zooner!"

HULK!

Queezac must now work even more ferociously, and without an assistant he can't lift much, so perforce must do his dirty work on the floor. He zips Zmitzy open and with the hands of an accomplished surgeon hollows out the skull, inserts the reconditioned electronics, as many of the plug-ins as possible, then injects the essence of his Eminence into Smitzy's dwarf carcass and *Voila!* – a brand new Executive Liaison for the Entire Northern Hemispheric Region is born! Even though the shark skin suit no longer fits, Queezac can at least replace his Eminence's bright white smile, for from his breast pocket he produces the set of nifty new dentures!

ZOOM! ZOOM! ZOOM! Peckler and the Scrapasawas come up quickly behind Chipper.

-RR ROW!

"No need to fret Betsy, you'h lookin at plastic and plasma and not much of nothin else."

Strange. Looks like a heavy metal act to her, and why is it Chipper's dallying so dangerously? Rev it up, get us out of *he-rrr!*

"Can't evah affohd to show feah, no mattah how dihe the situation."

-ro?

"Nope. See we'h nine tenths psychological, which means we've got to convince ouh enemy the fight ain't evah goin to be easy…"

How about the last tenth that's thin skin vulnerable?

"...we'll let them get in close, see..."

-*rulp*

"...like they ah about now..."

-*huhhuhhuh*

"...then real easy like..." Chipper leans over casually and strokes the Harley's belly, whispers something affectionate. "...hit it hahd!" And he does, a quick flick of the wrist and he goes blasting out toward open space.

-*huhhhhh...*

Chipper's so fast he vanishes.

Leaves the QuotLink patrol utterly baffled until — *FA-FOOOSH* — all balls he rides right up behind them, then peels away, leaves them chasing off after him in three different directions while he taunts them with coarse remarks about their mechanical origins — son-of-a-wrench or some such socket buster scum — gets them so riled the two prongs ride right over one another, shredding a leg of one and tearing a second bolt hole in his partner, neither injury unfortunately fatal.

"*Whoo-ee*, did you see the way they went bumpin into each othah?"

Don't gloat, wounded QuotLinks can still be plenty mean. These two screw down their helmets and lock onto their infra-red laser tracers, seems they can sniff out the ass-end of a target at up to 60,000 paces.

"Have a feelin this is goin to be fun."

Fun chum, I don't think so, not as they regroup and lock in.

"*Whoa-oh!*" It's one of the pincers riding up from behind. Chipper tries weaving. But the Scrapasawa snakes along. So Chipper opens his hog all the way — *FWOOOM* — gives him a momentary advantage, but never underestimate an Asian knock-off's ability to catch up.

Yipes, he's back! Which is when Betsy decides she's about had enough of this nonsense. She waits until the QuotLink's nose up, up, close up and she lifts that wiry tail of hers, lets go with one of her distinctive doggie scents — *FLAPTOOTIE* — gale force in the goon's face and out he goes, for not even a shell shocked QuotLink can take an ass blast that bad, cycle goes careening offside, flips over on its head and bounces — *YOUCH! YOUCH! YOUCH!* — pounds itself down into the ground.

"That a gihl!"

Better believe it.

Sight makes L.L. livid, a good man gone, and if there's one thing the Colonel cannot abide — and it ain't flits, ginks or chiropractors, it's them women libbers — vows to get the bitch back as he slows to assist his wounded corporeal.

Chipper seizes the opportunity to speed way out along the outer wall of the parking lot, as far away from the kids and the congestion as he can get.

CHIPPER! A clump of fans comes jumping at him out of nowhere, waves as he races by. Chipper has to swerve to avoid them, he slides close along a tall concrete barrier — *SCREE-SCR'SCR'SCREEEECH!*
    -rowww!
    "Hang on tight babydoll!"
    Tight. Betsy's claws are dug in deep, deep into his belt, her ears wrapped around her eyes, trying to ward off the dust he's whipping up — when what's what? The second pincer's pulled alongside, and in his mirror Chipper spots a flash off Peckler's chromed helmet. Colonel's on his tailpipe — and don't even bother with the fart trick, cause maybe a machine can't handle the stench, but Peckler's he-man military dormitory school insensitive to all varieties of gas warfare.
    Betsy can feel the tip of the prod tickling at her — *rulp!* — while the QuotLink on Chipper's left seems to care nothing for his own physical safety, edging nearer and nearer, pinching at Chipper's flank — *SCRR-RR SCRUB! SCRUB!*
    It's a fight for the survival of the fastest. And if an attack cycle to the left, another right behind, isn't terrifying enough, take a look in front of you — headlights, dozens upon dozens, bright white and yellow low down fog lamps approaching on the horizon. Chipper braces for the worst. Betsy scrambles up top his shoulders so she can get a better look.
    "Will you watch with those goddamn toenails!"
    Is it friendly fire or foe? And kicking up a shit load of dust — it's... Cissy Coombs and coming straight *at- at- at- at them...*
    -roh! Betsy's blinded by the light, but still she can hear as the sisters blow *pa- pa- passsst them...*
    Sight slows the Colonel down, as Cissy rides right on by him too.
    Whew! Relief all around. Cissy races onward to the rescue, to the rescue of the kids that is — with PT 13 catching the action direct from the field.

    The feed into the control trailer, however, has been suppressed by the dread QSS, Cub under the gun and the techies momentarily stunned.
    Sends Lou burrowing underground, man's on a mission as he crawls along the cables beneath the floorboards, groping blindly until he feels a sting along the live line from PT 13 — *zap zap zap* — some little known law of thermoelectronics, that when noise reaches a certain feverish pitch it travels at an accelerated ferocity — *zapzapzapzapzap* — Lou patches it straightaway through to the big screens on the stage and from there it escapes into the airwaves — with the devastating result that any autocracy, corporate or otherwise, fears the worst — the entire audience, including those on their sofas at home, rise to their feet as one.

CHIPPER!

Impact shakes the new quake-proof stadium to its foundations — globe wobbles some on its axis as well — and since shock waves mount, the blimp does a flip, tumbles the QuotLink Elders upside down — QUOT • LINK • INC • • TOSSED • IN • A • HEAP • • STOCK • PRICE • PLUM • METS • • IN • LATE • NIGHT • TRAD • ING...

While the kids start in with that old 68 rabble rouser.

THE WHOLE WORLD IS WATCHING!

Watching as Her Royal Highness stands, prepares for a hasty departure.

THE WHOLE WORLD IS WATCHING!

Kids rally, shout it from inside and out as they realize the strength in their numbers.

THE WHOLE WORLD IS WATCHING!

Watching an unarmed Liverpool street tough in the parking lot jump the back of one of the cycleclones, who might be machined mean up front, but in reverse he's utterly useless. Punk grabs hold by the helmet and gives it a tug — *thwoop-oops an-plunk-a-derplug* — about like a cork pulled out of a jug, punk's left holding the head of the lug!

THE WHOLE WORLD IS WATCHING!

...and rooting for the tie-dyes and the day tripsters out there in the trenches! And they're not without their resources, these kids, bare fists up against thick tire tread and cattle prods — "'Ere, 'av a taste a'these!" — like a spiked wristband in the face — "Na way u slugs can stop us if enough ov us dance wi'ou' fea." And while Peckler's been outfitted with his own peculiar shaft driven design, the rest of the Scrapskawas are chain trains which makes them entirely vulnerable to a deftly pitched beer can — *riptangle-ringrang dipdangle-rungrung* — once floundering on the ground, a sea of youthful bodies closes in, the QuotLink is tempest toppled and tossed, used chunks from man and machine torn from tippity top to piddling bottom and spread asunder — while...

THE WHOLE WORLD IS WATCHING!

Cissy too — CLANKCLANKCLANKCLANK — she's into the fray. Sisters aren't afraid of the QuotLinks' rotating mixer blades, solid steel soled boot is all it takes to put those boys out of commission, and as for the prods, take a look at what Cissy's sprouting, her very own boar's hide Viking helmet, Brunehilde with a squawking chorus in line behind her. She's locked horns with the biggest bull moose on the field while belting out an aria that drives the rest of the tone-deaf QuotLinks to distraction.

Remaining cycle squads get separated in the confusion when who else should arrive with a war whoop — *wowwowwowwow* — it's Red Feather and his tribe of rampaging steel climbers, swinging in on ropes hooked from the light poles overhead. *FWUMP!* One QuotLink rider has an unexpected pair of knees strapped around his neck, a squeeze of thighs and down he dies. Red Feather himself is riding on the back of another QuotLink recyclable, a chop to the neck, a crack down the spine and the fused suck slumps forward.

The QuotLink Mounted Motor Division is going gore-to-gore with these lasses and braves and losing, prods prone, pincers plucked, one is seen rushing to save a buddy who's been outnumbered, when he's cut off by a sister wielding a lug wrench, his trunk slumps overboard while the riderless Scrapskawa keeps heading dangerously out-of-control — until Red Feather runs, jumps the machine buster bronco style and reins it in.

A quick glance around the field and it just might be too late in the game for the QuotLinks to score, two squads down, a third reduced to stragglers, though the fourth's mostly intact, that's Peckler's chasing after Chipper.

SCREECHCREEPCREEPCREEP — the remaining QuotLink slice cycle angles in on Chipper, forcing him up against a wall. Chipper gulps what saliva he's got left, and Betsy can feel it slide dry from his throat down to his gut — SCRAPESCRAPE — "Hold on gihl!" Like what else can she do as Chipper bangs a hard right ride up the coved concrete barrier, defying all known laws of gravity, like a skate boarder he skims off the top and does a 180°, lands one wheel then another and goes grinding back along the edge directly above the Colonel's head.

CHIP- CHIP-

Man's a marvel, yet when he lands the slice cycle's back alongside.

"Damn!" He can feel the fan of the razor spokes on his ankle, as the QuotLink kicks over with a prepackaged leg, forcing Chipper further and further into the wall — SCRA-SCRA-SCRA-SCRAAACH — and Peckler tight behind touching tread to tread.

"Betsy baby, want you to know whatevah happens, it's been the best!"

-*rulp!* This is how the story's going to end?

WHOOOF —WHONG!!! Wrong! A grapnel fork comes flying through the air, snags the QuotLink slice cycle side of the head like a scalpel. There's a tug and a tussle and the creep's a usurpated fossil — plus the unstopped oil spout spins Peckler out.

"What the flyin fuck was that?"

"*wowowowow!*" Red Feather gives a shout as he rides by on his borrowed Scrapskawa.

"WHAT'S THAT YOU'H SAYIN?"

"IT'S YOUR SHOW FROM HERE ON IN PARTNER!"

Chipper's thumb's up!

And the kids rush from behind the barrier, drag the mangled remains of the QuotLink slice cycle off the pavement, because the last lap's not over, with Peckler back on track and stokin in his own peculiar fashion — ZOOMA ZOOMA — Colonel's gaining on Chipper — close and on the inside, it's Harley, it's Scrapskawa, it's Harley by a hindquarter, Scrapskawa still gaining, and into the stretch, it's Harley by a nose, Scrapskawa alongside, Harley, Scrapskawa, Harley, Scrapskawa, and coming down to the line — kids have stretched a cable taut across the finish — Scrapskawa pulling neck and neck, when it's up — IT'S UP! It's Chipper Stirbee letting loose with a back-packed emergency parachute — INSTA-STOP! — while L.L speeds across first — WHULP! — severs him at the throat! Colonel's a head of chrome rolling along on the ground, the rest of him in spasm still stoking at full throttle forward and toward, oh no, out the exit, back from whence he came and aimed directly at the QuotLink Security Command Center!

FOLKS, DON'T LOOK UP! AND GOOD GOD DUCK!

PWOOOOOM! BOOM-BOOM-GABLOOM!

Body spares and technical parts ignite, tissue toss and thumbnail snatches, pecs, flecks, specs, epaulets, hair conditioners, denture cleansers and nostril pairs in every ethnic configuration, kneely caps and fiddle toes — flung hither and thither! Have the forces for Good won one for once?

Yes Betsy, look up!

The blimp in the air is definitely disturbed — QUO • DINK • CLINK • • NOOSE • LOCKS • • STIR • PER • CHIPS • • A • LIE • FOR • LIFE • • COR • POR • ROT • • GONE • BER • SERK — scowling amidst the stars.

While deep down in the emergency room, the lights dim as Queezac throws a switch! It's not lightning exactly, but close, Smitzy's corpse bolts straight up and out of its coma — "WHAT?" There's a flutter about the eyelids, and another squawk.

"Eminenze? Iz zat you?"

"What's what... who? *Youscrubbedgrubofamadscientist!*"

"Yez, iz me, iz Queezac, un you're alive, you're alive, rightz here in my ever-lovink armz un az nazty az alvayz!"

"Quit blubbering over me, *yourabiduglyrun-...*" Which is when the former QuotLink Executive Liaison for the Entire Northern Hemispheric Region notices that he and Queezac are at eye-to-eye level.

"I'm zo happy I can'tz tell you..."

His Eminence stares down at a stubby hand. "What..." And he hasn't even had a chance to glance in the mirror at his brand new warthog smile.

"Iz a miracle I could brink you back at all."

But it's when the Executive Liaison attempts to stand — being barely a hair over three foot three — that he really loses it. "*Youmealymaggotymottle throatedmole!* WHAT HAVE YOU DONE TO ME!"

"It vaz ze only option handy."

The Liaison examines himself all over, stumps for arms and legs and hairy everywhere – and who's that in the mirror laughing back at him – Smitzy, that's who with his goofy grin – only this time not servile friendly, but a mocking revenge.

"Eminenze, I can exzplain…"

His Eminence has no patience for explanations, he's too busy kicking and punching, but to no avail, Queezac easily dodging each jab – "*You fumbledumbgardengrunt!*" – each jibe, which gets them wrestling about on the floor, knocking over tables and cabinets and crunch go the dentures so now the Liaison's not only a gnome but a toothless one as well – "What am I going to do!"

"Betzer a Zmitzy zan a common variety vegetable zproutzink on live zupportz, vouldn't you agree?"

"Not at all! A nobly tall stalk of asparagus or a jewel filled pomegranate would most certainly be preferable to a lowly balled onion, no, I shall never show this face in public, I shall withdraw, end my days as a recluse on some South Sea island, hidden from public view."

"Yez vell, you've tried ze Zoutz Zea izland dizappearanze act bevore to no avail, un vherever you go you're goink to have to take ze buz becauze ze Elderz have cut you ovv witzout a zent to your name. Only hope you gotz levt iz to come begginkg handzoutz vrom me."

"You! You're my underling."

"Not now. I'm at leazt vive injez taller un have been hordink gold ingotz underneatz my bedztead vor decadez…"

"So?"

"Zo bendz on over un kizz my ingrown toenailz!"

The mass of kids both outside and inside the stadium are jumping up and down with such force that the ground around Wembley is quaking 5.5 on the Richter scale.

CHIPPER! CHIPPER! CHIP- CHIP- CHIPPER!

For victory is sweet.

CHIPPER! CHIPPER! CHIP- CHIP- CHIPPER!

Crowd swells around him.

CHIPPER! CHIPPER! CHIP- CHIP- CHIPPER!

Surge lifts him high upon their shoulders as they deposit him atop a handy van. He raises his arms in his V-salute, and the kids, his most loyal following return the gesture…

vvvvvvvvvvvvvvvvvvvvvvvvvvvvvvvvvvvvvvvvvvvvv

whupwhupwhupwhupwhupwhupwhupwhupwhupwhupwhupwhup
"Stirbee! Up here!"
-rr rup? -rup wherr?
"Stirbee! Up here! Grab hold!"
"Titanya!"
Along with her terrific teats too — *whupwhupwhupwhupwhup* — dangling at the end of a rope ladder by her ankles, her arms stretched down toward Chipper and Betsy.
"You'h a sight fah sohe eyes gal."
And the guys in the crowd agree, they're up and trying to nab her.
"Will you grab on!"
Chipper lifts Betsy up like a baby overhead, and Betsy who doesn't much like heights has to do another rope trick upward, *huff huff*, until Scotty reaches a strong arm down and rescues her.
She collapses into his embrace, sighs relief.
CHIPPER! CHIPPER! CHIP- CHIP- CHIPPER!
"See you next time guys and gihls, and remembah the snail dahtah's motto — if it's all ovah fah the smallest, the biggest got nowheah to go swimmin neithah."
CHIPPER! CHIPPER! CHIP- CHIP- CHIPPER!
He's all over Titanya, arms, legs, can barely hold his grip, has to crawl inch by inch and smooch her, a real lip lap tonsil tonguer.
"What's that for Stirbee?"
"Just glad to see you gal, that's all."
"Let's go."
"H'yep, tryin…"
"Let's go."
"…tryin, don't know what's the mattah…"
"I can't keep hanging upside down like this forever."
"…seem to be stuck oah somethin…"
"Stuck?"
"…fool Hahley won't let go!"
Fool Harley nothing, machine has a mind of its own, war worn and weary, not about to be abandoned on the battlefield to souvenir seekers.
Scotty's sympathetic — *whupwhupwhup* — he lowers a hook off a winch, lifts the three of them effortlessly — Titanya, Chipper and Harley — *whup* up over the auto park locked arm-in-arm, and banking so gently flies low over the heads of the crowd, everyone below leaping arms upward in an attempt to reach high enough and touch him.
CHIPPER! CHIPPER! CHIPPER!
CHIPPER! CHIPPER! CHIPPER!

He raises his arms in his V-salute, and the kids, his most loyal following return the gesture…

"'At's 'it! 'At's the las' we'a eva' goin ta see a'im Abby, up there ridin through the sky on 'is 'Arley."

"Why? Wha' makes u say 'at?"

"Jus' this funny feelin I got down deep in the pit a'me stomach."

"Maybe 'at's not really 'im."

"Wha'? Like 'e's some so' a'ghost o' imposta?"

"Naw. Cou' be a stuntman. Lots a'sta's out in 'Ollywood gots doubles 'oo make all thei' public appea'ances fa'em."

"Chippa's not like 'at. 'E does 'is own tricks single'anded. They say 'e ain' afraid a'nothin, naw 'eights, naw depths, naw even the Devil!"

"Don' know. Looks can be so deceivin."

"Righ', bu' seein's believin!"

Just as Chipper comes flying directly overhead, giving Abby and Lucy a clear bottom's up view.

" 'At's 'im a'righ', 'at's no 'Ollywood double."

"Righ'. I'd recognize 'at beau'iful bum anyw'ere!"

CHIPPER! CHIPPER! CHIPPER!

"Zuj a zpectacle!"

"The scoundral!"

"Ztill, he'z zo beautivul to watch."

"He is nothing but a fraud!"

"Anyvay, ve don't have ze time to botzer aboutz him Eminenze, ve gotz to getz outz ov here, now, bevore zome inzernational corporate crimez commizzion comez investigatink."

"I care not about my name nor my future. My responsibility lies solely to my Cold War generation."

"Yez vell let'z go join your generation somevhere on ze beach in Zoutz America, janje our namez, ztartz up zome zort ov importz-exportz zcam un enjoy our declinink yearz in qviet luxury togetzer."

"Retire? With you? You presumptuous toad!"

"Yez vell you're not lookink zo good yourselv zeze dayz."

"Spiteful, that is what you are, resentful of what I once was and you could never have been."

"Un juzt vhere did all zoze ztuck up pretenzez getz you, down here on ze viltzy vloor vitz me."

They go nose to nose, overlord and underling, one more gnarly than the other, and mouths? You couldn't count two tooths between them, still they'll *gnaw gnaw gnaw* each other raw into retirement.

"Enough! We must forget our differences momentarily and connive.

This is our last opportunity to destroy this upstart rockstar!"

"Jezuz Eminenze, give it upz!

"Never! I shall have my revenge!"

"Vengeanze vill only deztroy ze man who attemptz it."

"Hogwash! Vengeance in the defense of righteousness is no vice."

"Vhat rightjouznezz"

"For the mighty must retaliate, it is our sacred duty, one bred into our very bones."

"Yez vell your bonez have been zhattered into itzy bitzy pizzas."

"As long as I have breath Queezac, I shall make it my business to rid the planet of this menace!"

"But ve've tried everytzink ve could ztink ov – ve even called in ze armored invantry!"

"Peckler?"

"Yez vell he vaz zertainly a dizazter."

"It was you who salvaged him from the battlefield back in Budapest after the 57 uprising when everyone else was resigned to his loss."

"All ze tzankz I gotz vor zat."

"He never knew it was you who adopted him."

"I only vanted a virzthand peek into ze military head-zet."

"And what was it you discovered?"

"Zey succeed by narrowink down zere optionz to vone zingle-minded objective."

"Which is?"

"You gotz to getz zem bevore zey getz you."

"What else would you have expected?"

"True, but ze obviouz drawback vitz suj a ztrategy iz ze lack ov conzern vor ze large zcale repercuzzionz."

"It is the burden of the strong to shoulder on."

"Remindz me ov ze peazant who vaz zo diztrezzed vhen a meazly mouze gotz into hiz rootz zellar."

"Not another of your annoying fairy tales."

"Yez vell ziz peazant, zee, he took up a zhovel un he ztarted bangink around avter ze poor creature – *bang bang bang bang bang* – un in ze prozezz he mazhed up hiz potatoez, he pulverized hiz turnipz, hiz applez, hiz onionz, hiz carrotz, zo muj zat vhen he vaz tzrough all he had levt vor ze vinter to eat vaz a pile ov pulp un a hungry little mouze in ze houze too."

"You consider me no better than a peasant, *youscalybacklizard*!"

"I'z a parable Eminenze, not your biogravy, bezidez your vatzer vaz a dentizt, not ze Grand Duke!"

"My father could at least sign his name to my birth certificate!"

"Mine vaz lotz zmarter, he znuck outz ze vindow – bezidez birzt'z an aczident, i'z live zat'z ze jallenge."

"My point precisely. With that rockstar nothing less than a mortal threat to our kind's very existence!"

"He'z an empty headed vool vor Chrizzakez!"

"Who has outwitted us every turn."

"Our vorzt enemiez are mere zhadowz on ze vall."

"I adhere to the adage of the French Revolution: Extreme times call forth extreme measures."

"Maybe zat or maybe vize-verza."

Scotty soars high above Wembley, then lowers, hovers over hundreds of thousand inside, Chipper aboard the chrome plated Harley and glistening in the glow of the stadium lights.

CHIPPER! CHIPPER! CHIPPER!

He does a handstand, one hand, and high signs with the other.

CHIPPER! CHIPPER! CHIPPER! CHIPPER! CHIPPER! CHIPPER!

It is his moment in time, dangling dangerously at the pinnacle, his hair ablaze, his smile golden. Betsy barks, and damned if Chipper doesn't do a vertical flip, lands standing on the seat, both arms upraised, fists clinched and pumping muscle for victory!

CHIPPER! CHIPPER! CHIP- CHIP- CHIPPER!

CHIPPER! CHIPPER! CHIP- CHIP- CHIPPER!

As Scotty gently delivers him front and center stage, oh so gently. Will Cook goes crescendo! Chipper's key. The instant he lands on the boards, he leaps high high up on his own and rebounds with a howl of beastial intensity — FIGHTIN! — *whoa-ho-hohoho-HO!*

FIGHTIN! The crowd roars back!

> FIGH-TIN!
> FIGH-*high-high-hightin!*
>
> FIGH-TIN!
>
> Fightin fah huh lo-hove
> Yah! Yah! Yah! Fightin fah huh love
> In the middle of the *niiiiiiiight!*

YAAAAAAAAAAAAAAAAAAAAAAAAAAAAAAAAAAAAAAAAAAAAAAY!

The million plus are out of their seats and stomping!

CHIPPER! CHIPPER! CHIPPER! CHIPPER! CHIPPER! CHIPPER!

The mood in the control trailer is subdued. It's Cub McCluff who is squirming in his swivel chair this go around, a QuotLink QSS specialist with penetrating green eyes has been posted closely over his shoulder. Cub fidgets with the levers and dials, some of the many hundreds arrayed on the console in front of him. He nudges Lou's elbow — Lou in wide-eyed alert mode, as in hyper-attentive to every movement in the trailer. Cub nudges him again, and Lou blinks over. Cub fingers two levers and motions to a red button way right, he moves his hands away and repeats the motion, never quite pressing the button in question. He then returns to his regular routine — "Alright guys, let's pull in tight, our boy Chipper's about to hit on it bigtime." There's a lack of the old *snap* in papa bear's demeanor — he is surrounded all sides by the dread QSS — but the techies on the floor are war-ravaged themselves and shoulder on without any shout of assistance.

The Queen and Her loyal retinue have returned to their box. Not only is the show about to resume, with the spectacular arrival of the star attraction, but without launching a massive rescue operation, Her Majesty is encircled by the spirited youth of Her grandchildren's generation, a generation nowhere near as deferential as that of Her own.

Figh-*igh-igh*-tin!
Fah my little baby's lovin / *Yeah Yeah*
Fightin!
In the middle of the *nigh-nigh-nigh*-night!

FIGH-TIN!

"SO YOU FOLKS TIHED OF JUST HANGIN OUT? YOU ABOUT READY TO SETTLE DOWN FAH SOME SEHRIOUS MUSIC?"

YAAAAAAAAAAAAAAAAAAAAAAAAAAAAAAAAAAAAAAAAAAAAY!

"AH YOU?"

FIGH-TIN!

"CAN'T HEAH MUCH OF NOTHIN WAY UP HEAH!"

FIGH-TIN!

"WHAT? WHAT? WHAT?"

FIGH-TIN! FIGH-TIN! FIGHTIN!

"That's right, 'cause sometimes you've just got to get in theah and duke it out — right?

RIGHT!

"You got to stand up fah what you believe is right — RIGHT?"

FIGHT!

And Chipper does this leap, way *high-high-hup*, fifteen feet.
YAY! YAY! YAY! YAAAAAY1 YAAAAAY! YAAAAAAAAAAAAAAAAAAAY! Like a freight train gathering up steam.
"AHRIGHT THEN, LET'S DO IT!" Chipper arches way back, pumps his arm — "THAT'S ONE, THAT'S TWO, THREE, FOUH!"
Danny T 'Drummer Dynamo' kick starts it, Will Cook revs up… with Chipper racing as usual to catch up…

Wait wait wait wait…

Everybody stops while Chipper walks right up into Bubba's face — and this kid is still hormonal and cut, New York City Italian street style tough.

> Don't push me too fah / man
> Cause I'll whip youh ash / can

Bubba doesn't back off, none.

> That chick is mine / Stan
> She's goin along with me / and

Chipper juts his chin way way out, daring him to take a swing.

> Cause I'm fightin fah huh lu / -uv
> Fightin fah huh lu / -uv
> Fightin fah huh luv
> TONIGHT!

Bubba flexes some, sends Chipper scampering back center stage — "That's a one, two, three and fouh!"
Danny T kicks in again, and the rhythmic pattern of this Loose Nuke classic is a simple **bump** bump bump bump, **bump** bump bump bump downbeat staccato, vintage Danny T, vintage '60s rough 'n' tumble rock 'n' roll — no frills, no add-a-track, nothing synced nor dubbed, with the melody line to this and to all the old Loose Nuke classics kept as basic as hell, has to be, has to accommodate Chipper stabbing fitfully at his guitar, although everyone assembled can notice a distinct improvement to his playing — but his voice? Imagine a steel file scratching over an amplified fog horn, and you have the near equivalent.

> Back off the line / guy
> 'Cause I'm steppin by / -yy
> Don't want nobody to die / -ie
> But gotta give sweet honey a try / -yy
> I'm fightin fah huh lu / -uv

> Fightin fah huh lu / -uv
> TONIGHT!

Bubba comes muscling in on Chipper's spotlight, arm flexed for some mean-stormin tiff — no, not another on-stage, off-stage feud between this historical duo!

> ***bambambambambambuumbuum-battabwambwam***

"Damn! That the best you can do young fella? Thought you wah as tough as youh old man?" Chipper grins, because he's got a mean riff of his own — but then hell, he's had fifty years off by himself to perfect his digits.

> WAA-WAAWAA-WAAAAAAAAAANH-WAAAAAAAAAAANH

> ***buuuuuu-buuuuuu-bwaaaanh-waaaanh-waaaanh
> -waaaaaaaaaaaaaaaaaaaaaaaaaaaaaaaaaaaaaaaanh!***

"Whoa!"

But before either one of them has a chance to reload, Molly steps in — wiggling in between, arms lifted high up and slapping at a tambourine — *chi' chi' chi' chi' chi' chi' chi'…*

> MOLLY! MOLLY! MOLLY! MOLLY! MOLLY!

And what is it about the appeal of the mature woman on the young male — but then there may be no need to generalize, this is the legendary Molly Dawkens on stage and in the flesh.

> Step a little closah / gal
> Eyes'ah bluhry with beeh / gal
> Give us a pretty little twih / -rrl
> Now ain't you just a peah / -rrl / gal
> And I'm fightin fah youh lu / -uv
> Fightin fah youh lu / -uv
> TONIGHT!

And what a marvel of show business preservation both these old-timers are, Chipper and Molly, Molly and Chipper. The teenie girls in The Pit at Chipper's feet gape up at his raw chiseled jaw, the one he juts at the world in eternal defiance, his face scrawled over with markings of endless fights, a mangy misfit biker type, always new to a town, lawless and lewd.

While Molly's the ultimate party girl, adventurous and sassy, the girl who can take care of herself, thank you, and's not out there shaggin after some wimp.

In the opposite corner is Bubba the Bod Two, built, brash and bursting his seams with effortless energy.

> ***buuuuuu buuuuuu-bwaaaanh -waaaanh-waaaanh***

-waaaaaaaaaaaaaaaaaaaaaaaaaaaaaaaaaaaaaaaaaaanh!

The girls in The Pit don't know which hunk to root for, and Molly, she wins no matter who loses. She chucks Chipper under the chin and then slinks over toward Bubba, leaving him whacking on that guitar of his, frothed up into a mad fit, Danny T thumping behind, biding his time just like the old days.

> Like a gal with plenty of sa / -ass
> Babe who can swing it fa / -ast
> Don't care so much about cla / -ass
> Long as she's a good piece of / *-yeah*
> *-yeah -yeah -yeah* / ya / -sss
> And I'm fightin fah youh lu / -uv
> Fightin fah youh lu / -uv
> TONIGHT!

There's a garage quality to the Loose Nukes' sound, old and new, a greasier all-American version of the Stones, some neighborhood punks hanging out back and making far more noise than music. Then toss in the female additives, and what a super heated mixture it is — the original Molly Dawkens sharing stage with the sun swipe-ripened fruits from the Île de Ste Ceçile — Mango, Tangle and Tamarind — juicy sweet for the plucking.

There are other creative tensions in the band as well. There's the eternal enmity between Danny T and Chipper over who sets the beat, all around artistic control, and Molly's affections of course.

Distant and above the scuffle hovers Will Cook, the one true musician among them, his place in the firmament permanent — besides he's the only one who can cover Chipper's voice, which floats off-key regularly. But Will Cook thrives on the unexpected, twitching as he is, in or on ecstasy — every eye switched to the big screens as his long slim fingers flit across keys, guy's ready to take off on any tangent, up half a third, down a diminished fifth, plays his own little riffs above, below, beyond the line — so quick he can do whatever he damn well pleases and rebound just in time, bears down on the song's key chord, so obvious even Chipper can sense it's a cue.

Except as he's about to belt out another verse, Bubba steps directly in between Chipper and Molly, his ax upraised and ready for combat. Chipper quickly dodges and meets and matches him, both guitars roused to a duel. Molly feigns fright, turns tail and scrambles up the steps of the stage set toward her sisters for back up — sweet Mango, tangy Tangle and prickly skin Tamarind...

> So don't go gettin in my way / bub
> Tossin me outta the clu / -ub

> All you jahks ah in fah trou / -oub
> Trouble tonight!
> Right!
> Cause I'm fightin fah huh lu / -uv
> Fightin fah huh lu / -uv
> TONIGHT!

Danny T's suddenly out from behind his drum mound. Will Cook picks up the beat with a lefty's ease while the 'Drummer Dynamo' circles in the shadows of the spotlight.

> Goin to be troub- troub-
> Trouble tonight!

Chipper spins around, round and around while Bubba and Danny T close in on him from both sides.

> Don't push me too fah / man
> Cause I'll whip youh ash / can
> That red-headed chick is mine / Dan /
> She's goin along with me / and
> And I'm fightin fah huh lu / -uv /
> Fightin fah huh lu / -uv /
> TONIGHT!

Chipper jerks wildly from side to side, facing down the one, facing down the other. Will Cook is making wailing sounds on the keyboard, screams and sirens, and Danny T and Bubba are crashing into things, smashing things, bricks through window glass, chains whipped across an anvil, Mack truck air whistles. And Molly and Mango and Tangle and Tamarind have stepped up a level, battling it out among themselves on thrashing tambourines, all four women whole body into it.

Chipper does a defiant jump, a good twenty feet straight up and out of the reach of either Bubba or Danny T. And lands kicking, kung fu style.

> Watch fah the dooh / crash
> Watch fah youh jaw / smash
> Out in the alley / head bash
> Like to stay but gotta da / -ash
> Hey I'm out heah fightin fah huh lu / -uv
> Fightin fah huh lu / -*huh-huh* / -huuuuv...

Bubba, Chipper, guitars raised way up and at 'em, Danny T banging onbongos, Will Cook locked onto one wired weird chord, high tops and junk backstage bashing, tambourines clashing.

I'm fightin fah huh lu / -uv
Fightin fah huh luv

Crowd's into it.

FIGHTIN FIGHTIN FIGHTIN

Whang whang whaaa-aaaa-AAAANG!

FIGHTIN FIGHTIN FIGHTIN

Whap, crash and doulder bash!

FIGHTIN FIGHTIN FIGHTIN

Jang! Jang! Janglllllllle 'n' jang!

FIGHTIN FIGHTIN FIGHTIN

FIGHTIN FIGHTIN FIGHTIN
Fightin fah the rest of the *nigh-nigh-nigh-nigh-*
Nigh-high-high / Nigh-high-high-
NIIIIIIIIIIIIIIIIIIIIIIIIIIIIIGHT!

And the Harley comes running out of the wings with Betsy aboard while Chipper executes a perfect free-standing back flip, lands smack on the saddle upright and just before the last chord closes in on him, arms up in V for Victory, he guides the machine off-stage with his big toe, spotlight trailing after him, and the stand-up, jump-up only crowd is shout-about-it OUT-OF-CONTROL!

CHIP- PER CHIP- PER! CHIP- CHIP- CHIPPER! CHIP- PER CHIP- PER! CHIP- CHIP- CHIPPER! CHIP- PER CHIP- PER! CHIP- CHIP- CHIPPER! CHIP- PER CHIP- PER! CHIP- CHIP- CHIPPER! CHIP- PER CHIP- PER! CHIP- CHIP- CHIPPER! CHIP- PER CHIP- PER! CHIP- CHIP- CHIPPER! CHIP- PER CHIP- PER! CHIP- CHIP- CHIPPER! CHIP- PER CHIP- PER! CHIP- CHIP- CHIPPER! CHIP- PER CHIP- PER! CHIP- CHIP- CHIPPER! CHIP- PER!

THE FINALE

THE WHOLE WORLD IS WATCHING!
THE WHOLE WORLD IS WATCHING!

The military situation outside Wembley is rapidly deteriorating. The youthful invaders are advancing while QuotLink Security is in a full force rout. The Antiques in the blimp have blacked out completely. British Specials are doing their best to contain the flow along the perimeter of the roadways, their objective to seal the area from any newcomers — no kid enters, no kid leaves — that part's simple. It's the contingency plan that gets complicated, four point five million strong up against London's famed 22nd Brigade who although they've seen recent combat outside Kabul have failed thus far to extricate the Royals.

Inside the stadium the kids are partying in the aisles. Without security the bleachers have emptied onto the ground floor and assembled in a thick throng at the base of the stage. Outside and in, the crowd's approaching something akin to critical mass.

Yet somehow a slew of reporters breaks through to interview Chipper, along with a photographer — *FLASH! FLASH!* — and naturally one of Cub McCluff's crack QuotNet readicam teams.

"Do you in any way sanction the rioting Mr Stirbee?"

"No ma'am, I am hohrified along with families watchin live wohldwide that this unfohtunate incident is occuhrin, even so…"

FLASH! Chipper has his eyebrows narrowed, man's serious serious.

"Your sympathies are with the rioters then?"

"You mean with youh kids and mine caught out theah defenseless in the streets?"

"Quite."

"I am sympathetic, both sides of the line. Don't want to see nobody young huht, eithah raw recruit oah cooked out protestah. Kids ah ouh futuhe, whethah you pack them off to school in nifty unifohms oah a ripped paih of jeans."

"Haven't these teenagers crossed the line here this evening?"

"Hey, let's heah it fah life's free spihrits, they get to have all the fun — fact that bums out those left on the sidelines somethin bullshit."

"Are you opposed to the use of force?"

"Fohce well… least the six billion watchin from home can't use the excuse they wah lookin the othah way duhrin a commahcial break, nope, tanks in the streets don't say much fah the cause of populah democracy, now do they?"

"What about the rule of law?"

"H'yep. Protect propahty ovah people, rich ovah pooh, pahrents ovah what few rights theih kids might have to privacy, and poachahs ovah any animal that happens to cross theih path…"

"Are you anarchist in sympathy?"

FLASH! Man's genuinely shocked.

"You mean of the anti-Christ piss-on-youh-shoe vahriety, no way, but then Congress does seem to take fahevah to delibahrate cahtain unpopulah measuhes like long-tehm unemployment benefits — I mean fahget about creatin real jobs so folks can have a secuhe futuhe oah buildin adequate housin oah the quality health cahe folks need. Then too theah's decent daycahe, puhe watah and why not free intahnet hook-up while they'h at it — but no, these kind of concahns don't go nowheah — yet somehow it's a political freebie fah the president to dial up 911 and call out the ahmy to intahvene wheahevah he pleases."

"Do you have anything to say directly to the rioters?"

"Go to. You might just get lucky, spahe the planet fah anothah genahration oah so — which ain't a half bad deal fah the rest of us eithah."

"And to the Army?"

"Got to figuhe who you'h aimin at, might be the neighbah kids down the street — and only a halfwit follows a blind man down a dahk alley."

"You're surely not proposing an insurrection within the ranks?"

"Soldiah has to face up to the consequences of his own action — only followin ohdahs won't wash befah a wah crimes commission any longah, noh guahrantee a full night's sleep neithah."

"Would you agree the authorities have an obligation to keep order?"

"Those who begrudge theih own children ah a sohry sight."

"Some say you're at the center of this incident? Can you comment?"

"Whoa! Way too heavy to hang on one lone troubadouh's shouldahs."

FLASH! Captures that fool smile Chipper can get.

"Isn't this sort of affair consistent with a certain nonconformist posturing you practice however?"

"Confohmity? Confohmity's what most folks eat fah Sunday suppah — me, I've got this hankahrin fah somethin a lot mah satisfyin."

"What precisely is that sir?"

"Least feed the hungry, don't wohk them to death fah a buck oah less an houh. See, evahryone of us is bohn to die, and the pooh man's as much afraid of what's comin as the rich."

"We must restore order."

"I agree, but…"

"But what?"

"…what soht of ohdah? Comes a time when even you media celebrahties have got to stand up and fight fah what you believe in, right? And the destruction of the atmospheah's about on a pah with all out nucleah wah, one's just a slowah tohtuhe than the othah. Plain cruelty to stand aside and watch while little crittahs shrivel and die."

"What do you propose to do?"

"Hey lady, I'm only heah to sing and play. What I do know fah suhe though is the futuah's up fah grabs and this is the only planet any of us will evah call home — but I'd bettah head, looks like I'm runnin late as usual."

"Still, wouldn't you admit your position is to the extreme?"

"Hey! If you don't like my kind of answahs, then don't ask me any mah questions."

FLASH! FLASH! Chipper gives them the old high sign and sprints.

"Eminenze, ve've gotz to getz outz ov here, bevore iz too late!"

"There is no time limit for revenge."

"Jezuz! Leave ziz zilly vool be. Iv you ignore a child long enouv, he'll vander ovv un botzer zomebody elze."

"NEVER!"

"But vazn't it Trotzky who varned Ztalin, never letz zome old grudge temptz you to var?"

"And look what happened to Trotsky."

"Like ze Giant Igva Bird, zhe vaz virtzually extinct, ztill zhe pecked un zhe pecked at all zhe could eat…"

"I am in no mood for one of your nonsense riddles."

"…zhe ate ze vrogz in ze pondz un ze birdz outz ov zer treez, ze rhinozerozez in ze mud un ze giravvez gratzink in ze tall grazz, zen zhe dove into ze zeaz un gobbled ze vhalez, un when zere vaz notzink levt zhe could eat, zhe ztarted nibblink on ze young in her nezt."

"THE MORAL BEING?"

"Ze moral iz qvite zimple, juzt becauze zomebody'z zo high up un mightzy today doezn't mean zey can balanze on vone vobbly leg vorever."

The Liaison takes umbrage at the allusion and attempts a drop kick, but winds up flat on his back instead. "YOUSNAPTRAPPEDTURTLETURD!" As Queezac and he scuffle in the dust.

"Yez vell, you're not lookink zo good yourzelv zeze dayz eitzer, zat un your vaunted military'z vorze zan uzelezz."

"Wars are won in the hearts and the minds of the people."

"Doezn't look likez you've zcored zo good at zat game neitzer."

"Then we must resort to terrorist tactics."

"You mean zneak attackz on revugee campz un bombink buzloadz ov innozent jildren?"

"By any means possible."

"Yez, un I betz you've gotz zomeztink zimply terrible in mind."

"The worst."

"Zat'z ze kind I like bezt." Queezac lets up on the dwarfed Liaison.

"A special commando unit of my own creation."

"Commandoz, zat'z a great idea bozz, but ve've already tried zoze out, un he can be zo zlibbery, zat Jibber Ztirbee."

"THAT NAME!"

"Zhutz my moutz!"

"THOUGH IN THE END NO ONE CAN ESCAPE MY CLUTCHES, NOT WHEN I SET MY MIND TO TASK."

"Puzh ze tazk button in zat brain ov yourz un it'z good-byez Jarlie."

"Once I have my hands clutched on his balls, I'll yank the life right out of him…"

"Yez!"

"…watch while his eyes extrude…"

"Oh yez yez yez!"

"…while his tongue turns blue…"

"Blue zen puke purplisch puce!"

"…he will never warble another note!"

"No never, un avter you getz tzrough vitz him, I getz my grabz, yez?" Queezac twists his tongue into a corkscrew point. "I'll fillet vhat'z levt un freeze dry ze piezez vor late vinter nightz znackz, you betz I vill!"

THE WHOLE WORLD IS WATCHING!
THE WHOLE WORLD IS WATCHING!

Cub McCluff's numbed, his eyes two red glazed donuts with no taste for coffee or colas. Seems QuotNet's premier location man's reduced to surviving off stored fat as he fingers the switches and dials on the master console before him. Lou watches, warily, glances back at the QSS Specialist, the one with the unwavering green eyes who's peering over Cub's shoulder. Room is ringed with a dozen lookalike robotics in nasty dress blacks and armed with automatics.

Cub taps his hand nervously near a red button to the far right on his console — he pauses, reflects, then continues to flip switches and wrench dials, only to return, to dally a split second longer at the ready red button. Time's at a standstill inside the control trailer, the techies too, bunkered in for the long wait to daybreak.

SHREEEEEK -SHREEK -SHREEK -SHREEEEEEEEEEK!
"Whoa-*hoa!* Wheah'd all you little sweetheahts come from?"

It's a pack of groupie girls from The Pit. Amidst the confusion they're running rampant backstage, and they've found Chipper momentarily unattended. "Hey, hold on now, don't go squeezin the plums unless you'h plannin on buyin the bunch."

They're hands all over him, pay whatever price.

"No free samples." Slapping at their sticky fingers doesn't stop them from diving for a bite. "Damn you youngstahs today, you'h so active so eahly." Chipper has to backstep, then go bolting out of there.

-rr will you slow it down some chum?

"Betsy babydoll!"

Let a member from your loyal old fan club catch up.

"Need you neahby beside me gihl, looks like tonight's the one."

A full moon howler.

"Time to reach out theah and touch those stahs."

Time to keep our feet planted solidly on the ground.

"And you know thing's always get dicey right befah the show's ovah."

Maybe if we slow down, take it step-by-step.

"Let's duck in heah fah a minute, got to catch my breath."

Duck in where?

Chipper wedges himself in the dark between two equipment trailers, with billows of steam venting out of a grate in the pavement.

-choke! -choke!

"Time fah a toke." He fishes a squished bone out of his back pocket, rolls it between his fingers, smoothes it out. "Tell the truth, I've been doin some sehrious thinkin."

While frying more brain cells.

"And I've concluded," he fires the sucker up, almost swallows it whole, "theah's this somethin about life that nevah ends easy, cause it takes so much effoht to get somethin done, somethin wohthwhile anyway…"

Especially when you're stoked out of your mind.

"…but in the end, you've just got to do it, got to get up theah and go fah it befah it's too late."

"Yo talkin 'bout time bro?"

"What?"

"Time things take an the payoff so slow it ha'dly seems wo'th the effo't."

"Who's theah?"

-rr rowl rowl

"Hush gihl."

"Cause time's a'ways playin a game a'catch up, creepin 'long a step behind yo 'til one day when yo don' neva suspects, it catches up an nabs yo by the throat, rattles the livin daylights out a'yo!"

"Salaam? I can heah you, but… wheah ah you?"

"Fin'ly fo'ces yo t'take action." He's a head's popped out of the steam grate, two white eyeballs peering through the smoke.

"How'd you get down theah?"

"Amazin how a man can travel the whole globe unda'ground, neva botha t'su'face, 'cept when he wants t'see what's what from the bottom side up a'cou'se — had to drop by, say hello bro."

"Hello nothin, it's mah like so long, been fun and…"

"An?"

"…this last trick ain't goin to be easy."

"Piece a'cake fo the likes a'yo, cause yo been doin trial runs most a'yo life, pahked thea on the edge, a'ways temptin fate."

"But nothin you can evah imagine, not in youh wildest whacked out nightmahes prepahes you fah live fihe."

"Ezperience, only benefit about growin old — yo fin'ly lea'ns when it's time t'duck an when yo can go pokin yo head up."

"Easy fah you to say."

"Hey bro, I done paid my dues, now's about time fo me t'reti'a, but not yo, yo the kind that neva quits."

You can say that, even kicks in his sleep.

"Hello too doggie-do, an yo ain' no betta, yo keeps taggin thea tight behind, encouragin him as he goes."

Somebody has to keep watch, do you have any idea how much trouble he can get himself into?

"Trouble? Chippa hea? He's mo mischief than trouble."

Mischief, trouble, what's the dif, both wind up in a barroom brawl.

"What ah you two doin? Spendin the shoht time I've got left rankin me on my faults? What about my vihrtues?"

About which both go mum.

"All I knows is whateva it is yo gots t'do, yo gots t'do it. Decision's all yo's though, can't go blamin nobody else. Individual's bo'n with one inalienable right, only one, the freedom t'choose, the will powa t'stand up an fight fo what he thinks best."

"You come this fah to tell me that?"

"Had to make cer'tain, didn't wan t'hea yo wimped out in the end."

"Wimped out!"

Don't egg him on.

"I known exactly what I'm facin."

"Glad t'hea that, yo don' need no confusion 'bout that, not when time's standin outside the doo waitin on yo."

"Besides theah ain't no choice to it. This is somethin I've got to do — heah, have a puff off my homegrown."

"Don' mind if I do."

-rr only thing worse than one fool wrecked out of his mind is two.

"You goin to step up out of that hole?"

Salaam draws deep. "I's fine whea I's at, thank yo. Seen so much, I don' need t'see no mo." He hands the joint back to Chipper who sucks what's left down to an ember — *whuufwhuuf* — holds it in.

"So this a plain case a'stage fright?"

"Nope, done plenty of grandstandin befah – *whuh- whuh-*…"

Then why is your face so pale?

"Question fah me is mah about what comes aftah – *whuuuuuuw!*"

"Like whea does the sta go afta the show's ova?"

"Don't know. Don't know."

"Could pa'ty with the crew."

"Only delays the agony."

"Hea say pain passes in time an afta that thea's this relief."

"Like keep the faith 'til the finish, that what you'h sayin? But what if a man discovahs his lifeline's been left undone when he's always hoped it would be tied up tight neah the end?"

"It's a fa fa betta wo'ld yo-…"

"You know I don't believe one wohd of that Salaam."

"Skeptic don' mean yo gots t'be downright pessimistic, maybe the futu'a holds a promise the past could neva fulfill."

"Been kickin around too long to be a true believah. Change is illusion. Progress a myth. Time's mehely the moment, a blink, a spahk at most, quick ignition and a flash fihe, evahrythin buhnt to a crisp, this ash cold clod driftin off inta space fahevah."

"Ha'd faith t'bea' bro, when thea's no hope fo tomor'ow."

"Plenty of hope fah tomohrow, anothah child bohn and anothah aftah that, but ovah time, see, the bah gets set highah and highah, least fah us stah jumpahs. Only chance we've got is that one day one among us fools might suhvive the leap, 'specially if the new guys've been watchin us old jokahs take a stab at it."

"What about yo? Why go on waitin fo somebody else t'come along? 'Specially if thea ain't no pie in the sky like yo believes, no big daddy arrivin in a solid gold Caddy just in the nick a'time t'squa things up?"

"I figuhe if... if maybe I can dance on that edge a breath longah, wait fah that pahfect second, then I could chance it."

"How can a friend help?"

"True friend offahs his hand, somethin steady to grab onto befah you take that last great leap."

Salaam reaches such a hand out from the underground, and there's a strong grasp between the two — then a *clang* down the grate as he vanishes amidst the vapors.

"Damn, that dude's elusive."

As in delusional pal.

STOMP! STOMP! STOMP! STOMP! The black heavy boots of a rogue QuotLink patrol marches past.

"Eminenze!"

"What is it now? Can't you see that I am busy?"

"Yez but — vhat in ze blazez are you doink!"

His Eminence is fastening a halter top on a sub-teen with sun-bleached gold curls, a dozen or more of a similar sort gathered around giggling.

"Vishink vitz jail baitz getz you top ov ze hour on ze evenink newz un ze rezt ov your live zpent in zolitary convinement?"

"There you go, my little darling."

"Little darlink!"

A pat on the ass sends her back to the queue as the next one steps up.

"Have you've gone ztark ravink mad!"

"Not at all. I too dabble in technical brilliance with the closest attention to comely detail."

"Zey look juzt like ze kidz vrom Ze Pitz!"

"Precisely. I ordered up boxed sets from our warehouse in Orlando."

"Vhy vould anyvone vant to clone mall ratz?"

Dozens and more as other sets of minatures in assorted colors and creeds strut out of the crate, sharing but one feature in common, next to nothing for clothes — bare shoulders and legs, exposed navals, ringed ears, eyebrows and noses — for sex sells best among the spring loaded.

"Next!"

"Vhat are you doink vitz your handz under zer zkirtz!"

"Winding them up." HANDCRANKCRANKCRANK! Seems the Executive Liaison is about to release his own designer line of sweet innocents, a QuotLink Kiddie Korps. "Impressive, yes? With the added advantage of being able to maneuver their way in close to a target and not raise the slightest suspicion — why look at them? Who could distrust a one?"

"Ze're cute, iz true, but vhat real damage can zey do?"

"Smile, my darlings. Show Uncle Queezac your pearlies."

Dazzling smiles indeed, smiles which disguise stiletto honed braces.

"Cutting edge. Now your nails."

Fetching fingies that conceal retractable claws.

"Our last line of attack, should our military options fail."

"Vail, zey didn't even make it outz ov ze gate, un now ve've gotz to contend vitz vhat'z levt ov zeze merzenary halvwitz."

"Afraid of your own machinations, are you Queezac?"

"Abzolutely."

"So you can appreciate my invention."

"Ingeniuz!"

"Coming from you, I consider that a compliment — and given Chi-...."

"Jibber'z."

"...his perverse predilection..."

"He juzt might vall vor it."

"While we simply sit back and watch history repeat itself on this, the most auspicious moment of his sixteen month comeback career."

"Zat'z right, zock it to a guy rightz when he'z mozt vulnerable."

"Precisely." The Liaison twirls each around for a final inspection. "Go forth and mingle!" He orders as he releases them — I-EEEEEEEECH! — they screech as they run off so playfully. "Hunt for Chi- Chimp- Chump-..."

"Jibber, Jibber Ztirbee — juzt zpitz it outz!"

"...him yes, and *crimphiscampycrispers* for me while you are at it!"

I-EEEEEEEEEEEEEEEEEEECH!

"Mind guidin the way gihl? It's like a madhouse back heah and I can't see shit wheah I'm headin."

A little unsteady on your feet, are you?

"Maybe if we aim fah the stage...".

She noses him along.

"...I'd feel a whole lot bettah up theah — and don't be so damn pushy!"

Problem is the stage is surrounded — fans, cameras, would-be friendlies and unknown foes — though the only safe haven where a rockstar can go.

"Leastwise up theah you know which way evahrybody is gawkin."

As long as you guard your backside.

"But out heah in the open I'd be a gonah fah suhe."

Such are the forces that swarm around him. There's these leftover QuotLink patrols for starters — STOMP! STOMP! — a new set of cuties in The Pit — I-EEEEEEEEEECH! — and Cissy Coomb's all girl gang lurking somewhere backstage too — CLANK CLANK

Although there are the forces for good too, the kids in the stadium and beyond, in the auto park, in the streets, shouting their lungs out…

THE WHOLE WORLD IS WATCHING!
THE WHOLE WORLD IS WATCHING!

…Lou in the control trailer center field, with this tearing ache in his gut as he twists in his chair, alert for any cue, any sign of resistance from among the techie crew, a blink from the dry-eyed QSS Specialist, Cub diddling with this fucking red button — like what does it do for Chrissakes, ignite some underground ballistic missile?

"Let's make a break fah it gihl, take ouh chances with the masses!"

Brave words for a doper who can barely walk, Betsy yelps while she noses out of the smoke…

"Noo soo fast deary. Surely yoo rememboor me?"

Let me see, fat bitch in tight cowhide with spiked nipple pins, not a sight one easily forgets — CLANK CLANK CLANK CLANK — *hmm*, whole gang load of you hooligans. Shaved heads, hairy armpits, chain mail stylishly draped down the front — the weight of the ages — what a study in cross generational protest you do represent.

"Hasn't been easy catchin uup with the likes oof yoo."

Meant to send a card, but guess we've both been on the run lately.

"Where's Chippoor Stoorbee at, he's the oone we've coome to see?"

What? Not me! After all the scrapes we've been through together, I'm insulted. Although female bondage is something I've never been into, better tea and scones with an old crone at three or salted peanuts and beer with the truckers until closing, but whichever I prefer a snack to a rumble.

"Hee's been leadin woomen like uus on too loong with all his suugestive lyrics and sexy gyrations."

He can be a charmer, no doubt about it.

"Buut noow hee's goin to have to pay uup. Pay plenty."

I guess being a man's not an easy occupation these days.

"Soo where is the blooke, oor doo we have to resort to sit-doown negootiations as uusual?" Cissy arches an inquisitively plucked brow.

Let me see, let me see, that means sit down on me, no, I barely survived the last confab, so -*roh* last I checked he was heading this-a-way, no, that-a-way — *ror* was it any-which-away?

"Wee doon't have time to play games with yoor kind noomore."

CLANK CLANK CLANK — broad-beamed sisterhood fences Betsy in.

-*rolp*. I catch your drift. But whatever you're intent on doing, you're going to have to wait your turn — see the groupie girls over there? Over there by the costume racks? He's in the middle of something with them.

"Where'd that be yoo'r pointin to precisely?" Cissy's down snout-next-to-snout with Betsy.

See the groupie girls from The Pit standing -*rrover* there?

"Thoose nappy boottomed tots?"

Them, the ones who could, God forbid, be your very own offspring.

"Buut they're harmless."

No, nobody's harmless, not in packs they're not.

"Can't make mooch sense oof what yoo'r tryin to tell me."

Must be my yank accent.

"Yoo sayin he's oover there in the middle oof them?"

Where else?

"Is soo like a man to be chasin after yoong girls, poor things, they're soo vulnerable at that age. We've goot to march oover there sistoors and set'em right on whoot men like him are oopto."

CLANK CLANK — the sisterhood unanimously agrees.

Do do, and you don't mind if I don't join you?

CLANK CLANK CLANK CLANK CLANK CLANK CLANK CLANK

Betsy watches while the oversize beauties hustle away — *roh-k* chum, coast is clear.

"You suhe?"

Sure I'm sure.

"Somethin about women on a mission makes my gonads contract."

Don't want that — as Betsy leads the troubadour onward, one step, two, ears perked, eyes, nose, tail, and a dash out of the shadows into the open.

STOMP! STOMP! STOMP! STOMP!

Bad timing.

STOMP!STOMP!STOMP!STOMP!STOMP!STOMP!STOMP!STOMP!

Quick, jump inside here — *slap slam shut!*

Both listen as the troopers poke around outside — STOMP! STOMP! Troopers sniff around, then rush on — STOMP!STOMP!STOMP!STOMP!

"Bunch of weihdoes puhsuin me to the vehry end."

-*sniff*? -*sniff* herself? Betsy's never been inside a sanitary potty.

"Anyway, this is as good a place as any fah us to talk, you and me, about somethin mighty pahsonal."

Please. I know what's what with the birds and the bees, and the moths and the spiders too. It's those vultures buzzing overhead who concern me.

"Will you quit muttahrin snide remahks undah youh breath and listen fah once — we've got to finalize a few things."

Snide remarks? Years of unheeded advice and all I get for my trouble is an insult.

"I mean theah ain't much we haven't been through togethah, and fun, we've had mah laughs than teahs, but this finale — looks like a man's got to go that one alone."

No way pal, you and I are glued at the heels.

"You don't undahstand babydoll, this is the trip with no retuhn flight."

Good. Then book us both becau-...

STOMP!STOMP!STOMP!STOMP!STOMP!STOMP!STOMP!STOMP!

They're back.

STOMP! STOMP! STOMP!

Betsy and Chipper cease to breathe.

CLANK CLANK CLANK CLANK CLANK CLANK CLANK

STOMP! STOMP!

CLANK CLANK

"I think we'h suhrounded."

No shit Sherlock.

STOMP!CLANKCLANKSTOMP!STOMP!CLANKSTOMP!CLANKCLANKCLANK — CLANKERCLANKCLANK — WHOMP! WHOMP! WHOMP! WHOMP!

"Damn, sounds like they'h whalin on each othah!"

STOMP!CLOMP!CLOMP!CLOMP!CLOMP!CLOMP! — CLANKCLANK — CLOMP! — CRANKERCLANKCLANK — STOMPBOMBERSTOMP!STOMP!STOMP! — STOMP! — CRR-LANK — STOMP!STOMP!

"Not that it mattahs much who wins."

CLANK — STOMP!CLANKSTOMP!CLANKSTOMP!CLANKSTOMP!CLANK — CLANKCLANKCLANKCLANKCLANK — STOMP!STOMP!STOMP!STOMP! — CLANK CLANKCLANKCLANK — STOMP!STOMP!STOMP!STOMP!

The sanitary potty is rocking back and forth as Cissy's gang and the QuotLinks go at it.

STOMP!STOMP!STOMP!STOMP!STOMP!STOMP!STOMP!

"Can't end up like this, trapped inside a crappah!"

CLANKCLANKCLANKCLANKCLANKCLANKCLANKCLANK

And *hups* and *hoo-hahs*, gurgling guts and a horrible odor. Must be a battle to the last stench when a couple of the brutes accidentally bump up against the sanitary potty — SLAM! — tip the damn thing over — SPLAT! — out pops the jack-in-the-box along with mighty mutt. Fighting stops instantly as both sides gather round to stare at the prize rockstar splayed froglegged at their feet.

-choke!
"Yoo!"
Betsy smiles wanly. *Moi.*
Bruised QuotLinks merely gape, this batch having been cranked out end of the shift with no reasoning apparatus installed whatsoever.
Leaves Chipper with the condemned man's only recourse.

> When he was a child
> A boy was taught a prayer to say /
> One he must repeat
> Each and every day //
> Father if you're far away
> And cannot save my ass /
> Then all I ask is that a passerby
> Walks handy by with a bloody ax!

Though the prayers of the nearly agnostic must be particularly futile — or maybe not. For as each side prepares to pounce... it's BOOM! BOOM! // STAND BACK! // STAN MAAX // BOOM! BOOM! // AX MAN! And single handidly STAN MAAX steps in. CLANKCLANK — the beastie babes get tossed aside while — STOMP! STOMP! — he grinds the QuotLinks into a pile of metal filings — best lesson gangland can learn is never mess with a leather queen when she's having a hissy fit, particularly not at Stan's height and girth, that's muscle mass from years on the free weights, no machine's man enough for her — *wha-whoof* — as Stan hooks one last QuotLink and clucks him a good twenty feet, embossing his chiseled profile into the metal side of an idling tractor-trailer.

Rude display of male musculature sends Cissy and the sisterhood bleating a retreat — CRANK CRANK CLAMBEROVERONEANOTHER CLANK. And good thing since the AD MAN's really riled — runaway stars, near cataclysmic collisions, the possible downfall of corporate consumerism along with all those lucrative ad accounts — then there's Chipper's last minute whimpering act — "SO GET OVER IT AGNES!"

"Agnes?"

"GET YOUR BUTT UP THERE ON THAT STAGE AND SING! WE'VE GOT THE HIGHEST RATINGS EVER RECORDED IN LIVE TELEVISION HISTORY — 6.3 BILLION AND MOUNTING!" Stan winds up a boot as Chipper and Betsy go scurrying. "YOU TOO, GIT!"

I-EEEEEEEEEECH! A covey of teeniechicks scatter every which way.

Chipper hies himself onto the scaffolding, this lively limbed monkey bounding about. Betsy prefers to stalk along the base in the shadows while a spotlight tracks Chipper's every twitch.

CHIPPER! CHIPPER! CHIP- CHIP-

He abruptly drops out of sight…

-*rulp!*

…in order to pay a visit to Will Cook high up on his protected perch —
TUH-TUH TUH DOOM!

"Just wanted to stop by and tell you this might just be my grand finale."

Will reaches over his keyboard, latches both hands onto Chipper's.

"I mean nothin's evah fah suhe in this life, but no way I'm evah goin to get much closah."

Will wraps his lanky arms around Chipper's shoulders.

"Plus what in the hell does a guy say to a friend's who's been right theah with him evahry step of the way."

Not much. They just hug, forehead to forehead exchanging pings in their deepest sonar recesses until they butt skulls and awkwardly part, each with his own role to play in the evening's enveloping drama.

CHIPPER! CHIPPER! CHIP- CHIP- CHIPPER!

Man swings from bar to bar and ends up dangling over the stage, a mere thirty foot drop with the big screen dangling directly above him. Camera zooms close-up and the boy and the boy projected on the screen above grin ear-to-ear — while indeed, the whole world is watching. So… he does a strong arm lift over a lateral bar, one quick, two quick half turns, followed by a toss — *hup!* — holding in a, yes, in a one fisted handstand…

YAY! YAY! YAY! YAY! YAY! YAY! YAY!

…30, 40, 50 seconds before he executes this flip, a perfect stutz…

YAAAAAAAAAAAAAAAAAAAAAAAAAAAAAAAAAAAAAAAAAAY!

…with count them, a six salto dismount that lands him — *fooooof!* — center stage with a spring on no less than bare toes!

YAAAAAAAAAAAAAAAAAAAAAAAAAAAAAAAAAAAAAAAAAAY!

"Hey!" HEY!

Man might be sizzled on his own homegrown, but he still holds the prize for on-stage acrobatics.

"Hey!" HEY!

"Hey! Hey!" HEY! HEY! HEY! HEY! HEY! HEY! HEY!

"What say? About time fah some old Loose Nuke tunes?"

HEEEEEEEEEEEEEEEEEEEEEEEEEEEEEEEEEEEEEEEEEEEEY!

"Figuhed as much."

Band's got to come running so Chipper limbers up some more — a half dozen cartwheels across the front of the stage, and with hardly a pause, back as many forward. "Hey! Hey! Hey! We about ready to rock 'n' roll?"

CHIPPER! CHIPPER! CHIP- CHIP- CHIPPER! CHIPPER! CHIPPER! CHIP- CHIP- CHIPPER! CHIPPER! CHIPPER! CHIP- CHIP- CHIPPER! CHIPPER!

"OK alright" — *snap* — as in snap out of it, Cub's himself again, on the edge of his chair and rummaging through stacks on his desktop for that flip box of Slug Rites. "Looks like it's show time, gentlemen — take everything we've got, aim it straight at our boy Chipper — *snap! snap!*"

Even the QSS sentries step to.

TA-TITTLE-LA TA! TA-TA! Will Cook's restless fingers, darting back and forth from keyboard to synthesizers to mixers and scramblers and samplers — one would think the London Symphony was performing in the orchestra pit. It isn't. The Pit is crammed with spawning youth flesh as usual — SCREEEEEECH! along with an I-EEEEEEEECH! contingent. Will Cook however is immune to such distractions, music his sole preserve, mesmerizing the multitude with his electronic wizardry, preparing the pathways — for it is Will Cook who must hold the crowd's attention, build anticipation while Chipper Stirbee and the Loose Nukes rush to prepare for the last act, their great vault into everlasting rock 'n' roll history.

"OK, let's pull in every spare readicam we've got and stay on Chipper! Don't want to lose him, not this close to the finish line — right Lou?"

Lou nods, he is wide wide awake and taking notes, mental notes of the position of every one among the QSS occupying force, particularly the green-eyed Specialist whose face is puckered up violet violent as he attempts to assess what must appear to be a rapidly deteriorating situation.

"That's ready on the downlinks! That's ready on Rome! That's *snap? snap?* DO I HEAR A READY ON ROME?"

"READY ON ROME!"

Sure enough, the Sistine Chapel comes into view, the Last Judgment swirls overhead with the Pope seated under the canopy of the high altar, awaiting His cue. A weary smile. His Holiness bemused if not thoroughly confused by the pandemonium He is witnessing at Wembley.

"So Lou, what's your take on Chipper, quick medley, no break and straight through to the finale?"

"*Uh-* let's hope." Lou hopes, hope does he hope, sweats, for there is only this one last chance to catch the QuotLinks up in the momentum.

"READY ON THE QUEEN?"

Her Highness is nowhere to be seen, only curtains behind an empty throne.

"Tibet?"

"TIBET'S A NO GO!" Color bars and tone.

"OK alright, how about Teheran?"

"READY ON TEHERAN!"

A flutter on the screen and the Imam Elect of the newly united Islamic nations nods in the direction of the camera, a young face, dark beard, intense eyes, and standing in solidarity behind Him the representatives from every branch and known splinter group of the one fifth of the world's population, while from above the call of a muezzin summons the faithful to prayer at dawn in the near east — *Allahu Akbar! Allahu Akbar!*

"JERUSALEM!"

"CONTACT!"

"OK ALRIGHT, BROADCAST!"

Atop the three screens at Wembley, a rare triptych, the Pope, the Imam Elect and the 98 year old Head of the ultra-Orthodox, Rebbe Isaiah Hoshkaim Himself from the Old City Itself, and to the consternation of His attendants He is straining to stand in His wheelchair, which He does. His eyes twinkle, His long white locks glow, and there's the Wisdom of Ages encased on His forehead. The three revered leaders greet one another warily while the techies at their consoles scramble to secure the remaining up and downlinks.

HUM! HUM! MU-MUM MU-MUM! Will Cook attempts a bit of musical diplomacy, plays the opening bars of *God Save Her Majesty* — works — somehow from somewhere behind the curtain the Queen re-emerges to assume Her proper place at this momentous occasion, the three dutiful princelings following along behind Her.

YAY! YAY! YAY! YAAAAAAAAAAAAAY!

As a few hardy voices start to warble the anthem, Will Cook squeaks and squeals away from such solemnity into another of his inexhaustible harmonic peregrinations, some **wah wah** hip hop chop to liven up the proceedings.

Despite the occupying force Lou feels the beat, starts to rock in his seat — and so what if he's feeling smug? Man's had to strive to get where he's at, and if only Gertrude could see him now, or Elli — for here he is, the evening's impresario, he who has arranged all this, the ecumenical media event of the epoch.

"Waco's ready on standby Cub."

"OK alright, let's… let's wait on Waco."

For out of the wings Bubba Two steps on stage, the youngest of the Loose Nuke hunks.…

YAY! YAY! HEY! HEEEEEEEEEY!

…guy walks nonchalantly over to his spot and **whaaaaank!** — without warning blasts away at Will Cook with a metallic salvo.

Whaaht? Takes Will a second to respond — WHAAAAAAACK BACK — and will somebody please, hurry and get that youngster a sound check!

HEY! HEY! HEY! HEY! HEY! HEY! HEY!

Will Cook squeaks and squeals away from such solemnity into another of his inexhaustible harmonic peregrinations

Place is beginning to buzz. Danny T 'Drummer Dynamo' is next, slips into his spot unseen, tunes a little — TIPPITY-TAP-TO-THE-TOP A BAMBAM AND PING PING PINGLEPANGLEDINGLEDANGLE!

YAY! YAY! YAY! YAY! YAY! YAY! YAY! YAY! YAY! YAY!

Crowd's about pumped up when this siren, this vixen, this red hair streaming comes struttin her stuff cross front.

YAAAAAAAAAAAAAAAAAAAAAAAAAAAAAAAAAAAAAAAAAAAAAY!

Raises the crowd up off their seats for the lady is larger than life herself — even the holy figures on the big screens can't fail to take notice of a good convent-bred girl the lineage of Molly.

YAY! YAY! gives way to wolf calls and whistles, because if Molly's not enough of a rise for the guys— HEY! HEY! HEY! HEY! HEY! HEY! — try out the tropical fruit pack who do backups — Mango and Tangle and tart tasty Tamarind.

CHIPPER! CHIPPER! CHIP- CHIP CHIPPER!

He's here, man's standing center stage and pumping his arms above the crowd, a supercharged superstud superstar! With Betsy along beside him and thumping her tail in time to the rhythm.

CHIPPER! CHIPPER! CHIP- CHIP CHIPPER!

"This is it Lou, the moment of truth!"

Lou's jumping in his chair.

Impatience is in the air — and out there in the skywaves awaitin his prompt, it's the Reverend Jimmy Clapperd, comin at you live from his own multi-million dollar television studio and spiralin stainless steel rocket launcher sanctuary in Waco, Jus' Plain Jimmy C, the charismatic leader of the fundamentalist Church of the Ascendant Majority who has been see-lected by President Billy Ray Bopps hisself to represent resurgent 'Merica's religious commitment to peace, prosper'ty an political he-gemony on this earth forever and after Amen!

"BROADCAST!"

Jimmy C easily takes over center screen, gives that familiar televangelical smile of his direct to camera, is about to speak when…

"That's one, two, three and mah! — Gotta!"

GOTTA!

Gotta getta Girl

YAH! YAH! YAH! YAH!

Need a girl / Alot alotta
Gotta gotta / Gotta getta girl

Wanna girl / Really wanna

> Need a girl / Any girl
>
> Gotta gotta / Gotta getta girl
>
> Really gotta / Gotta poppa
> Shouldn't oughta / But I gotta
> Gotta lotta / Gotta getta girl
>
> Gotta squirrel / Alot alotta
> Need a girl / Feel a girl
> Gotta poppa / Poppa lotta little girls

YAH! YAH! YAH! YAH! YAH! YAH! YAH! YAH! YAH!

"*Whoa hoe hoe hoe!* Heah we go!" As Chipper slides into another of the Loose Nukes' classic raunch.

> Lindy Ann she gets huhself a yeahnin'
> Yeah she does
> 'Specially when the moon is full
> Huh insides theah / they staht in chuhnin'
> Satuhday nights when TV is dull
>
> Gal hikes out to the roadside
> Thumbs the fihst lone truckah down
> Climbs right up and sits beside him
> Befah long she's doin' the clown
>
> Lindy Ann / Lindy Ann
> She does fah Stan / She'll do fah you
> Lindy Ann / Lindy Ann
> Gal's bettah than pay-pah-view

"Ain't no reason evahrybody can't sing along on the chohrus."

> Lindy Ann / Lindy Ann
> She does fah Stan / She'll do fah you
> Lindy Ann / Lindy Ann
> Gal's a whole lot bettah than pay-pah-view

YAAAAAAAAAAAAAAAAAAAAAAAAAAAAAAAAAAAAY!

"We smokin oah what tonight?"

YAY! YAY! YAY! YAY! YAY! YAY! YAY! YAY! YAY! YAY!

"Smokin what tonight?"

HEY! HEY! HEY! HEY! HEY! HEY! HEY! HEY! HEY! HEY!

"Hey baby!"

HEY! Gals in the audience shout back.

"Know what I need?" Chipper gets low down gravel and gritty.

WHAT?

"What's bettah than smoke, what's even bettah than rock 'n' roll?"

HEY! HEY! HEY! HEY! HEY! HEY! HEY! HEY! HEY! HEY! HEY! HEY!

"And I need some, I need some, I *nee- nee- neeeee-* need some!"

YAH?

"Needa needa needa whole lot a some…"

> Some of yuh lazy lovin / baby
> I say lazy lovin
> Some of yuh lazy lovin
> That'swhatI'vehadahankahrinfahevahsincesuppah
> That lazy lovin / That crazy lovin
> That kick back brand lazy lovin you've got

YAH!

> And I need some — TONIGHT!

YAH! YAH! YAH! YAH! YAH! YAH! YAH! YAH! YAH! YAH! YAH! YAH!

"And you know why?"

WHY?

"Cause I'm this Maine boy, see… backwoods bohn and bred bahefoot and nevah been housebroken — CAN YOU RELATE?"

YES!

> MAINE BOY / SHAME BOY
> Wheah'd you lose youh PANTS?

YAAAAAAAAAAAAAAAAAAAAAAAAY!

> MAINE BOY / SHAME BOY
> When you goin' t'leahn t'DANCE?

> Cause rumah is that BOY's been spendin NIGHTS OUT
> Sniffin tracks back DEEP theah in the WOODS
> Can't seem to LOSE the sweet scent, H'RIGHT SCOUT?
> Got that wet NOSE of youhs rub'd in real GOOD!

> MAINE BOY / SHAME BOY

Don't go and lose youh PANTS?

MAINE BOY / SANE BOY
You got t'leahn t'DANCE?

What's that he's chasin ROUND nights in such a HUHRY?
Looks like he's done TREE'D himself some fancy TAIL
Got somethin UP THEAH lookin mighty fine 'n' FUHRY
'Cept one fast WHACK 'n' even a Maine boy might FAIL!

"You bettah believe it!'

MAINE BOY / SHAME BOY
Don't go and lose youh PANTS?
MAINE BOY / TAME BOY
Not befah you leahn t'DANCE?

"Once again now — with feelin!"

MAINE BOY / SAME BOY
Ain't nevah lost his PANTS.
MAINE BOY / FAME BOY
You fin'ly got youh CHANCE!

YAAAAAAAAAAAAAAAAAAAAAAAAAAAAAAAAAAAAAAAAAAAAAAY!

BOOM!
BOOMBA- BOOM! BOOM! BOOM! BOOM!
There's these rockets flying overhead and chrysanthemum blooms, purple, green and gold.
AWWWWWWWWWWWWWWWWW!
Abruptly cuts the Loose Nukes off before they can belt out the infamous *Love Baby*.
BOOM! BOOM! *cracklecracklecracklecracklecrackle*
Streaks in the dark followed by flickering sparks.
BOOM! BOOM! BOOM! BOOM!
An entire galaxy so close they could all reach out and touch it.
OHHHHHHHH — WOW!
An unscheduled event which sends the remnants of the QuotLink storm troopers chasing for the source
-WHEEEE -WHEEEE -WHEEEE -WHEEEE -WHEEEE
Whistlers.
...*pop pop pop pop pop pop pop pop pop pop pop pop pop*...
It's the kids in the auto park who've snuck in the rockets, disrupting the show with a dazzling display of fire power. And nothing taunts QuotLink grunts as much as the scent of gun powder.
Taunts Betsy too, she crawls underneath Danny T's drum stand, his

banging above can get to her, but not like fireworks or worse gunshots, she covers her ears with her paws and howls, for it's enough to drive a poor girldog out of her hide.

BA-BOOM!!!

An enormous fountain, metallic gold and spilt silver, comes cascading over the stadium.

YAAAAAAAAAAAAAAAAAAAAAAAAAAAAAAAAAAAAAAAAAAAAAAAAAAY!

Except some extra *pop-pops* respond, ground level and neither festive nor friendly, automatic rifle fire, hopefully the rubber tipped variety.

BOOM BANG BLAH-BLAH-BLOOM BOMB KA-PLOOIE!

Kids send up a barrage that lights up the heavens right as a full scale riot erupts on the roadways outside the stadium — QuotLink irregulars firing canisters of gas, which reluctantly forces the SAS to intervene with water cannon, along with tanks in the streets of London and the Queen of England clutching a silk kerchief to Her face.

THE WHOLE WORLD IS WATCHING!
THE WHOLE WORLD IS WATCHING!

"**HEY WAIT WAIT — FOLKS! WAIT!**" Chipper's at the mike pleading. "This ain't what we came heah fah. We'h heah in the name of peace, love, the eahth itself — and all you brothahs outside theah, let's get a grip!"

Grip indeed. The QSS Specialist has his .09 pressed up against Cub's temple. "Pull the plug!"

Cub deflates upon contact.

"I said pull the plug — this is a military blackout!"

Which Lou without a second's hesitation preempts as he stabs at the ready red button — pull the plug, you bet, you QSS asslick — douses the lights in the trailer and disables the main console, sets all signal transmissions on auto pilot with one camera locked on Chipper and transmitting uninterrupted world-wide.

"What the flying fu-...!" As the Specialist fires a few shots into the darkness. Hits what, who knows, but sparks an uprising among the techies. There's this scuffle with shadows, Cub's meateaters who have seen swamp duty in Nam bare fists and pummeling the plastisized guts out of these yesteryear leftovers, automatics or no, for there's only so much a law abiding citizenry can take in strong arm tactics — whence the wall of QSS falls with a thud.

Lou meanwhile slips off his swivel and rapidly disappears through the trap door, combing his way among the thousands of cables underneath the trailer — *zip zap* — there's this feeling he's developed for electronic pulses and patches. He isolates the satellite transponders, makes sure they're functioning, and stumbles across the main power line coming in from the portable ginny — but it's the Zoomocrane™ feed he's after, got to catch Chipper when he starts in jumping.

-zcrunch -zcrunch — there's this rustling in the dark under there with him, a hulk the size of an overgrown raccoon with teeth, beady eyes — "Zo, ve meetz again do ve Ztarcrave?"

"You!"

"Yez, iz me, your mozt vorrizome adverzary."

Lou cringes at the sight of this turtle, standing upraised beak and claw.

"Look at you, down here tryink to zalvage ziz upztart'z zilly vinale vhile I'm aboutz to zabotage it utzerly." Creature creeps so close Lou gets sprayed with its hiss.

THE WHOLE WORLD IS WATCHING!
THE WHOLE WORLD IS WATCHING!

"Not vor long zey von't be!" Whereupon Queezac lurches at Lou, knocks him off balance. Grabs the thick cable at Lou's feet, cradles it in his warty palms. "Vhat'z ziz, ze veed to ze zattelite dizh?"

"No! That's the…"

"Yez it iz. I can tell you're lyink to put me ovv ze zcent. Vell zat ruze von't vork." And Queezac hacks at the damn thing with his incisors until — *zip zap-zap-zap zoom* ZAPLOOZIE! — he glows for an instant, then flares red face with sparkles for whiskers, quivers, quakes, and rolls over grilled on the half shell.

"Tha- that's the main power cable you just bit into!"

Guess so, though whatever Queezac did he will never know. The lights in the trailer blink back on, along with all the electronics. Place is a mess but functional as the techies toss the QSS remains out the door and resume their positions.

Pair of longhairs are standing outside the trailer, assessing the carnage.

"Hey dude, it's like déjà vu."

"Who?"

"Scene I saw back in Chicago 68, riots in the streets, bodies piled up on stretchers."

"Chicago's in America, this is some other country."

"Can happen anywhere."

"You sure?"

"I was there."

"Man, I don't know, protest's a downer."

"It's not like something you ever forget."

"Got to get over it. Go for the here and now, do some dope, chill."
"Happened back before your time."
"Like I say man, ancient history."

While out in the auto park Red Feather and the Injuns on horseback are rounding the QuotLink renegades into a corral. Casualties in the stand off between the kids and the corporates have been mercifully minimal, fatalities at least among the human kind nil.

SAS relents as well, douses the hoses, reins in the half-tracks. Kids soaked to the skin settle in to watch the end of the show, whereupon this collective sigh of relief — *whewwwwwwww* — arises from the stadium, even laughter when dozens of little gizmo girls bump out of The Pit and overrun the stage — I-EEEEEEEEEEEEECH!

"Do do my darlings." The Executive Liaison coaches. "Finish off that *rebelliousremnantofarockstar* once and for all!"

Chipper's quick, however, he senses a threat and vaults high up over their pretty little heads. Betsy drops low to the ground, assumes her attack stance, exposing the dormant Doberman inside her — *rrr* RAKRAKRAK RAKRAKRAK — this jaggy set of matched canines which came equipped for flaying at flesh not chewing nor savoring it. But before she can lay a fang on a one of them, she is waylaid by none other than STAND BACK! // STAN MAAX // BOOM! BOOM! // MAD MAN! // STAND BACK! // STAN MAAX — and something about Stan's mass — must be a knee-jerk reaction people feel against giant sized males — because even this bunch of specialty mouthed brats backs off, fact is, they turn and flee...

"NO, *YOUPUSSPOUTYLITTLEPRINCESSES* — EAT YOUR FILL!"

...they do, they bop back into The Pit and feast upon the very genius who created them — nibble the dour tasting Diplomatic Liaison to the bone — "*YOUINCESTUOUSINGRATES!*" — which is the imp's very last retort, though a little late for a scolding isn't it, when you're in the midst of digestion?

Leaves those at home watching with a staggering question, for what does this say about the future of our race — today him, tomorrow whom — which is the inherent difficulty in raising the really ravenous child, plucky puckers will turn on you when they run out of fast food. Even Cub with his hand ready at the switch — ready at the switch — ready at the switch — can't believe what he's witnessing.

Snap! Snap! Somebody sober in the control trailer orders up a commercial.

A maturing couple is seen strolling by a marsh at dawn in matching wool crew neck sweaters. He is the picture of a corporate executive, silvered close-cropped hair, tan from golf. She too is country club, chiseled fine features with a dirty blond rinse. Their eyes are forward, their step determined. A close-up reveals his hand tightly gripping hers, squeezing. A quick cut to his neck, the veins bulging. High blood pressure. Stress. Purple rage.

No, no more. Ask your physician for Dimzol™ by name – Dimzol™ – for continuous relief of stress caused by demanding clients, envious superiors, predatory colleagues, incompetent subordinates and slow drivers. Why suffer needlessly or turn to drink when 250 mg per day with meals will build up a tolerance over time against all things threatening?

Dimzol™ contains no narcotic and is not addictive in the pharmaceutical sense of that term. Dimzol™ Relieves with a slight numbing at the threshold of consciousness, like looking through the mist on an early fall morning – the rough edges blurred, outsized shapes textured, sounds muted – the stridency, the immediacy of other people's demands fading into the landscape.

Dimzol™ Treasure life's dwindling moments.

Known contraindications include dream suppression, slight to severe memory loss and a slurring of speech in some patients. Safe with alcohol and nicotine, however. Dimzol™ Trust your family physician to understand your needs.

And after that another! Bummer! Everyone's going to have to wait it through – Pope, peon or poet.

Some Berliner leftische group out with a video. Black and white high contrast artsy. Scene is a big city disaster, buildings burnt out, no trees, no grass, faces of the inhabitants dried out for lack of water, infants choking on dust.

Into their midst a mime troupe mounts a makeshift stage, dressed all in black with gaunt white masks, hollow eyes, they walk round aimlessly in circles, bang these metal pieces together, chant in the new international brand English.

NOBODY // sees the rain
NOBODY // remains the same
nobody // resists the pain
NOBODY // feels the shame

junk! -yungyungyungyungyungyung...
junk! -yungyungyungyungyungyung...

WAKE UP // to severe pollution
WAKE UP // to nuclear profusion
WAKE UP // to mass confusion
WAKE UP // to no solution

junk! -yungyungyungyungyungyung...
junk! -yungyungyungyungyungyung...

NOBODY // sees the rain
NOBODY // remains the same
NOBODY // resists the pain
NOBODY // feels the shame

junk! -yungyungyungyungyungyung...
yunk! -yank — — — — — — — — —

Cub cuts the gloom and doom off mid-frame because it's back live to the great stage at Wembley... the scarlet robed Chelmsford Abbey Boy Choristers have been filing noiselessly into place on a steel rigged loft constructed solely for their appearance tonight. Dr. Pedarazzi, the choirmaster, follows closely behind, takes his place facing the boys.

Beneath the chorus the ladies of The North Atlanta Women's Re-Reformed Baptist Choir, bedecked in long canary yellow, occupy a similarly rigged loft.

Beneath them: Mango, Tangle and Tamarind.

Lastly: Molly Dawkens.

Four tiers of angels ranked from the seraphic to the soul rending to the fun and funky ground level earthy, with everyone of them ready to rock.

Rock, you betcha. Will Cook is double handily playing a medley of Pink

Floyd, *American Pie* along with Jimi Hendrix's version of *The Star Spangled Banner* — a mighty orchestral prelude to the Finale of Finales.

"OK alright, *snap snap*, how have we routed Tibet?"

Through Peking, so it seems, and while a techie's finger dials them up, the Dalai Lama is seen proceeding into a carved wooden monastery hall to the accompaniment of soft windlike reed ripples…

"BROADCAST!"

…with rows of saffron-robed shaved-headed monks settled and bowed, a mighty gong suspended by woven yak's hair swaying above, ready to resound worldwide, mallet poised by strong-armed loin-girded Asiatic youth awaiting extra-terrestrial electronic cue…

"Alice Springs? Are we ready?"

Ready indeed. There's this long shot way outback Australia — zoom in on this shaman Chipper consulted while on vacay in the desert, baked skin, buck naked old coot with his dingo exposed. He waves from top of his dry mound, smiling toothless. Some hollow mournful sound and the man calls out in his native tongue, something that translates on screen — "Remember my sons and my daughters, this land is your inheritance" — but what's that close-up in his hand there — a joint!

"Pan! Pan to the landscape!"

Can't have any of that.

Crowd in the stadium caught it though. Many a hand is raised in fired-up fraternal salute.

"Quick, cue in Waco!"

"READY ON WACO!"

"Waco! We've got Waco!"

"What the hellfi'e's been the hold-up?" Jimmy C forgets hisself and cusses into an open mic. "Ain't I neve goin t'git any ai' time t'say my piece?"

Simply smile Jimmy C, it's when you open your mouth that people tune out, besides…

"Ready? Are we ready?"

"Ready."

"Are we really ready?"

"Ready as we'll ever be!"

"That's quadrants one, two, three, four. Side panels and a split — *snap snap* — BROADCAST!"

There high on the stage rigging, an electronic pastiche of the heads of the world's major religions bowing appreciative greetings at one another. The entire stadium, the Queen Herself and Her entire retinue rise to their feet smiling and clapping. The Pope raises both arms in welcoming embrace, Jus' Plain Jimmy C flashes that telegenic grin a'his, the Aborigine Elder waves a smoldering finger, the Dalai Lama gazes serenely upon the unbelieving while hammer and sinew strike the sacred gong — WONG'G'G'G'G'G'G'G — His Holiness intones a sound so ancient and so rarefied that even Will Cook cannot emulate it. The Imam Elect wails out a spiraling ascendant progression, and the Chief Rebbe bounces His head in animated enjoyment of the occasion, His own feet ready to dance for joy in revelation to the steady crescendo of drum beats rolling forth from the hands of Danny T 'Drummer Dynamo'… this voice from somewhere out of nowhere…

> …YOUR HOLINESS, YOUR HOLINESS, YOUR HOLINESS, YOUR HOLINESS, YOUR HOLINESS, YOUR ROYAL HIGHNESS AND FAMILY, ASSEMBLED WORLD LEADERS AND DIGNITARIES, LADIES AND GENTLEMEN GATHERED HERE WITH US THIS EVENING AT WEMBLEY AND EVERYWHERE WORLDWIDE — SIX AND A HALF BILLION STRONG — LET US WELCOME BACK FOR THIS GRAND FINALE, THAT ROCK 'N' ROLL LEGEND IN THE FLESH — CHIPPER STIRBEE!

"I know yuh'll nevah undahstand babydoll, nevah in a million yeahs, but theah's this thing I've just got to do…"

-raw!

"…I do. I've got to reach out theah, fah as any man evah can, reach out theah and touch those stahs!" He's down on the ground hugging her tight. "Got to — and got to go this one alone."

Betsy licks into his ear.

"No mattah what it costs, no mattah how much it huhts."

She bores in, slobbering and sucking those ears clean clear through.

"Time like this we've both got to be brave."

She looks him square in the eyes, then sadly away.

Chipper stands, scratches her on the noggin, straps his white polished Fenderbender on his shoulder. He is ready.

STAN MAAX is spinning his arm around — *go go go go go…* Betsy barks. Chipper runs a few feet, he just can't chance a glance back, he hurtles the last few steps of the stage ramp and…

YAAAAAAAAAAAAAAAAAAAAAAAAAAAAAAAAAAAAAAAAAAAAY! THERE HE IS! SPOTLIGHTS INTERSECTING AT THE APEX! CHIPPER STIRBEE! MAN LANDS, LOPES DOWN THE RUNWAY, RESPLENDENT IN GLOWING LONG GOLDEN LOCKS — slings the guitar back, raises both arms in his characteristic high arm V, this wide sucker smile wipes across his face — AND THE MASS OF TEENAGE GIRLS INSIDE, OUTSIDE, WORLD-OVER START IN SHRIEKING — no need for and unheedful of any cues from anybody anywhere — GETS THE LOOSE NUKES A'ROCKIN, AND EVEN THE QUEEN WHO HAS REMAINED STANDING IN RESPECTFUL GREETING STARTS TO STOMP.

Hey! Hey! Hey!

The Finale • 645

YAAAAAAAAAY! YAAAAAAAAAAY! YAAAAAAAAAY!

Will Cook hones in on Chipper's flat E key, Bubba's fingers clasp his six string Stratocaster, and with the chart busting familiar theme riff, Danny T hits the downbeat, one, two, three… and in sweet sweet unexpected lyrical rapture…

>Sun up against the MOHNIN

YAY! YAAAAAAAAAAAAAAAAAAAAY!

>Gulls stih above the WATAHS

YAY! YAY! YAY! YAAAAAAAAAAAAAAAAAAAAY!

>Race time to 'scape the STOHMIN
>It's all that even MATTAHS

YAAAAAAAAAAAAAAAAAAAAAAAAAAAAAAAAAAAAAAAY!

>Fah-*ah-ah-ahhhh*
>If I had WINGS
>I'd reach to touch the HEAVENS
>If I had WINGS
>I'd dive into the SKY
>If I had WINGS
>I'd float in endless OCEANS
>If I had WINGS
>I'd bid my eahth GOODBYE / BYE -EYE -EYE
>HIGH / HIGH / HIGH
>I WOULD TRY TO FLY!

The Chelmsford Boy Choristers chime in soprano…

>**High! High! Hiiiiiigh!**
>I WOULD TRY TO FLYYYYYYY!

Then the Baptist ladies turn it round to gospel…

>*Sun risin in the mo'nin // Yah! Yah!*
>*Risin in the mo'nin // Yah! Yah! Yah! Yah!*
>**High! High! Hiiiiiigh!**
>*Gulls hova 'bove the wata's // Yah! Yah!*
>*Hova 'bove the wata's // Yah! Yah! Yah! Yah!*
>**High! High! Hiiiiiigh!**

With a big orchestral burst Will Cook pulls in the assembled rockstars from London, Melbourne, San Francisco and…

>**RACIN TIME TO 'SCAPE THE STORMIN**

IT'S ALL THAT EVEN MATTERS

I WOULD TRY TO FLY! FLY! FLYYYYYY!

And Chipper does one of his jumps — *Whoa!* — man must clear thirty feet!

"S*nap snap* — back way off! Ready on the long shot gentlemen — who knows, boy's hot, might even set the world record tonight!"

Chipper rebounds with ease, right in time to sing close harmonies with Mango, Tangle and Tamarind, add a dash of reggae flavoring...

>   FLY HIGH
>   A'bove di watas
>   FLY HIGH
>   Inta di skies
>   FLY HIGH
>   An say good-bye
>   Bye / Bye / Bye
>
>   **High! High! Hiiiiiigh!**
>
>   Fah man's fouled his sacred RIVAHS
>   His fohrests and his STREAMS
>   Laid waste his only TREASUHES
>   Destroyed his children's DREAMS
>   And fah what? Cause remembah...
>
>   Each step's a deep IMPRESSION
>   Footprints along the SANDS
>   Each man with his POSSESSIONS
>   Rapes eahth with GREEDY HANDS

He punctuates each point with a leap, *high-hup* he goes and *high-hup* again — FIFTY FEET! SIXTY FEET! — has to be impressive!

>   **Greed! Greed! Greeeeed!**
>   *Fouled his only riva's // Yes / Yes he has!*
>   *Fouled his forests and his streams*
>   **Greed! Greed! Greeeeed!**
>   *Laid waste his very treasua's*
>   *Destroyed the children's dreams*
>
>   SO OHOHOHOHOHOH...

Which is when Molly Dawkens cuts in, whole earth mezzo, with a siren's call sounded across continents...

If I had WINGS
OHOHOHOHOHOH
I'd reach to touch the HEAVENS
If I had WINGS
OHOHOHOHOHOH
I'd dive into the SKY
If I had WINGS
OHOHOHOHOHOH
I'd float in endless OCEANS
If I had WINGS
OHOHOHOHOHOH
I'd bid my eahth GOODBYE / BYE-EYE-EYE
High! High! Hiiiiigh!
Yes I would / Yes I would / You bet I would
High! High! Hiiiiigh!
I WOULD TRY TO FLYYYYYY!

And on that ecstatic note the host of religious leaders and rock celebrities unite with Chipper Stirbee and The Loose Nukes in their unanimous plea, an Anthem for Peace and the Earth's Deliverance...

IF I HAD WINGS
I'D REACH TO TOUCH THE HEAVENS
IF I HAD WINGS
I'D DIVE INTO THE SKY
IF I HAD WINGS
I'D FLOAT IN ENDLESS OCEANS
IF I HAD WINGS
I'D BID MY EARTH GOODBYE
BYE HIGH / HIGH HIGH HIGH HIGH
I WOULD TRY / TO FLY!

"AND REMEMBAH MAN, IT'S THE MESSAGE, NOT THE MESSENGAH!"

Those the last words Chipper is to utter before he feels this surge in propulsion under his feet — and a scramble, a black furry creature comes racing at him... there's this inalterable attachment, man's most loyal friend in the universe with her teeth sunk solidly into one heel — "*Whoa-hoa-hoa! What the flyin fuck?*" — it's a kick off the boards, and they're aloft, long arm reach for the stars, stroking furiously freestyle in order to maintain the momentum... together they thrash... high-up high-up, over the nine story stage scaffolding... hundred feet, two hundred, when — *WHOOOF!* — a Maine boy booster blasts in!

High! High! Hiiiiigh!
Yes he does / Yes he does
High! High! Hiiiiigh!

OHOHOHOHOHOHOHOHOHOHOHOHOH

FLY HIGH
EV'RY'BO'DY
FLY HIGH
YAY! YAY!
FLY HIGH
An say good-bye-bye…

"TOWER ONE, TOWER ONE, KEEP TRACKING HIM, TRACK… TRACK… THAT'S IT… GET ON HIM! STAY ON HIM! SNAP! SNAP! SNAP! SNAP!"
THE WHOLE WORLD IS WATCHING!
THE WHOLE WORLD IS WATCHING!
Even the unbelieving.

As Chipper and Betsy scoot easily aside the blimp — QUOT • LINK • INC • • SPRINGS • A • LEAK • • CON • SUM • ER • BUST • • MAS • SIVE • DE • FLA • TION • • SINKS • THE • MAR • KET • • … • • … • • … — where the Elders stare out their remaindered sockets.

And something about the combination of a full moon and a high dive superstar does a number on the earth's gravitational pull, tugs at Will Cook, who switches from *Stairway to Heaven* to Beethoven's *Ode For Joy* without missing a beat — along with full chorale — *Alle Menschen werden Brüder / Wo dein sanfter Flügel weilt…*

"What in thee Hell!" The assembled leaders of the world's major religions might be standing by faces agape, but the Rev Jimmy C there in Waco, he's outraged! "Ain't right. Mainstream 'Merica's not about t'be second in the race t'evangelize outta space, not behind some heathen hippie!" Thankfully, Jimmy C has provided for just such a contingency. He peels back his Hong Kong tailored custom fit to reveal a jumpsuit — red and white stripes with blue stars naturally — "Gadnab it! Gang way!" — and he hightails it off the pulpit and straight for the rocket launcher installed in his very own home sanctuary, at the ready in case the Second Coming were to go holy haywire. Devoted ground crew handles the pre-flight while Jimmy C slips into the cockpit, no time for decompression, no sir, "Let's let her rip an git yur butts out the way down below!" BLOO-VWOOM! — lift off as the glass sheathed and stainless steel sanctuary walls fall away and Jimmy C goes barreling.

…when – *whooof!* – a Maine boy booster blasts in

Titanya and Scotty have escorted Chipper and Betsy to the limits their rescue craft can carry them. Makes them the last of humanity to wave so long. While Chipper, that old snake of a charmer, is busy molting, soaring through the stratosphere and shedding his skin — his shirt and a pair of really ripped jeans waft off and since the guy's known to eschew underwear, this missive can mean only one thing, man's ascending heavenward buff naked!

And Jimmy C, good ol' boy might as well give it up, he's trailing a distant second and besides, if he floors it any further he might just ... just might *BLOW-ROW-HISSELF-HUP!*

Hubble locks in on Chipper, beams back a picture of this pinpoint of tawny blond light arcing serenely out past Pluto and Charon, out past Orion and his loyal Sirius — why if this Maine boy can hold at warp speed, he's going to reach far beyond the outermost galaxies to the ever expanding frontiers of space — and of course drag his best buddy Betsy right along behind him — and her not terribly fond of heights either — far beyond time — far beyond knowing — to the very birthplace of stars...

WAY WAY OUT THERE IN THE DARKNESS

THERE'S THIS WHITE-ON-WHITE FLASH!

INSTANT ON IMPACT!

and after that nothing

except an interminable no news black out

TOM TRAINOR survived the 60s unscathed and lived through the rest of the century in stunned wonder. He resides with his mixed breed family on Cape Cod where he indulges in photography and sailing, but otherwise leads the ascetic life of the writer. His second novel *The Sous Chef* is due out spring of next year, and samplings of his short stories are available online at thewaryeye.com